STEWARDESS BOY 2:
The Wilder Blue Yonder

STEWARDESS BOY 2:
The Wilder Blue Yonder

A novel by
Henri Gustave

Cover design and illustration by
Rae Crosson

Forest Hills, NY

STEWARDESS BOY 2:
The Wilder Blue Yonder
© 2018 Henri Gustave. All Rights Reserved.

Published by (201) Press
Forest Hills, NY 111375

First edition December 2018

Please direct all inquiries to:
Publisher@201press.com

ISBN: 978-0982857823 (Paperback edition)

Cover design and illustration by Rae Crosson
Cover art © 2018 (201) Press. All Rights Reserved.

Printed in the United States of America

DEDICATION

To my husband, Bruce. Without his love,
support, humor, and unfailingly honest feedback,
Stewardess Boy 2 would still be in a holding pattern
somewhere over Middle America…

…and to Rae, whose illustrations for the book covers,
holiday cards, and promotional features (since Day One)
have so perfectly captured the spirit of the Stewardess Boy series

CONTENTS

BOOK ONE

CONTENTS

BOOK TWO

BOOK ONE

CHAPTER 1

Living the Dream

June 1991

Flight Attendant Eric Saunders was tired of talking about penises.

"I saw the captain's in the hotel steam room in San Diego last month," said one of his co-workers, a muscular blond with ice-blue eyes. He sat up and lazily dipped his toes in the pool. "It was *huge,* and he was playing Mr. Show Off with it—if you know what I mean."

"That is *hot,* David!" commented another, whose name was Eduardo. "You know who else has a big dick?" he asked, as he spread suntan lotion on his caramel-colored skin. "That mechanic at JFK with the snake tattoos on both arms. What the hell is his name? Roberto? Rafael?"

"It's Rino, the Italian one who works afternoons," said David. "And when did you ever see his dick, Eduardo?"

"I came to the plane early one day and found him sleeping in a first-class seat. He must have been having a *wicked* sex dream. That big ol' anaconda was twitching in his pants, baby! I just stood there and watched him, until the rest of the crew came down. He got me so worked up, I had to go in the lav and jack off before we started boarding."

"I love it! What about you, Eric? Who are *you* hot for?"

"Nobody I can think of… at the moment." Eric stood up and put on his sandals.

David looked up at him. "Where are you going?"

"For a walk on the beach."

"Now? Just when the conversation's getting interesting?"

"Please! We've been having the same conversation for the last two days." Eric reached for a baseball cap. "Big dicks, thick dicks. Cut and uncut dicks. Dicks that point straight up, dicks that curve over to one side. White dicks, black dicks, Latino dicks—"

"Well, *chica,* we are in Miami," said Eduardo, as a well-endowed man in a black Speedo strolled by the hotel pool. "What else should we be talking about?" he added, as the man paused and casually examined the trio of bronzed male crewmembers.

"You know what, Eric?" said David. "You're a little uptight for a new hire."

"So I've been told," said Eric. "Remind what time we have to leave."

"Our flight is at four, we have to be at the airport at three. So we're leaving the hotel at two-thirty."

"OK. I'll meet you guys in the lobby at two-thirty this afternoon."

"Are you through with the chair?" asked the man in the Speedo, who'd been hovering nearby. He began draping his towel over it before Eric even replied.

"Be my guest," said Eric, as his co-workers snapped to attention. "I'll see you guys later."

"Try to unclench that beautiful ass of yours," said David, slapping Eric's rear end. "You never know who you'll meet, especially on Miami Beach."

"Thanks," Eric replied. "I'll keep that in mind." He followed the signs leading to the beach. Once his feet hit the sand, he turned left and headed north. It was a perfect day for a solitary walk. The sun was high in the sky, and on his right, the Atlantic Ocean was an exquisite shade of blue. As a native Texan, the only shoreline that Eric had ever seen was the murky water of the Gulf of Mexico. There was simply no comparison.

Eric sighed with delight as the ocean breeze caressed his bare chest and legs. This is what flying is all about, he thought to himself. An easy two-leg trip to Miami. A lively debrief with the crew last night, with free-flowing liquor that was all 'compliments' of the airline. Non-stop stories about crazy passengers and even crazier flight attendants. And a twenty-four-hour layover in a city that was teeming with beautiful men. True, the constant conversation about sex, both on and off the airplane, was a little tiresome. But that seemed to be a phenomenon that occurred whenever gay men gathered.

He sighed again and told himself that he *should* try to be more relaxed about everything. He wasn't a prude; if anything, he was sexually frustrated. He was a recent graduate of the Mercury Airways Flight Attendant Training Program, which had entailed six weeks of near-isolation in suburban Chicago. The students were monitored by instructors and staff every waking moment. There were rumors of video cameras hidden all over the campus, including inside the dorm rooms. Unlike his ever-ready roommate Anthony Bellini, Eric had chosen to abstain from sex. It seemed like the sensible thing to do. Nevertheless, six weeks was a long time.

As he walked along, his shoulders began to sting. But Eric didn't care. He wanted to continue a little bit further before he had to turn back and start getting ready for work. It was so quiet here, compared to the hotel pool—no crewmembers babbling, no children shrieking, and no corpulent German tourists cannon-balling into the deep end. Lord, those Germans! The sight of their lily-white bodies, squeezed into ridiculously small bathing suits, would take some getting used to.

Mercifully, there were few people this far from the hotel. An elderly couple, who both had skin the texture of old shoe leather, lay inside a nylon windscreen. The man was on his side, lazily scratching himself. The woman was on her back, stark naked, with her legs spread wide open toward the sun. She caught Eric staring and jerked her head up. "What the fuck are *you* looking at?"

"Sorry," said Eric, "It's just that I've never seen a seventy-five-year-old vagina before." He hurried along.

Overhead, airplanes taking off from Miami International roared by in quick succession. Some of them immediately looped back over the water and headed west. Others turned north toward New York City and Boston. He watched a Mercury Airways 737 as it climbed to cruising altitude. That'll be me in a few hours, he thought, running out of club soda and tomato juice by the time I get to row 10. Passengers on the Miami-to-New York flight were a notoriously demanding group.

He was just about to turn back when he noticed, fifty yards away, a dark-haired man lying alone on a double-sized towel. The man was easily six feet tall, with enormous shoulders that tapered to a narrow waist. His skin was copper-colored and gleamed from a combination of oil and sweat. He wore a baseball cap and a tiny red thong that barely contained his genitals. As he applied oil to his chest, lingering over his erect nipples, the fabric of the thong seemed to be straining to the bursting point. Everything about him was perfect, including his large, wide feet.

Eric slowed to a crawl, trying to appear nonchalant as he passed by. He bent over and pretended to sort through some random stones at the water's edge. It's twelve o'clock, he thought. I have to be downstairs at 2:30. I need one hour to shower and pack. If this guy's interested, that leaves me just enough time to… He felt a sudden swelling in his groin.

The man looked up, smiled and waved. "Hi, Eric."

Jesus Christ. It was Javier Morales, Eric's favorite instructor from the training school.

"H-hi, Javier," Eric stammered, trying to cover his erection. "What are you doing here?"

"I have a few days off before my next class starts, so I hopped on the first flight to Miami this morning. You must be here on a layover." He eyed Eric's crotch. "Looking great, I might add."

Eric blushed. "Yeah, we got here yesterday afternoon. Gosh, it's so strange to run into you like this."

"That's flying for you," said Javier, grinning. "How long are you here?"

"Not much longer. I'm working the four o'clock flight back to La Guardia today."

"Well, we have a little time then." Javier patted the empty space next to him on the towel. "Come lie down here next to me."

Eric's heart began beating rapidly. "Are you sure?"

"Of course I'm sure. Why else would I ask?"

"That'd be great." Eric slipped off his sandals and lay down on his stomach.

"Not so far away, baby," said Javier, pulling Eric closer to him.

Eric winced. "Ouch!"

"What's the matter?"

"My shoulders."

"Oh, they're starting to burn. Let me put some lotion on you." Javier squeezed a glob of white cream out of a tube and began gently spreading it on Eric's shoulders. "There," he cooed. "You've had too much sun for one day, that's all."

"I know," said Eric. "I should probably be getting back."

"No, not yet." Javier pulled him close again. "We have a little time still."

Eric felt Javier's massive dick nudging his backside. "Oh, God, I can't believe this is happening."

"Shh, you don't have to say anything else," said Javier, nuzzling Eric's neck. "It's perfect just like this." He slipped his hand into Eric's bathing suit and wrapped his fingers, still slick with suntan lotion, around Eric's cock.

"Javier, what are you doing?"

Javier's tongue flicked Eric's earlobe. "What you've always wanted me to do, baby." He began pumping up and down. "My God, Eric, you're as hard as a fucking rock!"

"Oh, Javier, not so fast!" Eric sputtered. "It's been such a long time since I …wait, stop it, or I'm gonna…" Too late. Eric's body was wracked with uncontrollable spasms. "Oh, God!"

"That's it, baby, that's it," said Javier, still pumping Eric's dick. "Good boy."

"Javier, Javier," Eric moaned, as he fell back against Javier's chest. "This, this is…"

"I know," said Javier. "Bliss."

As Eric's breathing returned to normal, he rolled over to be face-to-face with the man of his dreams. "Now we'll take care of you," he murmured, reaching down.

"Don't worry about me," said Javier. "We'll save it for the next time." He kissed Eric gently on the lips. "There'll be *a lot* of next times for us, now that you're not my student anymore. We can do whatever we want. Now, shhh…"

***

"Wake up!" A calloused hand was roughly shaking Eric's shoulder. The sudden contact with his sunburned skin made him cry out in pain. He opened his eyes. The old woman he'd passed by earlier was kneeling next to him.

He jumped up and scanned the beach for Javier, who seemed to have vanished into thin air. "Where'd my friend go?"

"I dunno," said the woman. "But is that your flight back home?" She pointed to the sky, where a Mercury Airways jet was streaking northward at five thousand feet.

"Oh, shit! I must have missed pick up at the hotel." He grabbed his suitcase and his tote bag and began running.

"You'd *better* run!" She sat back on her heels and cackled. "You're gonna be in a shitload of trouble if you don't make that flight."

Eric tried to pick up speed, but the wheels of his suitcase kept getting stuck in the sand. The harder he tried, the more slowly he moved, and the higher the plane rose out of reach.

"Faster, boy! You gotta go *faster*!"

Eric dropped his luggage and began flapping his arms. If I flap hard enough, he thought. If I can just get some lift… His effort to become airborne was futile; he remained firmly rooted in the sand.

"Jump, boy, *jump*!" cried the old woman. "It's the only way you'll make it!"

With Herculean effort, Eric threw himself into the air. A moment later, he miraculously found himself inside the plane.

"Oh, Eric! Where have you been?" asked Lynette, his co-worker in first class. She was the lead flight attendant and wore a perpetual look of worry on her face. "You weren't in your jump seat for takeoff!"

"I'm sorry, I missed the hotel van. I'll get started right away."

She looked him up and down, making a clucking sound with her tongue. "Where's your apron? You're supposed to be wearing it for the service."

"It's in my tote bag."

"Where's your tote bag?"

"Oh, crap! I must have left it on the beach!"

"Well, you can't work in *that*!" She pointed to his bathing suit. "We can see your ding dong!"

"What'll I do?" asked Eric, panic-stricken.

"Look for an extra blanket, I guess. We can't wait any longer." A call light rang in the cabin. "Answer that, please, Eric, while I turn on the ovens. It's the man in 3B."

Eric stepped into the aisle. "Yes, may I help you?"

The skinny, sharp-nosed passenger looked up and leered. "Hey, kid, nice presentation." He slipped two fingers into Eric's waistband. "Do I get a *double* serving of warm nuts with my drink?"

Oh, God, thought Eric. I bet anything this guy's got a pencil dick. "Keep your hands to yourself, *sir*," he replied, with a firm slap. "Now, is there something else I can get for you?"

The man's demeanor changed instantly. "Bring me a Scotch and soda," he snarled.

Eric turned off the call light. "In just a minute. First I've got to go find—"

"Not in a minute. *Now.*" The passenger started ringing the call button repeatedly. *Ding, dong. Ding, dong.* "I want a Scotch and soda, and I want it *now.*" *Ding, dong, ding dong, ding dong, ding dong…*

***

"Hey… HEY! PHONE!"

Eric opened his eyes. He was nose-to nose-with a man who had a long, jagged scar running down one side of his face.

"What?" Eric bolted upright on the sleeper sofa and tried to focus his eyes.

"I said there's a call for you!" He dropped the phone into Eric's lap. "Asshole woke me up out of a sound sleep, whoever it is," he grumbled.

Eric grabbed the phone and covered the mouthpiece. "Sammy, shhh!" he hissed. "Do you want me to get fired when I just started?"

Sammy Bellini plopped his naked, hirsute body down on an armchair. "Who the fuck needs to call you at six o'clock in the morning?"

"Sammy, shut up!" Eric cleared his throat. "Hello?"

"This is Bob at Crew Scheduling, calling for Flight Attendant Saunders."

"Speaking."

"We have a trip for you today."

"Yes?" From the corner of his eye, he could see Sammy scratching himself.

"You're gonna be number three on flight eleven to LAX, sequence number four-two-two, departing JFK at eleven-hundred, sign-in at ten-hundred." The crew scheduler rattled off this information very quickly. "Please confirm."

Eric, still groggy, reached for a pencil and a notepad. "I'm sorry, could you say that again, please?"

The crew scheduler repeated himself, speaking just as quickly as before.

"That's a ten A.M. sign-in, right?" asked Eric.

The crew scheduler sighed. "That's generally what ten-hundred means. Please confirm your assignment. I have other crewmembers to call."

"Yes, sir. Confirming. I'll be there."

"Thank you." *Click.*

"You going somewhere?" Sammy's hand moved lazily from his crotch to his rock-hard stomach. His entire body was covered with thick, wiry black hair. Sammy was, in fact, the hairiest man that Eric had ever seen. Sometimes Eric just couldn't stop looking at him.

"I'm going to Los Angeles."

"Nice. Nice to get out of this fucking town for a day. Do you have a long layover?"

"I forgot to ask."

"Six o'clock in the morning," said Sammy, shaking his head. "Well, as long as we're awake, you may as well make us some coffee."

"Do it yourself. I have to shower, shave and pack."

"Shit, bitch!" said Sammy, getting up from the chair. "You get dropped into *my* apartment, out of fucking nowhere to live here for six months, when I don't even *know* you, and you can't even make me a cup of coffee?"

"Let's get a few things straight, Sammy." Eric tried to look menacing. "Number one, this is your brother's apartment, not yours. Number two, you're only living here until Anthony gets transferred back to New York, at which time you'll be dumped back at your mother's. And number three, I am not now, nor will I *ever,* be your bitch. Go make your own damn coffee." He stood up. "And for the last time: when you're in the living room, please put *something* between your bare ass and the furniture!"

***

Eric gave himself the once-over in the hallway mirror before he left for the airport. Shoes shined, club-stripe tie perfectly knotted, gleaming silver wings pinned on burgundy blazer. He was ready.

"You look good," said Sammy. "Really sharp."

"Thanks."

"Let me see that *culo.*" Sammy pulled up the back of Eric's jacket. "Oh, sweet!" He grabbed Eric's backside with both hands. "Wait'll the other guys see *this.*"

"Goddam it! Keep your hands to yourself, Sammy! I thought you were supposed to be straight, anyway."

"Hey, a beautiful ass is a beautiful ass. What time will you be home?"

"Sometime tomorrow night, I guess. I'll find out when I get to the airport."

"Tomorrow night?" He scowled. "You'd better call first. I might be busy."

"What am I supposed to do, hang out in operations all night while you and your friends watch *Goodfellas* for the hundredth time?"

"Don't get smart with me, bitch. Oh, sorry. I forgot. Hey, since you're going to L.A., why don't you stop at Dan's and buy me some of those pretzels stuffed with peanut butter."

Eric double-checked to make sure that he had his crewmember ID badge. "Who is Dan?"

"Dealer Dan's. Anthony used to get stuff for us there all the time on his L.A. layovers. You could also pick up some—"

"Another time, Sammy. I've gotta go. Wish me luck."

"*Buona fortuna,*" said Sammy, kissing Eric on the cheek. His stubble was razor sharp. "Knock 'em dead."

"By the way, Sammy, don't forget to give the superintendent a rent check today. Anthony told me it's the last day we can pay it without a fifty-dollar late fee."

Sammy rolled his eyes. "Around here, we just call him the super, OK? Christ, stop acting like an old woman. I'll take care of it. Now get going."

***

Eric walked to the 71 St. subway station in Forest Hills. He dropped a token into the slot, passed through the turnstile and carried his luggage down the stairs. A Jamaica-bound E train pulled into the station a moment later. Eric boarded the train and sat down. He was surprisingly calm about meeting the crew and working the flight to Los Angeles. For one thing, he'd be working in coach, which was fairly straightforward: serve drinks, serve lunch, pick up trays, offer coffee—done. For another thing, Eric had a more pressing matter on his mind: money. After paying his share of the rent, and for other miscellaneous expenses, he had exactly one hundred dollars in cash to last until he got his first paycheck. A week is a long time to stretch one hundred dollars, he thought. He hoped that there would be a meal left over on the plane. That would take care of lunch; then he'd only have to buy drinks, dinner and breakfast the next morning. *Only*, Jesus!

At the Kew Gardens station, he left the train and followed the signs leading upstairs to the Q10 bus. Between the exit and the bus stop, he was approached by a man wearing a turban.

"Taxi, sir?" the man said. "I take you right to JFK. Only fifteen dollars."

Fifteen dollars for a taxi: it was an unimaginable extravagance. "No, thank you."

"OK, OK, I take you for *twelve* dollars. Which airline you work for?"

"Another time, maybe." He ignored all other ride offers and walked around the corner to the bus stop, where several other people were already waiting. He took his place in line.

An elderly woman in front of him turned around and smiled. "Where are you off to today?" She wore a navy-blue uniform with gold wings.

"L.A."

"You're with Mercury, right?"

"Yes."

"Good for you! I *love* your new uniform. That burgundy blazer is such a nice change."

"Thanks. We like it, too."

"My name is Dee Dee. I'm with Global Airways," the woman said. "I'm going to London."

"I'm Eric. Wow, London! How nice. It sounds a little more exciting than L.A."

"Oh, well, after forty years it's all the same." Her bright smile turned into a grim lip line. "To tell you the truth, if we're still in business tomorrow when we land at Heathrow, I'll be happy." She leaned in close and whispered, "Bankruptcy rumors. *Again*. They're in the newspaper every day."

"Oh," said Eric. It was then that he noticed the frayed red piping on her jacket and the dull, scuffed flat shoes that she wore. "Well, good luck to you."

"Thanks, dear. You have yourself a nice trip."

As the bus approached, they gathered their luggage. Eric paid his fare and took a seat toward the back, discreetly distancing himself from Dee Dee. Maybe things aren't so bad after all, he thought. I may not have a lot of money, but at least I'm not in her shabby blue shoes. Still… one hundred dollars. He opened his wallet to count his money again, and almost fell off the seat.

Eric no longer had one hundred dollars. He had a single twenty-dollar bill and a crumpled piece of paper marked: *To Eric*. As he unfolded the note and read it, he was overcome with rage. *Eric: I.O.U. $80. I'll pay you back next week. Signed, Sammy.*

CHAPTER 2

The House Rules

BZZZZZZZZ! Jolted out of a sound sleep, Anthony fumbled to turn off his alarm clock. He squinted at the illuminated numbers and groaned. *Seven A.M. Jesus!* He forced himself out of bed, pulled the curtains open, and was struck in the face by blinding, white-hot sunlight. The sun had barely risen, and it was already at least 80 degrees in Dallas; he could tell by the heat radiating through the glass. He closed the curtains, and then reminded himself that the outside temperature didn't matter: his new home had central air conditioning. He silently repeated the three words to himself: *central air conditioning*. It was a magical phrase to a native New Yorker who was used to a lifetime of rattling window units. He could walk anywhere inside the four-bedroom house and it would still be a comfortable 72 degrees. *Fucking fantastic.*

After brushing his teeth and finger-combing his hair, he slipped into the kitchen wearing a pair of jockey shorts. Undisturbed, he juiced an entire bag of oranges. Then he brewed coffee, made an omelet, and toasted two slices of bread. Amazingly, all of the kitchen appliances could be plugged in at the same time; there were more than enough electrical outlets. More importantly, there was an abundance of *space*. Not just counter space; and not the kind of space that New Yorkers usually bragged about. This was no dilapidated loft in SoHo, with rats scurrying inside the walls and other tenants noisily renovating, day and night. This was *real* space, and even though it was communal, Anthony planned to enjoy every square inch of it.

As he ate breakfast, he skimmed through the local newspaper, noting wryly that there was little mention made of events taking place anywhere outside of Texas. Christ, he thought, it's enough to make you think that as far as Texans are concerned, the world ends at the state border. Then he chuckled. Actually, that line of thinking is OK. New York City, and everybody who's still there, can get along without me for a while.

After breakfast, he went into the bathroom. He consumed a fistful of vitamins, and then spent a few minutes in front of the full-length mirror examining himself from head to toe. Not bad for twenty-nine, he thought, greatly pleased by what he saw. He flexed his pectoral muscles. Wait a minute, what the hell is that? He leaned closer to his reflection and yanked a solitary grey hair from his chest. OK, so he was really thirty-two... but nobody would ever guess it.

Back in his bedroom, he changed into a pair of onion-skin shorts, a muscle shirt and a pair of sneakers. He walked out to the driveway where, thankfully, his car was parked in the shade. Using a putty knife, he spent thirty minutes scraping a faded '*TEXAS: LOVE IT OR LEAVE IT!*' bumper sticker from the rear fender. The former owner of the car, whose bedroom Anthony now occupied, had decided to leave Dallas after a six-month stint and transfer to Chicago. Maybe, thought Anthony, I won't be so quick to make up my mind.

He went back into the house and entered his favorite room: the home gym. It was almost as big as his entire apartment in Queens. The gym, which overlooked an outdoor pool, was furnished with a treadmill, a bicycle, a leg press, a bench press, a large selection of free weights, and one completely mirrored wall. He inserted *Donna Summer's Greatest Hits* into the CD player. Then he did a quick a warm up in front of the mirror and began psyching himself for the main portion of his work out: heavy weight-lifting. That would take at least ninety minutes. Today was his upper-body day. He got down on the carpet and began a grueling set of one hundred push-ups. Up, down, up down… focus, focus, focus. Tonight, for my date, I need every part of my body pumped up to the max. He was starting to break a sweat when the door opened.

One of his roommates, a sandy-haired, green-eyed former gymnast, stood in the doorway wearing only a pair of cut-off denim shorts. "Anthony, phone for you," he drawled. Drew was from Louisville, Kentucky.

"Can you take a message, Drew?"

"It's a long-distance call. Collect. Some guy named Eric."

Oh, fuck, not again. "Would you mind bringing the phone in here?"

"Of course not." Drew returned a moment later with the telephone. "Here you go, stud." He sat down on one of the benches and fixed his gaze on the bulge in Anthony's shorts.

Anthony picked up the phone. "Hello?"

"Hi, Anthony, it's Eric."

"I can barely hear you. Where are you?"

"I'm calling from a payphone at JFK."

"What's up?"

"I'll tell you what's up: your brother has been *stealing money* from me, right out of my wallet!"

"Oh?" Anthony watched as Drew grabbed a pair of dumbbells and began doing a set of wide-grip flies. Drew's bare chest was muscular and lightly covered with blond hair. "How do you know it was my brother?"

"He left me an I.O.U.!"

"I told you not to keep a lot of cash in the house."

"What am I supposed to do with my money, roll it up and stash it in my ass?"

"No, you're *supposed* to open a fucking checking account, like everyone else."

"I did. But my ATM card and my checks won't be here for another week. In the meantime, thanks to Sammy, I'm on my way to Los Angeles with exactly twenty dollars to my name."

"So? Do what everybody else does: eat leftovers on the plane and save your cash for necessities, like alcohol and cigarettes."

"Very funny. I suppose—"

"You didn't give Sammy *cash* for the rent, did you?" There was a long silence on the other end of the line. "Oh, *fuck*, Eric, I told you *ten times* before you left: give him a check *only*, made out to the building management company."

"And I told *you*: my checks won't come in the mail for at least a week. The rent was due five days ago. I had to give him cash."

"Let's hope he actually paid it," said Anthony, immediately regretting the remark.

"Oh, my God. What happens if he *didn't?*" Eric sounded even more agitated. "Am I going to come home to find the front door padlocked, and all my stuff—"

"Stop being such a drama queen. I'll call the super and follow up on it." He tried to remain focused on the conversation as Drew moved to the leg press and began pumping his steel-cut quadriceps.

"What about the *rest* of my money? I can't keep worrying about Sammy—"

"Eric, calm down. I'll call Sammy, too, and tell him to knock it off. He can always go back to swiping cash from my mother's purse." He kept talking to Eric but couldn't take his eyes off Drew. "Now, will that make you happy?"

"Yes. Thank you."

"Good," said Anthony. "Another crisis solved."

Drew, obviously enjoying his audience, hopped off the leg press and slipped out of his shorts. He was now wearing just a bathing suit made from four square inches of white mesh fabric, which he proudly modeled for Anthony.

Fucking little tease, thought Anthony. Give me five minutes alone with that southern show-off, and I bet he'll—oh, right: my workout. Gotta stay focused. "So, you're going to L.A., huh?" he said into the phone. "Not a bad trip for your first week."

"We'll see how it goes. I've heard that the L. A. passengers can be a real handful."

"Count your blessings. I'm leaving tomorrow for an eighteen-hour layover in Duluth, Minnesota."

Eric laughed. "Lucky you! Anyway, I have to go now, or I'm gonna be late."

"Have a good flight, Eric. Later." Anthony hung up the phone. "Listen, Drew, if Eric calls again this week and I'm here, just say I'm away on a trip, OK?"

"Sure," said Drew. "What was that all that about?"

"Eric was my roommate in training. He's living with my brother in New York for the time being, and he's having a few adjustment problems."

"How old is he?"

"Twenty-three."

And where's he from?"

"Austin."

"Let me get this straight: your roommate from Texas got based in New York, and you're from New York and got based in Texas. That doesn't make much sense."

"It's a long, stupid story don't have the energy to go into it right now. I just wanna finish my work out and spend some time by the pool before it's a hundred degrees outside."

"I'm headed out there right now." Drew admired himself in the mirror as he spoke. "Are you gonna join me when you're done?"

"I'll be at least an hour and half. I have a really intense routine planned for today."

"Don't worry about making me wait, stud." Drew turned around and squatted in slow motion as he reached for his shorts on the floor. "I can go all day long."

***

"Boy, you weren't kidding about taking your time," said Drew, as Anthony plopped onto the pool chair next him. "You're really dedicated."

"Fuck, I'm beat."

"Who wouldn't be, after all *that* effort? I could hear you grunting and groaning all the way out here. I'm surprised the neighbors didn't call the police."

Anthony reached for a tube of suntan lotion on the table between their chairs and suddenly stopped. "I gotta just lay here for a second. I don't even have the strength to grab my own dick, much less—"

"Here, just hold out your hand." Drew squirted a glob of lotion into Anthony's outstretched palm, and then ogled his roommate as Anthony began spreading it all over his chest.

"Oh, nice." Anthony sniffed his hand. "Is this Bain du Soleil?"

"*Oui. For ze St. Tropez tan*," Drew said, with a grin. He held the tube out again. "More?"

"Yeah, thanks." Anthony sat up and reached for the lotion. "Ow, ow, *ow!*"

"What's the matter?"

"I think I pulled a muscle in my back. I can't reach back there."

"Let me help you before you really hurt yourself," said Drew, moving his chair closer. He began applying lotion to Anthony's back in slow, circular motions.

"That feels good."

"Thanks. Where does it hurt, Anthony?"

"In my rhomboids, on both sides. They're the muscles—"

"I know where your rhomboids are, Mr. Universe. *I* was an athlete, too, you know. Hang on. Let me just apply a little pressure with my thumbs."

"Whew, that's good." Anthony relaxed his upper body. "You know exactly what you're doing, don't you, buddy?"

"Mmm hmm." Drew pulled Anthony's arm back and started gently rotating it. "Between gymnast and flight attendant, I was a physical therapist."

"So, you're sort of a jack of all trades, huh?"

"Jack of something, all right. It was just kind of a natural extension from being a gymnast, I guess." He giggled. "Speaking of natural extensions…"

"Hmm?" Anthony turned around and casually glanced at Drew's crotch. "Wow, look at you. You're a real show horse."

"I can't help it. The aroma from your armpits is making me crazy."

Anthony raised his arm higher. "You like the man smells, huh?"

"I could bury my face in there for the *whole day*." He inhaled deeply. "Oh, fuck! Either this suit is way too small, or I'm way too excited." He jumped up and shucked it off. "There, that's better." He lay back, completely naked, and displayed his fat, hard penis. "I'd better grease this up," he said, reaching for another handful of lotion. "That sun is fierce."

"Yeah, you don't want get that puppy burned. There's not enough Solar Caine in the world."

"Come on, Anthony," Drew said conspiratorially. "Get naked with me."

"Do you want to go skinny dipping?"

"I want to do more than that." He yanked Anthony's bathing suit down and gasped. "Holy shit! And you call *me* a show horse!" He took Anthony's cock in his hand. "Beautiful," he murmured. "How big *is* that thing?"

"Grab a ruler, buddy, if you can't eyeball it."

Drew threw his towel on the ground and kneeled on it. "Please give it to me, Anthony." His eyes were riveted to the phallus protruding only inches from his face. "Please. *Please*."

"You're sure the neighbors don't mind if, right here, in broad daylight, you suck my big cock?" Anthony loved talking like that. It got him even more excited.

"Fuck the neighbors. That's why we have an eight-feet-high privacy fence."

"What about the house rule: no sex between roommates?"

"We're home alone today. Justin and Craig are both on trips. I won't say a word."

"I dunno know…"

"Come on, Anthony, you know I've wanted you since the first time I met you. It's all I think about. That manly body and that beautiful face, and …

everything! I'm going crazy with you living here, especially with your bedroom right next to mine!"

"Yeah? Really?" Anthony stood up and slowly stroked his dick. "Tell me more."

"I fantasized about sneaking into your room last night. I could hear you in there, getting ready for bed. I pictured you naked, slipping between the sheets. My head started spinning. I had to jack off *twice* before I could go to sleep. *Please!*"

"OK." Anthony loved it when the muscle boys begged him for sex. "You can blow me." He bent down slightly so that his dick was perfectly aligned with Drew's mouth. "I'm not gonna shoot a load, though. I'm saving it for tonight."

"No load? But that's the best part!"

"Sorry. I have a date."

"But I *have* to see you shoot! Come on! You should be able to go three or four rounds a day with that monster cock!"

Anthony took a step back. "Look, do you want it, or not?"

Drew, still on his knees, immediately moved closer. "Yes, I want it!"

"Then shut up and start sucking."

"Yes, sir." Drew took Anthony's dick in his hand and gently pulled back the foreskin. "Is there anything else that I should know about you?"

"Like what?"

"Like, your HIV status?"

The question caught Anthony so completely off guard that he started to lose his erection. "My… what?"

"You have to know what your status is. You're from New York. Everybody knows what's going on up there."

Don't worry," Anthony said. He focused on Drew's full lips, and the pleasure they would bring him, and became rock hard again. "I only top, so it's cool."

"Good enough for me." The matter was apparently settled; Drew licked his lips in anticipation.

Anthony slowly pushed his dick inside Drew's mouth. "Oh … *yeah*," he groaned, as he heard gurgling sounds emanating from Drew's throat. After a few minutes, he pulled back slightly. "Look at me," he commanded, putting his hand on the nape of Drew's neck.

Drew tilted his head back. His eyes were moist at the corners and radiated a look of complete bliss.

"That's it, buddy," said Anthony. "I like it just like *that…*"

***

"That was really hot," said Anthony afterward. He and Drew lay side by side on their pool chairs, drenched in sweat.

"I can't believe you can get that worked up, and go at it for that long, without coming," Drew croaked.

"It's all about control." Anthony admired his own penis, which was still as rigid as a flagpole. "I can't believe you can shoot three huge loads in a row."

Drew shrugged. "I guess it's 'cause I'm a lot younger than you."

"*Bite* me, you punk."

Drew laughed.

"Man, Drew, you really know how to suck cock."

"Well, you know how Southern Baptists boys are," Drew said proudly. "We come out of the womb craving dick."

"Right." Anthony lit a cigarette. "And then you spend your whole lives trying to avoid actually coming in contact with one—"

"Even our own!"

"—which, fortunately, none of you seem to be able to do."

"Hey, I held off until I was twelve." Drew grinned. "What about you?"

"I was ten."

"God dammit, I *knew* you'd say that! Why do New Yorkers always have to be the first at everything?"

"As I recall, you were the first one to pop a boner this morning."

"Well, what'd you expect me to do—around you?" He reached over and began stroking Anthony's turgid dick.

"Christ, haven't you had enough?" said Anthony, laughing. "You really *are* a cock whore, Drew."

"That's the God's truth, Anthony. When there's a man as hot as you within reach, I just can't help myself."

"Yes. That's *quite* obvious, to EVERYONE!" a male voice thundered from above.

"What the *fuck*...?" Anthony was so startled that he dropped his cigarette.

"Both of you stay where you are," said the voice. "I'm coming down *right now*."

"Oh, crap!" muttered Drew. "Jesus is coming, and I'm not even dressed for it!"

"Since when did Jesus have a southern accent?" said Anthony, trying to fish out his cigarette out of the pool.

"My guess," said Drew, "is we're not home alone after all. Dammit."

"Just what I need!" said Anthony. "Who is it, Justin or Craig?"

"Craig," Drew replied. "Couldn't you tell?"

"No, what do you mean?"

"Craig always tries to come off sounding really butch, like he's Marshall Dillon on *Gunsmoke*. Of course, every time I see that big ol' apricot wig, I automatically think of Miss Kitty."

"Fuck, Drew, you *had* to mention the hair! If I start laughing when he comes out here—"

"It's all about self-control, remember? You said so yourself."

The glass door slid open. "Hello, boys." Craig stood in the doorway. He was a middle-aged man with curly, reddish-blond hair. He wore a Hawaiian shirt, navy blue slacks and black loafers. Sunlight glinted off the gold wings pinned to his shirt.

"Hey, Craig," Drew said casually. "We thought you were away on a trip."

"Obviously."

"What happened?"

"They canceled the flight and sent us home." Craig put his hands on his hips. "I guess I don't have to ask what happened *here* this morning."

Drew shrugged. "Anthony and I were getting to know each other. It's not that big a deal."

"In *my* house, performing oral sex in a public area is considered a *great, big* deal."

"That was fifteen minutes ago. How would you know what we were doing, unless you've been watching us all this time from the upstairs window?"

Craig bristled. "Why don't you two come inside, so we can discuss the situation."

Drew rolled his eyes. "I feel a lecture coming on. Maybe I should get dressed first."

"Yes," said Craig, scowling. "Or maybe I should just hose you down like a *dirty dog*."

"I think a quick dip will suffice," said Drew. He hopped in and out of the pool. "Anthony, hand me a towel, please." After drying himself off, he and Anthony followed Craig into the house.

Craig led them into the living room, where he poured himself a Scotch on the rocks from the wet bar. "I'll be brief: there is to be no sexual activity between housemates. That's rule number one. Anthony, I thought I made that quite clear when you signed the lease last week."

"You did," said Anthony, looking down at the carpet. "Sorry."

"Rule number two: no sexual activity or nudity *at all* outdoors, whether you're alone or not. I don't want any more trouble with the neighbors than I already have."

"But this is *Oak Lawn*," Drew whined.

"What does that have to do with anything?" said Craig, gulping Scotch.

"Oak Lawn is the gayest neighborhood in Dallas," said Drew. "There isn't a breeder around here for miles. If we can't let our boys hang out *here*—"

"Connie Bettinger isn't interested in the relative freedom of your testicles. Furthermore, she has the Dallas Police Department on speed dial." He poured another drink. "Now, these are the rules. You can live by them, or you can vacate the premises. In the meantime, consider yourselves both on probation for the rest of the month. One more slip up, and you'll lose the roof over your head *and* your security deposit. Have I made myself quite clear?"

"Yes," said Anthony.

"Yes, sir," said Drew.

"Good. I'm glad we understand each other." He smiled faintly. "Just to show that there are no hard feelings, I'd like to invite you both to come with me to Rich's for Happy Hour today."

"Yippie!" said Drew. "Two-for-one well drinks and free Cheese Doodles. Sorry, Craig, I can't. I have a trip tonight."

"And I already have plans," said Anthony. "Sorry."

"Well, some other time then." Craig looked disappointed. "I'll see you both later."

"Who's Connie Bettinger?" Anthony asked, after Craig left the room.

"The fucking uptight, busy-body Evangelical *bitch* who lives next door," Drew replied.

"Oh, funny, you didn't mention *her* earlier."

"She's the last hetero hold out in the gayborhood. She refuses to sell and move out."

Anthony nodded. "It only takes one Fundamentalist to spoil everyone else's fun."

"I *loathe* her. She reminds me of the people back home. Do you know that she once left one of those hateful, anti-gay religious pamphlets in the mailbox?"

"You're sure it was her?"

"Of course! Anyone else on the block would have left us some high-quality, slightly-used porn. By the way, why didn't *you* say anything when Craig was reading us the riot act? You just stood there, looking at the floor."

"I was trying not to laugh." He punched Drew on the arm. "Christ, his hair really is the same shade as Miss Kitty's!"

"I told you!"

"What's up with that tacky Hawaiian shirt with the navy-blue slacks and dress shoes?"

"Craig flies for Patriot Airways, remember? That's what the guys wear on the DFW to Honolulu flight."

"You've gotta be kidding me."

"The women's Hawaii uniform is *worse*. It's a Mumu made from the same print as the men's shirt. They wear red leather pumps with it."

"*Oy!* Whose idea was that?"

Drew shrugged. "You can't expect much in the way of style from Patriot. Their corporate headquarters are right here in DFW."

"That explains a lot."

"Craig's a very *senior* flight attendant. He's been based here for almost thirty years."

"I see," said Anthony. "Well, that explains *everything*."

CHAPTER 3

Up and Away

"May I have your attention in the terminal, please. Flight Attendants Saunders and Rickerson, please report immediately to gate number sixteen for the flight to Los Angeles. Once again, Flight Attendants Saunders and—"

Eric came to a screeching halt at gate 16. "I'm here," he panted to the agent behind the desk. "I'm a little late. There was a big hold up at security because of—"

"Who're you?"

"Saunders. Number three." He showed her his ID badge.

The agent checked his name off the list. "I don't think I've seen you before. Are you another new one?"

"Yes."

"God, they're popping you kids outta that school like it was a PEZ Dispenser. Well, you'd better get your ass on board. The purser is just about to give her crew briefing, and she likes a full house."

"I'm on my way." He reached for his jet bridge key and then fumbled with the door handle.

"Here, let me show you," said the agent. "Insert your key like this, and then turn it to the left."

"Got it. Thanks."

"Break a leg."

"Excuse me?"

"Actually, you don't have to worry about that. Sylvia Saks is the purser today. She'll break it *for* you." She smiled. "I'm joking. Go, have fun. And good luck."

Eric tried to calm himself as he walked down the jet bridge. Making a good impression on his first New York-based crew was crucial. He stepped over the doorsill of the wide-body jetliner and into the first-class cabin. The crew—six females and one male—were all seated, except for one woman who stood in front of the credenza with paperwork in her hand. She had shiny, slate-grey bobbed hair. Her tailored uniform fit like a glove, and her Ferragamo leather pumps shined like new. Sylvia Saks—of course, he thought. Eric had met her once before, on the flight that brought him from the training center to New

York the week before. "Hi, I'm Eric, the number three. I'm sorry I'm late, but—"

"Where have *you* been?"

"There was a big holdup at the security check point. A lot of passengers were running late for the Santo Domingo flight."

"*Bubbee*, I don't know how long you've been around. But for future reference, you've got to get yourself down to security a little bit earlier whenever your departure time is close to the Santo Domingo flight, understand?"

"Yes, ma'am."

She gestured toward an empty seat. "Sit down already and catch your breath. You look like you need a glass of water. Jacques, will you get this kid a glass of water, please?"

Jacques, an attractive man with salt and pepper hair, disappeared into the galley. He came out a moment later with a glass of water. He handed it to Eric and smiled.

Sylvia did a quick headcount. "Cripes, we're still missing one. Anybody seen—" She glanced at her paperwork. "—Rickerson? No? Well, we'll have to get started without her. OK, here's the drill: We're completely full. What else is new? No wheelchairs today, but there are two unaccompanied minors in 38A and B. We're responsible for them until their parents pick them up at the other end. Sally, make sure they don't run off the plane by themselves when we land, like that kid last week. I was sweating bullets until they found him in line at Burger King. Let me remind everyone that it's summertime. We'll have a lot of families with noisy, uncontrollable kids, just like any other summer day. So expect the worst, and let's just get through the flight. I'm happy to help resolve any customer service issues, but I'm not putting out any fires that you start, so *think* before you *speak*. Rhonda, that goes double for you. What else … If you want to come up to first class for leftovers, please wait until I call you to say that we've finished the service. Pick up tomorrow is at noon, so please be downstairs *in the van* at twelve sharp." She looked at her watch. "We may go out short today, if this Rickerson person doesn't show up, in which case—"

"I'm here, I'm here!" A disheveled young woman with an undulating mass of tightly-curled blond hair rushed through the door. "I'm Pavonia, number six. Sorry I'm late, but my commuter flight from DFW just got in." She began throwing her luggage—an extra-large suitcase, a tote bag, a duffel bag, a plastic shopping bag, and an overstuffed handbag—into the closet nearest the door.

Sylvia pursed her lips. "What do you think this is, Manhattan Mini Storage? That closet is for passengers to use. Haul all that crap to the back right this minute."

"This is my designated crew stowage area," Pavonia said testily. "I'm working here in first class."

"Not with that hair, you're not!" Sylvia pointed at Eric. "You! I'm switching your position. You're working up here with me. Pamona, or whatever your name is, you're going to coach."

"You can't do that!" cried Pavonia.

"Yes, I can. If you want to push it, I'll get a supervisor to come down and give you a grooming check. Let's see: wrinkled blouse, torn hose, Lilt Home Perm. I don't think you'll pass muster."

"But I—"

"Consider yourself lucky that I'm just swapping your position. If it were up to me, I'd send you home. Now, move it."

Pavonia snorted, but she followed Sylvia's instructions and began removing her luggage.

"That's all, folks," said Sylvia. The crew began dispersing. "Call me when you finish checking your emergency equipment and we'll start boarding. Eric, could you step into the galley for a minute? I want to go over the sequence of service with you and Jacques."

"Yes ma'am."

"Please stop calling me ma'am. Just call me Sylvia."

Once they were in the galley, to Eric's great surprise, Sylvia hugged him. "Welcome to the line, kiddo. It's nice to see you again."

"You remember me?"

"Who could forget that *punam*?" She pinched his cheek. "So eager to get started. Tell me, have the local girls broken you in?"

"No, this is my first flight. I mean, out of training."

"Ooooh, we get you on your virgin cross-country run. Did you hear that, Jacques?"

"Mmm *hmm*."

"Eric, this is Jacques. He's working the galley. You and I will work the aisle together. Just follow my lead and you'll be fine."

Eric and Jacques shook hands. "I hope that swapping positions isn't going to cause any friction with the rest of the crew," Eric said to Sylvia.

"Screw 'em. It's my prerogative, and one of the few benefits of being in charge of the flight. Besides, I like being surrounded by handsome men. Jacques, why don't you get Eric started with pre-departures. I need to call cabin service for some hangars." She darted off the plane.

Jacques smiled and then handed Eric a carafe of orange juice, a bottle of champagne and a bottle of mineral water. "Anything else you need?"

"Just some glasses and a tray."

"Here you go."

Eric took the items and began arranging them on the credenza. From the corner of his eye, he noticed that Jacques was still smiling at him.

"What is it?" said Eric. He looked down. "Is there something stuck to my shoe?"

"No, it's those silver wings of yours. They're so shiny, they're blinding me."

Eric shrugged. "Everybody has to start sometime."

"I'm just playing with you, sweetheart. Don't worry, you'll be in good hands today."

"Promise?"

"Oh, absolutely."

"Good. I'll hold you to that." Eric began quickly pulling the wire cage from the top of the champagne bottle.

"Whoa!" Jacques grabbed the bottle, keeping one hand capped over the cork. "Be careful with that. It'll shoot all over you."

"Oh, we wouldn't want *that*," Eric said with a grin. "By the way, do you have any plans for the layover?"

"Just dinner." Jacques leaned closer. "Why, what did you have in mind?"

"Well, I thought maybe we could go to West Hollywood and—"

"OK, break it up, you two," said Sylvia, placing a stack of hangers in the closet. "Geez, I leave you alone together for one minute, and you're sniffing each other's rear ends like a pair of Rottweilers."

"Can you blame me?" said Jacques. "Look at him."

"*Ach*, men!" She shook her head. "Do me a favor, Jacques, and keep it in your pants until we land." She picked up the interphone. "Ladies and gentlemen, it's showtime!"

***

Two hours after takeoff, the elaborate service was almost complete. Eric and Sylvia had served three rounds of drinks, appetizers, salads, and a main course to their fourteen passengers. "Here's the last dirty tray," said Eric, sliding it into a cart.

"Good," said Sylvia. "Jacques is brewing fresh coffee. We'll be ready to go out with the dessert cart in a minute." She took a peek at the cabin and then pulled the galley curtain closed. "I think they can live without us for five minutes." She plopped down on a jump seat and started thumbing through a copy of the *Post*.

"Sylvia, is there something on my face?" asked Eric.

"No."

"How about in my teeth?"

"Let me see: give me a big smile. No. Why?"

"Just checking."

"*Why?*"

"Well, it's strange, but not a single passenger has made eye contact with me since I took their orders after takeoff."

"And this bothers you because...?"

"It doesn't really *bother* me. It's just that ... I *have* been going out of my way to give them a really nice service. And to be friendly. You'd think they could at least acknowledge me."

"Oh, *bubbee*, don't head down that slippery slope. If you start looking for validation from them, you'll get nothing but heartache."

"I guess you're right," said Eric. "Speaking of *them*, I'm kind of surprised there aren't any movie stars on today."

Sylvia shrugged. "Sometimes there are, sometimes there aren't. It's different every day."

Eric sat down next to her. "I bet you've met a lot of celebrities over the years."

"Oh, yes." She reached for a ramekin of mixed nuts. "Just about all the big ones."

"Ask her about the time she met Zazu Pitts," suggested Jacques.

"Who?"

"Screw you, Jacques!" Sylvia lobbed cashews at him. "The silent film era was decades before my time and you know it!"

"Did you ever meet Joan Crawford?" asked Eric.

"Yes."

"How about—"

"Oh, *God*." Sylvia pressed her hand to her forehead. "D'you want the whole gay boy list? OK, here goes: Joan Crawford, yes. Bette Davis: yes. Marlene Dietrich: no. Judy Garland: almost—"

"Almost?"

"She was on a passenger list during my first month on the job, but at the last minute, she didn't show. Big surprise. Who else? Lana Turner: yes. Faye Dunaway: yes, *oy!* Barbra Streisand: no. She never flies commercial."

"She might someday," said Eric.

"I assure you, she *won't*," Sylvia said with finality. "Have I covered everyone that you'd ever hoped to meet, dead or alive?"

"Yes, thank you."

"Tell him your Bette Davis story," said Jacques, as he removed cellophane wrapping from a bowl of whipped cream.

"I'll save that one for dinner. Do I have time to reapply?"

"Always," said Jacques. "I'll wait to pour the coffee until you've finished."

Sylvia reached into her hand bag. "I never go out for the dessert cart without a fresh pair of lips." Peering into a compact mirror, she painted on a coat of rich, red color and then blotted her lips on a paper napkin. "Well, boys, how do I look?"

"Radiant," said Eric. "Like a young June Allyson."

"*Before* she started doing the Depends commercials," Jacques added.

"*That's it!*" Sylvia hissed. "No Bette Davis story."

"I think we can worm it out of her later," Jacques said confidently. "A couple of Margaritas is usually all that it takes." He poured fresh coffee into a silver pot. "The cart's ready whenever you're ready."

"Let's go, Eric," said Sylva. "If you don't mind, I'll be the silent partner."

"What does that mean?"

"You do all the talking and take the orders. I'll be on the back end of the cart, and I'll make the sundaes."

"Works for me."

"Good. Frankly, I've had enough of facing these people today. Do you mind pouring coffee? It'll be closer to you, on your end of the cart."

"That's fine."

By the time they reached the last passenger in the cabin, Eric had become tired of asking the same question over and over. "Would you like dessert, Mr. Atkins?"

The passenger, who was focused on a stack of paperwork, didn't answer.

Eric repeated the question, and still received no response. He tapped Mr. Atkins lightly on his shirt sleeve.

"What do *you* want?" Mr. Atkins snarled, finally looking up.

"I want to know if you'd like dessert."

"Of course I want dessert!"

"Would you like an ice cream sundae, or cheese and crackers?"

"Sundae."

"Which toppings would you like on your sundae?"

"Well, what do you *have?*"

Sylvia, obviously irritated, leaned over the cart. "They're the same toppings that we've had since 1965: hot fudge, butterscotch, strawberries, whipped cream and nuts. Just tell us what you *want.*"

"I want *everything*. Including a better attitude from *you.*"

Sylvia rolled her eyes. "Sounds like someone's blood sugar is a little low." She quickly prepared the sundae and passed it to Eric. "You'd better eat this fast."

"*Hrrmph*," was the passenger's only reply.

Eric placed the sundae on the tray table. "Would you like coffee?"

"Yes."

Eric stifled a sigh. "Do you take your coffee black?"

"Cream and two sugars."

Eric poured coffee into a china mug and then added a small amount of cream.

"What're you *doing?*" Mr. Atkins asked.

"I'm putting cream and sugar in your coffee, just like you asked me to."

"This is Mercury Airways! You're supposed to let me put in my *own* cream!"

Eric controlled his facial expression very carefully as he prepared another mug of coffee and passed the cream pitcher to the passenger. He said nothing else to Mr. Atkins and knew better than to wait for a thank you. "I think we've finished here," he said to Sylvia.

She nodded. "Right you are!" They rolled the cart back into the galley.

"What a *momser!*" Sylvia yanked the curtain closed. "Has he been like that the whole flight?"

"No," said Eric, still taken aback. "He was OK until just now, when I tapped him on the sleeve."

"What happened?" said Jacques.

Sylvia gave Jacques an abbreviated version of the story.

"Asshole," said Jacques, shaking his head. "Typical New York-to-L.A. *asshole.*"

"I'll be back in a second," said Sylvia. "I'm gonna see if anybody on the crew has some Visine. If Pig Face wants another cup of coffee, I'll bring it to him myself." She stormed out of the galley.

"I don't get it," Eric said to Jacques.

"A little squirt of Visine in coffee is tasteless and causes terrible diarrhea," Jacques explained. "We resort to it occasionally, for very important people."

"Oh! No, I meant: why would that passenger, all of a sudden—"

"Because that's what they *do*. That's what they *all* do: they turn on you when you least expect it. That's why you should never be too friendly or make yourself too available. It's not worth the effort. By the way, sweetheart, don't be so quick to answer the call lights. Otherwise, they'll start thinking of you as their personal in-flight servant."

"Good advice. Thanks, Jacques."

"It's sage advice. I guarantee it. Personally, I try to avoid dealing with them as much as possible."

"How do you do that?"

"I only bid galley positions. That way, I don't even have to *look* at them, much less talk." Jacques smiled. "Seniority does have its benefits."

"Well, that's something for me to look forward to, I guess."

A moment later, Sylvia returned. "No luck with the Visine! We'll have to figure something else out. Oh, Christ! Here come the moochers, right on my heels!"

Two female flight attendants entered the galley. One was Pavonia. The other was a petite brunette with a Buster Brown haircut and a cherubic face. Eric noticed that they both had a small gold crucifix pinned to their collars. "How are y'all doing up here?" asked the brunette.

"We just finished dessert," said Sylvia.

"Need any help?"

"You're about fifteen minutes too late, Darcy. Thanks anyway."

"Well, in that case, do you have anything left over?"

Sylvia pursed her lips, which was by now a familiar gesture. "We haven't even started picking up. I said I'd call you when we're ready for you to come up, remember?"

"We don't want to get in your way," said Pavonia, beaming a fake smile. "We just want a little salad and maybe some caviar."

"Yes, you *always* want a little salad and some caviar. I repeat: I'll *call* you when *we're* ready. Get the message?"

"Yeah, we *get* it," said Pavonia. "You know what, Darcy? I think I'll skip the airplane food today. We'll get some real food, some *high-quality* food, at Dan's once we land."

"Good idea," said Darcy. "Why should we pump this crap into our bodies anyway? It's just gonna make a big, smelly exit on the way *out*."

"You express yourself with such elegance," said Jacques. "Were you an English major in college?"

"I'd rather save room for Dan's," said Darcy. "Besides, I have a mile-long shopping list for this afternoon."

"Me, too!" exclaimed Pavonia. "We're having a big party at my house this Sunday, right after church."

"By the way," said Darcy, "how do the loads look for your commuter flight home tomorrow?"

"Awful! All of our flights to DFW are oversold. I'll probably have to resort to my back up—Patriot. They have three non-stops, but of course I'll be at the very bottom of the standby list after all of *their* commuters."

"Well, I tell you one thing," said Darcy. "I'm getting myself back to DFW tomorrow come hell or high water. I gave up my crash pad in Kew Gardens last month, and I am *not* spending the night in operations."

"*Oy!*" Sylvia rubbed her temples. "Jacques, is there an ice pick handy? Put it right through my eardrum. I want to end this misery."

"Well," said Pavonia, ignoring Sylvia's remark, "as far as spending the night in ops, nobody in their right mind *wants* to do that, but if that's we have to, we have to do it. God, being a commuter is hard!"

"Tell me about it," said Darcy. "Even so, it beats living in the Rotten Apple."

"Ladies, this discourse is fascinating," said Sylvia. "But since we're still working, do us a favor: take a hike."

Pavonia's hands flew to her hips. "Don't worry, we're going."

"Thanks for making us feel so *welcome,*" said Darcy. She and Pavonia left, muttering to each other as they retreated.

"*Schnorrers!*" said Sylvia. "That's my life today: s*chnorrers* and *momsers*." She smiled at Jacques and Eric. "Thank God I have you two, irreverent though you may be."

"I'm glad to be here," said Eric. "Although if we start flying together a lot, I may need a translator. What's a *momser*?"

"It's a Yiddish word that I shouldn't use in polite company," Sylvia replied. "But believe me, in this job, it comes in handy quite often."

***

Eric spent the rest of the flight trying to make plans with Jacques, but they were constantly interrupted. The pilots wanted lunch, and then wanted to stretch their legs and use the bathroom. Flight attendants from other cabins wandered up to first class to 'chat and chew'. Passengers kept ringing their call lights. Before too long, it was time to serve baked-on-board cookies. Finally, as the aircraft started to descend, and Sylvia was in the lavatory, Eric and Jacques were alone. "So," said Eric, "right before takeoff, we were talking about what we might do today."

"Oh, that's right," said Jacques, as he wiped down the counter. "Tell me again what you had in mind?"

"I thought we could go to West Hollywood and go clubbing."

"Clubbing?"

"Well, I don't mean clubbing, *per se*. I can afford exactly one drink. But it would be fun to go out and have a few drinks."

"Oh, you want to go cruising! I'm sorry to tell you this, but our hotel is nowhere near West Hollywood. It isn't even *in* Los Angeles. It's in Palos Verdes."

"Where is Palos Verdes?"

"It's so far from West Hollywood that it may as well be in another state."

"How much would a taxi cost?"

"There and back? Probably sixty dollars, if not more."

"Ouch. Is there a city bus?"

"Maybe, but we'd have to make a million transfers. By the time we got there, we'd have to turn right around and come back."

"I see," said Eric, trying to hide his disappointment.

"If a gay scene is what you're after, you'd be better off flying San Francisco or Miami trips. Or Chicago, even. Palos Verdes is pretty quiet."

"What *is* there to do around the hotel?"

"You can get a manicure, get a facial, or buy a cute sundress in one of the boutiques. It's a real kind of girly-girl layover."

"You don't strike me as the girly-girl type, Jacques. What are you doing on this trip?"

"Sylvia and I buddy bid. We fly the same schedule together every month. Plus, I live in Chelsea, so I have all the gay life that I need right outside my front door."

"Lucky you."

"Let's see, what else is there to do in P.V.? You can always go for a walk on the beach. Or ride a bike—they have free loaner bikes at the hotel. And of course there's Dan's."

"That's the third time today I've heard somebody mention Dan's. What is it?"

"Dealer Dan's. It's a local food emporium. They also sell wine and spirits at very reasonable prices. Dealer Dan's had a very devoted following of crewmembers from all over the country. Going to shop there is like making a pilgrimage."

"I think I'll skip that."

"Good. I have a better idea anyway. Sylvia and I would like to treat you to dinner."

"Oh, I couldn't let you do that," said Eric, resisting only out of politeness.

"Why not? You're a poor new hire, right?"

"Well, yes but—"

"We've been in your shoes, and we remember what it was like. Besides, we'd enjoy your company."

"Wow, that's really nice of you. Uh, are those women from coach coming, too?"

"Oh, *no*," said Jacques. "It'll just be the three of us, with a pitcher of margaritas and some great Mexican food." He smiled. "We like to keep it intimate."

"Well, if intimacy is what you're after, I'm your man."

"Perfect. It's a date. We'll meet downstairs in the lobby restaurant at five. And, sweetheart, keep our plans to yourself, OK?"

"You bet."

CHAPTER 4

The Layover

"So," said Sylvia, later at dinner, "Ms. Davis and I just happened to find ourselves alone together one day in the upstairs lounge of the 747, right before takeoff. I knew that she was going to be on the flight, but it was still a great thrill to meet her face to face."

"What was she wearing?" Eric asked, completely enthralled.

"A very chic wool jacket and matching skirt with a big diamond brooch on the lapel, and knee boots. And one of those pageboy wigs she always wore in the Seventies, with a small veiled hat."

"Cigarette too, right?" said Jacques.

"Of course! She was twirling it around in her hand, just dying for the 'no smoking' sign to be turned off. Downstairs, it was the usual bedlam involved in getting four hundred people through the door. She was standing over the railing, just taking in the whole scene. I thought it was curious that she was people-watching when she could have been relaxing in her seat. So I joined her at the railing and looked down, too. 'Anything interesting going on?' I asked. And she shook her head, still twirling the cigarette, and said, in *that voice*, 'Ugh, those *people*.' And I said, 'What about them?' And she looked at me and said, 'Wouldn't you like to just *shoot them ALL!*'" Sylvia burst out laughing. "Well, if I weren't a lifetime fan already, and of course I *was*, I certainly would have been after that remark!"

"That's a wonderful story," said Eric. "Oh, I wish *I* could have met her before she died."

"It was one of the highlights of my career, really," said Sylvia. "They don't make 'em like her anymore." She took the last sip of her Margarita. "Let's order another pitcher," she said gaily. "This is fun."

"What about dinner?" Jacques said, signaling for Julio, their handsome waiter. "We have to feed our young friend before he faints."

"Oh, yes, of course."

Julio brought a fresh pitcher of Margaritas to the table and began pouring.

"Eric, darling," said Sylvia, "I recommend the *enchiladas verdes*. Their *tomatilla* sauce is to die for." Once they finished ordering, she held up an empty basket. "Julio, would bring us some chips, please?"

"Right away."

"Be careful with all that salt, Sylvia," said Jacques. "Remember, you have a girdle to squeeze into tomorrow morning."

"I'll worry about that tomorrow." Sylvia sighed contentedly as she reached for her glass. "What a beautiful afternoon! And what good-looking men I have to share it with. I couldn't be happier. Oh, shit! Here comes the Double D Brigade." She ducked under the table. "Heads down, everybody!"

"Relax," said Jacques. "They're not coming in here. When they march through the lobby with those empty bags on their arms, they have only one thing on their mind, and it's not socializing."

"Who are you talking about?" said Eric.

"Pavonia and Darcy and the rest of the girls. They're on their way to Dealer Dan's."

Sylvia's head reappeared. "Imagine," she said, with utter disdain. "Flying all the way across the country to go grocery shopping. It's like going to Seattle just to bring back a one-pound bag of that bitter coffee."

"I think they like the exotic fare that Dan's has to offer," said Jacques. "They probably can't find that kind of stuff back home."

"What, they've never heard of Zabar's?" said Sylvia.

"You're assuming that they know their way around New York City," said Jacques. "Remember, most of them have never set foot on the island of Manhattan."

"Why not?" asked Eric.

"Because they're *commuters*," said Jacques. "All they know of New York is the one square block around their crash pad in Queens, and where to get the Q10 bus to the airport."

"Exactly!" said Sylvia. "You think they're gonna get on the subway and walk around the city, for even one day? God forbid! They could get raped or pillaged!"

"It seems so strange," said Eric. "Why do people live in other cities when they're based in New York? I mean, who in their right mind travels twelve hundred miles by air just to *get to* work?"

"On the standby list yet!" added Sylvia. "Remember that yammering we had to listen to, about their commute home? It'll go on all day on the flight home, like the world's longest broken record! And you know what's worse? They don't even *live* in Dallas, or Atlanta or Nashville. None of them live in cities. They all live in dip-shit small towns that are hours away from the closest airport, where all of their neighbors are just like them— white, illiterate and God-fearing."

"You're being a little harsh," Jacques said. "A lot of them are married with children, and city living isn't for everyone. They have to worry about school districts, property taxes, aging parents, etc. We're not all swinging singles who stay moored to New York City for our entire careers. Even for the ones who aren't married, I think basically they do it for the real estate. Seven hundred dollars a month goes a lot further in East Stump than it does on the Upper East Side. They can have a mansion back home for less than they'd pay for a studio apartment in New York. Not to mention, New York has always been a junior base. They hold a much better schedule here than they would at DFW."

"*Ach!*" said Sylvia, with a dismissive wave of her hand. "They all have little gold crosses pinned to their lapels and collars, where their union pins ought to be. I say it's anti-Semitism."

"Not to mention a step backward," said Eric.

"How so?" said Sylvia, eyeing him keenly.

"Well, I mean… why go to all that trouble to get this job and get away from that small-town life, only to rush right back to it once you can start flying for free?"

"Exactly!" said Sylvia. "Why bother leaving in the first place? Why not just stay there and get a job at Sears?"

"Because," said Jacques, "at Sears, they don't let you turn the bedding department into a flophouse after the store closes, just because you live fifty miles away."

"Bingo!" said Sylvia. She looked at Eric. "Have you been in operations late at night yet?"

"No."

"Well, you'll see. The commuters *without* crash pads take over, and it's not pretty."

"It's like a scene right out of *The Grapes of Wrath*," said Jacques, with a shiver.

Sylvia nodded. "*Oy*, who would ever have thought it'd come to *this?* Commuters. Crash pads. Crucifixes!"

"Hair-*don'ts!*" Jacques threw in.

"Wrinkled uniforms! Beat-up shoes and beat-up luggage! Three-hundred-pound heifers on international flights!"

"Really?" said Eric. "At *Mercury* Airways? How do they keep flying if they're over their weight limit?"

"Weight limit?!" Sylvia laughed. "Oh, *bubbee!* You really *are* fresh out of training, aren't you? I promise you, once you're off probation, they'll never put you on a scale again."

"Everything about this job has changed," said Jacques. "White gloves, weight limits and girdle checks seem like ancient history."

"Exactly!" said Sylvia. "That's the whole problem: nowadays, they hire flight attendants. Back in my day, we were stewardesses."

"What are *we?*" Eric asked, full of indignation. "Chopped liver?"

"Present company excluded, of course."

"Thank you. I'd hate to think you'd lump us in with those Flop House Florences!"

"Oh, so touchy! I think someone's blood sugar is a little low." Sylvia picked up a menu. "Let's eat!"

***

"That was a great meal," said Eric, as they left the restaurant. "Thank you both very much."

"You're very welcome," said Sylvia. "Just promise us you'll do the same for another newbie, once you've been here for a while and scrape a few bucks together."

"That may be a quite a while, but yes, I promise."

"I'm not worried about you. Some real estate mogul or stockbroker will snap you up in no time. Jacques, you'd better make your move while he's still available."

"Eric has too much integrity," replied Jacques. "He'll be a working boy for a good long while."

"Just what I wanted to hear," Eric said ruefully. "Well, what'll we do now?"

"Do *now?*" said Sylvia. "I'm off to bed. You two can do whatever you want."

"Didn't you say something about a walk on the beach?" Eric said to Jacques.

"Sure, we can do that," said Jacques. "Sylvia, why don't you come with us? The fresh air will be good for you."

"After that meal? No, thanks, I ate all my refried beans and I'd rather fart away in the privacy of my own room." She gave them both a quick peck on the cheek. "I'll see you in the morning, looking gorgeous as usual. Jacques, keep your hands to yourself."

"Why am I always cast as the big, bad wolf in these situations?"

"Because I've known you for fifteen years, that's why. Goodnight."

***

Eric and Jacques followed the road leading to the beach. The sun was just a tiny sliver of red, sinking into the ocean, as they arrived. The temperature had dropped considerably.

"This is nice," said Eric. "There's nobody else around. It's like we have the whole beach to ourselves."

"Well, how is your evening so far?" said Jacques.

"Really wonderful, thanks."

"I know we're not as exciting as bar full of gay men lusting after you, but—"

"That's not a requirement for me. I just thought it would be fun. Don't you go out to the bars at all?"

"I'm a little old for the S and M routine."

"What's that?"

"Stand and model. I just don't see the point."

"Do you see anybody right now?"

"No, not right now. What about you? Whose heart did you break when you left Texas?"

"Nobody that I can think of."

"That's good. It's better for you to be free and unfettered when you're just starting out. You shouldn't have to worry about—hey, watch it!" Jacques yanked Eric toward him as a man on roller blades, oblivious to the rest of the world, came whizzing by. "Bastard! How I *loathe* people like that. 'Out of my way! This is all *my* personal space.' "

As they resumed walking, Eric was pleased that Jacques didn't pull away. Instead, he kept his arm around Eric's waist.

"Look, there's the first evening star," said Jacques, pointing to the darkening sky. "Make a wish."

Eric closed his eyes and murmured to himself.

"What'd you wish for?"

He kept his eyes closed. "That every time I fly, I get to meet a man as handsome as you."

"Well, now, that's the kind of wish that should be sealed with a kiss." Without warning, he leaned down and sweetly planted his warm, soft lips on Eric's mouth.

"Oh, that was nice," said Eric, reeling slightly. "It's been a while."

"For me, too."

"I've been cooped up at the Charm Farm for six weeks. What's your excuse?"

"Let's just say that I haven't met anyone lately who's really rocked my world."

"Let *me* give it a try," said Eric, moving his hand down to caress Jacques' rear end.

"Eric, listen…"

"We've got not one, but *two* rooms waiting for us back at the hotel." Half-drunk from tequila, he boldly moved his hand from Jacques ass to his crotch. "We could start in yours, and finish in mine."

With a gentle tug, Jacques moved Eric's hand away. "Not tonight, OK?"

"Oh, I'm sorry," said Eric, feeling suddenly embarrassed. "Was that move too forward for Palos Verdes?"

"No. Just a little unexpected."

"Why? *You're* the one who kissed *me*. What did you expect me to do?"

"Sometimes a kiss is just a kiss. You'll find that out when you're a bit older."

"A little bit older? Who are you, all of a sudden? Ward Cleaver?"

"I'm sorry. That was a very condescending thing to say." Jacques zipped up his jacket. "Believe me, Eric, I know what I'm talking about. Crewmember entanglements are… complicated, to say the least."

"Christ, you are Ward Cleaver! All that's missing from this scene is a cardigan sweater."

"Let me update myself then. When flight attendants start fucking around together, it just leads to trouble. Jealously, suspicion, gossip—"

"Don't forget to warn me about 'the clap', too."

"I'm very sorry if you felt that I was leading you on. You're a handsome, bright young guy. If it makes you feel any better, I want you to know that it's not you, it's—"

"Don't say it!" Eric covered Jacques' mouth with his hand. "Let's just leave it at 'handsome, bright young guy,' OK?"

"With a beautiful ass," said Jacques, kissing the palm of Eric's hand.

"What the hell!"

"I may seem a little fatherly right now, but I'm not blind. Now, do you want to keep walking?"

"No. I'd rather just go back to the hotel."

"All right. Let's head back." He slipped his arm around Eric's waist again. "I hope this doesn't put a damper on what could become a very nice friendship."

"You probably ought to keep your hands to yourself." Eric pulled away and began walking a few paces ahead of Jacques.

"Oh, still a little huffy I see," said Jacques, quickly catching up with him. "Do you want me to buy you a drink in the lobby?"

"No."

"Do you want to go somewhere for dessert?"

"God, no!"

"Do you want to stop by my room to borrow some porn?"

Eric almost tripped. "*You* travel with a porn stash?"

"A small stash. I am a man, after all."

Well, since you offered… what do you have?"

***

After Eric left his room with a few choice magazines, Jacques noticed the red blinking light on his phone. Without even bothering to check the message, he dialed the front desk. "Would you connect me with Sylvia Saks, please?"

"Certainly."

She picked the phone up on the first ring. "Where've you been? I called you an hour ago."

"I was out with Eric."

"Doing what?"

"We went for a moonlight stroll on the sand. You were there when we left, remember?"

"Yes, of course I remember. And *then?*"

"And then I nailed him behind the Fat Burger on Pacific Coast Highway. Is that what you wanted to hear?"

"Don't get fresh with me. I'm old enough to be your mother."

"As if I could forget."

"Did you—"

"No, we didn't. And not because I didn't want to."

"Did he make a pass?"

"He… misinterpreted a gesture."

"Dear Jacques. You're always the gentleman, aren't you?"

"You know I don't kiss and tell."

"Of course he made a pass! One: you're too goddam good-looking and charming for your own good. Two: he's a horny twenty-something who's been cooped up in that Chicago hen house since April. Three: the moon is—"

"I hear ice tinkling in a glass. Are you still drinking?"

"It's only seltzer, I swear."

"Mmm hmm."

"I *could* use another drink though. I was just on a long phone call with Morty."

"Let me guess: was he begging you to bring home some treats from you-know-where?"

"No. He was telling me about being in court all day with Ronnie and the Bitch from Biloxi. I'm referring, of course, to Dennis Stadler's mother."

"What's the latest news?"

"She's still trying to get her hands on everything since Dennis died. Money, stocks, furniture—even the lease on their goddam apartment. She doesn't even *live* in New York! What should Ronnie do, go sleep on a park bench?"

"I don't think I can bear one more story about a relative dive-bombing in to swoop up the estate when she wouldn't even come to see her son before he died."

"She has no idea who she's up against. Morty made sure that Dennis signed all the right papers while he was still alive. Not to mention, he *relishes* handling this kind of case. He's like a pit bull. He loves telling women like Sandra Stadler that they're going back home without a fucking dime of the son's money. It serves her right, that holier-than-thou *cunt*." She sighed. "God, how I hate them all."

"Sylvia, let's be fair. We've met a lot of loving, devoted parents since the AIDS crisis started, too."

"I know. The whole situation just frustrates me."

"It's a good thing you have Morty around."

"Don't I know it? He fights the good fight and looks out for our friends. I'm a lucky woman. So what're you doing now?"

"The usual. Taking care of business and going to sleep."

"Oh, *there's* a vision I can take to my dreams! Don't you guys ever get tired of playing with yourselves?"

"Sylvia, dear, you're crossing that line again."

"Sorry, Well, then, my handsome friend, let me just say good night. And don't forget to wash your hands afterward! You're cooking for sixteen tomorrow—plus the pilots."

"I said, *good night!*"

CHAPTER 5

Anthony's Texas Two-Step

"This wine has turned," said Jim Sizemore. He was Anthony's date for the evening, and his tone was a little arrogant for Anthony's liking.

"I'm sorry, sir," said the waiter. "I'll bring you another bottle right away."

"Screw the Pinot Noire," said Jim, scanning the wine list for a second time. "Bring us the Cabernet Sauvignon instead."

"Yes, sir."

"How do you like *that*," said Jim, shaking his head.

"It happens," Anthony replied nonchalantly. "The point is that he's correcting the problem."

"Well, regardless, when I'm paying forty-five bucks for a bottle of wine, I don't expect it to taste like horse piss."

"Horse piss? That's a classy way of putting it."

Jim laughed. "Sorry. That's my Midland upbringing. It shows through sometimes. Well, I hope the *food* is better. I mean, come on. This is the Mansion at Turtle Creek. It's supposed to be the best goddam restaurant in Dallas." He reached for a piece of bread and slathered it with butter. "I hope their standards aren't starting to slip."

"When I was here for dinner *last* week," said Anthony, "everything was fine. So let's just relax." He looked closely at his date. Jim was a typically handsome, older gay Texan. He was well-built and stood over six feet tall. He had salt and pepper hair, blue eyes, and thick, dark eyebrows. His face was clean-shaven and his cologne smelled expensive. He was dressed in a starched long-sleeved shirt, pressed khaki slacks, and Italian loafers. Light from the ceiling fixtures glinted off his Rolex watch.

"This kind of thing would never happen at the Oak Room in the Plaza Hotel, I can tell you that," said Jim.

"Never?"

Never. I've been traveling to New York on business for the past twenty years, and I *know* New York."

"Let me guess," said Anthony. "The Plaza is the only New York hotel that you'd even consider staying in, right?"

Jim snorted. "I might go back to the Essex House—if they ever get a decent restaurant."

"Uh huh," Anthony replied, thinking: this guy's really good-looking, and has a lot of money, I don't think but he knows his A-train from a hole in the ground.

The waiter returned with a new bottle of wine and poured a small amount into a fresh glass.

Jim took a sip and nodded his approval.

The waiter, looking relieved, filled both their glasses.

Thank God Jim didn't swirl the wine around and start talking about its 'legs', thought Anthony. Otherwise, I'd have to split.

"Gentlemen," said the waiter, "have you decided what you'd like for dinner?"

"Yes," said Anthony. "I'd like—"

"Why don't you let me order for the both of us," said Jim. "The chef is a personal friend of mine." He rattled off two appetizers, two salads, and two main courses—all of which were the most expensive choices on the menu. "We'll discuss dessert later."

"Very well, sir," said the waiter. "Your appetizers will be served shortly."

After the waiter had left, Jim picked up his wineglass. "Cheers, Anthony."

"Cheers."

"It was fun meeting you in first class today," said Jim. "Is New York to DFW your regular run?"

"No. It just happened to be the last leg of the trip that I was on."

"But you usually work in first class, right? I mean, I can't exactly picture you slinging hash in coach."

"I work wherever."

"Coach," Jim repeated, even more disdainfully this time. "You'll never catch *me* riding back there."

"Never?"

"*Never.* I'm a million-miler with Mercury. I only fly in first."

"What about business class?"

"Are you kidding?" said Jim. "Glorified coach—all those yahoos are on upgrade tickets. They don't even know where to plug in their headsets. I'm a real premium passenger. I *pay* for first class. Fortunately, I have the means to do so." He seemed pleased to share this fact.

Oh, Christ, thought Anthony. You're one of those. I guess you're picking up the check. And you'd better be a good lay, too.

"Anyway," Jim continued, "it was nice to be served by a male flight attendant for change." He leaned closer. "Especially one as handsome as you. You're pretty new to the job, right?"

"Yeah, I've just been flying for a few weeks." At this airline, anyway.

"I thought so," said Jim. "I was surprised, though, when you told me you were based here in Dallas. Mercury seems to have a lot of crewmembers at this domicile, male and female, who are... how should I put it... past their prime."

"Yeah, I've noticed that, too." Anthony chuckled. "I can't complain, though. They've all been pretty nice to me."

"I *bet* they have," Jim said with a leer. "I mean, I know it's rough for y'all, money-wise, when you're just starting out, but..."

"But what?"

"Well, let's just say that, with a face and body like yours, you're probably not the kind of guy who's forced to stay home every night eating Ramen Noodles."

Anthony shrugged. "Myself, I'm happy with a peanut butter sandwich."

Jim laughed and poured another glass of wine for himself. "See! That's another thing I like about you, Anthony—that quick New York sense of humor. It makes me feel like I'm right back in the Big Apple." He refilled Anthony's glass, too. "D'you know who you remind me of?"

"I'm warning, you, buddy: if you say Rhoda Morgenstern, I'm walking."

Jim laughed again. "You and I are gonna get along like a house on fire. Oh, here comes our first course. Good." He discreetly squeezed Anthony's leg under the table. "I don't know about you, but I'm starving."

***

"How did you like your dinner?" asked Jim.

"It was wonderful," said Anthony.

"How about dessert now? Or a brandy?"

"I'll pass on dessert. I'll take a brandy, though."

Jim motioned for the waiter. "We'd both like Courvoisier. Make sure it's V.S.O.P."

"Yes, sir."

Do you ever order just the regular anything?" Anthony asked wryly.

"I order what I like. Why shouldn't I?"

"Do you want the truth? It seems like you're trying very hard to impress me."

"I don't need to impress anybody, especially you."

"Why especially me?"

"Because you're a—"

"Flight attendant?" Anthony pulled out his wallet. "Check, please!"

"What the hell are you talking about?"

"I may be just a working stiff, but I'm not a fucking idiot. I know when I'm being insulted."

"What's with the indignation, all of a sudden? If you had let me finish, then you'd know I was going to say you're a *date*, not a client. I work my *ass* off to impress clients. With a date, I should be able to relax and be whoever the hell I am. Fair enough?"

"Fair enough."

"OK, then." Jim clenched his jaw. "Christ, I'm just trying to show you a good time."

There was an awkward moment of silence as the waiter served them two snifters of brandy.

"Sorry, Jim," Anthony said. "I guess I jumped to conclusions."

"Let *me* jump to a conclusion: is it possible that you're just a little bit touchy about being a thirty-something-year-old man who spends his workday running up and down an airplane aisle serving drinks to men like me?"

"As *if*," said Anthony. "In case you didn't notice, I never run up and down the aisle. I take my sweet time."

"Yeah, I noticed. You like to give everybody in the cabin a good, long look at you. You had *me* snapped at attention from the moment I boarded your flight."

"I guess you've got my number, buddy."

"Enjoy it while you can. And take advantage of it. I guarantee you: ten years from now, nobody will give a shit. You'll be a *forty-year-old* man in the aisle, wearing an apron and comfortable shoes, with reading glasses perched on top of your balding head. And you know what that'll be? Sad. Guys like you don't realize—"

"Guys like me don't *own* 'comfortable' shoes. And no man in my family has ever gone bald. So there."

Jim downed his brandy in one long swallow. "If I were you, I'd drop the attitude, and consider what I'm saying as free advice from a reliable, mature source. How do you think I got to be where I am?"

Anthony rolled his eyes. "Thanks, Jim, but give me a break. You already told me that your family set you up in that design business, so you can drop all the Texas 'I pulled myself up by my own bootstraps' bullshit."

"Ouch," said Jim, pulling an imaginary dagger out of his back. "You've got me there."

"See?" Anthony grinned. "I'm never wrong."

"You fucking smart-ass," said Jim, as he squeezed Anthony's thigh again. "Will stay long enough to finish your brandy, at least?"

"Sure." Anthony tucked his wallet back into his pocket. "I didn't bring enough cash to pay for dinner, anyway."

Jim laughed. "I figured. I may be from West Texas, but *I'm* no idiot, either." Jim looked directly into Anthony's eyes. "Let's stop playing goddamn games. I know that you can have any man you want." He leaned back in his chair and spread his legs "I'm interested in you. Tell me honestly, Anthony: are you attracted to me? Sexually, I mean."

"I know what you mean." Anthony let his eyes travel downward, from Jim's handsome face to the sizeable bulge behind the zipper of the pressed khaki slacks. "Yes. I'm interested."

"All right. Let's go over to my place, have another drink, and see what happens."

"Sounds good."

Jim pulled out an American Express card. "I'm warning you though: at the risk of sounding like my old man, I think you need to be taken down a peg or two."

"Yeah?"

"Yeah."

"I guess we'll find out."

"The anticipation is killing me." Jim placed a chit on the table. "Here. Why don't you give this to the valet while I pay the check, and then wait for me outside. We'll drive over in my car. You can leave yours here tonight. I'll bring you back in the morning."

"Wrong again. I'll follow you in my own car."

"Why? Are you planning on making a quick getaway later? Should I have locked up all the good silver before I left the house?"

"No. I want my car there in case we're not a good match sexually. Sorry to be so blunt, but I've been down this road before, and I'm not spending the night on your sofa if the sex with you peters out." Anthony took the last swallow of his brandy. "Besides, you were the one who suggested that we stop playing games, right?"

"You don't seem to have very high expectations of me. Well, I wouldn't worry about that, Anthony. In the first place, I'm hotter for you than I've been for anybody else in the past five years. I guarantee you a good time. And in the second place, screw the sofa—I have eight bedrooms. You can take your pick. So drop the goddam attitude and give me a chance, OK?"

Anthony thought it over for a moment. "OK." He slipped the valet ticket into his shirt pocket. "But I'm still following you in my own car. And that's that."

***

Jim put on his turn signal in front of massive Spanish colonial-style house and turned onto the circular driveway. He paused and stuck his head out the window. "I'm going to pull into the garage in back. Just leave your car here in the driveway, Anthony."

Anthony nodded. He parked and got out of his car. "Are you sure you want me to leave my car parked in your driveway?" he asked when Jim reappeared a moment later.

"Sure, why not?"

"It's a second-hand Toyota Corolla. What will the neighbors think?"

"Fuck the neighbors. I'd let you park in the garage, but my other two cars are in there."

"What else do you drive?"

Jim grinned. "You sound more like a Dallasite every minute."

"Meaning?"

"That's an old joke. In Dallas, the first question a gay man always asks is, 'What kind of car do you want to drive?' Down in Houston, the first question is always, 'do you want to fuck me or not?' Anyway, my other cars are a Mercedes SL and an Alpha Romeo."

"What, no Learjet?"

"No," said Jim with a laugh. "You probably won't believe me, but those little planes make me nervous. I like big jetliners." He reached into his pocket for another set of keys. "Well, come on into the house."

House! thought Anthony, as they walked toward the front door. *I* live in a house. This place is a fucking mansion.

They entered the foyer. Jim led him past a staircase with an exquisitely carved banister, and into an enormous living room. The décor was modern, masculine, and austere to the point of minimalism. "Nice," said Anthony. "I like this room a lot."

"Some people find it a little sterile."

"No, I really like it. I'm a minimalist at heart, too. I'm kind of surprised how many gay guys in Dallas feel the need to decorate their home as though it were an exact replica of their grandmother's."

Jim nodded. "Lace doilies on the end tables and sofa arms, quilts on every bed, and a kitchen full of homemade preserves in mason jars." He shivered. "I can't *stand* that shit, and neither can most of my clients. Well, would you like the whole five-dollar tour?"

"Later, maybe," said Anthony, casually glancing at a monochromatic painting that hung over the fireplace. "Nice."

"Isn't it?" said Jim, beaming with pride. "That was painted by an artist named—"

"Yves Klein. His International Blue. I've seen his work in several homes."

"Oh, have you?"

"Yeah. Why don't we just head upstairs, or wherever the bedroom is."

"Right this way," said Jim, as he began climbing the staircase.

Fuck, thought Anthony, as he scanned the artwork lining the walls. Look at that! This guy has money—and it's not monopoly money. He has *real fucking money.*

"Do you like the Pollack?" Jim asked. "That's one of my favorites."

Anthony gestured toward another painting. "It's very nice, but I prefer the Rauschenberg."

"I'm surprised to hear that name coming out of your mouth."

"Why?"

"You just didn't strike me as the type who spends his free time strolling through the art galleries on West Fifty-seventh Street."

"I dated an art dealer in New York a few years ago. He only bought and sold high-end stuff."

"Oh. Whatever happened to him?"

"He opened a gallery in Paris, and things got complicated."

"I guess Paris' loss is my gain."

"For tonight, at least."

Jim led Anthony into a room on the third floor. It was a large, rectangular room. Like the rest of the house, it was decorated in a minimalist, yet masculine, style. The one luxurious item in the room was the plush carpeting. There'll be no rug burns tonight, Anthony thought, as he stepped into the room. This guy's thought of everything. Against one wall, there was a king-sized bed covered in black leather sheets, complemented by a black leather headboard. A small, maple nightstand was placed on each side of the bed. "Funny," said Anthony, nodding toward the bed. "I'd have pegged you for a guy who slept in red satin sheets."

"Oh, I have those, too," said Jim, slipping his arm around Anthony's waist. "But right now, they're on a bed in one of the guest rooms."

"Good," said Anthony. "I always sweat on satin sheets, and then I end up slipping right onto the floor."

"Ditto." Jim grinned. "That's why they're on a bed on one of the guest rooms."

The wall to the left of the bed was mirrored, yet it was a single, wall-sized piece of highly-polished glass, rather than mirrored tiles. The wall to the right was covered with floor-to-ceiling drapes that extended the length of the wall.

"What's behind that?" said Anthony, pointing a large maple panel in the wall directly across from the bed. "A jail cell with a leather sling suspended from the ceiling?"

"No, just a hi-fi system, a VCR and a wide-screen TV. As you can tell, I like the uncluttered look. The entertainment system operates via remote control. I generally never have the TV on in here, unless I'm watching the evening news or a movie or—"

"Porn," Anthony interjected, with a grin. "Speaking of which, I like that mirror-covered wall a lot. Just think, it you had ten guys in here for an orgy, it would seem like twenty."

"True," said Jim. "But that's not the only reason for the mirror." He picked up a remote control and pushed a button. The recessed lights in the ceiling immediately turned off. "Now, watch this." He pushed another button, which opened the curtains to reveal a stunning view of the Dallas skyline.

"Sweet," said Anthony.

"It's not New York City, but it *is* beautiful, nonetheless," Jim said with pride. "And see how it's reflected in the mirror on the other side?"

"Yeah, that is nice. It's kind of like we're floating among the skyscrapers."

"That was my intention," said Jim. "I designed the entire house, including this room."

"You should be proud of yourself. You did a great job."

"Thanks. Well, Anthony, if you're a good boy, maybe you'll get to come over here on a regular basis."

It was such a condescending thing to say that Anthony's immediate impulse was to say, "Fuck you," and head right down the stairs to his car. But he didn't say a word. One of the two men *would* be taken down a peg or two tonight, but it wasn't going to be Anthony.

"Make yourself comfortable," said Jim. "I'll go get us some brandy."

"Make sure it's Courvoisier V.S.O.P."

"I don't have any other kind in my house."

"How about putting on some music?"

"Sure. I think you'll like this." Jim pressed a button. "I had it custom-mixed by a DJ in the Pines last summer."

"Hey, that's nice," said Anthony, as he listened to the first song. "Good music for fucking."

"Yeah, that's exactly what I thought the first time I heard it. Go on, make yourself comfortable. I'll be right back."

As soon as Jim left the room, Anthony kicked off his shoes. He didn't even pay attention to where they landed. Then he unbuckled his belt and unzipped his jeans. He tossed the jeans over a chair next to the bed, and then pulled off his shirt. Underneath the jeans, he wore a white Bike-brand jock strap. He climbed onto the bed and opened the drawer in the nightstand to see what kind of supplies Jim had stocked. Inside, he found several wash clothes, a box of condoms, a tube of KY gel and a brand-new bottle of poppers.

Anthony examined the label on the bottle. It was Jungle Juice: the real stuff, from London—not the crap brand of poppers that was usually on sale at gay bookstores in the U.S. One whiff of Jungle Juice would practically blow your head off—and turn you into a cock-craving whore. If anybody was going to act like a cock-craving whore, Anthony decided, it would be Jim. He left the bottle on the nightstand and made himself comfortable on the bed. He gazed at his reflection in the mirror and was very pleased. He was magnificent from his curly brown hair all the way down to his beautifully-formed, size eleven feet. And he knew it.

A moment later, Jim came back into the room. "You won't believe this, but I'm out of Courvoisier. So I hope you don't mind I brought us some—Jesus fucking Christ!" The glasses in his hand fell to the floor. He stood, open-mouthed, as he took in the sight of Anthony lying naked in his bed.

Anthony stretched out and put one of his hands behind his head, making his melon-sized bicep muscle pop. With the other hand, he pulled the jockstrap to one side and enjoyed the sight of his six-inch flaccid penis growing to a full nine inches right before Jim's eyes. "What the fuck are you looking at?"

"I… this is gonna stain…" Jim stammered, as he his eyes darted back and forth between Anthony's penis and the brown stain on the floor. "This carpet cost me—"

"Fuck the carpet," said Anthony, taking his dick in his hand. "I know what you want."

"What do you think I want?" Jim's gaze was now firmly fixed on Anthony's crotch.

Anthony pulled back his foreskin, which made the head of his big cock swelled even more. "You want this, don't you?"

"I want to…" Jim crept closer. "Can I just… hold it in my hand for a minute?"

"Yeah, come on over here."

Jim crept toward the edge of the bed. "Would you mind moving closer to me?" he whispered.

"You want it, you come *here*." Anthony casually tugged at his enormous balls. Then he turned to look out the window as if he couldn't have cared less whether Jim stayed in the bedroom or went downstairs to make an apple pie. "Tell me what you want, fucker."

"I want…" Jim licked his lips. "I want your dick."

"This isn't just any dick, buddy."

"I want your big, fat, uncut Italian dick."

"Where do you want it?"

Jim tried to form the words, but apparently couldn't.

"I *said*, tell me where you want it."

"In my mouth."

"Yeah? Take off your clothes," Anthony commanded.

Jim stripped off his shirt so fast that several buttons broke.

"Good boy," said Anthony. "Now the rest of it."

Just as quickly, Jim removed his belt buckle, slacks, and underwear.

Anthony snapped his fingers. "The socks, too."

Hypnotized, Jim complied. He was now completely naked. "Give it to me."

"Fuck you. Don't order me. *Ask* me for it."

"Please, can I have your dick?"

"Try again."

"Please, *sir*, may I have your cock?"

"That's better. Now, get on your knees."

"I've got a bum right knee. Would you hand me a pillow, please, sir?"

Anthony tossed one toward him. "Here you go, old man. Prop yourself up."

"Can I have a hit of poppers, sir?"

"Yeah, you can have a hit." Anthony bobbed and weaved his dick in front of Jim's face. Then he reached for the brown bottle, unscrewed it, and held it under Jim's nostrils.

Jim inhaled deeply. His eyes rolled back in his head as he opened his mouth. "Please let me have it!"

"Have what?"

"Your cock, sir. That's all I want, and all that I need."

"What about your cars and your carpet and your eight bedrooms and all your fucking artwork?"

"Don't need 'em, sir." Jim's hand was furiously pounding his own sizeable dick. "I only need your cock… *please,* sir! I'm begging you!"

Anthony grinned as he pulled Jim's head forward. "That's just what I thought you would say."

CHAPTER 6

Big City, Small World

"Well, what do you think? Do you like it?"

With great trepidation, Flight Attendant Ginnie Jo Burke lifted her head and peered into the lighted mirror in front of her. As she took in the sight of her head crowned with long, cork-screw brick-red curls, she sighed with pleasure. "Oh, thank God. I have hair again!"

"It's a perfect match to your natural shade," said Fiona, her British hairdresser, spinning the chair gently from side to side.

"You're sure this thing will stay on, Fiona?"

"Yes, just make sure you pin it here and here and *here*."

"I bet this is gonna be hot on the airplane."

"Yes, dear, the passengers will all be completely enamored of you, just like the old days."

"No, I mean hot as in: I'm gonna *fry* in this thing all summer long."

"Well, darling, you can't keep walking around New York City with that crew cut. You looked like a tragic cross between Joan of Arc and a Lesbian Avenger."

"Yeah, I'm aware of that." Ginnie Jo carefully fluffed her hair. "I thought I could just get by with a little extra eye makeup, but—"

"There isn't enough Midnight Magic Eyeliner in the world for you to pull off that look. It's been almost a month, and you're still practically bald. Who did this to you, anyway?"

"Madge *fucking* Baxter."

"Darling, careful, you're spitting on me! Who is Madge Baxter?"

"The dried-up old bitch that runs the Mercury Airways Training Center in Chicago."

"But *why* did she scalp you?"

"We were doing a mock meal service one day, and I served her lasagna with a hair in it. It was *my* hair."

"Dear God in heaven." Fiona shook her head. "I will never understand the strange world of air hostesses, or what you'll put up with to start all over again at a different airline. The job simply *can't* be worth it."

"Initially, no. But in the long run, definitely."

Fiona picked up a teasing comb and tried to give Ginnie Jo more volume on the top of her head. "When is your next trip?"

"Hard to say. I'm on reserve this month. I was off today, but I go back on call at midnight."

"On call at midnight." Fiona clucked disapprovingly. "Like a real call girl."

Ginnie Jo rolled her eyes. "I assure you that the girls at British Airways sometimes start their workday at midnight."

"All right, darling, you do seem determined to make the best of a bad situation. Do you want to try out the new look right now? You should have a little practice run before your next flight. Believe it or not, this will take some getting used to."

"Sure. Where?"

"Right here. Take a stroll around the neighborhood. Catch your reflection in a store window. See whether any Madison Avenue men on are casting sidelong glances. Then decide if you really want to go through with this, or if you'd rather go *au natural* until your hair grows back."

"That is not an option. I'm wearing this damn thing for as long as I have to."

"Then go strut your stuff." Fiona glanced at her appointment book. "Come back in an hour if anything needs tightening."

"I beg your fucking pardon?"

"Relax, darling," said Fiona, eyeing her appointment book. "I'm talking about your *wig,* not your *whatsit.*"

***

Ginnie Jo left the salon and stepped out onto the street. At five P.M., there seemed to be thousands of people converging on the corner of 59th Street and Lexington Avenue, all racing for buses, cabs and the subway. She suddenly noticed a familiar, chestnut-haired young man about a half a block away from her. Eric Saunders was standing near the main entrance to Bloomingdale's. He looked dazed, as though he and his house had just been dropped by a cyclone into Munchkinland. She decided to save him from the horde of rush hour commuters before he was trampled to death. "Hey, you!" she said, as she walked over and grabbed him by his arm. "Tell me something: are you a good witch or a bad witch?"

He looked at her for a few seconds and then blinked. "Ginnie Jo! What are you doing here?"

"I live here too, remember?"

"Sorry, it's just such a surprise to run into here on the street." He looked at her closely. "You look so different. The last time I saw you, you didn't have any... I mean, your hair was—"

"Fooled ya. It's a wig. How does it look?"

"Great. I'd never have known if you hadn't told me."

What're you doing in this neighborhood?"

"Sight-seeing."

"On this corner? What's to see?"

"Bloomingdales. I've never been here before. I was in Central Park all day."

She couldn't resist. "Trolling through the Rambles, looking for a little action?"

"The what?"

"Never mind. What'd you see in Central Park?"

"Belvedere Castle. Bethesda Fountain. Strawberry Fields, and the Dakota Building. Did you know that Lauren Bacall lives there?"

"Yeah. I think everybody in the world knows that. Where else have you been since you arrived?"

"Uh, let's see: Rockefeller Center, Times Square, Macy's on Thirty-fourth Street, Battery Park and the World Trade Center, Chelsea, the West Village—a couple of times—Little Italy, and Chinatown, which I'll never set foot in again."

"No more Chinatown? You're gonna miss out on some good food."

Eric blanched. "I wouldn't even look at a menu in a neighborhood where grown men blow their snot right into the street—much less eat in a restaurant."

She nodded. "It's hard getting used to some people's habits. What else have you seen?"

"That's everything. It has only been a month."

"What about the Empire State Building and the Statue of Liberty?"

"I'm saving the big stuff for when Anthony comes back."

"You look thirsty. Do you want to go have a drink?"

"I'm sorry, but I can't afford it," Eric said sheepishly. "I'm trying to do New York on ten dollars a day, and I've already spent seven. I can buy a candy bar and a token for subway ride back to Queens."

"You're obviously hanging out in the wrong neighborhoods. There's a sugar daddy just waiting for you at the Townhouse Bar on East Fifty-third Street. Besides, it'd be my treat. I owe you an apology."

"For what?"

"For being an asshole to you on graduation day. When you invited me for coffee right before we boarded our flight to New York, remember? I'm sorry I was so rude. I just had to get the fuck out of there!"

"I felt the same way. We *all* did."

"No excuse for my behavior, though. Come on, let me make it up to you."

"In that case, Ginnie Jo, yes, I'd love a drink. Might there be some pretzels or something else to go along with it?"

"Follow me, Dorothy Gale."

***

She led him to a booth inside a dark, cool bar down the street, where she was friendly with one of the bartenders. "Eddie, bring me a Glenlivet up with a soda back. What'll you have, Eric?"

"I'd like a vodka martini with three olives, please."

"Any particular vodka?" asked the bartender.

"No, your well brand is fine," Eric replied.

"Make it Stoli, Eddie," said Ginnie Jo. "And bring us a big bowl of whatever you're serving for happy hour munchies."

"Coming up."

"Why three olives?" she asked after Eddie had left.

"Force of habit," said Eric. "Anthony always ate at least one."

"Gotcha," she said, pulling a pink leather Dunhill cigarette case out of her purse. "Old habits die hard. Want a smoke?"

"God, yes!" He eagerly reached for a cigarette, put it between his lips, and was about to let Ginnie Jo light it for him when he suddenly removed it. "Wait, wait!"

"What's the matter?"

"Let's wait for a second, until our drinks come."

Eddie appeared a moment later and set down two cocktails, along with a bowl of salted snack mix.

Ginnie Jo picked up her glass. "Did you want to make a toast or something?"

"Yes. Here's to running into old friends who are kind enough to buy you a drink."

"Cheers. I'm happy to do it."

Eric took a sip of his drink and then placed the cigarette expectantly back between his lips.

"Now?" said Ginnie Jo, ready to strike a match.

"Now." He inhaled deeply. "Oh, God… nicotine! I gave up smoking two weeks ago. I'm economizing, or trying to, anyway." He leaned back into the leather booth. "This is nice." He stretched his legs out. "It feels good to sit down. I didn't realize how long I'd been on my feet today."

"You gotta take a load off whenever you can," said Ginnie Jo. "Newbies always overdo it. Remember, you *live* here now. You don't have to see everything in the first month. So, have you worked a trip yet?"

"Yes, a couple: one L.A., one three-day Minneapolis-Chicago trip, one Miami layover, and several airport standby shifts where they didn't fly me anywhere."

"And?"

"L.A. was great. I went out with a couple of senior flight attendants for Mexican food and margaritas. Minneapolis and Chicago, I barely remember, we were on duty for so long all three days. And Miami was stiflingly hot. Thank

God it's not like that here." He took a drag from his cigarette and smiled. "I *like* New York in June."

"Just wait, sugar. The first of July is only a few days away." She took a sip of her drink. "Speaking of likes, how do you like the subway?"

"The New York City subway? It's the greatest invention in the world."

"Really?"

"Absolutely! Just think about it: you walk down a flight of stairs, look at the map, pay a dollar and fifty cents, and you can go anywhere you want in New York City. You walk up a different flight of stairs at the next stop, and you're in a whole different world. It's like a magic carpet ride that costs almost nothing."

"Uh huh," she replied, thinking: I guess he hasn't had a subway rat run over his foot yet.

"I love New York," said Eric, "and I love the subway system because you can get anywhere you want to go without putting cars in the equation. I hate cars. With the subway, you never have to worry about cars breaking down, or getting a flat tire on the freeway, or somebody forgetting to pick you up, or planning on how you're going to escape."

"Escape from what?"

"From suburbia. I was raised in the suburbs—of Texas, mind you—and I hate them. I hate strip malls and megachurches and bland subdivisions, where every street is named after a different tree, and you can never find your way out. You could drive around for hours and never find the goddam exit!"

"Then it's a good thing you're here. How's your living situation?"

"Queens is OK. I'm sure I'll be living in Manhattan by Christmas, as soon as—"

"Anthony comes back to New York. I know. In the meantime, how is it living with Sammy?"

"Oh, I forgot that you knew him. Sammy is pretty much what I expected. He's not very bright, he keeps the place like a pigsty, and his friends are all loudmouths who sit around every night drinking beer and bullshitting. I cannot believe that he and Anthony are brothers."

"But he's kinda hot, don't you think?"

"What do you mean?"

"I mean, if he tried to crawl into your bed one night, you wouldn't kick him out, would you?"

"Oh, please!" He started munching the snack mix. "If I wanted a guy with a jet-black pompadour and a gold crucifix nestled in his chest hair, I'd make a beeline for Pinocchio's."

"What's Pinocchio's?"

"It's the gay bar around the corner from the apartment. I've been there a couple of times."

And?"

"There are three distinct groups of men there: domestic flight attendants, who are only there because it's a two-for-one drink night; condescending international flight attendants, who try to act like they didn't come in just because it's two-for-one drink night, and who will not even consider speaking to a domestic flight attendant; and the local guys in ribbed-knit muscle shirts who look just like Sammy."

"Don't be so quick to brush off the locals. They can be pretty good lays."

"Sage advice," said Eric, gobbling up the last of the snack mix. "Oh, I'm sorry. I made a real pig of myself." He held up the empty bowl as he licked salt from his lips. "Maybe we could ask for more. I mean, if *you* want some."

She took the bowl from his hands and eyed him critically. "You've lost weight since the last time I saw you. At least five pounds, if not more."

"I have to watch my weight limit, like everyone else."

"Are you getting enough to eat?"

"Now and then. Could you ask Eddie for more snacks, please?"

"Fuck the snack mix. Let me pay up and we'll go to the French restaurant next door." She waved for the bartender. "You need some real food."

"I told you, I can't afford—"

"Relax. I'm buying."

"But I couldn't let you—"

"Stop!" She grabbed her hair in frustration. "Listen to me: you've got to stop acting like you're Anne Baxter in *All About Eve*. If somebody in this town wants to treat you to a meal, with no strings attached, let them *do* it. Believe me, it won't happen very often, even for a pretty boy like you."

"OK," said Eric. "I'd love that. I'm warning you, though, since there are no strings attached, I'll be ordering multiple courses."

"Good. I could use the company. I've been cooped up in my apartment for the last four days on reserve. Crew scheduling didn't call, and neither did anyone else. Today is my only day off. Where the hell is Eddie with that check?"

"I see him coming," said Eric. "Hang on a second." He reached across the table and tugged her hair firmly with both hands.

"What's the matter?" said Ginnie Jo.

"You pulled your wig askew a minute ago."

"Oh my god, I forgot! Thanks!" She dove for a compact mirror as Eddie approached the table.

"Anytime," said Eric. "Just looking out for you."

***

Oh, Lord! thought Ginnie Jo, throwing open her apartment door and running the bathroom. That's what I get for ordering *cassoulet* in the summer. She hoped Eric had made it back to Queens without having a bathroom emergency. The last place you'd want to be when nature urgently called was on a subway car traveling under the East River.

As she walked out of the bathroom, the phone rang. She debated whether or not to answer. Technically, she didn't have to be available to crew scheduling until midnight. Then again, if they were going to send her to Bismarck at five A.M., it would be better to know about it now. She picked up the phone. "Hello."

"*Ciao, bella.*"

"Oh, fuck. What do you want?"

The caller grunted. "Hey, nice way to greet an old friend."

"Sorry. What can I do for you, 'old friend'?"

"I heard you were back in town and wanted to call and say hello."

"Isn't that funny. I was just talking about you an hour ago. I ran into Eric on Lexington Avenue."

"So, how did everything go at training in... Dallas, was it?"

"Uh, do you mean *Chicago*? It was fine. Got my new wings and everything."

"Good. Welcome back. How's life on the Upper East Side?"

"Same as it always it." She lit a cigarette. "Except there're more fucking mothers with double-wide strollers on the street every day. They take up the whole sidewalk! I swear to God, I'm gonna start shoving them into moving traffic."

"It's the same all over. So, where've you been hanging out?"

"Right here, waiting for 'screw' scheduling to call. I'm on reserve. Where've you been hanging out, besides the Off Track Betting booth on Queens Boulevard?"

He laughed. "I branched out. I'm playing poker now. I've gotten pretty good at it. I'm thinking about turning pro."

She rolled her eyes. "Good luck with that. Let me know how it turns out. Well, it's been nice catching up with you, Sammy, but I've gotta go. I need to keep this line open in case they call me for a trip."

"OK. Hey, listen, before we hang up, can you loan me five hundred dollars?"

She snorted. "Please hold, sir, while I transfer your call to the psych ward at Bellevue Hospital."

"What the—"

"If you think *I'm* gonna loan you five hundred dollars, you're out of your mind."

"I'll pay you back by July first, I swear. Come *on*, I'm in a real bind here."

"No way. And do you know why? Because I'd never get it back."

"But I—"

"If you're really desperate for cash, then stuff your oversized *schlong* into a jock strap and head over to Man's World on Eight Avenue. Maybe they'll give you back that little dressing room where you used to do 'massages' between performances."

"*No*. I don't do that shit anymore. It's fucking undignified."

"Oh, excuse me! Well, if you're looking for a nobler pursuit, then you could try lifting wallets at the Port Authority Bus Terminal. Good location for you: Man's World is right around the corner, in case you turn out to be a lousy pickpocket. Or you could always place a new ad for body rubs in the local gay mags. You used to do pretty well doing that 'gay for pay' straight boy routine. Easy money."

"I can't believe you won't help me. Rent's due. I'm gonna be out in the fucking cold!"

"It's summertime, babe. You can sleep on a park bench."

"You know…" His voice took on a menacing tone. "If you fuck me, you fuck the hayseed, too."

She bristled. "Sammy, if Eric ends up without a roof over his head because you can't get your shit together, I'll personally come out to Queens with a baseball bat and knock your sorry ass all the way to Montauk."

"Relax, will ya! I was kidding. I'll figure something out."

"You'd better. I have to go now. What *are* you gonna to do about making that rent money?"

He sighed. "I guess I'll wash out my jock strap and go crawling back to the owner of Man's World. Maybe he will rehire me."

She giggled nastily. "You'd make more money wearing a stained one. The clientele there likes it down and dirty, remember?"

"Yeah, I remember. Well, that's that. I guess I'll talk to you later."

"One more thing, Sammy: as far as Eric is concerned, keep your fucking hands to yourself."

"Meaning?"

"You know what I mean. He's a nice kid. Getting mixed up with someone like you is the last thing he needs right now. If you get horny in the middle of the night and feel like playing grab ass him, go jack off in the bathroom and leave him alone."

"You make me sound like a real fucking pig."

"You are. Now I've really gotta go, Sammy. Later."

CHAPTER 7

Ultra Eric

"Hey, you! The Q33 bus is here."

"Huh?" Eric struggled to open his eyes. "What?"

"Wake up, sleepy head." He felt a little tap on his shoulder. "Aren't you going to La Guardia?"

"To *where?*" He was suddenly wide awake. It was completely dark outside. He was standing on a street corner, in uniform, with his head propped against a street lamp. "The bus to La Guardia! Did I miss it?"

"No," said the woman who had awakened him. "But you got 'bout thirty seconds to get on it before it does leave." She waived at the bus driver, who'd started the engine. "Hold on! You got one more."

"Wait, *wait!*" Eric exclaimed. "Where's my luggage?"

"It's right behind you."

"Oh! Thank you."

"You'd better start keepin' an eye on your shit, baby boy. You can't be sleepin' around here. There's all kinds of suspicious folks lurkin' about."

"My God," he said disbelievingly. "Who else in their right mind is even *awake* at this hour of the night?"

"*Morning,*" she said. "It's four-thirty in the morning. And these hoodlums will cut off your hand for a five-dollar Chinatown watch, much less a suitcase."

"Right," he said, as he boarded the bus. "Thanks for your help." He greeted the driver and paid his fare. Then he sat down and shoved his suitcase underneath the seat. He started to place the tote bag on his lap, then remembered it had been resting on the filthy pavement at the bus station. He placed it on the vacant seat next to him instead. "Sir," he said to the driver. "Would you please let me know when we arrive at the main terminal, just in case I fall asleep?"

"Not a morning person, are you?" The driver's voice was surprisingly pleasant.

"Not by a long shot."

"Where are you going so early?"

"To DFW and… I forget where else. They just called me out. All I know is that I have to be there by five A.M."

"You're pushing it."

"I know. But this is the earliest bus to La Guardia, and I can't afford a car service."

"The airlines don't pay you people shit, do they? You're lucky they didn't make you go all the way to Newark."

"I know. I'd have had to walk, I guess."

"You should get yourself a union job, like me."

"I *have* a union job. New-hire pay is still terrible."

The driver winked at him in the mirror. "Tell you what. You can snooze for the next twenty minutes. I'll keep an eye on you."

"Thank you," Eric replied gratefully. "I'm not sure, but I think I have a very long day ahead."

***

As Eric entered the terminal, he was surprised to see how many people were already lined up at the ticket counter. It was still dark outside; he'd expected a ghost town. The coffee shop was already open and full of customers. I'll stop and get a cup on my way to the gate, he thought. I'd better go to ops and sign in first.

Flight Operations at La Guardia was located behind the coffee shop. Eric opened the door and stepped into a long, dark, depressing hallway. The walls hadn't been painted in years. The carpet was threadbare and smelled of mildew. Broken wheelchairs and discarded cardboard boxes littered both sides of the hallway. How can they keep the terminal looking so nice, he wondered, and leave the employee side of the building looking so terrible? He took out his flashlight and lit a path for himself as he walked cautiously toward the end of the hallway. La Guardia ops was infamous for its rodent infestation.

He reached operations and opened the door. The light inside wasn't much brighter than in the hallway. He leaned his suitcase against a desk and walked toward a bank of computers in the corner. Another flight attendant was standing there, engrossed in the screen in front of her. "Hi," Eric said brightly, trying to summon an early-riser personality. "Are you going to DFW, by any chance?"

"Yes, I am," she whispered.

"My name's Eric. What yours?"

"Shhh!" The flight attendant gestured wildly toward the adjacent break room. "They're sleeping in there!"

"Oh," he whispered, wondering who 'they' were. He peered into the next room but could only see vague lumps covered with red coach blankets. He started to sign in on the computer next to her, but the room was so dark that he couldn't see his fingers on the keyboard. He reached for the light switch on the wall.

"Don't!" She grabbed his wrist. "What are you trying to do, start World War Three with the commuters?"

"I can't *see* anything. I have to sign in and pull up my paperwork."

"Be *quiet!*" someone yelled from the next room. The admonishment was immediately followed by a loud, sustained fart.

"Oh, my God! How can anyone sleep through *that?*" Rachael covered her nose with one hand, and with the other, she used a penlight to illuminate the computer keyboard. "Just sign in," she whispered, "and you can print up the rest of your paperwork at the gate."

"Thanks."

"Oh, Jesus," she said, gagging, "Let's get out of here!" They grabbed their luggage and headed out the door. "How I loathe flying out of La Guardia, especially early in the morning!" she said, as they stumbled toward a small patch of light at the end of the hallway. "Give me a JFK trip any day. I'm Rachael, by the way."

"Nice to meet you," he said as he held the door open for her.

Rachael was a pretty blonde with an elegant swing haircut who appeared to be around the same age as Eric. "Ah, this is better: lights, people, action!" She nodded toward the coffee shop. "Do you want to stop for breakfast? We have plenty of time."

"We get a crew meal today, don't we?"

She snorted. "If you can call it that."

"I think I'll hold off. But I'll treat you to a cup of coffee."

"Save your money. We can get all the free coffee we want once we're on the plane. Ugh! Look at the line for security. We'll have to plow through."

Eric sighed. "People make such a fuss when we cut in line."

"Too bad," said Rachael. "There should be an employee-only line. We're *working*." She scanned the crowd for the easiest entry point. "See that old lady in the wheelchair, with her husband standing behind her? She'll take forever to be processed and to get her chair scanned. Let's slip in front of them. Excuse us, folks. Excuse us, please, thank you."

'Hey!" yelled the husband. "That's not fair! We've all been waiting our turn!"

"Sorry, sir," Rachael replied, with a smile. "If we don't get there on time, *you* don't leave on time." She dropped her bags on the conveyer belt. "Tittie baby," she muttered, as she walked through the metal detector with Eric on her heels. "Let's see, I think we're going out of Gate 10."

"I didn't even get a chance to look at this trip when I signed in. Where do we layover?"

"Huntsville tonight, Little Rock tomorrow. The fun never ends!"

"Are we on a 737?"

"You wish. We're on an Ultra Jet."

"Really? What fun! This'll be my first flight on Ultra Jet."

"Didn't you work on one in training?"

"Only the mock-up, for a meal service. It wasn't like being on the actual plane."

"Well, there's nothing 'ultra' about this airplane. Hey, watch out for the stroller!" She yanked him aside. "That woman was coming right at you! Didn't you see her?"

"No. I didn't get much sleep last night. They called me out for this trip at one in the morning. I never got back to sleep afterward."

"What position are you?"

"Number two—coach galley."

"Lucky you. During boarding, at least, you can stay in the galley and avoid dealing with the passengers. And your jump seat is against the back wall, out of passenger view. My jump seat is right next to the galley. Passengers always want to chat me up during takeoff and landing."

As they reached the gate, the airplane was arriving from the hangar. The Ultra Jet was an updated version of a twin-engine airliner that had first gone into service in the 1960s. The engines were mounted on either side near the tail, which made for a notoriously noisy ride in the back of the plane. An emergency exit was built into the rear wall. As flight attendant number two, Eric would be responsible for opening it if an evacuation occurred. He remembered from training that the exit was tricky to operate. Opening it in the emergency mode required a complex set of maneuvers. The backup procedures, used in the event of a system failure, were even more nerve-racking. Performing that drill in training had resulted in the one assignment that Eric failed—twice—before he passed. "Do you mind reviewing the rear exit drill with me once we're on board, just in case?" he asked Rachael.

"No problem." They walked down the jet bridge and boarded the airplane. "Well," she said resignedly, "this is home for the next three days."

Eric stopped in the middle of the first-class cabin and was overcome by a terrible odor. "What is that smell?" he said, trying not to gag. "This doesn't smell like an airplane. It smells like the back of a goddam inter-city bus!"

"The Ultra Jet always smells like this. It's the disinfectant fluid they use in the toilets. Just wait until we get to the last row." They started walking down the aisle toward the back. "The coach lavs, of course, are right by our jump seats."

"Christ!" Eric exclaimed, as he clumsily bumped his suitcase against empty rows of seats in the airplane's narrow aisle. "It's hot on here!"

"We'll have to call maintenance to turn on the air conditioning. The pilots usually do it, but they're not here yet. Give me a second to stow my bags, and I'll go call maintenance. Gee, I wonder where the number one is. We can't start boarding without her."

Eric wiped sweat from his forehead. "Rachel, we can't board this airplane even if she were here! It must be a hundred degrees on here!"

"So take off your blazer and loosen your tie. Why are you buttoned up like Pee-Wee Herman, anyway? It's August, for Christ's sake!"

"I'm *supposed to* wear my blazer for boarding."

She shrugged. "Then leave it on and sweat to death. If you come to your senses, there's a hanger for you on the coat rack on the back wall. In the meantime, let's try opening all the air vents above the seats. That will help a little."

"What closet do we put our luggage in?"

"There's no closet back here," she said, tossing her suitcase into the last overhead bin. "Throw your suitcase up there, and we'll hide our tote bags in an empty cart in the galley."

"What if the passengers sitting in that row have luggage to stow overhead?"

"They'll have to use another bin. We're going to run out of room on every leg of this trip, so get used to it. These planes were built before everyone started bringing a suitcase on board with them. The people who come on last will have to gate-check their Rollaboards."

"It's ridiculous that this airplane has no closets. I was on a 767 to L.A. last week, and there were two closets just for first class."

She sighed. "How long have you been flying?"

"Six weeks."

"Really? Six weeks, and you're that fussy about the plane that you're working on? Listen, honey child, if you want to make it to six months and get off probation, you'd better get with the program. This is a crappy, junior, three-day narrow-body sequence—*not* a transcon. So take off that damn blazer, calm down, and accept it for what it is, OK?"

"Yes, ma'am."

"Hey, you guys," said another flight attendant walking toward them. "I'm Darlene, the number one. You must be Eric and Rachael. Shit, it's hot on here!" She pulled back her long braids and fashioned them into a ponytail. "Don't worry, I already called maintenance to come and turn on the AC. And to dump my lav, too. It smells like an outhouse up front! Have you checked yours yet?"

"No," said Rachael. "I haven't even opened the lav door. I don't want this one to pass out from the fumes." She nodded at Eric. "He's delicate. Hey, where's the rest of the crew?"

"We're *it*, girl," Darlene. "We have FAA minimum crew today."

"Just the three of us to serve breakfast to *all* these people this morning?" Rachael said indignantly.

"Probably for the whole trip! There's a system-wide crew shortage this month. It's the usual summertime bullshit: too many people on the sick list to cover all the trips. Sick, my foot. You *know* those stews are all sunning themselves at the Jersey shore. I'll hold off on serving breakfast in first class until you've finished in the back. Then one of you can come up front and help me."

"Don't count on it," said Rachel. "We'll be lucky if we finish picking up all the coach trays before we land. Eric's new, and on reserve, and he got no sleep last night—the poor thing."

"That's the best way to break him in," said Darlene. She glanced at a piece of paper in her hand. "Lordy, look at this standby list! We'll have to strap 'em to the wings. Don't be surprised if we have jump-seaters in the front *and* the back, on every leg of the trip. Hey, Eric!" She poked him in the ribs. "Do I need to prop your eyes open with toothpicks?"

"I'm sorry, I'm just not an early-morning person."

"Well, make yourself some coffee and let's get this show on the road." She turned and headed back to the front.

"I'm going with her," said Rachael. "I have to direct at the front door. Do you know how to set up the galley?"

"Of course. Hey, can we go over my exit operation and evacuation drill, please?"

"Oh, yeah, I forgot." She reviewed the complicated process with him step-by-step. "Any questions?"

"No. Thank you, Rachael."

"That exit scares me to death. God forbid you should ever have to use it. It'd be very easy to get trapped back here, and then trampled by hysterical passengers—the ones who're too busy to pay attention during the safety demo."

"Yes, I'm already familiar with that type of traveler."

"We're boarding," Darlene's voice crackled over the PA system.

"Coming!" said Rachael. "One more thing, Eric: if there's ever a fire back here, don't try to play the big hero and save everyone. Just get the hell out, whichever way you can. If anyone questions you later, you were *pushed* out the door by frantic passengers. Otherwise, you'll be the bottom crust of a crispy critter pie. It happened to a flight attendant at another airline just a few years ago during a runway incursion. He never had a chance."

"Thanks. I'll bear that in mind as we're hurtling down the runway for takeoff."

"Well, your eyeballs are open now! See you in a few."

                                    ***

Eric marched into the galley, picked up the crew phone and dialed first class. "Hello, this is Darlene."

"This is Eric," he said tersely. "There's no more room for bags back here. None! Not even for a purse."

"OK, baby boy, relax. I'll tell the agent. Send the passengers up to the front with their suitcases and we'll start gate-checking them. It's as simple as that."

"Thank you." He hung up the phone. "I'm sorry, sir," he said to the passenger standing in front of him. "But there's no more room for large bags back here."

"What do you mean?"

"I mean, sir, that there is no more room. All the overhead bins are full. Please take your suitcase up to the front, and it will be gate-checked to your final destination."

"Will they bring it right up to the door for me when we get to DFW?"

"No, you'll have to pick it up in the baggage claim area. I'm sorry that we can't accommodate you."

The passenger sighed. "Are you sure there isn't any space further up front?"

"There may be, but I'll have to ask you to look for yourself. We have FAA minimum crew on board, and for safety reasons, I'm required to stay within five rows of the rear exits."

"Oh, all *right!*" the man snapped.

Eric returned to the galley and tried to resume loading warped metal racks into the oven. Every time he tried to shove a new rack in, it pulled all the protective foil off the omelets on the rack below. *Ding, dong.* Another passenger call light went off. Christ, he thought. What do they want *now?* We haven't even taken off yet. He trudged forward to row 15, where a woman was waving from her seat. "Yes, may I help you?"

"Young man, could I have a glass of water, please? I need it to—"

"Take a pill?"

She smiled. "How did you know?"

"You're the fifth person who's asked me for one this morning," he snapped, instantly regretted it.

"Well, I'm sorry if I'm inconveniencing you." Looking wounded, she turned away.

"It's no inconvenience," said Eric, forcing a smile. "I'll bring it to you in just a moment."

"No, never mind! You know, it was bad enough when you and your *very* rude friend pushed your way in front of my husband and me at security. I *am* disabled, after all. But this—your need to punish me for *daring* to ask for water—this really is the last straw!"

As her voice increased in pitch, passengers seated nearby were suddenly watching the scene intently. "Ma'am, as I said before, I'd be happy to bring it to you. I'll be right back."

"Don't bother! I'll do without. I'm supposed to take my medication at a specific time, but I'll sit here and wait until you have nothing better to do!"

A classic 'victim' mentality, thought Eric. I will *not* reinforce that behavior. He kept smiling and turned off the call light above her seat. "As you wish."

A passenger sitting in row 17 grabbed him by the arm. "I think that's disgraceful."

"What's disgraceful?"

"That poor old lady asked you for a measly cup of water, and you won't bring it to her. It would take two seconds!"

"You're mistaken, Miss. I did offer to bring it to her. Twice."

"Yes, but you made her feel terrible in the process. What are *you* doing right now that's so important?"

"I'm trying to set up breakfast for one hundred and—"

"Save us your excuses!" The woman reached into her purse and brought out a small bottle of water. She tapped the man sitting in front of her and said, "Sir, would you please pass this to the lady right in front of you? It's still sealed. I bought it for myself, but she can have it. This steward is too busy to attend to customers."

"Whatever," said Eric, unable to keep from rolling his eyes.

"What the—did you just roll your eyes at me?"

"No, ma'am. It was very nice of you to offer your own water to that lady. Would you pardon me, please?" As he turned to leave, the man who'd had to check his suitcase came rushing toward him. "What are you doing *here?*" the man demanded.

"I beg your pardon?"

"You said that you had to stay within five rows of the rear exits, and that's why you couldn't help me find luggage space. This at least *ten* rows from the exit."

"I have to answer a call lights. There could be a medical emergency, or—"

"Oh, right," the man replied sarcastically. He shook his head. "I don't know what this airline is paying you, but whatever it is, it's way too much."

Eric wanted to shout, "I don't get paid a fucking *dime* until this plane pushes back from the gate!" Instead, he kept his mouth closed, retreated to the galley, and drew the curtain closed. It's five-thirty A.M., he thought, wearily leaning his head against the oven. How can people be so goddam unreasonable at five-thirty A.M.? A moment later, the curtain was pulled open. "Excuse me," said a female voice.

Stifling the urge to scream, he turned around and was confronted by a nightmarish sight. The woman standing before him was tall, disheveled, and wore a flight attendant uniform that was bursting at the seams. Raggedy blond curls framed her face, and a slash of pink lipstick was drawn up and over her natural lip line. She can't be a flight attendant, thought Eric. She *can't!*

"I'm Lynn, your jump-seater. Do you have room for my bag anywhere back here?"

"No, I'm sorry. There's no more room for bags back here. You'll have to take it up front and gate-check it."

"But I'm a commuter."

"There's no more room for bags back here," he replied again, robotically. "You'll have to take it up front and gate-check it."

"But I only have thirty minutes to make my connection at DFW! Are you *sure* there's no room back here?"

"Yes, I just *told* you—" His fingers twitched as a sudden rage tore through him. Be still! he told himself. Your hands would never fit around that fat neck anyway. "Excuse me," he said politely, as he stepped out of the galley. "I need to use the lav."

***

"Eric, are you OK?" There was an urgent knocking on the bathroom door. "Eric!"

He calmly opened the door. "Yes, Rachael, I'm fine. Is something the matter?"

She looked worried. "You've been in there since I came back, five minutes ago. We're leaving. Darlene just said 'prepare for departure' over the PA. Didn't you hear her?"

"No, I didn't. Let me get my door." He armed his door and picked up the microphone. "Aft exits are armed and cross-checked," he announced crisply. As he and Rachael gathered equipment for the safety demonstration, the commuter plopped herself down on Eric's jump seat and opened a large bag of cookies.

Eric motioned for Rachael to follow him into the galley. "Who is *that?*" he asked, as Darlene informed passengers about the flying time and the weather at DFW via the PA system.

"Her name is Lynn. She's a commuter. "

"I know that. But she's a mess! She looks like a life-sized Baby Jane doll— only fatter. How can she possibly fly for *this* airline?"

"She probably does the deep South America trips. On those international all-nighter flights, supervisors aren't quite as rigid with the grooming checks as they are on domestic."

"Rigid? Are they blind? She weighs at least two hundred pounds."

"Well, you know what they say: our uniforms come in three sizes—small, medium and international."

"She's taking up the entire jump seat! There's no room for me at all."

"I know. It's a tight squeeze for even one flight attendant, much less two." She snickered. "Just tell her she needs to 'moooove' over. Oh, gotta go! I have to start the demo at row one." She darted toward the front of the plane.

Eric stood near the wings, performing the choreographed safety demonstration. Since he was facing aft, he was forced to watch Lynn gobble one cookie after another as she sat splayed on the rear jump seat. God help me, he thought. I may throw up.

After he had instructed the last past passenger to raise her tray table, he sat down next to Lynn and tried to fasten his seatbelt and shoulder harness. "Could you move over a little, please?"

"Geez," she said, through a mouthful of Oreos. "I'm up against the wall as it is."

"Well, try harder, please. Half of my rear end is hanging off the seat."

"No wonder." She grinned. "That is a truly bodacious ass that you have."

"I beg your pardon?"

"That's a compliment," she said, wriggling around a little. "You want a cookie?" she asked, offering the bag.

He looked at her sticky, crumb-covered fingers. They'd probably come in contact with every other cookie in the bag. "No, thank you. I'll wait for my crew meal."

"That's how you stay so trim! Good for you. On international, we're *always* hungry. It seems like we never stop eating!"

"So I see."

"Excuse me?"

"The jet lag must wreak havoc on your body clock," he replied tactfully.

She shook her head. "I fly north-south. We don't get jet lag."

"Oh." He tried to shift his torso. His shoulders, pressed against hers, were already starting to ache. He looked at Rachael, who was perched on the single fold-out jump seat next to the galley. The passengers in the row next to her were all asleep.

"Ladies and gentlemen, this is Captain Martindale. There's quite a bit of early morning traffic out here. We're currently number fifteen for takeoff and expect to be airborne in about thirty minutes. We'll continue moving slowly but surely during that time, so please keep seatbelts fastened. Thanks for your patience."

"I can't keep this damn thing fastened for another half hour!" said Lynn, springing up. "I can barely breathe! Do you have a seatbelt extension back here?"

He pointed. "In the last seat back pocket," he said, with disdain. Using an extension while riding on a jump seat was strictly forbidden by the FAA

I'm just gonna stand here for a few minutes."

"Suit yourself," he said, grateful for the extra space.

God, it's hot back here!"

"Yes, it is." He reached for a safety briefing card and started fanning himself. "It was even worse when we first got on, if you can believe it."

"These fucking Ultra Jets: the worst piece of equipment in the entire fleet. And we have hundreds of them! The goddam AC never really works on the ground. And these lavs! You can *smell* that shit sloshing around in the tanks below us! Thank God we don't have 'em on international. But, Christ, how I *hate* having to commute back and forth to New York on these goddam planes!"

"Why don't you live where you're based? Wouldn't that be easier?"

"My husband and I own an equestrian center outside of Amarillo—a very profitable one. I ride, too. Do you have any idea how much that property would cost on the East Coast?"

"No." But I can imagine how many horses have to be to shot after *you've* tried to mount them, he thought. He closed his eyes and fanned the card faster, trying desperate for relief from the fetid cabin air.

"So, where do you go on this trip?" Lynn asked.

Oh, please, could I have five minutes of quiet? "Huntsville and Little Rock, three-day trip, four legs each day."

"To hell and back, you mean."

"Maybe there'll be something interesting to see on the layover. I've never been to either Huntsville—or Little Rock."

"I remember this kind of trip, from *w-a-a-a-y* back. All I saw ever saw was the lobby of crummy airport hotels. Oh, listen to me! I don't mean to spoil your fun. Who knows what might happen? You could meet the Razorback of your dreams, right there in Little Rock!"

"It's three days out of my life. I'm practically brand-new at the base. It'll be *decades* before I have enough seniority to hold the kind of trips that you do now."

Eric's sly reference to her age flew right over her head. "Well…" She pulled the last Oreo out of the bag. "You gotta pay your dues, I guess, like everyone else. We all did it."

"I know. Today, though, it feels like I'm paying them with my blood."

***

"Would you like Kellogg's Corn Flakes for breakfast, sir?"

"No," said the sour-faced man in 32F. "I want an omelet."

"I'm sorry, but we're out of omelets."

"How can you be out of omelets?"

"Because we're catered with exactly one meal for each passenger, and the omelets were very popular today, and you're in the last row, and all that I have left is cereal. I'm very sorry."

"I *still* don't understand why I don't get a choice."

"I just explained it to you."

"Your explanation is hogwash."

Eric took his hundredth deep breath of the day. "May I suggest, sir, that if having a meal choice is very important to you, that in the future you request a seat closer to the front of the cabin. We always start the service from the front. As for right now, all I have left is cereal."

"Maybe first class has omelets left."

"They do not. I've already checked."

"What about the pilots? Don't *they* get omelets for breakfast? You could get me one their omelets. I am a paying passenger, after all, and I want an omelet."

If you say the world 'omelet' one more time, thought Eric, I'm going to bop you on the head with an ice mallet. "Everyone on this airplane is a paying passenger, sir. Now, would you like the Corn Flakes nor not?"

"Fine!"

Eric set the tray on the man's tray table.

The man sneered. "Look at this! The banana's so green that it's inedible! Take it away."

"As you wish," said Eric, thinking: I bet *your* banana is so *over*-ripe that it's inedible, too.

"Oh, if he doesn't want that cereal, I'll take it," said the woman sitting next to him. "I like a *big* breakfast."

"With pleasure," said Eric, passing the tray to her.

"But she already has a tray!" cried the man. "And *she* got an omelet!"

"Yes," she said, "and it was delicious! I loved that biscuit, too: all nice and warm and buttery. Mercury has the best food of all the airlines."

I simply can't believe this!" said the old man. "I have the worst seat in the airplane! It doesn't even recline! There's an engine right outside my window, blocking the view, which is so goddam *loud* that I'll be deaf by the time I land. And to top it all off, now you're *starving* me!"

Another victim, thought Eric. I refuse to respond.

"Isn't that too bad," said the woman, happily eating the cereal. "You had your chance. As for you, young man, you're doing a fine job. And you're good-looking, too. Oh, how I love Mercury Airways!"

"I can't tell you how much I appreciate that." He knelt next to her seat. "Thank God my next flight is just a snack service," he murmured. "They all get the same thing: a turkey and Swiss cheese wrap, chips, and a slice of Entenmann's—or they go hungry."

"You know what I say, honey." The woman waved her spoon around like it was a scepter. "Let them eat pound cake!"

***

"God, I have to wash my hands right this minute!" said Rachael, after they'd picked up the last dirty tray. "What's left to eat?"

"Back here? Nothing. How about up front?"

"There's a teaspoon of raspberry jam, and a bagel that some old man sneezed on."

"How about our crew meals?"

She shook her head. "Catering puts them on the *next* flight."

"That's two hours from now! I'm starving!"

"I *told* you we should have stopped for breakfast in the terminal."

"I know. I was trying to economize."

Rachael gestured toward Lynn, who was asleep on the jump seat. "What about Baby Jane? Does she have anything else stashed in her bag?"

"Yes: six bottles of scotch and three bottles of gin."

"What is she, a bootlegger?"

"Of sorts. She buys duty-free booze on her layover and sells it to friends back home—at a fifty percent mark-up."

"That's some racket!"

"Tell me about it. Those goddam bottles haven't stopped rattling since we took off. Did both the pilots eat?"

"You didn't really ask that question, did you? I already called Darlene. Not a *crumb* left on their trays."

"Well, that leaves nothing for us, I guess."

"Can you make it to the next flight?"

"I suppose I'll have to. Oh, what I wouldn't give for an Oreo cookie now!"

***

"Christ, Christ, *Christ!*" Rachel muttered as she came down the aisle, right before departure time on their second leg. "Another full load. It was a madhouse up front! You're lucky you were back here."

"Oh, yes! I've been having a marvelous time! Seat dupes, separated family members, old people who can't lift their own luggage."

She tossed two small, grey plastic bags on the counter. "Well, here's what you've been after since six A.M."

"What are those?"

"Our crew meals."

He grabbed one of the bags and ripped it open. It contained an orange, a three-ounce can of tuna topped with a plastic cup, a single-serving tube of mayonnaise, and a package of Saltines. "Tell me you're joking."

"I assure you that I am not. See, you pop open the tuna, mix it with the mayonnaise, and *voilà!* Tuna salad."

"I don't fucking believe this!"

"Believe it. This is what is known as a flight attendant meal. Or 'snack pack,' as the company calls them. Not quite the same thing as the first-class meal that the pilots get on every leg, is it?"

"*This* is supposed to get me through a twelve-hour duty day, when there's no time to get off the airplane and buy some food in the terminal? It's inhumane!"

"Of course it is. Do you see now how much this company thinks of you, Mr. Super Stew? We'll have to resort to what we usually do: scavenge the snack baskets for unwrapped leftovers before we land. Amazingly, you *can* live for three days on chips and pound cake. Don't look at me like that. I'm not kidding. I also have a couple of protein bars in my purse, and I'm happy to share them."

"Anything else I should know before this day continues?"

"I hate to be the one tell you, but we have a jump-seater back here."

"You mean *I* have a jump-seater. Is it another commuter?"

"Ha! What do you think? God forbid anyone these people should live where they're based. That would make too much sense. This one's name is Chester."

"Is he fat?" he asked contemptuously.

"I'd call him… husky."

Well, that's just *perfect*."

***

"Jesus, it's a tight squeeze back here, isn't it?" said Chester, sat down for taxi-out. Chester was huge. "You have shoulders like a linebacker."

"I don't think my shoulders are the issue here."

"You're right. This jump seat should be wider." He sighed. "It's these damn lavs, pinning us in! Why didn't they put them in the *front* of the cabin when they designed this plane? That would solve so many problems." He looked at his watch nervously. "I hope we get into St. Louis on time!"

"Why? Is someone picking you up at the airport?" asked Eric, fanning himself with a now well-worn safety briefing card.

"No, it's that I only have twenty-seven minutes to make my connection."

"You're making a connection in St. Louis? To *where?*"

"Branson. That's where I live."

"Where's that?"

"In Missouri, silly."

"Do we even fly there?"

"Mercury Express does. I hope there's a seat for me one the three o'clock flight! Commuting is so hard, but doing a double-leg commute is the worst!"

Eric didn't even have the strength to bristle at Chester's irritating Midwestern accent. He just sat there fanning himself.

"I don't know why we can't just operate non-stops between DFW and Branson," said Chester. "Every other airline does, and those flights are full! We could be making tons of money on that route. But those fools at headquarters never ask *my* advice on how to run this company. If they ever did, would I give *them* an earful."

"Are you based here at DFW?"

"Yes."

He couldn't help asking. "Well, why don't you just live near DFW?"

"Oh, no! I could never be so far away from my family."

"Then, why fly at all?"

"It's a long story," he said. "You see, my ex-wife, who wasn't always the bitch that she is now, and I moved home to Branson right after we had our first baby. Then, a year later, we had a second baby. Then a couple of years later—"

"Ladies and gentlemen, we're now number one for takeoff," said the captain. "Flight attendants, please prepare for takeoff."

As the airplane swung around at the end of the taxi way, Eric stared straight ahead and placed his hands in his lap. He tried, unsuccessfully, to block out Chester's voice as he did a quick mental review of his emergency evacuation procedures.

"...*then* I found out that my wife was having an affair. With my brother, if you can believe that! And if you saw my brother, you wouldn't believe it. You talk about one ugly mother-fucker. It was strange, too, because at my wedding, the two of them got into a drunken brawl, right in front of God and everybody! They ruined the whole day! They're both hopeless alcoholics."

The engines started revving up. A moment later, as the takeoff roll began, and the engines were operating at maximum power, the noise was deafening. Chester kept right on talking. "My mother was the one who told me about the affair. On my birthday, of course, because she's the type of woman who loves to..."

The nose lifted off the ground, and a moment later they were airborne. Eric could hear nothing but the roar of the engines. Chester's mouth continued to form words, sharing private details of a sordid life—with a seatmate he'd never met before. Eric was starting to learn that many of co-workers simply lived their lives that way. Discretion seemed to be the last thing on their minds.

***

"This is Darlene up front."

"This is Eric in the back. There's no more room for bags back here. None." It was like a nightmare that reoccurred four times each day. "Start gate-checking everything."

"Are you sure? There's still quite a line of—"

"Listen to me: there's not one square inch of room! Start gate-checking!"

"OK, honey. Good thing this is the last leg of the day. We need to get a drink in you as soon as we land—or a Valium."

"Finally, something for me to look forward to! Thank you." He hung up the phone and looked up the aisle. A passenger was trying to shove his enormous suitcase into an overhead bin. He tried ramming it in first vertically, then horizontally, and then vertically again. He stared into the bin, as though doing so would magically make it double in size.

Idiot! Eric thought. Can't you *see* that it won't fit?!

As though the passenger was reading his mind, he came charging toward the back. "I need a space for my suitcase."

"Your suitcase is too large for the bin, sir. You'll have to take it up front and gate-check it."

"What do you mean, gate-check it? I travel on this airline almost every day of the week. *You* go find a space for it."

Eric slowly inhaled and tried desperately to control his tone. "Sir, as you can see, all of the overhead bins are full, and there is no more room for a suitcase as large as yours. I'm sorry that we can't accommodate you. If having your luggage with you is vitally important, then I suggest that in the future, you arrive earlier than five minutes before departure."

The passenger stepped closer. "Don't talk to me like I'm a moron. Just find a space for my goddam bag!" Half of the cabin turned around to stare.

"What's going on here?" demanded Rachael, making her way down the aisle.

"This guy has a suitcase doesn't fit in the overhead bin. I've asked him several times to take it forward and gate-check it, but he refuses to do so."

" 'This guy'?" the passenger repeated, with a snarl. "For your information, I'm a million-miler on this airline. And I'm telling you, I am *not* checking this fucking suitcase! Now, you two get off your goddam lazy asses and *do* something about it!"

"We certainly will," said Rachael. She grabbed the crew phone and furiously dialed the cockpit. "Captain, this is Rachel in the back." She snatched the boarding pass from the man's hand. "There is a passenger in 28E by the last name of Norell. He has an oversized suitcase, for which there is room, and he refuses to check it. He is being verbally abusive with the crew and is interfering with our safety-related duties. You should know that the 'F' word was used … thank you, I'll send him right up." She hung up the phone. "The captain is waiting to see you at the entry door. Be sure you take all of your belongings with you. I don't think you'll be traveling with us today."

"We'll see about that!"

Rachael stood nose-to-nose with him. "What *you'll* see, Mister," she said, so softly that only he and Eric could hear her, "is us waving goodbye as we leave you behind, *asshole!*"

"How *dare* you speak to me like that! I'm a million—"

"I don't care if you fly a hundred million miles a year. Once you become abusive with the crew, you lose all rights and privileges. Now, *go.*"

As the man stormed up the aisle, other passengers began applauding. "Oh, Christ," Eric muttered. He stepped into the galley and rested his head against the oven. "I can't believe what just happened. They didn't teach us how to handle someone like that at the Charm Farm. I'm grateful you were here, Rachael."

"I'm grateful we have a captain with balls. A lot of them don't. Besides, we don't have to put up with verbal abuse. Ever! That's federal law. They don't teach you that at the Charm Farm. Well, here's to a happy last-leg-of-the-day. One more snack service and we're done."

"I really need a drink. Will we get to the hotel in time for happy hour?"

"Not to worry. I've been saving a liquor stash since six A.M. I hope you like vodka. Hey, guess what? No jump-seaters on this leg!"

"Well, thank you, Jesus!"

***

"This feels so good," said Eric, leaning against the headboard. "Just to lie here, with a drink in my hand, and be quiet."

"That's the fourth drink you've had in your hand," said Rachael, with a giggle.

"And it should probably be your last," said Darlene. "That six A.M. wake-up call will come before you know it." She stood up and clumsily gathered empty potato chip bags that littered Eric's bed. "We'd better go get some real food. The restaurant downstairs closes in an hour. Do y'all want to share a pizza?"

"I'm in," said Rachael, slipping into her shoes.

"I still have two slices of pound cake," said Eric. "Just leave me another vodka."

"You'll regret it tomorrow," said Darlene. "Lord, will you regret it!"

"Sorry," said Eric. "I love you both, but I can't bear to be around any more people today."

Darlene snorted. "Who do you think you are? Gretta fucking Garbo?"

"Get us a table, Darlene," said Rachael. "We'll be down in a minute."

"You'd better be bright-eyed and bushy-tailed tomorrow," said Darlene, shaking her finger at Eric. "Flying with a hangover is a bad habit to get into, especially so early in your career."

"Don't worry about me!" said Eric, as Darlene left. He closed his eyes and tried to ignore the fact that the room was spinning. "Do you know what, Rachael? I can smell myself. I'm so grimy that I can *smell* myself. I put clean clothes over a dirty body because I was too tired to shower. I smell like..." He sniffed himself. "Ultra Jet lav disinfectant. I may throw up."

"It's gonna be like this for a good long time, you know: up and down, up and down, over and over, in a hot little hunk of metal. No food to eat. Whiners and complainers and commuters, who'll all suck the life right out of you. In short, nothing *but* people."

"It's not like that on the transcons."

"Forget the transcons, babe. You've been lucky to get as many as you have so far. *This* the real deal. You're new, and this is what you'll hold every line month, regardless of what you bid, so get used to it. Now get up and come with to get some real food."

He forced himself to stand up. "Can we at least get a corner table away from everyone else?"

Rachel rolled her eyes. "You're such a drama queen. We'll do our best, Miss Garbo."

CHAPTER 8

The Luck of the Draw

"Attention, please. Standby Flight Attendant Eric Saunders: please report to the M.O.D. desk."

Eric put down his copy of *The New Yorker* and trotted over to the desk of the JFK manager on duty. "Hi, I'm Eric."

"Hi, Eric. I'm Sheila. I have a trip for you this morning. Someone called in sick at the last minute."

"Oh, I hope it's a four-legger to Kansas City! I haven't been there yet."

She smiled. "I think we can do a little better than that. You're going to be the number nine on the ten o'clock flight to San Francisco."

His pulse began to race. "San Francisco? Really?"

"Yeah, you lucked out. This trip has a twenty-four-hour downtown layover." She glanced at the computer screen. "With quite a crew!"

"Who's the purser? Is it Sylvia Saks, by any chance?"

"No. Leslie Carson is your purser. She's right over there." She gestured toward a young woman strutting into operations wearing an exceedingly short skirt and black stiletto heels. Her long, crimped, blond hair bounced freely around her shoulders as she moved. "Oh, Criminey," said Sheila. "Look how short that skirt is! Hey, Leslie! Come here for a second."

"Hi, Sheila! What's up?"

"The hem of your skirt. Who's doing your alternations these days? Trina of Trollopville?"

"I can't help it," Leslie said. "This is only uniform skirt that I have. It got torn on a broken armrest last week. The tailor had no choice but to shorten it."

"Well, you better not hang around here too long. Phillip Hendry is in today, and if he takes one look at you, he'll pull you right off the trip—unpaid—and send you home."

"Just because my skirt's a little too short? That's ridiculous."

"It's not just the skirt, and you know it. Your hair is too long to wear it like that. It should be pinned up or pulled back. And you have an inch of dark roots showing. That's *three* strikes against you. They're one the warpath about grooming regulations this month. You'd better beat it before they see you."

"Thanks for the warning, Sheila. You're a doll."

"By the way, this is Eric. He's going with you. Denny just called in sick."

"Denny called in sick for a long S.F. layover? I'm shocked! Hi, Eric."

"Hi."

The phone on the desk rang. "Hello, this is Sheila ... Hi, Phillip." She glanced at Eric. "Saunders? Yes, he's standing right here. I just assigned him to flight twenty-five to San Francisco ... OK, are you coming out or should I send him in?" Sheila covered the phone and whispered, "Get going!" to Leslie, who immediately grabbed her luggage and headed for the exit. "Fine. I'll send him in. He has a few minutes before he has to go down to the gate." She hung up the phone. "Your supervisor wants to see you, Eric. Have you met him yet?"

"No, not yet. He was on vacation last month when I started flying."

"So pop in and say hello. He's right through that door, and in the first cubicle on the left."

Suddenly feeling nervous, Eric smoothed his hair. "Do I look all right?"

"Are you kidding? He'll adore you. Just smile and tell him how much you love the job, and then excuse yourself to catch your flight."

"Thanks, Sheila."

"One more thing." Sheila motioned Eric to come closer. "Don't offer him any unnecessary information. Got it?"

"No, what do you mean?"

"Supervisors are always trying to get dirt on senior flight attendants from new hires. It's like an obsession with them. Don't dish on anybody you've flown with, no matter what you've seen. Unless it's a serious safety violation, or someone shows up drunk to work a trip, whatever happens on the plane stays on the plane. I'm a flight attendant, too, just in case you were wondering. I'm working the MOD desk this week because I'm on light duty. I had foot surgery last month and can't come back to flying just yet."

Eric nodded his head. "Got it. And thanks for the heads up." He walked into the office and stopped at Phillip's cubicle. "Hi, Phillip. I'm Eric Saunders."

"Pleased to meet you, Eric. Have a seat." Phillip had the palest skin that Eric had ever seen. His face was covered with freckles. He had ginger-colored hair over an exceedingly large head. He wore a double-breasted navy-blue suit that partially hid his round, full stomach. "I have your employee file right here." He opened a manila folder and began flipping through it. His hands were covered with freckles, too. "So, how do you like flying so far?"

"It's been wonderful. I'm quite happy to be here."

"Are there any issues that you've encountered on a regular basis? Cabin service problems? Catering shortages?" He paused. "Problems with other crewmembers?"

"Oh, no," said Eric, maintaining a broad smile. "Everything has gone like clockwork on the trips that I've worked so far, and all the crews have been very nice to me."

"That's what we like to hear." He continued flipping through Eric's file. "Mmm, a B.A. in Psychology: that should come in handy on a daily basis. Oh, I see you haven't been weighed since your last week of training." He gestured toward a scale in the corner. "Would you mind?"

"Not at all." Eric stepped on the scale.

"One hundred and sixty pounds. You're within five pounds of the limit for your height. Bravo, let's keep it that way. May I see your hands, please? Ah, perfectly groomed. That makes such a nice impression when you're serving our passengers. And that shirt, so nicely starched. Not just yanked out of the dryer without a second thought, like some of your co-workers." He looked Eric up and down. "Everything about your appearance is just as it should be." He patted Eric on the shoulder. "Good job!"

"Thank you," said Eric, feeling vaguely like a steer on display at the Texas State Fair.

"So you're on your way to San Francisco. Lucky man." Phillip looked at his computer screen. "And such a diverse crew: three of a kind in first, three of a kind in business…" He scrolled down the screen and smiled. "And in your cabin, four of a kind, if I'm not mistaken."

"I beg your pardon?"

"Nothing. Just thinking out loud." He made a few notes and then closed the folder. "Oh, look at the time. You'd better get down to the gate."

"Yes, I'd better." Eric stood up and shook hands with his supervisor. "It was very nice meeting you, Phillip."

"Stop by anytime. I'm always here to address any concerns that you may have."

"Thank you. I appreciate that." He turned to leave.

"By the way, Eric: play nice with the other boys in coach today, but don't let them get you into trouble on the layover." He winked. "See you soon."

* * *

Eric arrived at the gate and boarded the plane. Leslie was stowing her bags in a closet in first class. "Oh, hi again!" she said. "Sorry I couldn't talk to you earlier. I had to make a run for it. God, those supervisors with their grooming regulations! I wish they'd focus their attention on something that really matters, for a change." She stepped into the bathroom, leaving the door open as she examined her face in the mirror. "Ugh! This lighting in here is terrible! It shows every single flaw! I'm like, hello! I didn't know that the Bride of Frankenstein was on this crew." She pulled her long curly hair behind her ears and frowned. "Fuck it! I *cannot* wear my hair pulled back or pinned up. Look at me. I'm all nose!" She fluffed her hair to maximum volume with her hands and then turned to Eric. "So, did you meet Pumpkin Head?"

"Who?"

"Philip Hendry. That's his nickname. Didn't you notice how his head looks like a giant pumpkin?"

"Oh, yes. I mean, yes I met him."

Did he ask you to spy on us?"

"No. Why would he?"

"Old habit. Supervisors love trying to use new hires to report back to them about stuff they see on the plane: if we're violating grooming regs, if we're take shortcuts on the service, or if we're stealing liquor. It's easier than flying with us to perform a check ride, even though they're *supposed* to do check rides. They hate having to leave their offices for that."

"No, all he did was weigh me and—"

"Good morning, Leslie!" chimed a pretty brunette coming through the door.

"Oh, hi, Julia!"

"It was murder finding a cab on Second Avenue today," said Julia, as she stowed her luggage. "I can't believe I made it here on time."

"Neither can I!" said Leslie. "I've been up since six A.M., rushing around like a maniac! But three hours, four espressos, and five different pairs of shoes later—I just couldn't decide which ones to wear—here I am, ready to meet the man of my dreams. You never know: he could be sitting right here in my cabin today. By the way, Julia, this is Eric. He's filling in for Denny."

"Denny won't be here?" said Julia. "That's too bad." She started giggling. "I bet you he snagged a man last night, and he's still going at it this morning!"

"*Who* snagged a man?" This query came from a stunning redhead who'd just walked on board. "And how come it wasn't me? I'm supposed to be the Queen of the Man Snaggers around here!"

"Hi, Madeline!" Leslie and Julia shrieked in unison.

"Oh, my God, Leslie!" said Madeline. "I *love* your hair like that! Did you get it permed?"

"No, I just stopped blow-drying it straight. It's impossible to keep it straight way in the summer anyway, with the constant goddam humidity."

"I love it that way too!" Julia said. "The long, blond curls say: Hey, Mr. Investment Banker in 3B, just in case you're wondering, I can be a wild child — when I want to be."

Leslie tossed her hair and grinned. "Sheila at the M.O.D. desk was harassing me for not touching up my roots. Actually, I love the roots showing. It's like I'm saying: I'm *not* a natural blond and I don't care who knows it."

"Honey!" said Madeline, squeezing her breasts together. "There's nothing natural about any of us!" This comment brought forth a gale of high-pitched laughter, followed by a three-way hug.

"I think I'll head to the back," Eric said, to no one in particular. It didn't matter, as no one was paying him the slightest attention.

He proceeded down the aisle toward the coach cabin. As he passed the midship business class galley, he stopped to introduce himself. A flight attendant, her face hidden by curly blond hair, was kneeling on the floor as she set up the beverage carts. "Hi, I'm Eric."

She looked up and scowled. "Oh, I remember you." It was Pavonia Rickerson, from Eric's first flight. "You're the guy who got me kicked out of first class on that L.A. trip last month."

"Well, technically, it was the purser who—"

"Well, look who's here." Darcy Usher stepped into the galley. "It's Mister Snooty Pants. I hope you're not planning on taking over business class today. The three of us are a well-oiled machine, and we don't need anyone butting in."

"I wouldn't dream of it," said Eric. "Today I'm in coach and quite happy to be there."

Can you believe this?" said a third flight attendant, entering the crowded galley. She was a chubby, middle-aged woman with frosted hair and coral lipstick. Her eyeglass frames were covered with tiny rhinestones. She spoke with the same East Texas twang that Pavonia and Darcy used. That's Kendra, thought Eric. She was working the flight that I took to go to training. Kendra wore a small gold crucifix on her lapel, just like Pavonia and Darcy.

"Believe what, Kendra?" said Darcy.

"There's not a single coat tag in the service kit. Well, of course, everybody in business class today will want their jacket hung up. So I stepped out on the jet bridge to call cabin service myself. I wouldn't dream of interrupting Leslie's mirror time, even though she's the purser and it's her *job,* but whatever. Anyway, I called and said to the guy who answered the phone, 'I need coat tags for flight twenty-five to San Francisco.' And the son of a bitch hangs up on me. So I called right back, and I said, 'Excuse me! I said we need coat tags for the flight to San Francisco.' And he hung up on me again! So I called a third time and said, 'Hey! What the hell is your problem, Mister? I need coat tags for flight twenty-five, and I need 'em before we start boarding!' Well..." Kendra began pounding her fist on the counter, unable to control her raucous laughter. "As it turns out, he thought I was askin' for Kotex! It embarrassed the hell out of him, and that's why he hung up! Ha ha ha!"

"Isn't that just typical?" said Darcy. "Even if you *were* asking for Kotex, what's the big deal? It's a perfectly normal request for a perfectly natural function. Half the world's population uses them every month."

"Yes, we all bleed, just like Jesus on the cross," said Kendra. Her lip started to tremble. "Only he bled from the crown of thorns that they cruelly jammed on his head."

"And from the wounds that they inflicted on him when they crucified him," said Pavonia.

"Five wounds. Five *holy* wounds, to be exact," said Darcy. "One on each hand, one on each foot, and one on his torso. Sometimes, when I think of the way he suffered and died to save us from eternal damnation, I cain't bear it."

"Let's take a moment to thank Jesus before we begin boarding," said Pavonia. She started to close the galley curtain as the two other women bowed their heads. "Do you *mind*, Eric?"

"Not at all. I'll see you later." As he finally reached the back of the plane, he was thrilled to hear male voices. There were three men in the galley. One appeared to be about forty years old. He was thick-waisted, with dark features and thinning black hair combed carefully across his head. The other two men seemed to be the same age as Eric. They were both trim, attractive, and blond, and had matching military-style haircuts. They were so similar in appearance that they might have been twins. "Hi, I'm Eric. I'm your number nine."

"*You're* the number nine?" said the middle-aged man. "Where the hell is Denny?"

"I think he called in sick at the last minute. I'm taking his place."

"Oh," he said, obviously disappointed. "That's sucks."

"Arnie!" said one the two younger men. "Where are your manners? Hi, Eric. We're Jim and Ted, and this bitter old man is Arnie."

"It's *Arnold*," the man corrected him. "You know I prefer to be called Arnold."

"Don't put on airs, girl, just because we have a new hire with us today," said Jim. "So, Denny called in sick for a downtown S.F. layover. Something must be up."

"Something's up, all right," said Arnie, with a leer. "There's probably an eight-inch cock rammed up his ass right now."

"You have such a way with words, Arnie," said Ted. "Still, I wish I could have been the crew scheduler on duty when *that* phone call came in."

"Yeah," said Arnie. "It was probably from the payphone of the West Side Club. 'Hello, this is Flight Attendant Molinovski. I've got a terrible sore ass—I mean, throat—and I won't be able to make my trip today. Put me on the sick list, please.' What the hell, more power to him. I should be so lucky. Do you know how long it's been since I've touched any man's cock, besides my own?"

"That's your own fault for living on Long Island," said Ted. "Nobody scores out there."

"Exactly," said Jim. "The city is the place to be, Arnie. Stop complaining and move into Manhattan already! Besides, we've offered to help you update your look a million times."

"You think I want a makeover from the two of you?" said Arnie. "Thanks, but I'll pass." He looked at Eric. "Well, if you're taking Denny's place on the trip, then you're taking his place on the layover, too."

"OK," said Eric. "What do you guys have planned?"

"We're going to the Castro for Happy Hour and dinner, if you're interested."

"Hallelujah!" said Eric. "A real layover at last."

"So, you're family?" Arnie asked.

"Isn't it obvious?" said Eric.

"I never assume anymore," said Arnie. "We've got a lot of young closet cases running around here these days. But once they come busting out of that closet, *bam!* Watch out!"

"Hey, guys," said Leslie, appearing in the galley. "I've been calling and calling you on the crew phone! Why didn't you answer?"

"It didn't ring," said Jim. "It probably needs to be reset. I'll take care of it."

"We were supposed to start boarding five minutes ago. I need a plucker outside and a director at the door *pronto*, please."

"Jim and I are coming up right now," said Ted.

"By the way, here's your briefing: it's completely full back here. You have one person on oxygen in 25B—he should be on low flow, but please don't forget to check his tank every hour. You have five wheelchair passengers, three lap children, and a ton of special meals. Here's all your paperwork. Let's get started." She turned and left the galley with Jim and Ted following right behind her.

"What should I be doing right now?" Eric said to Arnie.

"You stay here and keep an eye on the carry-on luggage while I set up the galley. Then once everyone has boarded, walk through and check off names on the special meal list. Make sure the name on the list matches the person in that seat. Otherwise it's pandemonium during the service." He handed the list to Eric.

Eric glanced at the paper. "Forty-five special meals?!"

"Uh huh. And it's not even Passover. Welcome to coach in the summertime."

***

"Ladies and gentlemen, we'll be pushing back from the gate now. Flight attendants, please prepare your door for departure."

Eric stopped to watch Arnie move a door arming lever on each of the back doors.

"Would you cross-check me, please?" said Arnie.

"You're cross-checked," said Eric, making sure that both levers were in the correct position. "Have you ever actually forgotten to arm your doors?"

"No, but I forgot to *disarm* them once after we landed in Phoenix, about twenty years ago. I blew a slide when the agent opened the front door. It was a big fucking deal. They had to take the plane out of service and cancel the outbound. I almost got fired. Thank God for the union—and for the station manager in Phoenix, who I was dating at the time. Anyway, ever since then I never fail to have someone cross-check my doors. Did you finish verifying all the special meals?"

"Yes, they're all here."

"Good. Now even more importantly: who's on the crotch watch list today?"

"I'm sorry, I don't know what that means."

"It's a little game we play to help pass the time. I'll show you how it works once we're at cruising altitude," Arnie said with a grin. "But for future reference, Eric, it's just as important as doing your emergency equipment check—and a hell of a lot more fun."

***

Once the plane leveled off, Eric and his three co-workers unfastened their seatbelts and stood up.

"Jesus Christ," said Arnie. "That little seat gets harder and harder every year. They could at least put some real padding on it."

"It's a shame you don't have any of your own," Jim said jokingly.

"Ha, ha!" said Arnie. "Let's see what *your* ass looks like at forty-five."

"Not to worry," said Jim. "If my ass ever heads south, I'll run straight to Park Avenue."

"And I'll be right behind you," said Ted.

"Our insurance doesn't cover butt lifts, you know," said Arnie. "You two better sell a lot of booze and headsets over the next twenty years."

"We're way ahead of you," said Jim, reaching for a large bag of headsets.

"Do you want me to start selling them from the back?" asked Eric.

Jim and Ted exchanged a look. "Oh, no. You stay here and help Arnie finish setting up."

"That's right, Eric," said Arnie. "You wouldn't want to cut into their nip-and-tuck fund. And just in case you were wondering, you and I will be serving the meals. *They'll* be selling drinks today and tomorrow."

"We all supplement this shitty salary in one way or another, Arnie," said Jim. "I know for a fact that your layover stash of Bombay Gin comes right from the liquor cart. I bet we're already out of gin, as a matter of fact, and we haven't served a single passenger yet."

"Please!" said Arnie, covering Eric's ears with his hands. "Not in front of the b-o-y."

"All right then," said Jim. "Let's get going."

***

Two grueling hours later, the service was just about completed. "Here's the last of the dirty trays," said Eric, pushing a cart into the galley.

"Do you need anything else before we sit down?" said Arnie.

"Yes. Either a fistful of sleeping pills or a sock stuffed with wet sand for the kids in row twenty-three."

"Ahhhhh," said Arnie. "You thought they were so *adorable* when they boarded. What happened?"

"They won't stay out of the fucking aisle! It's impossible to move the carts past them."

"What you need to do is roll a two-hundred-pound beverage cart right over their fat little feet. I guarantee you they'll stay out of your way after that."

"You wouldn't really do that, would you?"

"*Watch* me," said Arnie. "Accidents do happen."

"Girl," said Jim, pushing the beverage cart into the galley. "I am *done* with these people. I can't remember ever having such a needy crowd on a San Francisco flight."

"Speaking of the crowd," said Eric, "where are all the gay passengers?"

"What do you mean?"

"This is a New York-to-San Francisco flight. I just assumed that there would be a lot of gay men in the mix."

"Oh, right," said Arnie. "We usually have a planeload full of them—all dressed in tight t-shirts, faded jeans and work boots, writing their phone numbers down for us on cocktail napkins."

"Well," said Eric. "Something like that."

"Not to worry. We're heading to the Castro, and we don't have to get up early tomorrow, so you'll have plenty of time to hunt for your fantasy man. By the way, we never made a crotch watch list today."

"Oh, yes we did." Jim pulled a napkin out of his shirt pocket. "Eric, these are they seats that you want to pass by very slowly when you're doing a seatbelt check."

"Cross 32B off the list," said Ted. "He caught me looking right before takeoff and covered himself with a blanket. I don't think he'll be removing it until we land."

"I keep telling you, girl, you need to be a little more discreet," said Jim.

"What do you mean?"

"You're so obvious—like a vulture spotting its prey from the air. So, what's the plan for the layover?"

"Let's meet in my room for a drink around four," said Arnie, "and then we'll head for the Castro around five."

"A drink before we go out for drinks," said Eric. "I like that idea."

"Four o'clock might be pushing it for us," said Jim. "We have to work out and shave. That'll take at least two hours."

"Why are you going to shave again?" asked Eric. "You look fine to me."

"He means 'down there,' " said Arnie. "Ach! Just the *thought* of taking a razor to my pubes gives me the heebie-jeebies."

"It's the nineties, Arnie," Jim said. "Get with it: body hair is *out*."

"For your generation, maybe. I like men to look like men, not boys."

"Let's just plan on meeting you at four-thirty, OK?" said Ted.

"Fine," said Arnie. "I'm going to head up front to see if they have leftovers. I'm starving."

"Listen, Eric," said Jim, after Arnie left. "What are you doing this afternoon before you meet us?"

"I'm going sightseeing. The captain said the weather is supposed to be beautiful and I don't want to spend the whole day indoors. I want to walk up through Nob Hill and down to the water and back."

"Whew, that's a lot in one afternoon! Don't wear yourself out before we meet up. Take the cable car or a cab back to the hotel."

"Do you know if the bus is cheaper? I'm on a budget."

"Don't worry about that," said Jim, stuffing two twenty-dollar bills into Eric's shirt pocket.

"What's that for?"

"It's expense money for your layover. Just take it and don't ask where it came from. In return, can you do us a favor? Try to get to Arnie's room a few minutes early and make sure he's wearing something age-appropriate."

"I'm confused. Do you guys really enjoy hanging out with him? You haven't stopped sniping at each other since before takeoff. Would you two rather do be on your own today?"

"No, we love Arnie," said Ted. "As long as he doesn't drink too much—"

"Or pull out that *tired* photo album of his 747 days," Jim interjected. "He and Denny are truly a perfect match. They're both dark and hairy and stuck in a retro groove."

A vivid memory popped into Eric's head. "Does Denny have kind of a brooding, Slavic look? Great jaw and a chin covered with dark stubble?"

"That's him," said Ted. "Have you flown with him already?"

"Actually, yes," said Eric. "He was working the flight that I took to training. last spring. He was very nice to me."

"We love Denny, too. He's great fun. But put him and Arnie together with a quart of liquor and—baby, watch out!"

"He gave me his phone number during the flight and told me to call him when I got to New York," said Eric. "I have no idea where I put it."

"I'll give you his number if you want it. Just don't call too early in the day," said Jim.

"Or too late at night!" added Ted. "You never know who you or what you'll get at the other at the end of the line. Here comes Arnie. Eric, if you want something to eat in first, you'd better go now. Once the business class girls go up there, there won't be a scrap of food left."

Eric snorted. "With all the prayer power in *that* galley, you'd think they could perform the miracle of the loaves and the fishes."

"Girl," replied Jim, "That routine only works on the ground."

"Why are those devout ones here?" Eric asked. "This hardly seems like an appropriate line of work for them: wearing makeup, serving alcohol, being away from home, dining with pilots instead of their husbands, and having gay co-workers. It doesn't add up, practically speaking. So why the fuck are they here?"

"Honey, your face is so red all of a sudden that you look as though you're about to have a stroke. What's up with you and the Evangelicals?"

"I grew up in Texas. I was surrounded by Fundamentalists my whole life. When I was seventeen, I met another guy my age in a gay bar who lived way across town. His name was Kevin, and he was beautiful. We feel in love immediately. He used to drive an hour a half to pick me up so we could go to gay bars downtown, then drive me home, and then drive himself back home. It was like magic when he pulled up in front of my house on a Saturday night. Even if we could only be together for a few hours every week, it was worth it. His family was Church of Christ—a sect even more devout than Southern Baptists. One day, his mother was snooping around his room and found a love letter that I'd written to him. Sending letters was risky, but making too many phone calls was suspicious, too. Once they found out he was gay, they…" He had to choke back the tears. "They tortured him. They let the air out of all his tires so that he was trapped at the house. They wouldn't let him near the phone. Then they shaved off his long, beautiful blond hair—every last bit of it. Then they made him get up in front of the congregation the next Sunday and 'admit' to the terrible sin of homosexuality, and beg for their forgiveness. I got all this information second hand from his cousin, by the way. She used to come bar-hopping with us once in a while. I never saw or heard from Kevin again. I have no idea if he eventually ran away, or was forced to get married and have kids, or if he hung himself in the garage. *That's* why I despise the Fundamentalists and Evangelicals. They're such hypocrites. And they have no idea how much pain they inflict on us. They *ruin* lives— all in the name of Jesus. So let me ask you again: what the *fuck* are *they* doing *here?*"

Jim shook his head sadly. "Eric, that story breaks my heart. Is it any wonder that as gay teenagers, we all want to leave our hometowns and move to a big city, where we can feel a modicum of safety? As for those three working in business class today… God only knows why they fly, hon. You'd have to ask *Him.*"

CHAPTER 9

Buddies

Eric and his crew stepped out of the terminal at San Francisco International Airport and made their way to the hotel van. The boys squeezed themselves into the last row. The crew from business class was in the middle and the women from first class were in front, as though they were still on the plane. After loading all their luggage, the driver took his seat, and a moment later they were on their way to the Union Square layover hotel.

"We need some air conditioning, please!" Kendra said as she dabbed sweat from her upper lip with a tissue. "We're roasting in here!"

"One moment, please," said the driver. He set the air conditioner on high.

"Thank you!" said Kendra, moving her face as close to the ceiling air vent as possible. This action was immediately followed by the frantic closing of air vents over the first row, where none of the occupants had any measurable body fat.

As the van entered the freeway, Jim and Ted pulled Sony Walkmans out of their tote bags. "Time for a power nap," said Jim, as they both turned on their music players and closed their eyes. Arnie followed suit, but a moment later, he slapped himself on the forehead. "Damn," he muttered.

"What's the matter?" asked Eric.

"Dead batteries! This is going to be a very long ride."

Julia turned around and smiled sweetly at Eric. "Eric," she said, "would you like to be my buddy for this trip?"

"Your buddy?" Eric felt put on the spot by this invitation, especially since he'd barely spoken to her during the six-hour flight. "That's very nice of you, Julia, but I've already made plans with the guys."

Julia laughed. "Oh, no! I'm not talking about hanging out together. I'm talking about buddy-*bucking*. That means you tip the driver a dollar today, and I'll tip him tomorrow."

"In essence," said Arnie, "giving the driver fifty cents per person for loading and unloading all our luggage instead of a dollar, which is the standard tip." He shook his finger. "We're all supposed to give the driver a dollar each way. It's protocol, and it's fair. That buddy-buck system makes us all look like a bunch of cheapskates."

Leslie whirled around indignantly. "You've been flying ten years longer than we have, Arnie, and you make a lot money more per hour. Cut us some slack."

"If you Upper East Side girls can afford a cab from Manhattan to JFK, you can afford to give the van driver a dollar bill. *Case closed.*"

This stinging rebuke led to a great deal of urgent whispering among the crew from first class, including sly references to petty theft on the part of the main cabin crew.

"So," said Eric, trying to lighten the mood. "What's everybody doing today?" His query was followed by a sharp jab in the ribs from Arnie.

"I don't know about you boys, but we're going to have an *amazing* adventure," said Leslie. "First, we're going to the de Young Museum to see an exhibit of antique European shoes. Then, after we've been inspired by a couple of hours of shoe-worshipping, we're trekking back to Union Square to do some serious shoe-*shopping.*"

"As if we need inspiration!" said Julia.

"True!" said Madeleine, "although exactly *how* a new pair of Christian Louboutin pumps can compete with a pair of Marie Antionette's bejeweled slippers escapes me at the moment."

"Well," said Leslie, grinning, "there are shoes ... and then there are *chausseurs!*" This witty retort was lost on everyone except Eric, who was the only French speaker on the crew.

"What about you three, Pavonia?" said Julia. "I'm surprised to see you on this layover. We get back so late tomorrow night. You'll never be able to make your commuter flights home."

"We're here for a more honorable purpose," said Pavonia. "Reverend Michael Knight is holding one of his famous Family Values rallies tonight at the Moscone Center. We reserved front row seats."

"If that's not worth spending the night on an armchair in operations tomorrow, I don't know what is," said Darcy. "By the way, Susan Collins will be there, too. She left JFK on the eight o'clock flight this morning."

"Good ol' Sue!" said Kendra. "I knew she wouldn't miss this for the world."

"Who's Sue Collins?" Eric whispered to Arnie.

"She's a red-headed, Nineties version of Anita Bryant—who also happens to be a New York-based stew," Arnie whispered back. "She commutes to New York from Oklahoma City."

"You mean there are *more* like them?"

"You'd be amazed," said Arnie. "So, Darcy, you three came all the way to San Francisco to hear a fundamentalist preacher? I thought your hometown would have been the first stop on his tour."

"Believe it or not, Arnie," said Darcy, "people *do* come here for reasons other than to go cruising in the Castro."

"Of course," said Arnie. "We also come to cruise south of Market Street."

"I'm aware of every dingy street corner in this city where gay men gather to ogle each other," said Darcy.

"Been doing your gay community marketing research, have you?" said Arnie.

"Our church gets new literature all the time," said Darcy. "We know exactly what goes on in your so-called community."

"Just look at this!" said Kendra, pulling a gay newspaper from Dallas out of her tote bag. She opened it to the personal ads, some of which featured provocative photographs. "Talk about fifty *filthy* ways to meet your lover."

"Nothing shocks me anymore," said Darcy, waving away the newspaper. "It only makes me even more resolute in achieving my goal."

"Which is?"

"Never mind," said Darcy, looking straight ahead. "Let's just get to the hotel and, all go about own business."

"Christ," Arnie muttered to Eric. "Some people should just stay home."

"Not me!" said Eric. "I can't wait to get out and go exploring. All I need is a city map, my camera and the kindness of strangers in case I get lost."

Arnie squeezed his thigh. "That, my young friend, you'll have *no* trouble with."

***

At four o'clock that afternoon, Eric knocked on Arnie's door at the hotel.

"Come in," said Arnie, opening the door. "How was your sight-seeing trip?"

"It was—" Eric was rendered speechless by the sight of Arnie squeezed into a pair of tight jeans and a mesh tank top, but he quickly recovered. "It was exhilarating." He walked into Arnie's room. "Hey, look! You got a suite!"

"Seniority has its benefits. Tell me what you did."

"I walked all the way up Mason Street, through Nob Hill, and down to the bay. The view from California Street was spectacular."

"That's nice. Did you see all your landmark buildings?"

"Yes. I saw the Mark Hopkins Hotel, the St. Francis Hotel, and the Brocklebank."

"What's that?"

"It's a gorgeous high-rise apartment building at the intersection of Mason Street and Sacramento. It's where Kim Novak's character lived in the Hitchcock movie, *Vertigo*."

"That's nice."

"There was so much beautiful detailing on so many of the apartment buildings that I didn't know where to look first: the woodwork, the stonemasonry, or the elegant lobbies with their beautiful glass doors and marble floors. You know, where I come from, we have apartment 'complexes', not buildings, and they appear overnight on a formerly vacant lot, made from these dreadful prefab kits. My walking tour was such a treat! If I ever left New York, which I *won't*, the only place I'd consider moving to is San Francisco."

"I'm glad that you enjoyed yourself. That's what flying is all about."

"The only disappointing part was ending up at Fisherman's Wharf. It was kind of tacky down there: I could smell the fried clams from two blocks away."

"Yuck! That tourist trap. I can't remember the last time I was anywhere near there. Promise me you'll never go there for chowder in a sour-dough bowl, or I'll disown you."

"What are some of your favorite neighborhoods in San Francisco, Arnie?"

"Hard to say. I did all the sight-seeing stuff twenty years ago when I was new. Now, after a six-hour flight, I have to put my feet up for a couple of hours before I can even think about leaving the hotel."

"So what did you do this afternoon?"

"I went to the liquor store next door and bought us some snacks." He opened a small bag of potato chips, poured them into a bowl, and opened a container of onion-flavored dip.

"Gee, that doesn't seem like very much food for four people," said Eric. "Maybe I should run over there myself and—"

"Relax," said Arnie. "Those two queens haven't eaten an ounce of starch since their first Junior Miss pageant. Here, help yourself."

"I hate to ask a stupid question, but are Ted and Jim twins or not?"

Arnie laughed. "No, they're not twins. They're just the kind of gay men who only bond with other gay men who look exactly like themselves."

"I see," said Eric. "They must gravitate toward each other, sort of like rare-earth magnets."

"Yes. It's the new 'gay clone' look. We had the same phenomenon back in the Seventies, only it was with big mustaches and lots of chest hair showing. These days, the smoothies rule. But the pendulum will swing back to 'furry' one day. That's just the way it goes." He pulled a bottle of wine from an ice bucket. "Here's some Chardonnay from first class." He handed the bottle and a wine opener to Eric. "Help yourself."

"Thanks. What are you drinking, Arnie?"

"Gin and tonic." He emptied the last few drops from a mini into a glass filled with ice and tonic. "Fuck. That takes care of my stash."

"I guess you didn't bring very much, huh?" said Eric.

"I started tipping a little early today," said Arnie. He pulled a wastebasket from under the desk and shook it, which produced the sound of rattling plastic bottles.

Eric looked inside the basket and counted six empty minis.

"Sometimes, it just makes the evening a little easier to handle," said Arnie. "I may have to run back downstairs to the liquor store before Les Girls arrive."

"If you don't like them, why do hang out with them?"

"Who says I don't like them?" Arnie seemed genuinely surprised by the question. "They're my friends, and they're great guys."

"Oh. Well, the way you keep making those little digs, it sounds like—"

"I hate their flat, little tummies that *stay* flat even after flying all day. And their gravity-defying asses, that's all. I know it's silly, but it's true."

Eric nodded. "It sounds like you have Margot Channing Syndrome—and one too many Eve Harringtons hanging around."

"Yeah, and counting you, that makes three." Arnie laughed. "See, when Denny's around, he kind of balances things out. He's halfway between my age and theirs. But don't get the wrong idea, Eric. I think you're fucking adorable and a hell of a nice guy, and I'm glad that you're here." He rattled the ice in his glass. "Man, I really would like another drink."

"Why not have some wine?"

"I never mix."

"Do you want me to run to the liquor store for you?"

"Do you mind?" Arnie reached into his tote bag for his wallet. "Let me give you—oh, wait." He smiled and dug out two more minis. "Ah! I forgot all about my emergency supply. That'll do for the next half hour. In the meantime, let's make ourselves comfortable." He refreshed his drink and sat down on the sofa so close to Eric that their knees were touching.

"I got some great pictures today," Eric said, as he sipped Chardonnay. "The lighting was perfect."

"If you're into photography, I have some pictures you may be interested in."

"Sure, I'd love to see them."

Arnie reached for a battered scrapbook and handed it to Eric.

"What's this?" asked Eric.

"Just look," said Arnie, reaching for his drink.

Eric opened the scrapbook. The first page featured a faded color photograph of a young, dark-haired man with a thick black mustache, wearing a navy-blue uniform with a wide club-striped tie. He was posed on a ramp stand in front of a gleaming four-engine jetliner.

"Is that you, Arnie?"

"Yep. That was on my very first trip— a 707 from JFK to San Francisco."

"What year was this picture taken?"

"I started in 1976. God, what that a great year!" He pointed to the next page. "See, here's a copy of the original crew list, and a picture of all of us crammed together in the galley."

Eric scanned the faces. He didn't recognize any of them, except one. "Sylvia Saks?" he said, dumbfounded. "Your first trip was with Sylvia Saks?"

"Uh huh. And she was a senior stew even back then: she'd been around ten years already. Nowadays, ten years seniority is nothing."

"My God, she hasn't changed at all, has she?"

"Nope. I think she came out of the womb with that bobbed haircut and scarlet lipstick."

Eric flipped a few more pages. "Who are these guys?"

Arnie reached for a pair of reading glasses. "My friends Chuck and Eddie. We used to buddy-bid on the 727 when we couldn't hold transcons." He smiled. "With the right crew, you can have fun anywhere. Even in Buffalo! And boy, did we get to know Buffalo—and Rochester and Syracuse, too. Thank God for all the 'curious' college boys in upstate New York."

"They're both so handsome." Eric turned the page. "All these guys are!"

"That's Rex and me, and our friends Nancy and Josie. We're in first class on a 747. See how elaborate that cart is? We used to carve the roast beef right in the aisle. The ding-dongs they hire nowadays would probably slice their own fingers off instead. Not you, of course. I'm sure you know your way around a large piece of meat."

Eric flipped to another page and saw a pamphlet that featured a color photograph of a very young, sexy Arnie standing on the wing of a 747. Two beautiful black females were seated together below him inside the cowling of one of the plane's massive engines. "Hey, I saw this picture in training! It was part of a slideshow about the history of in-flight uniforms."

"It's a little campy, I know That was a promo for the recruitment department. There was a big push one year to start hiring more men and more minorities."

"It's not campy at all! I love it." He continued flipping through the album. "Look at this picture. Who are all these hot, half-naked guys lounging around the pool?"

These three are Reggie, Blake, and Todd. We took a share on Fire Island with those four guys from Global Airways during the summer of seventy-nine. I've forgotten the names of the Global guys."

"I see what you mean about the mustaches and chest hair."

"Yeah, well, that was the look then." Arnie sighed fondly. "It was one of the best summers I ever had. I'd never so much sex in my life! Of course, crew scheduling was ready to kill us all. They could never get hold of us when we were on reserve! Beepers weren't allowed in the Meat Rack; they spoiled the mood."

"They all seem like great guys. I hope I get a chance to fly with some of them. Are they all still based in New York?"

"Nope," said Arnie sadly. "They've all moved on." He quickly flipped toward the back of the book. "Let me show you just one more picture." He pointed to a photograph of swarthy, hairy-chested young man strutting across a small stage in white bikini briefs. "Do you recognize this guy?"

"Yes. It's Denny. I met him on my flight to training, remember? God, Denny just exudes sex. Was he a stripper before he became a flight attendant?"

"No, we were on a layover once when he was new, and he kept complaining about how dead broke he was. We were kind of drunk, so I dared him to enter the underwear contest at the Manhole. He won first prize: a hundred dollars and free drinks for all of his friends."

"I may have to follow his lead if my finances don't improve soon," said Eric.

"I hope you didn't take this job for the money, baby. You won't have any in the bank for a long time." There was a knock on the door. "One minute, please!" Arnie shouted, closing the scrapbook. "Here come Frick and Frack. Would you let them in, Eric? I need to pop in the john."

"Sure." Eric opened the door.

"Hi, Eric." Ted and Jim walked in, wearing matching leather jackets over skin-tight Lycra t-shirts and 501 jeans. "Don't you look cute in that polo shirt!" said Ted, handing Eric a bottle of red wine so that he could take off his jacket. "I just knew you'd be a preppy out of uniform."

"But why now show off those nice biceps of yours, sugar?" said Jim, pushing Eric's short sleeves further up his arms. "If you got 'em, flaunt 'em! Where's Arnie?"

"In the bathroom."

"How is he dressed?" whispered Ted, reaching for the wine opener.

"Very casually," Eric said. "Why don't you guys sit down? Would you like some chips?"

"Oh, God, no!" said Jim, raising his shirt to reveal a sculpted abdomen. "Look at me! I'm fat as a pig!"

"We both are!" said Ted.

The bathroom door swung open. "Hello, boys." Arnie glanced at Ted and Jim. "You're looking a little puffy. Have you put on weight recently?"

"Arnie, what on earth are you wearing?" said Ted.

"What, this? It's just a muscle shirt. What's wrong with it?" He flexed his pectorals. "At my age, you gotta show off your assets."

Ted looked horrified. "Since when is silver chest hair poking through mesh fabric considered an asset?"

"I guess I could always let my dick hang out of my zipper."

"You may as well, those jeans are so tight. And not in the right places!" Jim folded his arms across his chest. "Arnie, I refuse to walk into *any* bar in the Castro with you dressed like that."

"I agree," said Ted. "We didn't spend two hours at the gym this afternoon just to be the laughing stock at Headquarters."

The scene reminded Eric of a day in high school when he'd seen two cheerleaders mocking a homely, overweight student as she scurried past them in the hallway. He'd loathed those former classmates ever since that day, and at that moment he felt the same way about Ted and Jim. "Listen, you two, why don't you—"

"Stop! Everybody *relax*," said Arnie. "I only wore this shirt to get a rise out of you. I was going to change before we left. I haven't gone out to the bars dressed like this since 1985!"

"Oh," said Ted, looking at the carpet. "Sorry."

"Forget about it," said Arnie, looking rather satisfied. "I love to watch the two of you go ape-shit about appearances, but I didn't mean for it to go that far. Let's all kiss and make up. Eric, pour them some wine. Ted, put on some music, and I'll go put on something that'll help me blend into the walls." As he walked out of the room, he started to pull the shirt over his head. "Just remember, my friends," he said, showing them his hairy back and shoulders. "This'll be you in twenty years!"

Ted and Jim exchanged a look as Arnie closed the bedroom door.

"Never in a *million* years!" Ted whispered fervently.

"Never!" his best friend agreed.

***

"I'll take another round for us, please," said Eric. "Two Greyhounds, one Tanqueray and tonic, and one vodka martini—"

"With three olives. I remember," said the bartender, with a wink.

"That's right." Eric was feeling no pain after having a glass of wine at the hotel and two martinis at Happy Hour. He steadied himself by propping one foot against the chrome rail and ogled the bartender. "Tell me your name again?"

The bartender, wearing only leather combat boots and a well-filled jockstrap, obviously enjoyed the attention. "I'm Wayne."

"Wayne from Wichita!"

"That's right." Wayne had emerald green eyes, a shaved head, and a stubble-covered jaw. The blond hair on his chest, which extended all the way down to his waistband, was carefully trimmed to show off the musculature of his torso. "And you're Eric from Austin."

"*Formerly* from Austin. I live in New York now."

"Right. You told me. You're here with those guys from Mercury."

"Yup. I know this is impossible, Wayne, 'cause this is my first time here, but I swear I've seen you somewhere before."

"It's not impossible," said Wayne, grinning slyly. "I do a little film work once in a while." He lazily ran a hand all the way down his torso. "That's why I have to clip all this. Otherwise, I'd look like a blond gorilla." Wayne's smile was slightly lopsided—a minor imperfection in an otherwise beautiful male specimen. Eric found this trait so endearing that he wanted to lean over the bar and kiss him.

"Well, here you go," said Wayne, dropping three olives into Eric's drink.

Eric reached for his wallet. "How much do I owe you?"

"Nothing, if you'll lose that fucking polo shirt."

"Seriously?"

"Seriously. It's a little out of place in here. Otherwise, you owe me twenty bucks."

Without a second thought, Eric peeled off the shirt. "How's that?"

"Beautiful. Some of us still *like* hairy guys. Hand me that shirt. I'll fold it and keep it behind the bar for you. You can pick it up on your way out. Now you better get going with these drinks. The ice is starting to melt."

"Thanks, Wayne."

"Come right back to me when you're ready for the next round. I'm here until eight."

"What are your plans for later tonight?"

"I'll be in bed and asleep by nine. I'm doing a shoot tomorrow morning at ten, and I have to go to the gym and pump up beforehand."

"Too bad."

The bartender scribbled a phone number on a cocktail napkin. "Look me up next time you're in town. You can catch me here every Monday through Thursday this summer. And in your local video store next month. In the *premium* section, not the sale bin."

"Thanks." Eric folded the napkin and put it in his wallet. "Does your movie have a title yet?"

"No, but just look for me on the box cover."

"Hey," said Ted coming up behind Eric at the bar. "Where've you—hey, look at you! Nice nips." He tugged Eric's left nipple. "I see you're getting into the Headquarters groove." He reached for two of the drinks. "We thought maybe you got lost."

"No, I was just talking to Wayne." They moved a few feet away from the bar. "Damn, he's hot!"

Ted laughed. "His boyfriend thinks so too."

"He didn't mention a boyfriend. And he was flirting with me!"

"Oh, so what? It's all just for fun. Anyway, please come back and join the group. A friend of mine wants to meet you, and we need to be rescued from Story Time with Arnie."

"How do you mean?"

"He's loaded, and he's telling nonstop retreaded tales of his glory days on the 747." Ted shook his head. "When's the last time that something *new* happened to that guy?"

"I think he needs to expand his horizons."

"Expand *something*, besides that waistline. I need to introduce him to the treadmill before he becomes a completely lost cause."

Eric and Ted joined a small group of men gathered near the back wall. "Eric, this is our friend Toby," said Jim. "He works in the financial district."

Toby was a handsome, clean-shaven, slightly older version of Ted and Jim. Boy, thought Eric, shaking Toby's hand, talk about gay men traveling in packs.

"Toby has a great penthouse apartment up in Twin Peaks," said Ted, "with a fantastic view of the whole city."

"It's hardly a penthouse," said Toby, with a grin. "But the view is very nice. Maybe you'll get to come over and check it out sometime."

"That'd be nice," said Eric. "I haven't been to Twin—"

"There you are!" said Arnie, putting his hand on Eric's shoulder. "I just went to look for you in the bathroom. I thought maybe you'd found the man of your dreams at the urinal."

"No, I was—never mind. Here's your drink, Arnie."

"Thanks. Where's your shirt?"

"A friend is keeping an eye on it for me."

"Ugh! Another show-off," said Arnie. "Let me see how far I can suck in my gut, and maybe I'll join you, Betty Jo and Bobbie Jo in the water tower."

"Join who in the what?" said Ted.

"Don't you remember *Petticoat Junction*?" said Arnie. He jerked his arm as though he were pulling a train whistle. "Woo, woo!"

"It was a Sixties sitcom about three sisters living in a small, rural town," Eric explained. "In the opening credits, a train would pass by a water tower where the sisters were always swimming together."

Ted rolled his eyes. "Sorry, Arnie: another cultural reference wasted on the eighteen-to-twenty-nine-year-old demographic. Not to mention: swimming in the town's water supply— how disgusting."

Arnie looked at his watch. "Well, you guys, Happy Hour is just about over. Do you want to think about moving along to another bar?"

"Oh, no," Ted said. "We all just got fresh drinks. I think we're going to hang here for a while longer. But if you want to head over to the Midnight Sun or someplace else on Eighteenth Street, feel free. We can catch up with you later."

"And bust up this quartet? Not a chance. In fact, I'd like to say something." Arnie held up his glass. "Here's to you guys. I know we rib each other a lot, and that sometimes you think I'm from another century. But I love you guys. It means a lot to me have some gay friends to hang out with, instead of wandering around the Castro on my own. You know, the last few years have been—" He choked back a sob. "Nope!" He took a deep breath. "I'm not going to go there tonight. Let me just say... thank you for being my friends. Oh! And I want to officially welcome Eric to the group and to the line. I know he's going to be another great friend and one of Mercury's finest stews!"

"Oh, Arnie," said Eric, genuinely touched. "That's so sweet!"

"You know we feel the same way about you, Arnie," said Jim.

"Well then show me, you guys!" said Arnie. "Come over here and give me a hug."

"Of course," said Jim, hesitating slightly before he moved closer.

"This is a special moment," said Arnie, as the four men embraced.

"Yes, it is," said Ted. "But I'm warning you: if you slip over to the DJ booth, and request the *Golden Girls* theme song, we're out of here."

"Fuck both of you!" said Arnie. "You just can't stand any *real* intimacy, can you?"

"Hello, boys. Am I interrupting anything?"

"James!" said Jim. "What are you doing here? And don't you look hot!"

Eric looked up. Another man had joined the group. He was tall and muscular and had a shaved head. He wore a leather sash across his bare torso, faded jeans and police boots. Even in the darkened corner of the bar, his tanned skin and sinewy arms attracted the other patrons' attention immediately.

"I thought I saw you guys at the airport today," said James. "I was checking people in for the Chicago flight. I tried to say hello, but you were making a beeline for the hotel van."

"Eric," said Ted, "this is our friend, James Hayes. He's an agent at SFO. And as you can see, Mister Leather something-or-other. What exactly is your title?"

"Mister California Rawhide, two years in a row," James replied, with pride.

"Aren't you a little overdressed for Happy Hour?" Arnie asked derisively. "I mean, a string of pearls and a sweater set would have been fine."

"I have a fundraiser to go to at eight o'clock," said James. "I'd invite you, Arnie, but I doubt that you'll still be on your feet by then."

"Whatever your cause is, James, I bet that you'll raise a million dollars just by walking in the door," Eric said.

"Eric just graduated from the Charm Farm," said Jim. "He's here on one of his first layovers. And I think you know our friend, Toby."

"Sure! Hey, boys," said James, shaking hands all around. Then he wrapped one arm around Eric's shoulder and looked directly into his eyes. "Tell, me, Eric, since you just graduated—"

"You can ask me anything."

"Do you by any chance know a guy named Anthony Bellini?"

"*Know* him?" Eric was thunderstruck. "Anthony was my roommate in training. I'm living in his apartment in Queens right now."

"What a fucking unbelievable coincidence!" said James. "I met him when he was deadheading back to the Charm Farm after a training flight. He said he was going to be based in DFW, but I had the impression he wasn't thrilled about it."

"Yes, he is based at DFW. But I haven't spoken to him in a while, so I couldn't tell whether he's thrilled or not."

"I gave him my phone number and asked to call me sometime. But I haven't heard from him yet. Have you—"

"Anthony meets *so* many people who are interested in him," said Eric, as resentment suddenly bubbled forth. Did Anthony *always* have to be the center of attention, even when he wasn't physically present? "He's kind of hard to pin down these days. The next time I talk to him, I'll be sure to remind him to call you."

"I don't know what it is about Anthony," said James, "but I can't seem to get that sexy, Italian mother fucker out of my mind."

"Fuck this Anthony guy, whoever he is," said Toby. "*I'll* help you get him out of your mind. And I'll provide the space too, after your fundraiser. Let's make it party time in Twin Peaks!"

"That might be just the ticket, Toby!" James wrapped his other arm around Toby's shoulder. He smiled as though he were posing for a publicity shot. "Look at these two handsome men on either side of me. Who else here is interested in—"

"Look no further!" said Jim. "We're always good for a round of *that*."

"Good!" said Toby, drawing everyone closer. "Let's work out the details."

"Hey, Arnie," said Ted. "Are you OK?"

"I'm… fine," said Arnie, who had slumped against the back wall of the bar.

"You don't *look* fine," said Jim. "You need a little fresh air. Eric, would you mind taking Arnie outside for a few minutes? I know that look. Believe me: he's reached his limit for the night."

"Sure," said Eric.

"Don't give him a cigarette, no matter how much he begs you," Ted added. "He quit smoking six months ago."

"OK." Eric and Arnie began moving toward the door, with Arnie in front.

"*Psst!*" Jim whispered into Eric's ear. "We'll take care of everything party-wise on this end. Just be cool about everything, OK? Come back in about five minutes."

"Sure." Eric pushed Arnie ahead of him. "Oh, it's cool outside," he said, once they were on the sidewalk. "And quiet, too. That's nice." He reached for a package of cigarettes in his back pocket.

"Give me a cigarette," Arnie demanded churlishly.

"Didn't you quit smoking six months ago?"

"Fuck it. I'll quit again tomorrow. Just give me one, please."

"Suit yourself," said Eric, offering him the pack.

"Let's sit down for a minute."

"On the sidewalk?"

"Yes, what's the big deal?" He sat down and leaned against the side of the building. "It's not like we're panhandling in front of Walgreens. I just need to get off my feet for a minute. Here, put my jacket behind you so your back doesn't get all scratched up." He lit a cigarette. "Oh, that's good," he said, puffing away. "God, I can't remember the last time I smoked while I was getting plastered."

"It's just like old times, huh?"

"No, not really. It'll never be like old times again for me." Arnie took another long hit and exhaled through his nose. "My old friends... the ones whose pictures I showed you... they're all dead, you know."

"Excuse me?"

"All those guys. Chuck and Eddie, my former buddy bidders. And the other Mercury guys from Fire Island, and the Global guys too. And a bunch of other great men that you'll never get to meet. All dead from AIDS."

"Arnie, I'm sorry."

"Do you have any idea what's that's like?"

"Yes, I do."

"No, you *don't*." Arnie's nostrils started flaring. "How old are you?"

"Twenty-three."

"And you're from Texas, right?"

"Yes, that's true, but I've lost friends to AIDS too."

"How *many* friends?" Arnie snorted. "I bet you can count them on the fingers of one hand! You have no fucking idea what it's like to be a gay man at my age and deal with—"

"Don't try to pull gay rank on me, Arnie. I've been out since I was fourteen, and I was screwing around before anyone was preaching about safer sex and condom use. I've seen the horrors of AIDS close up and personal, and like everybody else, I've been trying to cope with this goddam crisis in whatever way I can."

"You still don't *get* it." Arnie's anger suddenly gave way to a torrent of tears. "All my friends are dead. Not just some, but *ALL OF MY FRIENDS ARE DEAD!* Or *dying*. In a couple of weeks, I'll probably have to cross the last name out of my phone book." He leaned his head against Eric's shoulder and sobbed. "Why do you think I'm hanging with those two ding-dongs who make me feel like the world's oldest homosexual? There's nobody else left! Well, except for Denny."

"I'm sorry for your loss, Arnie," he said in a soothing tone. "But maybe you should start considering yourself lucky to be alive and to live in New York City. There are probably a million other gay men in the same boat, and there are dozens of organizations in desperate need of volunteers. That's a great way to meet people. Maybe it's time for you make friends outside the bar scene. "

Arnie shook his head sadly. "I live in Long Island and I fly. I can't—"

"Arnie, stop making excuses." Eric dropped the soothing tone from his voice. "There's GMHC—they always need Buddies. There're ACT UP meetings at the Gay and Lesbian Center. There's probably even a Long Island AIDS group where you could volunteer. Jesus, there are millions of isolated gay men in small towns all America who would love to have the support that's available in New York City. Dry your eyes and do something!"

All right, all right." Eric's words seem to have knocked the wind from Arnie's sails. He wiped the tears from his eyes with the back of his hand and crushed his cigarette.

"Feel better now?"

"Yes, thank you."

"Are you ready to go back inside?"

"Yes. I'm going to walk right into the bathroom and splash some water on my face. I'll meet you guys in a minute." He managed a grin. "Let's see what this Twin Peaks shin-dig is all about. And maybe you should think about getting your shirt back on, toots, before your nipples freeze solid."

"Good idea."

They walked back into the bar. After picking up his shirt from Wayne, Eric rejoined Jim, Ted, and the others.

"Where have you been?" Jim demanded. "I thought maybe you'd decided to go someplace else."

"We were just talking," said Eric.

"What about?"

"Life in general."

"Arnie likes you," said Ted. "That's nice. He could use new people in his circle. It's been getting smaller and smaller lately."

"So he said."

"Listen," said Jim, "here's what we have planned. We're heading over to the Midnight Sun at ten. That's when Jim's fundraiser will be over. He's going to meet us there. We'll have quick drink, and then grab a cab and head to Toby's for a J.O. party."

"What kind of party?" Eric asked.

"A jack off party," said Ted.

"It's the latest thing here in San Francisco," Jim explained. "We know all the people involved, we're all attracted to each other, and it's one hundred percent, completely safe sex. No fuss, no muss. We'll have a few drinks, watch some good porn on a widescreen TV, and pass around the lube and poppers. Everybody gets off with a willing, sexy partner—or partners, depending on the chemistry. Then we all shake hands and go on our merry way, which will probably back to the hotel. You're interested, right?"

"Well, I—"

"You *did* say you were ready for a real layover, didn't you, Eric?"

"Yes."

"We figured you'd be chomping at the bit, especially after being holed up at the Charm Farm for a month and a half," said Ted, with a grin. "Consider this your special welcome to the line. It's not the Mile High Club, of course, but first things first."

"Besides," said Jim, "the newest party member at Toby's always gets the most attention, if you know what I mean." He slipped his hand inside Eric's shirt. "Especially one with a chest as nice as yours."

"All right, I'm in."

"Great!" said Jim. "There's just one thing we need you to do."

"Stop at Walgreens and buy a large canister of Handi Wipes?"

"No. It's a little trickier than that. We need you to ditch Arnie."

"You mean he's not invited?"

"Of course not," said Ted. "In the first place, he's drunk. In the second place, participants at Toby's J.O. parties have to maintain certain appearance standards. I mean, if just anybody off the street was invited to attend, then it wouldn't be a special event."

"Oh, I see," said Eric. "We're talking about exclusivity—deciding who's in and who's out. Do you have any idea how depressed Arnie is right now? Telling him that he's not invited will probably send him into an emotional tailspin."

"We *are* taking Arnie's feelings into consideration," said Ted. "Can you imagine how he'd feel taking his clothes off in front of us? He'd be mortified to expose that big belly and that hairy back. Nobody would have a good time. We have to keep a certain vibe going or the whole thing is a bust. Besides, I'm sick to death of that broken record playing, 'Boo hoo, all my friends are dead, what'll I do?' "

"Oh," said Eric. "I didn't know that you'd heard that song before."

"Every layover, for as long as we've known him," said Ted.

"Well, how do you want me to get rid of him? He *knows* about the party."

"Just come with us over to the Midnight Sun," said Jim. "Get a few more drinks in him. Then, when he's had enough, and he's about ready to fall down face-first, walk him outside and hail a cab to take him back to the hotel. Here's ten bucks. If he starts squawking, just give the money and the hotel name to the cab driver. Problem solved."

This will be one of those experiences that you'll remember for your entire career," said Ted. "I'd hate for you to miss out on it."

"I don't know," said Eric. "The whole setup seems very mean to me."

Ted sighed. "Eric, in this job, reputations are built in an instant. Now, do you want to be known as a sexy party boy who goes with the flow, or a sad alcoholic stumbling around the Castro until last call?"

Eric took a deep breath before he responded. "I'll let you know at ten o'clock. How's that?"

"Oooh! A man of mystery!" said Ted, grinning. "We *like* that!"

CHAPTER 10

Picture This

God dammit, thought Ginnie Jo, as she dragged her luggage through the busy concourse at JFK. How I LOATHE early-morning trips! The whole chain of events leading up to her 0600 sign-in had put her in a rage before she even got to the airport:

3 A.M. Knock alarm clock off nightstand, force self out of bed, and walk straight into a wall on the way to bathroom. Make mental note for future reference: four fingers of Scotch at bedtime is not an ideal sleep aid. Torture self with cold-water shower in useless attempt to open eyes.

3:30 A.M. Try to avoid *gouging* eyes while putting on mascara, and breaking neck while struggling into pantyhose.

4:15 A.M. Finish dressing, grab luggage, congratulate self for leaving right on time, and head downstairs.

4:20 A.M. Realize that wig is still pinned to wig stand on vanity and run back upstairs, cursing all the way.

4:35 A.M. Rush back downstairs and try to hail a cab on deserted corner of 71st Street and York Avenue. Driver, who finally stops, reeks of God-knows-what and refuses to help lift my suitcase into trunk. But at least he understands, "Park Avenue and Forty-second Street, Mister, and *floor* it!"

4:50 A.M. Get in line for airport bus. While waiting, avoid at all cost making eye contact with the up-all-night freaks who're still roaming the streets. (They're probably all harmless fuckers, but hey—I read those stories in the *Post*.)

5:00 A.M. Board bus and stow bags. Tell myself that this ride will be infinitely better than taking the E train to the Q10 bus, and absolutely worth the extra money. Pray to God, as we pull away from the curb, that there won't be any chatterers riding to JFK at this hour. Thirty extra minutes of sleep will make all the difference in the way that this day goes.

5:05 A.M. Realize that, as usual, prayer will go unanswered. They're *here*.

5:15 A.M. Resist the urge to yell to chatterers: "Would you two *please* shut the hell up!" Instead, pray that their plane crashes as payback for keeping all of us awake.

5:55 A.M. Get off bus at Mercury Airways terminal and realize that, ironically, chatterers are working the same seven A.M. flight to Orange County.

6:00 A.M. While signing in for trip, revise last prayer: if our plane *does* crash, chatterers will be toast, but I'll walk away without a scratch. Will then sell story to *The Enquirer* or *People* —whichever pays more — and then I'll never have to get up for work at three A.M. again.

After passing through security, she stopped in front of the massive flight information board. Her mind was still in such a fog that she kept forgetting her gate number. As she stood there trying to focus her eyes, she had to steady herself against the hoard of people rushing by in both directions. *Ugh*, summer travelers! she thought. Why the hell do all these people need to fly to so goddam early? Holding firmly onto her luggage, Ginnie Jo forced herself to concentrate: Orange County, flight 167, gate 42. Go!

Hurrying along the concourse, she burped, quite unexpectedly, and caught a whiff of Scotch. It was a faint whiff, granted, but it was noticeable— and it came out of her mouth. Shit! She ducked into the ladies room to quickly rinse with Scope and then popped a breath mint, just to be sure. Introducing herself to co-workers while reeking of booze was not the ideal way to start a trip.

She arrived at her gate and noticed an animated crew of flights attendants who were looking a photo album. She plastered a big smile on her face. Be nice, even to the chatterers, she reminded herself. Keep all this bullshit in perspective: I'm starting all over again and there's no way around it. It's my second airline, second probationary period, and second time to pay my dues. By Christmas, I'll be off probation. And by next summer, I'll be able to hold what I like: afternoon flights with the Wall Street types who want to relax with a few stiff drinks, flirt with a pretty woman, and invite her out for dinner. At that point, 'pre-dawn sign-in' will never be part of my vocabulary again. "Good morning. My name's Ginnie Jo. I'm the number four in coach."

"Hi, Ginnie Jo!" chirped a young woman with platinum-blond hair. "I'm Sally, and this Betty and Pauline." Sally was also a blonde. Betty and Pauline were both brunettes but couldn't have looked more different. Betty used dramatic eye makeup, including false eyelashes, and wore her hair in a retro flip. In contrast, Pauline's skin was so pale that she looked as though she'd been white-washed. Her hairstyle was a short, no muss-no fuss affair that required no combing at all. A bobby pin held her limp bags off her forehead. Christ, thought Ginnie Jo. This chick couldn't look any less appealing if she tried. "Nice to meet you all," she said, resisting the urge to grab her make-up kit and slap some blush on Pauline's cheeks.

"Ginnie Jo, do you want to see something adorable?" asked Sally, thrusting the photo album toward her.

"Sure, Sally." Oh, joy. What could it be? She's too young to be a cat lady.

"This is my son, Taylor, eating his first birthday cake. I set it down in front of him and let him have at it. The first-birthday-cake free-for-all is a time-honored tradition in my family."

"He's adorable all right," said Ginnie Jo.

"Isn't it *hilarious* how he has icing smeared all over everything?" said Sally. "He really let it fly! I swear to God, it's been over a month and I'm *still* cleaning chocolate off the kitchen walls."

"I warned you, Sally!" said Betty, with a big laugh. "Their first cake should always be plain old vanilla. White frosting blends right into the wallpaper."

"My son Jackson didn't *have* a cake for his birthday," said Pauline.

"No cake?!" said Sally. "Why not?"

"Because he's never had a single taste of sugar in his life, and he never will," Pauline said self-righteously. "How many times do I have to tell you? Refined sugar is pure poison. I don't allow it in my house."

"Well, it's gonna cross your threshold sometime, Pauline," said Betty. "Just wait until his first Halloween. You can't dress him up in a cool costume and then not let him out trick-or-treating!"

"I'm not worried. In the first place, I'd never let my kids go from door to door begging for candy. That so-called rite of passage should be left to the children from welfare families. And in the second place, I have a tofu recipe for every major holiday."

Oh, bite me, thought Ginnie Jo. I hope this uptight broad isn't working with me in coach. I'd just as soon put up with the chatterers. Who'd have believed that an hour ago? "So, it is just us four girls today?"

"No," said Sally. "Denny is working in coach with you and Pauline. He's the galley today. He's already onboard, setting up."

"Setting up?" said Pauline, with a scowl. "If I know Denny, he's out on the catering truck, smoking."

"Oh." Ginnie Jo grabbed her cigarette case from her purse. "In that case, I think I'll get on right now and see if he needs a hand."

Sally and Betty exchanged a knowing look and then started laughing. "Look out!" said Sally. "I can tell we have *double* trouble in the back today!"

Pauline scowled. "I swear to God, if I smell one *whiff* of cigarette smoke when I get back there, I'm going to——"

"Shhh," Betty said. "Pauline, honey, you have got to start loosening up. Breathe, relax, meditate, start drinking again—do something just for yourself!"

"But second-hand smoke is——"

"We know, we know," said Sally. "Let's all get on board and get this party started, OK? Save that energy for the women you meet who feed their babies formula instead of breast milk."

Ginnie Jo walked toward the back and shoved her suitcase into an overhead bin. She noticed that the aft galley was flooded with sunlight, which indicated that one of the doors was open. Oh, please, please, please, she thought. She stepped into the galley, cigarette in hand, and sniffed. Oh, I do smell smoke, thank God! There was a catering truck parked next to the rear door; a catering rep was busily wheeling carts into the galley. She nodded hello to him and then noticed a flight attendant crouched in the back of the truck with a cigarette in his hand. "Hey there." She stepped carefully across the small ramp that connected the plane to the truck. "You must be Denny. I'm Ginnie Jo."

"Hi."

"Mind if I join you?"

"Not at all."

"Make it a quick one, you guys," said the catering rep. "I'm just about finished here, and I gotta haul ass to another flight."

"We will," said Denny, as he lit Ginnie Jo's cigarette.

"Oh, that's good," said Ginnie Jo, inhaling deeply. "What a treat! I didn't think I'd get to have another of these for hours."

"Fringe benefit of working in the back," Denny replied, with a grin. "You've just got to check with the cockpit first to make sure that we're not getting fueled. Otherwise, you know, the minute you light up: ka-BOOM!"

"Right!" replied Ginnie Jo, as she puffed away. "Sometimes, I feel like I'm the only smoker left in the world, know what I mean?"

"Yeah, most of the other stews who still smoke have gone over to international. But smoking will be banned eventually on those flights, too. It's just a matter of time."

Ginnie Jo studied Denny as they smoked. He appeared to be in his early thirties and of Eastern European descent. He had strong facial features, including a prominent brow and a square jaw in need of a shave. His thick hair, heavy eyebrows and piercing eyes were jet black. Together, these features gave him a sinister, sexy look. He wore the male summer shirt with epaulets. Denny's short sleeves had been altered to hug the crest of his biceps. As he stood up to put out his cigarette, she noticed that his uniform pants had also been tailored with great care; they were snug in all the right places. "Look at you," she said. "You're a real stud muffin."

"Thanks."

"But you're gay, right?"

He chortled. "You had to ask?"

"I just figured. The straight guys never look so pulled together." She sighed. "Too bad."

"My boyfriends don't think so," he replied, without missing a beat.

"You got a brother, maybe?"

"Yep." He grinned. "He's gay, too."

"Damn! Oh, well. My loss."

"You can't have *every* man you want. That wouldn't be fair to the rest of us."

She laughed. "I can tell one thing already, Denny: we're gonna get along great."

"You know it, sister! Be glad that I'm bringing some male energy to this crew. These other girls are all very nice, but this is a real 'Mommy' trip. The early morning flights always are. It's gonna be 'baby this' and 'baby that' all the way to California. Especially from Pauline."

"What's up with her, anyway? She seems a little tightly wound."

"A little? She's like spin top on steroids. Any day now, she's gonna spin herself right off the planet."

"Hey, speaking of Pauline, here she comes."

"Quick! If she asks what you're doing on the layover, tell her that you have plans. I always have that expression on the tip of my tongue when she's around, just in case she asks."

"What *do* you have planned?" she asked, as Pauline stopped to check emergency equipment in the overhead bins. "From what I remember, Orange County is one of the most boring places on earth."

"It still is. That's why they named the airport after John Wayne: it's strictly Dullsville."

The caterer shooed them off the truck and pulled the ramp away.

"Thanks, Juan, see you next time," said Denny, as he closed the aft door. "I'm lucky. I have a date this afternoon."

"What kind of date?"

"What kind do you think?"

"Oh, really? Hey, that's nice!"

He shrugged. "It'll probably be a quickie. They're all married or closet cases in O.C. But it helps to pass the time on a layover like this."

"What *are* you doing on a layover like this?"

"This is an overtime trip. It's all that was available. God, I *hate* early sign-ins."

"Me, too. Is the hotel near anything?"

"Yes: a major freeway and mall. But there's also a great little joint for drinks and burgers nearby that nobody else seems to know about yet. It's called Sheila's."

"I love little joints."

"Great we'll go for Happy Hour after my date leaves. We can walk there. It's right across the street."

"Wonderful! Things are starting to look up."

"Remember, not a word to Pauline. I need her tagging along like I need a hole in the head."

"Not to worry. Mum's the word."

***

Two hours after takeoff, Denny and Ginnie Jo collapsed onto their jump seats. "Whew! Thank God that's over!" Denny said, pulling the galley curtain closed. "This plane is the *worst*: one narrow aisle, one hundred and sixty passengers, and only three stews to serve them. I can't believe we use it on a coast to coast flight."

A moment later, the curtain was flung aside by Pauline. "What's this? Are you on break already?"

"Yes," said Denny. "We're sitting down for ten minutes. It might get bumpy. I can feel it."

"Excuse me, but the service isn't over until it's *over*. I need more drinks: three apple juice, a Diet Coke, two coffees with—"

"Tough shit," said Denny. "We just went through with the beverage carts a second time when we picked up the trays. I'm not lifting a finger for the next hour."

"Never mind! I'll just do it myself, as usual."

"Go right into your martyr act, girl. We're done."

Ginnie Jo propped her feet against a cart. "I thought JFK-Orange County was supposed to be one of our 'high-end' markets. It's more like an Orlando trip today. What's with all the goddam kids on this flight?"

"They're the precious off-spring of all those 'high-end' passengers," replied Denny. "They're traveling for free on their parents' frequent flier miles. Obnoxious little fuckers, too. I hate 'em all."

"You said it!" said Ginnie Jo, noticing that Pauline's face was beginning to redden. "The only people I hate more are the parents who do nothing to control their kid's behavior. Don't they teach them anything these days? Like even saying 'please' or 'thank you'? Not to mention the jumping up and down on the seats and the screaming and yelling. I'd like to shove 'em out the window. I bet they'd *really* scream on the way out!"

"They all should all be sedated before boarding starts," said Denny.

"Hey, good idea!" said Ginnie Jo. "Do you think I'd have trouble getting a can of chloroform through security?"

"I can't believe what I'm hearing!" said Pauline.

"What's the matter with you?" said Ginnie Jo.

"All of this anti-family sentiment. It sickens me. Neither of you has children of your own, am I right?"

"Are you kidding?" said Denny. "I come from a family of eight. It was total *bedlam*, twenty-four hours a day. My mother used to say, right before she locked us outside in the summer, 'If any of you ever come home and tell me that you're getting married and having children, I'll *kill* you.' So I came home and told her that I was gay instead."

"What about you, Ginnie Jo?"

"No way. My womb will remain fetus-free until I take my last breath."

"It's so typical of non-parents to judge the way that other parents raise their children," Pauline said indignantly. "Kids aren't little wind-up toys, you know. You can't turn them on and off whenever you want."

Denny flipped a newspaper open. "Hey, Pauline, that coffee's starting to get cold. Maybe you should save yourself another trip and head back out with that tray."

"I'm just saying that as a parent, and as someone who *writes* about parenting, you two should think twice before you open your big mouths. You know nothing about handling children. And cut the parents some slack, please. Those high-end passengers *do* pay our salaries, you know!" She left the galley in a great huff.

"Is she really a writer?" asked Ginnie Jo. "She didn't strike me as the type. What does she write—books, a column, a newsletter?"

"Don't make me laugh! A few years ago, she got a letter to the editor printed in *Working Mother Magazine*. You'd think she won the goddam Pulitzer Prize. She still carries a tattered copy with her wherever she goes. By the way, what do you want for crew juice today for the ride to the hotel?"

"You make crew juice? Oh, my God. That's the first time I've heard that expression since I started flying at this airline. What are my choices?"

"Whatever you want. That's one good thing about breakfast flights: there's always a lot of booze left over."

"The other girls won't mind?"

"No, they're cool. Even Pauline, believe it or not. You and I can park it in the last row of the van and sip away while they write out their Dealer Dan shopping lists."

"There's a Dealer Dan's in Orange County?"

"Yeah, it just opened and it's within walking distance to the hotel." He gestured toward the front of the plane. "They're all so excited that they're about to wet themselves. Anyway, I'll make a us an Evian bottle of champagne and OJ for the ride."

"I'm not a huge fan of mimosas, but whatever."

"I know. You're a Scotch drinker."

"How'd you know?"

"I could smell it on you this morning."

"Why didn't you say anything?!"

"Don't worry, I'm discreet." He opened the liquor cart. "Here. Take some minis for later. The mimosas are just for the van ride. I want to get a post-flight buzz before my date."

"I'm still on probation. I'm a little leery of stashing minis in my purse."

"Not to worry." He opened a cupboard. "I kept all the empty Evian bottles and caps from the service. The trick is to transfer a handful of minis into an empty bottle before we land."

This is just like the old days, she thought happily. "Oh, Denny, I *knew* that I'd love flying with you!"

"Ditto. Meet me in the lobby at five, and aw-a-a-ay we'll go."

***

At five P.M., feeling pleasantly intoxicated, Ginnie Jo stepped off the elevator and into the hotel lobby. There's nothing like a nice buzz in the afternoon, she thought. As long as I have a few drinks and a little fun to look forward to at the end of the work day, I really can get through anything. The long flight, the noisy children, and even Pious Pauline were already a distant memory.

"Excuse me," a smooth male voice said behind her. "Are you Ms. Burke?"

She turned around. It was the front desk clerk who had checked the crew in earlier. He was an angelic blue-eyed blond whose name tag identified him as 'Samuel from Salt Lake City, UT'.

"Yes, that's me."

"I have a message for you. Mr. Malinovski is running a few minutes late. He'd like you to wait for him here in the lobby. He said he'll be down as soon as he can."

"Still screwing, is he?"

He tried to hide a smile. "He didn't give me any reason for the delay. Would you prefer to wait in the bar?"

"Oh, no, I'm fine right here. Thanks, Samuel."

"My pleasure."

As she lit a cigarette, she imagined Denny upstairs with his date. Obviously, they were still going at it. Lucky SOB, she thought. She wondered what kind of man Denny liked, and decided that his date would be handsome but in a bland way, like Samuel. Denny probably relished using his sinister appeal to lure a certain type of man: the kind who spent his entire life fighting his most primal physical needs. That always made for the hottest sex—or so she'd been told by many gay friends.

A moment later, the elevator chimed and opened, but it wasn't Denny who appeared. It was Pauline.

"Oh my God!" said Pauline, racing into the lobby. "I'm late. I'm LATE! Did you see them?"

"See who?"

"Betty and Sally! We're going shopping together. I was supposed to be down here an hour ago! But I overslept. God dammit!" Pauline was wearing a 'Got Milk?' t-shirt, plaid shorts and sandals. Jesus, thought Ginnie Jo. This chick has the whitest, stoutest legs that I've ever seen.

"As soon as I got into the room, my husband called," said Pauline. "He couldn't figure out the carpool schedule for the kids' afternoon activities. I had to spend *thirty minutes* going over it with him. The whole time I'm thinking, as I'm trying to maintain consciousness: Christ, Keith! How can you be that incompetent? I mean, you have a doctorate in math and you can't figure this out without my help? I finally told him, 'I have a migraine and have to go to bed. Don't call me for any reason. I don't care *what* happens!' Then I called the front desk and told them to put a Do Not Disturb on my phone. Then I overslept, and now my day is ruined!"

"That sucks, all right. Do you see now why there's a No Vacancy sign on my reproductive parts?"

"Believe me, Ginnie Jo, sometimes I think to myself: if I could go back seven years, I'd—never mind. So what are you doing down here?"

"Uh… nothing. I'm just having a smoke and trying to decide—"

"Sorry I'm so late," said Denny, bursting through the elevator door. He skidded to a halt when he saw Pauline. "Oh, hi, Pauline. I thought you were going to Dealer Dans."

"She overslept," Ginny Je Jo explained. "Betty and Sally already left."

"Where's your friend, Denny?" Ginny Jo asked.

"He slipped out the back exit. It's closer to the parking lot."

Of course he did, she thought. Closet cases always slip out the back door.

"What are you guys doing?" Pauline asked.

"We're going out for a drink," said Denny. "In a dive bar, with seedy people who will be smoking cigarettes. I'm sure you wouldn't want to—"

"A drink sounds wonderful. Can I join you? Please? *Please!*"

She looked so pathetic that Ginnie Jo couldn't say no. "Sure, Pauline," she said, avoiding a murderous glare from Denny. "I think a cocktail or two might do you some good."

***

"Well," Ginnie Jo said approvingly. "This is a joint, all right."

"Isn't this perfect?" said Denny. "It's cool, quiet, and family-free." He waved a laminated menu in the air. "See: there's no kiddie menu! I love this place. Here comes Sheila, the owner. She's ultra-cool."

Sheila approached the table. She had long, sun-streaked hair and wore frosted lipstick. A ribbed-knit tank top showed off what she must have considered as her best feature: her breasts. "Hey, Denny. You brought some friends, huh? Nice. What'll you have?"

"The usual, Sheila: a vodka and soda."

"Coming up." Sheila looked at Ginnie Jo. "You?"

"Glenlivet up, with a water back."

"Call liquors aren't on the Happy Hour menu, FYI."

"Not a problem."

"What about you, hon?"

"I'll have a Long Island Iced Tea," said Pauline, without hesitation.

"That's *definitely* not on the Happy Hour menu."

"Not a problem for me, either."

Ginnie Jo nudged Pauline. "Do you know how much liquor is in one of those?"

"Yes. And the faster that Shelia brings it, the faster I can start *drinking* it."

"OK," said Sheila. "I'll be right back."

Pauline watched Sheila closely as she walked away. "Remarkably firm breasts for a woman her age."

"Yes, but I don't think they're real," remarked Ginnie Jo.

"It doesn't matter," said Pauline. "They still look nice on her."

"Boobie talk!" Denny said with great disdain, as he lit a cigarette. "I may as well be out drinking with the pilots! All that's missing from this table are the golf shirts!"

"Oh, relax!" said Ginnie Jo. "We can't talk about dicks *all* the time. By the way, how come you're on a first name basis with the waitress? I thought you hardly ever did this trip."

"I don't, but whenever I do, I always come here."

Sheila returned with a tray of drinks and served Pauline first.

"Well," said Ginny Jo, picking up her shot glass. "Here's to—"

Slurp! "Oh, that was good!" said Pauline, sucking the last few drops through a straw.

"Jesus fucking Christ!" said Ginnie Jo. "Denny and I haven't even touched ours. Take it easy!"

"I warned you," said Denny. "I knew her before she became Mother of the Year."

Pauline waved Sheila over. "Bring me another one."

"Already? I just served you one."

"This is probably the one day this year I'll get to feel like a grown up. *Bring it.*"

Sheila cast a quizzical glance at Denny.

"It's OK," he said resignedly. "She's with us, and we're staying right across the street. We'll make sure she gets back to the hotel in one piece."

"Whatever," said Sheila. "Just don't let her cross the street by herself."

"Let me have one of those, too," said Pauline, reaching for Ginnie Jo's cigarettes.

"You're not even a smoker!" said Ginny Jo.

"I used to be. I used to do a lot of things." She removed a cigarette and looked at it lovingly. "Do you know how long it's been since I've held one of these in my hand?"

"Probably as long as it's been since I've held a nice, fat eight-incher in mine," said Ginnie Jo.

"You can have my husband's. I don't want it coming anywhere near me, ever again." Pauline lit the cigarette and inhaled deeply. "Oh, my God!" she whispered, as her eyelids drooped. "There's nothing like that first hit. This must be what heaven feels like."

"You have an eight-incher waiting for you at home and *that* feels like heaven?" Denny shook his head in disbelief. "*Vaya con Dios, chica.* Just remember: it'll be *your* funeral on the flight back tomorrow. That five A.M. wake-up call is going to kill you."

She slammed her fist on the table. "Let me *be,* will you? Just let me be one of the crew, for one fucking layover."

"OK, OK, don't get all excited," said Ginny Jo. She placed her cigarettes on the table between them. "Do whatever the hell you want. Drink, smoke, dance topless on the bar. We'll be your guardian angels for the day."

"Thank you," Pauline replied gleefully, as Sheila served her second drink. "And by the way Ginnie Jo, you're a very pretty woman. If it's been a long time since you fondled an eight-incher, then you're doing something wrong."

***

"My first pregnancy was easy," said Pauline. "I never had morning sickness, not even once. Things didn't get complicated until I got to the hospital. One of the first things they do when they prep you for the delivery is to give you an enema. One of the nurses stuck a rubber hose up my ass and told me to take in as much water as I could hold. I mean, my husband was right there in the room!"

"How appalling," said Denny.

Pauline finished her fourth cocktail and clumsily set the glass on the table. "And then they take you in the rabor room, where you're supposed to get the shinal shock, but I—"

"They take you *where* to get the *what?*" Denny was clearly irritated. "I can't understand a word you're saying. Sit up straight and stop slurring, for Christ's sake."

"I think she meant the *labor room,* where they're supposed to give you a *spinal block,*" said Ginnie Jo.

"What's that?" asked Denny.

"It numbs you … *down below* … before the kid starts coming out." Ginnie Jo began discreetly looking for an escape route.

"Oh, no you don't!" Denny clamped her arm with an iron grip. "You're the one who invited her to the party. You're staying until the bitter end."

"But I didn't *get* a spinal block," said Pauline, "because—"

"Do you guys want to order some food?" asked Sheila, suddenly appearing at the table.

"In a minute," said Denny.

"You've been drinking for almost an hour straight. I think you should eat something."

Pauline banged her fist on the table. "Would everybody stop interrupting me while I'm trying to tell my goddam story?"

"OK, girlfriend." Sheila picked up Pauline's empty glass. "No more alcohol for you."

"I don't think I'm gonna eat right now anyway," said Ginny Jo. "I may order from room service later." She stood up. "If you guys don't mind, I'm going to head back to the hotel."

Denny's big black eyes narrowed into two little slits. "If you leave right now, I'll follow you with the biggest, sharpest knife that I can find in the kitchen and cut you to ribbons."

"Damn you, Denny!" shouted Pauline. "How dare you talk like that, after what happened to me!"

That's it!" said Sheila. "You're all cut off. Either order some food or pay up and get the hell out of here."

"Three cheeseburgers with fries," said Denny.

"Coming up," said Sheila. I'll bring your check with the food."

"So go on, Pauline," said Denny. "You were saying you didn't get a spinal block, right?"

"No, I did *not!* The baby came too fast! What I got instead what an episiotomy!" She grabbed her purse and began fumbling through the contents.

"What's an episiotomy?" Denny asked.

"Don't you know *anything?!*" She grabbed a small photo album. "It's where they slice you open before the baby RIPS YOU APART on the way out."

"Oh… oh, no," said Ginnie Jo, as the room started spinning. "Please don't tell me that this story comes with illustrations."

"Look! Look at this!" Pauline shoved the open photo album at her. "THIS IS WHAT BABIES DO TO YOU!"

"Oh my fucking God!"

***

Suddenly, everybody was shouting. "Get her up! Get her up off the floor!"

"No, don't move her. If she broke anything, you'll only make it worse."

"Is there a doctor here?"

"In here? Are you kidding?"

"Ginnie Jo, can you hear me?"

She felt two slaps across her face. "What? Yes, I hear you." She opened her eyes and saw Denny looming over her. "What the hell happened?"

"You fainted."

"Bullshit. I've never fainted in my life."

"First time for everything. Can you get up?"

"Of course I can." She clumsily stood up and sat back down in her chair.

Sheila appeared with a middle-aged man by her side. "You won't believe it, but there *is* a doctor in here. Oh, wait, she's up now. And she didn't break her neck? That's good." She slapped down a check. "There's a cab waiting for you outside. Pay up and leave."

Denny reached for his wallet. "We don't need a cab. Our hotel is across the street."

"Listen to me," said Sheila. "I served you alcohol. In fact I over-served you, and I'm liable for damages if you walk into oncoming traffic. Now get up, get your friends into that fucking cab, and don't come back here. Ever." She crossed her arms in front of her chest. "From now on, Mercury crews are *banned* from this establishment. Get out!"

***

The flight back the next day was miserable. They had barely finished the service in coach before they hit a patch of turbulence that sent Ginnie Jo and Denny scrambling for their jump seats. They buckled up just in time to see an insert go flying off the counter and onto the floor, creating a nasty puddle of juice, coffee, tea, and cocktail napkins.

"Fuck, talk about just in time," said Denny. He pointed to a lumpy mass covered with a blanket next to Ginnie Jo. "How Pauline can sleep through this is beyond me."

"Mothers." Ginnie Jo shook her head. "They're immune to all commotion, I guess."

"Talk about a party pooper!" Denny remarked. "I don't care what happens: she is never coming out me with me again. And I'm never *covering* for her again, either. Lucky for her she's flying with cool people. Any other crew would have turned her in for showing up so hungover that she can't even stand up straight."

"God, that picture!" said Ginnie Jo. "I can't get it out of my mind. The little head and shoulders, squeezing out through her—I've never been so traumatized in my life. I mean, who the fuck shows a picture of her baby *coming out* to a person she barely knows?"

A piercing wail filled the air. Pauline bolted into an upright position. "What the hell was that?" she demanded, as she pulled off the blanket.

"That's the four-year-old in row twenty," said Denny. "Now, *there's* a reason for carrying a Taser on every flight! The mother is useless. She won't even keep him buckled up when the seatbelt sign comes on. But I tell you what: if that little Bridgeport Bomber comes flying down the aisle one more time, I'm going to knock the shit out of him."

"Excuse me," said a woman, timidly poking her head through the galley curtain. "I'm very sorry to bother you, but could you please do something about that woman and her two children sitting behind me?"

"What's the matter?" asked Ginny Jo.

"Her little boy is constantly kicking my seat, jumping up and down, and shrieking for no reason at all. I mean, if it were a baby crying, I wouldn't mind so much, but his mother is taking no responsibility at all."

"Are you in row nineteen?"

"Yes."

"We'll take care of it as soon as we can get up," said Denny. "In the meantime, the last row is vacant. Just have a seat there and buckle up, please. It's not safe for you to be out walking about right now."

"Oh, thank you!" The woman looked greatly relieved as she turned to leave.

"What are we gonna do?" said Ginnie Jo. "That mother is a real bitch. I almost ran over that kid twice with the cart and she acted like it was my fault. I'm on probation, you know. If I say anything else to her, she'll write a bad letter, and I'll be screwed."

"*I'll* handle this one," said Denny. "I refuse to be terrorized by that self-absorbed cunt—or her kids."

"You awake now?" Ginnie Jo asked Pauline, who appeared to be coming out of her haze.

"Yes," she replied. "I see it's finally smoothed out. Is it time for us to start the breakfast service?"

Ginnie Jo rolled her eyes. "It's done. You've been asleep for two hours."

"Oh. Thanks for covering for me."

"You owe us big time, Pauline."

"I know," Pauline replied remorsefully. "I was so out of control last night. I don't remember a thing after that first drink! That's why I should never start. Well, anyway, right now I need for this flight to land. All I want to do is get home to my kids."

"Cut!" said Denny. "Let's do it again and this time, say the line like you mean it. Take two!"

Ginnie Jo took a peek up the aisle. "Hey, Denny, that kid is racing up and down the aisle again. Let's see if you're a man of your word."

Pauline stood up. "What's that child doing up, in this turbulence? Isn't the seatbelt sign on?"

"Duh!" exclaimed Denny. "I just said: the mother's oblivious!"

"Why is he *screaming* like that?" Pauline screeched.

Denny dropped his newspaper. "I've had enough of this for one day." He stood up and positioned himself between the galley and the aisle. "Watch, Ginnie Jo. This is how you fake an accident."

No," said Pauline, pushing him out of the way. "Let *me* teach that child and his mother a fundamental life lesson." She stood watching from the corner of her eye. At the last possible moment, she stepped into the aisle. Her collision with the toddler was violent.

"Oh my God!" shouted the woman in the last row, as Pauline stood immobilized over the bloodied, screaming child. "Why are you just standing there? Get some paper towels! Get some bandages! Get a doctor—move!"

Ginnie Jo sprang out of her seat. "I'll get the first aid kit, Denny. You page for a physician."

"Oh, Christ," muttered Denny, as he picked up the interphone. "Here comes the mother in hysterics, acting like all of a sudden like she gives a damn. We're going to get a letter about *this* one, that's for sure!"

"I... I couldn't help it," Pauline sputtered. "It was an accident! I mean, the seatbelt sign *is* on. That little boy came charging at me from out of nowhere. It was all just a terrible, *terrible* accident."

CHAPTER 11

Puttin' on the Herb Ritts

"Push it," Jim commanded.

"I am pushing!" Anthony replied, almost out of breath.

"Come on, be a man, *push* it!"

"I can't go any further! And would you lower your goddam voice?"

"Don't use that tone with me, you son of a bitch. I'm trying to help you."

"By drawing a crowd? Yeah, that really helps."

A man next to them grunted. "Do it, man. *Do* it. It's fuckin' thing of beauty to watch."

"Bite me," Anthony replied.

Jim spread his legs and lowered himself until he was practically straddling Anthony. "Come on, baby," he whispered. "Can't you give me just a little more?"

"I... said... I... can't!" Anthony panted, as his entire body heaved. "Watch it, watch it!"

"Hey!" Jim jumped back as the dumbbells fell with a resounding thud. "You almost broke my foot!"

"I warned you!"

"This is the last time I ever spot you."

A muscular man in a body-hugging t-shirt came running toward them. "Gentlemen, we'll have none of that here, thank you very much." He placed his hands on his hips. "Grunting and groaning is one thing, but there is to be no dropping of weights on the floor. You're not at Gold's Gym, you know."

"Thanks," said Anthony. "I'll try to work on my grunting and groaning instead. Jim, when I say I can't take any more weight, I mean I can't take any more. Got it?" He grabbed his towel, pushed his way through the onlookers, and stormed off to the aerobic area.

Jim was right on his heels. "You've been on the forty-five pounders for a month. You've got to keep increasing if you want to gain muscle mass."

"I've got plenty of muscle mass," said Anthony, as he hopped on a treadmill and set the controls.

Jim pressed the stop button. "No cardio today. We have just enough time to hit the steam room and shower before brunch at Heinrich and Deiter's."

"We'd have had plenty of time today if we'd worked out at your place. You have a complete gym at your house. Why do bother keeping a membership here?"

"I make a lot of connections here. It's good for business."

"And why is it so crowded on a Sunday morning? These queens should all be at home, sleeping off their Mining Company hangovers."

"This isn't the Mining Company crowd. These men have grown-up lives. Fitness is an important part of that. Besides…" He affectionately whacked Anthony on the ass. "I like showing you off. Come on, let's hit the steam room. And remember what I told you about the way to wear your towel."

"Are you expecting me to put on a little show for your buddies?"

"There's nothing little about you, Mr. Bellini, and you know it," Jim growled, as he slipped his hand into Anthony's onion-skin shorts.

Christ, thought Anthony, that sensation—like a bolt of lightning! Jim could be so obnoxious at times, but all it took was the touch of his hand and Anthony was hard as a rock. "I could say the same for you, buddy."

Jim grinned. "That's why we're so good together. We're evenly matched."

"All right," said Anthony, making no attempt to cover his erection. "We can do a quick steam. How much of me do you want them to see?"

"Well, it's not a porn video. But I wouldn't mind if they got a good look at your nine-incher. It's fun to watch 'em sweat and salivate at the same time."

"And if a strange hairy hand starts making its way up my thigh…?"

"Oh, no," Jim said. "They can look all they want, but only *I* can touch."

***

At one o'clock, they arrived at the home of Jim's friends, Heinrich and Dieter. They lived in a massive yet sparsely furnished house in the exclusive Highland Park area. The house was set far back from the road at the end of a long, wooded drive. The exterior was so imposing that first time they went there, Anthony had expected a line of liveried servants standing at attention in the foyer. As the house came into view, Anthony spotted an available parking space right near the front. "Hey lucky, you. Put her in right there."

Jim scowled. "God dammit. Why didn't François tell me that he'd be driving his Mercedes today?"

"What, he has to ask your permission?"

"No, of course not. But if I'd known, I'd have driven the Alfa Romeo. I can't park my Mercedes behind his. This is absurd."

Anthony tried not to laugh. "Is that like the two of you showing up in the same dress?"

"As a matter of fact, Mister Wise-ass, it is."

"Well, look, at least yours is a different color."

"Now I'll have to park way over there, and we'll have even further to walk to get to the front door in this fucking August heat."

"We could have driven my car today."

"Are you kidding? They wouldn't have let us past the security gate in that jalopy of yours."

"That jalopy is paid for and it's the first car I've ever owned," Anthony said with pride. "Anything wrong with that?"

"No, not if you're in your senior year of trade school. Forget about your car. We'll take care of that in due time, too."

"Too? What else are we taking care of?"

"Living arrangements." He grinned. "I think it's time you left that stew zoo in Oak Lawn."

Alarm bells sounded in Anthony's head. "Why should I move? It's a nice house and they're decent guys. It's fun living with other flight attendants."

"That's all well and good for now, but you've got to think about your future, Anthony. You'll get nowhere in life living with those clowns—except Sunday Beer Bust at JR's."

"You're moving too fast, Jim. I've only known you for six weeks."

"Then you know I like to take the bull by the horns. But we'll talk about that later. As far as the car, I'm calling in a favor from a friend who owns a Maserati dealership. I'll make sure you get a few bucks for Chitty Chitty Bang Bang when we trade her in."

"Who says we're trading it in?"

"*I* say," said Jim, as they got out of the car. "I want you to have something that's a little more luxurious. I can't let your million-dollar ass riding around Dallas on leatherette seat covers."

"Appearances count for a lot with you, don't they?"

"Appearances count for everything. That should have been the first thing you learned when you moved here."

"Speaking of which, I hate being a guest in someone's home and walking in empty-handed. We should have stopped for flowers or dessert or something."

"This is brunch in Highland Park, not a potluck dinner in Oak Lawn. You don't just waltz into a million-dollar home with a cardboard box from the House of Pies." Jim's arrogance always revved up a notch in social situations. "Did you bring the Speedo that I bought for you last week?"

Anthony thumped his gym bag. "Got it right here."

"Believe me, darlin', that's all they care about you bringing. The party shifts outside to the pool right after lunch, and everyone's going to be looking at you."

"Remind me again which one is Heinrich and which one is Deiter."

"Heinrich has dark blond hair and a goatee."

"So does Deiter."

"Heinrich has a slight German accent."

"So does Deiter. As I recall, one of them *is* German, and the other is American but tries to sound like he's German. But I can't remember who's who. I've only met them once."

"They both have big dicks, but Heinrich's is uncut," Jim said, as he rang the doorbell.

"Thanks. That'll help me tremendously as they're passing around the Waldorf salad."

"Waldorf salad… in *this* house." Jim shook his head. "Bite your fucking tongue!"

***

Waldorf salad was not on the menu at Heinrich and Deiter's. The elegant hosts guided their handsome guests to an antique Biedermeier dining table laden with sumptuous dishes. "Does everyone have a glass of champagne? Come, we'll have our meal now," said Heinrich. "Deiter, ask André to bring in another bottle of *Krug Grande Cuvee*." He observed the guests' half-empty glasses. "Wait! Tell him to make it two."

Anthony noticed that Heinrich had trimmed his goatee and now wore only a thick, dark blond mustache. The mustache would have looked dated on another man but it gave Heinrich, with his perfect Teutonic features, a sexy, retro look. "Now sit, down, everyone, please. Deiter has given his all for us today." He gestured at the gleaming white porcelain platters and sterling silver trays. "Just look at all these beautiful dishes he has prepared for us."

"I did have a little help from André," said Deiter, full of false modesty.

"Nonsense!" said Heinrich. "He may have passed you an ingredient or two, but this is all your handiwork and you should be proud of it. Now, this is spinach and gruyere quiche. We also have fresh steamed asparagus with toasted almond slivers; Macedonian fruit salad; red bliss potatoes topped with sour cream and caviar—"

"Ooh, is that Sevruga?" asked Jim, eyeing the dish appreciatively. "That's my favorite. Anthony, you're gonna love it."

"Beluga would have been our *first* choice, of course," said Heinrich, "but as I said to Deiter, 'Darling, is it worth selling the Lamborghini just to impress our friends?'"

Deiter grinned. "*Unt* I replied, 'For dinner maybe, but not for brunch!'"

As everyone else laughed heartily, Anthony took a big gulp of champagne.

"Now, we also have a plate of miniature *pain au chocolat*—but none for you, Albert, you little piggy!" Heinrich immediately moved the plate away from the red-faced guest to his right. Albert was the only person in the room carrying an extra ten pounds—and it showed. "But these little sweets are just for show. Dessert and coffee will be served afterward. And finally, in honor of Anthony, our new friend from New York, we have bagels and lox."

Bradley, handsome young man with long black eyelashes, looked suspiciously at the last dish mentioned. "What's that?" he said, pointing. His older boyfriend, who was greatly embarrassed, covered the pointing finger with his own hand.

"What are *lox?*" Deiter looked at the young man as though he were a Kurdish refugee.

"Isn't that Jewish food?" said Bradley. "I'm not sure if I should eat that."

"Bradley, darling, it's salmon," said Deiter.

"Not just any salmon," said Heinrich. "That is *Wild Baltic* salmon."

"Forty dollars a pound," Jim whispered to Anthony. "You'd better enjoy every bite."

Bradley looked at the tray more closely. "Is it *raw* salmon?"

"Bradley, *mein schoen Blume*," said Deiter, "do you know anything at all of seafood, besides the menu at Red Lobster? It's *smoked* salmon."

"Oh," said Bradley, turning pink. "I've never had it before."

"There's a first time for everything," said Anthony, feeling a sudden need to protect the youngest, most vulnerable man in the room. "I had my first chicken fried steak last week on a layover in Houston, and loved every bite of it."

"Chicken fried steak? In *Houston?*" said a horrified man wearing a heavily starched button-down shirt. "Where on earth were you eating?"

"At the Black-eyed Pea," said Anthony, enjoying the sight of Jim visibly cringing. "It came with mashed potatoes and fried okra, and everything was covered with white cream gravy."

"Ugh!" said Deiter, with a wave of his hands. "Those awful Texas *chain* restaurants, with their cheese biscuits, and gallon-sized glasses of iced tea, and perspiring waitresses, and—"

"Deiter, please!" said Heinrich. "Everyone at this table is a guest in our home. It is not our place to insult anyone's heritage, no matter how humble it may be." He removed a linen napkin from its silver ring and put it in his lap.

The guests followed suit. Then they all paused for a moment to appreciate the efforts of their hosts. The food had been meticulously prepared and beautifully presented. The background music featured a variety of artists, tempos and moods suitable for any topic of conversation. And best of all, there was a seemingly endless supply of champagne. A great deal of money had been spent on a single meal for twelve privileged men. Anthony noticed Bradley nervously eyeing the *Ravinvet d'Enfert* flatware. He prayed that the young man wouldn't drop a fork and be swiftly banished from the house.

"Gentlemen," said Heinrich, "we are delighted that you are here." He nodded graciously toward his guests. "Let us be— *Mein Ghott in Himmel!* Your glasses are practically empty! André! Bring more champagne. *Schnell, schnell!*"

***

After having a sliver of dessert, Anthony excused himself, changed into his Speedo, and quietly slipped outside. The enormous backyard was beautifully landscaped and surrounded by a ten-foot-high privacy hedge. The grass was still verdant, despite the relentless ninety-five-degree heat. Lounging chairs and plush towels were arranged around an Olympic-sized pool that included both a low and high diving board. Small tables and chairs, arranged in groups of two and three under large shady trees, allowed intimate conversations. It was an idyllic place to spend a Sunday afternoon. Anthony noticed one of the other guests seated at a table, thumbing through a magazine. His name was Craig. He was smooth-skinned and had curly blond hair and blue eyes. Anthony noticed an ashtray on the table next to him and began strolling in that direction. "Do you mind if I join you, Craig? I think you have the only ashtray on the property."

"Oh, dear God."

"If it bothers you, I'll take the ashtray and move to another table."

"No!" said Craig. "I was going to say, 'Oh, dear God, there's someone else here who smokes!' Can you spare one?"

"Sure."

"Then have a seat and let's indulge. But holler if you see my hubby coming. I'm a closet smoker."

Anthony took out a cigarette and then offered the pack to Craig.

"No, light it for me, Anthony. Do it like Paul Henreid did for Bette Davis in *Now, Voyager.*"

Anthony sensually lit two cigarettes at once and passed one to him. "How was that?"

"Heavenly," said Craig, as he took a deep drag. "And probably the closest I'll ever get to your lips touching mine—what a shame."

"Never say never. I'm a sucker for big blue eyes."

"Don't torture me, you hairy beast." Craig held up the magazine he was reading. "Do you believe this? A house full of interior decorators, and there's nothing to read but home furnishing rags." He tossed it onto the table. "I came out here for a reprieve from the world of decorators."

"Careful, buddy. You know they prefer to be called designers."

"Right now, it's just the two of us. We can let our hair down."

"Please!" Anthony set his drink on the table. "I'd be happy just to put a *glass* down without getting the stink eye from Heinrich. Is he afraid I'll leave a ring? Put out some coasters, for Christ's sake!"

"That's not it. Our hosts are minimalists. The thought of placing random objects on bare surfaces causes them tremendous anxiety."

"They're *all* minimalist," said Anthony. "They've got these huge fucking homes and practically nothing inside them. Don't they get tired of that stark look? I mean, this is Texas—the land of over-the-top everything."

"It serves a purpose, darling. *They're* supposed to be the center of attention in a room—not the furnishings."

"Oh. I hadn't thought of it that way."

"But you're right. Heinrich does get wound up so easily." He took a sip of his drink. "Well, at least the bar is always well-stocked. I'll give 'em that."

"I've been to two of these Sunday brunches so far. Is it always the same group of guys?"

"Pretty much," said Craig. "Unless there's some hot, new boy toy being introduced. You caused quite a stir when Jim brought you over on the Fourth of July, but I'm sure you know that."

"I don't think of myself as Jim's boy toy," Anthony said testily. "And neither does he."

"Boy toy, flavor of the month, eye candy—it's all a matter of semantics. And speaking of eye candy, look what's heading our way."

Anthony followed Craig's gaze. Three beautiful young men in tiny swimsuits were passing through the sliding glass door. They walked languidly toward the pool, as though they were instinctually aware of being watched. The trio arranged themselves on fluffy white towels and began applying sunscreen to their already-bronzed bodies. They lay in a row, glistening, with their faces turned up toward the sun. A few minutes later, the bathing suits were teasingly slipped off and tossed aside.

"Like clockwork," said Craig. "Out comes the oil, off come the bikinis, and out pop the big, floppy dicks."

"Heinrich doesn't mind? Somebody might leave a skid mark on one of his Ralph Lauren towels."

"A skid mark? These boys? Never!" said Craig. He stripped off his own suit and proudly displayed himself. "Besides, in this crowd, minimalism only counts when the topic is decor."

***

By four o'clock, the entire brunch party, along with *après-midi* invitees, were gathered in and around the pool. Anthony surveyed the men one by one as he sipped another cocktail. Aside from the requisite six-pack abs and oversized penises, each guest displayed something special: an exquisite profile, sculpted cheekbones, a high round ass, or a magnificent head of hair. Even among the older men, there wasn't one inch of sagging skin or even a hint of a pot belly. "Unbelievable," he said to Craig, shaking his head. "It's like stumbling onto the set of a Herb Ritts photo shoot."

"That's a perfect analogy," said Craig, framing the scene with his hands. "Over-the-top, completely unattainable, male beauty… captured for just a moment in time."

"Except at this house, the moment never ends. Hey, why isn't Heinrich naked? He's got a great body, too. Look at that ass on him, and he's pushing fifty."

"He *is* a demon at the gym." Craig leaned closer. "But he gets a little help from the International Male catalogue. That particular swimsuit has padding in the back. Oops! You didn't hear that from me!" He snorted. "Sorry, I get bitchy sometimes when I've had a few." He refilled his glass from a bottle of cognac that he'd stashed under his chair.

"Well, I still can't believe this is where I'm spending my weekends." Anthony was pleased. He was getting more than his fair share of attention. "You know what? It feels fucking *good* to be a part of it."

"Oh, come on, Anthony. You're no stranger to this kind of scene. I bet you *ruled* Fire Island back in New York—in the Pines, of course. You've probably never set foot in Cherry Grove."

"I've strayed in that direction once or twice."

"Straying into the Meat Rack at midnight doesn't count, you satyr!"

Anthony laughed. "No, this scene isn't new to me. I just didn't know that it existed in Dallas, too."

"There's a gay 'A' list wherever you go. Right now, in Missoula, Montana, the twelve most beautiful men in town are sitting down to eggs Sardou in a five thousand square-feet log home that the hosts built with their bare hands. They even cut down the trees, using a crosscut saw that belonged to Great-great Aunt 'Jimmie'—a pioneer gal, who was known to dress like a lumberjack."

"The cabin has been featured in *Architectural Digest*," Anthony added, "although, in the article, no mention was made of the fact that the owners are a couple."

"Oh, mercy, no! They're always 'business partners.' "

"Speaking of couples, how long have you and Peter been together?"

"Ten years—which is five years past my shelf life."

"Your what?"

"My *expiration date*." He leaned closer again and lowered his voice. "I'm over thirty, believe it or not. And I've outlasted every other shop girl who's come slinking by this pool to show off her assets." He raised his glass. "Here's to me! Or to my genes, my trainer, my colorist, and my aesthetician, I should say."

"Ah, Christ," Anthony muttered. He turned away in disgust and lit a cigarette.

"What's the matter?"

"I hate it when a gay man talks about himself like he's—"

"A commodity?"

"No, a woman. One who's afraid that the minute her tits start sagging, her husband's going to trade her in for another model."

"Trade her *up*, you mean. And that's exactly what happens to people like you and me—straight or gay, it doesn't matter. Eventually, we all get traded for a newer, shinier model. What you have to do is keep your fenders free of dents for as long as you can. *And* make sure you get a piece of the action while Daddy still gets a hard-on every time that he sees you. By action, naturally, I mean a legal share in whatever he happens to own—*in writing*. Verbal contracts get you nowhere in court. Any such documents should be tucked away in a safe deposit box, for which there is only one key. That key must be hidden somewhere other than the bottom of your underwear drawer."

Anthony laughed. "Christ, it's like getting advice from *The Gold Diggers of 1933*."

"Facts are facts. In any relationship, the man with the money is the one who calls the shots. All these bathing beauties have a shelf life, whether they know it or not. Did you notice Albert, the only one here with love handles?"

Anthony nodded. "That scene with the *pain au chocolat* must have embarrassed him, poor guy."

"He'll be hiding inside all day, too mortified to show himself at the pool, even in a Maillot. I guarantee you that by next summer, there'll be a new man stepping out of Trent's Jaguar—some strapping young lad, fresh out of Southern Methodist University, who needs just a bit of 'molding.' Poor, pudgy Albert—if only he'd gotten his name on something earlier in the game. You're lucky that Jim likes 'em a bit older."

"*Excuse* me?"

"Speaking of Jim, how come you weren't here with him last week?"

"I was working."

"On a Sunday? What do you do?"

"I fly for Mercury Airways."

Craig's eyes widened. "Wow, are you a pilot? That's a sexy change of pace."

"A pilot?" Anthony laughed. "No, I'm a flight attendant."

"Oh," said Craig. "We've had a lot of those come and go over the years. I think that job title had a little more cachet before you-know-what came along."

"Christ, don't be so delicate. Or don't *y'all* know how to say AIDS here in Dallas?"

"Of course. But trust me—nothing crashes a party faster than uttering that acronym. Now, let's get back to you. What are your long-term plans?"

"Is this just between you and me?"

"Scout's honor."

Anthony shrugged. He had to talk to *somebody*. "Who knows? I haven't known Jim for very long. And I don't get a lot of weekends off. It's tough to start a new job, in a new city, and date someone new all at the same time. I don't even plan on staying here for a year. I'll probably be back in New York by

December." He thought of Eric suddenly, and couldn't remember the last time he'd returned one of his phone calls. "I'm supposed to be going back, anyway."

"Back to New York? I hope you haven't mentioned that to Jim. You'd be a fool to walk away from that man. Do you have any idea how much he's worth?"

"I know exactly how much he's worth. But like I said, I really can't control my time off until I get some seniority. Everyone's just going to have to be patient."

"I used to have a career, too. I made fifty thousand a year as a personal shopper at Neiman-Marcus. That's where I met Peter." He waved to boyfriend, a sandy-haired man who stood ready to dive off the high board. Jim was on the ladder right behind him. "Now, *I* have a personal shopper, and I spend twice that much on my own wardrobe every year."

"There's one goal worth working toward, I guess."

"This could be your life too. Think about what I said. Jim can offer you the world on a silver platter, just because you're so goddam beautiful." He nodded toward the pool. "I don't know how committed you are to your career aloft, but I wouldn't let Jim come here alone too many Sundays in a row. As you can see, he's very popular."

The crowd cheered as Jim did a perfect dive and sliced into the water without making a ripple. He surfaced a moment later, shaking water from his hair. Several younger men immediately swam closer to him, talking excitedly, and hands suddenly disappeared under the water. "See? Right in front of your nose, those baby sharks are circling."

"Thanks for the advice, but I'm not worried. I can hold my ground for as long as I want. That's the way it's always been for me."

"Have it your way. I'm sure you know what you're doing." He reached for his glass. "Nosey old me. I should mind my own business." He clumsily tilted the heavy crystal tumbler and spilled Courvoisier all over his chest. "Shit!" he yelled, as the tumbler fell out of his hand and shattered. He stood up and started trying to pick up shards of glass.

Buddy, thought Anthony, you just officially passed your expiration date. As twenty heads swiveled in their direction, He pushed Craig back into his chair. "Sit down! You're drunk. If you cut yourself and start bleeding on these *Pietra Firma* tiles, you'll be shopping for your fall wardrobe at J.C. Penny."

André scurried over with a small broom, a dustpan and a look of utter disdain. He eyed the bottle of cognac as he took over the clean-up job. "*Alors! You're* the one who stole it from the liquor cabinet. Dieter has been looking for it all afternoon. Give it to me." He snapped his fingers. "*Donnez-la-moi, immédiatement.*" He marched through the yard with the dust pan in one hand, and the bottle of cognac tucked securely under his arm.

"How *dare* he!" said Craig, full of righteous indignation. "That *whore* from Montreal, posing as a Parisian major-domo!"

Well," said Anthony, laughing, "there's helping yourself, and then there's *helping* yourself."

"You're right," said Craig, hanging his head in shame. "I bet that I'm going to scolded for *this* when we drive home today."

"Or maybe even before."

"Oh, dear God. I just had a terrible thought." He grabbed another cigarette and lit it. "What if we don't get invited back next week?" He began nervously puffing, oblivious to the look of rage on Peter's face as he jumped out of the pool and stormed toward the house.

"Maybe no one else noticed."

"Incidentally, Anthony…" The cigarette was calming Craig down. His voice had taken on a sweet, syrupy tone. "If you're looking for a rug weaver, I know the best one in Dallas. He's a true artist. I'd be happy to refer you to him."

"Thanks, Craig," said Anthony, stymied by the offer, "but in my house in shabby old Oak Lawn we have wall-to-wall carpeting."

"No, darlin', I'm not talking about that. I'm referring to that little bald spot on the top of your head."

"My… *what?*" Anthony sputtered, forcing himself not to reach upward.

"Shh! It's barely noticeable. You're so tall. I didn't even realize you had one until you bent over a moment ago. I'd jump on that ASAP if I were you, before Jim notices. Speak of the devil!" he exclaimed, as Jim suddenly popped out of the water right next to them.

"Hi," Jim said, gripping the side of the pool. "Remember me?"

"Sure," said Anthony. "You're the guy with the *blue* Mercedes, aren't you?"

"Fuck you!" said Jim. He laughed as he splashed Anthony with water. "You two have been thick as thieves all afternoon. What's going on?"

"I'm trying to figure out a way to steal all your money. Craig was giving me a few pointers."

"Sorry, buddy," said Jim. "The cash is out of my hands. It's all family money, you know."

"Five million in cash rolled up in a cotton sock and hidden under your father's mattress?" said Anthony.

"Something like that." Jim examined his arms. "I'm getting sunburned. Are you about ready to leave?"

"Whenever you're ready."

"Nice to see you, Jim," said Craig. "I hope we'll see you both next week."

"You're going home too," Jim said. "Peter is bringing the car around right now."

"Is the party over already?" Craig tittered nervously.

Jim nodded. "For you it is. Everyone else is invited to stay until sundown. And here's a tip for you, Craig: people who can't handle their liquor should keep their hands off *other* people's liquor."

"Thank you for the advice, Mr. Sizemore. I'll take that for what it's worth."

"It's damn good advice," said Jim. "If I were you, I'd take it to heart."

***

"Are you hungry?" Jim asked on the drive home.

"Not really. But we can stop for a bite, if you like."

"How about Long John Silver? I hear their tartar sauce is outstanding."

"No valet parking, though."

"Shucks. I guess we'll have to go elsewhere."

"I wouldn't mind a drink."

"Good. I know the perfect place."

"Are we going slumming with the Beer Bust crowd?" Anthony asked.

"I had something a little more refined in mind."

"Can we skip the tufted leather chairs, just this once?"

"Nope. I have my reputation to think of."

"OK, whatever. Would you mind stopping someplace so I can pick up some cigarettes? I left mine with Craig."

"Anthony—"

"Not a word, Jim. I'm a grown man. If you take me, you take the whole package."

"That's what I want to talk about."

"Now? Today?"

"There's no time like the present."

***

The bar was cool inside and nearly empty. "We'll have two beers, please," Jim said to the bartender. "Do you have Lone Star?"

"Naturally, sir."

"Oh, good," said Jim. "I was afraid you might only have imports."

"I'll take a shot of Jack Daniels with mine," said Anthony. "And would you bring us an ashtray, please?"

"Once the drinks were served, Anthony took a long swallow of beer.

"Did you enjoy yourself today?" Jim asked.

"Yes, as a matter of fact, I did. Are we going back next week?"

"No. We're hosting next week. It's only fair that we rotate. Otherwise, we're just freeloaders, swilling Heinrich's champagne and pretending to enjoy that ghastly mocha *mille-feuille*."

"What if I have to work?"

"I'm glad you brought that up. I wanted to talk to you about that."

Here it comes, thought Anthony. "I'm on call next weekend. I may be flying."

"You don't *have* to be on call."

"Jim, I'm not quitting my job."

"I'm not asking you to quit. I'm just talking about making a phone call once in a while to a friend who works in crew scheduling."

"Does he owe you a favor, too? How many times can you play that card?"

"As often as I please. He's a very good friend."

"Well… as long as I'd still get paid."

"Yes, you'll still get your five-hundred-dollar check. Isn't that about what you clear after taxes every two weeks?"

"Have you been snooping around in my flight bag?"

Jim laughed. "No, but I've been down this road before. You're not the first flyboy that I've ever dated. But how long are you going to keep doing it?"

"Why are you asking me that? You know I just started."

"For the second time. You said you flew before, right?"

"Yes, I flew for Atlantic Coast Airways. We went belly up a few years ago. I'm sure you read about it in the papers."

"I was in the Atlanta airport the day that it happened. I remember the looks on the employees' faces. They—"

"Hey, you don't have to tell me. I *lived* it."

"That's just my point."

"Mercury isn't going to bankruptcy court anytime soon. It's a solid company. I'm lucky they hired me."

"Still, you must have some type of long-term plan for the future. Every man should."

"I know that every man should have a long-term plan. I have a lot on my plate at the moment. Right now, I'm focused on the present."

Jim rested his hand on Anthony's. "I know that you worry about money. But you don't have to. There's no reason on earth why a man like you should ever have to worry about money."

"Why are you talking to me like I'm a hustler?"

"I'm not. Maybe deep down, you think of yourself that way, but I don't."

As much as he wanted to gulp the shot of bourbon to steady his nerves, Anthony sipped slowly, the way that any gentleman would. "Let's get it all out in the open, Jim. What do you really want from me?"

"You know what I want. I don't want to 'date' you. I want to make this a permanent situation."

"We've only known each other—"

"It doesn't matter how long. I'm in love with you."

Anthony averted Jim's gaze. "Please don't say that."

"Why not? It's true. I *am* in love with you." His voice cracked. "Do you think it's going to take a year before I know for sure?"

"No, it's too much, too soon." He tried to pull his hand away, but Jim held it even more tightly.

"I've never felt about anybody else the way I feel about you," Jim said, in a tone of voice that Anthony had never heard before. "You feel the same way. Don't deny it. Come on, you're the one who wanted to get it all in the open. *Look* at me. I want you to come and live with me."

"I... I could feel the same way about you, Jim. But I have to be truthful. The timing couldn't be worse. I was on unemployment for a year, and then I spent six weeks in training with Mercury. I just started all over again. I'm not even supposed to *be* here in Dallas. I'm should be in New York. If I hadn't been late to class the day that we turned in our base preference sheets—that one *fucking* day—and my instructor hadn't caught me in a lie and decided to punish me by sending me to DFW, I'd be there right now. I already put my name on the transfer list. I'll be based in New York by December, as soon as I'm off probation. That's only four months away."

"Why go back? You said yourself that were starting all over again. Can't you see that going back would be a huge step *backward?*"

"But I have commitments. I made promises."

"To whom?"

"To Eric, for one. He's in my apartment, with my brother who, for all I know, could be hauled off to jail any minute for God-only-knows what crime."

"To hell with Eric. Put the lease in his name and let him figure out things for himself. He'll either sink or swim. If he swims, he'll be better off for it."

"I have a second lease in Oak Lawn. I put down a security deposit."

"I'll pay it off for you. Naturally."

Stall, stall, stall! "You'll have to give me time to think about it."

"How much time?"

"I don't know!"

"Anthony, how old are you?"

"You know how old I am. I'm thirty-two."

"I'm *forty*-two. You have no idea how quickly time passes. You won't— until it's too late to go back and make up for lost time. Just look at some of the older guys you work with: spending night after night in second-rate layover hotels. Bidding their lives away, month by month. Getting all pumped up because they can hold San Francisco layovers and go drink themselves blind in the Castro. Doesn't that ever get tired? Those gay disco dollies from the Seventies—where are they now? Where will *you* be in twenty years?"

"Who are you, the Ghost of Christmas Yet to Come? Threatening me with a shitty future isn't the way to my heart."

"Let's focus on the present then and face facts. One: we have hot sex. We can't keep our hands off each other. Two: except for the money, we're evenly-matched in every way. You don't give yourself credit for half the things you could do. Three: I know that I'm in love with you, and whether you admit it or not, you feel the same way. Four: we're both HIV negative. If we're monogamous, we can do whatever the hell we want to sexually. I can fuck you 'til the cows home, and vice-versa, without worrying about condoms or AIDS. Think about what I'm offering you, Anthony. And then decide whether you want to make a life with me or keep putting yourself out there."

Anthony waited a few minutes before he responded. He thought about what Craig had said earlier, and decided that it might have been good advice after all. He finished the shot of Jack Daniels and set the glass down. "Those are all valid points. I *am* thinking about my future. But for me to take this chance—to even seriously consider it—I need some type of assurance that in ten years, you'll feel the same way about me that you think you do now."

A triumphal smile spread across Jim's face. "Well, if that's all your worried about, Mr. Bellini… I'll just have to find a way to sweeten the offer."

CHAPTER 12

A Hot August Night

"What you want tonight?" asked the smiling waitress. She spoke with a heavy Greek accent.

"I'll have the roast half-chicken dinner with a small salad, hold the onions, please," said Eric. "And I'll have a dry baked potato and steamed broccoli for my sides."

"Very good. You know the whole menu almost by heart."

"I should," said Eric with a laugh. "I'm here often enough."

"You want wine? It comes with the special."

"Yes, a glass of white wine."

"No, white wine is *terrible* tonight," she said as she took the menu. "Tastes like dirty socks. You try red wine. Nice Chianti."

"OK, thanks for the warning."

Eric had become a regular patron at the Mykonos Diner on Queens Boulevard, not far from his house. While not the most glamorous place in the world, the portions were generous and the prices were reasonable. East Coast diners were a new phenomenon to him. He was amazed at the variety of food that could be ordered at any one time. Doubting the freshness of many of the available choices, however, he tended to stick to either the breakfast special or the daily dinner special.

As he waited for the wine, he studied the blue and white paper placemat, which featured a lesson in Greek history and culture. He was semi-engrossed in a quiz at the bottom when he heard a commotion behind him.

"Hey! Close the goddam door!" the manager screamed at an incoming patron, who had paused in the doorway to speak to the woman behind her. "Do you think I'm paying to air condition the sidewalk?"

Eric was happy to be sitting in a back booth, as far from the door as possible. New York was experiencing an endless round of August heat waves. At 7 P.M., it was still stiflingly hot outdoors. Going down into the subway later would be even worse—akin to self-torture. But he had to get out of Queens, even if just for a few hours, and into the company of other gay men.

"You're not flying today?" The waitress set a glass of Chianti and a basket of bread on the table.

"I came in this afternoon from Orlando."

"Ugh! Florida in summertime. Even worse than here."

"You're telling me," said Eric. He sipped his wine. It wasn't very good, but it *was* free and it would help him to relax. He leaned back in the booth and reviewed the events of the day. A La Guardia-Orlando turn-around in coach in August: surely there wasn't a viler trip anywhere in the system. He'd spent the entire day on an airplane packed from stem to stern with the demanding parents and their overly-stimulated children. The meal choice on the return leg was either garlic chicken or black olive rigatoni, both of which gave all one hundred and thirty passengers foul, uncontrollable gas. The cabin temperature was at least ninety degrees during boarding because the on-ground air conditioning system was inoperative. And to top it off, everyone was dressed in the official uniform of the central Florida leisure traveler: a t-shirt, ratty shorts, and a pair of rubber flip-flops. Not even sandals! No, he thought: wearing sandals would require too much effort. Passengers would have to bend down to unfasten the ankle strap. Flip-flops could be removed effortlessly the moment they sat down. Then they could prop their bare feet on the nearest available surface: the bulkhead wall, the armrest, or their neighbor's tray table—anywhere but the floor. They even walked barefoot into the bathrooms, for God's sake! He took a big gulp of wine. Pigs, all of them!

"Here is your salad," said the waitress, interrupting his reverie. "Hey, you finished that wine fast!"

"Oh, look at that, I did." He smiled. "I think my nerves are shot."

"You want another one?" She leaned closer. "On the house," she whispered. "My treat, because you're always a good tipper."

"Thanks, I appreciate it. They really wore me out today." God dammit, he thought. This is *not* what flying is supposed to be all about.

***

After finishing his meal, he walked to the subway station. He instinctively covered his nose before going down the stairs. Oh Lord, here it comes, he thought. Try as he might, there was no way of avoiding the unbearable stench. It was a putrid combination of urine, vomit, and God-knows-what-else that had been baked into the concrete over the past hundred years. To make matters worse, the station was unbearably hot and humid. He immediately started sweating, and unbuttoned his cotton shirt. Christ, he thought. I'll be soaked through in less than a minute. Why did I even bother taking a shower?

As he stood on the platform fanning himself, he peered into the darkened tunnel. He prayed to see a pinpoint of light at the far end, which would indicate that a train was coming. He made sure to look only into the tunnel, and not down on the tracks. The tracks would be covered with refuse and rats— enormous rats with unbelievably long tails. They scurried day and night, seeking every scrap of rotting food strewn below, and yet somehow managed to avoid killing themselves on the electrified third rail. Of course, Eric thought wryly: they're New York City rats. They can survive anything.

His neck started to hurt from the strain of being turned for so long. Despite his fervent wish, there was no train in sight. He sat down on a wooden bench, carefully checking first to make sure that it wasn't soiled with unidentifiable muck. Last week, he'd sat in something so foul that he had to go back home and change clothes. Sammy wouldn't even let him in the apartment; he'd been forced to strip down to his underwear in the hallway. A brand-new pair of jeans, completely ruined. Eric sighed. In a span of only six weeks, his magic carpet ride had been transformed into Dante's *Inferno*.

A waft of putrid air suddenly blew past him. The train was coming—finally! He jumped up as an F train thundered into the station, but he was careful not to move too quickly toward the platform edge. That was vitally important to remember. At any moment, some psycho could sidle up to him and, without any warning, try to push him in front of—No. It was too gruesome to even think about it. Just get on the train.

He boarded and sat down. Mercifully, the subway cars were air-conditioned. At eight o'clock in the evening, there were few other passengers, so everyone had a little breathing room.

Ironically, a construction worker wearing filthy boots entered the train and sat down directly across from Eric. He placed a Styrofoam container on his lap. As he opened the lid and started eating a fried chicken dinner, the smell of grease filled the car. The man ate voraciously; between bites of chicken, he shoveled forkfuls of gravy-covered mashed potatoes and a biscuit into his mouth. That must be the first meal that he's had all day, thought Eric.

The man caught Eric watching him and stopped chewing. "You want some?" he asked, as grease ran down his chin.

"No, thank you. I just ate."

"Then what the fuck are you looking at?"

"Sorry." Eric moved a few rows away and studied the posters on the wall. One was an advertisement for a dermatologist. It featured a 'before' picture of a young woman suffering from a hideous case of acne. Under the 'after' picture, which showed considerable improvement, she profusely thanked the doctor for saving her skin—and her life! Another ad, for a podiatrist, graphically illustrated the trauma of corns, bunions and hammertoes. Dear God, thought Eric, looking at the floor. Couldn't the GAP or some other major company pay for an underground campaign?

The train began slowing down as it reached the Roosevelt Avenue station. From the corner of his eye, Eric noticed that the construction worker had finished eating and closed the lid of the Styrofoam container. As the train came to a stop and the door opened, the man leaned over and tossed it onto the platform. A woman in sandals shrieked as the lid flipped open and her feet were splattered with gravy, gnawed bones and bits of chicken skin.

A garbage dump, thought Eric. This entire city is a living, breathing *garbage dump*. Why couldn't the man have waited and carried his trash off the train at his stop? There are garbage cans on every platform, for God's sake! As the train pulled out of the station, Eric pictured the poor woman rushing toward the exit before the rats started chasing her with tiny pink tongues darting out of their mouths. He banished the image from his mind and tried to focus on the evening ahead. He'd have a couple of cold beers in a nice quiet bar (without a single child in sight), listen to some music, and enjoy the company of other gay men.

He got off the train in the West Village and made his way over to Christopher Street. He could have left the subway sooner and gone to Chelsea. Even on a weeknight, Chelsea would have a more animated crowd. But Eric wasn't looking for obnoxious muscle boys or dance music blaring from the speakers. He just wanted to drink, relax and maybe meet a man.

He walked into a small bar that advertised itself as 'a West Village tradition since 1969.' The cool, dark interior was a welcome retreat from the heat and noise on the sidewalk. Eric ordered a beer and then, after scanning the room for a place to stand, took a vacant spot near the window. The bar was three-quarters full, but none of the men were talking to each other. Most had their gazes fixed on the TV screen above the bar, where music videos alternated with soft-core gay porn.

Eric stood around for a few minutes, sipping his beer. Well, he thought, I wanted a low-key evening, but this place is like a funeral parlor. On a nearby shelf, there was an assortment of local gay magazines. He considered picking one up that featured a calendar of weekly events, but then decided against it. There are some good-looking men here, he thought. I doubt they'll try to strike up a conversation if my nose is buried a magazine. Besides, it's impossible to compete with half-naked models on the cover.

A short while later, a man with a beer bottle in his hand came and stood next to Eric. "Hey."

"Hey," said Eric, pleased to be approached. "How are you doing?"

"Doing OK," the man replied. He appeared to be in his thirties and had dark brown hair and blue eyes. He wore a plaid shirt with the sleeves ripped out. His biceps and forearms were well-defined and covered with sinister-looking tattoos. "Do you believe this fucking heat?"

"It's awful," said Eric. "I hope it doesn't stay like this until the fall."

"It might. This is turning out to be one of those summers. Well, at least we have a nice, cold beer to cool us off." He took a long swallow. "Man, am I glad to be out!"

"Out of what?"

"School."

"Long day?"

"Brutal. Last day of the last session of summer school."

"What're you studying?"

He laughed. "You're a few years off, my friend. I teach at a private school for boys here in Manhattan."

"What subject?"

"Does it matter? None of them pay attention. All they think about is getting out at three o'clock, getting high, and getting into their girlfriend's pussies."

Eric grinned and extended his hand. "My name is Eric, and I promise you a pussy-free conversation."

"I'm Tyler."

They shook hands. Eric was captivated by the tattoos. None of my teachers ever looked like that, he thought enviously. I wonder if he has to keep his arms covered with long sleeves when he's in the classroom? "Do you teach all year long or just during the summer sessions?"

"All *fucking* year long."

"I just graduated last December. It'll be strange not to start a new semester next month."

The man grinned wryly. "You just graduated from what? High school?"

"No, college. I went to U.T. Austin."

"Funny, you don't sound like you're from Texas."

"I know. I get that a lot."

Tyler put one leg up on the bar rail above the floor. The new pose accentuated his crotch in a very flattering way. "So, what'd you study at U.T.? Animal husbandry?"

"I think you're confusing U.T. with Texas A. and M. I have a B. A. in Psychology."

"Are you here on vacation?"

"No, for work."

"Uh huh." Tyler scanned the crowd as he spoke. "So, what's a young guy like you doing in this dump on a Monday night?"

"Just hanging out, relaxing." Eric shifted his weight from one foot to the other. His feet hurt from standing all day and he wanted to sit down. He glanced around at the bar. He noticed a man with wavy brown hair and brown eyes seated next to the only empty stool. He smiled at Eric. Eric wanted to return the smile, but he thought it might seem rude when he was already engaged in a conversation.

"There're lots of other places you could have gone." Tyler picked up one of the magazines on the shelf and began flipping pages. "Look: there's drag show, a jockstrap contest, and male strippers—al within three blocks."

"I already told you. I'm not looking for a scene. I just want to relax."

"Does that mean you're not looking for any action?"

"I didn't say *that.*"

"Good. Let me buy you a beer."

"OK. Thanks, Tyler."

"I'll be right back."

Eric watched Tyler walk over to the bartender. He noticed the man with the wavy, brown hair was still sitting next to the vacant stool. The man smiled at him again. This time Eric returned the smile.

The man hopped off his barstool and started walking toward him. When he saw Tyler returning with two beers, he changed course and walked toward the bathroom instead.

"Here you go," said Tyler.

"Thanks."

"So, Eric, do you live around here?"

"No." Here it comes, he thought. I'm gonna get the brush off because I don't live in Manhattan. "I'm a 7-1-8."

"A what?"

"I live in Queens."

"Oh. I'm a 2-0-1 myself. I live in Hoboken."

"Where's that?"

"Right across the Hudson River, in New Jersey. It's the birthplace of baseball and Frank Sinatra."

"I love Sinatra. *Come Fly with Me* is one of my favorite songs."

Tyler grinned. "D'you want to come over and check out my place? I'm on the sixth floor. The view of Manhattan is fucking fantastic. Hoboken is just one stop away on the PATH train."

"What's the PATH train?"

"It's the subway system that runs between New Jersey and New York. It runs twenty-four hours a day, just like yours."

"Would it be OK if we just hang out here for a while?"

Tyler smile disappeared. "Sure."

"I've been doing a lot of running around all day. It'd be nice to get to know you a little and—"

"Decide if I'm hot enough for you? You don't have to explain." They drank in silence for a few minutes. "So, what are you into?"

"Into?"

"Yeah, what kind of scene?"

"Nothing in particular. I'm just trying to meet people. I've only lived here for a few months and I don't really know anybody yet."

"Gotcha. Are you into groups? 'Cause there's a group of guys I sometimes hook up with on Monday nights, right here in the Village. We could go check it out if you're interested in playing."

"Playing what?"

"The original cast album of *Gypsy*. What do you think? I'm talking about a J.O. party, dummy." He leaned in closer. "Or more, if you're interested in sucking or fucking. But for that, we'd have to go to someone else's place afterward. They're very strict at this party: safe-sex only."

Eric grinned. "Jack off parties must be popular these days. That's the second one I've been invited to."

"Where was the other one? Chelsea?"

"No, San Francisco."

"What were you doing there?"

"I was there for work, just a couple of days ago."

"What did you say you do for a living?"

"I didn't," said Eric. "I'm a flight attendant for Mercury Airways."

"A flight attendant!?" Tyler snarled. "If I'd known that, I would never have even bothered *talking* to you!"

"Why not?" asked Eric, completely flabbergasted.

"Because you're all a bunch of whores, that's why." He looked at his watch. "Shit. To think I wasted almost an entire evening talking to a fucking air mattress!"

Eric was so shocked that he couldn't think of a single thing to say. He put down his beer and left without uttering another word.

***

Late that night, Eric stewed in his bed as he played the scene with Tyler over and over in his mind. 'Well, professor, I'll be partying in San Francisco again next month. You'll be sharpening pencils and listening to *pussy* tales from your pimple-faced students. A little jealous, perhaps?' No, that wasn't it.

'So, *you* invite *me* to a sex party, and then call me a whore. That's the pot calling the kettle black.' No, that still wasn't right. Try again.

'Well, I may a be flying 'ho', but at least I'm not an asshole from *Hoboken!*' Eric jumped off the sofa bed. "Yes, that's it!" he yelled. "That's what I should have said!"

"Hey! Sammy bellowed from the bedroom. "Pipe down out there!"

"Ah, go fuck yourself," Eric muttered. He wiped sweat from his forehead. Shit, he thought, it's hot in here! He tried moving the floor fan closer to the sofa bed. It was pointless; the fan did nothing but blow hot, moist hair around. Goddam that Anthony! He had failed to mention that there was only one window unit air conditioner in the apartment, and that it was installed in the bedroom—where Sammy slept.

Eric contemplated what else he could do. There wasn't any more clothing to take off. He had already stripped down to his underwear. I can't fucking stand this! he thought. It's like trying to sleep in a tomb! He walked over to the window and tried to raise the sash higher. Another wasted effort: it was still broken. Despite the super's promise to repair it days ago, the upper portion could only be held a few inches above the sill by a thin wooden dowel. He reached for a book and placed it under the dowel to try to prop it up higher. The dowel immediately slipped out, and the heavy window smashed down on his fingers.

His shriek of pain brought Sammy running, naked as usual, out of the bedroom. "What the fuck is going on in here?" he demanded, as he stood scowling in the doorway. Dim street light coming in through the open window glinted off the gold crucifix that he always wore on a chain around his neck.

"I hurt myself, that's what!"

"At two in the morning? How?"

Trying to prop open the fucking broken window!"

"Are you bleeding?" Sammy crossed the room and reached for Eric's hand. "Let me see."

"Don't touch me!"

"Calm down. Can you wiggle your fingers?"

"Yes."

"Then I don't think anything's broken. I'll get you some ice." He walked into the kitchen and returned a moment later with ice cubes wrapped in a towel. "Stick your hand in this before it starts swelling up."

"Thanks."

Sammy wiped his own forehead. "Jesus Christ, it must be a hundred degrees in here!"

"I know! That's why I was trying to open the window higher."

"Why the fuck don't you just come and sleep in the bedroom?"

"Thanks for the offer, but I'll manage out here."

Sammy shook his head. "Suit yourself." He went into the kitchen again and returned with another towel soaked in cold water. "Come here. Let me put this on the back of your neck."

"Thanks," said Eric, surprised at the gentleness of Sammy's touch. "That feels good." They stood together silently near the window, their bare chests almost touching. Eric was hypnotized by the crucifix that adorned Sammy's chest. And he had such a beautiful chest, too! It was muscular and covered with black hair. Sammy had beautiful dark nipples that were always erect, regardless of the ambient temperature. Eric felt such a strong desire to touch Sammy's chest that he had to force his hands to remain at his side.

"Relax, for Christ's sake," said Sammy, shifting on his feet. "Just relax!"

Eric shut his eyes. All that he could sense now was Sammy's palpable body heat and sure, steady breathing.

"Let me put this on your forehead now, Eric."

"OK." As Sammy raised his arm higher, Eric could smell a musky odor emanating from his hairy armpit. Without thinking twice, he moved an inch closer and inhaled deeply.

"What the fuck do you think you're doing?"

"Shut up, Sammy. Just for a minute, stand there and shut up." He was surprised when, rather than pushing him away, Sammy raised his arm higher.

That's good, isn't it?" said Sammy. "Yeah, buddy. Relax and breathe in that man smell."

Eric felt a surge of white-hot energy run through his entire body. Anthony had always called him "buddy," too. Anthony, who had paraded himself naked in front of Eric over and over while they were roommates in training. Anthony, who was now fifteen hundred miles away and who hadn't returned a phone call in two weeks...

"Look at you," said Sammy. "You're still sweating."

To Eric's great surprise, Sammy leaned down and licked a bead of sweat from his forehead. "Oh!" Eric exclaimed, as Sammy's tongue came in contact with his skin.

"You've got some here, too." Sammy let his tongue slip to the side of Eric's face, first near his earlobe, then near his jaw.

"Sammy..."

"You know what the problem is?" Sammy growled into his ear. "You've got too much fucking clothes on. That's why you're so hot." Without warning, he yanked Eric's underwear down to his ankles.

Eric gasped. "Oh, Jesus!"

"Yeah, that's it, buddy. Let that big cock of yours fly loose." Sammy's hot hands were suddenly everywhere at once: squeezing Eric's nipples, tugging his balls, and slapping his ass. "Look how fucking excited you are."

Eric was speechless and so overcome that he dropped to his knees.

Sammy stood looming over him with his huge dick only inches away from Eric's face. "You want it? You want it, buddy?"

"Yeah..." Eric croaked. "I want it."

"Then let's go in the bedroom." Sammy pulled him up off the floor.

"OK." Eric started to pull up his underwear.

"Leave 'em! You don't need your fucking tidy-whities right now!"

"Wait a minute, Sammy. Before we go any further, we have to negotiate what kind of sex we're going to have. I only play—"

"I know all about how you white-bread guys like to play. Now, leave your fucking underwear out here, get into that room, and get up on my bed."

"Yes, sir. I'm coming."

Sammy laughed wickedly. "You bet your sweet *ass* you are."

CHAPTER 13

A Member of the Club

"There's my young friend, looking debonair as always!" said Dee Dee, as she saw Eric getting online for the bus to JFK.

And here's my little storm cloud, thought Eric, blotting out the sun wherever she goes. "Hello, Dee Dee."

"Where are you off to?"

"L.A., on the DC-10. I'm in coach today. And you?" It was only polite to ask.

"A Fort Lauderdale turnaround on a ratty old DC-9. Do you believe it?"

"I take it you're not a fan of turnarounds."

"It's all I can hold anymore! Thirty years with Global and I can't even *touch* a two-day. And the European flying—forget about it! Those women are so old, they're dropping dead in the aisle. I'm not kidding So, off I go to Lauderdale." She shrugged. "At least it's not spring break, in which case I'd shoot myself."

"You'll get through it. It's just one day."

"I know. This damn airline could be out of business by the end of the day. Rumor has it there isn't enough cash on hand to make payroll next week. How much longer can we go on like this? Beat up old airplanes, one delay after another, one *pay cut* after another, and employee morale in the toilet. Cripes, my *uniform* is older than you are. I don't know how much longer I can take it." She started to hyperventilate. "If only we could merge with another airline—or even be bought outright. So what if we ended up working for someone else? At least we'd have job security, instead of worrying every day about being tossed out on the tarmac. You can't imagine what it's like to have that constantly hanging over your head—especially at my age." She grabbed his sleeve. "You're so lucky to be *young*, Eric, and just starting your career, and to work for a great airline! You guys get new airplanes and new routes every week! Oh, if only I'd applied at Mercury in '61 instead of at Global! Think where I'd be now!"

Eric tried to picture Dee Dee as a young woman—one without scuffed shoes, reading glasses on a chain, and a frayed canvas bag hanging over her stooped shoulder. All three accessories were *de rigueur* for the Global Airways corps, whose heyday as flying fashion icons was long-gone. "It is hard to believe," he said, pulling his arm free. "But... well... at least you had a good, long run. I mean, when I was a kid, yours was the premier airline. I even remember the TV commercials: 'Global Airways: the most *distinguished* way to fly.' "

"It *was* the most distinguished way to fly," she said, with a wry smile. "And we all thought it would last forever. Goddam Airline Deregulation Act! That was the beginning of the end for us. We just didn't know it at the time." As the bus approached, she gathered her luggage. "Take a good look, my friend," she said, climbing up the bus steps with great difficulty. "This could be you in thirty years!"

That couldn't be me in *fifty* years, thought Eric. At the very least, my shoes will always be shined.

***

As he walked to his departure gate, he stopped for a moment to appreciate the hub-bub in the terminal. The large overhead information board listed flights to cities all over the world. Excited passengers, boarding passes in hand, were lined up at each gate, where sleek, new airplanes would whisk them away to exotic destinations. Flight attendants greeted one another enthusiastically as their paths crossed. Even those who didn't know Eric smiled and nodded at him. I am fortunate, he thought. Poor as a church mouse, but fortunate to have been hired by such a great company. And who knows whom I'll get to meet on the plane today? Maybe this will be the one time this decade that Barbra Streisand flies a commercial airline. Of course, she'd never be sitting in coach.

As he approached the gate, he saw a group of jovial flight attendants sitting near the window. "Hi," said a pretty brunette. "My name is Lorraine. I'm the purser. You must be Eric. I've heard such nice things about you from my friends Sylvia and Jacques."

"They were on my first trip," Eric said. "They made it very special. We had great fun together."

"Let me introduce you to everybody, Eric. We have a wonderful crew today—no whack jobs, for a change! This is Joan and Glenda, they're working in first, and…" She continued with the business-class crew, and finished with the rest of the coach crew: Nancy, Josie, and Mary.

Much to Eric's delight, they all seemed to be warm, friendly people. "Am I the token male today?" he asked.

"No. Zack Pendergast is working the lower lobe galley. He's already down there, setting up. You'll have to pop down to meet him. He only comes upstairs to sit in his jump seat for takeoff and landing. He's in charge of setting up carts and cooking food for the entire airplane. He almost never stops working, the whole flight."

"Thank God they didn't call *me* out for that position," Eric said with a grin. "This is my first DC-10 flight. I'd be in hysterics and the service would be a disaster."

"Oh, no, we'd never subject you that torture. I'd swap you right out and put someone else in the galley."

It's better for you to work upstairs, Eric," said Mary. "We like to have the eye candy in the cabin, where it can be appreciated."

***

"OK, that's all the info that I have for you right now," said Lorraine, as she concluded her briefing. "Oh, wait! One more thing: when we get to L.A., the entire crew stays on the plane until *all* the wheelchair passengers are off, and all parents have claimed their gate-checked strollers, got it?"

"That won't be a problem today," said Josie. "Edna MacAllister isn't here."

"Yeah, and you know what else?" said Nancy. "There may actually be some food left over for the rest of us!"

"It's like a MacHoliday!" said Mary.

These catty remarks brought howls of laughter from the rest of the crew.

"Who's Edna MacAllister?" Eric whispered to Nancy.

"She's a scrounger and a trouble-maker. You'll meet her one day if you keep working the transcons."

"We'll start boarding in about ten minutes," said Lorraine. "Eric, let me give you a quick tour of the service center so that you'll know where everything is."

The service center was located between first class and business class and functioned as the nerve center of the DC-10. It contained coffee makers, supply drawers, stowage spaces for carts, an intercom system, and two elevators which led to the galley beneath the main deck. "I'll be in here the whole flight, coordinating the service," said Lorraine. "It seems like the carts never stop coming up and going back down. This is a high traffic area, so please avoid coming in here unless you absolutely need to."

"In other words," said Josie, "if you don't want all your toes broken, stay the hell out of here!"

"Once the service is over, you're welcome to eat up here or down in the lower lobe," said Lorraine. "There's usually food left over."

"Speaking of the lower lobe," said Eric, "do I have time to meet Zack before we start boarding?"

"Sure." She opened one of the elevator doors. "Step inside and I'll send you down." She pressed a button. "Don't be too long," she said, as Eric began descending.

He stepped out of the elevator. The galley was a large space lined with carts and ovens on both sides. At the far end, near the sink and mirror, there was an escape ladder. Eric remembered having to climb the ladder during training and subsequently pop out, like a jack in the box, through a panel in the floor in first class. He secretly hoped that he'd get to do that one day—but only if there were passengers on board.

Zack stood in the middle of the galley, loading racks of meals into the ovens. He had dark wavy hair, blue eyes, and a muscular body. He was wearing the short-sleeved uniform shirt without a tie; hints of dark chest hair were visible at the base of his neck.

"Hi, I'm Eric."

Zack looked up. "Oh, hey. I thought I was the only guy working this flight."

"I just got this trip a few hours ago. I'm on reserve."

"So you're new."

"Pretty new, yeah."

"Welcome to the base." Zack stopped loading meals to shake Eric's hand. "We love new hires, for obvious reasons."

"Oh?"

"Yeah. It keeps the rest of us from having to fly reserve. The more there are of you, the further away we move from the reserve list, see? Besides, it's always nice to have another guy on the crew." He pointed upward. "All that female energy can be a bit much, you know what I mean?"

"Sure," said Eric, feeling guilty for agreeing with such a misogynistic remark.

"Plus you're a hot man, Eric—as if you didn't know it."

"Thanks. The feeling's mutual. Zack, that hair sticking out of your shirt... does it go all the way down?"

"Want to see? Go open the elevator door for a second. As long as the door is open, they can't operate the lift from upstairs. Make it fast."

By the time Eric had opened the door and turned back around, Zack had unbuttoned his shirt. His torso was covered with dark hair, including a prominent line snaking all the way down to his navel. His large nipples were pierced with silver rings. "You like?"

"Yeah, I like," Eric replied, as reached over to touch Zack's chest.

BZZZZZZ! Eric jumped back at though he'd touched an electric fence.

"Hey, you two, stop screwing around down there," Lorraine said over the intercom system. "I need Eric upstairs. We're boarding."

Zack laughed and started buttoning his shirt.

"What the hell!" said Eric, turning beet red. "Is there a camera down here?"

"No. Lorraine knows I like to flirt. You'd better head upstairs."

"I'll come back later."

"No rush. We've got six hours. Hey, after the service is over, let all the girls come down to eat before you do. You come down last, so we can have some privacy."

"Sounds like a plan." He started walking toward the elevator.

"Hey, Eric, when you do come back down, make sure they have everything they need upstairs so that nobody bothers us. And be sure to leave that door open."

"Yes, sir."

***

"Flight attendants, prepare for takeoff."

Eric took his jump seat next to the over-wing exit and smiled at the passenger sitting across from him. She was an older woman with harshly dyed black hair and evidence of a recent facelift. She wore a pink tracksuit and silver sneakers.

She smiled back at him. "Are we going now?"

"Yes, ma'am. We'll be airborne in just a moment."

"Do you live in Los Angeles?"

"No, we're based here in New York."

"Lucky you. I live in Los Angeles now. I *used* to live in New York. I'm from Queens originally."

You didn't have to tell me, thought Eric. I can see just see you pulling a shopping cart along Austin Street.

"My son lives in L.A.," she said. "He wanted me nearby and bought me a house out there, so I moved." She leaned closer. Her facial skin was as smooth as glass. "I don't like it there," she whispered. "Nobody walks anywhere and they don't talk to each other. Ever. I don't have anyone to *kibbitz* with."

"What about your son?"

"*Ach!* He's always off somewhere, making a movie. You've probably met him. He travels back and forth between New York and L.A. all the time."

Before she even mentioned her son's name, Eric realized who she was. Of course, he thought. I've seen her on TV lots of times. Yikes! Close up, her facelift was almost too much to deal with. He casually glanced out the window as the plane lifted off the runway. "We have a beautiful day for flying," he said, as they passed over Belle Harbor and then turned and began climbing back toward the West Coast.

"Are you working up front today, with all the real celebrities?"

"No, I'm working here in main cabin."

"Do me a favor: if you go up to first class later, and my son happens to be on board, tell him to come back and say hello to his mother."

"Sure, but wouldn't he know if you were on board the same flight?"

"You'd think so, wouldn't you?"

"I understand. I'll keep an eye out for him."

"Thank you." She pulled a magazine and a wallet out her purse. "How soon does that drink cart come by?"

"In just a few minutes."

"I'll start with a double rum and Diet Coke." She handed him a fifty-dollar bill. "Run a tab for me, please. Whatever money is left over at the end, you can keep for yourself."

"Thank you, ma'am, but we aren't allowed to accept tips."

"Oh, sweetheart," she said, laughing. "It's the Nineties. Get with the program already!"

***

Well, this seems like a nice crowd," said Nancy, as they gathered in the back of the plane after takeoff. "Are there any movie stars sitting in first class today, Eric?"

"Yes, I met a few when I was out pulling tickets out at the gate, but nobody to get excited about. It's funny how different they all look in person, compared to the way they look up the big screen."

"That's the magic of lighting and make-up," said Nancy. "Nevertheless, meeting movie starts in a nice part of this job. That's one thing I never get jaded about. I keep thinking that one of these days, Harrison Ford will walk right through that door."

"What will you say?"

"Nothing. I'll just faint dead away. Hopefully, he'll catch me as I fall. It's too bad so many actors fly on private jets nowadays. The Seventies and Eighties were great for movie star sightings. On the 747s, we had everybody on board and it was a non-stop party all the way to L.A." She sighed. "I miss those days."

"Why don't you work in first class, then? You're senior enough to hold it."

She shook her head. "It's not the same anymore. Too many people from the *business* end of show business sit up there nowadays. A lot of them are real assholes. It's the same scenario in business class—worse, actually. Me, I'm happy camping in coach. Drinks, dinner, movie—done."

"Speaking of drinks and dinner," said Mary, "You're working with me, Eric. Would you rather do the drink cart or the meal cart?"

Oh, beverages, please! No one's ever asked me before. They usually just point to the meal cart and say, 'that's yours.' " He shrugged. "I'm pretty familiar with the routine already: senior stews are always in charge of liquor and headset sales, for obvious reasons."

"You don't have to worry about us, Eric," said Mary. "Today, you're working with the plaid jumper brigade."

Oh? Was that your first uniform when you all started flying?"

"What? Oh, no!" She laughed. "I meant, we're all Catholic school girls. See, around the time that we were interviewed in the Seventies, the company was only hiring Catholic school graduates—out of New York, at least. We were already used to be terrorized by the nuns, so they figured we'd follow the rules and do everything by the book."

"Or so they thought!" said Josie.

"Now, the New York City public school girls they hired before us, in the Sixties—*they* were trouble," said Mary. "Talk about a rough bunch of women. They scared the hell out of me when I first started."

"I don't think I've met any of them yet," said Eric.

"They've all went over to international years ago and mostly fly the Caribbean routes," said Josie. "People buy a lot of liquor going to the islands."

"Good place for them," said Nancy. "You *need* tough flight attendants on those flights."

"Now, Eric, there are a few exceptions to the liquor and headset money debacle," said Josie. If your flight lands after midnight and you don't feel safe going home on the subway, take twenty bucks for cab fare. You think the company gives a shit if you get stabbed on the E train? They don't. You have to look out for yourself. But don't make it a regular habit."

"Thanks for the advice."

"We've got your back," said Mary. "Hey, you know what, Eric? You fit right in with us today. We're all Catholics school graduates and you've got a face just like an altar boy!"

"Gee, thanks. That's the image I'm trying to project for sure."

***

Two hours after takeoff, the service in coach was over. "That wasn't too bad, huh?" said Eric.

"Smooth as silk," said Nancy. "No drama today. That's the way we like it."

"I can't believe you've only been flying for such a short time, Eric," said Mary, as she emptied coffee pots down the drain. "If you hadn't mentioned it, I'd have thought you'd were an old pro. I like the way you look, too. Isn't it nice, girls? Not like some of the bums we fly with out of New York."

"Oh, those lazy straight boys!" said Josie. "I'm not mentioning any names, but—"

"Beau Thompson!" Nancy and Mary crowed in unison.

"Why does that one name pop up again and again?" said Josie.

"Because he *is* the laziest straight male flight attendant on the planet." The crew phone rang. Mary picked it up. "Hello, it's Mary … OK, I'll spread the word." She hung up the phone. "That was Lorraine. They're all finished up front, and Zack has a buffet with leftovers set up downstairs. Who wants to go eat?"

"I'm starving," said Nancy.

"Me, too!" said Josie. "I didn't have time for breakfast today."

"Why don't the three of you go eat," said Eric, "and I'll keep an eye on the cabin. I don't mind going last."

"He's such a gentleman!" said Josie. "We hit the jackpot today."

So did I, thought Eric, as he anticipated what would happen with Zack in the lower lobe.

***

A half hour later, he stepped out of the elevator downstairs. Zack was sitting on the jump seat near the sink, reading *The Advocate*.

"Hi," said Eric, making sure to leave the door open.

"Hey," Zack said, stuffing the magazine into his tote bag. "I was wondering when I was gonna see you."

"I wanted to make sure the coast was clear. I checked before I came down. They don't need a thing upstairs. Jesus, it's cold down here!"

"That's my trick for keeping the yackers away. I have my own thermostat and I keep it set at sixty-two degrees. It's funny: the skinniest ones are the ones who yack the most. Keeping it that cold sends 'em back upstairs in a hurry." He reached to turn up the thermostat. "It'll warm up in just a second."

"Don't you get cold?"

Zack grinned. "I've got my fur to keep me warm."

"Oh, right."

"Everything OK, Eric? You look a little tense."

He was a little tense. This was new territory for him, but he didn't want Zack to know that. "I think I pulled a muscle moving the beverage cart."

"A groin muscle?" He stepped closer.

"No, shoulder."

"I'll give you a good rub down at the hotel. In the meantime, if you want anything else, let's get right to it."

Eric grinned. "I didn't come down here for leftovers."

Zack started unbuttoning his shirt. "Take off that apron."

Eric quickly removed it and put on the jump seat.

"Now the tie. That's good." He grabbed Eric by the waist. "Come here." He planted a wet, salty kiss on Eric's lips. "I've wanted to do that since the minute you came downstairs before takeoff. And to touch that ass, too." He unbuckled Eric's belt and pulled his slacks down. "Jesus, that's beautiful!" he said, as he fondled Eric's rear end.

"Your chest," said Eric. "I've got to feel that chest again."

"You like that goody trail, huh?"

"Yeah, I love it." Eric ran his hands all over Zack's torso, he then tugged on the silver nipple rings.

"That's it, baby," said Zack. "Pull 'em, but not too hard. God, you've me so fucking excited!"

"Pull out your dick, Zack. I want to see it."

Zack unzipped his pants and hauled out a fat, rock-hard cock. Eric moaned as he wrapped his fingers around it.

"Use a little spit, man," said Zack. "Lube is the one thing I don't have handy."

"Do the same for me."

"Fuck, what a nice piece, Eric!"

Eric couldn't believe it. Right above his head, passengers were watching a movie, and his co-workers were chatting and flipping through magazines. Yet, there *he* was, half-naked and having sex at 36,000 feet!

"I'm getting close, man," Zack said, panting.

"Me too."

"Give me your load, baby, right here in my hand. Give it to me now, and if you want, I'll fuck you later until you can't walk."

That put Eric over the edge. "I'm cumming!"

"I'm right there with ya!" He and Zack exploded into each other's hands.

Eric couldn't believe the size of Zack's load. "Hey," he managed to stammer as he stepped back. "Not… on… my uniform!"

Zack's breathing finally slowed down. He laughed as he reached for a stack of paper towels next to the sink. "I didn't get any on your pants, did I?"

"No," said Eric, standing with his arms out at his sides as he examined his trousers. "I'm good."

Zack wiped Eric's hands for him and turned the water on in the sink. "Was this your first time having sex in the air?" he asked, pumping liquid soap from the dispenser.

"Yep."

"I thought so. That makes you an official member of the club."

"Which club?"

"The mile-high club."

"God, you're right!" said Eric, drying his hands. "I hadn't even thought about it."

"And I got to initiate you. Hot *damn!*"

" Have you done this a lot?"

"I'm the president of the eastern division," Zack said with pride.

"I'm honored."

"It helps when you fly this position. On any other plane, there's really no place to go except the coach galley. But it has to be very late at night, and you need a light load and another flight out to be a lookout."

"What about the bathrooms?"

"Nope. Never have, never will. I leave that to drunken passengers."

They were interrupted by the buzz of the intercom.

"Hey, Zack, it's Lorraine. I'm trying to get the lift to come up. Is the door open down there?"

"What do you need?"

"Do you have any more club soda?"

"Yeah. I'll send it up with Eric."

"Thanks."

"I guess I have to go back to work now," said Zack. "Time to start baking the cookies."

"Thanks again. That was hot."

"Will you be up for round two later, at the hotel?"

"Sure," said Eric.

"Will you let me have that ass?"

He fondled Zack's still-turgid penis through his pants. "As long as we play safe, I'll give you anything you want."

"Not to worry. I travel prepared. See you on the ground."

***

Where've you been?" Mary asked when Eric returned. "You were gone for quite a while."

"I was downstairs, eating."

She looked him up and down. "You want to fix yourself up a little bit?"

"What do you mean?"

"I mean, little altar boy, that your hair is mussed up, your tie is crooked, and your shirt tail is sticking out of your pants."

"Oh!" He didn't know what else to say. "I guess I better go comb my hair."

"Yes. You do that."

He made a beeline for an empty lavatory and emerged a few minutes later, looking as neat and tidy as he had when they boarded.

Mary was waiting outside the lav door. "You made it with Zack in the galley, didn't you?"

"Well, I—"

"You like flying the friendly skies? Well, *watch* yourself, Eric. Some of these guys aren't as selective as you think. Zack's one of them. He'll fuck anything that moves."

"Thanks a lot. That makes *me* feel special."

"Did you let him screw you?"

"Are you crazy? Of course not!" He tried laughing it off. "I mean, what if we hit turbulence? Somebody could get hurt."

"Go ahead, make jokes. I'm trying to be serious, but never mind."

"You won't say anything to Nancy or Josie, will you?"

"No. But like I said: watch yourself. Why do you think we're hiring so many people? A lot of the guys that used to work here are out of commission—on long-term medical leaves. Or *dead*. You know what I mean?"

"I appreciate your concern. But you don't have to worry about me, Mary. I'm very careful."

"Did you wash your hands afterward?"

"Yes, of course we did."

"*Boys.*" She shook her head. "You'll do it anywhere, won't you?"

"Let's change the subject."

"OK. Gimme ten dollars."

"What for?"

"The party fund."

"What party? Nobody invited me."

"You must have missed that conversation while you were downstairs. Nancy and Josie are going to make a run to Dealer Dan's for wine and snacks. We'll meet up by the pool this afternoon and relax for a while. Then we're going out for Mexican food. You're welcome to join us for both."

"I'd love to meet you by the pool. I'm not sure about dinner, though. Can we play it by ear?"

"Sure. It's *your* layover. So lay over with whomever you like."

***

As the crew waited in front of the terminal, Nancy impatiently tapped her foot. "Where the hell is that van? We always have to wait for it. It's not like they don't know that we're coming."

"I just called dispatch," said Lorraine. "The driver is on his way and should be here in about five minutes." She did a quick head count. "Anyone seen Zack?"

"He forgot his galley gloves," said Josie. "He had to run back to the plane."

Five minutes, thought Eric. I have just enough time for a smoke. He took out his cigarettes.

"Ugh!" said Mary. "You *smoke?!* Who smokes anymore?"

"I do," Eric said defiantly as he put a cigarette between his lips.

"Over there," said Lorraine, pointing to the end of the sidewalk. "That's the designated smoking area. Don't worry, we won't leave without you."

"I can't believe that you smoke," said Mary. "You didn't strike me as the type."

"Oh, Mary, get off his back," said Nancy. "You used to smoke *pot*, back in the days before drug testing."

"Hey, Cindy Brady! Nobody likes a tattletale," said Mary.

"We all used to do a lot of things before drug testing," said Nancy. "Go enjoy your cigarette, Eric. I'll watch your bags for you."

Eric slunk over to the smoking area. He lit the cigarette and enjoyed the rush of nicotine that came after a six-hour abstinence.

"I'll take that," said Zack, suddenly appearing at Eric's side.

"What the hell?" said Eric, as Zack pulled the cigarette from his lips. "Am I going to get a lecture from you, too?"

"No, I just wanted a drag for myself," said Zack. "Oh, man, is that's good!" He handed the cigarette back to Eric.

"Are we still on for later?" Eric asked.

"Absolutely."

"Are you coming out to the pool with us?"

"No. I'm dead meat. I'm going right to sleep and then I'm going to hit the gym for an hour."

"Well, how do you want to arrange this?"

"Let's see, it's four o'clock now. Why don't you call me around seven and we'll take from there? If I don't answer, leave me a message and I'll call you when I get back."

His proposal was a bit too casual for Eric's liking. "Zack, you're not going to flake out on me, are you?"

He grabbed Eric by the shoulders and planted another big, wet kiss on his lips. "Does that seem like flaking out to you?"

"Hey, you two!" shouted Mary. "Get a room!"

"That's just what we have planned," Zack replied, taking the last drag from the cigarette. "Don't worry, Eric. Go have drinks with the girls and call me at seven. We are *on*, OK?"

***

"Eric, your glass is empty," said Nancy. "Would you like a refill?"

"Yes, please."

"Which red are you drinking?"

"The cabernet sauvignon."

"Oh, I love it when you say it like that. Do it again."

"Cabernet sauvignon," he repeated in perfect French.

"Look," said Nancy, raising her sleeve. "Goose bumps!"

"God, I can't believe this," said Eric, as he began drinking his third glass. "Who knew you could get so much wine for so little money?"

"Why do you think we go to Dealer Dan's? It ain't for the chips and salsa."

"Good," said Mary, madly scooping up salsa with one tortilla chips after another. "More for me."

Eric looked at his watch. Shit, it was 6:50! He hastily finished his wine and stood up. "Well, ladies, thank you very much. I've had a wonderful time."

"What about dinner?" said Josie.

"I'm not hungry anymore. I filled up on chips and salsa. I'll meet you for breakfast tomorrow though, if anybody's going."

"All right, girls," said Josie. "Let's give him his parting gift."

"Here," said Nancy, passing Eric a rolled-up airsickness bag.

"Thanks, but I didn't have *that* much to drink," said Eric.

"I know. Look inside. These are some party favors we collected for you."

Eric opened the bag. Inside there was an assortment of condoms, a small tube of lubricant and a bottle of hydrogen peroxide.

"That's spermicidal, water-based lube," said Mary. "It's the best kind. Use the hydrogen peroxide after oral sex. You should gargle with it."

"Thank you."

"Why are you getting all red in the face?" said Josie. "We know all about safer sex."

"I guess it's a topic that I've never really discussed with women before."

"What do you think, that we were *born* in our forties?" said Nancy. "We were all single once, doing the party scene in Manhattan. We've been around the block, and we're simply looking out for your well-being and your sexual health."

"I'm touched," said Eric, "but believe me, I can take care of myself."

"Oh, honey, you're *so* young," said Nancy. "There're a lot of people who'll try to take advantage of that."

"I'm twenty-three years old. I'm a grown man!"

"We know. We're just trying to help you make it to *thirty*-three, OK?"

Eric sighed. "I don't think you all know what it's like nowadays."

"Sweetheart, you're so wrong," said Josie. "We know exactly what it's like. We've spent a lot of time visiting gay friends in hospitals over the past few years. We think you're terrific, and we want to you to be around for a long time. If we didn't like you so much already, we wouldn't bother to say anything."

"Well, thank you very much." He closed the bag. "I'll put this stuff to good use. And now I really should get going."

***

Doom and gloom, he thought, as he walked into his room. Why does everyone have to rain on my goddam parade? He tossed the bag on the desk. They're very sweet and they really do care. But I *can* take care of myself. As he reached for the phone, he found himself becoming agitated. Christ, I'm not a hick from the sticks! I know how to have safe sex with other men. What do they think, I just came out yesterday? "Could you please connect me with Zack Pendergast? Thank you." I didn't become a flight attendant to go shopping at Dealer Dan's, he thought. I want a walk on the wild side and that's exactly what I'm going to have.

Zack answered on the first ring. "Hello?"

"It's Eric."

"Oh, hi. I was wondering if I was going to hear from you."

"Here I am. Are you ready?"

"Uh, yeah, but there's been a slight change of plans."

You mother *fucker!* Thought Eric. If you try to break our date, I'll—

"I ran into a friend at the gym," said Zack. "He's a pilot for another airline. He's built like a brick shit house and has a big fat dick. Don't you, Tony?"

"Is he there in your room right now?" asked Eric.

"Yes."

"So let me get this straight: you're ditching me for *him?*"

Zack laughed. "No, you idiot! I told him about you and we want to know if you're interested in a three-way. If you're not, I'll send Tony back to his room and catch up with him another time. He knows that you have priority. So what'll it be, hot shot?"

"Tell Tony to stay. I'll be right there. What room are you in?"

"Eight thirty-three."

"I'll be there in five minutes," he said, grabbing the bag from the desk. "And this won't be a quickie."

"Hell, no," said Zack. "We've got all night. See you in five."

CHAPTER 14

Wheels in Motion

"Well, do you like it?" asked Jim.

"What's not like?" Anthony replied, as he began stroking the hood of a red Ferrari Testarosa. "She's a beaut."

"Stop that!" Jim reached out to pull Anthony's hand back. "You'll leave finger prints."

A glare was all that it took to stop the hand in mid-air. "It's a car, Jim. It's a fucking car."

"It's a two-hundred-thousand-dollar car, buddy boy."

"It'll get rained on. Birds will be shitting on it, for Christ's sake."

"Not if I can help it," said Jim. "Get in. I want to see how you look behind the wheel."

Anthony folded himself into the front seat. "I think I'm a little too tall. Maybe we should look at something else."

"No, it's a perfect fit: classic male Italian beauty in a classic Italian sports car. This is the one. Let's take it."

"I don't know. I'm going to feel a little pretentious pulling into the employee lot in this."

"You won't be 'pulling in.' You'll be arriving in style." He laughed. "I can just see those DFW rich bitches. They'll be *green* with envy. Imagine, a New Yorker showing them up."

"Yeah, not to mention showing up in my driveway. What'll the guys say?"

"I think they'll say, 'Anthony seems to be doing very well for himself. Maybe we should start looking for a new roommate.'"

The front seat suddenly felt claustrophobic. Anthony stepped out of the car. "Jim, let's take this road trip one mile at a time, OK?"

Jim's smile evaporated. "Are you kidding me? You're still not sure, after all the talks that we've had?"

"Don't get all excited. I—"

"I didn't ask you to throw your shit into a U-Haul and try it out at my place for a few weeks, you know. I invited you to *share my life*. There's a lot at stake here. There are documents to sign and property to settle. My attorney is already putting pen to paper—all to protect *your* interests, I might add. If you're starting to get cold feet—"

"I'm not getting cold feet. It's just…"

"Just what?"

"It's the whole package: you and the house and the weekend trips to the Coast and the personal shopper at Neiman Marcus and *everything*. Sometimes it feels like too much."

"I'd hate to call you an ingrate, but I know a lot of boys who'd be overjoyed just to have the personal shopper."

"I'm not a boy, or a boy *toy*. I'm a man."

"I'll say you are." Jim playfully pushed him against the car. "You're *all* man. And you're all mine."

Anthony squirmed. "Jim, I don't think the salesman will appreciate you copping a feel on the showroom floor."

"Considering how much money I'm spending, I could *fuck* you on this showroom floor and he wouldn't bat an eye."

"Gentlemen, have you made a decision?" The salesman had appeared from out of nowhere. His name was Paul. He wore a charcoal suit with a persimmon-colored tie.

"I, uh…" Anthony stammered.

"We'll take it," Jim said with finality.

"Excellent choice," said Paul, looking Anthony up and down. "I assume you have the title for the vehicle you want to trade in?"

"Yeah. It just came in the mail this week." Anthony reluctantly pulled an envelope out of his pocket. "I almost hate to part with it. It's the first car I ever owned. I thought I'd be keeping it longer than just a few months."

"Not to worry," said Paul. "We'll find a good home for it. A used car like yours in good condition and with such low mileage—it'll be perfect for the raffle at my mother's church bazaar. You can write it off as a tax deduction."

"Don't bother," said Jim. "Just sell it for scrap."

"Hey, guys, show a little respect, please," said Anthony.

"I remember my first car," Paul said, dreamily. "A brand-new Mustang Fastback. It was a present for my sixteenth birthday. I used to tote the quarterback home from football practice every day. Oh, if that back seat could talk! On Homecoming Night, after we dropped off our clueless 'dates,' we—"

"I wish we had time for a trip down memory lane, Paul," Jim said, forcing a smile, "but Anthony needs to be somewhere by two o'clock."

"OK. Come into the office and we'll discuss terms."

"No terms to discuss," said Jim. "I—I mean, *we*—are paying cash. No monthly payments"—he looked directly at Anthony as he spoke—"and no strings attached." He took out his checkbook.

"I'm sorry, Jim," said Paul, "but we'll need a certified check."

Jim's face reddened. "You're kidding me, right?"

"Of course, I'm kidding. If I know one man in this town who can put his money where his mouth is, it's Jim Sizemore."

"That's my name."

"And how he loves the sound of it," said Anthony.

"Speaking of which," said Paul, "do you want both your names on the title?"

"No, just one," said Jim. "This vehicle will be the sole and exclusive property of Mister Anthony Bellini. B-e-l-l-i-n-i."

"Wait a minute," Anthony started to protest.

"The car is yours," Jim said matter-of-factly. "I said no strings attached and I meant it."

"What about insurance?" said Anthony. "The monthly premium on this baby is going to be—"

"I'll take care of the insurance, naturally." Jim turned to Paul. "Can you start the paperwork now, please?"

"Fine. Why don't you have a seat in the lounge? My secretary, Kathy, will be right in to offer you refreshments."

"Same old Folgers Coffee and Dunkin' Donuts?" asked Jim.

Paul laughed heartily. "I think we can do a little better than *that* for you, Mr. Sizemore!" said Paul. "Folgers coffee. Ha!"

***

"Do you want a cappuccino?" Jim asked Anthony, as Kathy prepared one for him.

"No, thanks."

Jim perused a tray of French pastries. "How about an éclair?"

"You know what I'd like? A cup of Folgers coffee and a donut."

"No can do," said Jim.

"A La Marzocco cappuccino machine in a car dealership," Anthony said derisively. "That's the Texas textbook definition of 'too much.' "

"I keep a package of Ding Dongs in my purse," Kathy drawled. "Would you like one?"

"That's the *other* Texas textbook definition of 'too much,' " Jim grumbled.

"I'd love a Ding Dong," said Anthony.

"Kathy, would you excuse us, please?" Jim said, in a tone that sent her scurrying out of the room. "Anthony, how long are you going to keep this up?"

"Keep what up?"

"The proletariat act. The feigned scorn and sly digs about my money, my friends, my business associates, and my life in general—which, by the way, you take a very active part in." His jaw was so tight that the skin blanched. "Despite what you may think, my assets weren't handed to me by my parents on a silver platter. It's true that I started my company with some family money, but that was just seed money. I've worked my *ass* off for everything that I have. All the wealth that I've accumulated over the last twenty years I owe to my brains, talent, ambition, goddam hard work, and nothing else. Yes, my family lived nicely. I'm going to live *very* nicely. I've established certain standards for myself, and I won't settle for anything less." He threw his checkbook down on the desk. "Nor will I tolerate any attitude from a *goombah* like you who doesn't even have a pot to piss in. I don't give a shit *how* big your dick is. Have I made myself clear?"

"Yes. I'm sorry, Jim. I didn't realize I was being such a jerk."

"Well, now you know."

"The plain and simple truth is that I just wasn't brought up this way. You know how I've struggled over the past few years, especially during the strike at ACA. I never took a dime from anyone. If anything, I've gotten used to *not* having very much."

"For someone with your looks, that a completely absurd situation to be in— and an even more absurd situation to stay in."

"I need time to adjust. If we could…" He chose his words carefully. "If we could just tone it down, if we could simplify things, I'd be more comfortable."

"What do you want, a weenie roast in the backyard? Or a Pyrex dish of lasagna slapped down on the kitchen table for dinner? That's not going to happen. If that's the kind of life you want, then haul your jalopy back to the stew zoo in Oak Lawn and stay there. Or better yet, drive it all the way back to Queens. It's your choice." He took out a silver pen. "Now," he said calmly, "am I writing a check for the car or not?"

"Write it," Anthony said. The words came out of his mouth so fast that Jim's mouth dropped open. "Write it, Jim, and let's move on."

Jim recovered quickly. "Good," he said, as he scribbled out a check for $200,000. "I'm glad that's settled. By the way, what time do you get to L.A. tonight?"

"Around four, I think."

"You'll call me as soon as you get to your hotel room, right?"

"You mean, the minute I walk through the door?"

"Yes, the very minute."

"Why? Are you afraid that I'll meet somebody between the lobby and the elevator?"

"You don't get it, do you? I'm not keeping tabs on you. I trust you implicitly. I want to talk to you right away because sometimes, darling, I can't bear for us to be parted." It was rare for Jim to use terms of endearment. He smiled as he took Anthony in his arms. "Aren't I allowed to indulge in something as mundane as missing my lover when he's away from home?"

"Yes," said Anthony, getting an erection the moment that Jim's hand cupped his rear end. "You certainly are."

***

Several hours later, Anthony pulled the Ferrari into the employee parking lot at DFW. He could barely see where he was going. Every aisle was full of pickup trucks and SUVs that towered over him. He finally found a space and parked. He hopped out and gently closed the car door. Then he stood there for a moment to admire the vehicle and remind himself that he owned it. The Ferrari was more than a car: it was a work of art.

"Wow-wee! That is some set of wheels!"

Anthony looked up. A beautiful flight attendant with platinum hair was sitting behind the wheel of a gun-metal grey Hummer.

"Thanks," said Anthony, as he took out his luggage.

"Can I make a suggestion, hon?" Her Texas twang was heavy. "Don't park it here. The doors'll be so dinged when you get back that you'll want to shoot yourself."

"Where else is there to go?"

"Follow me to the back lot. It's a longer wait for the bus to the terminal, but I guarantee you'll be glad that you did."

"OK." He got back in the car and followed her for five minutes to a remote area that was only half-full. She pulled in between two parking spots. Anthony noticed that most of the other cars in the area were parked the same way, so he followed suit.

The woman opened her door. She wore shimmering hose and four-inch stiletto heels. As she stepped out, Anthony was sure that she'd fall straight to the pavement below. Watching her exit the vehicle, though, he realized that she'd had a lot of practice.

The woman was stunning. Her tailored jacket revealed a perfect hourglass figure. Her makeup had been painstakingly applied, and her long, manicured nails glistened in the sun. Her jewelry sparkled. She sore an immense diamond ring on her left hand, a diamond bracelet and diamond earrings. She even had diamond pins nestled in her hair. She opened the back of her car, where a set of Louis Vuitton luggage was neatly stacked inside. "It's not regulation, I know, but everything else about me is." She grinned. "And if a supervisor asks, my Travelpro is 'in for repairs.' "

"Let me help with you that." Anthony reached for her suitcase.

"Aren't you nice!" she said, as Anthony put it on the ground. "God damn, it's hot out here!"

"It sure is," he said, taking off his jacket.

"Ooh, baby, look at you! Sculpted!" she said, eyeing him. "But I'll ogle you later. We need to seek cover immediately before my face starts to run. Come on, this way." She led him to a bus shelter where they shared a dime-sized patch of shade.

"It must be ninety-five today," said Anthony.

"I *loathe* summer," she said, dabbing her neck with a handkerchief. "I swear, today is the last time I drive myself to DFW until Halloween. Would you excuse me for a second, please?" She removed a phone from her purse and dialed a number.

Get *her*, thought Anthony. A flight attendant with a cell phone.

"Hello, Marty, it's me," she drawled. "I just parked the car and I am *frying* out here. It should be a crime to be this hot! From now on, I want James to drive me to and from the airport—every trip ... Well, I'm sorry if you have meetings all over town every day, but I'm the one wearing a hundred dollars' worth of Guerlain makeup ... So hire a second driver, you can afford it ... Honey, don't fight me on this, you know that I'll get my way in the end ... Ah, thank you, darlin', of course I'll make it worth your while. Oh, here comes the bus! Gotta go! I'll talk to you later." She hung up. "See how easy that was? Problem solved."

"I like your style."

She shrugged. "If you never ask, you'll never get. Where are you heading, by the way?" she asked, as they boarded the employee bus.

"The three o'clock to L.A."

"What a coincidence, so am I." She pulled at the collar of her blouse. "Christ, this bus is as bad as the parking lot! I'm melting! Driver, can you crank up the AC, please! Thank you!" She turned to Anthony. "My name's Lana."

"I'm Anthony. I'm working up front, Lana. Where are you?"

"Oh, honey, as if you had to ask." She patted her bejeweled hair. "I don't wear Harry Winston to impress the folks in coach. Are you from New York?"

"Yeah."

"Let me guess: from Queens?"

"Jesus, am I that obvious?"

"I *knew* it! Be still, my heart! I love your accent. My husband's from Queens too and the sound of his voice makes my pussy *purr*."

Anthony grinned. "This is going to be a hell of a trip."

"Oh, yes! And because you're such a gentleman and helped me with my luggage, dinner tonight will be my treat. And I'm not talking about the In-and-Out Burger on Sepulveda. I mean, a real dinner in a nice restaurant. That is if you don't have any other plans."

"I have no plans at all."

"Good. I want to hear all about you, Anthony. And the first thing I want to know is: what you had to do to get that gorgeous automobile."

"Just lucky, I guess."

"Bull! There must be more to that story. Let's finish the service quickly up front today, OK? You and I have some talking to do."

As they exited the bus, Lana's phone rang. "Oh, God. What now? Hello? ... Marty, I just spoke to you five minutes ago! ... Where do you think I am? I'm getting off the bus! What do you want?... Oh, you silly! I love you, too!... Yes, I'll call you before takeoff. Bye!" She shook her head as she hung up. "There's nothing like a man in love, is there, Anthony?"

"No, nothing."

***

Anthony stood at the entry door as passengers began filing down the jet bridge. The first-class passengers were the usual group of harried, pasty middle-aged men. They were all sweating in their suits and ties. The air conditioning system on the jet bridge was simply no match for the brutal Texas heat. Five minutes later, the coach passengers arrived. They were a little friendlier; they acknowledged him as they entered, at least. Nevertheless, he was struck, as always, by the sheer number of obese people flying out of DFW. Even though lunch would be served in both cabins, many passengers were carrying large, greasy paper bags of fast food. The smell of burgers and fries, combined with jet fuel and the heat, started to make Anthony feel nauseous.

"Full boat?" asked Lana, as she finished setting up the first-class galley.

"Just about," said Anthony. "There are still two open seats in the last row of first."

"I'll be ready to start pre-departure drinks in a just a sec," she said, as she struggled with a champagne cork. "Anyone worthwhile on here today?"

"Define 'worthwhile.'"

"Don't play dumb, hon. You know what I mean."

"No, not really. Besides, what would Marty say?"

"There's nothing wrong with making new friends," she said, as the cork finally came out with a pop.

A gate agent came huffing and puffing down the jet bridge. "Are y'all just about ready to close up?" she asked, as she handed the final paperwork to Anthony.

"Yes," said Anthony. He gestured toward the cabin. "Is this everybody?"

"I have one runner," she said. "Well, if only he *would* run. He's coming from the Club and he's taking his sweet time. Of course, I can't say anything. God forbid I should offend a VIP! But I'll still be the one who gets hollered at if this flight doesn't get push back on time. Oh, here he comes now. Good. Hey, Lana, can I get a glass of something cold, please? It's so hot today, I'm like to pass out..."

As Anthony saw the last passenger arriving, the agent's voice faded into the background. The man was so good-looking that Anthony became weak in the knees. He was even taller than Anthony, and had tussled blond hair and sky-blue eyes. In sharp contrast to the other passengers, he wore a crisp white linen suit and loafers without socks. His blue shirt was unbuttoned a quarter of the way down, revealing tanned skin. His only luggage was a Vuitton weekend bag.

He walked on board casually, as though it were perfectly natural to keep one hundred and thirty other passengers waiting for him. "Hey, Lana, check this guy out," Anthony said.

"Oh my God," she said, as the man strolled by, smiling broadly at Anthony. "He's…"

"Gorgeous," said Anthony. "And look: his luggage matches yours. It's kismet. You better call Marty and tell him not to hire that second driver yet."

"Oh, Lord, that reminds me!" She grabbed her cell phone and dialed. "Hello, Marty, it's me. We're just about to push back. I'm calling to say goodbye. I'll talk to you as soon as we land." She pulled the galley curtain closed. "Yes, I *know* where you'll be," she said, greatly exasperated. "I *will* call you. Now honey, you have to let me go! I'm working!"

Anthony stood watching as the last passenger stowed his luggage overhead. As the blond man removed his jacket and revealed a perfect torso, Anthony suddenly realized that he'd seen the man before. But he couldn't remember where. On another flight? At one of Jim's parties? In a movie? In a magazine? Yes, that was it! He was a *Stallion* model—the epitome of the type, in fact. Only the most beautiful men in the world modeled for *Stallion*, which was known everywhere as the slickest, sexiest and most expensive gay porn magazine available. *Stallion* models, by virtue of the gifts bestowed on them by Mother Nature, had a lifestyle that most other gay men could only dream of. Anthony had been approached more than once by the owner of *Stallion* to appear in the magazine, with a guarantee that he'd be on the cover. He'd politely declined each offer. Once your junk was out there, it was out there. There was nothing left to the imagination, which in the long run was counter-productive.

He vividly remembered one of the photographs that he'd seen of the passenger. He was standing naked and alone in a beautiful, sunlit room, looking like a Rodin sculpture that had come to life. His skin glowed. His arms and legs were lightly covered with blond fuzz. He was gazing lovingly at his gargantuan, veined penis. It curved downward and slightly to the left. He was reaching for it with his right hand … his fingers were about to make contact with the perfectly shaped, uncircumcised head. In his solitude, he needed nothing else—except, perhaps, for someone to watch him.

"Excuse me!" The agent said. "I asked you if I could close the door now. We're *past* departure time."

"Oh, sure," said Anthony, "we're good to go." As the agent swung the heavy door closed, Anthony grabbed a hanger. "Lana, would you mind arming the forward doors, please? I'm going to offer to hang that gentleman's jacket."

"Sorry, honey, but I don't kneel on a dirty carpet for anyone—even Marty. Besides, you should never ask anyone to arm your doors for you. You know better than that." She snatched the hanger from Anthony's hand. "I'll take care of that," she said, as she stepped into the cabin.

"Gee, thanks. You're a real team player." He kneeled carefully, as the carpet *was* rather dirty, and armed the left-hand and then the right-hand door.

Lana came back a moment later. "He's all yours," she said. "Pretty boy plays on your team."

"How do you know?"

"I offered to hang up his jacket and all he said when he looked up was, 'Where's the other one?' Meaning you." She snorted. "Not even a thank you!"

"Well, you are spoken for, Lana." He reached for the flight information sheet and the microphone as the plane began moving forward.

"And what are you, friend?" she asked, as she took out equipment for the safety demo.

"To tell the truth, I haven't quite made up my mind."

"I suppose that Ferrari just appeared under your Christmas tree last December?"

"It *was* gift, but a more recent one. 'With no strings attached.' Those were the giver's exact words."

"Right," Lana said, with a dark laugh. "Keep telling yourself that, darlin', and let me know how it turns out."

***

After takeoff, as Anthony served beverages and lunch, he noticed that as usual, the first-class passengers were completely self-absorbed. Other than an occasionally grunted "thanks" for refilling a glass, no one paid him the slightest attention—except the man in 5A. His name was Chasen de Biers, and his sky-blue eyes followed Anthony wherever he went. Chasen's penis seemed to follow Anthony, too. It seemed to be in a permanent state of erection. Anthony had first noticed it right after takeoff, when he went to close the first-class divider curtain. An hour later, it was still erect and straining against the fabric of his pants. Since he was in the last row and the seat next to him was vacant, Chasen made no attempt to hide it. Occasionally, as Anthony spoke to him, the penis would shift slightly as though it were a python stalking its next meal.

"Would you like more champagne?" Anthony asked.

"You don't have to ask," said Chasen. "Just keep it coming." His voice was deep and husky.

"Yes, sir." Anthony refilled Chasen's glass and then stood with the bottle in his hand.

"Perfect," said Chasen, as he stared at Anthony's crotch. "This is just the way I like it."

It had been a long while since Anthony had been so blatantly cruised by a passenger. He forgot what a turn on it could be. Jim's friends flirted with him all the time, but that was harmless fun. This man was serious—and Anthony liked it. Christ, it's great to be back in the air, he thought.

"How about some dessert, Anthony?"

"Sure. What would you like on your ice cream sundae?"

"Screw the sundae. I want a big banana split."

Anthony grinned. It was such a cornball line, but it didn't seem so corny coming out of Chasen's mouth. "Sorry, but we don't have those on the menu today."

"Don't you ever let people order off the menu? I am a million-miler, after all."

A million-miler. Oh God, you're pushing your luck with that tired line, thought Anthony. "Once in a while. It just depends."

"Well, let's be sure to discuss it before we land." He lowered his hand into his lap and squeezed his dick through his pants.

All right, thought Anthony. I don't mind flirting a little. He shifted his stance, making it clear that Chasen wasn't the only show horse on the flight. "Yeah, we can talk about it." *Ding, ding.* Anthony glanced up. The passenger in 3E had rung his call light and was glaring in Anthony's direction. "Hang on, let me answer that call light." He walked over and turned it off. "Can I help you, sir?"

"Yes, I'd like another glass of wine. I've been sitting here for ten minutes with an empty glass. Are you serving the entire cabin, or just the last row?" he asked snidely.

"I apologize for the wait. I'll get that for you right away." He promptly returned with the man's glass refilled. "Is there anything else you'd like right now?"

"Just keep an eye on *all* your passengers, please."

"Yes, sir." He took a quick walk through the cabin and returned to row five. Chasen was thumbing through a stack of glossy eight by ten photographs. "Oh, good, you're back. Tell me, do you ever get layovers in San Diego?"

"Sometimes," Anthony replied. "We fly everywhere from DFW."

"Do you like the beach?"

"Sure." Here comes the pitch. So I'd be stepping out on Jim once… Big deal. There's no ring on my finger yet.

Chasen handed Anthony the stack of photos. "I have a beach house in La Jolla. It has a pool, a Jacuzzi that fits ten, a houseboy, and a master bedroom that looks right out over the ocean. Why don't we arrange a visit sometime? I mean, if you're completely free—and you don't have some god-awful four A.M. wake-up call the next day."

'Completely free.' That was an odd choice of words, and it immediately put Anthony on guard. "It's a very nice offer," he said casually.

"I'd pick you up at the airport or your hotel and bring you back the next day. And, of course, it would be just the two of us in the Jacuzzi," he added with a wink.

"What about the houseboy?"

"I'd give him the night off. But he'd be back to serve us breakfast the next morning."

"I see," said Anthony, as he casually thumbed through the stack. The house looked vaguely familiar. "It's funny, but it feels like I've seen this house before."

"Do you read *Architectural Digest*? My house was featured in a recent issue." He pulled a photo from the bottom of the stack and handed it to Anthony. "Here's one picture they didn't include in the article, for obvious reasons. I thought you might enjoy it." It was a picture of the master bedroom. Through a large window at the foot of the bed, framed by billowing curtains, the Pacific Ocean shimmered under a clear blue sky. And on one seagrass-covered wall, there was a large, framed photograph of Chasen—completely naked, erect, and gazing down lovingly at his massive penis, his hand outstretched as though he were just about to touch it.

It all came to Anthony in a flash. Chasen *was* a *Stallion* model, but *Stallion Magazine* wasn't the only place where Anthony had seen him naked. He'd seen this picture of the bedroom before. In fact, he knew every room in the beach house. It had been renovated six months ago, for a considerable sum of money, by Jim Sizemore Design. Jim had shown Anthony the same series of photographs right after they met.

"Very impressive," said Anthony. He handed the photograph back to Chasen, thinking: you phony. You big-dicked, goddam phony. You might live at the house, and you might lay around the pool all day, but you don't own it. Jim had done the job for a divorce attorney—a very wealthy older gay man, as Anthony recalled. Chasen was probably his trophy husband. Well, why not? What else was a former porn star qualified to do? He obviously wasn't a million-miler. If he were, he'd look more like all the other pasty, middle-aged men that traveled in first class.

It was too much to be a coincidence. It was a trap—set by Jim—and Anthony had almost walked right into it. Fortunately, Chasen was so full of himself *and* champagne that he didn't know where to draw the line. So much for Jim's implicit trust, Anthony thought, as his blood began to boil.

"Well," Chasen said triumphantly. "It looks like we have the where. Now all we need to talk about it the when."

"It's a very nice offer, but I really can't. I'm seeing someone right now."

Chasen laughed. "Oh, come on, we're all seeing someone. The important thing is to be discreet about it. And I'm *very* discreet."

Anthony kept smiling. He'd never let on that he knew about the setup. "Do you want more champagne?"

"No, I want you to say that you'll come and spend time with me at my beach house."

"Sorry, Chasen, but I'm not available."

"Here. Take my card—in case you do become available. I can be very persuasive."

"OK, if you insist."

Chasen seemed pleased. "I'll look forward to hearing from you, Anthony. And I think I will have one more glass of champagne if there's still time."

"Sure." He retrieved the bottle and poured the remains into Chasen's glass. "Enjoy." As the plane began to descend, the seatbelt sign came on. "I have a few things to take care of in the galley. I'll check on you before we land."

Anthony walked back to the front jump seat, where Lana sat reading *The Robb Report.*

"You're not dumping me for dinner, are you, Anthony? I hope you didn't get a better offer from Lover Boy."

"Not a chance. Hey, Lana, if I wanted to find out some information about a passenger, how would I go about doing it?"

"Well, their basic info is on the final paperwork that we get right before takeoff."

"No, I don't mean just their name and their 'elite' status, I mean if I wanted more personal information."

"That's easy. When we land, ask the agent to print a copy of their PNR. It's a file that lists every single piece of information associated with the reservation—who made it, the credit card used to purchase the ticket, business and home phone numbers—everything."

"The agent will just give me all that info?"

"Sure. Tell her that the passenger left something on the airplane and you want to make sure it gets returned to him. It's less work for the agent if you take care of it. Get it?"

"Good to know. Thank you."

***

As the passengers deplaned, Anthony stood by the front door waiting patiently for Lana to call Marty. When she finished, he said, "Do you mind saying goodbye to the folks while I pop out to see the agent?"

"No problem."

The agent readily printed a copy of Chasen's PNR for Anthony. He read all the details as he walked back down the jet bridge to get his luggage. The ticket had been purchased in Chasen de Beer's name—but it had been paid for by Jim Sizemore using his American Express card. Anthony's blood started to boil again.

***

In front of the terminal, Anthony and the rest of the crew waited for the hotel van. Anthony said nothing as Lana answered another call from Marty. "Yes, we're waiting for the van … I don't *know* how long I'll be here. I'll call you as soon as I get to my room! Can't you wait even ten minutes until…."

Christ, he thought. It's like she's tethered to him by an invisible leash. And to think that I almost ended up the same way. I'm sure that a cell phone would have been Jim's next gift.

The girls from coach rolled their eyes as they listened to Lana go on and on. "What are you doing tonight, Anthony?" one of them asked.

"Going to dinner with Lana. Do you want to come?"

"Lana's taste is a little rich for our blood. We're going to the In and Out Burger."

"No, come with us." He pulled an American Express card out of his wallet. The card was in his name, but the bill went straight to Jim's accountant. "My treat."

"We can't let you do that. You hardly know us!"

"Yes, you can. If I wanted to, I could charge fifty thousand dollars on this card. Let's meet in the lobby at six for drinks. That'll be my treat, too."

***

Anthony wasted no time once he got his hotel room. He threw down his luggage, poured himself a large Scotch and soda, and placed a call to Dallas. "Hello, Jim."

"Hi! I saw that you arrived right on time. How was the drive to the airport in the Ferrari?"

"Fine." Anthony took a sip of his drink.

"Did anyone notice you in the car?"

"Oh, yeah. I got noticed. But that was all part of the plan, right?"

"Well, sure. Hey, if my lover is going to be seen, he should only be seen in the best that money can buy."

"Your generosity floors me sometimes."

"I'm always generous to the men I love. Wait, let me be more specific: to the *man* I love. And that's you, Anthony. How was the flight?"

"Nice. I got noticed on the plane, too." Watch your tone, he thought to himself. Don't let on that you know what he did. Save it until you're ready to come in for the kill.

"Of course you got noticed," said Jim. "Who wouldn't notice you? You're gorgeous. God, I wish you were here. I can wait for you to come back tomorrow. Hey, was it a smooth ride today? I saw there were some big thunderstorms over West Texas this afternoon."

"Oh, yeah, everything was smooth, right up until the very end."

"Excuse me?"

"You sound like you're in good spirits, Jim."

"I am. I'm in exceptionally good mood today, except for the fact that I miss you like hell."

Anthony took another sip of his drink. "Then I guess you received your report already and you know that I turned him down."

"What are you talking about?"

"Don't play dumb with me, Jim. I'm not one those eighteen-year-old nimrods that your buddies snatch up the minute they get off the bus from Midland."

"Anthony, what the hell are you talking about?"

"The setup. You set me up with Chasen de Biers."

"Who?"

Anthony slammed his drink down on the desk. "I said *don't* play fucking dumb! You put a great-looking, big-dicked guy on my flight and tested me to see if I'd take the bait. All less than four hours after you gave me a big hug, told me that you trusted me implicitly, and sent me on my merry fucking way to DFW. What a fucking laugh. And what an idiot I was to believe you. You're an arrogant, self-centered, insecure control freak, just like I always thought you were."

"Anthony, I swear I don't know what—"

"You liar. You're lying to me right now! You paid for his fucking ticket! I have proof right here in my hand. I guess you didn't think that I'd have enough brains to check it out."

"Christ, oh Christ!" Anthony loved hearing the panic in Jim's voice. "I'm sorry, Anthony! I'm sorry, I'm sorry. It's just that I love you so much, and you're so goddam beautiful, and I—"

"Skip it! Here's what I want you to do: go back to your friend Paul and get my car back for me. I want it parked in *my* driveway at *my* house when I come home tomorrow. I'm dropping the Ferrari at your house and then taking a cab home. And I don't want you to be there when I drop it off."

"But—"

"I'm only doing that because you have no way of accessing the employee parking lot at DFW, and I don't want you to get any further involved than necessary. I'll send both your house keys and the car keys via FedEx overnight. And then I don't ever want to see you again."

Jim was sobbing now. "Anthony, you can't leave me, not for one lousy lapse in judgment."

"You think I'm gonna stay with someone who pulls this kind of shit on me? My mind is made up. There are a million guys just as handsome and generous as you, only they're not fucked up like you. I don't think I'll be lonely for very long."

"I'm begging you." Jim sounded like he was thirty seconds away from having a complete breakdown. "Don't leave me! *I'll change*. I'll go to counseling."

"No. We're through. And I'm hanging up now."

Anthony, wait! I'll do whatever I have to keep you with me and to make amends. I'll even up the ante."

"What the fuck do you think I am, some whore that you're bidding on at a frat house auction? Goodbye, Jim."

"Anthony, listen to me a minute! I love you! I can't live without you! I'm willing to do whatever it takes for you to forgive me. I invited you to share my life, right? So I'll *give* you half my life: half of my house, half of my money, and half of my business. We'll change the name on the company letterhead. You'll be my full business partner. The contracts will be ironclad and in your favor. You can work with me as much or as little as you want to until you're ready to stop flying. Please, Anthony. Just think about it. Come home tomorrow. I'll make a nice, simple dinner for you—roasted weenies or lasagna." He laughed weakly. "And for dessert, I'll serve you Folgers coffee and a donut."

After a long pause, Anthony said, "That's a lot to think about. And I will think about it later. But for now, I'm hanging up. I'm going to meet my crew for a lavish dinner. And you're footing the bill for all of us."

"Of course, that's why I ordered that American Express card in your name. Get a bottle of *Dom Pérignon* and leave an outrageously big tip. Will you call me later tonight?"

"No, I don't think so." I'm not letting you off the hook that easily, he thought. A little punishment will go a long way. "I'm so angry right now that if I could, I'd run right over you with that goddam Ferrari. You really fucked up, buddy boy."

"I know I fucked up. I'm just asking for one shot at redemption from the man who means more to me than anything else in the world. *Please.*"

"I'll call you tomorrow before I leave L.A. and let you know my decision."

"Thank you. Good night, Anthony." Jim seemed calm again. "I love you."

"Good night." Anthony hung up the phone and finished his drink in one long swallow. He poured himself another one, put his feet up the desk, and began grinning from ear to ear. What a fortunate set of circumstances: Jim fucks up in a big way, then he gets caught and realizes that he's about to lose me. As a result, he hastily makes an offer that he knows I can't refuse. And that was exactly what Anthony had wanted all along.

Fifteen minutes later, the phone rang again. He debated whether or not to pick up, but decided that if it was Jim calling, he'd simply hang up on him. "Hello?"

"It's Lana. Are you still coming? We're downstairs in the bar waiting for you."

"Sorry, I got sidetracked. I'll meet you in the bar in thirty minutes. In the meantime, order a bottle of champagne. The most expensive one they have."

"Ooh, I like where this is going!"

"It's been a long day. Let's get this goddam party started."

CHAPTER 15

The Pied Piper

"Hello?" Denny croaked into the phone.

"Good morning. This is Shirley from Early Bird. This is your wake-up call."

"Sorry, *who's* this?"

"It's Shirley from the Early Bird Service and this is your requested five A.M. wake-up call. How many damn times do I have to repeat myself?"

"It can't be five o'clock, Shirl," he mumbled. "I just went to sleep a few minutes ago."

"Well, it is. And I have to get you out of that bed as usual. Now, sit up, put both feet on the floor, and walk across the room."

"I am walking across the room."

"Liar! I want to hear those big, bare feet slapping against hardwood floors, and then I want to hear water running in the sink."

"How do you know I have big feet?"

"Believe me, after all these years I know what kind of racket you make getting out of bed. GET UP!"

OK! I'm up." He turned on a lamp. "I forgot where I'm flying today. Did I mention it when I made the request last night?"

"Who am I, your personal assistant? Call crew scheduling if you can't figure it out. I've done more than my job, Denny. The rest of your day is of no concern to me."

"Geez, you could at least wish me *bon voyage*."

"*Bon voyage*. And you better get with the program, Mister. I'll be on vacation the next two weeks, and the other girls here aren't as devoted to you as I am. Understand?"

"Yes, ma'am."

"I'm signing off now. Buh-bye!"

"Hey, that's supposed to be *my* line."

***

As soon as he reached operations, he printed a copy of his trip sequence. One leg to Chicago, followed by a second leg to Seattle. Not too shabby. And an eighteen-hour layover, to boot. Well, that was something. He glanced at the crew list. He knew the two women working up front and liked them. He didn't recognize the fourth name, but he could tell by the employee number that it was someone relatively new. Good: he could always count on new hires to do the heavy lifting. Now if he could just stay awake for the eight hours that it would take to get to Seattle. Then he'd have a nap, then drinks at Happy Hour, and then… who knows what could happen?

"Good morning," he said to Karen as he entered the 737.

"Good morning. You look like shit."

"Thanks. I love hearing that when I've just opened my eyes."

"What happened to you last night?"

"I didn't get any sleep. I'm out of sleeping pills. And muscle relaxers, too. All I have left is a few Xanax and I'm saving those for an emergency."

"Oh, Denny. You and those goddam pills. You're such a tragic figure. When are you going to get off that shit?"

"When I can the hold first-class galley on an afternoon transcon and hide behind the blue curtain for six hours."

"What are you doing on this early trip, anyway? I've never seen you at work before noon."

"I forgot to bid for this month. Do you believe it? Five years of flying and I forgot to bid. So crew scheduling has to make up a schedule for me as the month goes along. And honey, I am flying *crap*."

"It only takes once. It's like being woken from a dead sleep in a hotel room and hearing the purser say, 'We're all downstairs in the lobby, waiting for you. The limo is leaving in two minutes. Why are you still in your room?' After you have experienced that horror once, it never happens again."

"True. Well, fortunately the month is already halfway over. Hell, it's already time to bid for September. And this trip isn't too bad: we have a long downtown layover in Seattle. That's nice."

"Not to mention that Danielle and I are here. You know you can count on us for a good time—unless you decide to ditch us for the bars on Capitol Hill."

"Who else is along for this joy ride?" he asked, ignoring the dig.

"Some new kid named Eric. He seems pretty sharp—although he's a bit of a yammerer. He knows you, by the way."

"From where?"

"He didn't say. Have you hooked up with any button-down types lately?"

Denny did a quick mental review. "Not that I can recall. But the last couple of weeks are hazy. You know, with all the early sign-ins and—"

"Honey, your whole *life* is a haze. Whatever—go and say hello to him. "

"If I did screw him, I hope I made a good impression."

"You must have. He's excited about flying with you. Now, move it. We're boarding in five minutes."

The new hire was making coffee in the coach galley. He had thick chestnut hair and brown eyes. He looked vaguely familiar, but Denny couldn't quite place him.

The new hire looked up and smiled as Denny approached. "Hi, Denny! It's great to see you. I'm Eric Saunders. Do you remember me?"

"Kind of. Have we flown together before?"

"Yes, once, about four months ago. We were on the same plane, only you were working, and I wasn't. It was an early Sunday morning. I was on my way to training. The other two flight attendants were named Kendra and Barbara." He spoke quickly, but his voice was well-modulated, so it was only mildly annoying. "One of them women on your crew that I was a ghost-rider. She made you come back to my seat to check me out and we started chatting. I showed you my acceptance letter from the recruitment office, and then we had a long talk about what I should expect in training."

"Oh, yeah, I remember you now. You're the 'fly me' guy!"

"Excuse me?"

"You had all your paperwork in a leather binder that someone gave you as a going-away present. There was a small gold plate inside, engraved with the words 'I'm Eric, fly me.' "

"Oh, that's right." Eric blushed. "It was from my boss. You must have thought I was a big goober."

"No, I got a kick out of it. You were so excited about everything."

"Anyway, you gave me your phone number, which I misplaced and could never find. I was hoping that I'd get based in New York and that I'd get the chance to fly with you, and here we are."

His face was so open and eager that Denny couldn't help liking him. "I'm glad you got your wish. It's such a drag working with people who don't want to be in New York. Bitch, bitch, bitch, all the time."

"I know. I've flown with a few of them."

"Hey, tell me: did you ever get laid in training?"

"No. My roommate did, but that's a story for later in the day."

"Good. We have something to look forward to after breakfast."

"Right." Eric looked up the aisle. "Here come the passengers."

"Lord," said Denny. "Give me strength."

***

"Why do you keep trying to get up the aisle during boarding?" Denny asked"

"Because," said Eric, "these people have obviously never put a suitcase in an overhead bin before. We'll be here all day if I don't help them."

"Let them learn. You're just asking for an injury on duty."

"Aren't the agents supposed to stop them at the door if they have too much luggage?"

"Dream on, dumplin'."

"Dumplin," Eric repeated. "That's sweet. It reminds me of home."

"Where are you from?"

"Houston."

"I'd never have guessed that in a million years."

"I know. I like it that way."

"Did you live in Texas your whole life before you left for training?"

"Yes. I went to college in Austin. That was better, but it was still Texas—the redneck capital of the world. Do you know what I mean?"

"Oh, absolutely. Are you moving back to Texas after you get off probation?"

"Are you out of your mind? Why would I do that? I'm here for good."

Denny grinned. "That's nice to hear. I hate to break-in new friends, only to have them bail for their hometowns six months later."

"Where are you from, Denny?"

"Shawnee, Oklahoma."

"No way! You sound just like a native New Yorker."

"Thanks." Denny smiled. "See, I never picked up the hometown accent either."

***

As they taxied out to the runway, they sat on the double jump seat in the back of the plane. Denny, having already run out of steam, sat with his eyes closed and his head propped against the wall.

Eric was talking a blue streak about his dire financial situation. "I tried picking up a Miami turnaround to make some extra money, but it wouldn't go through. The crew scheduler I spoke with told me that I wasn't legal for the trip. He said it was a thirty-in-seven problem, but wouldn't explain what that meant. He just hung up."

Denny opened his eyes briefly. "You can't fly more than thirty hours in a seven-day period. It's contractual, to protect reserve flight attendants from being abused when manning is tight. Otherwise, the company would fly people a hundred hours in a week if they could."

"But doesn't the company care that I'm not making enough money to live on?"

"No. The company doesn't care about any of your needs—including your financial needs or your physical well-being. Mercury a major American corporation. Their only concern is having an ass in the jump seat for takeoff and landing because the FAA *makes* them." He rested his head against the wall again.

"Well," said Eric, "while we're on the subject, another thing I want to know is—"

"Are you going to be like this the entire day?"

"Like what?"

"You talk a lot, and you talk fast."

"I'm sorry, I tend to do that when I'm trying to stay awake. The one thing I'm not good with is the early sign-ins. After I got the call for this trip at one A.M., I never got back to sleep. I was sure that I'd miss the alarm going off."

"Honey, that's what modern medicine is for. You need a prescription sleeping pill."

"Where would I get that?"

"From a doctor, dummy."

"I don't have a doctor in New York yet."

"We'll take care of that. My doctor's great. He's gay too, and he understands everything about the lives of gay men and flying. He's the only person in New York who does care about our physical well-being. And he'd love to have you as a patient, I'm sure."

"In the meantime, maybe I could go to the company doctor for a prescription. It would save me the cost of a regular doctor's office visit."

Denny shook his head. "Let's think that through. Would you go to the company doctor if you got the clap from some guy you picked up on a layover?"

"No, I guess not."

"Good answer. Don't go to the company doctor for anything, unless you trip over someone's briefcase in the aisle and dislocate a shoulder. The less the medical department knows about you, the better."

The captain's voice came crackling over the PA. "Ladies and gentlemen, I'm afraid we're caught up in the early morning rush hour traffic here at La Guardia. There are about fifteen airplanes ahead of us. We'll probably take off in thirty minutes or so. Thank you for your patience."

"Oh, Christ," said Denny. "Just wait! Here come the frantic inquiries about connections!"

A call light went off at that moment.

"I'll get it," said Eric.

As Eric walked up the aisle, Denny's eyes followed him. That is one nice ass, he thought. He watched Eric's interaction with the passenger. He listened attentively, nodding up and down, and then patiently answered the passenger's question with a smile on his face. He returned a moment later. "Just like you said—someone had a question about their connection." As soon as he sat down, another call light went off.

"I'll get this one," said Denny.

"No, really, I don't mind. It helps keep me awake."

"Stop!" said Denny. "You'll end up repeating yourself fifty times before we take off. Let's solve all this with one call to the cockpit." He picked up the crew phone and dialed the cockpit. "Captain, we have a lot of passengers who are anxious about their connections. Would you mind making a PA, so we don't have to answer a thousand call lights? ... Thanks, we appreciate it." He hung up the phone and reached for his tote bag. "Now, you and I can get on with more important things—like planning our layover." He took out a copy of *Seattle Gay Times*. "Are you interested in going out tonight?"

"Oh, God, yes, count me in. I've been cooped up with slam-clickers all week. I wish I had one some of those local gay newspapers." Eric reached into his suitcase and pulled out a battered copy of *The Dameron Gay Guide to the USA*. "This weighs a ton. It helps when I'm on reserve though, and I could end up anywhere in the country."

"I used to schlep one of those myself. Now I try to keep city-specific guides with me—for the major cities, at least."

"I'm working on that. I've been dragging this for a month. I bought it second-hand from a guy who's transferring to international."

"Bought it?" Denny eyed the dog-eared pages. "Cheap bastard. He should have given it to you for free."

"I'm glad to have it. I hate asking hotel desk clerks if they know of any gay bars in the area."

"Yeah, I know. I hate that blank stare they give you. It should be their *business* to know where the gay scene is in their town—if there is one. Do they think everyone wants to spend their layover shopping for Garanimals at Target?"

"Hey, that's nice," said Eric, pointing to the shirtless model on the cover of Denny's gay periodical. "Look at that hairy chest!"

"He is hot," said Denny. "You like the furry guys, huh? That's good. I'm a furry guy too."

"I like all kinds of guys," Eric said. "He took the magazine from Denny. "I like him, and him, and him too"

"That's quite a variety."

"Wait, let me show you something." Eric reached into his own tote bag and pulled out a photo album. He opened it and began flipping pages.

"Is that your Charm Farm photo album?" Denny asked.

"How'd you guess?"

"Every new hire carries one for a year or so. Then they find a spot on a bookshelf at home and forget about it—unless you happen to be Arnie, the Queen of the 747."

"I know who you're talking about. I've flown with him." He stopped flipping pages. "Here. This is the man who makes me melt." Eric pointed to a man in a photo with him. He was a muscular Latino with cappuccino-colored skin and a thick mustache. His enormous hands were resting on Eric's shoulders.

"Wow," said Denny. "Who's that?"

"Javier Morales, one of my instructors. He could have pulled me around by my nose and I wouldn't have cared. God, I'm so hot for him!"

"Does he know it?"

"I think I was pretty obvious."

"But you didn't get anywhere, huh?"

"No. I think the feeling was mutual, but he was strictly by the book—no messing around with students. There was a lot of eye candy in my class. Want to see some more?"

"Hang on a second." Denny jumped up and looked out the window. "Yeah, we still have at least six or seven planes still in line ahead of us."

Eric flipped to another page. "This really good-looking blond guy is Dillon Hightower. He was another instructor."

"Christ, where do they go looking for instructors nowadays— Chippendales?"

"Forget it. He's beautiful, but he's straight—and a self-centered asshole."

"Yeah, you can kinda tell just by looking at him."

"This is Alexandra Hallsey, our lead instructor. She was wonderful, but boy, talk about going by the book. You wouldn't want to get on her bad side. And this is—"

"Anthony!" He tore the album from Eric's hands. "Anthony Bellini!"

"Good Lord, how do you know him?"

"I was working on one of his training flights. Well, I didn't really *work* that day. I just sort of… showed up. Actually, I was a complete, fucking hung-over *mess*. I should have called in sick. Anthony was supposed to be deadheading, but he pulled my ass out of the fire by working my position on the flight. He probably saved my job and I'll be eternally grateful to him. Were you two in the same class?"

"Yes, in fact we were roommates in training. And now we're best friends."

"You lucky bastard!" Denny began hurriedly flipping through the pages. "Do you have any shots of him out by the pool?"

"I think so. Let see… Yeah, here's one."

"Oh, look at that *perfect* body! Jesus, I'd give up my apartment to have sex with him just once. And I'm in a rent-controlled one-bedroom!"

"That's me, right next to him," Eric said, tapping the photograph. "I thought *I* looked pretty good that day too."

"Yes, yes, you're adorable. Where is Anthony? What is he flying? Does he live in the city? I gave him my phone number, but I haven't heard from him yet."

"He's based in DFW."

"What the fuck? Why?"

"Oh, I'm *so* tired of telling this story."

"We have one minute before takeoff. Tell me."

"Here's the short version: he was late to class the day we had to turn in our base preference sheets. Alexandra gave him what was left over. She knew damn well he wanted to back to New York, but she sent him to DFW anyway."

"She screwed up his life for being ten minutes late? That seems not only cold-hearted, but completely fucking irrational too. Why didn't he complain to somebody higher-up?"

"Because Alexandra caught him in a lie. He went off-campus for a date and didn't get back until the next day. He said he'd been sick that morning, but she knew that he'd been off the property. On her way to work, she'd seen him stranded on the side of the road with his date from the night before. They had a flat tire."

"So she stranded him in Redneck-ville. Nice."

"He's lucky she didn't fire him on the spot." He sighed. "If only Anthony had—well, never mind. I've been down that road too many times to count. It is what it is."

"So when's he coming back?"

"In December, as soon as he gets off probation. I'm living in Anthony's place with his brother right now, until he comes back."

"What's that like?"

"Like waiting for Godot."

"You can tell me over drinks," Denny said, as the plane swung around at the end of the runway. "I think we're leaving now."

At that moment, they heard the captain say, "Flight attendants, prepare for takeoff."

Eric put away his photo album and fastened his seatbelt.

"Can I see those pictures of Anthony again later?"

"Sure," Eric replied testily.

"What's the matter?"

"I get tired of playing second banana to Anthony wherever I go."

"You don't have to," Denny said, slipping his hand over Eric's thigh. You're hot too."

Eric promptly removed it. " 'Adorable,' you said. That's hardly the same thing."

"Dumplin', you do need a nap—and a drink." He nibbled Eric's ear. "When we get to Seattle, I'll show you exactly how sexy I think you are."

***

"It's so nice to be here early," said Karen, as they waited for the crew van in Seattle.

"And so nice not to be hot!" said Eric. "The cool air is delicious."

"Delicious: that's so cute," said Danielle. "But it's true. The humidity in New York has been unbearable lately."

"Where the hell are the pilots?" said Denny, as the van approached. "How long are we supposed to wait for them?"

"They're going to the short layover hotel," said Karen. "They leave at the crack of the dawn tomorrow on the first flight to Chicago. We go back with different pilots."

"Are you two going right out today, after we check in?" Denny asked.

"Of course," said Danielle. "We're taking a long walk in the Arboretum, and then we're going to the Asian Art Museum, and then we're going over to Pike Market to buy salmon. I'm having company for dinner on Friday night."

"That sounds like a busy day," said Denny. "I admire people who can jump right into their civvies and out into the streets. Myself, I need to be horizontal for a while."

"I take it you and Eric won't be joining us today?"

"Well," said Eric, "we—"

"We'd love to join you, but we already made plans," said Denny. "We both desperately need a nap. Then we're going to eat an early dinner, and then I thought I'd take Eric for a walk up to Capitol Hill."

"You've got to be kidding me," said Danielle. "You guys are going to waste a beautiful afternoon sleeping, and then hang out in dingy gay bars all night?"

"Yes, ma'am."

Karen and Danielle exchanged a look. "Suit yourselves," said Karen. "But you'd better show up on time for pick-up for tomorrow. In your uniform, ready to work, and on the van at twelve o'clock sharp."

"And don't be hungover, Denny," Danielle warned. "I'm not coming back to coach to help out because you're both in a self-induced stupor."

"Not to worry," said Denny "We'll be fine tomorrow"—he winked at Eric—"by noon."

They arrived at the hotel thirty minutes later. The front desk clerk had their sign-in sheet and room keys ready. Denny immediately grabbed keys for the only two rooms that were adjacent to each other. He took one and gave Eric the other.

"Well, you two have become fast friends," Karen said.

"Birds if a feather," Denny said with a smile.

"If anything changes for tomorrow, I'll give you a call. Come on, Danielle, let's get going."

"Have a good time," said Denny. "I'm going to pop into the lobby store to see if they have club soda. There wasn't any left on the plane, and I'm parched."

"I bet there wasn't any vodka left either," said Karen.

"No, there wasn't," Denny said with a straight face. "We had a lot of drinkers on the last leg."

"Yeah, I could tell by the twenty dollars you turned in for liquor sales." She turned to Eric. "Don't let him get you into trouble."

"I won't," said Eric. "I'm still on probation and I'm a very responsible person."

"I can tell that you are," said Karen. "But Denny has a certain way about him. He's like a gay pied piper."

"What she's saying," said Denny, "is that I'm a bad influence. Stop clucking, Karen, and get going on your citywide tour. We'll meet you two for breakfast tomorrow, how's that?"

"Fine. Meet us in the lobby at nine. I know a great place just a few blocks from here."

"OK," said Denny, steering Eric toward the gift shop. "We'll see you then."

"Why don't we go with them?" Eric asked. "We can go out to the bars later tonight. It sounds like they have a lot of fun things planned. This is my first time in Seattle. I'd like to see as much as I can."

"What are you, an old lady? You have twenty years to trot around to parks, museums, and fish markets. Besides, we're both dead on our feet. We *need* naps, so that we can look good tonight."

"What's happening tonight?"

"It's a surprise," said Denny, as he paid for the seltzer. "Leave the details to me. Let's meet in the lobby at four o'clock. Does that give you enough time to do everything you need to do?"

"Sure."

"See you then. And no jacking off in your room, no matter how horny you get. You need to save your energy for later."

"Yes, sir!"

"Tap on the wall if you can't sleep. I'll come over with something to help you relax."

***

Once inside his room, Denny started stripping off his uniform before he'd even turned on the lights. Then he opened his suitcase, removed his layover clothing, and hung it up in the closet. He liked looking casual while out and about, but not rumpled. From his tote bag, he removed an Evian bottle filled with vodka and put it on the desk next to the bottle of seltzer. That was for later; he would consume no alcohol before five P.M. Then he took his Dopp kit into the bathroom. He shoved the hotel's perfumed toiletries aside and arranged his own non-scented products on the counter. He turned the shower on and stepped inside. He groaned with pleasure as the scalding hot water began washing away every olfactory trace of the airplane: burnt coffee, Bloody Mary mix, cheese omelets... He scrubbed every part of his body except for his armpits and his crotch. Tonight, when he walked into the bar, he wanted to smell like a *man*. Then he reached for a pumice stone and scrubbed his feet until they were smooth as a baby's behind. That part of his post-flight ritual was essential. It didn't matter how manly he was: no one liked scratchy feet in bed.

After toweling off, he called the front desk and asked for a 3:30 P.M. wake up call. Then he set his own alarm clock as a backup, turned the air conditioner down to 65 degrees, and pulled the blinds closed. The room was cool and dark—perfect. He'd sleep for ninety minutes and wake up raring to go. He slipped between the sheets, closed his eyes and prepared to drift off.

Except that he *couldn't* drift off. He was wired for sound, as always, after a long day on the airplane. The sights, the sounds and the problems of the day just wouldn't go away.

He tried everything. He took deep, controlled breaths. He imagined himself floating on a cloud. He pretended he was nestled deep in the woods, listening to bird calls and a babbling brook... and still no sleep. He *had* to sleep, or else he'd walk into oncoming traffic later without even realizing it. It had happened before, more than once. His feet started twitching under the covers. Christ, the brocade bedspread was heavy! He thrashed around and finally pulled it off the bed completely. That was better. But God dammit, he still couldn't sleep!

He knew what he needed: a pill. A one-milligram Xanax would do the trick. Even a half of one, just to take the edge off. He got up and started to reach for his tote bag. No! He had to learn how to go to sleep like a normal person. He'd gone to sleep for twenty-five years *without* pills before he started flying. Besides, he had only two left. They had to be kept in case of emergency—which could happen anytime he was on duty. He returned to bed and tried not to think about the Evian bottle on the desk, but he couldn't help it. It was right there. He started to reach for it. No, no, no! The vodka was for later, and only to be consumed in the presence of another person. To drink alone in your hotel room meant... well, when you get right down it, it means that you're sleep-deprived and nothing more, he reasoned. He did some quick math. The bottle, which he had brought to share with Eric, contained the equivalent of twelve vodka minis. If Denny had two drinks now, and they each had two drinks before they left the hotel, there would still be roughly four drinks for Denny to have later—just enough to make him sleep that night. Before he knew it, he was out of bed and reaching for a glass. He poured a modest amount of vodka and added seltzer.

Then he slipped back into bed, propped himself up against a pillow, and took a big swallow.

Relief was almost instantaneous. Every cell in his body started to relax at the same time. The hubbub of eight hours in the air receded into the background. The room was dark and quiet except for the pleasant hum of the air conditioner. It was heavenly. This is what the end of every workday should be like, he thought, as he luxuriated in the sensation of cool, clean sheets against his naked body. Right now in New York, five million sweaty people are getting on the subway, heading home to their miserable spouses and mush-mouthed teenagers. Meanwhile, here in Seattle, I'm lying naked in a hotel room with a drink in my hand and a willing twenty-something right next door. He thought of Eric's fresh, clean-shaven face and dark brown eyes... the carefully-combed hair begging to be mussed... his high, round butt that looked like two ripe melons that needed to be squeezed, slapped, and then spread wide open.

Denny could feel his dick swelling. He pulled the sheet back and admired it. It was long, uncut and rose up like a baseball bat from a thick matt of jet-black hair. He pictured Eric naked, on his knees, looking up at him in wonder as he opened his mouth. The young guys were all the same: one taste of Denny's dick and they went wild. He started lovingly stroking it, all the while thinking: no, no, no! I should save it for later. God dammit, I should be able to control at least *one* fucking thing! But fuck! Eric's right on the other side of that wall! All I'd have to do is knock and I bet he'd come bolting right through the connecting door. With his free hand, he took a big gulp of vodka and seltzer. He felt so fucking *good* now! A loud, sustained moan escaped his lips, as he thought of Eric's lips on his cock... those sweet young lips, only ten feet away.... Then he heard a tapping sound coming from the other side of the wall.

"Yeah?" Denny grunted. He got out of bed and walked over to the door. "D'you want something?"

"What're you doing in there?" he heard faintly.

"Hang on a second. I'll call you." He grabbed the phone and dialed. Eric answered on the first ring.

"Are you awake?" Eric asked.

"Yes."

"I thought so. I heard you thrashing around. I can't sleep!"

"Neither can I."

"Do you want to head out now instead of later?"

"No, it's too early. We'll be dead by six o'clock."

"Well, what do we do?"

"What do *you* want to do?"

"I don't know. I'm all wound up." Eric cleared his throat. "You promised you'd bring me something to help me relax. Does that offer still stand?"

"Absolutely. Do you have some ice?"

"Yes."

"Give me a minute and I'll be right over."

Denny smiled and mentally commanded his dick to go back down to normal size; there was no sense in overwhelming Eric all at once. He hung up the phone, and then hurriedly threw on jockey shorts, jeans, and a t-shirt. He shoved his size-twelve feet into a pair of leather flip-flops, taking a moment to admire them. His feet were beautiful: at Foot Fetish parties, men always went crazy over them. He slipped a bottle of poppers, a condom, and a vial of lube into his pocket. Then he grabbed the vodka and the seltzer and knocked on the connecting door. "Open up," he said. "Here comes the Sandman."

"*Entrez.*" Eric was wearing jeans and a white t-shirt. His hair, not surprisingly, was carefully blown dry.

"No wonder you can't sleep," said Denny. "Your hair is too tight." He reached over and began to muss it.

"Stop that," said Eric, visibly annoyed. "I can't help it. My hair practically combs itself."

"All right, we'll worry about that later. First things first. How many fingers do you want?"

"I beg your pardon?"

He held up the Evian bottle. "I mean, how big a drink do you want?"

"Is that *all* vodka?"

"Of course."

"Make mine a double, with a little seltzer added."

"I thought so." He poured out two drinks and handed one to Eric. "*Skol.*"

They sat on the bed together. "Oh, that's good," said Eric, after taking a big gulp. "That's *wonderful.* I feel better already."

"Why couldn't you sleep?"

"I don't know. I just couldn't wind down. This passenger's voice from the last flight started bouncing around in my head and it wouldn't stop. It was that older woman who asked me twenty times if she'd have a wheelchair waiting for her in Seattle. It was such a raspy, grating, voice, too: 'Excuse me, sir, are you *sure—*' "

"*Shh, shh, shh.* You need to learn to leave all that bullshit on the airplane," said Denny, feeling like a first-class hypocrite. He scooted closer to Eric. "Here. Put your head on my chest and relax."

"How can I put my head on your chest and drink at the same time?"

"I'll sit up a little bit." With his free hand, he began massaging Eric's shoulder. "Jesus, you're tight! What else is going on?"

"I don't want to talk about it. I'm supposed to be relaxing."

"Sometimes it helps to verbalize things."

"Well... it's just that I have no money."

"New hires never have any money. You're supposed to be poor."

"I don't think you understand: I have NO MONEY. I went back downstairs right after we checked in to see if I could cash a check. The desk clerk snidely informed me that the hotel will no longer cash personal checks for crewmembers."

"Flight attendants bounce a lot of checks trying to play 'beat the bank' before payday. But what else are you guys supposed to do? Your salary is shit for the first few years."

"So I came back upstairs and scraped all the spare change from the bottom of my tote bag. It looks like I can go out for a hamburger at MacDonald's. A *single* hamburger—no soda, no fires, not even any cheese on it."

Don't worry about money. Tonight is my treat. For right now, I am *ordering* you to drink up and relax. We're gonna have fun later, I guarantee it."

"You're the boss." Eric gulped the rest of his drink and held out his glass. "I feel better already. Make me another."

"You bet." Denny slipped out of bed, freshened both their drinks, and slipped back onto the bed, gently putting Eric's head's back on his chest.

"Oh, Christ this is nice." Eric nestled closer. "What're we doing tonight, by the way?"

"We're going to Bare Chest Night at the Squeeze Inn."

"What's the Squeeze Inn?"

"It's a leather-and-jeans bar up in the gayborhood. Usually, there's not too much going on there during the week. But on Bare Chest night, it's packed—cheap drinks, good music, and hundreds of hot, shirtless men."

"Sounds great."

"By the way, do have another shirt to wear?"

"Why?" Eric sat up. "What does it matter if it's Bare Chest night?"

"It matters. I know it sounds dumb, but they do care about what you're wearing when you walk in. Bars like the Squeeze Inn all try to maintain a certain atmosphere."

"Oh, Christ, another gay establishment with petty rules and regulations. How does anybody ever get laid these days?"

"Come on, just play the game. It'll be worth it. I think I have a Mineshaft t-shirt that you can borrow."

"OK."

"Good." Denny finished his second drink and ignored the instant desire that he felt for a third one. God dammit, why was it always like that? Once he begin to feed a craving—whether it was for alcohol or pills or sex—he never felt satisfied until he was past the point of no return. He turned his attention back to Eric, who, for the moment, seemed relaxed at last. "Feeling better, baby?"

"Oh, yeah." His eyelids were beginning to droop. "I'm a little drowsy now. Maybe we could have that nap now."

"Yeah, let's cuddle up. I'll set an alarm, just as a backup."

"Good idea."

"Hey, let's get out these jeans first. We'll both be more comfortable."

"Sure… comfortable… that's a good thing." They both unzipped their jeans and tossed them onto the floor. A moment later, they were curled up together. Eric once more had his head on Denny's chest. "I bet you've got a great chest, Denny," he said dreamily. "Are you really hairy?"

"Oh, yeah, I'm, like 'Seventies gay porn star' hairy."

"Lemme see."

Denny ripped his t-shirt right off, leaving him only in a pair of boxer shorts.

"Oh, damn, you weren't kidding," said Eric.

As Eric made lazy circles with his hand in Denny's chest hair, Denny grinned to himself. Without very much effort, he had Eric right where he wanted him. "D'you wanna see more?"

"Sure."

"Let's *both* take our shirts off."

"Fuck, let's take everything off," said Eric, slipping his t-shirt over his head.

"Not yet," Denny growled, as his hard dick strained against the fabric of his underwear.

"Why not?" Eric panted, with his hand on the waist band.

"Because I said so." A second later, he had Eric flat on his back and his arms pinned down. He looked into Eric's eyes, which were now wide open.

"Oh," Eric murmured. "Oh, Denny, *please* let's get naked."

"Shh, shh, shh." Denny leaned forward and kissed him. Eric's lips were soft. He immediately opened his mouth for Denny's wide, warm tongue. Denny slightly released his vice-like grip on Eric's arms.

Eric immediately wrapped his arms and his legs around Denny. "Denny, Denny, why are you making me wait?" he panted. "Let's get NAKED, right now!"

"Nope," Denny replied, as he squeezed Eric's nipples. "This is just a preview. I want us to keep the energy up for later tonight."

"Fuck, I'm twenty-three! I can go three or four rounds in one day!"

Eric was so ready to give himself up that Denny could barely control himself. But Denny had to. He wasn't twenty-four. If he shot his wad now and then had more to drink, he'd be a drunken, sloppy mess by sundown. If I don't start being more careful, he thought, I'll end up just like Arnie. The fear of that happening raced through his brain, even as Eric reached into his underwear and grabbed his huge throbbing cock. "Oh, my God, Denny!"

"We're waiting, we're waiting!" Denny panted. He bent down again, his face only an inch away from Eric's. "I want you to want my dick. I want you to spend all day today craving it. I want to walk into that bar thinking about nothing *but* my dick. I want that beautiful ass of yours. I'm fucking torturing myself not taking it right now. But when I do, I want it to be wide open. Fuck, I want it to be throbbing."

"Jesus Christ," Eric moaned. "It already *is* throbbing. Open the drawer right there. I have lube and condoms and everything else. But before we go any further, I need you to know that I only play safe."

"Yeah, of course you do. Me, too." He pulled the drawer open. "The important thing is that we're *fucking*." He suddenly remembered the bottle of poppers in the pocket of his jeans. "You like poppers, baby?"

"Oh, hell yeah!"

"Good." He jumped off the bed and grabbed the bottle. "Because you're gonna need 'em!"

***

"Feel good?"

"Oh, yes," Eric murmured. "That was great."

Denny started to get up. "Let me get you a washcloth."

"Thanks."

After they cleaned up, Denny took Eric in his arms and pulled up the sheets. "Wanna sleep? Can you sleep now?"

"For a hundred years."

"D'you want me to stay?" asked Denny, as he nuzzled Eric's ear.

Eric nodded.

"OK. Let's make sure that we're not disturbed." He reached over and unplugged the phone. Then he finally began to fade away, thanks to the perfect combination of fatigue, alcohol, and sex. He closed his eyes, and for the first time in more than thirty-six hours, he slept.

CHAPTER 16

Sleeping in Seattle

"Eric, wake up."

"What time is it?"

"It's five o'clock."

"In the morning?"

"No, in the afternoon." Denny struggled to open his own eyes. "Come on, we've got to get up."

"No. Sleep." Eric pulled the covers over his head. "Need to sleep."

"But we have the whole evening ahead of us."

"Go on without me."

"Like hell I will." He pulled the covers back down. "Get up. You'll feel worse if you sleep all day."

"Denny, please, go if you want and have a great time, but I'm telling you that I can't move!"

There was an inch of slushy water in the bottom of the ice bucket. Denny picked it up and poured it over Eric's head.

"Fuck you, you *asshole*!"

"You say that now, but you'll thank me later. Now, shake those bones It's time to rise and shine!"

***

God dammit, it's bright out here!" Eric said, squinting, as they left the hotel. "Which way are we going?"

"Right up that hill," said Denny. "That's the way to the gayborhood."

"Are we walking or riding?"

"Whichever you like. Just FYI, it's practically straight uphill and there's not much to see on the way."

"That's OK," said Eric. "We'll go on foot. I need to clear my head."

They started walking. After a few minutes, Denny noticed that Eric was zigzagging. "Hey, you look a little wobbly."

"I am a little wobbly. I'm not used to drinking in the afternoon."

Denny cupped his ass. "How about fucking in the afternoon?"

"I'm sorry to say, Denny, but you're not the first."

"Yeah, I could tell."

"Don't be a pig. Hey, which way is the Space Needle?"

Deny pointed behind them. "In the other direction. We can have a look after breakfast tomorrow if there's time before we leave."

"That'd be great," said Eric, taking another glance back at downtown. "I'd like to say that I saw at least one thing that was unique to Seattle on my first—"

"Hey!" Denny grabbed him as a car horn blared. "Watch it!"

"What's the matter?"

"You almost walked right in front of that SUV. It was his light."

"In New York, pedestrians have the right of way at all times," Eric said huffily.

"Oh, brother. Let's get you off the street. Look, there's a bus coming right now, and I have exact change." He pushed Eric through the door and paid their fares. "Have a seat." Ten minutes later, he said, "This is us," and pulled Eric to his feet as the bus came to a stop. "Welcome to Capitol Hill!"

"A new adventure," said Eric, smiling, as they hopped off.

"Stick with me, dumplin', and I'll show you the world. Now, first things first. We could both use a jolt of joe."

"A what?"

"Coffee. A cup of strong coffee."

"Are we going to Starbucks?"

"No. As long as you're with me, you will never set foot in any chain establishment, not even a local one. We're going a funky little coffee house where they make a great cappuccino. Then we'll get something to eat. And then we'll pick up the party where we left off."

"Sounds like a plan."

***

"How was that cappuccino, Eric?"

"Good. I feel more alert now. I was really out of it."

He wiped a bit of foam from Eric's upper lip. "That was the afterglow of being with me."

"That was fun," said Eric, smiling. "I hope we get to do it again."

"We will. So, how do you like this place?"

"I like it." Eric leaned back in his chair and surveyed the room. "I like the atmosphere, and the men here."

"Yeah, there's a lot of hotties in this town."

"It's not just that. They're more casual than the gay men in New York. Everyone seems more relaxed. And I like all the facial hair and flannel shirts."

"Refreshing, isn't it? Nobody's hulking around in a t-shirt that's two sizes too small, pointing his big steroid tits in your face. Jesus, those queens in Chelsea! I avoid that fucking neighborhood altogether."

"Where do you live, Denny?"

"In the East Village."

"I haven't been there yet. What's it like?"

"Like this, in a lot of ways."

"Is there a gay scene in the East Village?"

"Oh, yeah. There's a lot of underground stuff, too. The new mayor and his goons haven't discovered the East Village yet, and tried to shut down every sex-related business like he's doing in Times Square—thank God. There're still a few good backroom bars in my neighborhood. So, is your head clear now?"

"Yes, I'm much better."

"Then let's get going. There's a great burger place just a few blocks from here. And then it's time for a drink."

Back out on the street, Eric continued to observe the locals. "Does everyone here wear a flannel shirt over a t-shirt and jeans?"

"It's the grunge look. It started here in the northwest. I like it to a point, because you never have to iron anything here. The men in suits are all back downtown but believe me that's strictly a nine-to-five business scene." He stopped in front of a bar with a faded eagle on the door. "Hey, do you want to stop in here for a minute?"

"What for?"

"For a drink."

"What about food? I haven't eaten since breakfast."

"Come on, ten minutes—just for a quick drink and to say hello to the bartender. He's a friend of mine. I bet you he'll comp a round for us."

"All right, one drink. But then we have to get something to eat."

"I promise," said Denny, pushing the door open. "Just one."

The interior was dark and gloomy. The walls were covered with the requisite sexy posters advertising leather events around the world. Men with huge crotch bulges, stubble-covered jaws, and smoldering eyes stared down at them from the illustrations. Unobtrusive house music thumped from speakers mounted in the corners. Denny and Eric were the only patrons in the bar.

"This place is dead," said Eric. "Let's go. Maybe we'll come back later."

"Eddie already saw us," said Denny, waving to the bartender. "We'll stay *ten* minutes. It's only six o'clock."

"Hey, Denny," the bartender said. He was in his early forties, with a slight paunch, a bald head, and piercings in both eyebrows.

"Hi, Eddie. This is my friend, Eric."

Eric and Eddie shook hands. "Is that really your Mineshaft t-shirt?" Eddie asked.

"Why wouldn't it be?" Eric replied.

"Truth be told, you don't look like a typical Mineshaft man."

"Well, I…" Eric seemed to be at a loss for words.

"Come here, Eric," said Denny. "Take off your shirt."

"What the hell—" Eric sputtered, as Denny pulled it up over his head.

"Look at that Eddie," said Denny. "Remember when you used to look that good?"

"Nice," said Eddie. He reached across the bar and squeezed Eric's nipples.

"What the *fuck?*" said Eric. He grabbed the t-shirt from Denny and put it back on. "I'm out of here. Denny, tell me where that burger place is and you can meet me there."

"Don't worry, I'll come with you. Eddie, you have the manners of a pig."

"Aw, don't leave, guys," said Eddie. "Except for the panhandlers, you're the first people who've walked through that door all day. Come on, stay. I'll buy you a drink."

Denny looked at Eric. "Well?"

"All right, we'll stay," said Eric. "For one drink."

"But only if you have one with us, Eddie," Denny said.

"I can't drink on duty. That's against the house rules, and you know it."

"Who's gonna know?" said Denny. "We're the only ones here. C'mon. Join us."

"OK, but keep it quiet. What'll you boys have?"

"Two shots of Jägermeister," said Denny.

"What's that?" asked Eric.

"It's an aperitif," said Denny. "It'll help stimulate your appetite."

"Aperitif, my ass," said Eddie. "I'm happy to pour whatever you want, but isn't it a little early for the hard stuff?"

"It's all right," said Denny. "We just drank way too much coffee, and one of us could use a little loosening up."

***

"Don't you love this?" said Denny, as they relaxed together on the patio. "Having a nice drink, after having great sex, at the end of a workday. I fucking love it. And look: a few interesting men are starting to come in."

"It's deriscious ... I mean, *delicious.* But my face is starting to go numb."

"That's because you drink too fast. Remember, you *sip* Jägermeister, you don't knock it back like tequila. Speaking of which, don't ever drink tequila within ten feet of me. I got so drunk on Cuervo once on a layover in Mexico City that I threw up for twelve hours straight. Just the smell of it makes me want to retch."

"I'll remember that," said Eric, take a tiny sip of his second shot. "Hey, speaking of layovers, could you do me a favor?"

"Sure what?"

He reached into his knapsack and pulled out a bid sheet. "Could you show me how this thing works? Crew scheduling made up a schedule for me my first month and I'm reserve this month. Next month is my line month, and the first time that I'm bidding on my own. I want to make sure I get a good schedule."

Denny stubbed out his cigarette. "The first rule of bidding is: never pull a bid sheet out in a bar. It's anti-social. You may as well sit down, pull a pencil from behind your ear, and start doing a crossword puzzle."

"Two minutes, that all I'm asking."

"All right." He patiently went through the bidding process, step by step, and taught him everything he needed to know about choosing the best trips, best layovers, and the best days off. "After you've finished prioritizing your choices, you enter your bids on the computer, chew your nails for a few days, and then *voilà*—bids are out, and you have your schedule for the next month. Have got all that?"

"Yes, that makes perfect sense. Thank you."

"Good." Denny folded up the bid sheet and tucked it back in Eric's knapsack. "Now, forget everything I just taught you. You're new, and it doesn't matter where you want. You'll pretty much get whatever is left over, meaning the shitty trips that no one else wants to fly. Say hello to Chicago and Toronto turnarounds. You'll hold a decent line eventually, as senior people transfer out and more new hires transfer in. It'll take a year, at least." He lit another cigarette. "In the meantime, you'll have to pay your dues."

"I'm OK with that. At the very least, I'll be up in the air."

"Come again?" said Denny. He was distracted by a bearded man with a shaved head and a muscular, hairy chest, who bore a striking resemblance to one of the models on a poster inside. He wore a flannel shirt with the sleeves ripped out, snug 501 jeans, and police boots. He had a large nose, which made for a great profile. *Oh, Daddy!*

"I meant: I'll be flying for a living," said Eric. "That's all I ever wanted to do, ever since I was a kid. I love to fly. I'd rather be on an airplane than anywhere else in the world."

"I know," said Denny, trying to redirect his attention from the new arrival, who was lighting a cigar. "I could tell watching you earlier today."

"It's funny," Eric said. "Nobody ever asks pilots why they want to fly. It's a given that they're obsessed with it. But with flight attendants, it's always supposed to be a diversion—something we play around with for a few years after college until we decide what we really want to do with our lives. But not me. I plan on being here for a very long time."

"Let me see your hands," said Denny, grabbing them.

"Do you read palms?"

"Yes. It's a skill that I picked up from my grandmother. Are you left- or right-handed?"

"Left-handed."

He examined Eric's hands intently. "Yep, you're here for life." He traced a line across Eric's left palm. "It says so right here." He looked into Eric's sweet, determined young face. "So you're living out your dream. That's great."

"Yes, it is," Eric said proudly. "And it's not just that I got the job of my dreams, Denny: I escaped, too."

"From where? Prison?"

"No, Texas."

"Same thing."

"I couldn't wait to get Out of there. I hated it. I hated *all* of it: that shit-kicking, gun-toting, redneck mentality…"

"That terrible, twangy country-western music playing everywhere," Denny added. "Where I grew up in Oklahoma, was the same thing. Eighth-grade boys in big, stupid cowboy hats who dip chewing tobacco on the school bus, and then spit it into a puddle on the floor for everyone have to walk through. Fuckin' pigs! And women with hairdos ten feet high, who can't cut their hair even if they want to because Jesus wouldn't like it. You remember their motto? 'The higher the hair, the closer to God.'"

"Oh, the *Evangelicals*," Eric hissed. "Don't even get me started. The Southern Baptists and the Pentecostals and all those other *fucking* fundamentalists who try to impose their God-fearing, undereducated worldview on everyone. Not to mention the parents who throw their gay kids out on the street or lock them up in a psych ward—or worse." His face was turning purple. "Homophobia *kills*, you know—figuratively and literally."

"Thank you, Harvey Milk, but you're preaching to the lavender choir. Been that, seen that, and now I do whatever I can to help fight back in my own way." Denny drained his shot glass. "And by the way, there's no need to kill the nice buzz that I have going on."

"What? Oh! Sorry, I didn't mean to get so worked up. I can't help it sometimes."

"Hey, Eric, you weren't talking about your own family just now, were you? I can't imagine you being raised in that kind of home."

"Oh, no! My family is great. I was raised Catholic and both my parents are lifelong Democrats. But sometimes it seemed like there were six of us and five million of *them*. Anyway, the important thing is that I got out."

"Congratulations," said Denny. "We both did. Now let's celebrate with another shot. I'll get it for us. By the way, don't ever repeat this, because it would ruin my reputation, but I feel exactly the same way about flying that you do."

"I had a feeling." Eric smiled. "Birds of a feather."

***

Walking through the door of the Squeeze Inn that night was liking entering a different world. The bar was packed with sexy, bare-chested men. Some were engaged in quiet one-on-one conversations; others were dancing in groups to the music blaring from the speakers. Everywhere Denny looked, fingers and hands were moving—stroking pumped up shoulders, tugging on erect nipples, traveling down furry-covered torsos. The sexual energy was palpable and intoxicating. "Oh, this is a great crowd," said Denny "Hey, check it out: that Daddy from the patio at the Eagle is here too. And he's looking right at us. Oh, what fucking *luck* to get this layover today! I may forget to bid more often."

"What do we do with our t-shirts?" asked Eric.

"We can tuck them in the waistband of our jeans, like this." After they'd taken their shirts off, Denny grabbed Eric's face in his hands and kissed him on the lips. It was a long, sloppy kiss.

"What's that for?" asked Eric.

"To let people know that we're open to playing together."

"Well, swing the man by me for a look-see before you make any major decisions. And Denny, FYI, I don't play with cigar smokers." Shirtless, they walked up to the bar and ordered two drinks.

"God, what a great crowd," Denny repeated, looking around. "Oh, fuck, no. Not tonight."

"What's the matter?"

"See those two good-looking guys with big hair, chatting underneath the neon Budweiser sign? One has a mustache."

"Yeah. What about them?"

"Their names are Jefferson and Theo. They're Atlanta-based stews and all they ever want to do is talk shop. I am *not* here to talk shop. Let me know if they start heading this way and I'll make a quick exit to the patio."

"What am *I* supposed to do?"

"You can stay here with them and debate the merits of Aqua Net versus White Rain, or join me on the patio. If you come out though, be forewarned: the lights are turned off at ten o'clock and it can get pretty wild."

"Thanks, but I do have some experience groping my way around in the dark. Hey, Jefferson and Theo are coming this way."

Denny pulled out a twenty-dollar bill. "Here, buy yourself a couple more drinks. If I'm not back in fifteen minutes, come and look for me. You're cool if we end up with other people tonight, right?"

"You're quite the fair-weather fuck buddy, aren't you?"

"Well, I hate to waste a good opportunity, and you said you don't like cigar smokers."

"Go," said Eric, with only the slightest hint of irritation. "I can handle myself. I'm from Texas and I'm well-versed in all major brands of hairspray."

***

Denny found the bearded man in a quiet corner of the patio, puffing on a cigar. He walked right up to him, put out his hand and introduced himself. "How's it going, man? My name's Denny."

"I'm Hank. Good to meet you Denny." Hank had a rich, deep voice.

"What brand of cigar do you smoke?"

"*Hoyos*, from Cuba."

"Aren't those illegal in the U.S.?"

"Yeah." Hank chuckled. "But I'm not the one carrying them into the country."

How do you get them?"

"A buddy of mine flies for Air Canada. He brings them in through Vancouver, and then gives 'em to me when he's in Seattle."

"That's a little risky."

"I make it worth his while," Hank said, puffing. He shifted from one foot to the other. As he did, the bulge in his jeans moved right along with him.

"I work for an airline, too," said Denny.

"Pilot?"

"No, flight attendant."

"Where're you based?"

"New York."

"I figured as much."

Denny wasn't sure what Hank meant, but he decided to take the remark as a compliment. "Do you live here in Seattle?"

"Just a few miles north, which is almost out in the country here."

"Not into city living?"

"No, it's not that. I need a lot of space for my work."

"What do you do?"

I'm a furniture designer and builder. All custom-made stuff."

Hot damn, thought Denny, a man who used tools to make his living. Can't get any sexier than that.

"Cool." Denny kept his eyes on Hank's face. "You must have all kinds of beautiful wood to work with here."

"Oh, yeah," said Hank, casually stroking himself.

Denny had to look down this time. "What's your favorite? Wood, I mean."

"Are you really interested?"

"Yes. I have a good friend in New York who's a furniture dealer. I have a real interest in original pieces."

"Maybe I'll bring you to see my space sometime." His 'maybe' hung heavily in the air.

"That'd be cool," Denny replied nonchalantly. The trick to scoring with a man like Hank was never to seem too eager. "I get out here to Seattle once in a while."

"That's good," said Hank, moving a little closer to him. "I like visitors. No complications."

"And I like visiting." Denny reached up and touched Hank's beard. "Great beard. Nice and thick."

"You look like you'd have a good thick one, too." Hank traced a finger along Denny's stubble-covered cheek and jaw. "Why don't you?"

"I have to be clean-shaven for work. It's a real drag."

"Only if you were dragging that jaw across my balls. You'd scratch the shit out of 'em."

"We wouldn't want that," said Denny, then he added, "I bet you have a nice big pair of low hangers."

"Oh, yeah." Hank grinned. He leaned over and kissed Denny on the mouth. Denny groaned. "Oh, Christ, that tastes good."

He rubbed his jaw against Denny's. "You don't mind the cigar smoke in my beard?"

"No, I love it."

"Want some?" He offered the lit cigar.

"Yeah. *Fuck,* yeah." Denny puffed expertly. "That tastes good. I haven't done that in a long time."

They stood quietly for a moment, sharing the cigar and the silence. Several other men had come outside and were eyeing Denny and Hank. Forget it, guys, Denny thought smugly. Tonight, this man is all mine.

"You smoke weed?" asked Hank.

"Nah, I can't. I get drug trusted at work."

"What if I told you I had something at home that guaranteed you wouldn't fail a drug test?"

"I'd say let me think about it."

"OK. It's not a deal breaker. There's other things we can do if you want to come over."

Denny was buzzing from head to toe. He couldn't remember the last time he'd felt so good. "Of course I want to fucking come over!" he blurted. "Why else would I have followed you out here?" Well, there was no sense in playing hard to get now. Hank had him, and he knew it.

Hank grinned again and extinguished the cigar.

Denny stared at Hank's hands. They were large and hairy. His fingertips were calloused and stained with wood finish. Man hands, thought Denny, like none that I've never seen.

Without warning, Hank grabbed Denny roughly by both nipples and steered him deeper in the corner, out of view of the other patrons. Then he unzipped his jeans. In the perfect stillness, the sound was like a grenade going off. Every head on the patio turned in their direction. Hank pulled a massive penis out of his jeans. "Think you can handle that?"

"Yeah," said Denny. "I can handle that."

"You suck?"

"Absolutely."

"Swallow?"

"Maybe. What's your status?"

"Don't be a downer. You fuck?"

"Oh, yeah."

"Top or bottom?"

"Semi-versatile. I usually only top, but for you I'll break my own rule."

"Sure you will. 'Semi-versatile' guys all say that." He stuffed his dick back in his jeans and zipped up. "You ready to go?"

"You'll drive me back to my hotel, right? And not too late. I need to be up by eight tomorrow morning."

"Don't stress about the time, man. And don't worry about anything else. If I get too fucked up, I'll put you in a cab. My treat."

"OK then. Let's go."

"What about your friend?"

"Who?"

"That kid that came in with you. Isn't he joining us?"

Shit! Denny had forgotten all about Eric. *What kind of fucking friend am I?* he thought, but then pushed the guilty feelings out of his mind. Eric would be fine. He couldn't get enough discussion of the airline business; he was probably plying Jefferson and Theo with questions about the Atlanta base. "No, I don't think so. He doesn't like cigars."

"Too bad. I was hoping to work *both* of you over tonight."

"Well… I can ask him. But heads up: I think he's pretty vanilla."

"That's what so tempting. I want to throw his hot little ass into the mix and see what happens. *Ask* him." It was more of a command than a request.

"All right. I'll introduce you." As Denny expected, he found Eric at the bar talking to Jefferson and Theo. The trio had evidently moved past shop talk. They were conversing in hushed tone, and Jefferson was playing with Eric's nipples.

"Hey, Jefferson, hey Theo. Nice to see you guys. Eric, sorry I was gone so long."

"Don't worry about it," said Eric. "I've been having a very nice time with my new friends."

"I can see. Eric, this is Hank."

"Hi, Hank."

"Listen," said Denny. "Hank has invited us back over to his place. He's got his car right outside. How about it?"

"He's invited *us* over? Why?"

"For a drink and… whatever."

"Just like that?"

"What do you mean, 'just like that'?"

"Thanks for the offer," said Eric. "But Theo just bought us a round of drinks."

"Well, uh, we could wait for you to finish."

"I don't think so," said Eric. "Maybe some other time. Nice meeting you, Hank."

"You don't know what you're missing, kid," said Hank.

"The two of you might find this hard to believe," Eric said frostily, "but I'm not interested. Denny, I'll see you tomorrow. Goodnight."

Oh fuck, thought Denny. Now I've done it. "Hang on a second, Hank." He tapped Eric on the shoulder. "Could I speak to you for a minute?"

"Sure. I'll be right back, guys."

Denny led him to a pair of vacant stools at the end of the bar. "What's the matter?"

"Nothing, why?"

"Because you're acting all haughty—like Celeste Holm in the ladies' room scene in *All About Eve*."

"I don't know what you mean."

"Christ, stop being so indignant and just tell me why you're pissed off."

"All right. I'm pissed off because we're supposed to hanging out together. I know this isn't a date, but we *are* out together. You spent the whole afternoon talking about what a great time we'd have tonight. Then as soon as we got here, you ditched me for that big-dicked arrogant asshole, making it clear that getting into his pants was your top priority. You left me on my own for forty-five minutes. Then when the two of you are all revved up and ready to go, you interrupt my conversation to invite me to a three-way. *Then* to add insult to injury, you offer to wait for me to finish my drink, so that I can hop in a car with you and a stranger and drive off to God-knows-where to do God-knows what, as though we were twenty-dollar hookers working a waterfront saloon. *That's* why I'm pissed. So fuck off, Denny. You're not the kind of friend I'd thought you'd be. You're an asshole."

"You're right. I am an asshole." He eyed Hank, who was gesturing impatiently. "And a lousy friend, too. I'll tell Hank that I've changed my mind. You and I can go and get a slice of pie or something."

"Don't *even*, Denny! Just go!"

"All right, I will." He signaled Hank. "But in all fairness to me, I did ask you if you minded. You said no. If you *did* mind, you should have said so."

"Well—"

"And there's one more thing you should consider. I know that you're new, Eric. But when male crewmembers go out together, we move more independently of each other than females do. We don't perch together, for hours on end, like crows on a power line."

"You can rationalize your behavior any way you want, but... fair enough."

"Still friends?"

"I haven't decided yet."

Deny stifled a sigh. "Why don't we meet for breakfast and talk about it then?"

"I may go sightseeing. I'll leave you a voicemail on your phone when I get back tonight. Now if you'll excuse me, I'm going to rejoin Theo and Jefferson." He weaved a little as he stood up and grabbed his drink.

"How many of those have you had?"

"Don't worry. I'm sharing a cab back to the hotel with the boys. They're staying at the Sheraton, too."

"All right. See you tomorrow."

***

"Where to?" a cab driver asked Denny, several hours later.

"Sheraton downtown."

"Whoa! That'll cost you."

"I know." Hank had given him $50 to pay for the ride. "It's more than just a couple of miles, isn't it?"

"Yeah."

The driver turned on his meter. "Hey, man, do you mind rolling down that back window?"

"Iz zere a problem?" Shit, stop slurring. "Is there a problem?"

"Yeah. You reek."

"Of what?"

"What do you think? *Weed*. The smell makes me nauseous."

"I didn't think anyone in Seattle minded that smell."

"I'm in recovery, dude."

"Sorry." Denny rolled down the window. The fresh air felt great. Gotta clear my head, he thought. It's one A.M. now. Not *too* late. If I'm in bed and asleep by two A.M., I'll still be in good shape to meet Eric and the girls for breakfast. Nobody will know a thing. I've just got to remember to take that stuff that Hank gave me before I go to bed, and then again when I get up in the morning. Christ, I hope it really will hide the pot in my system, just in case I get popped for a drug test tomorrow.

He started to feel anxious, despite the tremendous buzz. He was still stoned, but the fear lying just beneath that buzz reared its ugly head, as it always did. Not only had he smoked pot: he'd also let Hank fuck him without a condom. It had seemed so exciting at the time, so goddam *dangerous*, but now that it was over, he was chastising himself. Why the fuck do I have to keep crossing that line? Well, there's no going back now. I can't get un-fucked. But at least I can erase the pot-smoking, according to Hank. That's one less thing to worry about.

He opened his knapsack and fingered the box reassuringly. Hank had guaranteed him that it would throw a positive drug test result, without a trace of monkeying around. Denny hoped so. Getting busted for drinking on the job was one thing: a thirty-day stint in rehab and he'd be back to work. People did it all the time. The gay rehab center in Minneapolis had a revolving door just for flight attendants.

But getting busted for drugs was a different story. He'd be fired with no recourse. The termination would go on his Department of Transportation record, and no other airline would hire him. Shit, shit, shit! As he tried to quell the panic, he realized that he was also ravenously hungry. The munchies were setting in. There was nothing in his hotel room but flat seltzer water and four fingers of vodka. Wait, fuck, he didn't even have that! He had left it in Eric's room. Well, he'd have to go without it. He couldn't very well barge into Eric's room and say, "I'm back from whoring around. Can I please have what's left of my vodka now?" He should have something to eat, though. It was hours since he'd last eaten anything. "Hey," he said to the driver. "Is there any place around the hotel to get something to eat?"

"At one A.M.? Let me think… maybe 7-11."

"That'll do. Can we make a pit stop?"

"Sure. It's your money, man."

Denny licked his lips in anticipation. Some chips, a sandwich, and one of those mini fried apple pies with hard sugar coating would satiate him. Christ, he thought, as the driver pulled up in front of the store. Talk about old habits dying hard. I'm walking into in a 7-11 at one A.M. with a raging case of the munchies. I may as well be back in high school. How pathetic is that?

***

He'd eaten almost an entire large bag of Doritos before entering the hotel lobby and finished it while riding up in the elevator. His stomach was rumbling all of a sudden. He felt an urgent need to go to the bathroom. As the elevator door opened on his floor, he began racing down the hall. He fumbled with the room key, tossed the 7-11 bag on the bed, and flew into the bathroom. Whew! He made it just in time. When he emerged from the bathroom, he noticed the red message light blinking on his phone. Eric had already left a voice mail.

Somebody wants to make peace, he thought with a smile. But it was too late to call. He'd deal with Eric in the morning. First things first: he'd take the supplement to clean out his system, and then get into bed and go right to sleep. He sure wouldn't need a pill tonight! After all that booze and pot, he was lucky to still be standing. He looked at the clock. It was almost two A.M. Six hours of sleep would be plenty. He'd wake up refreshed in the morning and ready for a good breakfast. He reached for his knapsack.

Fuck. The knapsack wasn't on the bed. There was just the paper bag from 7-11, containing an empty Doritos sack, a half-eaten ham and cheese sandwich, and an apple pie. Maybe in the bathroom? Fuck, no, it wasn't there either. He ran into the hallway. Maybe he'd dropped it running from the elevator to his room. No luck. Where the hell could it—oh, no! He must have left in in the cab! He'd have to call and see if the driver would bring it back to him. But which cab company had he used? He couldn't even remember the color of the cab, much less the name of the company. He rummaged through his pocket for a receipt, and then remembered that he hadn't asked for one. Why would he? Hank had paid for the ride.

Fuck me running! he thought. But there was nothing he could do about it. Of course, he was too stressed now to go to sleep. He'd have to take a pill to calm himself down. He rummaged in his tote bag, found a one-milligram Xanax and swallowed it. Thank God it worked so quickly. A few minutes later it came: that wonderful floating feeling! This is the last time I take chances just for the sake of some good sex, he thought, as he felt the pill take effect. He stopped worrying about the drug test. Tomorrow, I'm turning over a new leaf. No booze, no cigarettes, no pills, and no fucking around. It'll be a brand-new me. As he drifted off, he realized that he'd left his favorite poppers (the $30 bottle from the leather store in San Francisco) in his knapsack. Damn! Well, never mind, I'll get a new bottle in San Francisco next week…

***

Christ, that noise was loud! He swatted the alarm clock next to his bed, but it wouldn't turn off. No wonder: it wasn't the alarm, it was the telephone. He opened his eyes. The room was pitch black. There wasn't even a crack of light coming in between the drapes. Who the fuck could be calling so early? "Hello?"

"Denny, it's Karen. What are you still doing in your room?"

"What do you mean?"

"We're downstairs in the van waiting for you and Eric."

"What for?"

"What for?! For pick up! Come on, we're going to be late for sign-in."

"But…" His tongue felt so goddam thick. "We're not supposed to leave until noon."

"Noon?! Pick up is right now!" she said impatiently. "We've been reassigned to work the seven A.M. flight to Chicago!"

"What the fuck?"

"Goddammit, I called you *both* last night, and left you *multiple* voicemail messages when I couldn't reach you."

"I saw the red light, but I thought it was—" He jumped out of bed and fell right on the floor with the phone still in his hand. "Oh my fucking God. We'll be downstairs in fifteen minutes. Tell the driver to wait."

"No dice, Denny. There's another crew in the van. They're going to be late, too. We're leaving."

"But you have to wait!"

"Listen to me! Get Eric up, get him dressed, and get yourselves a taxi to the airport. And you'd better be there by departure time. If this flight gets delayed, or God forbid *canceled,* that kid will be out on his ass. And it'll be all *your* fault, Denny." *Click.*

Denny raced to the connecting door and frantically pounded on it. "Eric, get up, get up! It's an emergency!"

"What?" Eric pulled the door open. He was dazed and stark naked. "What's the matter? Is there a fire?!"

"Worse! We're late! We have to leave right now! We've been reassigned to work the seven A.M. flight to Chicago."

"They can't do that!" he said stupidly.

"They can and they *did.*" He flipped on the light switch. Eric's room looked like a disaster area. "Put on your uniform and throw everything else into a suitcase. Don't shave, don't comb your hair, don't even brush your teeth! There's no time." He glared at Jefferson and Theo, who were lying in a stupor in Eric's bed. "Don't just lay there, you idiots! HELP HIM PACK! We're going to miss our flight!"

***

"How much further is it?" Denny asked the taxi driver.

"About ten minutes. You guys are lucky there's no traffic at this hour."

"Can't you go any faster? We're in a *big* hurry."

"If he drives any faster," said Eric, "I'm going to hurl all over the seat." He grabbed the strap handle as the driver made a sharp turn. "This is insanity. Why didn't you check your messages if that goddam light was blinking when you got back?"

"Why didn't you check *yours?*"

"I didn't have one!" snapped Eric. "You unplugged my phone yesterday right after we had sex, remember?"

"Jesus, your breath!" Denny turned away. "Did something die in there?"

"You told me not to waste time brushing my teeth."

"I know, but don't you have a mint or something in your pocket? It's making me nauseous."

"Here!" The driver tossed a pack of Dentyne over the seat. "Take that."

"Thanks." He handed a piece of gum to Eric. "How much did you have to drink last night?"

"A lot. Jefferson and Theo came to my room with a bottle of Jack Daniels. Jesus! Those southern boys can put it away."

"Yeah, I bet I can guess right where they put it, too."

"Please! Spare me the innuendo and help me tie my tie."

As Denny reached over, he noticed the driver eyeing them suspiciously in the rear-view mirror. "Something the matter, mister?"

"You guys aren't pilots, are you?"

"No."

"But you are crewmembers, right?"

"Don't worry, we're deadheading, not working the flight." He was proud of his ability to lie so smoothly. "We just overslept."

"Good to know," said the driver. He shook his head. "I wouldn't want to be a passenger on *any* flight that you guys are working today."

***

"Now listen to me," said Denny, as they entered the crowded terminal. "We've got to haul ass. Let's go right to the front of the security line. I don't care who we have to push aside. Don't look anyone in the eye, don't say excuse me, don't even open your mouth. Just flash your ID, throw your bags on the belt and run through. Well, what are you waiting for? Move it!"

"Hang on! I'm just checking the board to see what our gate number is. Oh, look, we're delayed by thirty minutes! Thank God."

"Yeah, it's delayed because *we're not there!* And when we get to the gate, remember, same drill: head down, flash ID, get on the plane and go straight to the coach galley. Because it anyone gets a good look at either one of us, we're dead."

"This is a big deal, isn't it?"

"That's just now dawning on you, Einstein? Yeah, it's a big deal! You're lucky I'm with you. If you were by yourself, and late enough for sign-in that a flight got delayed, you'd be fired the minute they opened the door in Chicago. As it is, we'll both get written up, and having one more bad letter in my file is the last thing I need. So whatever happens, keep quiet and let me do the talking. That's the one thing I'm good at."

"God, get me through this," Eric muttered, looking upward. "Get me through this and I swear I'll never drink again on a layover again as long as I live."

"Forget it," said Denny. "God's heard that promise from flight attendants so many times that he just laughs when he hears it."

As they approached the gate, there was no sign of either Karen or Danielle, who were undoubtedly on board already. But both pilots were standing there, and they were fuming. Oh, fuck, thought Denny. Why didn't I introduce myself to them yesterday? They're always nicer in these situations when they at least know your name. "Hi, guys. Sorry we're late. There was a bit of mix up. We never got the notification about being reassigned."

"Well, this doesn't look good at all," said the captain. "We only had forty-five minutes on the ground in Chicago to get to our next flight. Now we'll misconnect for sure."

"We're fucked," the first officer snarled. "God knows where they'll send us now. And I've got a thing at my kid's school tonight."

"We can board this flight in fifteen minutes," said Denny, grabbing at straws. "And maybe we can make up some time in the air."

"Not very likely," said the captain. "We just canceled."

"W-w-w-hat?" Eric stammered. "Just because we're fifteen minutes late?"

"No, because this airplane's out of service," said the captain. "There's a goddam hydraulic leak, which I wrote up in the logbook myself when we brought the plane in yesterday. They should have fixed last night, but they didn't. Assholes."

"Whew!" said Eric. "Thank God."

"What was that?" said the first officer.

"Nothing. I was afraid—"

So, what now happens?" said Denny, cutting Eric off.

"Karen just went to call crew scheduling. It's anybody's guess."

Karen arrived a moment later. "Hello, boys," she said with a smile so fake it could have lit up Times Square. "I'm glad you could make it."

"What's the word?" said the captain.

"Scheduling wants you to call them directly, Jim," said Karen. "As for us, we've been reassigned again. We're going to the Doubletree here at the airport and working the red-eye to JFK tonight."

"We're going to the hotel?" said Denny. "Right now?" Hallelujah!

"Yes. Pick up should be around eight-thirty tonight. No sense in hanging around here. Let's go."

"Hey," said Denny, "why should we be stuck at the Doubletree all day if we're not leaving until tonight? Can't we go back downtown? I bet they haven't even cleaned our rooms yet."

"Denny," said Karen, who was obviously at the end of her patience, "pick up your fucking bags and start walking *that* way. Now!"

***

By the time they reached the hotel pick up point, the sun had risen. "Jesus Christ!" said Karen. "In broad daylight, you look even *worse*, if that's possible."

"And you stink, too," added Danielle.

Karen shook her head. "I'm not sure why this turned out the way it did, but for some reason, you two idiots have been given a reprieve."

"Well," said Denny, "as my mother used to say, 'There's a God in heaven who looks out for fools like you.' "

"She got the fool part right!" said Karen. "This could have been much worse. Denny, you'd have had a lot of explaining to do. Eric, you'd have kissed your brand-new wings goodbye."

"In our defense," said Denny, "crew scheduling never spoke with either one of us on the phone. Technically, if they didn't make first person contact, we're not responsible for—"

"Denny, shut up. You've pushed your luck as far as you can. I guarantee you that the next time, you won't get off. This is the kind of crap I expect from a twenty-year-old. What're you, thirty? Get your shit together and spare us all the goddam drama."

"Karen, you're absolutely right," said Denny. "I apologize to everyone. It won't happen again."

Karen turned to Eric. "You seem like a nice guy. If you want to keep this job, I suggest that you be a little more selective about picking your friends. Understand?"

"Yes, ma'am."

"Good," said Karen, as the van pulled up. "That's all I have to say."

"You all get on the van," said Denny. "I'll make sure the driver gets all of bags stowed."

"Thank you," said Karen. She and Danielle climbed aboard with Eric right on their heels.

"Not you," said Denny, grabbing him by the arm. "You have some explaining to do. What were Jefferson and Theo doing in your bed at five A.M.? I want to hear everything, right now. Come on, we'll grab a seat in the last row."

"Well," said Eric, a few minutes later, as the van began moving, "We were in the taxi going back to the hotel. I was sitting in the middle, and they each had a hand on one of my legs. And then…"

CHAPTER 17

The Observation Ride

"Pardon me! Excuse me! Pardon me!" Flight Attendant Rose McElroy tried to appear composed as she raced through DFW. It was hard to rush anywhere in two-inch pumps, especially while dragging a heavy tote bag perched on top of an off-balance suitcase. One of her suitcase wheels was wobbling precariously; she prayed that it would last through the end of her three-day trip. And it was a brand-new, company-issued suitcase, too. Damn!

She felt a bead of sweat trickling down her face. The temperature inside the terminal had to be at least 85 degrees; so typical of DFW in August. Hoping that she wouldn't be spotted by a supervisor, she took off her uniform hat and shoved it into her tote bag. Lord, she thought, as she smoothed her hair. Just get me to the gate on time, please.

She couldn't help overhearing snippets of conversation as she zigzagged through the plodding crowd of summer travelers, some of whom would suddenly stop in their tracks, blocking the walkway.

"I'm completely lost, y'all!" said a woman in short-shorts and sandals. "*Now* which gate are we leavin' from? They keep changin' it every five minutes!"

"Oh, how I *hate* goin' through DFW!" said an elderly man, who limped along using a cane. "This airport is just too damn big! Where's one of them damned handicapped carts when you need one?"

"Hey, Mama, there's a Mi Casa Restaurant!" said a rotund teenager. His extra-large Texas Rangers t-shirt didn't quite cover his pale belly. "Let's go and get us some jalapeño poppers."

"You just keep right on walkin', J.J. They're gonna feed us on the plane."

"But Momma, they fill 'em with cream cheese before they fry 'em." He smacked his lips. "I gotta have some!"

"Don't you sass me, boy!" She shook a bony finger at him. "Enough is enough. Besides, you had a whole mess of food right before we left the house."

The familiar sound of Texas twang made Rose feel homesick. Her own mother used expressions like "a whole mess of food." But it was a fleeting feeling. Her more immediate concerns were getting something to eat and not being late for her flight. She looked at her watch. It was 11:40. Her flight to Albuquerque was leaving at 1 P.M. from Gate 39. She had to be there by noon, and she was only at Gate 5. I have twenty minutes, she thought. That leaves me just enough time to run to the food court and pick up something for later. I *have* to do it. I can't even look at one more bag of honey-roasted peanuts, and I can't afford all those sugary calories anyway.

Trying to find healthy food options in an airport, especially in Texas, was tricky business. Pizzas, jalapeño poppers and Big Macs were all *verboten* to a new-hire who was within one pound of her weight limit. Scouring the limited options at the food court, she chose a salad with fat-free dressing. It consisted of iceberg lettuce, under-ripe tomatoes, and ossified carrot slices. Criminey, she thought, as she reached for the salad and took her place in line. It's 1991. Isn't it about time Texans ate something in a salad besides iceberg lettuce?

"Hey there!" said a gravelly voice behind her.

Rose turned around. The weathered-looking man who had addressed her was decked out in a Stetson hat, a silver-and-turquoise belt buckle, and cowboy boots.

"Hello," she said, smiling pleasantly. Sometimes, her face ached from smiling so much.

"Where are you off to?"

"I'm going to Albuquerque."

"Well, what do you know!" he said excitedly. "I am too!"

"What a coincidence."

"Albuquerque is home to me." He moved closer. "Is that your regular run?"

She kept the smile on her face. This query seemed to serve as every man's opening line with female crewmembers. "No, I don't have a regular run. I'm too new."

"I can tell." He whistled appreciatively. "And I gotta say, it's mighty nice to see a stewardess who looks like a *stewardess,* and not like my Grandma Ida."

She wanted to say, "We're called flight attendants, sir. No one uses the word 'stewardess' anyone." But it hardly seemed worth the effort. "Thank you for the compliment."

"So do you have plans tonight?"

"No, sir. I have a very short layover. I'm leaving at the crack of dawn tomorrow to go back home to Chicago." Could this line move any slower?

"Too bad. I was hoping to show you the sights."

"It's very nice of you to offer." She started to say, 'another time, maybe', but there was no sense in encouraging him.

"Well," he said, "we can at least get acquainted during the flight. Are you working in first class or coach?" His chest swelled with pride. "I'm sitting in 3B, myself."

"Oh, I'm in the back today. Isn't that a shame?" Mercifully, she had reached the front of the line. "Excuse me for a moment." She placed her salad on the counter. "Do you have any grilled chicken you could throw on top of this?" she asked the woman behind the cash register.

"No, hon, I don't," the cashier replied. She wore a hairnet, and a hangdog expression on her face. She reminded Rose of the cafeteria ladies in the training center. Poor thing, Rose thought. I'm sure I'd look the same way if I had to wear a hairnet and stand rooted in the same spot all day long.

The cashier gestured toward the chiller compartment in front of her. "I could give you a scoop of tuna salad."

Rose mentally calculated calories. "Is it fat-free, by any chance?"

"Fat-free tuna salad?" The cashier shook her head. "No, hon."

"All right. I'll take it anyway, thanks." She reached for her wallet.

"Here, let me get that for you!" said the man behind her. "You new girls don't make diddly-squat. I know that for *a* fact."

"Oh, I couldn't let you do that, sir." She quickly paid for her food. "Thank you just the same. Nice chatting with you."

"Don't forget, I'm counting on you to come up to first class and visit me, Miss…?"

"I'll do my best, sir. Now, I really have to skedaddle." Oh, God, listen to me. It's as though I never left this damn state! "Have a good flight."

A few moments later, she arrived at Gate 39 and was surprised to see no one there but a lone ticket agent. "Hi, I'm Rose McElroy, flight attendant number three. Where is everybody?"

"You're awfully early. The flight to McAllen doesn't leave for ninety minutes."

"McAllen?! I'm going to Albuquerque!"

"Let me see." The agent typed quickly on her keyboard. "There was a gate change. You're going out of Gate 21. I'd hurry if I were you. They'll start boarding in five minutes."

"Shoot! Would you do me a favor? Would you please call that gate and tell them that I'm on my way?"

"I'll do better than that." She waved to a man driving by in a cart. "Hey, Sam! Hold on a minute. Would you give this girl a ride to her next flight? She's in an awful hurry."

"Of course I will. Hop on, little lady."

Little lady, Rose thought ruefully, as she stashed her bags and climbed aboard. At six-feet tall, that's one thing she'd never been called. "Thank you, sir."

As they arrived at Gate 39, and the driver stopped the cart and removed her luggage, she stepped down. "Thank you very much for the ride."

"You're welcome," he said, tipping his hat. "I wish you a safe and pleasant flight."

I will say this for the men of Texas: they are exceedingly polite, she thought. I do miss *that* sometimes… but not much else. She walked up to the agent at the desk and pulled out her crew ID badge. "Hi, I'm McElroy, the number three."

"You're *late*," the agent said accusingly. "Everybody else was here twenty minutes ago."

"I'm sorry," said Rose, fumbling in her purse for the jet bridge door key. "I'm afraid I didn't hear the gate change announcement."

"It's already unlocked," he said, jerking his head toward the door. "You'd better get right on down there and send the plucker out ASAP."

"Will do."

"And if this flight doesn't get off the gate on time, *y'all* are gonna be charged with the delay, not us."

Nothing like teamwork, thought Rose. "Yes, sir." As she walked down the jet bridge, one of her co-workers came rushing out to meet her. "Rose, honey, where've you been?" Ricky was a muscular young man with a blond crew cut and blue eyes. "We're just about to start boarding."

"I know, I know! I was getting some food. No big deal. Just let me stow my bags and we'll get started."

"No big deal, ha! There's a supervisor waiting for you in the back. You're getting a check ride in coach today."

"Shoot! Well, better a check ride than a ghost ride, I guess. At least I know she's here. Just give me a second to turn on the old McElroy 'country girl' charm."

"Save it, sister. It's a *he*, and he's a condescending queen from New York Flight Service. They're the worst! Impossible to please. Quick, give me that salad. I'll put it in the galley up here. Now, listen: you're late because you were waiting with a passenger from the inbound flight who needed a wheelchair and no other reason. That's an FAA regulation and he can't fight you on it. Understand? Hey, where's your hat?"

"Right here in my tote bag."

"Give it to me." He placed it expertly on her head.

"How's my lipstick?"

"Barely there. But you can reapply before takeoff. Just lick your lips a little for now."

"For *him*?"

"Girl, for once, would you just take my advice, please?"

"Here I go! Wish me luck."

"Tell Jennie to go out and pull tickets while you watch the luggage in the back and Dahlia sets up the galley."

"Will do."

She and Jennie crossed paths as Rose walked down the aisle. "I'm so glad you made it!" said Jennie, with a big smile. Jennie was a pretty, hardworking brunette from Urbana, Illinois. "Don't worry, I've had that supervisor on before for check-rides, and he's not as bad as he seems."

"Thanks, Jenny."

The supervisor, a stocky man of medium height, was standing, arms crossed, next to the coach galley. He had an enormous head covered with wavy, bright-orange hair. His face, his neck, and every other inch of pale, exposed skin was covered with freckles. "Ms. McElroy, I'm Phillip Hendry from La Guardia Flight Service."

I don't believe it, thought Rose. I know who this is: he's Eric's supervisor, Pumpkin Head! "It's very nice to meet you, Mr.—"

"Are you aware of the regulations stating that boarding on a narrow-body aircraft should begin thirty minutes prior to departure?"

"Yes, sir. I'm sorry I'm late. I was waiting with a passenger from my inbound flight who needed a wheelchair. The agent called again and again, but it took forever for the wheelchair to arrive."

"Oh, I see."

"I couldn't very well leave the passenger stranded on the jet bridge," she said, with a wide smile on her face. "That would be against regulations, too." She placed her suitcase and tote bag in an overhead bin. "Fortunately, I am here right on time for boarding." She stood calmly in front of him, with her hands folded.

"Yes, of course… in that case…" he stammered, obviously uncomfortable with the fact that Rose towered half a foot above him. "I'll be observing you throughout the flight today. You're required to have at least three check rides before you complete your probationary period." He consulted the clipboard in his hand. "Accordingly to your file, you've only had two. No infractions noted yet, but that's why *I'm* here. We do out-of-base check rides from time to time. We try to make sure that we offer a consistently superior service system-wide."

"I guess I'd better be 'on my toes' then, no pun intended. Tell me, do you by chance know my dear friend Eric Saunders, who's based at La Guardia?"

His demeanor changed completely. "Oh, yes! Eric is in my supervisory group. How do you know him?"

"We were in the same training class. Isn't he a delightful young man?"

"Yes. He's made quite an impression at the base."

"I've no doubt," said Rose, thinking: I bet his beautiful little butt has made an impression on you too.

"Well," Phillip said, "any friend of Eric's must be as professional as he is. I'm sure that I'll be giving you a perfect score today."

"I hope so. Here come the passengers. That elderly woman looks like she could use help finding her seat. Excuse me, Mr. Hendry."

"Call me Phillip. I'll take my seat now, Rose. By the way, please make sure that your safety manual is handy. I'll review it for discrepancies before we land. The same goes for the rest of the crew: standard operating procedure."

"I'll be sure to let them know."

***

Twenty minutes later, Dahlia stuck her head out of the galley. "Hey, Rose, is everybody here?" she asked in a lilting Jamaican accent.

"I think so. We should be leaving in just a few minutes."

"Let's get these overhead bins closed then before we hear about *that*, too." Dahlia's lip curled. "Where's the fat man?"

"What fat man?"

"The ugly, little fat man with the clipboard."

"He's sitting up in row eighteen, near the window exit."

"Well, that's *something* to be grateful for," Dahlia muttered. "Usually they sit in the very last row and watch every flippin' move we make." She slammed an overhead bin shut. "Just my luck: because *you're* getting a check ride, now I'll be getting one, too."

"Sorry, Dahlia. I guess we'll have to do everything by the book. For this leg, at least." After the bins were closed, she followed Delia to the aft galley.

Dahlia snapped the curtain closed. "He already fussed at me about not having my hair pulled back. You know what else he said to me? 'Your skirt is too short and much too tight across your rear end.' Then he looked down his nose at me and asked, 'When's the last time you had a weight check?' Do you believe it: the ugly, little fat man chastising *me*, with that potbelly hanging over his belt? I wanted to ask him, 'When's the last time you saw your own dick?' Man, I bet he can't even *find* it." The crew phone rang. Dahlia picked up it immediately. "This is Dahlia the Fat Ass in coach … yes, hang on a minute." She passed the phone to Rose. "It's for you."

"Hello?"

"Rose, it's Ricky. Come up to first right away. There's somebody here that you should see."

"If it's that old man with the gaudy belt buckle, I'll pass."

"Who? Oh, no. Not *him*. It's someone else. Come on up and make it fast."

She quickly walked toward the front. Ricky stepped into the galley and motioned for Rose to join him.

"What's up, Ricky?"

"The man of my dreams is sitting right here in my cabin. Take a look."

"My boyfriend doesn't like me to ogle strange men."

"Yes, yes, Rose, we *all* know that you that have a boyfriend, and that he's on the Chicago police force, and that he's a great, big, hairy he-man. I'm not asking you to give someone a blow job, for God's sake, just sneak a peek!"

"Which passenger is it?"

"The silver-haired daddy in 4F."

Rose casually looked down the aisle. "Oh, he's handsome, all right. He looks pretty fit, too—for a man his age."

"Fit? He's built like a brick shithouse."

"Quite a beautiful head of hair, too. Do you think it's his own?"

"Absolutely. That was the second thing I checked out."

"Well, I know how quickly you work. Does he have your phone number yet?"

"No. I think he's on my team, but I'm not positive."

"What happened to your infallible gaydar?"

"Sometimes, really masculine men throw it off completely." He handed her a champagne bottle. "Here. Go offer to refill his glass. Chat him up a little and tell me what you think."

"All right. But you'd better keep that cowpoke in 3B busy. I'm not getting trapped into another conversation with him." She approached the passenger in 4F and smiled. "Would you like some more champagne, sir?"

"Yes." He held up his glass without looking at her. "And bring one for my partner, too."

"Your partner?" Rose was confused. The aisle seat next to him was empty.

"My business partner. He's at the newsstand, getting me a copy of the *Times*, which, by the way, *you* should be provide to passengers in first class."

"I see. Will he—I mean, is he nearby?" She looked at her watch. "I think we're just about to close the door."

He finally looked up at her. "Well, you'll just have to leave it *open* until he gets here," he said arrogantly. "I'm a Titan."

Ugh, one of those, thought Rose, taking an instant dislike to him. "I'll alert the whole crew, sir," she said, refilling the glass. "We'd hate to disappoint a VIP." She turned around and almost collided with a late-boarding passenger. When she saw who it was, she was so shocked that she almost dropped the champagne bottle. "Anthony!"

"Hi, Rose," Anthony said casually, as though he'd just seen her the day before. He looked resplendent in a navy blue suit and silver silk tie.

"Well, don't just stand there!" said Rose. "I haven't seen you in months! Give me a hug!"

As she and Anthony embraced, the man in 4F started drumming his fingers on the armrest. "Did you get my newspaper, Anthony?"

"Yes. Here you go. Jim, this is my friend, Rose McElroy. Rose, this is Jim Sizemore."

"Nice to meet you," Jim said curtly.

"Likewise." She turned and gave Anthony a real smile. "So, what are you doing on this flight? Are you deadheading, or non-reving, or—no, you couldn't be non-reving yet, we don't get our travel benefits until December."

"We're *full-fare* passengers," said Jim.

"Oh," said Rose, still beaming at Anthony. My God, she thought. I forgot how beautiful he is.

Jim cleared his throat. "Miss, perhaps you could step aside, so that Mr. Bellini could *take* his seat?"

Anthony whipped around. "Rose. My friend's name is *Rose,* Jim. I just introduced her to you."

"Sorry, Rose," said Jim. Could you—"

"Yes, of course. Buckle up, Anthony, and I'll bring you a glass of champagne."

"Are you working up front?" Anthony asked, as he slipped past her.

"No, I'm just helping out for the moment. I'm in the back today. Maybe we can catch up later."

"Anthony and I have a lot of work to do," said Jim. "I doubt that he'll have time."

"I'll *make* time," said Anthony.

Jim grunted in response and buried his nose in the business section.

Rose dashed into the galley and returned with a glass of champagne for Anthony. "The agent's closing the door now. I'll see you before we land, I hope." As she leaned down to put the glass on his armrest, she whispered into his ear. "Anthony, you are still flying, aren't you?"

"Of course I am."

"Good. I thought for the moment that maybe you'd... well, never mind. Enjoy the flight."

As she brought the tray back into the galley, Ricky stood tapping his foot. "Well, what was all *that* about?"

"We're moving now, Ricky. Aren't you going to arm your doors?"

"What? Shit, I almost forgot!" He picked up the microphone. "Flight attendants, please arm your doors and cross-check." He knelt on the floor to arm the entry and galley doors. "Yuck, this carpet is gross! From now on, I'm going to start carrying knee pads whenever I fly number one." He stood and reached for a towel to wipe the grime from his hands. "What'd you find out about the Daddy in 4F?"

"Dream Man *is* on your team. But don't waste your pretty blue eyes on him. He's an arrogant asshole."

"Whoa! When *you* use language like that, I'll take your word for it. Hey, who's the hunk sitting next to him? You acted like you know each other."

"We do know each other. We graduated from training together this spring."

"He's a flight attendant?"

"Yes. He's based here at DFW."

Ricky grabbed the manifest and began scanning it. "James Sizemore and Anthony Bellini. How come Anthony's not listed as an employee?"

"Because they're both full-fare passengers." She shook her head. "Mr. Sizemore is full of something, all right."

"Well, what are they doing together?"

"Lord, Ricky. Do I have to draw you a picture? They're *together*. And not only that: he referred to Anthony as his business partner. I wonder what the hell that means?"

"Leave it to me, girl. If it's pointless for me to cruise either one of them, I'll do some detective work instead. This is just like an episode of *Charlie's Angels*. I'll be Jill Munroe, naturally."

"Be discreet. And take good notes. I'll want to know everything."

"Don't worry. I'm on the case."

***

An hour after takeoff, Rose breathlessly returned to the forward galley. "Do you need some help, Ricky?"

"Of course I do! We're landing in twenty minutes, and I haven't even offered coffee yet. You know what: screw the coffee service, we don't have time. How'd it go with the check ride?"

"Fine, I think. He said that he'll give me some notes after we land—"

"Notes?! Who does he think he is, Martin Scorsese?"

"—but he promised he wouldn't hold us up getting onto the hotel van. He knows we have a short layover."

"Well, that's considerate, which is more than I usually expect from a check rider. Grab the trays from the last two rows, would you? And don't make any eye contact with anyone! If you do, they'll order something else just for the hell of it."

"Right away." She returned a moment later with two meals trays. "Now, tell me what you found out about Anthony and Jim."

"Well, for starters, they've spent most of the flight looking over a set of blueprints for a house that they're building in Santa Fe. A *big* one."

"Is it going to be *their* house?"

"No. It's a house that Sizemore's working on for a client. They have a meeting with the client this evening. Jim has his own design firm in Dallas."

"How do you know that?"

"When I set their trays down, he was showing Anthony a copy of a business letter that he'd just sent to another client. His name was on the letterhead. Anthony's name is listed next to his. Incidentally, Jim's 'business partner' doesn't seem to know jack shit about either architecture *or* design."

"I still don't understand why Jim referred to him that way."

"Do I have to draw you a picture? Anthony's got himself a Sugar Daddy."

"That's a terrible thing to say! You make it sound like a male prostitute."

Ricky chortled. "If the twelve-hundred-dollar Armani suit fits…"

"Ricky!"

"Let me make it more palatable for you: Anthony is for show and tell. He's the eye candy that Jim brings along to impress the clients. After the meeting, there's probably a chilled bottle champagne in a silver bucket right next to the hot tub. Get it? Champagne flowing, steam rising, hot men stripping off—"

"I get it. But I don't like it. Besides, Anthony shouldn't be mixed up with anybody right now. He should bide his time and focus on getting the hell out of Texas. My friend Eric is depending on him."

"To do what?"

"To transfer to New York where he belongs and move back into his old apartment in Queens. Eric's living there with his Anthony's brother right now, and from what I hear the brother is a real hoodlum."

"If I were your friend, I wouldn't count on that. Jim and Anthony do squabble a bit, but there's real chemistry between them. You can feel it. I bet they have *fantastic* sex together. Not to mention, Jim's obviously loaded. All that money must be tempting to a new hire making eighteen grand a year. How does anyone even think of living on that in New York on our paltry salary?"

"I don't know. I guess Eric eats a lot of tuna casserole."

"Exactly. Why do that, when someone will buy you *filet mignon*—and a lot more?"

"Nevertheless—"

"How old is Anthony?"

"I'm not sure. Late twenties?"

"Ha. Thirty-something is more like it, which is another point to consider: he may not have many more chances like this one. When opportunity knocks, Rose, you have to answer the door. I don't blame Anthony one bit. I'm always on the lookout myself. You don't think I'm doing this for the rest of my life, do you?"

She rolled her eyes. "Oh, good Lord."

"I only foresee one problem with those two," said Ricky. "Jim doesn't strike me as type who'll tolerate midnight phone calls from crew scheduling. Or to wait around for lover boy to come home from a three-day trip, reeking of Ultra Jet lav spray. I bet he's already putting the squeeze on Anthony to quit flying."

"Over my dead body. If I have to—" *Ding, dong, ding, dong.* "I'll get that." She picked up the crew phone. "This is Rose up front."

"What the hell are you doing up there?" It was Dahlia. "Didn't you hear the captain say to prepare for landing? We'll be on the ground in eight minutes!"

"No, we didn't!"

"Well, tell Ricky to make the PA *right now*, and you'd better get out in the aisle. The little fat man has been writing up a storm, and he's on his way up there."

"I see him coming. Thanks for the warning." She hung up the phone. "Ricky, we're about to get in trouble. Make the 'prepare for landing' PA. Quick!"

Rick peeped through the galley window. "Oh, shit! I can see tree tops!"

As Ricky made the announcement, Rose opened the closet and began reaching for passenger jackets.

"Pardon *me*," said Phillip, as he charged into the cabin. "Exactly what is going on up here?"

"We were just starting the coffee service, but we ran out of time," said Ricky.

Rose nodded her head up and down. "This flight is shorter than I realized!"

"And the captain is a bit of a mumbler," Ricky added. "We didn't hear him tell us to prepare for landing."

"Spare me your excuses. I heard the captain loud and clear over the PA system." His face was becoming redder by the second. "I have excellent vision, and I can spot a pair of galley gossips from fifteen rows away."

"Excuse me, Phillip, but I'd better pass these jackets back quickly," said Rose. "I don't want passengers to have to wait for them on the ground."

"So much for your perfect rating today," the supervisor said snidely.

"Can we discuss this a bit later, please?" said Ricky, as he frantically latched galley compartments closed. "The landing gear just came down."

"We'll debrief as soon as the last passenger deplanes. I hope, for your sake, that your safety manuals are up-to-date. Otherwise, you may both find yourselves in hot water."

"Yes, sir."

***

"Well," Rose said later, as they waited for the Sheraton van outside the terminal. "That debrief with the supervisor went faster than I thought it would."

"Only because the fat man's return flight was leaving in fifteen minutes," said Dahlia. "otherwise, he would have kept talking shit for an hour. They *all* talk shit."

"Thank God our manuals are up-to-date," said Rose.

"And thank God that Phillip has the hots for your friend Eric. It's the only reason he cut you some slack." Ricky laughed nastily. "Not that it will get him anywhere. Jesus, that face!"

"I'm ready for a drink," said Jenny. "I hope we haven't missed Happy Hour. Hey, weren't those two guys on our flight?" She pointed toward the private car pick up area.

Rose looked over and saw Anthony and Jim standing together. "Yes, they were."

"The younger one is a friend of Rose's," said Ricky.

"Really?" said Dahlia, obviously impressed. "What's his situation?"

"Unfortunately," Rose replied, "he seems to be taken."

As Jim began impatiently punching numbers into a cell phone, Anthony sat down on one of their suitcases and calmly lit a cigarette.

"Oh, Daddy's not going to like that," said Ricky. "*Never* sit on Vuitton."

A quick admonishment from Jim brought Anthony to his feet immediately. "See what I mean?"

A moment later, a Mercedes with tinted windows pulled up in front of Jim and Anthony. The driver jumped out and immediately began to load their luggage into the trunk. Anthony started to reach for the passenger door, and then pulled his hand back.

"Anthony is better trained than I thought, Rose," said Ricky. "At least he knows enough to let the hired help to their job."

"Oh, shut up," said Rose, as she watched the driver open the door for them.

"Aren't you going to wave goodbye to your friend?" asked Jenny, as the car sped off.

"No!" She ripped her uniform hat off. "Where *is* that goddam van? It must be a hundred degrees out here!"

Here it comes," said Dahlia. "Rose, you need a drink, too. A big one! Let's sign in quickly at the front desk and then all meet downstairs right away."

"I'll catch with you guys a little bit later," said Rose. "I need to call Geneviève, my roommate back in Chicago."

"Can't it wait until later?"

"No. Geneviève is friends with Anthony and Eric too, and I need to talk to her now—*right now.*"

CHAPTER 18

Entitlement

Eric was at home packing for a trip when he received an unexpected call from his supervisor. "Good afternoon, Eric. I see that you're on the five o'clock flight to L.A. today. Could come to the airport a few minutes early? There's something I need to discuss with you."

Eric was immediately on guard. "Sure, Philip. Is everything all right?"

"Yes, why wouldn't it be?"

"I thought maybe I'd received a bad passenger letter or something like that."

"Oh, no." Phillip laughed. "That's one thing I'll never have to worry about as far as you're concerned. I need to share some information with you about a new program that we're implementing. Just pop into my office around three-thirty, if that's convenient."

Like it wouldn't be 'convenient', thought Eric. "Sure. I'll see you then."

***

When he reached operations, the receptionist promptly directed him to Phillip's cubicle. Phillip was in a heated phone conversation and didn't see Eric. His face was so flushed that it almost matched his hair color. "Well, Miss Johnson, let me tell *you* something: I find it hard to believe that you can't remember a single detail about the incident, considering that it happened just last week. I've spoken to several of your co-workers on that flight, and they know exactly what I'm talking about. So I suggest you think it over again, and have some details ready when you come in for our meeting tomorrow … Yes, you should definitely bring a union rep with you. I'll see you at nine A.M. sharp. Goodbye." He hung up the phone and began scribbling notes.

Eric knocked on the cubicle wall. "Hi, Phillip. Is this a good time?"

"Eric, how nice to see you." Phillip pasted a big smile on face and pushed his notes aside. "Sit down, please."

Eric eyed the scale in the corner. "Aren't you going to weigh me first?"

"No, you look fine." Phillip wiped beads of sweat from his forehead. "I wish all the people in my group were as well-groomed as you. Some of our flight attendants are getting out of control. Especially the females. Why should *I* have to remind grown women what a regulation hairstyle is? Do you know that sometimes I fantasize about running through the terminal with a large pair of scissors and going snip, snip, snip!"

Although Eric often had the same fantasy, he smiled and said nothing.

"Given our huge financial losses over the last three quarters," Phillip continued, "you would think that all employees would do everything possible to retain our valued customers— including adhering to grooming regulations. It goes without saying that passengers do *not* want a meal tray served to them by a woman whose untamed hair is dangling an inch above their chicken Kiev."

"No, I'm sure they don't."

"Now, Eric, the reason I asked you to stop by is that we're making an exciting change to our frequent flyer program. There's a handout in your mailbox already, but it's my responsibility to make sure that everyone in my group is familiar with it. Let's take a moment to review first. As you know, the Titan frequent flyer program began five years ago and has been wildly successful. Can you guess how many Titans we have enrolled worldwide?"

Eric mentally reached for figures that he vaguely remembered from training. "Five million?"

"*Ten* million. And we can't let them think that they're enrolled in just *any* frequent flier program. We've decided that it's important to recognize our *very* frequent flyers by adding tiers based on actual miles flown. Effective today, anyone who initially joins will still be referred to as a Titan. There's a certain amount of cachet associated with that title alone, of course. Middle-tier customers, those with between five hundred thousand and one million miles, will be known as Mighty Titans. And our top-tier customers, those with a million miles or more, will henceforth be known as..." He paused dramatically, as though he were about to announce the Best Picture of the Year. "*Almighty Titans.*"

It took everything in Eric's power to keep from laughing. "That's very catchy," he managed to say.

"It is, isn't it? This new component is vital to our continued success. As I mentioned only a moment ago, you know what a competitive business this is. It would be terrible to lose even *one* valued passenger to another carrier." Reading from a full-color brochure on his desk, Phillip began outlining the various perks available to each tier of customers.

As Eric listened, he noted that as a flight attendant, he would be involved with almost none of the details, which mainly consisted of cabin upgrades. The upgrade process was tightly controlled by the reservations department and by and gate agents.

When Phillip had finished reading aloud, he looked up. "Do you have any questions?"

Eric squirmed. He had to come up with a response, if only to prove that'd been paying attention. "Just one. What perks will be available for these top-tier customers in-flight?"

Phillip's face went blank. "In-flight?"

"Yes. I mean, will they get first choice of entrées over other passengers, or amenity kits like those we offer on international flights, or something along those lines?"

"Nothing quite so... tangible as that," said Phillip. "The most important thing is to recognize them when they're on board and to make them feel like true VIPs, because they *are* VIPS. If the opportunity to go above and beyond should present itself, please jump at the chance. The future of our company depends on their continued patronage."

Oh Jesus, thought Eric. How much company Kool-Aid has *he* had to drink?

"Confidentially," said Phillip, "I have a friend who flies for Global. You know what terrible financial shape *that* company is in. His paycheck bounced last month. Can you imagine? He couldn't pay his rent." He sighed. "I'm sure it won't be very long before Global goes the way of Atlantic Coast Airways. Tragic, isn't it? Another of America's most prestigious airlines forced into liquidation. They might still be in business today if only they'd taken better care of their customers."

It wouldn't be a pep talk, thought Eric, without throwing in the fear factor. He was surprised at how much he'd learned in just a few months: the answer to every customer service issue at the airline was to blame the frontline employees.

"At any rate, Eric, I'm pleased to tell you that an Almighty Titan will be on your flight today. Here is his name and preliminary seat assignment. He booked at the last minute. He's in coach as of right now, but he'll surely get an upgrade to business, as we had one cancellation. I hope I can count on you to deliver the level of service that he'll be anticipating. And I'll look forward to reading his comments about whether or not we met his expectations. Can I count on you?"

Oh, Lord, thought Eric. Three more months until I'm off probation, and then I can start tossing these bullshit handouts right into the recycling bin. For the moment, he smiled and slipped all the paperwork into his tote bag. "Yes, Phillip. Of course you can."

***

Eric boarded the 767 and stowed his luggage. He had been assigned to work in business class. Business-class service on transcon flights was a relatively new phenomenon at Mercury Airways. A tiny mid-ship coffee bar in the coach cabin had been converted into a full-service galley. It was awkwardly located next to the window exit rows—rows which were always requested by top-tier fliers who wanted the extra leg room. Unfortunately, the constant rearrangement of carts, the clanging of wine bottles, and the non-stop galley chatter often resulted in exit rows filled with highly annoyed top-tier flyers. Eric reminded himself to be extra careful moving carts in and out of the galley. Unfortunately, he would have no control over crewmember chatter.

A few minutes later, he met the rest of his crew in business class. The other aisle flight attendant was named Carol. She had a long, white ponytail and was slightly stooped-over. Stacey, who'd be working in the galley, had dark circles under her eyes and smiled at neither of her co-workers. Carol seemed warm and easy-going. Stacey made it clear that she was in no mood for pleasantries. After introducing herself, she tied her apron, entered the galley, and snapped the curtain closed.

As Carol and Eric readied the cabin, Eric made sure to have a large stack of hangers ready. Based on previous experience, he knew that every passenger would have a suit jacket and insist on having it hung up before they even sat down. He'd only worked in business class twice before, but it was already his least favorite cabin. Passengers in that cabin were the most demanding people in the world. They wanted everything on the menu and more, and they wanted it all *now*. They guzzled cocktails before dinner and then wine with dinner, snapping their fingers for a refill before their glasses were even half-empty. Every cabin on the airplane had its challenges, but Eric truly loathed business class.

He noticed Carol walking through her side of the plane and placing a hanger in each seat pocket. "That's a great idea," said Eric, following suit.

"It's the only way," said Carol. "I can't bear it when they stand there waving their coat at me like it's on fire. What am I supposed to do, swim upstream while the coach passengers are trampling me? This way is easier. We'll collect them all at one time, right before we leave."

"Heads up. We're boarding," the purser announced over the PA.

"Let's get into our holding pen," said Carol. Their assigned boarding position was behind a small partition between the last row of seats in business and the mid-ship lavatory. It was an awkward place to stand, but there was nowhere else to go. Eric steeled himself as his passengers charged down the aisle. They immediately began shoving their suitcases into overhead bins, not even paying attention to whether or not they fit. Eric watched a young woman on Carol's side struggle to lift a heavy suitcase. It slipped out of her grasp and crashed to the floor, barely missing the head of the man seated next to her. She haplessly whirled around and fixed her gaze on Carol and Eric.

"Oops! Time for the disappearing act," said Carol." She jumped into the bathroom locked the door.

Dammit, thought Eric. Why didn't I think of that?

The woman waved at Eric. "Can you help me with this?"

Eric reluctantly walked to her row and eyeballed the suitcase. "I really don't think that's going to fit up there, ma'am."

"Oh, it will fit," she said. "I travel with this suitcase every week. It's just too heavy for me to lift. Give me a hand, would you?"

Other passengers, trapped behind her in the aisle, were becoming visibly annoyed. Eric reached for the suitcase and tried to lift it. It was absurdly heavy. "This is too heavy even for me to lift, Miss."

"I don't believe it." She sat down and pulled a large stack of magazines from her purse. "A strapping young man like you!"

"Here, *I'll* help you with that, son," said a middle-aged man in the aisle. "That way the rest of us can get to our seats."

"Thank you, sir," said Eric, as together they managed to shove the suitcase into the bin.

The man glared at the woman. "Miss, if you can't handle your own carry-on luggage, you should check it. It's no one else's responsibility to lift *your* luggage."

Eric beamed. He couldn't wait to get off probation and be able to speak so directly to a customer.

"Amen," said the man seated next to the woman. "She almost killed me with that goddam thing."

She merely shrugged. "Steward, bring me a vodka and tonic, please."

"I can do that right after takeoff," said Eric. "In the meantime, we'll offer champagne, water and orange juice as soon as the aisles are clear."

She snorted. "I've never had a problem asking for a cocktail on the ground before." She thumbed through the pages of *Women's Wear Daily*. "This *is* business class, isn't it?"

You *bitch*, thought Eric. Well, at least she wasn't on his side the plane; after takeoff, she'd be Carol's problem. "One moment, please. I'll see what I can do." He stepped back toward the galley.

Stacey glared as he opened the curtain. "What do you want?"

"Can I get a vodka and tonic, please?"

"Are you kidding me? I'm *busy*." She picked up a mallet and began viciously breaking up a bag of ice. "They get standard pre-departures on the ground, and I haven't even opened the champagne yet. Come back *later*." She yanked the curtain closed again. If Eric's nose were any larger, she would have cut it off.

Eric walked back to his boarding position, where Carol had just stepped out of the bathroom. "You're going to *love* the woman in 11H," he said. "She's a real piece of work."

"Ha!" said Carol, with a wave of her hand. "Not to worry, sonny boy. I never let them get under my skin."

Eric noticed a passenger on his side of the cabin trying unsuccessfully to lift a heavy bag. Without even thinking about it, Eric ducked into the bathroom. "My turn now."

"Good boy!" Carol replied. "You're learning. I'll knock when the coast is clear."

There was brief lull before departure time. Eric heaved a sigh of relief and began closing the overhead bins, already crammed to the bursting point with luggage. Eric forced them closed anyway and prayed that they wouldn't hit any heavy turbulence after takeoff. He was just about to distribute menus when a Passenger Service rep came scurrying down the aisle. She was followed by a very handsome, well-dressed man with salt and pepper hair.

The man stopped in the aisle, looked at his seat and glared at her. "Row eleven, next to *bathroom?* This is the best you can do for me?"

"I apologize, sir," she said obsequiously, "but everyone else in business today is full-fare. Their seats were already reserved. This is the only seat we have left."

"Oh, this is gonna be just *great!*" said the man. "He opened an overhead bin and grimaced when he saw that it was full. "Now where the hell is there room for *my* luggage?"

"One moment, Mr. Sizemore." She looked at Eric. "I'm Connie with Premium Passenger Services," she said breathlessly. "*Please* tell me you have room somewhere up here for one more suitcase for an A.T."

"For a what?"

"An *Almighty Titan!* Didn't you get the handout?"

"Yes, but we're about to close the door. These bins are all full. I'm afraid there's no more room available."

"Mr. Sizemore was waiting for upgrade. Otherwise he'd have been here sooner," Connie said.

"You don't owe him any explanation," said Mr. Sizemore. He glared at Eric. "You. Go *find* me a spot."

Eric started walking toward the back. "Let me see if there's room in coach."

"No, *not* back in coach. I don't have time to wait for it once we land."

"Please, please!" Connie whispered to Eric. "Can't you do *something?* She was trembling with fear.

Eric knew, at that moment, that in the future he would do everything possible to avoid working in business class. He called the purser. "Do you have any room left up there for a suitcase?"

"I have space for just one, in the closet, if it's not too big."

"Wonderful." He hung up the phone, greatly relieved. "Sir, if you'll just take that suitcase forward, the purser has room in—"

"I'm going to take my *seat,* if you don't mind." He sat down imperiously and took out a cell phone. "I have business to care of. You two can deal with it."

"Let me be of service," said Connie, reaching for the suitcase. "I'll take it."

"No, *I'll* take it," said Eric, afraid that if he didn't remove himself immediately, he would break a wine bottle over Mr. Sizemore's head.

Connie followed him up the aisle. "Oh, thank you! I'm eternally in your debt. I know that Mr. Sizemore's not the most gracious man in the world, but please extend every courtesy that you can. We have a lot riding on this new program."

"Not to worry." Eric slammed the suitcase into a corner of the closet, hoping that it contained fragile items. "I'll make sure that he gets everything he deserves."

***

After takeoff, before the plane had even leveled off, call buttons began ringing. Eric sighed and unbuckled his seatbelt.

"Don't get up," said Stacey, who was in a jump seat right behind him. "We're not even at ten thousand feet yet."

"But Carol's already answering call lights on her side."

"So? Let her. We're not trained seals. Whatever they want, they can fuckin' *wait*."

A few minutes later, Eric joined Carol in the aisle to take entrée preferences—the worst part of working in that cabin. Invariably, before they got to the last row, they would run out of one choice or the other, resulting in open-mouth stares of disbelief. "What do you *mean* there's no more beef? Do you know how much I paid for this ticket?"

Fortunately, by the time Eric reached the last row, it had all worked out. And he didn't have to worry about Mr. Sizemore. He'd fallen asleep right after takeoff with his cell phone still clutched in his hand. Hopefully, he would stay asleep until they landed.

Preferences taken, Eric and Carol waited patiently as Stacey finished setting up in the galley. Heads kept swiveling in their direction as passengers waited for their first drink.

"You look stressed, Eric," said Carol, as she changed into a pair of clunky black sneakers. "What's the matter?"

"We've been in the air almost twenty minutes," said Eric. "We're supposed to serve the first drink by fifteen minutes after takeoff."

"Oh, relax," she said. "Why get yourself into such a dither? Do what *I* do: answer all call lights, tell them you'll be right out, and lull them into a false sense of security. They all think they're VIPs, and believe me, they are: very *impatient* people. They'll get their money's worth before the flight is over—if you just let them think it."

***

By the time that they finished serving dessert, Eric's patience was wearing then. He was just about to deliver a sundae to the last passenger when Mr.

Sizemore woke up. He shook himself fully awake, grabbed his menu, and waved at Eric. "When are you serving dinner?"

"We already did. We're serving dessert."

"Oh. Well, I'd like my dinner now. I want the filet. You can leave off the potatoes and skip the bread. And I'll have vinaigrette dressing on my salad."

"I'm very sorry, Mr. Sizemore, but there is no more filet. I can offer you three-cheese ravioli."

"What do you *mean* there's no more filet?"

Here we go, he thought. "We took main course preferences right after takeoff. You were sound asleep."

"Why didn't you wake me?"

"It's company policy not to wake people up to ask them about meal preferences."

"Screw your policy. I want a steak. Besides, I know the rest of these jokers are all upgrades."

"As a matter of fact, sir, *you* are the only upgrade today, as Connie mentioned when you boarded. These passengers all paid full fare."

Mr. Sizemore locked eyes with Eric. "Don't get smart with me, kid. It doesn't matter *how* I got the seat. I'm an Almighty Titan. The last that I heard, that's supposed to mean something at this airline." He started to raise his voice. "First you seat me next to the goddam bathrooms, and *then* you tell me I can't have what I want to eat."

"Mr. Sizemore, I am very sorry, but—"

"Why the *hell* are you people promising to deliver the goods when you *can't* deliver them?" he shouted.

Stacey opened the curtain, glanced in their direction, and then quickly pulled the curtain closed again.

From out of nowhere, Carol appeared at Eric's side. "Is there a problem?" she asked in a syrupy voice. "Can I help?"

"He'd like a steak," said Eric, trying to keep his voice steady, "but as you know we're all out of steaks."

"I want protein," said Mr. Sizemore. He turned on his laptop computer. "I will *not* eat your intestinal-binding pasta, under any circumstance. So you two go and figure it out. And bring me a glass of Cab Sav, while you're at it."

Eric bristled. If there was one thing he could not tolerate, it was Americans who abbreviated the names of French wines—usually because they couldn't pronounce them.

"One moment, please, sir. "Carol smiled. "Let me see if we can accommodate you. We'll be right back."

Eric followed her in the galley. "Why are you rewarding that kind of behavior? He's a fucking asshole!"

"Calm down, Eric. I saw the X next to your name on the crew list. That means you're still on probation, right?"

"Yes, but—"

"You're not going to risk losing your job over something so silly. Watch and learn. Let's see if the pilots will help us out." She picked up the crew phone. "Jim, this is Carol in business class. How are you? And how is your lovely wife? I haven't seen her in a coon's age. Margaret and I used to fly together all the time … Yes, I bet those boys of yours *are* a handful! Thank God I'm barren. I'd never be up to the task."

"Do you *mind?*" Stacey said, through gritted teeth. "I am trying to put all this crap away! I've been up since five this morning so that I could get my kids off to camp, and then get my commuter flight, and I'm *done*."

Carol covered the mouthpiece. "Control yourself, please, Stacey. I'll just be a minute longer." She resumed her conversation with the pilot. "Jim, have you eaten yet? … Oh, good. Listen, we seem to be short one steak. I know that you guys are catered with one steak and one pasta. Could I ask you to help us out and both have pasta tonight? It would make our lives so much easier … Oh, you're a living doll! Thanks, Jim. I'll be up later to say hello." She hung up the phone. "Problem solved! Stacey, I'm going to run up to first class to get a steak. Would you mind plating it for us?"

"I don't believe this," said Stacey, as she finished clearing the counter of debris. "I've had enough. *I'm* going to the back to take a break. You two brownnosers can do whatever you like."

"Fine, we're quite capable," said Carol, as Stacey stormed out. "Oh, my. Those Pittsburgh commuters: always so rough around the edges! Eric, tell your VIP to sit tight. I'll be back in a flash." She returned a moment later with an aluminum tin marked *beef* and a china plate. "Here we go, about to exceed all his expectations! First, we close the curtains all the way. Then we make sure the steak isn't overcooked. That would never do." She opened the container and poked a finger against the filet. "Oh, it's cooked perfectly!" Eric watched in horror as she turned the container over and dropped the steak onto the galley floor. Then she dragged it around underneath her shoe. "Nothing better than pepper steak for this maneuver. Those tasty bits of God-knows-what on the floor only *add* to the flavor." She picked up the steak, plopped it onto the plate, dribbled sauce over it, and added a side of grilled vegetables. "Who'll take it out to him, you or I?"

Without a second thought, Eric reached for the plate. "Please, let me."

"Have at it." She picked up an open bottle of Cabernet, coughed all over the rim, and then licked it. "I'll follow you with his wine. We must make sure to set this bottle aside for *his* use only. We can always open another one for the other passengers." She grinned. "You see? That's how we cope with catering to an asshole's needs, and still manage to sleep at night." She opened the curtain. "You go first, honey. I love to watch them take the first bite."

***

Later, as the crew traveled to the hotel, Eric was filled with remorse. In all the time that he'd worked as a waiter in college, no matter how obnoxious a customer was, he'd never done anything so vindictive—or unsanitary. Then it occurred to him that, working in a busy restaurant, with so many other people in the kitchen, he'd never actually had the chance.

"You're so quiet," said Carol.

"What's to say?" he replied, waving a hand at the rest of the crew. Despite the late hour, they were all engaged in a loud, no-holds-barred discussion about their unbearable schedules, unreliable husbands and ungrateful children. Even Stacey had found her second wind. "I couldn't get a word in edgewise even if I wanted to."

"So don't bother," said Carol. "We have one more ordeal to go through before we're tucked in for the night: the fuss over the sign-in sheet at the hotel."

"What's there to fuss over? Our layover is only fifteen hours."

"Oh, darling boy, what you don't know about your co-workers. When we get to the front desk, stick with me at the back of the line. You've put up with enough nonsense already today."

At the hotel, as soon as the clerk produced the crew sign-in sheet, Eric's co-workers swooped down like vultures. They looked up a moment later in stunned disbelief.

"We need at least two adjoining rooms," said a coach flight attendant. "None of these rooms is even on the same floor!"

"Not to mention there's not even one room over the pool *or* with a balcony!" This complaint came from Stacey.

"I know these room numbers," said another, pointing. "They're all right next to the elevator. No, no, no!"

The clerk, whose name was Alex, patiently explained that there was a large convention at the hotel and that there were no other rooms available.

This explanation only made the crew even more indignant. "Why do we always get treated like crap, just because the company's paying a corporate rate? It's just not fair!"

"Oh, for heaven's sake," said the purser finally, as he took a room key. "We're leaving before noon tomorrow! Just sign in, take your key and step aside!"

"So simple," Carol murmured from her spot in the back of the line. "That would be so simple, wouldn't it?"

"Carol, help me," said Eric. "I'm about to blow my top."

"Ssh," she said. "Just wait. I'll get a couple of nice rooms. Besides, I have a treat for us." She unzipped a tote bag, revealing an unopened bottle of red wine.

The other flight attendants, still bemoaning their fate, began noisily moving toward the elevators.

Carol gestured for Eric to follow her to the front desk, where she introduced Eric to Alex. "How do you do it, Carol?" asked Alex. "How do you put up with them month after month? If they worked here with me—God forbid—I'd kill them all!"

"I'm a very patient woman," said Carol. "I've learned to let it all go in one ear and out the other." She picked up a pen and the sign-in sheet.

Alex grinned. "Oh, no darling, don't take those crummy rooms. I just happen to have two adjoining rooms, with balconies, above the swimming pool. Just give me a second to make you a new room key for each of you."

"You are an angel!" said Carol. "We both appreciate it."

"My pleasure," said Alex. "It's such a delight to do something special for people who deserve it."

Eric smiled and thanked Alex, and then headed for the elevator. He was grateful for both Carol and Alex. At last, someone was looking out for *his* needs for a change, and not the other way around.

***

"Isn't this nice?" Carol said later, as they sat together on the balcony. "I can't remember the last time I saw such a beautiful full moon!" She reached for a cigarette and lit it while Eric opened the wine.

"It's spectacular," said Eric, pouring out two glasses. "What should we toast to? A quiet flight back tomorrow?"

"Hell, no," said Carol. "Let's not waste it on that. Let's toast to our new friendship. I love meeting charming, handsome young men."

"Perfect!" said Eric. "There is nothing quite as nice as making friends with a charming, beautiful, and very senior stew."

"Why thank you, sweet thing. I'm glad to know that I've still got it." She arched her back, crossed one sandaled foot over the other, and exhaled dramatically. "Hiya, big boy. I'm Carol. Fly me!"

"Hey!" Eric said, with a laugh. "That's supposed to be *my* line."

"It's good to see you smile, Eric. See? This is how it works: once the day is over, we have a nice glass of wine, and a cigarette, and we forget all about the people on the plane—the passengers *and* the crew."

Eric's smile disappeared as the scene with the Almighty Titan flashed through his mind. "Oh, no, darling. If I live to be a hundred years old, that's one face—and one fucking name—that I'll *never* forget: Sizemore."

CHAPTER 19

The Messenger

On a late-summer morning, at exactly the wrong moment, the phone rang in Eric's apartment. "I'll get it!" he said, reaching across the bed.

"You... gotta be... kidding me!" said his bedmate, huffing and puffing.

"It might be crew scheduling. You know I'm on call." Eric picked up the phone. "Hello, this is—"

"Why didn't cha let the goddam machine pick it up?" A large, hairy hand smacked Eric's rear end. "Fuck, I was *that* close!"

"I'm sorry, could you hold for just a moment, please?" Eric quickly covered the mouthpiece. "Sammy, would you shut up! It's not going to kill you to wait for two minutes!"

Sammy retreated, glaring.

Eric cleared his throat. "Hello, thank you for waiting."

"Eric? *C'est toi?*"

"*Geneviève!* I can't believe it. How wonderful to hear your voice! Where are you?"

"I'm in Chicago. I'm so glad I reached you! They just called me out for a trip with a long New York layover tonight. Can you meet me for dinner?"

"Sure! I'm on call too, but I could try to get them to release me for the day. Where are you staying?"

"The Grand Hyatt on Forty-second Street. I'll be with crew of flight 134 from Chicago. Shall we meet in the lobby at six P.M.?"

"Perfect. If I do get a trip, I'll leave a message for you at the front desk. Otherwise, I'll see you then."

"Wonderful! I can't wait to see you."

"Me neither. *A bientôt*, Geneviève."

She giggled. "Tell your friend I'm sorry for interrupting! *A six heures, mon cher.*"

"Who was that?" Sammy demanded, as Eric, red-faced, hung up the phone.

"Geneviève. A friend from my training class, who's based in Chicago. I'm meeting her for dinner in the city tonight."

"Am I invited?"

"No, you'd be bored. It'll be a lot of yackety-yack about flying and people you don't know."

Sammy snorted. "As usual, I'm only good for one thing around here."

"That's right. And it's not for picking up your dirty socks." Eric started to get out of the bed. "I'd better call crew scheduling right now to see if they'll release me. I took a trip for them on a day off last week when they were desperate. Thank God they owe me a favor. I hope I have a clean shirt. I think I'll wear my—"

"Talk about yackety-yak. Why don't *you* stop yacking!" Sammy grabbed him by the ankle. "Get back over here and finish what you started." With his free hand, he took the phone off the hook. "Crew scheduling can fuckin' *wait*."

***

"There you are, darling!" At six o'clock, Eric looked up and saw and saw Geneviève floating toward him, blond and beautiful, wearing a white sundress and silver sandals. He was happy to see an old friend that he almost wept. "*C'est incroyable!*" he said, embracing her tightly. "I'm so happy to see you!"

"It *is* unbelievable!" replied Geneviève. "The two of us, together, in New York City of all places!"

"Do you realize that we've never seen each other anywhere besides the training center?"

"Oh, darling, don't even *mention* that place. That was the longest six weeks of my life. I still have nightmares about the food." She stood back for a moment. "Here, let me look at you. I've never seen you in such a tight-fitting shirt. Have you been spending a lot of time at the gym?"

He grinned. "Does it show?"

"*Mais oui.* You were always very trim, but you're much more muscular now."

"*C'est de riguer ici.* Every gay man in New York has a gym membership. That expense comes before food or clothes or anything else."

"Why?"

"Because the competition here is so fierce."

"Competition for what?'

"For other men."

She rolled her eyes. "*Oh, Mon Dieu!*"

"Now, let me look at *you!* Your hair is so much longer. What a change from that pixie cut! I love those soft curls."

"I started letting it grow the minute after we graduated. Luckily, my supervisor isn't a fanatic about hair length—or anything else. She uses good common sense and treats me like a human being. But Rose! Oh, *la pauvre!* She got stuck with a real Nazi, who's torturing her about her weight. I pray every day that she'll make it through this stupid probationary period without being fired. All these petty, senseless rules and regulations! Thank God we only have a few months to go." She sighed. "Only in America do they treat crewmembers like kindergarteners."

"I know, I know. Now, I want to hear everything—about Rose, and the fabulous penthouse apartment, and life in general. Are you hungry?"

"Starving. Where should we eat?"

"Gee, I don't know this particular neighborhood very well. Do you want to walk around for a bit until we find someplace that we both like? I'm open for anything but cheap Chinese."

"Sure. Lead the way!"

***

"*Eric, attends-moi!*"

He stopped and turned around, only to realize that she was half a block behind him. "Oh, Geneviève, I'm sorry!" He stopped to wait for her. "I was blathering on so much, I didn't realize that you weren't beside me anymore."

"You walk so fast now!"

"Force of habit. You have to move quickly here. There're just too many people on the street to go strolling." As he reached her, he pulled her against the façade of a building. "And whatever you do, don't stop in the middle of the sidewalk. They'll roll over you like an army tank."

"My savior!" said Geneviève, laughing. "It's that way in Chicago, too. I'm usually more alert. Right now, I'm just weak with hunger." She glanced at the awning above the doorway. "Trattoria Verrasso. Hey, look! A nice, little Italian restaurant, with air conditioning. And it's not too crowded. Shall we give it a try?"

"I'm game, but let's look at the menu first. I want to make sure it's not too, uh…"

"Pricey?"

"Well, yes."

"Darling, *don't* be shy. We're all living on the same terrible salary. I'd be happy to share a pizza and a carafe of good red wine."

"Perfect. *Allons-y.*"

***

"Don't you want some of these breadsticks, Eric?" Geneviève asked, as she nibbled. "They're delicious! Homemade, and dusted with fresh Parmesan cheese."

"No thanks. I'm trying to watch my starch intake. We have that pizza coming, you know. Now, first of all, tell me about Rose and how the two of you are getting along with your friend, Danielle."

"Well, the apartment is wonderful. It's a corner unit. The views alone are *spectacular.* The living room looks out on Lakeshore Drive. From the bedroom, downtown is laid out like a tray of Cartier jewels. At nighttime, it's sublime. Sometimes I sit and stare out the window for hours."

"That sounds wonderful. From my living room, I see an Indian restaurant across Queens Boulevard."

"Ah, but for you, Manhattan beckons! It's just a subway ride away—*quelle chance!* You know, today was the first time that I've ever flown into La Guardia. We went right up the East River. To see that skyline from the air—not in a movie or on TV—but the *real* thing, right below you... it's breathtaking."

"I know. After three months, I'm still glued to the window on final approach. I always wait until the last possible moment to take my jump seat. Of course, downtown Chicago is wonderful too. Have you been exploring on your days off?"

"Certainly. I've already been to the Art Institute three times. And the Sears Tower, and the Aquarium. I've taken several fascinating architectural tours too. Chicago has a great deal to offer."

"You and Rose must be having a grand time. Do you manage to get a lot of days off together?"

She shrugged. "Occasionally. Rose is a little less adventurous than I thought she'd be."

"That sounds like a diplomatic way of saying 'lazy.' "

"Don't put words in my mouth! Wait until I've had a little more wine. What about you? Is New York everything you dreamed it would be?"

"Absolutely! I'm in the city all the time on my days off."

"What do you do?"

"A lot of walking around mostly. I don't have money for much else. It doesn't matter. Just to be living here is such a thrill, and so different from what I'm used to. The flying here is great, by the way. I get a lot of transcons on reserve. I love flying the wide-body airplanes. Granted, L.A. isn't too exciting, but San Francisco is wonderful. I've been there twice. And I had a terrific long layover in Seattle last month."

"Oh, how exciting!" Her smile disappeared suddenly. "I've spent the summer 'touring' the Midwest. Whoever knew that it was so vast? Last month, I had three layovers in Rochester, Minnesota. A minimum of fifteen wheelchair passengers on every flight. The Mayo Clinic is there, you know."

"That doesn't sound very stimulating."

"It's not. Not to mention, the layover hotel used to be a mental hospital for the criminally insane."

"You're joking."

"I assure you that I am not. The rooms still reek of antiseptic cleanser. When I come home, it takes days to get that odor of my suitcase."

"Don't you get any Montreal trips? You're a French speaker, after all."

"Yes, once. It was part of a four-leg turnaround." She was looking more depressed by the moment. "I made all the French PAs. A Canadian passenger stopped me in the aisle to tell me that my French was unintelligible. *A Canadian*, complaining about the way I speak my native language! *Tu crois ça?*"

"*Un imbécile*," Eric replied, with a wave of his hand. "There's one on every flight."

"Just the same. I wish... never mind. Tell me more about you."

"New York isn't perfect, you know," he said, trying to cheer her up. "I don't always get the glamorous destinations. I've had my share of Ultra Jet trips, too."

"The Ultra Jet," Geneviève repeated contemptuously. "That's almost the only plane that we fly out of Chicago. What a perfectly ridiculous name for that horrible contraption!"

"It is a silly name, isn't it? You just know that some big queen in the marketing department came up with that one."

"It's so cramped and noisy in the back! I'll be deaf before I'm thirty. Not to mention the terrible smell from the lavatories, which, of course, are right next to our jump seats. We can't even sit in them after the service is over because of the endless line of people waiting to relieve themselves. It's the worst."

"Darling, I hate to say this, but you sound very unhappy."

"I'm not *miserable*. I know that we're still brand-new, and that the flying will get better. But... oh, Eric, I'm so envious of you! I wish that Rose and I had picked New York as a base when we had the chance in training!" She finished her second glass of wine and poured another. "Our living situation isn't working out as well as I thought it would."

"I'm sorry to hear that," said Eric, trying to conceal his satisfaction. He had hoped that they would all come to New York together, but Rose and Geneviève had chosen Chicago. Geneviève's friend, Danielle, had invited them to live with her rent-free and they couldn't pass up the opportunity .

"*Menteur!* You're so obvious! Please stop smirking when I'm about to pour my heart out."

"Sorry. Go on."

"Well, as you know, Danielle is one of my oldest friends. When she invited Rose and me to move in with her it was like a dream come true."

"It did seem like a Cinderella story."

"It didn't turn out that way. It seems we're around more often than Danielle thought we'd be. I had explained to her that we'd be on call, but I think Danielle thought that we'd be away for days at a time. I mean, come on! It's not like we fly to Patagonia. From Chicago, you can go to Milwaukee and back three times in one day and still be home for dinner. Sometimes she'll come home from work and say, 'Oh, you're still here?' as though I were a spoiled piece of fish that she forgot to throw out. Do you know what that feels like?"

"I'm sorry to say I know exactly how that feels."

"*Pauvre toi!* You'll have to tell me all about life with Anthony's brother. Anyway, at the beginning of August, Danielle suddenly switched jobs. She's no longer working for the French government, and *they* are no longer paying her rent. Guess how much that apartment goes for a month."

"A thousand dollars?"

"*Tu es fou?* On Lakeshore Drive?! Try *twenty-five hundred* dollars."

"Dear God! That's almost—"

"Nine hundred dollars apiece! Obviously, we'll have to move—and soon."

"But where will you go?"

"If Rose has her way, straight to the suburbs. *Mais je refuse!*"

"The suburbs?! Why?"

"Why else? *Le flic.*"

"*Quel flic?*"

"Darling, have you forgotten everything? You see, this is what happens when we don't make a concerted effort to stay in touch."

"I can't help it. You're never home when I'm home, and vice-versa."

I'm talking about Chuck. He's that policeman who was a passenger on your training flight with Rose, remember?"

"Oh, *him*. The big guy, with the beautiful furry forearms. I knew he was going to ask her out. I didn't know they had become an item."

"Well, they have. They're inseparable. It was love at first sight for him, and he hasn't let her out of his sight since we arrived."

"That could be good or bad."

"It's bad!" She pounded the table with her fist.

"Calm down, darling, before the waiter takes our wine away!"

"Sorry," she said, surprised by her outburst.

"You need to eat." He stroked her hand. "Look, our food is coming now."

"Here's your pizza," said the waiter, placing an aluminum pie stand on the table.

"Oooh!" cooed Geneviève. "Look, Eric! It's thin crust! They've never even *heard* of thin crust pizza on Chicago. All they like there is deep-dish; it's so goopy. Thank you, sir, this looks lovely. Would you bring us another carafe of wine, please?"

"Right away."

"Here, let me serve," said Eric. "Pass me your plate. Now, you were saying about Rose and Chuck?"

"It's bad, I tell you. Let's start at the beginning. Rose escapes from that small town in Texas, becomes a flight attendant, and starts a brand-new life, with a brand-new look, in Chicago. Yet, wherever she goes, there's a six-foot ape in a football jersey hovering nearby. She lets him monopolize all of her free time. I can't get her to a museum or a concert or anywhere else interesting."

"Well, he is quite handsome. I can see why someone like Rose would be smitten. I don't think she's dated very much. What's he like as a person?"

She rolled her eyes. "With him, we have to stick to three subjects: crime, the terrible Chicago winters, and the Bears."

"Which bears?"

"*Which* bears? They'd probably incarcerate you, Eric, just for asking that question! The Bears are the Chicago football team. Everyone there is obsessed with them, including Chuck and his friends—who are all cops, naturally—and their girlfriends. I spent an evening with them once. I was the only woman in the room wearing a skirt and high heels. The girlfriends wore acid-washed jeans and sneakers and they all have that same, terrible American hairdo—the long, frizzy perm with the bangs."

"Oh, how I hate that look! Were they nice at least?"

"Yes, but was a sports-themed party," she said, with great disdain. "We watched a videotape of highlights from the Bears' last season. The men brought cases of beer and the women brought food. You've never seen such a mountain of unhealthy food. Everything was deep-fried, even the cheese! These people exhibit no self-control at all. It's a completely toxic environment for Rose, don't you see?"

"Oh, dear God. And why is she considering moving to the suburbs?"

"Because *he* lives in the suburbs, and because it's so much cheaper than downtown. Eric, you can't believe how few flight attendants live in the city. Most of them don't even live anywhere near Chicago! They all commute to O'Hare on tiny airplanes from horrible little towns that I've never even heard of: Joliet, Bloomington, Travers City! They talk about nothing else but their commute the whole time that we're away. Then at the end of the trip, they will knock you down to get off the plane first." This all came out in a great jumble of words. "And what's worse, they seem to have no interests in life, other than their husbands and children. On the layovers, they lock themselves in their rooms with insulated food bags and a stack of magazines—always Hollywood gossip magazines! I don't know why they took this job in the first place. I can never get anywhere to go exploring with me." She looked as though she might burst into tears. "Needless to say, I'm always on my own."

"Say no more. We have the same appalling situation in New York. 'Gang way, y'all! I gotta get to my Nashville flight!' Or Rochester or Pittsburgh: just change the regional accent accordingly. I'll never commute! I chose New York, and I'm staying in New York. OK, maybe Queens isn't the most sophisticated neighborhood on earth. But I've got it all worked out. I'm saving every penny I can. Anthony will be back before Christmas, and we'll find a great apartment together in Manhattan. And once that happens, I'll be right where I want to be and living exactly the kind of life that I always wanted."

"Are you sure that you can count on Anthony to follow through with your plan?" she asked, raising one eyebrow.

Her tone of voice had changed so abruptly that Eric almost choked on his food. "Of course I can count on Anthony! Why on earth would you ask?"

"No reason in particular," she replied smoothly.

"Has something happened? Have you seen him? Or spoken to him?"

"No, I haven't seen him. But Rose has—just once, and she didn't really get a chance to talk to him. Nevertheless, I think you should have a backup plan, just in case."

"In case of what?"

In case of any unforeseen circumstances."

"Do you have a backup plan?"

She shrugged. "We're free to transfer after six months. You may be seeing a lot more of me."

"You mean, you're coming to New York?! Oh, how wonderful!"

"I'm merely considering it. Don't say a word to Rose if you talk to her."

"Why not? We're all friends. I hate keeping secrets among us."

"Nothing is definite yet."

"I see."

She patted Eric's hand. "Don't worry, I won't abandon Rose. I'll make sure she's settled in a decent apartment with a couple of nice girls. I'll do whatever I can, in fact, to put some space between her and Chuck. She needs some room to spread her wings. Oh, did I really say that? What a terrible pun. But it's true."

"You're a loyal friend, Geneviève."

"You are too, Eric. We're both loyal people. What a shame that we can't always expect the same from others."

He felt a chill run up his spine and helped himself to the last bit of wine in the carafe. "I still think there's something that you're not telling me."

"Darling, stop being so dramatic. It's just life. Sometimes things work out the way you want them to and sometimes they don't." She picked up the empty carafe. "Look at that. Not even one little drop left! Just as well. I'm a little drunk, and there's nothing worse than flying with a hangover." She motioned for the waiter. "Now, let's see what they have to offer for dessert."

***

Eric impatiently waited for the elevator in the lobby of his building. It had to be the slowest elevator in the whole city. After a few minutes, he decided not to wait and began running up the stairs. He *had* to go to the bathroom. He raced up four flights, frantically unlocked the door, and ran right into Sammy.

"Christ, what're you trying to do, kill me?"

"Sorry, bathroom emergency!" he blurted as he ran through the hallway.

"How was your dinner?" asked Sammy, following him.

"Very nice," said Eric, through the closed door. "Oh, God! Just in time!" He emerged a moment later, feeling greatly relieved. "Too much wine. I've had to pee since nine o'clock. I waited almost a half hour for the E train."

"That's what sucks about going out drinking in the city—having to piss like a mother-fucker on the way home."

"Why are the bathrooms in the subway stations always closed? It's ridiculous! I mean, why are they even *there* if they're never available?"

Sammy rolled his eyes. "Believe me, a bathroom in the subway station is the last place you want your dick hanging out. Well, I'm leaving, and I won't be back until late, so don't wait up for me."

"Where are you going?"

"Poker game around the corner."

"Another one?"

"My regular business has been slow."

"Sammy, please! Don't blow your rent money. It's due on Wednesday."

"Too late. I blew it last night. That's why I'm going back." He scratched the hair on his chest. "Do you have a trip yet for tomorrow?"

It's just like Genevieve said, thought Eric. They always want to know if you have a trip for tomorrow. "No. I'm on ready reserve. They'll call me if they need me."

"Oh, great. That means at five in the morning, right?"

"Just unplug the phone in the bedroom, Sammy, and keep your door closed. That way you won't be disturbed."

"So, you're sleeping out here tonight?"

"Yeah. I have a lot on my mind."

"Suit yourself. It's gonna be a scorcher."

"I'll live. Incidentally, Sammy, I don't think we should start making *that* a regular thing."

"What do you mean? You get me off once in a while when I'm horny. What's the big fucking deal?"

"Don't make it sound so one-sided. We get each other off. I just don't think—"

"End of subject. I'm outta here." He grabbed a package of cigarettes from Eric's shirt pocket. "You don't mind, do you? I'll pick some up later."

"Would you leave me a few, please, and maybe think about buying your own?"

He put three cigarettes on the coffee table. "You smoke too much."

"I'm quitting as soon as I get off reserve. I'm under a lot of stress right now."

Sammy snorted. "What fucking stress do *you* have? Christ, you should listen to yourself sometime. 'Should I party in the Village tonight or in Chelsea? When is scheduling going to call me with a trip? What should I say when I finally meet Liza Minnelli on a flight?' "

"Well, granted, I'm not relying on strangers to stuff my jock strap with cash for a living but—"

"I'm just saying be fucking grateful for what you do have that I wish I had. I don't even have health insurance. Do you know what happens to me if I break my leg?"

"Yes. The manager of Man's World has to call in your understudy. I bet you'd still do OK in the dressing room. Isn't that where you make the big bucks, anyway?"

Sammy's fist was suddenly an inch from his face. "That fat mouth of yours is gonna get you in trouble one day."

"Don't threaten me, you big goon. Your parole officer's number is taped to the refrigerator."

"Christ! I'm going. I hope you get your pantyhose untwisted by the time I get back."

"Don't rush. And if you're coming home broke, Sammy, don't come back at all. Why are you fucking with the rent money anyway?!" He heard the desperation in his voice and immediately regretted it.

Sammy had a dangerous gleam in his eye. "It'd be funny, wouldn't it, if we ended up with our asses out on the street and nowhere to go?"

"Hilarious. Don't forget to buy cigarettes. And not the generic brand."

"Nag, nag, nag," Sammy muttered on his way out the door.

Eric watched out the living room window until he was sure that Sammy had left the building. Then he sat down and nervously made a phone call to Dallas.

"Hel-looooo?" The man who answered the phone sounded drunk.

"Hello, can I speak to Anthony, please?"

"Oh... *Anthony*. He's not here."

"Can I leave a message?"

"Why, of course you can. We are his fulltime answering service, after all."

"Would you please—"

"We spend all day long taking messages for Mr. Bellini. Let me get another l'il slip of paper. What is your name, please?"

"This is Eric."

"And your last name?"

"Saunders."

"Next question: how much money do you make and what kind of car do you drive?"

"Excuse me?"

"Mr. Bellini must prioritize his calls. You don't expect him to call back just anybody, do you?"

Eric heard howls of laughter in the background. Then a man with a heavy southern accent said, "Give me that damn phone!" After a brief scuffle, a new person was on the line. "Hello?"

"Hello, this is Eric. I'm trying to reach—"

"Oh, hi, Eric. This is Dale."

"I remember you, Dale. How are you?"

"Fine."

"Who was that who answered the phone?"

"That was Craig, one of our other roommates."

"And the owner of this goddam whorehouse!" Craig yelled in the background.

"We just got back from a very long Happy Hour at the Mining Company," Dale explained. "Everyone's a little tipsy."

"Did Anthony go with you?"

"Anthony at the Mining Company?" Dale laughed. "That would be like asking Rockefeller if he wants dinner at Taco Bell."

"I take it he's not home."

"No, he's not."

"Is he on a trip?"

"I couldn't tell you. I haven't seen him for quite a while."

"Is he flying a lot?" Eric asked, trying to sound casual.

"No, I don't think so. We're a little overstaffed here at DFW. I only have thirty hours so far and it's almost the end of the month."

"Well... he's still *living* there, isn't he?"

"His stuff is still here."

"That's good to know," said Eric, somewhat relieved. "So I guess he's doing OK."

"*More* than OK. Anthony is *very* popular here. The phone never stops ringing. We're thinking of asking him to put in his own line."

"If you wouldn't mind taking one more message, would you tell him I called?"

"Sure. I'll leave it right on top of the stack in his bedroom. I'm walking in there as we speak. Boy, it's dusty in here. Hey, guess what he has on his dresser."

"What?"

"That picture you sent from the top of Empire State Building. He framed it. It's a great picture. But you look so sad!"

"Only because I was hoping to share that experience with him."

"You're awfully cute, Eric. Why don't you come on down here? We could get you matched up with a millionaire, too."

"Too? What do you mean by that, Drew?"

"Whoops! That's the other line. Gawd, I hope it's not crew scheduling. I won't be sober until noon tomorrow. I gotta go, Eric."

"Be sure to leave Anthony my—" *Click!* He stared at the phone for a moment, then hung it up and reached for a cigarette. As he lit it, he felt a drop of sweat fall from his forehead. He felt he was in a sealed coffin. He ran to the window and opened it as high as he could, thankful that the super had finally fixed it.

On the street below, there wasn't a soul in sight. They may as well roll up the sidewalk here at ten P.M., he thought. Even Pinocchio's would be dead; unless it was two-for-one night, that bar was like a graveyard. Besides, there was no sense in spending ten dollars for a cocktail when he could have one at home for free. He walked into the kitchen and poured himself a large glass of vodka on the rocks and then sat back down and lit another cigarette. He ruminated over his conversation with Genevieve. An alternate plan, he thought. I never *planned* on the need for alternate plan. What'll I do if Anthony doesn't... What if?... What *if?*

CHAPTER 20

The Great Divide

Boom, boom, boom! There was a loud knocking on the front door.

"Who the hell is that?" Eric asked, sticking his head out of the kitchen.

"I'll get it, I'll get it," said Sammy, running to answer the door. As Sammy opened it, Eric saw Santiago standing there, scowling as usual. The building superintendent was one of the most repulsive-looking men that Eric had ever met. He had a terrible comb-over and a huge pot belly that strained against the buttons of his blue work shirt. To make matters worse, he reeked constantly of marijuana and/or cheap cigars. "Hey, Santi, buddy! How're you doing?" said Sammy. Before Santiago could open his mouth, Sammy pushed him into the hall and closed the door behind them.

That's weird, thought Eric. Sammy never greets Santiago like that, and certainly never chats with him out in the hall. Something's up. Eric tiptoed to the front door and put his ear against it. No luck: it was solid metal. All that he could hear was a muffled conversation. As soon as he turned away, the two men began raising their voices. "And you know what's gonna happen if you don't have the money by tomorrow?" This was Santiago talking, obviously; Sammy always owed somebody fifty or a hundred dollars. Fortunately, Eric had learned right away never to leave his wallet within Sammy's reach.

"Shhh! Give me a fucking break, Santi, would you? I told you I'm good for it tomorrow."

"You better come through tomorrow. You have until five P.M. and not one minute later. I'll padlock that front door so fast, your greasy head'll spin."

"Fuck you. You can't do shit. We have a signed lease."

Alarm bells started going off in Eric's head. Whatever they were fighting about, it involved more than fifty or a hundred dollars.

"That's true," said Santiago. "But there's nothing to stop me from changing the locks. I've got rights, too, as the super of this building and so does the management company. They'd *love* to break your fucking lease. They could rent this place for twice what you're paying—or *not* paying, since July to be 'zact."

Eric's stomach dropped all the way to the floor.

"You better get that money to me, and fast. Or else you'll both be sleeping on the sidewalk tomorrow night." Santiago laughed. "I can just hear Eric crying like a baby, 'cause he can't get inside. I bet that stupid little shit don't even know what's going on."

Eric threw the door open. "What the hell *is* going on here?"

"That's what I'd like to know!" Their next-door neighbor, Mrs. Goldstein, had poked her head into the hallway.

"Nothin', Mrs. Goldstein," said Santiago. "I'm taking care of some building business. Sorry we bothered you."

"If this racket doesn't cease immediately, I'm calling the management office. I've had it! This was a *decent* building before they moved in. Get rid of those *bums!*" She slammed the door.

"Get back inside there, both of you," said Santiago. "And keep it down for the rest of the day." He smirked. "Eric, I think Sammy has some explainin' to do."

Eric resisted the urge to slam the door as hard as he could. "This is bad news, isn't it?" he asked, once he and Sammy were back inside.

"There's something I gotta talk to you about. Sit down."

"Should I make myself a drink first?"

"No, we both need clear heads right now. I'll buy you a beer later." As they sat down on the sofa, Sammy helped himself to one of Eric's cigarettes. "Here's the deal: I'm behind on the rent."

"That's impossible. I've dropped off both our rent checks myself for the past two months."

"I know. The thing is, I wrote a couple of bum checks." He said this as casually as though he'd stolen a packet of gum from the drugstore.

"And how is it that—"

"That you didn't know? You haven't been around when the late notices came. I've done a good job of covering. And Santi's been cool about keeping this just between him and me—until now."

"Well…" Eric took a deep breath. "They don't call you Sammy the Snake for nothing. How much are you behind?"

"A thousand dollars."

"A *thousand* dollars?"

"Yes. If I don't have it by tomorrow, *which I will*, Santi's going to lock us out, or so he says. That's the whole story. But don't get all excited, because I will have that money, every penny of it."

"How are you going to come up with a thousand dollars by tomorrow morning?" His voice had become so shrill that he didn't even recognize it.

"Don't get all excited. Christ, you act like such a fucking fish wife sometimes! I'll have it by tonight."

"What's happening tonight?"

"A poker game with these three *dumbassimos* from Long Beach. It's a sure thing. They're all lousy players. There's no way I *can't* win. I just need to borrow a couple of hundred dollars to get into the game. Could you—"

"Are you crazy? I'm not lending you a goddam dime!"

"Then get ready to start panhandling with me in front of the Chase Bank."

"You're not dragging *me* into this mess. Call Anthony and ask him for the money."

"God, you're so fucking dense. How is Anthony gonna loan me that much? He makes the same shitty salary that you do."

"Then get on the phone and start calling your johns."

"What johns?"

"Your 'body rub' clients. I've seen your ad, Sammy. Granted, your face wasn't in the picture, but I know that torso like the back of my hand. And I've answered the phone a couple of times while you were out. I know how you make money when you need fast cash."

"There's nobody to call. It's the end of August. My regulars are all out of town. Besides, *they* call me. I don't call *them*."

"Then you better think of another option, and fast."

"OK. Here's one solution. How about a modeling gig?"

"What modeling agency are *you* signed up with?"

"I know a guy who's been after me for a while to take some pictures. He does really classy stuff. He'd pay double for the two of us. You wouldn't even have to show your face. I mean, you could wear a baseball cap pulled down over your eyes, and—"

"You want me to do *porn* to pay *your* rent?! No, no, no!" Eric jumped up. "You listen to me: ever since I moved in here, I've lived on practically *nothing*. I've gone without basics. I've stayed here at night or splurged on a few beers at that shithole on Queens Boulevard instead of going into the city. I've taken food off the airplane for my layovers and eaten canned tuna at home until I was ready to puke, because the rent comes first—*cardinal rule!* I was being responsible, which I promised your brother I would be. If you think I'm going to be locked out, or evicted, or that I'm going to hole up in operations at JFK until you get this mess straightened out, you're out of your fucking mind." Spittle was flying out of his mouth. "You get that goddam money, or I swear to God I'll kill you. And I'm not kidding, Sammy. I'll slit your throat and enjoy every moment of it."

Sammy didn't flinch. "The poker game is my only option. That's *it*."

"Wait a minute," said Eric. "Why didn't I think of this in the first place? Call your parents."

"My parents? *Now* who's out of their fucking mind? No way."

"Why not?"

"Because it's useless. They'll say no. They always say no. They think I'm a bum, too."

"Who can blame them? But you're going to try anyway. This is an emergency. They wouldn't let their own son get thrown out on the street."

"That's what you think."

"Eric tossed the cordless phone at Sammy. "Call them, right this minute."

"You don't *call* Italians and ask for money. You go grovel for it in person."

"Then get going."

"Not unless you come with me."

"I don't even know them!"

"No, but you're a friend of Anthony's. He's always been their fucking favorite. Maybe, just *maybe*, if you're there, it'll be harder for them to say no. But it's a slim fucking chance."

"All right. I'll come with you. Put your shoes on. We're going right now."

Sammy slapped himself on the forehead. "Christ, I can't believe I'm doing this… again! Give me ten minutes to wrap my head around it."

"No. Stop stalling. *Now*."

"I'll need a drink afterward. A big, fucking drink. Anyway, what are we gonna do if they do say no?"

"Don't even *think* that. Are we taking the bus or the subway?"

"We're walking. They live just a few blocks from here on 108th Street."

"That close? Then how come we never see them?"

"Christ, Eric, haven't you figured *that* out by now?"

***

They waited at the corner for almost five minutes to cross to the north side of Queens Boulevard. But wait they did: jaywalking across the eight-lane thoroughfare was not only illegal, it was suicidal. Pedestrians were killed by speeding cars on a regular basis. Newspapers referred to it as 'the Boulevard of Death.'

As an oddly-dressed woman lugging a shopping cart passed by them, Sammy shook his head. "Christ, this neighborhood *sucks*."

"Why do you say that?"

"Look around you! Nothing but freaks living here. Butt-ugly *freaks*. I mean, I know they're old, but don't these hags even look in the fucking mirror before they leave the house?"

On a certain level, Eric had to agree. Since moving to Queens, he had never seen so many disheveled women in one place in his life. Wigs were askew. Patterned sweaters and plaid woolen skirts, worn even on the hottest summer days, clashed violently. Tan stockings were rolled down past the knees.

Collectively, they wore the ugliest shoes ever manufactured. To be fair though, thought Eric, elderly men in the neighborhood didn't dress much better.

They crossed the boulevard and turned onto 108th Street. Two blocks later, Anthony stopped in front an apartment building. "Well, this is it." It was a two-winged high-rise with a circular driveway, neatly trimmed hedges, and landscaped flowerbeds. The grounds were immaculate; there wasn't a cigarette butt or a scrap of paper anywhere. The entrance was protected by a large green awning. Across the awning, *La Marseille* was written in white cursive lettering.

"Your parents live *here?*"

"Yeah, what about it?"

"This is nice. I mean, it's a *named* building. We only have a street numbers above our entryway."

"Big deal. It just means they charge you more rent."

"Have they lived here very long?"

"Since I was a kid."

"Wow. Your father's restaurant must do very well."

"Listen, don't make any dumb comments like that in front of my folks, all right?" He stomped out his cigarette in the street. "Now, let's plan our strategy. First, we got to get past the doorman."

"There are doormen buildings in Queens?"

"You don't know anything, do you? Of course there are." He jerked his head toward a hawk-nosed man standing in front of the entrance. "That's Reggie, in the white shirt and black pants. He works the day shift."

"Why isn't he wearing a braided uniform jacket, like the doormen in Manhattan?"

"Because he's a doorman in *Queens.*"

"Well," said Eric, "his shirt's tucked in, at least."

They stood for a moment and watched Reggie go inside.

"Let's go," said Sammy. "Just play it cool and let me do the talking." They entered the spacious lobby. "Hey, Reggie," said Sammy, as they approached the front desk.

"You're still around?" said the doorman. "Gee, I thought you'd be dead by now. Or locked up, at least."

Sammy ignored the remark. "I'm here to see my mom."

"You called first, right? Mrs. Bellini doesn't like drop-ins, especially when it's *you* dropping in."

"Funny guy. Just buzz her and tell her I'm coming up, would you? Come on, Eric." He started walking to the elevator.

"Hold it right there," said the doorman. "I have strict orders to follow. Before I can let you up, I'm supposed to call first." He picked up the phone and dialed. "Mrs. Bellini, this is Reggie at the front desk. Samuel is here with—" he looked suspiciously at Eric "—a young man."

"Tell her that he's Anthony's friend from the airline."

Reggie relayed the information. "All right, I'll tell him." He hung up the phone. "You'll have wait. For how long, I don't know. She'll call me when she's ready for you."

"What, I'm supposed to just hang around the lobby all day?"

Reggie shrugged. "She's probably looking for a new place to hide her purse from you. Have a seat."

Fifteen minutes later, they were finally in the elevator headed for the 10th floor.

"I guess you're still doing all the talking, huh?" said Eric.

"No, you can talk. She likes clean-cut guys." He made 'clean-cut' sound like a dirty word. "It's *me* she doesn't like. I'll ask about the money, but I'll play that by ear."

They exited on the top floor and started walking down the long, carpeted hallway. "They're in 10M, all the way at the end," Sammy said. Eric was still surprised that the Bellinis lived in a luxury building. Anthony hadn't spoken much about his family while he and Eric were in training. Nevertheless, Eric had always pictured them living in a cramped apartment, one floor above the family business. Mr. Bellini would be eternally in the restaurant, wringing his hands over the lack of customers on slow nights. His mother would be chained to the stove in their apartment upstairs, wiping sweat from her brow as she stirred an enormous pot of marinara sauce. He imagined Anthony and Sammy fighting over the remote control in the living room and breaking a $25 lamp from Sears during the ruckus. The younger sister would be hiding on the fire escape, writing about her dreary life in a leatherette-bound diary and praying for something, *anything* to change.

As they reached the end of the hallway and Sammy rang the doorbell, Eric had no idea what to expect. He certainly wasn't prepared for the door to be opened by a slim, attractive brunette wearing a red sequined pantsuit and satin pumps. Mrs. Bellini stood rather theatrically in the doorway, with one hand on her hip and the other resting on the door handle. Her pageboy haircut framed her face perfectly. Light from the hallway sparkled off the sequins. "Hello, Samuel." Her voice was low and husky, like Anne Bancroft's. Eric was immediately enthralled. "Well, what do you want?"

"Aren't you going to ask us in?"

"I'm very busy right now. Who's this with you?"

"This is Eric, Anthony's friend from training. You know, he's been living with me until Anthony comes back."

"It's nice to meet you, Mrs. Bellini."

"How do you do," she said curtly.

"*Now* can we come in?"

"For five minutes only. I already told you, I'm busy." She stepped aside, allowing them to enter. "And whatever you want, Samuel, the answer is *no*."

The apartment was enormous and elegantly decorated. Beautifully framed artwork graced the walls. An entire wall was lined with books about art, theatre, and dance. Mrs. Bellini invited them to sit down on the large sectional sofa and perched herself across from them on the edge of an armchair. Eric noticed an ashtray on the large glass coffee table. "May I smoke?"

"Out on the terrace," she said. "But it's very hot out there in the afternoon. We face west."

Wow, thought Eric, a west-facing terrace on a high floor! He started to stand up, but then realized that it might appear rude to leave the room so soon. "Thank you. I'll wait."

"Aren't you going to sit down?" Sammy asked, as his mother continued to perch.

"I can't. I'm pinned together."

"Nice outfit," said Sammy. "A little splashy for daytime, don't you think?"

"This isn't an outfit. It's a work of art. Your sister designed this. It's her summer project at Parson's."

"She's still at that, huh?" he asked skeptically.

"How dare you use that tone. Your sister has an incredible talent. You couldn't even *conceive* of something this beautiful, much less execute the final product. That would require effort on your part."

"The detailing is extraordinary," said Eric. "I can just see you wearing that to the Met Gala."

"What a lovely thing to say," said Mrs. Bellini. "I'm sure she'd appreciate hearing it." She turned her head. Her profile was magnificent. "Angelina! Come out here for a moment."

Eric heard a door open. "I'm right in the middle of something, Mother."

"*Now.* I want you to meet someone."

"Just a second." A young woman entered the room. She was short and plain-faced with dark hair pulled back in a ponytail. The contrast between mother and daughter was almost shocking.

"This is Eric. He's a friend of Anthony's from the airline."

"Oh?" said Angelina. "How is Anthony? We haven't heard from him in quite a while."

"To tell you the truth, I haven't either," said Eric. "It's hard to stay in touch when we're both flying all the time."

She grunted. "We never hear from Anthony even when he *isn't* flying."

"Never mind," said Mrs. Bellini. "Angelina, Eric paid you a very nice compliment about your work. Why don't you show him your studio? It seems that your brother wants a word with me, anyway."

"OK." Eric followed her down a hallway and into a bedroom that had been converted into a design studio. Angelina had a sewing machine, a professional dress form, and a three-way mirror. Swatches of fabric and design sketches were pinned to the wall. A collection of evening gowns hung on a rolling rack. "This is impressive," he said.

"My parents have been very generous. They believe in my talent."

"Well, it's obvious that you're very talented. Those gowns are beautiful."

"Thank God I have *something* to offer."

"What do you mean?"

She smiled weakly. "Please don't play dumb. Everyone always compares me to them. Don't tell me you didn't do it the minute you saw me. My brothers got the good looks—both of them—from my mother. All three of them are so goddam beautiful. Even Sammy, with that hideous scar. My girlfriends were always chasing him in high school. I take after my father. Nobody chases me."

"I'm sorry," he said, not knowing what else to say.

She shrugged. "I used to wail about how unfair it was, but that's the way it goes. In the fashion world, it works in my favor. The customers are the ones who are supposed to look great in the clothes, not me." She pulled an evening gown with a plunging neckline from the rack and showed it to him. "This is one of the newest. I couldn't wear it in a million years. But my mother was born for clothes like this. She models for me all the time. She was a dancer before she got married—with New York City Ballet. She still looks and carries herself like a dancer. That's what makes her such a great model."

"They're fantastic designs," said Eric. "I'm sure you'll have a very successful career."

"Thanks. That's nice to hear. So why are you hanging out with Sammy the Snake?"

"We're just roommates. It's temporary. I'm waiting for Anthony to come back."

"I wouldn't wait too long. Anthony is just as bad as Sammy. It just takes people a little longer to catch on. If I were you—"

"*Basta!*" Mrs. Bellini shouted from the living room. "I said no! And that's final."

Eric's heart sank. "I think it may be time for us to go."

"I have work to do anyway. Nice meeting you."

Eric walked back into the living room, where Mrs. Bellini stood with her arms folded across her chest. Sammy was still sitting on the sofa, looking down at the floor. He had no expression on his face at all.

"Samuel, before you leave, I want you to go and spend two minutes with your sister. Say something nice to her for once. Eric, come out on the balcony. You can have your cigarette and look at the view."

Eric followed her onto the terrace.

"Have a seat," she said, as she sat down at the small patio table. "May I have one of your cigarettes?"

"Sure." He passed one to her. They smoked quietly together, admiring the view of the Manhattan skyline. Although it was a bit difficult to see through the haze, it was still beautiful.

"It's always hazy like this is in the summer," said Mrs. Bellini. "But in the fall and spring, on a clear day... my God, you'd think you could reach right across the river and touch the skyscrapers. I miss Manhattan."

Eric nodded. "I'm looking forward to moving there—eventually."

"Then you better start saving every penny you can. Manhattan is not for poor people."

"In this city, every facet of life seems to come down to having money—or the lack of it."

"That sums up life in general. By the way, Samuel told me everything. But I'm not giving him any money. I'll never be paid back, and in three months he'll come back asking me for more. My husband and I are tired of being treated like an ATM."

"I understand," he said, although he didn't understand at all. What the fuck! She *knows* we'll be out on the street!

Mrs. Bellini sighed. "Samuel... one of my own. What a wasted life! Nevertheless, Eric, I do understand the situation that you're in through no fault of your own. You must keep a roof over your head. Tell me, have you paid next month's rent yet?"

"No. It's not due until tomorrow."

"Then don't pay it. Get out right now. You don't owe my son any loyalty. Find yourself a crash pad in Kew Gardens. There are always notices posted in the crew lounge. You could move in tomorrow, live very cheaply, and start saving."

"Mrs. Bellini, do you know what it's like living in an airline crash pad?"

"Yes, I do. When I was starting my career, I lived with five other dancers in a railroad apartment in Hell's Kitchen. It was a fourth-floor walkup with a bathroom in the hallway and no air conditioning. We survived because we *wanted* to be there." She put out the cigarette. "If you want to stay in New York and have the kind of life that I think you want, you'll have to do it the hard way like everyone else. And that's all the motherly advice I have for you today."

"What about Anthony's furniture and other stuff?" he said, playing what he thought was his trump card. "It'll all be locked up in storage somewhere."

"Let Anthony worry about that. He's made some poor decisions, too."

"Don't you worry about what's going to happen to Sammy?"

"I gave up worrying about Samuel years ago." She opened the terrace door and followed him inside. "Thanks for the cigarette. Good luck. And now my daughter and I have to get back to work."

***

"Well," said Eric, as they walked back to the elevator, "at least you—"

"Shut up, Eric," said Sammy. "Just shut up. Don't make me say 'I told you so.'"

They rode down to the lobby in silence. Once they were back on the street, Eric stopped and turned to Sammy. "I just want to say I know that was hard for you and I'm sorry you walked away empty-handed."

"Not completely empty-handed."

"Oh, Christ, what did you steal, and how? I was there the whole time."

"Nothing." He held out his hand. "She gave me this."

"*This* is what your immediate future is riding on? A New York Lottery scratch-off card?"

"See what she thinks of me? She wouldn't even give me a fucking dime to scratch it *off* with."

"I give up," said Eric, shaking his head. "I'm heading home."

"Would you buy me a beer on the way?"

"You said you were buying *me* a beer. If you want a drink, there's a little vodka left in the house."

"Dream on."

"God damn you, Sammy!"

"Would you buy us some cigarettes at least?"

"Oh, Lord! Does that hand of yours *ever* stop reaching into other people's pockets?"

***

As Eric sat on the stoop, smoking a cigarette, he heard the front door open behind him. Mrs. Goldstein stepped out in a flower print dress and high heels, clutching her purse. "Excuse me," she said, walking past him.

"That's a lovely outfit," Eric said, immediately feeling like Eddie Haskell complimenting Mrs. Cleaver on a sweater set and pearls.

"Don't leave your cigarette butts on the stoop!" she replied, without turning around. "Take them out to the street."

A moment later, the door opened again. It was Santiago. With a loud groan, he sat down next to Eric and lit a foul-smelling cigarillo.

Christ, thought Eric, as the noxious cloud of smoke hit him in the face. Everything about that man stinks!

"How you figured out what *you're* gonna do?" Santiago asked.

"I thought you might give me a break, Santiago. I *have* followed the rules and paid my share of the rent."

"Oh, so now *you* want a favor from *me*, huh? What you have ever done for me?"

"Exactly what were you expecting?"

"Think about it: what did you say every time I asked you to bring me back a bottle of Dewars from the duty-free shop at the airport?"

"I told you every time: I fly domestic. I can't buy liquor in the duty-free shop."

"That don't matter. You could have taken the hint. You could have bought me even a pint of Dewars at the liquor store around the corner, just to be nice. Instead, what did you bring me over and over? Those goddam, greasy leftover cookies from the airplane."

"I thought you liked them. My co-workers said that everyone loved our baked-on-board cookies."

"What am I, a fuckin' pig in a trough? I don't eat that shit. You know what I used to do with those cookies? I'd throw 'em right in the trash." He laughed nastily. "I hope you got someplace to go, at least temporarily. I don't think the Snake is going to pull through this time."

"I'm already—"

"Eric! ERIC!"

Eric looked around. Who the hell would be yelling his name on Queens Boulevard?

"Over here!" It was Sammy, who was jumping up and down on the other side of the street. Eric had *never* seen him jump up and down, for any reason.

Sammy yelled something, but Eric couldn't hear him over the roar of passing traffic. He cupped his hands to his mouth and shouted, "I can't hear you!"

"It paid! It paid BIG!!!"

The scratch-off card. No, that's impossible, thought Eric. That kind of thing only happens in movies.

"PROBLEMS SOLVED! *THREE FUCKIN' G's!*" Sammy started running across the street. "Hey, Santiago! Go *fuck* yourself, you dickhead! We're staying right—"

Eric watched as Sammy went flying through the air, still clutching the scratch-off card. The black SUV didn't even stop. The driver, a young woman with long blond hair, covered her mouth and hit the gas pedal. She was gone before Eric could even try to read the license plate. He turned away as Sammy hit the ground with a sickening thud. He sat glued to the stoop, unable to move or even utter a sound. In a millisecond, all of his recent emergency training had fled, rendering him completely useless.

"Go to the bodega next door, call 9-1-1," Santiago shouted, as he bolted down the steps. "Move it, MOVE IT!"

Eric ran to the store on the corner. "Ambulance! We need an ambulance!"

"I already called," said the clerk, who was standing in the doorway. "I saw the whole thing. Oh my God, oh my God! The carnage on this street! When will it ever *end?*"

***

An hour later, after the paramedics had taken Sammy away and the police had finished questioning him, Eric was finally back inside the apartment. The police had given him none of Sammy's belongings because they'd found nothing on his person: no wallet, no ID, no cash, not even the scratch-off card. Unfortunately, for everyone involved, Santiago had gotten there first.

Eric picked up the phone and dialed Anthony's house in Dallas. After four long rings, someone finally answered.

"Hello?"

Eric recognized the voice immediately. It was Craig, the older roommate—the one who drank. "Craig, this is Eric. I—"

"Hey, Drew, get this!" Craig yelled. "It's the Crisis Queen from Queens on the line! Well, Eric, it's been a while since we've heard from you. How's every little thing up there?"

"Craig, I need to speak to Anthony. It's urgent. Is he there?"

"No, he's not. Hang on a sec. Drew, pour me another Jack Daniels and Coke, would you? Make it a double this time!"

"Craig, this is an *emergency*. Is Anthony away on a trip? Do you know where I can reach him?"

"Sorry, darlin', but I can't help you. Anthony doesn't live here anymore."

"What?! Since when? Did he—"

"Whoops, there's another call coming in. Gotta go. Nighty night, Eric."

"Craig, wait! Please!"

Click.

"Hello! *Hello?!!*"

CHAPTER 21

The Reality Check

Two days later, after spending a sleepless night in his hastily arranged new home, Eric was on a dreaded 5:00 A.M. standby shift at JFK. He signed in, drank a large cup of black coffee, and then sat bolt upright in a chair trying to stay awake. The room was almost pitch black. In order to accommodate the spillover of commuters from the sleep room, the lights in operations were never turned on until 6:00 A.M. By 5:30, he was sound asleep. He didn't even stir when he was paged over the loudspeaker. A few minutes later, he was roused by someone gently tapping his arm.

"Wake up, Sleeping Beauty."

He opened his eyes, squinting from the glare of fluorescent lights. A uniformed stranger was standing over him. "Are you Eric?"

"Yes."

"Sorry to disturb you, sugar, but you have a trip."

He immediately sat up, surprised at how quickly he became alert. "Where to?"

"You're on the seven o'clock to L.A. My name's Sue. I'm the purser. You're my galley up front. It's just breakfast, so it'll be easy as pie. We're heading down to the plane right now. We'll see you in a few minutes. Gate 42."

"I'll grab my suitcase and come with you."

"Maybe you want to freshen up a bit first."

He was horrified. "Oh, God, what is it? Hair bump, stale breath, something in my nose?"

She laughed. "A little mouthwash rinse and you'll be fine."

"Candi, *hi!*" someone shrieked from across the room.

"Carrie, Jill! I'm so glad you made it!"

He looked over and saw three women in a group hug.

"Where's Joanne?"

"She's right behind us."

"I thought you were gonna be no-shows!"

"We almost *didn't* make, Candi. There was a jack-knifed eighteen-wheeler on I-95. The cops had three lanes merging into one. It was insanity!"

"Hey!" someone yelled from a sofa in the corner. "Do you mind? I'm trying to *sleep* here!"

"Sorry!" said Candi. "*We* just happen to be *working* flight attendants!"

"Oh, dear," said Sue. "Obviously, those three got to bed very early last night."

"Where are they going?" Eric asked.

"They're coming with us to L.A. But don't worry, they're back in coach. And we have business class as a buffer. You won't even know they're there."

"Thank God for small favors."

Sue nodded. "He does work in mysterious ways."

***

Once the crew had boarded, Sue called everyone to the front for a pre-flight briefing. As she rattled off details about the flight, Eric noticed that as usual on early morning flights, he was the only male. It seemed that most gay men in New York preferred flying later in the day. Nevertheless, the eight flight attendants seemed friendly and made him feel like he was a welcome addition to the crew.

After takeoff, Eric and Sue served breakfast efficiently with a minimum of extraneous conversation. As soon as they had finished, Sue dimmed the cabin lights. Eric was just about to sink a fork into a leftover omelet when Candi came tearing into the galley.

"Don't eat that junk, Eric!" she exclaimed. "We have a whole buffet set up in the back. We all brought stuff."

"Candi, *shh!*" said Sue. "Everyone's sleeping here."

"Oops, sorry!" said Candi, covering her mouth.

"I heard you talking about the buffet earlier," said Eric. "But I got this trip at the last minute and I didn't bring anything to contribute."

"What difference does that make, baby boy? We have *tons* of food. You come back right now and eat something."

"Do you need some plates?" asked Sue.

"Oh, no, thanks," said Candi. "I brought Chinet plates, plastic cutlery—the works. The only thing I need from y'all is a real knife. Well, that and a pitcher of mimosas, *tee hee!*"

Sue handed her a knife. "Before we land, I'll make some crew juice for the van ride. No one is drinking champagne here in first today."

"Perfect!" said Candi. "See you in a few."

"Do you want to go back first?" Eric asked Sue.

"No, you go right ahead," she said, picking up a copy of *The Post.* "I've flown with those chatterboxes two months in a row, and I get enough of them on the layover. But bring me back a muffin. Candi does make fabulous homemade muffins."

Eric put his untouched omelet back in the oven. As he walked from first class all the way back to coach, he noticed that almost every passenger on the plane was asleep. Well, that was *one* benefit of working a 7 A.M. cross-country flight.

The flight attendants in coach were all abuzz over the selection of food displayed on the galley counters. There was a large bowl of mixed fruit; a tray of assorted bagels with three kind of cream cheese; a platter of sliced salmon, tomatoes and onions; a box of glazed donuts; and a basket of blueberry muffins tagged with a label that read: "Baked with love in Candi's Kitchen!"

"Is everything ready?" Candi asked excitedly.

Joanne opened the oven door and reached inside. "One more minute for the quiche," she said. "Why don't you all start with some fruit salad?"

"I think we should wait for the girls in business class," said Jill. "It will look rude if we start without them."

"That's silly," said Joanne. "We can't *all* fit in this galley at one time. Besides, they haven't offered us so much as a croissant from their own oven today. And you *know* they've already all had at least one apiece, if not two."

"I'm off starch completely," said Jill. "Not even a cracker has passed through my lips since Memorial Day."

"Check the quiche again, Joanne," chirped Candi. "I just can't WAIT to taste it."

"It's ready!" said Jo Anne. She pulled a pie tin out of the oven and proudly set it on the counter.

"That," said Candi, "is the most *beautiful* quiche I have ever seen! I want a great, big slice!"

"You may want to wait a minute," said Jo Anne, with a grin. "I have a surprise for you." She removed another pie tin from the oven. "Ta da!"

"Oh my God!" said Candi. "You baked two?!"

"Yes. This quiche is asparagus and mushroom. And *this* quiche is spinach and sun-dried tomatoes."

"Oh, Lord!" said Candi. "How am I going to decide which one to have?"

"I'm in a bit of quandary myself," said Joanne. "Personally, I like spinach and mushrooms together. I'm not crazy about either asparagus *or* tomatoes."

"Then why didn't you make a spinach and mushroom quiche?" Eric asked sensibly.

"No, I couldn't!" said Jo Anne. "One of these recipes is my mother's. The other is my aunt's. Heaven forbid I should mix the two!"

"I know what you mean," said Candi. "I have three hand-written recipe books at home. One is my mother's, one is my grandmother's, and the third is my great-grandmother's. And *Lordy*, do those women know their recipes! If I'm cooking for a family dinner, and I substitute even *one* ingredient, watch out! It's like starting World War Three! I remember last Thanksgiving I decided to make stuffing with–"

"Oh, yes, you told us that story on the last trip. Twice," said Joanne. "Well, dig in everybody."

Thank God Joanne interrupted her, thought Eric. I have a feeling that story would have gone on forever.

"Oh, wait!" said Joanne. "I just realized. I have to slice them first! Now, let's see: should I cut each one into six slices or eight slices?"

"Gosh, I guess it depends on what people want," said Carrie. "Do you think one quiche will be more popular than the other?"

"You can never tell," said Jo Anne. "Some people don't like asparagus, but they do like mushrooms. And then, some people *love* asparagus and *hate* mushrooms."

"I like fresh, steamed asparagus," said Jill. "The trick is not to overcook it." She sighed. "I've never learned that trick."

"Ha!" said Candi. "I'll give you my grandmother's recipe. It's foolproof!"

"Now let me see," said Joanne, with the knife still in her hand. "There are nine of us altogether. If I cut each one into six pieces, that's twelve slices. If I cut them into eight, that's more variety for everyone, but they'll be much smaller slices. I wonder how hungry everyone is."

"I'm pretty hungry!" said Candi.

"I might nibble a little of the insides, but I can't have any crust," said Jill. "I'm off starch completely, since–"

"Memorial Day," said Eric.

"Hey, you have a good memory!"

"Well," said Joanne, "I suppose I could always bring the leftovers to the hotel. I forget, are there refrigerators in our rooms at this hotel?"

"Yes," said Candi. "On floors one through five."

"No, honey, that's at the Marriott," said Jill. "We're at the Westin today. Those Westin rooms don't have refrigerators. I mean, there's not one in the room, but the front desk will send someone up with a mini-fridge if you ask them. Of course, it takes forever to get the darn thing delivered, and then you have to plug it in, and wait for it get cold, and–"

"If you're worried about leftovers," said Eric, as his temples throbbed, "maybe you could offer some food to the cockpit."

"Oh, no!" said Joanne, "they get REAL crew meals, and God forbid they ever offer them to us. No, the pilots are not getting one single bite of *my* quiche today!"

"Tell you what," said Eric. "Why don't I run up to business and see which type they want? Then you'll know exactly how many slices of each to cut."

"Oh no, don't do that!" said Candi. "By the time you get back, the quiche will be cold!"

If I hear the word 'quiche' one more time, Eric thought, I'm going to pick one up and hit somebody over the head with it.

"Besides, you know how Betty is," said Joanne. "The minute that I've finished slicing, she'll change her mind."

"Excuse me," said a passenger. "Could I have a glass of orange juice?"

"We just went through the cabin twice, sir," said Joanne. "Didn't you get anything to drink then?"

"I was asleep."

"I'll get it for him," said Carrie, pouring out a glass.

"That looks delicious," said the passenger, pointing to the pie tins. "Is that on the bill of fare this morning?"

"No, sir," said Jo Anne. "We made all this at home and brought it for ourselves."

"What did you serve to us poor slobs in the cabin?"

"Cheerios with a banana and a blueberry muffin." She pulled out a tray for him. "Here you are."

"Cheerios? That's it? Don't you have anything hot?"

"We had omelets, but we ran out of them by row twenty. Cheerios are what we have left over."

"I'd rather have something hot."

"We don't *have* anything hot."

He pointed to the quiche. "*That's* hot."

"Yes, but that's for us. We *made* it at home and *brought* it for ourselves."

"*Four* of you are going to eat all that?"

"It's for the whole crew. Now, sir, if you want this cereal, please take it to your seat."

"This *sucks,*" he said. He took the tray and left, grumbling all the way.

"Now, where was I?" said Joanne

"You were about to cut the quiches," said Candi.

"I hope they're still warm. Don't flip out anybody, my hands are clean!" Joanne felt the edge of the crust. "Oh, no! Now they're cold! I'll have to put them back in the oven."

Resisting the desire to slam his head against the wall, Eric put down his plate and spun around.

"Where are you going?" said Carrie.

"To eat my omelet in first class."

"But we have all this good food!" said Joanne.

"Save me something. I'll have it later."

"Which quiche do you want us to save for you?"

"Surprise me." He walked back up to first class, where Sue sat knitting a sweater.

"How was the smorgasbord?" she asked.

"It's bedlam back there. Where do they get the energy to talk so much and with such fervor about *nothing* so early in the morning?"

"They're wired differently than we are, " she said with a grin. "Did you bring me a muffin?"

"Oh, hell. I forgot!"

"Don't worry, I'll call Candi and ask her to save me one. What did you have to eat?"

"Nothing. I'll settle for my omelet."

"Oh, I'm sorry, honey, it's gone."

"Gone where?"

"The captain called and wanted to know what else we had to eat. You went to enjoy the buffet in coach, so I gave him your omelet."

"You're kidding me. Didn't the pilots already eat their *own* meal? We don't even get a crew meal on transcons, and they're scarfing what little food we have left over?"

"I'm really sorry, Eric. Next time write your name on the container before you put it back in the oven. That means 'hands off,' regardless."

***

Before landing, Eric was summoned to the back by Jo Anne. "Come and get it before we have to start putting everything away."

"Which quiche do you have left?" he asked, when he reached the galley.

"None, I'm afraid."

"None? No quiche? No quiche *at all?* What happened to the quiche? Did you cut each quiche into four slices instead of six or eight? Or did you drop a quiche on the floor? Or did that passenger who wanted an omelet come back and *steal* my slice of quiche?"

"Ha ha! You're so funny. Well, the business class girls came back, and you know what they're like. They each had two slices. There was still one slice left, but the captain called to see if we had any write-ups and asked if we had anything left to eat, and—"

"You *didn't!*"

"*I* didn't. Darla did."

"Who's Darla?"

"One of the girls from business. She just happened to pick up the phone, and she can never say no to the pilots. But we still have Cheerios. And some fruit salad, although the apples are starting to turn brown, so you'll have to pick them out. And no one touched the donuts , surprisingly. So help yourself."

"No, thank you. I don't want anything."

"Now, don't despair. As soon as we check in at the hotel, we're going to meet at the pool. Darla and Candi are running to Dealer Dan's to get us some wine and snacks."

"Speaking of snacks," said Candi, as she picked up a sheet of paper and a pen. "What kind of chips do you like, Eric? Potato, sweet potato, tortilla or blue corn?"

"Let's not forget about dips!" said Joanne. "Do you prefer salsa, guacamole, ranch, or fat-free sour cream? So far, we have three requests for—"

"I don't want anything!" he blurted.

Both women reacted as though he'd slapped them.

"Sorry," he said. "I just meant to say that I won't be joining you this afternoon."

"Why not? Do you already have plans?" asked Joanne.

"No. I want some downtime."

"But, honey, you're too new to be a slam-clicker."

"Thank you for the offer. But I really need some time to myself. I'm living in a crash pad in Kew Gardens. I just moved in. There was a lot of commotion last night, and I didn't get much sleep before this trip."

"Nothing doing," said Candi. "It's all for one and one for all with this crew!" She laughed. "We're like the Nine Musketeers."

Eric looked her right in the eye. "It's very nice of you to include me, Candi," he said evenly, "but I will *not* be joining you. Some other time, yes, but not today."

"Don't fight it, baby boy." Candi had a big smile on her face. "We'll just get your room number and keep on calling until you come down to the pool, *tee hee*."

Oh, yeah? Eric thought. Just *try* me.

***

As soon as he reached his room, he called the front desk. "Hi, this is Mr. Saunders in room 1019. I just checked in with the crew of flight twenty-three from JFK. Would you please put a hold on all phone calls coming into my room until my wake-up call at seven A.M. tomorrow?"

"Certainly. I'll put a 'do not disturb' on your phone line. Any incoming calls will go straight to voicemail. Have a nice rest."

"Thank you." After he'd hung the phone, he immediately stripped off his uniform, jumped in the shower, and then slipped into clean underwear and a clean t-shirt. Then he lowered the window shade and reached for a stash of eight vodka minis that he'd swiped from the liquor cart while Sue was in the cockpit. He hadn't even bothered transferring them into a water bottle. He cracked open two bottles (how he loved that sound!), poured the contents into an ice-filled glass, and laid down on the bed. The only sound he could hear was ice tinkling as he raised the glass to his lips. It was peaceful... it was mind-numbing... it was heaven on earth.

Fifteen minutes later, the red light on the desk phone began flashing, indicating that someone had tried to call and been transferred immediately to his voicemail. He smiled and poured himself another drink. To hell with you Candi, and everyone else. To hell with your quiches, your poolside parties, and your shopping frenzy at Dealer Dan's. This is *not* what I signed up for when I took this job.

But what *had* he signed up for? Seemingly, it was crushing poverty; a miserable home life; the endless, sweltering New York heatwaves; and incessant co-worker chattering. How long would it take before he'd finished paying his dues and have a decent flight schedule? Was a downtown layover in San Francisco (once every three months, if he was lucky) worth putting up with all the bullshit the rest of the time? Where were the great, new friends that he was supposed to be making? And speaking of friends, where *the hell* was Anthony?

He knew that he was feeling sorry for himself, but he didn't care. As he continued drinking, he ruminated on the big dreams he had on graduation day when he received his coveted silver wings. Three months later, those dreams seemed to have evaporated as quickly as a cirrus cloud on a hot summer day. Eventually, he ran out of ice and drank the vodka straight until it was gone. He closed his eyes and let his mind drift. By seven o'clock that evening, he'd fallen into a deep, heavy sleep.

***

He was dreaming about the day of Sammy's accident. In the dream, as the SUV hit Sammy and sent him flying into the air, Eric jumped off the stoop and bolted into the street. Without a thought for his own safety, he dodged oncoming vehicles and raced to Sammy's side. Ignoring the horror of Sammy's battered and bleeding face, he knelt on the street and immediately began administering mouth to mouth resuscitation.

A moment later, Sammy opened his eyes. "Oh, thank God for you, Eric. You saved my life." Then he burst into tears. As the shrieking ambulance approached, Eric held Sammy tightly in his arms, praying that Sammy would pull through somehow...

A moment later, he woke up and realized that the telephone was ringing. He picked it up, panic-stricken, not knowing where he was or how long he'd been there. "Hello?" he groaned. Jesus Christ, who's been stomping on my head?

"Mr. Saunders, this is Joyce at the front desk. I know that you asked us to hold your calls, but there's someone on the line who says he must speak with you immediately."

That goddam Candi! "Please tell her that I'm not—wait a minute, did you say 'he'?"

"Yes. His name is Anthony Bellini. He said it's urgent that he speak with you."

He sat up so quickly that he almost fell off the bed. "Put him right through."

"One moment, please."

"Hello?"

"Eric, it's Anthony."

"Where the *hell* have you been?"

"I was on a long layover in Guadalajara. I'm back in Dallas now."

"Do you have any idea—"

"Yes. I know everything. I finally got the message you left with crew scheduling."

"Then why didn't you call me?"

"Calm down. *Please*. I have enough to deal with right now. The phone system at the layover hotel was all fucked up. I didn't get the message until right before we left for the airport this morning. I just got back to DFW a few hours ago."

"Then why didn't you call me?"

"I've left you three voicemails so far today. Why don't you answer your goddam phone?"

"Because I asked the front desk for a—never mind."

"You sound fucked up. Have you been drinking?"

"Yes. A lot."

"Oh, perfect timing."

"Don't cop an attitude with me, Anthony. I'm not the one who disappeared. Where the hell are you *living*? When I called your house—"

"Listen, let's both knock it off. I don't have much time to talk. I'm on my way to New York right now to see Sammy and my folks. My supervisor gave me an emergency leave."

"How are you getting there? We don't have our travel benefits yet."

"A friend is letting me use his miles. I'll only be there overnight. I'm going right to the hospital from the airport. What time do you get back to JFK tomorrow?"

"Four-thirty in the afternoon."

"OK. Our return flight leaves from JFK at six tomorrow night. I'll meet you at your gate. I gotta go, Eric, they just announced final boarding for our flight. We'll see you tomorrow."

"See you, Anthony." Feeling slightly stunned, Eric sat for a moment looking at the phone in his hand. "We'll see you tomorrow," he repeated out loud. "Who the hell is *we?*"

***

The next afternoon, as the passengers deplaned in JFK, Eric hid in the galley trying to wipe a large Half and Half stain off his uniform. While tidying the galley during a bumpy final approach, the pitcher had spilled all over his pants. "Why won't this shit come *out?*" he hissed in frustration, as he rubbed both pant legs repeatedly with a hot, damp towel.

"Half and Half is the worst," said Sue, between 'goodbyes' to passengers. "Imagine what it does to your arteries! You'll have to take your pants to the dry cleaners. Lucky for you it's the end of the trip."

"I know that. But the coffee stains on my shirt cuffs are bad enough. And now this! I don't want to look like a slob walking through the terminal."

"Honey," said Sue, "stop worrying. People don't pay that much attention. Get yourself home, have a glass of wine, and call it a day."

After the last passenger had left, Eric gathered his luggage and left the airplane. As he walked up the jet bridge, he was overcome with emotion about seeing Anthony again. Despite the rage he'd felt at Anthony over the last few days, he had missed him terribly. Eric knew that they would pick up right where they left off. They'd straighten everything out. And they'd get their plans back on track to move to Manhattan and really begin their flying careers. His heart was racing as he stepped into the terminal and started looking around for his best friend.

"Hi, Eric." There was Anthony, in the flesh, smiling at him.

"Oh, Anthony! I—" Eric stopped in his tracks. Anthony was not alone. Standing right next to him was the most arrogant, self-centered passenger that Eric had ever met in-flight: Jim Sizemore. From the way they stood together and the way they were dressed, it was apparent that they were a couple. Between the two of them, they were wearing at least five thousands of dollars' worth of clothing, shoes, and watches. They were every bit the power couple on the cover of a glossy gay magazine. Standing there in his filthy uniform, Eric hated them on sight.

Anthony stepped forward to hug him. "You look good. Really good."

Yeah, I look great drenched in Half and Half. "You, too."

"Eric, this is Jim. Jim, this is—"

"We've met," Eric said icily.

"We have?" said Jim, obviously have no recollection of him.

"Yes, on a flight from JFK to Los Angeles. You're an *Almighty Titan*, aren't you?" He spat the words out.

"You have a good memory."

"I remember *everything*."

"Jim, why don't you give us a few minutes alone," said Anthony.

"OK, I'll check about our seats," said Jim. "Thank God we're the first ones on the upgrade list. This airport is a fucking zoo, as usual. Nice to see you again, Eric."

Eric said nothing at all.

"We'll go sit over there," said Anthony, leading Eric to a pair of empty seats in the smoking area.

"What's the latest news on Sammy?" asked Eric, as he lit a cigarette.

"He's still in ICU, but he opened his eyes this morning when he heard my voice." Anthony choked up a little, then took a deep breath. "It's going to be a long haul, but he might make it."

"I can't believe he wasn't killed. Does he remember what happened?"

"We don't know. He can't talk yet. His jaw is wired shut."

"Oh, God, that beautiful face."

"He's lucky to be alive. And lucky that my folks have a few bucks stashed away. He'd never be able to afford the hospital bill."

"One less thing for *you* to worry about." He meant for the words to come out with the same hostility that he felt, but Anthony didn't take the bait.

"So, I guess you moved all your stuff out of my place already?" Anthony asked.

"Yes. The day after the accident. Santiago made it clear that I had no other options. I'm living in a crash pad in Kew Gardens until something else comes along."

"Christ, I'm really sorry you couldn't reach me beforehand."

"Why? What would you have done?"

"I'd have helped you figure something out. Made some phone calls, or–"

"I'm fine. It's very cozy in Kew Gardens. There are fifteen of us—or twenty, I can never keep track—in a two-bedroom basement apartment. I don't know what we'll do if we're all ever home on the same night. Sleep in the bathtub, I guess. But they're very nice people. Most of them are DFW commuters who felt sorry for me and took me in. How ironic is that? Commuters helping *me* out after I've done nothing but dish them since I started flying. I'm grateful to them. I had nowhere else to go. So, what happened to you?"

"I had a big blow up with one of my roommates—Craig, the guy that owns the house. He turned out to be a drunk and real asshole. I had to leave in a hurry. It was the same day as the accident. Fuck, what timing!"

"And where are you staying now?"

"At Jim's place."

"That figures. How many bedrooms do *you* have? Ten? And how many dogs do you have? And do each of the dogs have their own room?"

Anthony still refused to react. "It's a nice place. And there's just one dog."

"Is it serious between the two of you?"

"Yes."

Eric forced himself to ask the next question. "Does he that know that you're planning to come back to—"

"I'm not coming back to New York in December. I'm not coming back at all."

"I know," said Eric, trying to contain the rage seething within him. "I knew it the minute that I saw you together. Are you aware, by the way, that your boyfriend is a complete *asshole?*"

"I know Jim can come off as a little arrogant, but he's different when you get to know him. You'll see. We'd like you to come and visit us soon."

"I don't think so," said Eric, trying not to cry. "I just bought my fall wardrobe at J. C. Penny. I doubt that I'd fit in with the crowd in Armani-ville."

"I hope that you change your mind. Dallas is OK. And Jim has some very nice friends I could introduce you to."

Eric wiped his eyes and put out his cigarette. "Don't do me any favors."

Anthony's easy-going manner vanished. "I thought I *had* done you a favor. You came to training with hardly any money at all, remember? I offered you a roof over your head, in the most expensive city in the world, for five hundred dollars a month. And I didn't even ask you for a fucking security deposit. What the hell *else* would you have done once you got here: set up an army cot in operations?"

"But you *promised* me!" Eric shouted. "My life's been on hold for months, waiting for you! We had it all worked out!"

"Christ, lower your voice. You're in *uniform*. People are looking at us."

"We had it all worked out," Eric repeated in a hoarse whisper. "We were going to be best friends, and fly together, and move into Manhattan, and be... *real* New Yorkers."

"I *am* a real New Yorker. And you know something? It sucks. It *sucks* to try to live here on this salary. Why do you think so many people transfer out as soon as they can? Because they can have a better life somewhere else. Even if you *do* have money, it sucks here. The noise and the traffic and the crowds and the filth, and these stinking homeless people begging for money on every street corner. There's no getting away from it. Even Jim can only take it for a few days at a time, and he's loaded."

"Yes, that's quite obvious."

"I've had it with this goddam city. I just didn't realize it until I moved away. Anyway, stifle it for a minute. Here comes Jim."

"Sorry to interrupt you," said Jim. "Anthony, they're boarding our flight."

Anthony looked at his watch. "We've still got plenty of time."

"I know, but I want to stow our luggage before they run out of space in the overhead bins. You know how I hate waiting for it at baggage claim. Let me take your suitcase with mine. And here's your boarding pass."

Anthony slipped the boarding pass into his shirt pocket. "Thanks, Jim. I'll be there in a minute. Order me a vodka and tonic, would you?"

"Will do. Eric, nice to see you again. I hope we'll be seeing you in Dallas soon."

As Jim walked away, Anthony glanced at his boarding pass.

"First class?" Eric asked.

"Yes."

"Well, naturally," said Eric. "It's the only way for you two to fly."

Anthony slung a Vuitton bag over his shoulder. "Look, I've gotta go in a minute. I'm sorry I lost my temper just now. I know you're upset. But let's not leave it like this. Eric, you may not believe me right now, but there's a part of me that feels terrible for the way that everything turned out. You've been a good friend since the first day we met, and I let you down. I hope you'll let me try to make it up to you." He reached into a side pocket and took out an envelope. "I hate to think of you living in that crash pad for too long. Maybe this will help."

Eric opened the envelope. Inside, there was a personal check made out to him for an outrageous sum of money. "A thousand dollars? You're in a position to give someone *a thousand dollars?*"

"Not just someone: my best friend. And yes, I am. Please take it."

Eric wasn't sure what to do first: tear up the check or slap Anthony across the face. Then he looked at the check again and realized that it was written on a joint account. "I can't accept this." He handed it back.

"Why not?"

"For two reasons. One, my friendship is not for sale. And two, just knowing that this is really Jim's money is enough to make me *puke.*"

"I'm sorry you feel that way." He stuffed the envelope back into the bag and took out a small silver case. "Here, take this business card at least. Our office and home numbers are on it."

"What for?"

"Because like I just said, we can't leave it like this. Let's stay in touch."

Eric took the card and put it in his shirt pocket. "You'd better go or you'll miss your flight." He stood up and reached for his luggage. "I'm tired. I'm going home, right now."

"Come here, buddy." Anthony tried to hug him.

Eric pulled away. "Go, Anthony. Just *go.*"

"Will you call me? Promise?"

Eric nodded as he turned and began walking up the long concourse. As he reached the exit door, he stopped just long enough to tear up the business card and toss the pieces into the nearest trash can. Fuck them— *both* of them. He walked outside and slowly made his way to the public bus stop. In his entire life, he couldn't remember ever feeling so deflated and exhausted.

BOOK TWO

CHAPTER 22

The Art of Storytelling

Denny waited outside the supervisors' office with his hands folded in his lap and a serene expression on his face. I am the embodiment of a poised, professional flight attendant, he told himself. There's no need for me to sit here looking guilty. I've committed no crime. It was more like... a transgression.

The receptionist, who was seated behind a glass partition, answered a call on the intercom and slid the partition open. "Denny, that was Miss Lansing, whom you'll be seeing today. She's running a little behind, but she'll be out in a minute."

"Thank you, Judith."

She eyed him curiously as she scooped up a forkful of chocolate layer cake. "What are you in for?" she asked, as though she were a prison guard interrogating a new inmate.

"Miss Lansing needs some information about a flight that I was working earlier this month." Nice try, Missy, he thought. As if I'd go blabbing to you!

"Are you in some kind of trouble, Denny?"

Oh, geez, he thought. Don't you have your own life to worry about, Porky Pig? Then he quickly reminded himself to watch his temper; that's the reason why he was there in the first place. The only graceful way out of the conversation was to change the subject. "That's a beautiful piece of cake, Judith." He approached the booth. "Look at all that frosting! How about cutting off a sliver for me?"

She quickly pulled the plate out of his reach. "No way!" Though her curiosity was piqued, she was not inclined to trade baked goods for gossip. "Have a seat, Denny."

Denny laughed as she closed the partition. Then he forced himself to regain his composure when he remembered why he'd been summoned to the office: a passenger complaint letter. He'd recently had an altercation with a passenger, and it had been a real doozy. He *knew* that the passenger was going to write.

Some people threatened to write, and then forgot about it the minute they stepped off the plane. But not *that* guy.

Idiot, he chastised himself. I walked right into that situation. If only I'd been able to maintain a modicum of self-control. Well, that's what I get for going bar-hopping the night before a trip. My resistance was down, and as usual, I couldn't keep my big mouth shut. What was it my mother used to say? "Denny, one of these days, that mouth of yours is going to get you into *real* trouble." What do you know: she was right! The task facing Denny now would be to talk his way out of an unpaid two-week suspension. He wasn't worried, though: over the last five years, he'd had considerable practice.

A woman who looked vaguely familiar walked into the reception area. "Hi, are you Denny? I'm Debbie Lansing." She held out her left hand for him to shake since on her right arm was covered in a plaster cast and protected by a sling.

"It's a pleasure to meet you, Miss Lansing. How are you today?"

"Call me Debbie. I'm doing pretty well, I guess, considering that I've had this contraption on my arm for two weeks. Would you come with me, please?"

"Sure." He followed her down the hallway and into Phillip Hendry's cubicle. "Where is Phillip, by the way?"

"He's on a leave of absence. Family emergency. I'm subbing for him until he gets back."

"I haven't seen you in the office before," said Denny, "but I'm sure I've seen you in the terminal or somewhere else."

"Yes, you probably have. I'm a flight attendant, too. I'm out of sick time, so the base manager arranged for me to work in the office until the cast comes off."

Oh, goody, he said to himself. She's one of us. This will be even easier than I thought.

Debbie opened a manila folder on her desk. "Now, Denny, do you remember an incident on a flight to Los Angeles earlier this month?"

"No, nothing in particular. Could you be a little more specific?"

"It involved a first-class passenger's carry-on luggage. The passenger's name was Carnes. Does that ring a bell?"

"Not right off the top of my head. May I see the letter?"

"Later, perhaps. First, I'm supposed to—I mean, first I'd like to hear your side of the story, exactly as you remember it."

I see, thought Denny. Standard operating procedure: she's supposed to make me squirm a little. Fine. I can play along. "When exactly was it?"

"It was the seventh of September, on a flight to L.A. Any of this sound familiar at all?"

"I seem to remember a *minor* incident that occurred around that time. There was a passenger who refused to comply with crewmember instructions, which as you know, is a violation of Federal Air Regulations." Under the circumstances, it was wise to mention FARs from the get-go. A flight attendant could never go wrong if he backed himself up with government rules.

"Tell me more."

"The passenger was sitting in a bulkhead row in first class. He had an enormous briefcase on the floor which he wouldn't stow overhead, despite my repeatedly asking him to do so. I explained to him that for safety reasons, all bulkhead row luggage had to be secured overhead for takeoff. By the time that we were ready to push back from the gate, he still had not done so." He relayed this information calmly, but his blood pressure began to rise as the incident played itself over in his mind. Mr. Carnes had been a complete fucking *jerk*.

"So then what happened?"

"After the safety video, I went through the cabin to do my compliance checks and I noticed that the brief case was still on the floor. As you know, crewmembers can be personally fined by the FAA if they don't make sure that luggage is properly stowed. Not to mention, it's a safety hazard in the event of an evacuation. I politely but firmly asked him once more to stow the briefcase." What Denny had actually said was: 'Hey, mister, what's your problem? I've asked you *four times* to stow your briefcase. We can't take off until you do. So I suggest that you get up and stow it now before I do it *for* you.' Fortunately, for Denny's sake, there were no witnesses; first class had been almost empty that day. "Unbelievably, the passenger still wouldn't budge."

"Is it possible that he was hearing impaired?"

Here we go, thought Denny. That's the classic reaction of anyone sitting behind a desk in this office: give the asshole customer all the leeway in the world. Wow, they sure trained *her* in a hurry. "I don't think so," he replied. "I think he was more preoccupied with the *Hustler* magazine in his lap. *Hustler* is one the more graphic men's magazines, just in case you're not familiar with it."

She frowned. "I'm familiar with it."

Denny smiled. "I assume that Mr. Carnes didn't include that detail in his letter."

"No, he did not."

"You should have seen him, Debbie. His eyes were glazed over, and he was practically drooling over the centerfold. I was shocked, to tell you the truth. Then the captain announced that we were next in line for takeoff. So I picked up the briefcase, despite the passenger's objections, and placed it in an overhead bin. I explained for the *fifth* time that it was a safety hazard and it had to be stowed or we couldn't leave. Then I took my jump seat and that was that."

"Mr. Carnes claims that you *threw* it into the overhead bin, damaging his laptop."

"That is a patently false statement. I'd never intentionally throw anyone's luggage."

"He went right to Baggage Services at LAX after he landed and filed a complaint. He said that the screen had been cracked."

"Perhaps the laptop was already damaged and the whole thing was a ruse on his part." He chuckled. "It wouldn't be the first time a passenger tried to scam the airline, would it?"

Debbie chewed the inside of her cheek. "I can't help thinking that there's more to this than meets the eye. Can you think of *any* other reason why he'd write a letter like this?"

"I'm afraid that's all there is to say about the incident. I guess you'll have to decide whom you want to believe: a fellow crewmember who is trying to ensure compliance with federal regulations, or a grown man who sits reading hard-core pornography in first class. By the way, he left the magazine behind when he disembarked. I have it with me."

Her mouth dropped open. "You took it with you?"

"I had to. The cabin cleaners in Los Angeles wouldn't touch it and I couldn't very well leave it on the seat for the next passenger! I was going to throw it in the garbage can in my hotel room but decided not to. What if the maids found it and reported me? Can you imagine what trouble I'd be in?" He reached into his tote bag, pulled out a large Ziploc bag with the magazine inside, and handed it to her. "Here it is."

She reluctantly took it from him and peered at the cover. "*Ewww!* That's disgusting!"

"The plain brown wrapper, with his mailing address label attached, is tucked inside. But don't touch anything unless you have a pair of rubber gloves handy," Denny warned. "Some of the pages are... stuck together, if you know what I mean."

Debbie made a low, gurgling sound and dropped the Ziploc bag into a wastebasket.

"Is there anything else you'd like to know?" Denny asked.

"I don't think so." She gestured toward a bottle of hand sanitizer on the desk. "Give me a squirt, would you please?" She looked at the letter again and sighed. "Oh, Lord. The traveling public! Well, Denny, I'm sure that the company will pay for the damaged laptop. But as far as your role is concerned, given your statement and the evidence you provided, we'll consider the matter closed. So don't worry about the letter. I'll make sure that it doesn't remain in your personnel file."

Crisis averted. Denny smiled. "Thank you, Debbie."

"Do me one favor." She pointed to the wastebasket. "Take that with you, and get rid of it *after* you leave the building."

"Will do. Thanks again."

"You're welcome. Nice to meet you, Denny. Fly safe."

***

A few minutes later, he stood in front of a computer, happily entering his bids for October. I *am* a resourceful man, he thought. Maybe a B. A. in Theatre Arts hadn't been a complete waste of time and money after all. The mention of the plain, brown wrapper had been a brilliant bit of improvisation. He *knew* that Debbie would never stick her hand inside the bag to check. He was so delighted with his performance that he started giggling. Then he yelled, "Ouch!" as a passerby pinched his rear end.

It was Sylvia Saks. "I love it when you scream like that. You sound just like a little girl. Hey, look at you in your good suit! How come you're all *fahputzed?*"

"I had to come in to discuss a bad passenger letter. I thought this would make a better impression than jeans and sneakers."

"Is Phillip after your hide again?"

"No, Pumpkin Head is out on leave. Someone on 'light duty' is filling in for him."

"Really?" Sylvia looked suspicious. "Who?"

"A red-head from international named Debbie Lansing. Do you know her?"

"Oh, God, yes. She's a hoot. If you ever fly with her and Mavis Bean, her buddy bidder, look out. Anything could happen. So what is Debbie doing on light duty? She gets hives just from walking by entrance to the supervisors' offices."

"Nursing a broken arm, out of sick time, light duty, blah blah blah."

"If I know Debbie, she probably fell off a barstool. Or Maybe Mavis *pushed* her off. So, was she cool about the letter?"

"*Very* cool. She listened to my side of the story and told me not to worry about it."

"So, don't worry about it."

"So, who's worrying? I have more important things to think about. Where are you off to, Sylvia?"

"The two o'clock to San Francisco. Jacques and I had to switch it up for September. We're sick to death of flying with the same people over and over again. Hey, Denny!" She nudged him. "*Tuchus* alert!"

Denny's head whirled around in ten directions at once. "Where?"

"Over there, by the bulletin board."

"That *is* a nice ass." Denny took a second look. "Hey, wait a minute! That's Eric."

"You know him?"

"Yeah, we did a long Seattle layover together, just about a month ago."

"I was the purser on his very first trip in June," Sylvia said. "He's a real sweetheart. Delightful to work with, too."

"Yes," said Denny, remembering their afternoon together in Eric's room. "He's delightful, all right."

"Look, he's all *fahputzed* too. It's a sign. Go ask him out."

"What do you mean, 'it's a sign'?" Sylvia could be such a *yenta* at times.

"Isn't it obvious? Here you are—two gorgeous men, all dressed up, who've already met—who just happen to run into each other on a beautiful September day in New York. You were meant to be together. Go invite him to lunch."

Denny shook his head. "I should be so lucky as to have an extra fifty bucks to *pish* away on lunch."

Sylvia pursed her lips. "You know, when you talk like that, you sound just like my Aunt Rose from Bayonne. She was a penny-pincher, too."

"He probably already has plans anyway: dinner at Le Cirque with a fifty-year-old investment banker and then orchestra seats to *Les Misérables*. Why else would he be dressed like that? Certainly not just to hang around here."

"Oh, for heaven's sake. He's a wonderful young man, he's almost brand-new, and probably still dead-broke. You march over there right now and invite him out!"

"All right, already! I'll do it."

"Take him someplace *nice*, Aunt Rose." She wagged a finger at him. "No diners and no coffee shops."

"I'll come up with something, don't worry."

She looked at her watch. "*Oy*, I've gotta run. I can't be late for my own briefing!" She stuffed paperwork into her tote bag. "I want a full report the next time that I see you. And by the way: keep your grubby paws off him. Just be a *friend* for once."

"Yeah, yeah." He kissed her on the cheek. "Get going."

"I'll call you tomorrow night. Bye!"

He walked over to the bulletin board, where Eric stood intently scanning roommate notices. Denny tapped him on the shoulder. "Hi, sexy. Remember me?"

"Hi, Denny." Eric removed a card, glanced at it, and tacked it back up. "It's nice to see you."

"That's it? 'It's nice to see you.' No hug?"

"What? Oh, sure. Come here." Eric gave him a quick hug. "Sorry, I'm a little preoccupied today."

"How come you're all dressed up?" Denny asked.

"I came in to look for something on the bulletin board."

"For *that* you put on a suit and tie?"

"They told us on our first day that any time we come into operations out of uniform, we should have on business attire."

Oy, Denny thought. He's still *so* new.

"What about you?" Eric asked.

"I had a meeting with a supervisor. No big deal. What are you up to?"

"I'm looking for a new roommate, but there doesn't seem to be much of anything available right now."

"A new roommate? Why? Did Anthony's brother go to jail?"

"I'd rather not talk about it. I'm not living there anymore. Let's leave it at that."

"But isn't Anthony transferring back just a few months? How is he, anyway? Hey, did you ever give him my—"

"I wouldn't *know* how Anthony *is*," Eric hissed. "And frankly, I don't give a shit."

"Jesus, really? I thought you guys were best friends. What happened?"

"Are you deaf? I said I don't want to talk about it!"

"OK, OK. You don't have to talk about it. Let's see about finding you a new roommate. That's one of the *easiest* things to do at around here."

"Ha!" said Eric. "Have a look."

Denny took a card from the bulletin board and read it aloud. " 'One-bedroom apartment to share in luxury high-rise on Upper East Side. Washer, dryer, doorman, balcony. Please call Annika at—' Oh, 'females only'. And that's *underlined*. Well, you wouldn't want to live on the Upper East anyway." He pulled down another card. " 'Studio in West Village, available for immediate occupancy. Current tenant travels extensively and is looking for part-time roommate.' Hey this sounds perfect for you! 'Call Danielle at—' Wait! 'Non-smoking females only.' Damn!"

"They're all like that, every single one! Females only."

"You can't be the only gay man in New York who's looking for a roommate."

"I'm telling you, I've checked them all. There is nothing up there!"

Denny pulled an index card from the very top. "Well, if you're that desperate, how about this: 'Cozy space available under large kitchen table in Kew Gardens. Very convenient location on Q10 bus line. Electrical outlet available daily one hour per day. Bathroom privileges negotiable. Please note: you should not be a light sleeper: my husband and children are noisy eaters. Call Grace W. at—' "

"You think this is *funny*? It's not funny!"

"I'm sorry, but this one *is*. It's a real ad!"

Eric grabbed the card and ripped it to shreds. "Here's something *else* that's funny: I'm living in a crash pad in Kew Gardens with so many other people that I've lost count. Last night, I had to sleep in the bathtub. As heavenly as that may sound, it's only a temporary situation: I have to find another place by October first. That's ten days from now! I have no options, and I know no one. And to make matters worse, I *still have no money!*"

"But we just got paid a week ago."

"Christ, do *any* of you remember what it was like to be new? You've been here five years, Denny. *I've* been here for four months. My paycheck was barely five hundred dollars! I can't live on this fucking salary!"

Denny put a hand on Eric's shoulder as heads started turning in their direction. "Whoa, baby, calm down."

"Don't tell me to calm down. This is impossible! How am I supposed to pay for rent and food and two student loans and get myself to the airport on less than a thousand dollars a month? It *cannot* be done!" Eric's shoulders began to heave and then tears started spilling down his face. "I'm going to have to quit flying and go home to Texas, Denny. To *Texas!*"

"Shh, shh, not in here," said Denny. He took Eric by the arm and firmly steered him to the exit. "Don't ever let *them* see you like this," he said quietly. "I guarantee they'll hold it against you later." He led Eric out of operations and down the hallway, and then shoved him through the door of the men's room. He motioned for Eric to remain silent as he checked under the stalls for prying ears. "I think we're OK, for the moment. Now let's get one thing straight, and please remember that I use *that* expression in only in dire circumstances: you're not going back to Texas. You're a New Yorker now. You work and *live* in New York City. *Capisce?*"

"But Denny, how am I going to—"

"Stop stressing, right this minute. It will all work out with a little help from your friends. And I'm your friend." He handed Eric a wad of tissue. "Blow your nose. Good boy. Now, what are your plans for the rest of the day?"

"I don't have any." Eric splashed his face with cold water, being careful not to splatter his starched white shirt. "I figured I'd just go back to the crash pad, roll myself into a little ball in the bathtub, and have a nervous breakdown."

"I have a better idea. Why don't you let me treat you to a decent meal and a couple of drinks? And you can fill me in on what's been happening."

Eric eyed him warily. "Do you mean a *real* meal this time? Actual food?"

"Yes. I swear to God. We'll start with lunch first and then progress to drinks."

"Somewhere in Manhattan?"

"No, I thought I'd buy you a six-incher at the Subway on Queens Boulevard." Denny rolled his eyes. "Of course we'll go to Manhattan."

"Dressed like this?"

"Absolutely not. We'll stop by your trailer park so that you can change. Then we'll hop on the subway, pop into my place so I can change, and take it from there. Are you flying tomorrow?"

"No, I'm off."

"Good. Pack an overnight bag. You're staying with me. Hey, you been to the East Village?"

"No, not yet."

"Great. Tonight is Underwear Night at my favorite bar. That doesn't start 'till eight o'clock, but there's another bar that opens at noon with happy hour prices, so we—"

"Oh, no! I haven't forgotten that Bare Chest Night fiasco in Seattle. I don't care where we go, but we're eating first. I'm starving."

"Yes, I know, I already promised—"

"I'm not kidding, Denny. I'm *starving*."

Eric had a look on his face that Denny had never seen before: pure desperation. "Jesus Christ, you're serious, aren't you?"

Eric nodded. "You won't believe the things I've done, just to be able to fucking *eat*."

"Wow," said Denny. "Let's get going. I want to hear *all* about it."

***

"This looks beautiful," Eric said at the restaurant as the waiter placed their food in front of them. "Thank you."

"Do you want another drink?" Denny asked.

"Sure."

"Could you bring another round, please?" Denny asked the waiter. "Thanks. Now, Eric, tell me your tale of woe."

"Don't get me wrong, Denny," said Eric, as he began attacking his food. "The summer started with a bang. I love flying even more than I thought I would. God, when you have a good crew and have nice long West Coast layover, there's no better job in the world!"

"But…?"

"It all started going downhill in August. I was on reserve, and I got nothing but Chicago turnarounds the whole month. They stink! No expense money, you work your ass off, and the trip is barely worth five hours of flight pay! And then this month, which is my line month, I *held* Chicago turnarounds, when I didn't even bid them! I wanted layovers."

"Chicago turnarounds," Denny said, "are strictly for single mothers who want to be home every night, and that ain't you. But like I told you in Seattle: you're new, and you'll get what's left over. I do have a suggestion for you: on your line months, bid relief schedules for the senior women who fly part-time. You'll get a much better schedule for at least half of the month anyway."

"I don't even know what that means."

"Crew scheduling takes the schedules of two people who each only two weeks out of the month and make in a one month's schedule that you can bid for. They're always senior stews who fly only transcons, so buh-bye to Chicago turnarounds. I guarantee you'll be much happier with your trips and you'll make more money than you are now."

"I should have asked more questions about the salary at the interview. You know, eighteen dollars an hour seemed like a pretty good starting pay, but when you're only getting paid for seventy-one hours a month, it's *nothing*."

"I know. Even in training, they never really explain how we get paid. If they did, nobody would stick around long enough to graduate. I'm sure, though, that at some point we all said to friends, 'I just want to fly. I'm not doing this for the money.' We didn't know it at the time, but we weren't kidding. Now, tell me about this horrible crash pad you're that you're living in."

"It's a roof over for my head, and I'm grateful to the commuters who took me in. But they're nuts. They all hate New York with a passion. Half of them have never been to Manhattan or even know to use the subway. They sit around the apartment, day and night, talking about only two things: when they think their transfers come through to DFW or Miami, and who has the worst commute to New York. It's like a pissing contest every single night."

"I know, I know. They do it on the plane too. Are there any cute guys living there at least?"

"There are a few dumpy, middle-aged pilots. Their conversation is just about as scintillating."

"What about basic amenities? Phone, cable TV, air conditioning?"

"There is air conditioning, but only in one of the bedrooms. If you don't manage to snag a space in that room, you can set your cot up in front of an industrial-strength floor fan in the living. That bad boy runs twenty-four hours a day."

"Jesus, Eric, it sounds awful."

"It is. Between the commuter clacking and the floor fan, the noise just about drives me crazy. Last week, just to get away for the evening, I went to Pinocchio's on Queens Boulevard. I thought maybe I could hook up with someone who has AC."

"Pinocchio's?! That dump is still open? Geez, I haven't been there in a million years."

"Hey, don't knock it. They have two-for-one drink specials on Sunday and Tuesday, and it's the only gay bar in the neighborhood."

"So did you score?"

"I closed the place down, along with four other guys, all locals. Two of them were a couple: a hot older guy and his twenty-something boyfriend, named Saul and Ray. They invited everyone who was left back to their place for an after-hours party."

"Did they have air conditioning?"

"Yes."

"So you scored *and* you got a good night's sleep. Good for you."

"No, it was awful. By the time we got back to their place, two of the guys were too drunk to get an erection and passed out within five minutes. And Saul and Ray were at each other's throats from the minute we walked in the door. It was like a scene right out of *Who's Afraid of Virginia Woolf?* I should have left right away."

"Why didn't you?"

"I was drunk, it was three o'clock in the morning, and I had no idea where the hell I was. By four, the other guys left. They lived right around the corner and stumbled home. Saul and Ray let me sleep on the sofa."

"That was nice of them."

"Yes. It would also be nice if they kept a spare toothbrush on hand for overnight guests. Thank God they had some Listerine."

"Did they make you breakfast, at least?"

"If you want a call offering me a can of Schlitz as 'breakfast', then yes. The younger one, Saul, kept making eyes at me at the table, which Ray didn't like one bit. He made me leave the apartment with him at eight o'clock. In broad daylight, by the way, Ray wasn't the least bit hot. He looked *terrible*. As we were walking to the subway, he turned to me and said, 'If you sneak back there and screw around with Saul while I'm at work, I'll find you and slit your fucking throat.' "

Denny groaned. "Stop! I can't listen to anymore! Waiter! Can we get those drinks, please?"

"Wait, that's not the worst of it. Last week, I came home from an Orlando turnaround—"

"What the hell were you doing on another Orlando turnaround? Isn't Chicago bad enough?"

"I picked it up to make a little extra money."

"Ugh! Orlando: the lowest of the low-rent passengers. Go on."

"My brain was fried when I got home from that trip. As usual, the apartment was a zoo. Some asshole had eaten the sandwich I left in the refrigerator with my name written on the box. There was no other food in the house. I *had* to get out. But it was three days before payday and I only had five dollars to my name. So I decided to go to Pinocchio's for a beer and free bar snacks."

"Pinocchio's again! Go on: tell me what tawdry situation you got tangled up in this time."

"It was a quiet night, but the bartender was nice and comped me a few drinks. Instead of relaxing though, I started getting more and more panicky about money. Around midnight, this drunk Korean guy started chatting me up and offered to buy me a drink. God, was he drunk! He kept pawing me and calling me 'pretty boy.' All of a sudden, the bartender announces he's closing early because it's so dead. I had no money and couldn't bear the idea of going back to the crash pad. The drunk guy invited me to his place. He wasn't bad looking; he had beautiful skin and a very nice smile. I decided to go home with him, only because… oh, Denny, I can't tell you! I'm so ashamed of myself."

"Spill it, sister. I've seen every *Movie of the Week* that Linda Blair ever made. Nothing shocks me."

"When he took out his wallet to pay for our drinks, I noticed that it was stuffed with cash. This terrible idea popped into my head, but I was so beside myself that I decided to follow through with it."

Denny put down his fork and knife. "Should I guess what happened next or do you want to tell me?"

"We walked to his building. The doorman gave us a dirty look, but we ignored him and got right in the elevator. It was a very nice apartment. He made us both a drink. We kissed a little, and then laid down on the bed. Thirty second later, he passed out. Dead drunk, thank God. All of a sudden, I felt like I was on autopilot. I got up, reached for his wallet on the dresser, took forty dollars, stuffed it in my pocket, and let myself out. I casually strolled past the doorman when I got to the lobby. Then once I got outside, I bolted. I started running and kept running until I got back to my apartment."

Denny didn't blink an eye. "Why did you stop at forty dollars? That's chump change."

"I didn't want to wipe him out. That would have been shitty of me. We all have bills to pay."

"So there is such a thing as honor among thieves. That's good to know." Denny raised his glass. "Now, may I suggest an alternative way of earning extra cash?"

"Please do."

"Until your financial situation becomes more stable, try to work in coach as often as you can, and push the cocktails and headset sales."

"Denny, I am not going to get into the habit of stealing liquor and headset money. I know that once people start, it's a hard habit to break. There's a stew on Long Island Sound with a boat named Headset, for God's sake! Not to mention, I'm on probation. If I get caught, I'd be fired on the spot."

"How would you get caught? On a wide-body aircraft, there are two hundred passengers in coach. Even if the company wanted to, they couldn't put enough ghost riders on board to record every cash transaction that takes place."

"What happens if someone on the crew gets wise and turns me in?"

Denny laughed. "Do you honestly think that you'd be the first flight attendant to supplement his income that way? It's a matter of survival. We all do what we have to do, and we mind our own business. That's part of *our* code of honor."

"To each his own, I suppose." Eric sighed. "Oh, Lord. I wonder what my mother would have to say about this. She raised me better than to pilfer from my employer."

"What would she say about you rolling drunks for pocket change? That's hardly a nobler endeavor."

"You have a point."

"Besides, if our employer paid you a living wage as a new hire, it wouldn't *be* an issue. So fuck management and take care of yourself any way you can. Do you want dessert?"

"Not if we're still going to the underwear party. I'll be sucking my stomach in all night just from the burger and fries."

"We'll go walk it off. You'll love this area. The East Village is one of the few neighborhoods in Manhattan that hasn't been gentrified—yet. But before we leave, I want to know what happened between you and Anthony. That's one story you still haven't shared."

"Do I have too?"

"I just bought you lunch and two rounds of drinks, dumplin'. Start squawking."

Eric sighed. "Anthony bailed on me. He met a rich, handsome guy from Dallas, whom I happened to meet by coincidence on a flight before I knew they were together. This guy is such an asshole I wouldn't piss on him if he were on fire. But Anthony seems happy with him and decided to stay in Texas. It's a very cushy situation for him. He could probably quit flying tomorrow if he wanted and never worry about money again." He smirked. "I wish them every happiness in the world. They deserve each other."

"So, he chose to whore himself out instead of keeping his promise and maintaining his friendship with you. Well, it happens." Denny shrugged. "One door closes, another opens. That's life in the big city." He pushed back his chair. "Order us some coffee, would you? I'm going to go make a few phone calls on your behalf."

Eric perked up immediately. "What about?"

"You'll see." He squeezed Eric's shoulder. "I said I was your friend and I meant it. Just have a little faith and your troubles will be resolved, I promise."

***

The Underwear Party at the Tool Shed was just getting started when Denny and Eric arrived. As they waited in line, Eric watched as the man ahead of them stripped down to his socks and underwear and put all his other clothes in a Hefty bag. Then, after putting his police boots back on, he handed the Hefty bag to the coat check staff. They gave him a claim check so that he could pick up his clothes when he was ready to leave, or the when party ended—whichever came first.

"See? It's a very efficient system," said Denny, as they began taking their clothes off. "Just don't lose that claim check or you'll be walking home in your tightie-whities."

"What should I do with my wallet?"

"Take out whatever cash you have and stick in a sock. Same for the claim check. The wallet is safe in your Hefty bag with the coat check staff, anyway."

"How far will ten bucks get me tonight, drink-wise?"

"With that ass of yours, sugar, don't worry about it. The bartenders will probably comp your drinks all night." He handed Eric a wad of singles. "Here, take these to tip the bartenders."

"Thanks, Denny."

The Tool Shed was quickly getting crowded as attendees passed from the entryway into the main bar. It was an indoor Easter parade of jock straps and work boots, thongs and sneakers, briefs and deck shoes. Some men strutted toward the bar, ordered a drink, and claimed a prime spot that would assure them maximum visibility. Others slunk in, avoided looking at themselves in the mirror behind the bar, and opted for the safety of a darkened corner. A pecking order, based on body type and general level of attractiveness, was established early in the game.

"I feel a little dorky in these sneakers," said Eric. "I wish I had a pair of work boots."

"Forget footwear," said Denny. "Tonight is all about the way you look in those white briefs, which I've got to tell you is damn *hot*." He patted Eric's rear end. "By the way, I invited a friend to join us. You'll be particularly interested in meeting him. Hey, there he is now. Michael! Hey, Michael! Over here!"

A man turned around, saw Denny, and smiled. "I'm ordering a drink. I'll be right there." A moment later, with a beer in his hand, he walked over to Denny and Eric. Michael was tall and trim, and bald. He had a nice furry chest and a friendly smile. He was wearing a pair of printed jockey shorts. As he came closer, Denny realized that the jockey shorts were emblazoned with the Global Airways logo.

"Where did you get those?" Denny asked.

"I had them custom made," Michael said with a grin. "I'm trying to drum up new customers for the airline. Times are *tough*, baby. I don't know how much longer we'll be around."

"Eric," said Denny, "this is Michael Powers. He flies for Global."

"I figured," said Eric, smiling. "Nice to meet you."

"Michael lives in Forest Hills Gardens, right off of Seventy-first Street."

"I'm on Queens Boulevard, not too far from you," said Eric.

"Howdy, neighbor," said Michael. He raised his glass. "Here's to a happy harvest for all of us this evening."

"Here's something else that you should know about Michael," said Denny. "His roommate just moved to New Orleans last week—without much warning. So Michael's looking for a new roommate *pronto,* and he wants a gay male flight attendant only. The rent is five hundred dollars a month."

"What do you say, Eric?" said Michael. "I'm in a bind, and it sounds like you are you, too. Denny told me all about your situation, and he also told me what a nice person you are. Now, it's only a one bedroom. You'll have to buy a futon and share the bedroom with me when we're both home the same night, which I'm sure won't be too often since we both fly. You can move in tomorrow if you like. I own the apartment. There's no lease to sign and no security deposit required, since you're a friend of Denny's. Are you interested?"

Eric responded by bursting into tears. "Yes, I'm interested! Oh my God, thank you!"

"No tears," said Denny, grabbing a handful of cocktail napkins. "It spoils the party mood."

"Thank you, Michael. You'll never know how grateful I am."

"You should thank Denny," said Michael. "He was the one who thought to call me this afternoon. I'm glad that I was still at home. I was going to put up a notice in operations tomorrow."

Eric threw his arms around Denny. "Thank you, thank you, thank you. Denny, you're the best friend that a boy ever had."

"You're welcome," Denny said. He picked up his drink. "Now, boys, let's go see what kind of trouble we can get ourselves into tonight."

CHAPTER 23

Uno, Dos…Tres.

At noon on a glorious October day, Eric walked out the front door of his new apartment building, heading for La Guardia Airport. As he reached the sidewalk, he stopped for a moment to look back and admire the façade. It was nothing at all like the plain, red brick edifice that he'd formerly occupied on Queens Boulevard. His new home, in Forest Hills Gardens, was an elegant six-story Tudor. Each architectural detail blended perfectly with every other structure on the street. Of all the details, Eric loved the main entrance in particular. The arched double door was carved from solid oak and framed with intricately detailed stonemasonry. Small leaded glass windows kept the spacious lobby hidden from passersby.

The house was set far back from the street. There was no stoop and no foul-mouthed superintendent lounging about, complaining of the summer heat and the constant demands of tenants. Instead, two small steps led to a long brick walkway, which then led to the sidewalk. The grounds were planted with shrubbery and flower beds, all of which were fastidiously maintained by the staff. Eric grinned from ear to ear. No matter how many times he entered or left the building, he could not believe that he was lucky enough to live in such a beautiful place—all thanks to Denny and to his new roommate, Michael.

"Hello there, Eric!" It was Mrs. Grossman, Eric's next-door neighbor, who'd walked up behind him. She was dressed to the nines in a two-piece suit and ruffled blouse. Her handbag matched her leather pumps. As always, her hair was meticulously coiffed. In the Gardens, leaving the house with one's wig askew, or wearing a mismatched sweater and skirt, was simply unheard of. "Are you coming or going?"

"I'm flying to Miami today, with a long layover on the beach."

"Oh, how wonderful. Weren't you just in Vancouver just the other day?"

"Yes, on Sunday."

"I'm green with envy! To be young again and see the world!" She said it without a trace of malice. "I wish *I'd* been a stewardess when I was younger."

"It's never too late," he said, smiling. "You'd be perfect for the job."

"Ha! My husband would burn the house down just trying to make toast. No, I'd better stay put. But you get going and have a wonderful time."

Eric rounded the corner on 71st Street, past the charming railroad station, which always reminded him of Santa's Village. December was only two months away. Soon he'd get to experience his first-ever snowfall. But that could wait. For right now, the beautiful autumn leaves and the crisp breeze blowing through his hair around were reward enough. The God-awful New York summer was over at last. He loved his new apartment and his new roommate. He was flying better trips and making new friends. Life was definitely on the upswing.

***

Two hours later, he boarded the Miami-bound flight gasping for breath. "Hi, my... name's... Eric," he panted, as he stumbled through the entry door.

"I'm Chrissie," said the flight attendant standing in the first-class galley. She had blond hair and was an obvious sun worshipper. "Are you all right? You look like you're about to pass out."

"I caught got up in an incredibly long line at security. I've never seen anything like it! I had to run all the way so that we could start boarding on time."

"Oh, honey." She hurriedly poured a glass of water for him. "Never run *anywhere*, especially in the airport. You'll fall and break something, it happens all the time. We'll start boarding when we're damn good and ready."

"Thank you." He gulped down the water. "My God, it's a *zoo* out there!"

"What'd you expect? It's a flight to Miami."

"I take it we're full today?" he asked warily.

"Of course we're full. After you stow your bags, come right back up here, please. We're going to have a quick briefing. Let Richard and Rebecca know in the back, please. They got on before me and I haven't had a chance to speak to them yet."

"Sure." Eric had almost reached the back of the plane when Chrissie's voice came over the PA system. "Can I get everybody up here for a briefing *now*, please?"

Eric sighed and shoved his suitcase into the nearest bin. Jesus, he thought, as he marched back to the front. Who has a briefing before a Miami flight? What is there to say besides, "This is going to be pure hell!"?

He sunk into a first-class seat. A moment later, Rebecca and Richard joined them. Rebecca was exotic and beautiful. She had a mane of dark curly hair that was pinned in the back with a lovely silver clip. Richard was pale-skinned. He had auburn hair that hung a few inches past his shirt collar and bright blue eyes. The length of his hair was a definite violation of appearance standards, but it was so beautiful that Eric immediately wanted to tousle it. Richard's face was covered with stubble. That was another grooming violation, but it suited him perfectly. Rebecca sat down and crossed her long legs. Richard sat on the armrest of the same seat and draped his arm around her.

"Hi, you guys, this is Eric," said Chrissie. "He's working in coach with you." She glanced disapprovingly at Richard. "Richard, you're still going for the ultra-casual look, I see."

He shrugged. "I left my razor in our hotel room in Bangkok yesterday. I didn't realize it until we were re-packing at home a few hours ago."

"I *like* him this way," said Rebecca, gently stroking his cheek. "It's so manly!"

"Isn't it scratchy?" Eric asked, trying not to sound envious.

"Yes… in all the right places," Rebecca purred.

"People: let's focus," said Chrissie. "This flight's going to be a double-whammy today. For starters, half the plane is connecting through Miami to the islands. They'll be *locos*, as usual. And to make matters worse, tomorrow is the first day of Rush o' Shawna, or whatever the hell that holiday is called, and you know what that means."

Rebecca's eyes darkened. "It's *Rosh Hashanah*," she said, carefully pronouncing each syllable. "And tell us, what *does* that mean, Chrissie?"

"It means that the beanie people will be out in full force," Chrissie replied.

"If you're referring to the skull cap that Orthodox Jewish men wear, it's called a *yarmulke*," Eric said with disdain. "And before you go any further, the side locks that the Hassidic Jews wear next to their ears are called *payot,* not 'curly-cues.' "

"I don't care what you call it. I'm not putting up with shit from *anybody*."

"Not to worry," said Richard. "We're professionals. We can handle anything."

"And we can do it without the need to pigeon-hole anybody," Rebecca added.

"Whatever," said Chrissie, with a shrug. "I'm gonna run out to have a word with the agent about carry-on luggage, and then we'll start boarding. Battle stations, everybody." She hurried off the plane.

"She's something, isn't she?" said Eric.

"She's what my grandmother would call a real piece of work," said Rebecca. "Are you Jewish, Eric?"

"No."

"Then how do know about *yamulkes* and *payot*?"

"I believe there are certain basics that all New York crewmembers should be familiar with," he replied, pleased that she had asked. "You either know something about the world in which you live, or you know nothing."

"I'm impressed," said Rebecca.

"I was impressed the moment I saw him," said Richard, smiling.

Chrissie came back a moment later. "Oh my God, it's mob scene out there! They may have to call the cops before we even start to board! Eric, you go out and pull tickets. Elena, the agent, is working by herself, and she's gonna need all the help she can get. You'll have to maintain complete control of the situation."

"I can handle it," he said, emulating the relaxed manner of Richard and Rebecca. He stepped off the plane. As he began walking up the jet bridge, he heard a loud *psst!* behind him.

"Eric!" It was Rebecca. "Don't let my people drive you crazy!"

"Which ones are yours: the Jews or the Islanders?"

She grinned. "The former, smart ass. But be ready for trouble from both."

"Don't worry. I've been around for a while now. I don't let *anyone* drive me crazy." He passed a conga line of ten elderly women in wheelchairs. Each one had an enormous, unwieldy suitcase sitting on her lap. Ladies, he thought smugly, good luck getting someone to lift *those* backbreakers overhead for you. For once, it won't be me.

As the agent picked up the microphone and announced that rows 20 through 30 could begin boarding, one hundred and fifty people jumped up and immediately started rushing toward the jet bridge door. "Rows twenty through thirty *only,*" Eric said loudly in Spanish, to no avail. The next thirty minutes were absolute bedlam as he tried to cope with verifying boarding passes, monitoring outrageously oversized carry-on luggage, and jumping back when eight-to-ten-year-old children in baby strollers were almost pushed over his feet. There was a constant stream of semi-hysterical passengers trying to push past him. They acted as though they were fleeing from mercenaries intent on killing their entire family.

In a vain attempt to maintain some semblance of order, Eric repeatedly put his hand up and asked them to form one single line. *"Una sola línea, por favor, una sola línea!"* moment by moment, his stress level increased to the breaking point. As yet another boarding pass was thrust in his face and almost sliced through his eyeball, he lost it. He turned to the agent and screamed, "If you don't get these *fucking* people to form one *fucking* line, and wait their *fucking* turn, I will close this *fucking* jet bridge door, and no one will go *fucking* go anywhere! Do you *fucking understand me?*"

The agent rolled eyes at him. *"Aye, Diós,"* she muttered. "Get back on the plane, and I'll finish this myself. Do me a favor, *mi hijo*: don't bid Miami flights anymore, OK?"

Eric didn't even bother to answer her. He walked onto the plane, still unhinged, and headed straight for the back. He completely ignored a request from a shivering heavyset woman for an extra blanket. That's what you get for wearing a halter top and short shorts on an airplane, he thought. He also ignored a woman in an aisle seat, who appeared to be traveling alone. She sat muttering to herself in Spanish and shaking her fist at the ceiling, her withered face streaked with tears. Another 'woman on the verge.' There were many on board.

Rebecca smiled at him as he entered the galley. "Is that every—Eric, honey, what's the matter?!"

"I can't even talk about it! It was insanity! I've never experienced anything like it!"

"You're shaking!" She pushed him onto the jump seat in the corner. "Take off that blazer and loosen your tie. Dick, made him a drink, quick!" As she pulled the galley curtain closed, Richard made a vodka and tonic and handed it to Eric.

Without even thinking about it, Eric gulped the cocktail. He felt better almost instantly. "Thanks. God, I've never done *that* before."

"You needed it," said Rebecca. "I can only imagine how awful it was out there. It was nuts on here too, just trying to get them to stow their luggage and sit down."

"God, I hate Miami," said Eric. "I *hate* it!"

"Shh, turn around," said Richard. He leaned over Eric and began kneading his back and shoulders.

"Oh, Jesus," said Eric. Richard's touch was so heavenly that he almost fell off the jump seat. "Richard, your hands are incredible."

"Thanks," said Richard. "Beck and I are both licensed massage therapists. We were just in Thailand, taking a class together. We learned some great new techniques." He worked his hands all the way down to Eric's lower back and then started working his way up again. "And call me Dick. All my friends do."

"Will do, Dick," said Eric, fantasizing about being naked on a massage table with Dick spreading warm oil across his shoulders, and then down his back— and then between his legs.

"God, it's hot on this plane," said Rebecca. "I'm gonna call the captain and ask him to crank up the air conditioning."

"Why don't you take off that God-awful sweater first?" said Dick. "You know I can't stand to see you wear that *schmata* anyway."

"Duh, why didn't I think of that?" She pulled it off and tossed it onto her jump seat. "That's better already."

"Now, that's what I like," said Dick. "Eric, look at my beautiful girlfriend," he growled into Eric's ear. "Doesn't she have amazing tits?"

Eric glancing up at Rebecca, who playfully thrust out her chest. "Yes. They're spectacular," he replied.

"Flight attendants, prepare for departure," Chrissie said over the PA system.

"Oh, I forgot that we're supposed to be working," said Eric.

"Yep, it looks like we're going," said Rebecca. She opened the galley curtain as Dick armed the doors and Chrissie began the welcome aboard announcement. "Thank God this airplane has a video system. I loathe doing manual demos."

"For some reason, I never mind doing a safety demo," Eric said. "I love all that flight attendant *schtick*." He mimed pointing out the emergency exits.

"That's because you like people admiring you in the aisle," Dick said, with a grin. "And I bet I know just what they're admiring."

"We both noticed it," said Rebecca. I've never seen a man look so good in uniform pants. Would you send Dick to your tailor, please? He needs help from *somebody*."

"It wouldn't make any difference," said Dick. "I've got no ass. I'm carrying everything up front."

"Oh, Dick, you have a delicious little behind," said Rebecca. "It's true though, Eric. You wouldn't *believe* what he's hauling between his legs. I almost fainted the first time I saw it."

Eric sat straight up and opened his eyes. Both Dick and Rebecca were smiling at him. It wasn't his imagination; the sexual energy in the galley was palpable. "You shouldn't talk that way in front of a gay man," he said, finally. "It gives us strange ideas."

"*Ach!*" Rebecca waved her hand. "Gay, straight. Who cares? They're just labels. They don't mean anything."

"That's not what they told me when I came out in my senior year at high school."

"Where are you from, Eric?"

"Texas."

"Oh, *fuck* Texas," said Dick. "Except for Austin, that entire state is a shithole. I was on a layover in Dallas once, and this asshole redneck cop—"

"Ladies and gentlemen, this is your captain speaking. Luckily, we had a very short taxi today, and we're currently number two to take the runway. Flight attendants, please prepare for takeoff."

"Oh, shit!" said Eric, jumping up. "My jump seat's all the way up at the front. I'd better do my compliance check and haul ass."

"We'll take care of that," said Dick. "You just run up front and buckle up."

"Yeah, run, stewardess boy," said Rebecca. "We'll be watching."

***

The climb out was exceptionally bumpy, forcing the cabin crew to remain seated for the first half hour. "Shit," Eric said to Chrissie, who sat next to him reading a Carnival Cruise brochure. "Now we'll have no time for the service. And it's full back there!"

"So?" said Chrissie, without looking up. "If you don't finish, you don't finish. We can't work miracles. I'm not risking a broken leg just to serve these jokers a chicken boob."

The plane suddenly dropped a least a hundred feet. Eric gripped his shoulder harness so tightly that his hands became chalk-white. "God, if it's this bad up here, imagine how bad it must be in the back. Poor Dick and Beck!"

"Dick and Beck, huh? You've gotten chummy with them fast."

"They're nice people."

"Yes, very extroverted, both of them," said Chrissie. "Are you going out with them tonight?"

"I don't know. They haven't asked me yet."

"Well, if you *do* go, be sure to bring some protection."

"What do you mean?"

"Nothing," she said with a smirk. "I just meant that it's been a little chilly in Miami this month and they always like to take a long stroll on the beach at night. Bring a jacket."

"Oh, right," said Eric, as the crew phone rang.

"I've got it." Chrissie grabbed the phone. "Chrissie here, what's up? ... OK, I'll tell everybody. Thanks." She hung up the phone. "We should be in the clear now. We're finally on top of the clouds."

"Do you need me to help you up here?"

"Oh, no. I can do this service with my eyes closed. You go help your friends in coach." She took off her high heels and slipped into a pair of well-worn flats. "You look a little stressed. You want half a Valium?"

"Thanks, but I'd better not."

***

The atmosphere in coach was surprisingly calm compared to the chaos that Eric had experienced during boarding. But the crew was still rushed to finish the service. There was barely time to serve drinks, much less drinks *and* a hot meal. Eric could feel the time pressure, even as they reached the last five rows. Dick was on the beverage cart, Rebecca was on the meal cart, and Eric was floating in between the two.

"This cart is empty," said Rebecca, as she reached row 25. "I'm going to run back for the last one. You help Dick make drinks until I get back." She leaned across the cart and whispered, "I just served the last chicken. It's going to be pasta for everyone else. Get ready for some drama."

"Oh, great!" While he waited for her to come back, Eric spent a few minutes making drinks. As he poured a glass of orange juice, he blissfully ignored a man two rows away who was making a hissing noise to get Eric's attention. Hissing, as far as he was concerned, was just as vulgar as snapping one's fingers; he refused to respond to either behavior.

Rebecca returned a moment later and started stacking ceramic casseroles filled with lasagna on top of the cart. "Well, this part will be easy," she said. "It's all the same."

"Here, let me have some of those," said Eric. "We're caught up on drinks for the moment." He set three trays of lasagna down at once.

"*Qué es esto?*" said the woman in the aisle seat, frowning.

"*Es pasta,*" Eric replied.

"*Pasta?! Yo quierro pollo!*"

"*No hay,*" he said. "There isn't any left."

"*Pollo! Pollo!*" The woman started stamping her feet. "*Dáme pollo!*"

"*No hay pollo!*" he snarled. "*Es pasta o nada! Comprende?*"

"Eric," said Dick, "turn around for a second. I need to talk to you."

Eric whirled around. "What?!"

"Dude, don't argue," he said softly. "It's a battle you can't win. Just set the tray down, smile and move on. Don't give them a chance to make a fuss. And for Christ's sake, don't let on that you speak Spanish. Understand?"

"I understand," said Eric, trying to stop himself from shaking.

"Take a beat and breathe. If you let passengers get you this wound up over the lack of a frigging meal choice, you won't last a year."

"Thanks for the advice," said Eric, smiling tightly, as the seatbelt sign came on. "Now let's get finish this damn service. I think we're starting to descend."

***

Twenty minutes later, he trudged into the galley with a large bag full of trash.

"You can put right in here," said Dick, opening a cart door.

"Is there any Courvoisier left?" Eric asked.

Rebecca and Dick looked at each other. "For who? A passenger?"

"Yes. Someone just asked me for a Courvoisier and Coke. Can you imagine? I almost threw up."

They started laughing. "Sorry," said Rebecca, "but I used all of the cordials, and just about all the other leftover booze, to make crew juice." She showed him two large water bottles filled with amber-colored liquid. "This is for the ride to the hotel."

"What's in that brew besides Courvoisier?" Eric asked.

"Can't tell," said Rebecca, with a wicked smile. "It's a secret recipe that I learned from an Air France crew."

"I'll say this, though," said Dick. "It'll kick your ass before you know it, so don't drink it too fast. When we go to dinner later, we'd rather you were still on your feet. You're joining us for dinner, right?"

"Sure, I'd love to. Is it just us or is the whole crew going?" Eric wasn't sure if he was up for an evening of chit-chatting with the pilots. Their conversation invariably revolved around the same three topics: their miserable commute, their overly-crowded crash pad, and their ex-wives' incessant demands for more alimony.

"Absolutely not," said Dick. "It's just the three of us, so keep that to yourself. We're going to stop by a great little Cuban place for dinner, and then we'll go for a walk on the beach."

"*Little* dinner, Dick," said Rebecca. "I'm still stuffed from last night. Eric, you should have been at our place last night. Dick made *flunken tsimis* and *latkes* for my whole family. They were in town, visiting from Pittsburg. He made everything from scratch. He even grated the potatoes by hand!"

"It's true," said Dick, "I have the knuckle scars to prove it. Do you know how many potatoes you have to grate to make *latkes* for eight people? Next time, Beck, we buy frozen."

"Bite your tongue!" said Rebecca. "It was all worth it. Everything was delicious. My grandmother was a little suspicious when we sat down at the table, but by the end of the meal, she was *plotzing*. 'Where did a *goy* learn to cook like that?' she said."

"I'm a man of many talents," Dick said humbly.

"Is there *anything* that you can't do?" Eric asked.

"No," said Dick, looking him straight in the eye. "Nothing."

***

On the way to the restaurant that evening, Dick sat up front with the driver, chatting away in Spanish. Eric and Rebecca sat in the back seat. Rebecca was radiant in a blue-and-white print halter top, a short skirt and sandals. Her skin was so moist and luscious that Eric had to fight himself from squeezing her arm. Eric and Dick both wore cotton shirts and shorts. They kept the car windows rolled down for the entire ride. The balmy night air was a welcome change from the autumn chill back in New York.

The restaurant was small, lively, and popular with locals. Aside from the three crewmembers, there wasn't another *gringo* in sight. They were greeted warmly by the owner and seated at a table right away. Dick ordered food and beers for all three of them in rapid-fire Spanish.

Three large, ice-cold beers were promptly served. "Gee, I'm not sure if should drink this," said Eric. "I'm still pretty buzzed from that crew juice."

"I told you," said Dick, grinning. "But you have to drink at least one. It goes so well with the food."

"What did you guys do with that second bottle of crew juice?" Eric asked.

Rebecca patted a large tote bag on the seat next to her. "It's right here. This is for later. We travel prepared."

"Are you trying to get me drunk?" Eric asked.

"Hey, you're a grown man," said Dick. "You should know by now what you can and can't handle." He and Rebecca raised their beers. "Here's to new friends. Eric, we're happy that you're with us this evening."

"Ditto." As he smiled and raised his own, Eric took a moment to admire Dick. His shirt clung nicely to his torso, and there was a nice patch of auburn chest hair poking through the open buttons.

The food was delicious and portions were generous. Rebecca ate her entire meal and part of Dick's, and then, eyeing Eric's plate, said, "Are you going to finish all that?"

"Hands off," he said. "You wanted a small dinner, remember?"

Dick laughed. "Oh, my friend, what you don't know about Jews and food."

Rebecca's fork was still poised in mid-air. "Come on, Eric, let me have just a little."

He finally relented. "All right, go ahead."

"Thanks. I just can't seem to get enough food in me these days."

"Wow," said Eric, as she greedily scooped forkfuls of rice and beans from his plate. "You'd think that you were eating for two."

She started gagging and spit food into her napkin. "God forbid!"

"That's not part of the plan," said Dick. "Maybe someday, but not right now."

"Not now, not *ever!*" said Rebecca. "I'm not giving up my life to become one of those women who can only fly turnarounds and has to be home by three-thirty every afternoon. That is *not* why I took this job, and not why I hooked up with Dick, either." She leaned back and slipped her arm around his waist. "Oh, honey, you'd better start cutting back a little bit. You're getting a tummy."

"Ah, leave him alone," said Eric, who was tired of gay men who obsessed with their bodies. "Dick is all man, and you're lucky to have him."

"I know," said Rebecca. "We just like to tease each other a little."

"You guys are so laid back, even on the plane," said Eric. "Nothing seems to bother you in the least. I love that about you."

Dick finished his beer and sighed contentedly. "Because *this* is why we fly. We come to work, put in a few hours, get off the plane, and then we have a twenty-hour layover in Miami. Cold beer, great food, great company, and all day tomorrow on the beach. OK, so occasionally we have to put up with some bullshit from passengers along on the way. Once you learn not to let them get to you, it's all cake, see?"

"Oh, cake!" said Rebecca. "Dick, order some *dulce de tres leches* for dessert!"

"No," he replied. "We're going to have to roll you out the front door as it is."

"I'll try to remember what you said about passengers the next time I'm working business class to L.A.," said Eric.

"Oh, *fuck* business class," said Dick. "That's the one thing I cannot tolerate. I know my limitations."

"The other reason that we love flying is the travel benefits," said Rebecca. "Getting our employee travel cards after six months on the line was like getting a golden ticket. We've been all over the world, to places I'd never even heard of before I started flying."

"The thing I like best," said Dick, "is that we can be completely spontaneous. Sometimes when we have a few days off, we each pack a small bag, head for the airport, check to see what flight has a couple of open seats, and we're off. No guidebooks, no hotel reservations, no preconceived notions." He smiled and squeezed Rebecca's hand, which was resting gently on his leg. "I wouldn't trade that freedom for anything."

"I can't wait to get my employee travel card," said Eric. "I only have one month to go."

"You'll be a real world-traveler then," said Dick. "Speaking of which, why aren't you flying international routes? With your language skills, you're being wasted on domestic flights."

"One step at a time," said Eric. "I need a little more seniority first."

"I need to walk," said Rebecca. "Let's get the check. There's a full moon tonight, and I can't wait to see it."

"Full moon over the ocean," said Dick, motioning for the waiter. "Makes me want to *howl.*"

***

The moon was spectacular that night. It was a harvest moon, huge and orange; it hovered just above the nearly deserted shoreline. "I can't believe there aren't more people here," Eric commented after they had walked half an hour without seeing anyone.

"That's why we prefer North Miami Beach to South Beach," said Rebecca. "It's usually like this during the week."

"Oh, *fuck* South Beach," said Dick. "It's all Eurotrash. I've never seen so many phonies in one place. Hey, Beck, I'm getting tired—and thirsty, too. Can we park it here for a minute?"

"We can stop for longer than that," said Rebecca. She set the tote bag down and pulled out a large, rolled up blanket. "Give me a hand with this, guys."

They searched for a level spot and found one halfway between the water's edge and a row of seemingly empty beach houses behind them. They spread the blanket, kicked off their sandals, and sat down. Rebecca pulled the bottle of crew juice and three plastic glasses from the bag.

"Wow, this is living," said Eric, as she poured a drink for each of them. "Stick with us, babe," said Rebecca, leaning happily into Dick's chest.

Eric sat so close to them that he could feel the heat emanating from their bodies. He was overcome by the urge to reach over and touch them—both of them—but wasn't sure exactly how to proceed. He'd never found himself sexually attracted to a woman before. He'd been attracted to many heterosexual men, naturally. But he'd never given a minute's thought to the idea of trying to 'convert' a straight man. That was strictly the stuff of gay erotica. He decided to play it safe for the moment, rather than make an awkward move. He was content to enjoy their company and the beautiful locale. The moon was passing in and out of the clouds; every few minutes, the beach would turn pitch black. But he could still hear the waves rhythmically crashing against the sand. It was a perfect way to end the day; he couldn't remember ever feeling more relaxed.

"God, it's warm tonight," said Dick. He took off his shirt and folded it on the blanket. "Oh, man, does that feel good. I'm working up a sweat. It must be from the chili peppers in the food."

"You're just showing off," said Rebecca, giggling. She started running her hands across his chest, lingering for a moment to squeeze his nipples.

"Hey, what are you trying to do?" Dick said. "You know my nipples are wired to my dick."

"Everything's wired to your dick," said Rebecca, tugging gently.

"You look comfortable," said Eric, pulling off his shirt. "I think I'll join you."

"Wow, nice!" said Rebecca, admiring Eric's bare torso. "Now who's showing off? See, baby, if you'd spend a little time at the gym, you'd have a flat belly like Eric."

Dick shrugged. "I'm happy with myself exactly the way that I am."

Rebecca let go of one of his nipples and, with her free hand, began playing with Eric's chest hair. "I'm so glad you don't shave, Eric. I *hate* it when men shave their body hair."

"Never," said Eric, his mouth starting to get a little dry. A woman had never touched him like that. Her long, tapered nails and smooth fingers felt strange but pleasant on his skin.

"You boys are so lucky," Rebecca said petulantly. "You can take off your shirts wherever and whenever you want. I'm jealous."

"There's nobody else around," Dick said. "Who's stopping you?"

She smiled and slipped off the halter top. Her bare breasts were magnificent. They were round and firm, with large pink nipples. Dick took her left breast in his hand. "My God, I *love* these." He squeezed her nipple, making it instantly erect. "Eric, feel this, man."

Eric inched closer and nervously reached for Rebecca's right breast. Rebecca sighed as Eric's hand made contact with her body. Eric and Dick sat quietly for a moment, fondling her beautiful breasts. A moment later, Dick leaned forward, put his mouth on her nipple and started sucking it. As Eric watched, fascinated, Rebecca put her hand on the back of his head and guided him to her other nipple. As Dick and Eric both began sucking, she threw her head back and groaned.

Eric felt like he was in a dream, never imaging that he'd find himself in such a situation. He certainly never expected contact with woman's breasts to give him an erection. As he continued sucking, he reached over started caressing Dick's back and broad shoulders. When Dick didn't resist his touch, Eric slipped his hand around Dick's torso and began stroking his chest. Dick's nipples were just as responsive as Rebecca's. The contrast between their two bodies—hers was soft and smooth, his was solid and hairy—was extraordinary. A moment later, he felt Dick's hand exploring his chest. The sensation of Dick's slightly calloused hands on his skin made his dick so hard that he started leaking pre-cum.

"Oh, Jesus, this is wonderful," said Rebecca. "You're both such beautiful men."

"*You're* beautiful," said Dick. He cupped Rebecca's face in his hands and kissed her softly.

She responded by kissing him forcefully, and then opening her mouth and running her tongue around his lips. "Fuck, I love this," she said. "Are we taking this a little further, boys?" Before Eric could say anything, she reached for his crotch and started tugging at his zipper. He was thrown off-balance by her assertiveness, but quickly found himself reaching down to help her. He'd already gone this far; he was ready for a new kind of sexual experience. Besides, he knew that if he got naked, he'd get to see Dick naked too. And that was all the motivation he needed. As he slipped out of his shorts and underwear, his penis slapped against his stomach with a loud whack. The warm ocean breeze felt wonderful on his bare skin.

A moment later, Rebecca was naked too. The only one still wearing any clothing was Dick. "Come on, baby," said Rebecca. "We've been waiting for this all day." As Dick stood up, she knelt in front of him. Eric joined her, filled with anticipation. Dick, with his hand on the zipper, looked down at their eager faces and smiled. Without saying a word, he unzipped and stepped out of the shorts.

Eric couldn't believe the size of the penis that lay trapped in Dick's white cotton briefs. It was so big that it pushed out of the waistband and up past his navel. "Jesus Christ," he murmured. "Look at that thing."

Dick teasingly pulled his underwear down bit by bit, hesitating every few seconds, as though he was doing a striptease for them.

Rebecca, tired of waiting, yanked his briefs all the way down and grabbed his penis. "Look," she whispered to Eric. "I can wrap *both* my hands around it, and still not cover it completely." She moved one hand down the shaft until she reached the base. Encircling Dick's cock and balls, she squeezed hard, making his dick appear even bigger. Then she moved to the side a little bit and began stroking Eric's neck while slowing guiding his head forward. Eric closed his eyes and opened his mouth.

"Uh… hold it." He felt Dick's hand on his shoulder.

Eric opened his eyes. The throbbing, penis was only an inch away from his face. "*What?* What's the matter? Jesus, don't tell me you've changed your minds! I think it's a little late in the game for that."

"No, dude," Dick said. "It's just that I'm so hard right now, I'm afraid I'll come in two seconds if you start sucking me."

"Oh," Eric said, feeling slightly embarrassed.

"Damn," said Rebecca. "The wind's starting to pick up." She crossed her legs tightly. "The last thing I want right now is sand up my vagina."

"Believe me," said Dick. "That's the last thing that *I* want too."

"Do you guys want to go back to the hotel?" Eric asked, hoping that he hadn't spoiled the mood.

"No need," said Dick. "We have keys to that house right over there—the one with the wrap-around porch. It belongs to a friend of ours who's out of town."

"We can use it whenever we want," said Rebecca. "He has a great music collection, the fridge is always stocked, and there are clean sheets on the bed."

Eric grinned. "How convenient that you picked this particular spot to get the party started."

"What do you think we are?" said Dick, as he started getting dressed. "A couple of amateurs?"

"Listen, Eric, there are a few things we have to discuss," said Rebecca. "We should have brought them up right away, but you know how spontaneous we like to be."

"What is it?"

"Have you had an HIV test recently?"

He wondered if she asked the same question when they played around with heterosexuals. "Yes. Three months ago. It was negative."

"OK. Have you had any unsafe sex since your last test? Any anal sex without condoms or swallowing semen?"

How strange that her demeanor was so clinical, only three minutes after offering him her lover's penis. "No. I'm religious about practicing safer sex. I've been that way for a long time now."

"Good," said Dick. "We know what a drag it can be to talk about this. But we should mention boundaries, too. Basically, we're open to anything sexually, with two exceptions. One, no kissing—"

"Oh, I see. You don't kiss other men?"

"*Neither* of us kisses other people. And the other thing is: I'm the only person who fucks Beck without a condom."

"Not to worry. I don't think I'm ready to take that plunge yet anyway."

"Then it's all settled," said Dick. "Let's go."

"I've got to say," said Eric, "I like the way that you two discuss everything so openly."

"Agreed," said Dick. "It's always nice, though, when that conversation is out the way. Now let's move this party inside."

***

At midnight, Eric returned to his hotel room. He ripped off his sweaty clothes and fell naked onto the bed. His mind was reeling from the sights, sounds and smells that'd he'd just experienced for the first time. The most vivid memory of the evening was the moment when Rebecca was ready for Dick to enter her. By that point, the three of them had all driven each other to a near-frenzy; eager hands and mouths had been everywhere for what seemed like hours: squeezing... stroking... exploring... touching... tasting. As Rebecca laid back on the bed and Dick climbed on top of her, Eric positioned himself right behind Dick, leaning on his elbows. If this was going to be the one time in real-life that he watched a man fuck a woman, he was going to see it close up. He watched Dick slowly guide his penis into her, inch by inch. For a split second, he was insanely jealous of Rebecca. Did she realize how lucky she was to be able to feel a man's penis inside of her without a condom? For the last several years, that was all that Eric had experienced; skin-to-skin contact seemed like a distant memory. But then he quickly lost himself, watching the couple in rapt fascination. For some reason, he expected Rebecca to lay there passively until Dick was ready to take her. Instead, she took complete control. She wrapped her legs around Dick and slammed herself against him repeatedly, forcing him all the way inside. Each time that he slowly pulled out, trying to tease her, she pulled him right back in again. The two lovers began grunting, sweating, and establishing a sexual rhythm. They rocked back and forth so hard that the bed shook and Eric almost slipped off. Rebecca ordered Eric to come closer, and so he moved up and laid down next to them. He began stroking his own rock-hard cock each time that Dick thrust into Rebecca until the three of them were perfectly in synch. And finally, the three of them climaxed together, making loud, primal noises that Eric had never heard before. To his great surprise, the sound coming out of his mouth was the loudest of all.

***

He awoke to his phone ringing at nine o'clock in the morning. It was Dick calling. "Hey, Eric, are you up for breakfast?"

"Sure. I need to shower first. Give me about a half hour."

"No problem. Meet me in the lobby at nine-thirty. Beck's not coming, so it'll just be the two of us."

"What's up with Beck?"

"Dinner didn't agree with her last night." He chuckled. "Don't worry, buddy. Everything else agreed with her—just not dinner."

"OK. See you soon."

***

Dick was sitting in the lobby, dressed in a long-sleeve shirt, board shorts and a large-brimmed hat. As Eric approached, Dick stood up and hugged him.

"Is that Coppertone I smell?" Eric asked.

"Yeah, SPF 75. I burn like a mother-fucker in direct sunlight. This is how I spend all day on the beach and keep my lily-white skin. I am *not* going to end up like that lizard-skinned Chrissie. So, there's a great breakfast place about three blocks from here. You up for a little walk?"

"Sure."

"Do you mind walking on the shady side of the street?"

"Not at all." Eric held out his arm, which was still moist from applying suntan lotion. "SPF 50 for me. I don't want to end up looking like Chrissie, either."

***

"So, how was last night for you?" Dick asked, as soon as their coffee was served.

"It was great. I loved it."

"Were you surprised when we made a pass at you?"

"No. I had a funny feeling about you two right after we met. It's hard to explain."

"Was this your first three-way?"

"No, but it was my first time having a three-way with a woman."

"I know. We both got off on that."

"I surprised myself. I didn't know how I'd react, once we, uh… got down to it."

"How do you mean?"

"I was a little nervous that Beck would start making those noises."

"What kind of noises?"

"You know how in straight porn movies, as soon as a man starts fucking a woman, she begins moaning and squealing in a high-pitched voice? And then she starts talking dirty-talk, but all of a sudden, her voice is like a little girl's? I can't *stand* that. It ruins everything. I always have to turn the volume all the way down at that point."

Dick laughed so hard that he almost spit up his coffee. "That only happens in porn movies. That's not how real women have sex."

"Well, that's all *I* know about the way women have sex. I learned something new last night, I guess."

"Tell me, Eric, do you play around with a lot of other crewmembers?"

"Once in a while. I don't necessarily go out looking for it. If it happens, it happens."

"But when you do mess around, you keep it to yourself, right?"

"Absolutely. You know what they say: 'telephone, telegraph, tell a flight attendant.' My business is *my* business, and nobody else's."

Dick nodded. "It's amazing how narrow-minded some of our-co-workers are, especially the Southerners. I wonder why some of them are even here. It seems like they'd be much happier working a nine-to-five job and being home every night. Fuck, just become a greeter at Walmart and call it a day."

Eric studied Dick's face. He was so striking. And he seemed to be just as at ease alone with Eric this morning as he'd been last night. Suddenly, he felt the need to feel Dick's skin again. He slipped off his sandal and rubbed his bare foot against Dick's hairy leg under the table. "Dick, do you think we could try it alone together sometime, just the two of us?"

"Sorry." Dick smiled as he slowly pulled back his leg. "We don't do one-on-ones. And we don't do repeats either."

"Why not?"

"It makes things complicated. People start getting attached to one of us, or both of us, or one of us starts feeling attached to someone else. It causes all kinds of problems. So that's where we draw the line—to protect ourselves, I guess."

"I see. So, what are you: pretend swingers?"

"I guess you could say we're *half-assed* swingers. We like playing. Sometimes, I think it's because we're not ready to make a total commitment to each other. Whenever the subject comes up, one of us always seems to get cold feet."

"Well, since you're not committed, and since you and I like each other, why can't we—"

I don't consider myself bi, Eric," Dick said. "I like experimenting, *love* experimenting, in fact, but without the need for—"

"Labels." Eric's smile evaporated. Jesus, it was the classic straight male morning-after response. "I know. Rebecca mentioned it last night."

"Don't look so disappointed. That only strokes my ego. I tell you what we would like, though: we'd like to have you as a friend." He squeezed Eric's hand. "And I'm not saying that to let you down easy, or for any other bullshit reason.

We choose our friends very carefully, and we haven't met anyone like you in quite a long—"

"Excuse me," said their waitress, interrupting them. "Is one of you Dick Williams?"

"Yes, I am," Dick said, his hand still entwined in Eric's.

"I have a message for you for someone named Rebecca." She handed him a folded slip of paper. "She called a minute ago to see if you were here."

As Dick read the note, his eyebrows furrowed. "Oh, Christ." He threw a twenty-dollar bill on the table and grabbed his hat.

"What's the matter?"

"Beck's sick. She needs me back at the hotel. I've gotta go."

"Your breakfast is ready," said the waitress. "Do you want me to pack it up so you can take it to go?"

"No, thanks, I'll grab something later. Eric, I hope you have a big appetite this morning. I'm sorry, but you'll have to eat alone."

"I'll bring your order right out, sir," the waitress said to Eric.

"Do you want me to come with you?" said Eric, standing up.

"No." He shoved his sunglasses into his shirt pocket. "I don't think it's life-threatening. But I'll call you if we're not going make the trip today. Otherwise, we'll see you at four this afternoon. I've really gotta go now."

Eric sat down as the waitress returned with his breakfast on a tray. "Is everything all right with your friend?" she asked as she served him.

"I hope so." Breakfast smelled delicious. He hadn't realized how hungry he was until just that moment, and he dove into the food. "We're from out of town, and his girlfriend is sick today."

"His *girlfriend?*" she said skeptically.

Oh, thought Eric. It's because she saw us holding hands. Typical, narrow-minded Southern mentality. What else should he expect? "Yes, his girlfriend."

"Poor thing," said the waitress. "There's nothing worse in the morning than being sick. That can just *ruin* your whole damn day."

Eric almost choked on his eggs as three words started racing around in his brain: *Girlfriend. Morning. Sick.* Oh, shit.

CHAPTER 24

The Company You Keep

"JFK, Terminal ten," the driver called out. "Mercury Airways domestic and international flights."

As the bus slowed down, Eric grabbed his luggage and started pushing his way to the rear door. Before he'd even reached the exit, the bus was in motion again. "Hey!" he yelled. "Back door!"

"Back door!" hollered another rider, who was closer to the front.

Slam! Eric lunged for the nearest pole as the bus screeched to a stop.

"Jesus Christ!" said a woman, as she lost her footing. "Where do these mother fuckers learn how to drive?"

"They'll kill us all someday," Eric muttered as he hopped off the bus. As he reached the terminal entrance, he saw Ginnie Jo getting out of a taxi.

"Hey."

"Hey." She turned to the driver. "How much do I owe you, sir?"

"Forty dollars even, Miss."

"Here's fifty. Keep the change."

"Nice way to travel," said Eric. "Did you marry a millionaire since the last time I saw you?"

She laughed and took her cigarette case out of her purse. "No. The taxi ride was compliments of my date from last night. He's very generous."

"I see. Did he slip you fifty dollars for the powder room?"

"What? Oh, no. The guy that I'm dating lives across town from me, on the Upper West Side. He wanted me to spend the night, but I told him I'd only do it if he paid for my cab to the airport today." She plopped her tote bag on top of her suitcase. "It's the *schlep* factor, you know?"

"Tell me about it. I just got off the bus. It's like being crammed into a can of sardines."

"I remember when I was a new hire at Atlantic Coast, living in Queens and taking that bus to the airport. Thank God that shit is over." They watched as a limousine with tinted windows glided to a stop near them. "Now *there's* the right way to travel."

"I bet it's a movie star," Eric said excitedly, as the driver got out and opened the trunk.

"You never know. Let's wait a minute and see."

"Where are you going today?"

"L.A., on the two o'clock flight," she said.

"Me, too! What cabin are you in?"

"I'm in business." She sighed. "I can already hear the fingers snapping."

"I'm in coach. I can hear the babies wailing."

"Wanna trade?"

"Absolutely not."

"Never hurts to ask." She put out her cigarette. "Well, will you look at that." A handsome male flight attendant stepped out of the back seat of the limousine. He exchanged pleasantries with the driver as the driver stacked his luggage on the curb. "He doesn't even have to lift a finger. He probably *did* marry a millionaire. That type usually does."

"What type?"

"Duh! Tall, blond, beautiful. Built like a brick shithouse."

"*Ach*," said Eric. "I find blond men boring."

She snorted. "Like *you'd* toss him out of bed."

"How would I get him there in the first place?"

She patted his rear end. "Oh, you have your ways."

"His uniform jacket is a little snug," said Eric, as he watched the man walk through the automatic door. "And so are his pants. You know who he reminds me of? Dillon Hightower—the way he used to strut around the training center like Foghorn Leghorn. I couldn't *stand* him."

"Please! Don't ever mention that name in my presence. Having sex with him was one of the biggest mistakes I ever made."

"So you *did* have sex with Dillon!"

"Did you hear what I said? I don't want to hear his name!"

"Just tell me one thing, Ginnie Jo: did he have a nice penis?"

"What do you think?" She shivered. "Come on, let's get going."

***

They walked into operations together. "Geez, it's like a ghost town in here," said Ginnie Jo. "Where is everybody?"

"There aren't too many flights leaving at this time of day. It's an off hour."

"Are we full?"

"Yes, but to tell you the truth, I don't care. I'm just grateful to be on a transcon. I couldn't stand one more four-leg day on the Ultra Jet this month."

"I thought you loved all those takeoffs and landings."

"I do, but twelve hours straight on the Ultra Jet? Believe me: the thrill is gone."

"I shouldn't be so picky myself, having started all over again. Oh, well." She slung her Fendi purse over her shoulder. "I'm going to the food court to grab a salad. Want one? My treat."

"Sure."

"What kind of dressing?"

"Anything low-fat."

"You're counting calories? Why?"

"Because of this." He pinched an imaginary inch of fat on his waistline. "I've got to lay off the sundaes for good."

"Oh, God. You're getting as bad as the girls! See you at the gate." She blew him a kiss as she walked out the door.

As he blew a kiss back, he suddenly heard a disturbing noise. "*Brr-brr-blacccch!*" It sounded like someone was vomiting. He looked over and saw a lone male flight attendant standing in the corner. He was tall and exceedingly thin; his arms hung like matchsticks from beneath the shorts sleeves of his shirt. Perched on top of his head was one of the worst-looking hairpieces that Eric had ever seen.

"Are you all right?" Eric said.

He sneered, and then mouthed a three-syllable word. Eric couldn't decipher it, but it was clearly not a compliment.

Eric put down his paperwork and began walking toward him. "Is something the matter?" he asked, trying to look stern.

The flight attendant picked up his suitcase and marched past Eric without saying another word.

What the *hell*, thought Eric, is his problem?

***

"Did you pull up a crew list?" Ginnie Jo asked as they walked down the jet bridge.

"Yes. I know the purser, Sylvia Saks. She's great. I didn't recognize any other names."

"I don't know what everybody else is doing this evening, but I'm up for a drink after we land. I found a great little bar near the hotel that makes kick-ass margaritas. Are you interested?"

"Absolutely."

Sylvia was waiting for them at the entry door. "Where've you been?" she asked impatiently. "You missed my briefing."

Eric looked at his watch. "We're right on time, aren't we?"

"Yes, but the agents want to board early. We've got a full boat and they're hocking me to get the flight out on time."

Eric noticed that the handsome blond from the limousine was working in the first-class galley. "Who's that?" he asked.

"His name is Chaz," said Sylvia. "You can meet him later."

"All right, let us stow our bags and we'll be ready to board in one minute. Sylvia, this is Ginnie Jo."

"Hello," Sylvia said, rather coolly, to Ginnie Jo. Then she shooed them toward the rear of the plane. "The passengers will be here in a minute. Get going already."

"You go first, Eric," said Ginnie Jo. "You're all the way in the back."

"Thanks. I'll see you after takeoff." As he neared the business-class galley, someone abruptly shoved a cart into the aisle. "Ow!" he yelled, as he smashed his knee into it. A head popped out of the galley. It was the flight attendant with the terrible hairpiece.

"Sorry about that," he said, not sounding the least bit sorry. "Are you hurt?"

"What do *you* think?" said Eric.

He grabbed a rubber mallet and started breaking up a bag of ice. "Do you want an ice pack?"

"Don't bother. I'll get one in the back."

"Suit yourself."

Eric stood in the aisle, rubbing his knee. "Would you mind *moving* this cart so I can *get to* the back?"

The surly man put the cart away. "You should always be careful walking past this galley. It's a high traffic area."

"Thanks. I'll keep that in mind," said Eric, as he hobbled back to coach. He stowed his suitcase and was just about to introduce himself to the crew when he felt someone frantically grab his shoulder.

It was Ginnie Jo. "Trade with me," she said.

"What?"

"Trade positions with me, *please*."

"Nothing doing. I don't know who that asshole is in the galley, but I'm *not* working with him."

"Come on, I bought you salad!"

"No."

"You'll have the better jump seat, up at the front. You'll be sitting right next to that hot blond for takeoff and landing. I bet you'll *love* getting to know him."

"No! Look at those jerks in business class, already waving their jackets around like they're on fire. They can't wait even *three seconds* to have them hung up."

"Eric, I can't explain right now, but I am begging you. *Please*."

He looked into her eyes. For the first time ever, he saw raw, stark fear. "Oh, all right."

She looked immediately relieved. "Thank you!"

"But *you* deal with those passengers during boarding. I'm not setting foot in that cabin until after takeoff."

"Deal."

***

After the safety demo, Eric walked up to first class and sat down on his jump seat in the galley. He was only inches away from Chaz, who up close was even more handsome than he'd realized. Sylvia introduced them and said to Eric, "That redhead who boarded with you, she's a *close* friend of yours?"

"I wouldn't say 'close.' We were in the same training class."

"Do you know she used to work for another airline?"

"Yes. She was with Atlantic Coast before they ceased operations."

"And do you know that she crossed the picket line when they were on strike two years ago?"

"Yes, but how do you know that?"

"Because Brick used to fly with her at ACA."

"Who's Brick?"

"The business-class galley. Strange name for a *meskite,* I know, but—"

"Oh, him. What a jerk. And what's up with that toupee? It's *awful.*"

"Be grateful that you have such nice hair, darling. One day it could start falling out in handfuls."

"Never!" said Eric.

Chaz looked up from his glossy magazine. "You do have beautiful hair, Eric. Which shampoo do you use?"

"Bumble and bumble."

Chaz leaned over a took a whiff. "Nice."

"Gentlemen, let's focus, please," said Sylvia. "Brick has the scab list from their strike and her name is on it."

"I know all about their strike," said Eric. "Ginnie Jo wasn't the only person from ACA in my training class."

"Well?"

"We discussed it months ago. She knows it was the biggest mistake she ever made and said she'd never do it again."

"Don't be so naïve. Scabs are never to be trusted, regardless of what they say." She wagged a finger at him. "If I were you, I wouldn't be so chummy with her."

"I already know her. What should I do, completely ignore her?"

"I'm just saying that you should pick your friends very carefully. You have a sterling reputation at this base, Eric. Cherish it. We're just about to start a contract negotiation with the company, and things will heat up very quickly if it doesn't go well."

"I know that. I read our union newsletter every month and I listen to the hotline every Friday. I'm very well-versed in the negotiations process."

"If it looks like we *are* heading toward a strike, emotions will start running very high. People will either be pro-union or pro-company. I'd hate for anyone to think that you were in the wrong camp."

"Sylvia, I truly appreciate your concern," he said, "but I am a proud, well-informed, dues-paying member of our union. No one will ever have to worry about *me* crossing a picket line."

"Good," said Sylvia. "Keep it that way."

"What do you think about all this Chaz?" Eric asked.

Chaz looked up again. "Oh, I'm sorry! I wasn't paying attention. I'm trying to decide which new hardwood floors to install and I can't make up my mind." He showed Eric two samples in the magazine. "Which one do you like better?"

"The maple herringbone pattern. It's beautiful."

"You're putting new floors in your apartment again?" said Sylvia. "Didn't you guys just do that a year ago?"

"Not in the apartment," said Chaz. "In the beach house."

"Which one?" Sylvia asked. "East Hampton or the Pines?"

"East Hampton."

"Hoo-ha!" said Sylvia. "It must be nice."

"Where's your apartment?" Eric asked Chaz.

"We live on Central Park West, just a few blocks from the Natural History Museum."

"I was just there a week ago and at MoMA the week before."

"I'm impressed!" said Chaz. "A flight attendant who takes advantage of all of that New York has to offer."

"I love it here," said Eric. "I try to spend all my days off in the city."

"Well," said Chaz, "since you're around so often, maybe Aaron and I will have you over one night. Tell me: are you single?"

"Yes."

"Oh, what fun! We could introduce you to some very nice people if you're interested."

"I'd love it!" Eric said, amazed at his good fortune.

"Now, see, Eric?" said Sylvia. *"This* is a friendship you should be cultivating!"

***

After takeoff, Eric went back to business class. Brick and a petite brunette were standing in the galley. "Hi," said the brunette, smiling. "I'm Jackie."

"I'm Eric. Nice to meet you." At least *she* seemed friendly.

"Where's Scabrina?" asked Brick.

"Who?"

"Scab-rina," Brick repeated with relish.

"She's working in coach today," said Eric. "*I'm* working here."

"Fine by me," said Jackie. "Do you want to pass out menus, Eric?"

"Sure."

Brick had already divided the menus in half. "Here you go," he said, passing a stack to Jackie. "Jackie, you have two kosher meals in row seven." He passed the other half to Eric. "You, scab lover, you don't have any special meals today."

Eric's hand froze in mid-air. Three syllables: *scab lover*. That's the phrase that Brick had muttered in operations. "Jackie, would you excuse us a second, please?"

"Sure."

"Thanks." Eric pulled the curtain closed. "Listen, I don't know what your problem is. And I don't give a shit about your history with Ginnie Jo. That's your history, not mine. But if you think you're going to treat *me* like a piece of shit for the next two days, you're out of your fucking mind." He was shocked at the words coming from his own mouth. He'd never spoken to another crewmember that way, but then he'd never found it necessary to do so. It felt wonderful. "Knock it off, or I'll rip that goddam wig off your head and shove it right up your ass. Got me?"

"You'd better be careful the way you talk to me," Brick managed to stammer. "You're still on probation. I'll go right into the office and get you fired like *that.*"

Eric inched closer, enjoying the look of fright on Brick's face. "I figured you for a little chicken shit who'd go running to the office for protection. If you don't want that reputation, I suggest that we settle this ourselves like grown men, right now."

"Here's how we'll settle it," said Brick, trying to regain some of his bluster. "Unless it involves the service or the safety of this flight, don't talk to me at all."

"Fine by me. The less I have to say to you, the better." He opened the curtain. "Jackie, we're ready to get started now."

***

For two hours straight, Eric and Jackie never stopped running. The requests were endless. Brick did his job quietly and efficiently, saying as little as possible. Eric and Jackie worked well together. They maintained a steady stream of conversation over Brick's head, which to Eric's delight seemed to annoy him greatly.

"Here's my last dirty tray," said Jackie, coming into the galley.

"The dessert carts are just about ready," said Brick. "Jackie, would you call the back and ask them to send up a couple of people to help out?"

Two young females came up a moment later. Ginny Jo was not one of them. The four flight attendants pulled the dessert carts into the aisle, only to be barraged by another round of special requests:

"Can I have extra fudge on my ice cream? A little more... a little more... a little *more*, please."

"I'm a purist. Just pour a double shot of Courvoisier over mine."

"I don't eat ice cream. Give me *two* plates of cheese and crackers."

"I'll take coffee, one-third regular and two-thirds decaf with a lot of skim milk and just a few drops of cream. No, no, you put in too much cream! I can't drink that! You'll have start all over again."

By the time that he'd dealt with the last special request, Eric wanted to strangle them all. As soon as he finished, he called Sylvia. "The service is over. Do me a favor and dim the lights in business."

"Thank God," said Jackie, as the cabin went dark. "I've never poured so much wine in my life. Maybe they'll all pass out now."

"They'd better," said Eric. "I refuse to go out there again until it's cookie time."

"Hey, can I ask y'all something?" said one of the flight attendants from coach. Her name was Glenda.

Brick sighed. "If it's about what we have left over to eat, you'll have to *wait.* I haven't had five minutes to—"

"No, it's not about that," said Glenda. "Hang on. I'll be right back." She returned a moment later with the latest issue of the union newsletter. "This just came in the mail yesterday. I tried to read it but I'm totally confused."

Brick stopped working immediately. "What about?"

"Well, there's a long article about the contract negotiation. It seems like a big deal. I've only been working here for a month, and I can't make heads or tails of it. See, I'm from Mississippi. We don't have unions there. My father always says the ones in the Northeast are run by the Mafia. Could one of y'all tell me what's going on?"

Brick snorted. "Simple: this negotiation is going to be a shit show and we'll be on strike by next Easter."

"A strike?" said Glenda. "Why would we go on strike?"

Brick smiled for the first time that day. "To shut this mother-fucking airline *down.*"

"Oh, my God!" She turned pale. "You mean I'll lose my job? But I just started!"

"Oh, you can keep your job—if you want to be a *scab.*"

"What does that mean?"

"A scab is someone who crosses the picket line and goes to work while the rest of are outside *walking* the picket line—fighting the company for our jobs, our futures and our lives."

"I don't think I'd ever do *that*," said Glenda, wide-eyed.

"Let's see," said Brick. "It's November now. If you're brand-new, by the time that Easter rolls around, you'll still be on probation, right?"

"What difference would that—"

"Don't you get it?" said Brick. "That's why they hired you. That's why they hired *all* of you last year—to cross the picket line in order to maintain the operation while the rest of us are out on strike."

"Are you saying I wouldn't have a choice?"

"Yes, you'll have a choice. As a probationary, you can walk the line with us, in which case the company will fire you for not reporting for work. Or you can cross the picket line and be known as scab for the rest of your career."

"Oh, *stop* it, Brick," said Eric. "What you're telling her is utter nonsense. Glenda, the negotiation process has barely begun. All we've done so far is elect flight attendants to represent us on the negotiating committee. We still have a very long way to go." He calmly explained each step of the arduous process per the outline in the newsletter. "It will take a year, minimum. Even if the talks completely break down at the end and the union calls a strike, everybody who participates is covered. You cannot be fired for going on strike, even if you're on probation. It's a violation of federal law."

"Eric is right," said Jackie. "And I ought to know."

"What makes you think you know so much, Jackie?" said Brick.

"Because I'm one of the people who was elected to be on the negotiating committee, and I have a strong background in labor relations."

"Well," he said, smirking, "you all can delude yourselves all you want. But this airline has lost money every quarter for the past two years. Senior management would *love* a strike. That way, they can get rid of all the senior people who earn the highest pay, and replace them with new hires who make diddly squat. Knowing how incompetent our union is, the whole thing will be a disaster. They have no idea what they're doing. Like I said: shit show."

"Thanks for the vote of confidence," Jackie said warily.

"Nevertheless," said Brick, "I'll be out on strike too if it comes down to that. I'd *never* cross a picket line."

"Oh, golly," said Glenda. "I don't know what to think!"

"If you *do* cross, Glenda," said Brick, "you'll keep your job, but I guarantee you that you won't want it anymore. The strikers will know what you are and we'll make your work life a living hell." He smirked. "Go ask Ginnie Jo. She'll tell you all about it" He took off his apron and tossed it on the counter. "Whew, I'm spent. I need a change of scenery. I'll be up in the cockpit if anybody needs me. Leftovers are in the oven."

"I should head back," said Glenda. "They're probably wondering where I am. Thanks, Eric, I feel a lot better."

"Any time. Let me know if you have other questions."

"How long have you been flying, Eric?" Jackie asked.

"Almost six months."

"Wow, I'm impressed. How'd you get to be so well versed so fast?"

"I read a lot." He grinned. "It's something to do while you're on a twenty-hour Tulsa layover."

"It's not just that. You're very bright. You understand the process and you explain it very well. Listen, we're about to start recruiting volunteers at each base for a new program called 'The 4-1-1.' Are you interested in joining?"

"What would I do?"

"You'll wear a special pin that identifies you as a member of the program. People can come to you with any questions they might have. You'd get updates from the union before they go out to the general membership, along with talking points. The rumor mill is already flying, as you can see. We want people to have the facts. This program will help to keep everyone informed—and unified, which is something we desperately need."

"Sure, I'd be happy to. Although I don't understand why more people don't just read the newsletter. It's all there in black in white."

"Unfortunately, many of them won't take the time. Half of them didn't even bother vote for union president in the last election. Don't they know what kind of message that sends to the company?" She let out a long sigh. "Lord. I hope we can get through this process without any major drama."

"What's your gut feeling?"

"Confidentially, I'm afraid we're in for a rough ride. On that note, Brick wasn't so far off. But the future isn't quite as dire as he predicts. That's why it's so important to disseminate real information."

"I'd love to get involved, Jackie. You can count on me."

"Great." She picked up the crew phone as it rang. "Hello? ... Yes, he's right here." She passed the phone to him. "It's Sylvia."

"Darling," said Sylvia, "have you eaten?"

Not yet."

"We have plenty of food left over. And we're looking at some nice pictures of Chaz's. Why don't you come up? And bring that layover photo album of yours." She giggled. "I want him to see how you look in civvies."

"I'll be right there."

***

Looking at Chaz' photo album was like thumbing through an issue of *Vanity Fair*. "Here we are at Opening Night of the Metropolitan Opera this year," said Chaz. "Doesn't Aaron look wonderful in that new tuxedo?"

"Absolutely," said Eric. Aaron appeared to be about ten years older than Chaz. He had a full head of beautiful silver hair, blue eyes, and a square jaw. "Does he wear anything *but* tuxedos?"

Chaz laughed. "Oh, yes. We've just been very busy socially this year. He's forever dragging me to one black-tie event or another. Now, here's a more casual shot from last summer. In Greece." In the photograph, Aaron and Chaz were standing together at the water's edge. Despite the difference in their ages, it was difficult to say who had the more beautiful body. Aaron's chest was broader, and his shoulders were wider. He was hairy chested and deeply tanned. Chaz was leaner and his body was completely smooth but he had muscles popping out from head to toe.

"Wow, that's breath-taking," said Eric. "I've never seen water that color. Where are you? In Mykonos?"

"Oh, heavens, no. I'd never get Aaron to visit such a tourist trap. We were on…" He mentioned the name of an island, but Eric didn't quite catch it.

"I've never heard of it," said Eric. "Where is that?"

"It's another island in the Aegean."

"Wow," said Eric. "I should put that place at the top of my list. In two weeks, I'm getting off probation, and I'll finally get my travel benefits. How do you spell the name of that island?"

"You might want to think a little smaller if you're traveling on your own," said Chaz. "That's a private island, accessible by invitation only. We happen to be friends with the man who owns it."

"Oh," said Eric, feeling waifish. "Then maybe I'll consider a few days in Fort Lauderdale this winter instead."

Chaz grinned. "Remember, I said on your *own*. I can think of several men right off the bat who would love to have you as a traveling companion. All on their dime, of course."

"Don't be vulgar, Chaz," said Sylvia, as she finished the last bite of filet mignon. "Eric's not the gigolo type."

"Maybe not. But when he does settle down, wouldn't you like him to be partnered with someone who has a few assets?"

"Of course, but he's not going to be a kept man. Now, Eric, show us some of your pictures."

"Well, I don't have that many," he said, as he presented a small photo album. "Remember, I've only been here six months. Let's see… here I am in San Francisco."

"The Golden Gate Bridge at sunset," Chaz said politely. "Isn't that nice? A must-have snapshot for any new hire to share with friends and family."

"It is very nice," said Eric. "San Francisco is my absolute favorite layover city. Then here I am in Los Angeles… and here I am in Seattle… and here I am in Boston."

"Hmm," said Sylvia. "These are mostly interior shots of bars." She pursed her lips. "Is that where you're spending all of your layovers? In bars?"

"Not every layover," said Eric. "I try to see the sights, too, depending on where we are."

"Which museums have you been to in San Francisco?" asked Sylvia.

"None, I'm afraid. They all seem to be kind of far from the layover hotel."

"Not true. For starters, there's a city bus near the hotel that will take you straight to the de Young."

"Where is that?"

"In Golden Gate Park. Don't tell me you haven't even been to the park? *Oy!*"

"Well, lots of times, after a long flight, it's nice just to be able to sit down and have a drink somewhere." He took the album from Sylvia's hands. "Look, here are nice photographs of downtown Philadelphia. That was a wonderful layover. Isn't that a great shot of City Hall?"

"Let me see that," said Chaz. He frowned. "Is that Denny Malinovsky you're with?"

"Yes."

"You're friends with him?"

"He's my best friend. We try to fly together whenever we can. It's not easy at my seniority, but we manage. Do you know him very well?"

"Yes, I do," said Chaz. "We invited him to a dinner party a few years ago. He showed up drunk, made a pass at Aaron in front of all our guests, and almost knocked a Lalique vases off an end table."

"That Denny," said Sylvia, shaking her head. "He's a nice man, but he has a problem."

"He's been very generous to me," Eric said defensively. "He's treated me to dinner many times, and shown me how to get a better schedule, and even helped me find an apartment when I was living in a real hellhole. We enjoy going out together. We have a lot of fun."

"No one's saying that you shouldn't have fun, sweetheart," said Sylvia. "But you get into certain habits with certain people, and they can be hard to break. Too many flight attendants spend their careers inside bars. What a *waste* of a golden opportunity."

"I'm going to give you an opportunity right now, Eric," said Chaz. "Are you free on November eighteenth?"

"I'll have to double-check my schedule, but yes, I think so."

"Good. How would you like to come with us to a benefit at the Guggenheim? Aaron's firm paid for an entire table. There's one vacant seat, and I'd love to put you in it."

"Oh my," said Sylvia. "Talk about starting him at the top. What's the dress for this shindig?"

"Black tie optional," said Chaz.

"What does that mean?" asked Eric.

"It means that if don't have a tuxedo, you can wear a very nice dark suit," said Sylvia. "You could probably wear the one you wore to your interview last spring."

"A fair number of people will be coming right from their offices, including a gentleman that I want you to sit next to," said Chaz, smiling. "You'll be just fine."

"I'd love to come."

"Good," said Chaz. "I hate to think of you languishing in sleazy bars night after night when you have so much to offer. You should take advantage of your youth *and* your connections, Eric—if you're fortunate enough to have connections."

"It's very nice of you to invite me, and I look forward to it," said Eric. "Just the same, I don't know if I'm ready to settle down completely. I still have plenty of time for that."

"In this job," said Chaz, "a year goes by in the blink of an eye. And it will suck the very life out of you if you spend too much time at it. I only fly one trip a month, if that often. I drop all of my trips through a trip-trade service." He picked up the magazine again. "There are so many other more important things on my agenda."

There was just enough condescension in his voice to make Eric rethink accepting the invitation. "How nice for you. Chaz, just out of curiosity, who did you vote for in the election for union president?"

"When was that?" Chaz asked, without looking up.

"Just a month ago," said Sylvia. "I'm curious to know who you voted for too."

"I'm afraid I missed that one. Where were we in October? Oh, now I remember. We were at a ranch near Albuquerque. Aaron's sponsored an entry in the balloon festival this year. Oh, look at this beautiful mid-century dining table! It would be perfect for the house in East Hampton. And it's a steal at only five thousand dollars!"

Sylvia shook her head. "I swear, it's like flying with Doris Duke!"

A moment later, Jackie walked into the galley. "Hey, Eric, are you ever coming back? I could use a break myself. Those call lights still haven't stopped ringing."

"Of course. Sorry, Jackie. I'll head right back."

"And don't forget to give me your phone before the trip is over," said Chaz. "I'm expecting you at that benefit."

"I'll keep the date open."

"Good," said Chaz, still admiring the dining table. "Don't take this the wrong way, Eric, but from what I've seen, your circle of friends needs a little widening."

***

"So what do you think of Chaz?" Sylvia asked, as she and Eric walked through the terminal in Los Angeles.

"He leads quite a rarified life."

"Did you give him your phone number?"

"Yes. I was surprised that he didn't rescind the invitation when he saw my Queens area code."

"I know that he comes off as a little full of himself, but his heart's in the right place. He and Aaron hosted a fundraiser for our team in the AIDS Walk last year *and* gave us a check for twenty-five hundred dollars to boot."

"That's very generous."

"He does know a lot of interesting people. And you could do him a world of good too. He needs a few more down-to-earth friends. You'd complement each other very well."

"You're quite the matchmaker, aren't you?"

"There's a method to my madness. I also need someone to keep him in the loop about what's happening to those of us who do work full time. Ditto the Connecticut housewives married to lawyers and stockbrokers, who barely fly at all. It's impossible to get their attention even when they are here. Jackie told me you're going to become a 4-1-1 rep. I'm thrilled. You'll be great at it. So, what are you doing tonight?"

He nodded toward Ginny Jo, who was walking alone a few feet ahead of them. "I was going to have a drink with Ginny Jo, but she changed her mind. She said she'd rather spend the evening by herself."

"She may be doing a lot of that," said Sylvia. She shook her head. "Poor thing. But she did bring it on herself. One poor decision made, and it will follow her for the rest of her career."

"Yes," Eric agreed tersely. "That *is* unfortunate."

"Oh, that tone! Is something the matter?"

"No, I'm just ready for a new topic of conversation."

"Agreed. Listen, Jackie and I are meeting for dinner later. Want to join us?"

"Sure, as long as we talk about anything but the bid sheet, the union or this airline in general."

"That," said Sylvia, "would be a genuine pleasure. Meet us in the lobby at six."

CHAPTER 25

The Looking Glass

"Do you want another beer, Leander?" Eric asked.

"No, this one's still half full," his friend replied. As he looked around the bar, the halogen lights overhead gleamed off of his bright red hair. "I think I'm going to head home. I have an early sign-in tomorrow, and this place isn't my scene. Aren't you and Denny flying tomorrow too?"

"Not until the afternoon, so I think I may stay a while longer."

"Are you sure you want too? You don't look like you're enjoying yourself."

"I'm all right." Eric signaled the bartender for another cocktail. "I feel like a bit of a wallflower today. In fact. I'm starting to feel like a wallflower every time I go out in New York City." He surveyed the crowd. "How many men do you think are in here right now?"

"Two hundred, easily."

"Well, look, I want to ask you something, and I'm not begging for compliments. But I'm... reasonably attractive, aren't I?"

"You're adorable. Good body, great hair and a pretty face."

"Then how come I can't get a conversation started with a single man here?"

"Easy," said Leander. "Because you're competing with *that*." He pointed to the center of the room, where a muscular stripper with a shaved head and smooth, copper-colored skin was crouched on the bar, thrusting his pelvis into the air. He was very tall and had enormous hands and feet. Eager men were lined up ten-deep to shove money into his jockstrap, which looked as though it might burst open at any moment from the strain of its contents.

"Are you kidding?" said Eric. "Nobody can compete with that."

"I know. But that's what everybody wants. Sorry, Eric, but you should have been here five years ago. The tide has turned: the clean-cut look is out, and the Blatino is in."

"The what?"

"Men like that stripper. Half black, half Latino, and built like a proverbial shit house. Add a chunky gold necklace and tattooed knuckles, and you have the perfect fantasy man."

"The kind you don't take home to mother."

"That's the whole point. Everyone's tired of playing safe. They want forbidden fruit. They want *dangerous*."

Eric watched the stripper jump off the bar and start strutting toward the back of the room. The crowd cheered as they followed him with dollar bills in their hands. "Wow," said Eric. "There are no gay men like that where I come from."

"He's not gay, he's straight. Allegedly."

"Then what's he doing in a gay bar, teasing men with his big, allegedly unavailable dick?"

Leander laughed. "He's here for the money, what else?"

"That seems completely exploitative to me. Why are these guys getting all worked up over someone they can never have? It just reinforces that same tired, old idea that all gay men really want to do is convert a straight man."

"Oh, honey, you're reading way too much into it. We get a cheap thrill, and he makes some quick cash. It's a fair trade."

"Money," said Eric, shaking his head. "Once again, it comes down to *that*."

"Yes, which brings me to the second reason you're not scoring— in this bar anyway. If the men our age can't have a hunky Blatino, they want a sugar daddy. This city's impossible to live in if you're poor, as you well know. Once they find out that you're a 'trolley dolly' who makes eighteen grand a year, they run in the other direction. They can be poor all by themselves. In real life, misery does *not* love company."

"I give up. I'm ready to go home too. Why don't you stay, Leander? You're getting cruised left and right."

Leander shrugged. "It's my red hair. That's the other exotic feature that seems to be in demand this year. But I don't want to start something I can't finish. So, where are you and Denny off to tomorrow?"

"A three-day trip to Indianapolis and Akron."

"What on earth is Denny doing on a trip like that at his seniority?"

"He enjoys flying with me. And now and then he likes to be reminded how the other half lives. He says it keeps him humble."

"Wow," said Leander. "If I were you, I'd hang onto *that* friendship for dear life."

***

"Hi, sweetheart," said Denny, walking over Eric in operations the next day. "Ready to head to the gate?"

"Yep." Eric pointed at Denny's chest. "Did you know you have a big stain on your tie?"

"Where?"

"Right there. You can't miss it."

"Oh, shit." He scratched the spot with a fingernail, which only made it worse. "I think it's tomato sauce. This stain will never come out of silk."

"Go see the M.O.D. Maybe she can give you a loaner."

"Eh," said Denny. "Who's going to notice?"

"Everyone will notice. It looks like you were in a meatball fight."

"God, you're fussy." He eyed Eric carefully. "Don't you ever have a loose thread? A scuffed shoe? A little ring around the collar?"

"No. I don't. I like being that way."

***

"So, what are we doing tonight?" Eric asked as they walked through the terminal.

"We're going out, of course."

"Does anybody else go out on Wednesday night in Indianapolis?"

"We shall see." He pinched Eric's rear end. "If not, we always have each other."

"I'm glad we have a late pickup tomorrow," said Eric. "Just the same, let's not drag ourselves back to the hotel at four in the morning." He remembered Sylvia's warning about spending all of his layovers in bars. "I want to do some sightseeing, too."

"Sure. We'll start at the V.F.W. National Headquarters and go from there."

"Oh my God," said Eric, as they approached the security checkpoint. "Do you see that?" Standing in front of them was the sloppiest crewmember that Eric had ever seen. A cranberry-colored sweater, dotted with lint, was casually tied around the waist of her uniform dress. She carried an enormous, overstuffed backpack on top of her suitcase and wore clogs. Her hair, a patchwork quilt of various shades of blond, was piled on top of her head and secured with a banana clip.

"I hope she's not a smoker," said Denny. "One tiny spark and that bale of hay would go up in flames. Where do you think she's flying to?"

"Orlando," Eric replied with a sneer. "It *has* to be Orlando. She'll fit right in."

"You really loathe that city, don't you?"

"Don't get me started." Eric watched as she struggled to lift her heavy luggage onto the conveyer belt. "Look at that suitcase. It's like a Winnebago! Who packs that much shit to go to work? Never mind, I know: commuters." He sneered again. "She *has* to be—"

"Eric, you're starting to repeat yourself. You need to get a new *schtick*."

"She can't even contain all of her stuff. Look, a sandwich just fell out of her backpack!"

"Maybe she doesn't know. Excuse me, Miss," Denny said to the flight attendant. "Do you know that your backpack is open?"

"What? Oh, yeah, the zipper is broken," she said. "I've only got, like, a hundred magazines crammed in there."

"No doubt the *National Enquirer* is at the very top of the pile," Eric muttered.

"Where are you guys going today?" she asked.

"Indy and Akron," said Denny.

"No kidding! So am I! My name's Marla. I'm the number one."

"I'm Denny, and this is Eric."

"OK, I'll see you guys down there. I gotta stop at Hudson News and buy some gum." She grabbed her luggage and ran.

"She's going to be disappointed," said Eric. "I don't think they sell watermelon-flavored Bubbliscious there."

"You're on a roll today," said Denny. "It's a good thing you're not working up front with her."

"I won't even be going up for leftovers," said Eric. "I can only imagine what her galley looks like when she's through with the service."

"Oh, God, would you *please* stop making that face."

"What face?"

"Have you ever seen *The Prime of Miss Jean Brodie*?"

"Of course. It's a classic."

"Remember the brittle, prune-lipped headmistress who keeps trying to get Jean fired?"

"Yes."

"*That* face."

***

In Indianapolis, as they waited for their hotel rooms, Eric was so obsessed with Marla's horrible hair that he didn't hear Denny talking to him.

"Eric! Are you listening to me? I'm trying to tell you about our options for tonight."

"Sorry, I was preoccupied."

"With what?"

He nodded toward Marla, who was twirling a long, multi-colored strand while she talked on the pay phone. "I'm trying to count exactly how many unnatural shades of blond there are on her head."

"Christ, why do you care? You're not her supervisor."

"Because she's a *mess*," Eric replied, surprised at his own anger. "Because she drags the rest of us down. Because people see her in uniform and think, '*This* is who Mercury is hiring these days? Their standards are falling right off a cliff.' And yet no one says anything to her! That's what pisses me off the most. Where are the supervisors who put me on the scale and checked me over from head to toe every week like I was a fucking five-year-old?"

"Have they done it since you got off probation?"

"They certainly—well, no. They haven't."

"Of course not. Unless you're a new hire and they have to do it, most supervisors don't have the time to run around doing grooming checks. That's the first problem. The second problem is that some people don't give a shit about their appearance. And if there's no one around to hound them about cleaning up their act, they don't bother. It's like I told you when I first met you: play the game for your first six months and then anything goes. Unfortunately, it's a double-edged sword."

"Then why should *I* bother to—"

"Oh, God, I know. *Everyone* knows: 'Eric Saunders exceeds all expectations. Never a hair out of place or a gravy stain on his sleeve, even after a twelve-hour day.' You're the best of the best. Maybe they'll give you an award for impeccable grooming someday—although I wouldn't hold my breath. As far as everybody else is concerned, *drop* it. Frankly, I'm sick to death of hearing you complain."

For some reason, Eric couldn't let it go. "So what you're saying is that the entire flight attendant corps should be able to come to work looking like slobs, without any repercussions at all."

"There! That's *your* problem, Eric. You talk about everybody else's faults, but you don't even realize how aggravating *you* can be. Using expressions like 'the flight attendant corps.' Nobody talks like that! This isn't 1965. Nobody wears a bouffant hairdo, or a girdle, or gets swept off her feet by Cary Grant in first class on the 707. This is a *job* that people keep because of the twelve-day monthly work schedule, the health insurance. and the free travel benefits. And that's all, got it?"

"I'll never mention it again, Denny. Or anything *else*, for that matter."

They signed in for their rooms and took their keys. "How much time do you need to get ready?" Denny asked.

"Get ready? I'm not going *anywhere* with you."

"Oh, yes you are, buddy boy. I didn't pick up this lousy three-day trip to go trolling through Middle America on my own."

"You should have thought about that before you insulted me."

"Now you're acting like a five-year-old. Get upstairs, get out of that girdle and meet me back here in forty-five minutes. Otherwise, you can find another patsy to fly these dog trips with you. I'm *done*."

"All right," Eric said, finally relenting. "But you're buying the first round."

"So, what else is new?"

***

"Where to?" asked the cab driver.

"We're going here," said Denny, showing him a downtown address. "It's pretty close, right?"

"Ten minutes," said the driver, as he turned on the meter.

"Is there anything special going on there tonight, Denny?" Eric asked.

"Yes. Like I was trying to tell you in the lobby, it's Disco Night. The guy at the front desk said if there are any people out, that's where they'll be."

"He's right," said the driver. "Indianapolis isn't exactly rocking mid-week. But it'll be a nice crowd. Hey, if a guy named George is tending bar, tell him Joe said hi and that I'll stop by this weekend."

It was then that Eric noticed the decal on the dashboard. "I like your rainbow flag, Joe."

"It pays to advertise." He looked at Eric and Denny in the rearview mirror. "Where are you guys from?"

"New York," said Denny.

"Oh, boy," said Joe, laughing. "I hope your expectations aren't too high."

Eric liked him. He was beefy and had bushy eyebrows and a nice face. "We're just looking for some nice people to hang out with. We like Midwesterners. They're so friendly."

"That we are," said the driver.

"Are you stopping by for a drink after your shift?" Eric asked.

"Naw, I'm working until three A.M."

"Who's out on the street at three in the morning in Indianapolis?" asked Denny.

"You'd be surprised." The driver stopped in front of a nondescript two-story building. "Well, here you are. The bar's on the second floor. That'll be seven dollars, please."

"I've got this," said Eric, reaching for his wallet. "Here's ten. Keep the change."

"Welcome to Indianapolis, guys. I hope you have a great time." Joe smiled at Eric as he started to get out of the car. "Wait a minute. Here's my card. Give me a call me if you need a ride back to the hotel."

"Thanks, Joe, I will."

"What's your name?"

"Eric."

"Nice to meet you. Don't lose that number."

"Don't worry, I won't."

"Hey, Eric, come on!" Denny shouted. "It's cold out here."

Eric joined him at the front door. "This place doesn't look too promising."

"Let's keep an open mind," said Denny, pulling the door handle. As they started climbing a long, steep staircase, they could hear *Ring My Bell* blaring over the stereo system. "It's Disco Night all right."

"Oh, God, does this song take me back!" said Eric.

"It takes *you* back? To when—the fourth grade?"

"I know all of these songs by heart. I hope you're ready to dance your ass off."

"Honey, you know I have two left feet. I'm not promising anything."

"Well, if even just for the music, this should be a fun night. I'm glad we came. Sorry if I was being a baby earlier."

"It's forgotten. You look great, by the way. Your t-shirt is just tight enough, and those jeans fit you perfectly. Hell, I may keep you all to myself tonight."

"We'll see about that. I might want to make a new friend."

As they entered the dimly lit main room, they saw fifteen middle-aged men seated around a brass-railed bar that was decorated with miniature blinking lights. A few of the men glanced up at Denny and Eric and then went right back to sipping their drinks. To the right of the bar, there was a small stage with a glitter-painted microphone in a stand. In front of the stage, there was a small parquet dance floor, which at the moment was empty.

"Well," Denny said under his breath. "Which one of these Romeos do you want on your dance card first?"

"Whichever one isn't wearing acid-washed jeans."

"Then you're shit outta luck. The bartender is good-looking though. Let's go order a drink."

"Hi, guys," said the bartender. At least *he* was smiling. "What'll you have?"

"One gin and tonic and one vodka and soda, please," said Denny. "Make them both doubles. Is your name George, by the way?"

"Yeah. Why?"

"Joe the cab driver says hi and that he'll be in this weekend."

"Oh, good. Too bad he's not here tonight. Kind of a grim crowd so far, as you can see. But it's early still." He set their drinks on the bar. "That'll be ten dollars, please."

"Ten dollars for two doubles?" said Denny. "Honey, I'm home!"

As the last refrain of *Ring My Bell* faded away, George picked up portable microphone behind the bar. "Gentlemen, please welcome to the stage, for a special announcement, the entertainer who has more talent in her *schnozola* than Cher, Madonna, and Bette Midler combined ... Indy's very own 'greatest star' ... Miss Barbra Alarma!"

A drag queen wearing a silk sailor blouse and a bobbed brunette wig stepped up on the stage and picked up the microphone. "Hello, boys, I'm he-ah!" she brayed in Brooklynese, only to be drowned out by the screech of feedback. "Goddammit, Kenny, would somebody come and *fix* this fucking thing?!"

Denny sighed. "No, *please*. No amateur drag tonight. I don't have the strength."

Eric nudged him. "Don't be rude."

A man came scurrying onto the stage and adjusted the microphone. "Thank you, Kenny," said Barbra. "Remind me to show you later how grateful I am for *all* of your efforts… with a swift kick in the *tuckus*. Well, boys, I'm sorry I'm late, but I had a little business to take care of—out in the back alley. OK, I lied: it was *big* business. *Very* big business. About—" She held her palms twelve inches apart. "—*that* big!"

"Ba-*dum*-bump," said Denny.

There were a few weak chuckles from the bar.

"Oh, come on now! A girl's gotta make a living. And I can't do it on the tips that *you* cheap bastards shell out!" This remark was met with a long stony silence. "*Oy vey!* Lighten up, boys! Geez, I haven't worked a crowd *this* hard since I was in the back alley just now." The entertainer looked around the room and set her gaze on Denny and Eric. "Well, what do we have here? I've never seen you two before. Hello, gorgeous and *gorgeous!*" She flicked her hair back with a ridiculously long fake fingernail. "It's been so long since we've had any new customers in here—I mean, you know, under the age of forty. Ha *ha!*"

"Rule number one when you're on stage," said Denny. "Never laugh at your own jokes."

Eric, who didn't want to appear like a big city snob, smiled and said nothing.

"I think it's a sign, fellas," said Barbra. "Maybe things are gonna start changing for the better. It's possible, just *possible*, that…" She smiled a crooked smile and started singing *Happy Days Are Here Again.*

Someone slammed his fist on the bar. "Don't start with that maudlin shit! It's Disco Night! I wanna hear *I Will Survive.*"

"*Sweetheart*, with that pickled liver of yours, you won't survive until the first night of Hanukkah. Anyway, I'm not here to perform tonight. I'm just taking a moment to remind everyone about the benefit show for AIDS Alliance, taking place right here on December seventh and hosted by yours truly. We want to give the clients of that wonderful agency the best Christmas they've ever had. And I expect all of you to all dig deep, *deep* in your pockets and show how much you care. As a kickoff, I'm also here to sell raffle tickets for our grand prize: an all-expenses-paid weekend trip for two in Chicago. We'll start the sale as soon as my lovely elfin assistant shows up with the tickets." She peered across the room. "Darren, oh Dar-ren! Where *are* you, darling?"

"He's here," said George. "He's in the bathroom changing. He'll be out in a second."

"Ah, there's Darren," said Barbra. "Come on up here, sugar!"

Eric expected a dwarf in a green velvet suit and matching green pointed slippers to hoist himself onto the stage. He was surprised when a strapping, shirtless young man wearing tight red velvet pants, buckled black boots and a Santa hat rushed by him. Eric was smitten immediately.

"Sorry, Barb!" Darren said breathlessly, as he jumped up on the stage. "I was halfway here when I realized that I'd forgotten the tickets at home!"

"Well, where are they?"

"Right here in my back pocket."

"And don't they look *nice* tucked in there! Darren, show the people your back pocket." As Darren self-consciously turned around, Barbra gazed lovingly at his rear end. "I gotta say, honey, you really put the 'ass' in assistant. How can you say no to *that*, boys?" she said as she patted it lovingly. "Now, wait, I'm just going to reach in—*oy*, they're packed in there so *tight!* —and pull out a handful for some fortunate, generous customer. Five bucks a ticket, boys, let's get started."

A heavy-set man at the bar stood up and waved a five-dollar bill. "I'm perfectly capable of pulling my own ticket of those sweet cheeks, Barbra!"

"Uh... no touching!" Darren said nervously, as the man leered at him. "Or I'll have to put you on Santa's naughty list."

"Sweetheart," said the man, "I've been on the naughty list since the day I was born. Now, if you want to make a sale, walk it on over here *now."*

"Oh, God," said Denny. "This is like a scene is right out of a bad movie."

"Add me to the naughty list, too!" another man said, as he and every other patron started reaching for their wallets.

"We've gotta do something!" Eric said. "They're going to eat that poor kid alive!"

Denny whistled loudly. "Hey, Darren!" He held up a fistful of cash. "I've got a hundred dollars here and I don't need change." He had obviously sold a lot of headsets and liquor that week.

"Sold!" said Barbra. "Darren, give the handsome man his tickets."

"I'm coming!" Darren looked greatly relieved as he stepped off the stage.

"Well!" The heavy-set customer glared at Denny. "Merry *Fucking* Christmas to you!"

"Nice work, fellas," said George. "Your next round is on the house."

Ten minutes later, Darren joined Denny and Eric at the bar and introduced himself. "Wow, I sold every ticket I had! Thanks, guys, for getting the ball rolling. You have no idea how much I appreciate it."

"I'm glad we could help out," said Denny. "Just so you know, this was all Eric's idea."

"It... sounded like a very worthy cause," said Eric.

"It is," said Darren. "And personal one, too. My older brother, Peter, gets a lot of help from the Alliance. This year has been pretty grim for him. A big, blow-out Christmas dinner with all of his buddies will lift his sprits like you can't believe. It makes getting into this Santa suit worth it."

"What, that's not your regular outfit for the holiday season?" Denny asked.

"Are you kidding? I'd never have the nerve. This was Barb's idea. She volunteers her time for anything and everything that has to do with the LGBT community. When it comes to fundraising, she knows how to sell an event."

"She sure does," said Eric, ogling Darren's chest.

"She and my brother are very close friends, so she's going out of her way for this one in particular. By the way, will you guys be here on the seventh? Because if not, you should give us your number. You don't have to be present to win. Do you live in the neighborhood?"

"Sorry, Darren, I'm afraid we won't be here on the seventh," said Denny. "We're from out of town and just here for tonight."

"Oh, damn, I knew it was too good to be true. Where are you from?"

"New York."

"New York? Oh, gosh, how exciting! I've *always* wanted to go to New York. What do you do there?"

"We work for Mercury Airways," said Eric. "We're flight attendants."

"Oh, my God!" Darren got up so fast that he almost knocked over his drink. "This is kismet! I just applied with Mercury last month to be a flight attendant, and I have an interview scheduled on January fifteenth. I can't believe it! I want this job more than anything I've ever wanted in my life. You have to tell me all the ins and outs of getting hired. George, can I have a piece of paper and a pen, please? I want to write all this down."

"I'll let Eric walk you through it," said Denny. "He's a newbie, so it's probably fresher in his mind. George, is there a cigarette machine in here?"

"It's broken," said George. "But there's a convenience store two blocks away. Just turn left out the front door."

"I'll be back in ten minutes."

"Take your time," said Darren. "Eric and I have a lot of ground to cover. Now, Eric, for my interview, I'm going to wear a navy-blue suit and white shirt, of course. But I can't decide what color tie to wear. I have a burgundy tie that matches the color of the logo perfectly. But maybe that's overdoing it. Would a club stripe be better?"

"Hang on, Denny," said George, grabbing his coat. "I'll come with you." He turned to the bar back. "Kenny, take over while I'm gone. Remember, cash *only*, and don't run any tabs. I don't care who asks for one."

"I can handle it," said Kenny. "Take your time with the big spender."

***

"Hi, Eric," said Joe, as Eric and Darren climbed into the back of his cab two hours later. "Where's your friend Denny?"

"He's coming back later, after the bar closes. He and your friend George hit it off. Joe, this is Darren."

"Hi, Darren. Love your Santa hat. Where to, guys?"

"Back to the hotel."

"Gotcha." He laughed as he watched Eric slip his hands between Darren's legs. "Well, I'm glad *somebody* got lucky tonight."

"Lucky doesn't begin to describe it," said Darren, beaming at Eric. "Just get us there *fast*."

***

"Nice room," said Darren. He looked around while Eric hung the Do Not Disturb sign and latched the deadbolt. "Do you have this whole suite to yourself? What luxury!"

Eric laughed. "It's not always this luxurious. We're usually in standard rooms. This must be a quiet week in Indianapolis."

"It's *always* a quiet week in Indianapolis. How many rooms are there in here?"

"Just this sitting area with the TV, and the bedroom and the bathroom."

"Wow. Does the airline always put you up in four-star hotels? I mean, I could get used to this!"

"It depends on the city," said Eric. "Sometimes, you know, it's the Holiday Inn in the middle of nowhere."

"Well, wherever you are, I'm sure you're never lonely. You *or* Denny." Why don't you take off your jacket and put it on that chair?"

"Thanks. Hey, do you have anything to drink?"

"Yeah, I think there's some vodka, and maybe some mixer, too." He reached into his tote bag on the desk and pulled out four minis and a can of tonic water. "Vodka and tonic OK?"

"Just some tonic, please. I've had enough alcohol tonight."

Eric brought Darren a glass of tonic and then started to run his hands all over Darren's hairy chest. "God, that's beautiful," he groaned. He wasn't in the mood for any more conversation. He was drunk, horny, and ready to get down to business. He shoved Darren's pants and underwear down to the floor and then ripped off his clothes. Eric was so horny that his dick was bobbing back and forth. "I hope you like sucking," he said, pushing down on Darren's shoulders. He was surprised a moment later to feel Darren pushing himself back up.

"Wow," said Darren, looking a little embarrassed. "You don't waste any time, do you? I mean, aren't we gonna kiss for a little while first?"

"Oh, sure." He planted an open-mouth kiss on Darren's lips and then cupped his ass. Darren's ass was perfectly round, warm, and lightly covered with fuzz. Oh, God, Eric thought, I hope he likes to get fucked.

"Wait," said Darren. "I meant, kissing on the bed."

"Yeah. If that's the way you like it. Right this way," he said, leading Darren by the hand. "Oh, hang on one second." He reached into his tote bag again and took out a condom and a bottle of lube.

"If that's what I think it's for," said Darren, "you should know I don't get fucked, even with a condom."

"You don't?"

"No. I only play *very* safe. You would, too, if you saw my brother lying in his hospital bed. He weighs, like, ninety pounds and his whole body is covered with purple KS lesions."

"I get the picture," said Eric, as he started to lose his erection.

"Sorry, I didn't mean to be so graphic. But I think it's best to set limits right from the get-go. That way, there're no awkward moments later." He grinned. "I teach a class on negotiating safer sex every month. I'm the star instructor."

"Don't worry, Darren," said Eric, trying every sexual image that he could think of to keep his erection. "We'll play very safe, and I'll have you back home before your mother even knows that you've left the house."

"Back home?" The easy grin vanished. "Aren't you going to ask me to spend the night?"

Oh, fuck a duck. "Yeah, sure, if you want. But be forewarned, I have an early sign-in tomorrow. You'll have to get up with me at—"

"No, you don't. You're not leaving until tomorrow afternoon. You told me so in the bar. The *third* day of your trip is the early sign-in: oh-six-hundred hours in Akron."

Me and my big mouth, thought Eric. "That's right. Good memory. You know it's hard to keep my hours straight sometimes. You'll find out for yourself when you start flying."

"I'm glad we can take our time. Let's make this a special night." He kissed Eric sweetly and then started nuzzling his neck. "Wow, you smell good!" He looked meaningfully into Eric's eyes. "I think I'm ready for you to make love to me."

Make love? Oh, shit, thought Eric. I could have jacked off with some porn and been asleep by now. This sex better we worth it.

＊＊＊

"That was really nice," Darren said afterward.

"Here's a washcloth. Careful. It's hot."

"That was some load," said Darren, as he wiped off his chest and stomach. "You must have been super-horny."

Eric climbed back into bed with him. "I was."

"I think I need another washcloth, please."

"I'll be right back." He trotted to the bathroom and back.

"Thank you for not coming on my face, by the way," said Darren.

"Like I told you earlier, I'm good at following directions." He handed Darren a second wet washcloth. "I'm ready to go to sleep. How about you?"

"Yeah, I am too."

"I should call the front desk and ask for a nine A.M. wake-up call."

"I'll do it." Darren picked up the phone next to the bed and dialed. "Hello, this is room 622. Could we please have a nine A.M. wake-up call? Thank you, Miss, and have a pleasant evening." He hung up the phone. "Am I invited to breakfast with you and Denny?"

"Sure," said Eric, struggling to stay awake long enough to end this seemingly endless conversation. "The more, the merrier."

"And you'll show me how you look dressed in your uniform tomorrow?"

"Yes. I promise. But I'll have to press my shirt first."

"I'll do it for you. Put a steam iron in my hand, and I'm like a Stepford wife."

"OK, fine. For right now, Darren, would you turn off the light, please?"

Darren turned off the light and snuggled close to him. "Goodnight, sweetheart."

Eric didn't feel like cuddling, but to push Darren away, at this point, would seem downright rude. "Good night."

***

The next morning, Eric woke up with a dull headache and an acrid taste in his mouth. He opened his eyes and looked at the clock on the nightstand. It was 6:45. Still early. Now all he had to do was figure out which city he was in. Placed next to the phone was a copy of *Where* magazine, featuring a cover story about trendy restaurants in Indianapolis. Well, there's a contradiction in terms, he thought. Then it all came back in a flash: Disco Night with Denny and the late night with Darren, the would-be flight attendant. Sex with him had been pleasant, if not very exciting. The whole experience had turned out to be a series of conflicting intentions. For Eric, it was about the release of pent-up sexual energy. For Darren, it seemed to be the start of something big, even though Eric lived almost eight hundred miles away. Darren had wanted to spend the night. Eric preferred sleeping alone, but didn't have the heart to ask him to leave after they had sex. Darren tried to cuddle with him the entire night. Eric finally had to push him away at one point so that he could finally fall asleep.

Darren was in the middle of the king-sized bed now, hugging a pillow and sleeping peacefully. He looked sweet and natural lying there, with his dark hair tousled and his mouth slightly open. Well, thought Eric, I hate to admit it, but it is nice to wake up with a warm body next to me, especially when I have a hangover hard-on. Maybe Darren would be up for another round of sex before breakfast. If so, Eric decided that he'd try to connect with him emotionally this time. He leaned over and softly kissed Darren on the neck.

Darren mumbled something and reached for Eric, slipping his hand between Eric's legs. "Mmmm," he growled happily. "D'you know how much I love that beautiful penis of yours?"

Eric grinned. Now that Darren knew him a little better, perhaps he'd be more receptive to the idea of getting fucked. "Hang on," Eric whispered. "I'll be right back." He slipped out of bed and into the bathroom, quietly closing the door behind him. He splashed cold water his face and took a big swig of Listerine, and then studied his face in the mirror. He wasn't pleased by what he saw: his skin was pale and haggard-looking, and his eyes were bloodshot and puffy. He soaked a washcloth in cold water, placed it over his face, and sat on the edge of the bathtub. What did it mean, he wondered, that he had *decided* to try connecting emotionally with a sex partner? Had he become so jaded in half a year that to consider doing so was a novelty? Was he starting to behave like most of the other men he'd met in New York? Would he go through the motion of trading phone numbers, knowing that the encounter was a one-night stand and that he'd never see Darren again? Or was he keeping him at arm's length because there was no real chance of getting involved? Yes, he decided, that was the more likely scenario. It's a matter of being practical. Once I build up some real seniority, how often will I be hip-hopping the Midwest in an Ultra Jet? Never, if I can help it. By next summer, I'll be off reserve and flying nothing but transcons. And maybe in another year, and I'll be senior enough to jump over to international. *Bonjour,* Paris! Flying overseas: that was his motivation for taking the job in the first place, wasn't it?

"Eric," he heard Darren say through the door. "Are you coming back or what?"

He removed the washcloth and looked at himself in the mirror again. His appearance was much improved: his color had returned and the puffiness around his eyes had diminished. "I'll be right there, Darren."

***

When he woke up the next time, it was almost nine o'clock. He automatically reached over to squeeze Darren's ass, and then realized that the other side of the bed was empty. He must be in the bathroom. No, the bathroom light was turned off, and he didn't hear water running. "Hey, Darren, where are you?" There was no response. He sat up and turned on the lamp. Maybe Darren was watching TV in the other room. Naturally, he'd left the door to the bedroom closed so that Eric wouldn't be disturbed. He's just that kind of considerate person, Eric thought with a smile. Then he noticed that the closet door in the bedroom had been left wide open. To his horror, was completely empty: his uniform, his suitcase, and even his dress shoes were gone. He couldn't believe it. Jesus, Christ, he'd been robbed—by a Midwestern twink! He yanked open the drawer in the nightstand. His wallet was still there, thank God, but where the *fuck* was his uniform?! What kind of sick person would *steal* a uniform? How the hell was he supposed to go to work that afternoon? In a blind panic, he grabbed the phone and dialed the front desk. Maybe Darren had just left and hotel security could catch him on the way out. God, how fucking sordid is *this*: robbed by a trick on a layover. Could there be anything more embarrassing?

"Hello, this is Julie with Guest Services. How may I help you?"

Oh, great, thought Eric, a woman! I can only imagine what's she going to think. "This is an emergency. I'm calling from room 622. I've been—"

There was a knock on the bedroom door. "Good morning, Mr. Saunders." It was Darren. "This is your personal nine A.M. wake-up call."

"Never mind, Julie," he said into the phone. "I was mistaken. Sorry to trouble you." As he hung up the phone, the bedroom door opened.

"Well, are you ready to come fly with me?"

Eric stared in disbelief. Darren was standing in the doorway, smiling proudly, dressed from head to toe in Eric's uniform. The jacket looked as though it had been tailor-made for him. He'd even clipped Eric's ID badge to the lapel. The tie was perfectly knotted and the white shirt was freshly pressed. "Do you believe how perfectly this fits me?" said Darren. "We wear exactly the same size, right down to the loafers. We could be twins!" He flipped up the back of the jacket. "Look how great my ass looks in these pants. Their eyes will be *glued* to me when I walk up the aisle. By the way, you had a little blob of something icky on your shoes, but it came right off with a damp cloth. Now wait, he's the best part. Follow me."

Eric jumped out of bed, open-mouthed. In a daze and still completely naked, he followed Darren into the next room.

"Now watch this," said Darren. He grabbed the raised handle of Eric's suitcase and started walking back and forth across the room, pulling the suitcase behind him. "Can't you see me strutting through JFK on my way to LAX? I'm a natural!"

Eric couldn't speak. It was like standing in front of the mirror in his dorm room on the day that he graduated from training. The hairs on the back of neck stood straight up. He'd never been so mortified in his life.

"Watch how fast I can take corners, and still never trip myself up!" As Darren whirled past him, the suitcase caught the base of the ironing board, sending it crashing to the floor and the iron flying. The iron's heavy electrical cord smacked Eric right in the testicles. He immediately doubled over and fell to the floor.

"Oh my God, I'm sorry!" Darren let go of the suitcase and rushed over to him. "I'm really sorry! What can I do for you?"

As Eric curled into a fetal position, writhing in pain, the phone rang. "Answer the goddam phone, would you?"

"Yes, of course. Hello? … Hi, Denny, this is Darren! Eric, it's Denny."

"Take a message!"

"Eric can't come to the phone right now. Can I take a message? Uh huh … meet you downstairs for breakfast in thirty minutes. I'll tell him. We'll see you then. Bye! Oh, Eric. I'm so, *so* sorry."

"It's all right, I know it wasn't intentional. Look, grab that ice bucket on the desk. There's an ice machine at the far end of the hallway. Bring me lots and lots of it. Take my key. It's right there on the desk. You'll need it to let yourself back into the room."

"I'll be back in a flash!"

As soon as Darren left, Eric pulled himself onto the bed, grabbed the phone, and dialed Denny's room. "Denny? It's me. Listen up, because I have to talk fast. I can't meet you for breakfast. I've had an accident. Nothing serious, I just need to ice my balls … Very funny. Listen! I need you to do me a favor. I've got to get Darren out of here right now. I'm on overload and I can't take one more minute of him. Take him to breakfast, tell him a few good airplane stories, and then get rid of him. Will you do that for me?… Thank you." He heard the door opening. "I've gotta go. Call me an hour before pick up."

"Sorry that took so long," said Darren. "The ice machine on this floor was broken. I had to go up to the seventh floor."

"Darren, I feel like shit today. I hope you don't mind, but I'm not going to breakfast."

"Oh no, and it's all my fault!"

"No, it's not. I had too much to drink last night and I have a terrible hangover. But Denny would love for you to join him. His treat."

"I hate to leave you by yourself."

"Don't worry about me. It's better if I stay here and get some sleep."

"Well… if you're sure."

"I'm sure. I had a great time with you, and I'll see you next time I'm in town."

"When is your next flight here?"

"I don't know. I don't have any more Indy layovers more this month, but I'll call you next time I have one on my schedule."

"Let me give you my phone number. Where should I write it down on?"

"There's a pad and a pen right there on the nightstand."

Darren wrote his number down and tore off the top page. "Here you go."

"Thanks."

Darren stood expectantly next to the bed. "Aren't you going to give me your number?"

"Of course. Hand me the pen and pad. Here, this is my home number. You can always leave a message if I'm not there."

"Don't worry, Eric. I'll find you, wherever you are." He sat down on the bed. "I want to tell you something. Last night was one of the most special nights I've had in a long time. You're one of the nicest, most handsome men I've ever met."

"I feel the same way, Darren." Play along, he thought, even just for another minute. The quicker you get him out of here, the quicker you can go back to sleep. At five P.M., your flight will take off and you'll probably never see him again.

"I hope you don't think of me as a one-night stand," Darren added.

"Of course not."

"And I can call you with any last-minute questions before my interview, right?"

Absolutely."

Darren bent over to kiss Eric goodbye.

"Darren, before you leave…"

"Yes?"

"Would you please take off my uniform?" He forced a smile. "I'll need it later today."

"Oh, my God! I almost walked right out the door in it! Wouldn't that have been hysterical?"

"Yeah, a riot. You'd better get going. Denny's a real bear when he's hungry."

"All right." He quickly changed clothes and hung Eric's uniform in the closet. "Bye, Eric."

"Bye."

After Darren left, Eric got up, took a quick shower, swallowed two aspirin, and brushed his teeth again. He climbed back into bed, feeling exhausted. It was almost ten o'clock, yet he couldn't fathom leaving the room for anything. He didn't want to meet Denny for lunch, compare notes on last night's sexcapades, or tour the VFW Headquarters. For the next few hours, he wanted to tune everything out.

He reached into his tote bag and took out a small envelope. Inside were six white pills that Denny had given him last week after a horrific Tampa turnaround. "Here. From my private stash. Pop one on the way home and you won't give a shit what happened on the plane today. They're great for taking the edge off. Keep them with you in your flight bag, just in case. I never leave the house without a few in my pocket." When Eric had balked, Denny shoved the envelope into his shirt pocket. "Just take them! You never know when they'll come in handy. Besides, everyone in New York takes *something*. How else do you think we maintain our sanity?"

Eric decided that Denny's stash was just what the doctor ordered. He swallowed two, set an alarm clock, turned off all the lights, and closed his eyes. As usual, whenever he tried to relax, his mind started spinning. The scene with Darren preening like a peacock in his uniform played over and over again. Christ, he thought, is that what *I* look like in front of my co-workers? I could be the laughing stock of the base and not even know it! Well, not anymore. It's going to be a whole new me, starting right now. He tossed and turned in bed as his mind raced uncontrollably. If I could just get my brain to turn off for five *goddam*—

And then, *everything* turned off. Every muscle in his body relaxed. Time seemed to have come to a standstill. He was floating through an azure sky on a puffy, white cloud without a care in the world. What a delight, for the first time in months, to not be concerned about a single, blessed thing. Nothing mattered at all except this delicious, new sensation of euphoria.

Right before he fell into a deep sleep, he remembered was Leander had said to him about his relationship with Denny: "If I were you, I'd hang on to *that* friendship for dear life." Oh, yes, he thought, right everything went black. Abso-*fucking*-lutely.

CHAPTER 26

Austerity

On an afternoon in mid-December, Eric walked down the hallway to his apartment. His suitcase glided effortlessly over the terracotta floor. Sunlight flooded the arched hall through a large window at the other end, bouncing off the smooth white-tiled walls. There wasn't a stroller or a shopping cart to be seen anywhere on the floor. His apartment was like oasis at the end of a trip, no matter where he'd been. With each passing week, he felt more and more at home there. As he reached his front door, it was suddenly opened from the inside. Michael stood in the doorway, wearing jeans, boots and a black leather jacket that Eric coveted.

"Oh, you're home!" said Michael, holding the door for him. "Thank God. Do you have a cigarette? I was just stepping out to buy some."

"It's nice to see you, too," said Eric.

"Oh, honey, you know I love ya," said Michael. "*Do* you have a cigarette?"

"Yes. Let me just set my luggage down and put something in the fridge."

"Sure. By the way, did you bring home some toilet paper from the hotel, like I asked you to?"

"No." Eric took off his blazer and draped it over the back of a dining chair. "I did not."

"Oh, well. Bring it next time for sure. Hey, do you mind if I smoke in the apartment?"

"What do you mean, do I mind? It's your non-smoking apartment and your rule. I've never smoked in here, not even once, I swear to God."

"I know. But I don't want to seem like a hypocrite, since I always make you go out in the back stairwell to light up. It's just for this once, OK? Now let me see, we need an ashtray." He started opening kitchen cupboards. "Do I even have an ashtray?"

"I think there's one behind that bottle of Jamison's."

"Hey!" Michael pulled the bottle out. "Have you been drinking my Scotch?"

"I've had a few nips," said Eric.

"A few nips? This bottle is almost empty! I didn't think you even liked Scotch."

"Denny was over here last week while you away were on a trip. He helped."

"Oh, that explains it. I love Denny, but that boy is a real liquor whore."

"I'll put a bottle of Jamison's on my shopping list."

"Fine. Here we go: one ashtray." Michael examined it closely. "Hmmm, this is from the George Cinque in Paris. I must have swiped it when I was a new hire. That hasn't been our layover hotel for at least fifteen years. But then, at the rate we're going, I guess we're lucky they don't try to book us into some whorehouse in Pigalle." He set the ashtray on the table next to a stack of Christmas cards and opened the window over the sink. "What's that you have?" he asked as Eric took a blue, round container out of his tote bag.

"It's caviar."

"Caviar?! You won't bring home one lousy roll of Charmin, but you bring caviar?"

"I'm sorry, Michael, but I refuse to swipe toilet paper from the hotel. It's so…"

"You can say it: cheap."

"I was going to say frugal."

"Then you'd better add *that* to your grocery list, too, buddy boy. Along with some Kleenex. I've been schlepping both toilet paper and Kleenex home for months, and I can't do it anymore. Security is doing spots checks on our luggage before we leave the hotel. It's so humiliating, especially when we get caught. Let me see that caviar." He grabbed the tin and read the label. "Wow. This costs fifty bucks an ounce—retail."

"I know what it costs."

"Where'd you get it?" Michael asked sarcastically. "Were they having a sale at Dealer Dan's?"

"You know where it came from."

"I can't believe it: Mister Goody-Two-Shoes swiping caviar," said Michael.

"I just did it this one time!"

"Nor can I believe that, in this economy, you guys still serve gourmet food in first class."

"Caviar is our first course on transcon dinner flights, right after the cocktail hour."

"Do you know what *we* serve as our first course to Paris? Frozen puff pastries. They're not even made by our chefs at JFK. They're frozen and come in a big box marked Swanson's. Do you still serve champagne, too? *Real* French champagne?"

"Of course."

"We don't. We serve sparkling wine. I think it's Annie Green Springs."

"Oh, Michael," said Eric, laughing. "They don't even make that brand anymore."

"Well, whatever we serve, it's just as bad! A passenger asked me to show him the bottle yesterday. He read the label and laughed right in my face. God, it just gets worse and worse. Where's that cigarette, by the way?"

"Here. Light one for me too, while I wash my hands. Those subway poles are so gross! God knows what germs I picked up on the way home.*"*

"Why don't you walk home from the bus stop, like I do? Think of the extra money you'd have at the end of the month."

"I'm not schlepping my luggage all the way from Kew Gardens to Forest Hills to save a dollar-fifty on subway fare. It's the little things in life that count."

"Suit yourself. Did you bring home some champagne to have with the caviar? We could pretend that we're a couple of Park Avenue high society matrons today."

"No, the hoarder got to that before I did."

"What hoarder?"

"The purser that I worked with, in first class. Her name is Diedre. She's been flying for twenty-five years. She lives in Scarsdale, drives a BMW, wears a three-carat diamond ring, and steals everything in sight. I mean *everything*: champagne, wine, salad greens, sugar, sweetener, swizzle sticks, even coffee packets—all gone. Can you imagine someone even *wanting* to brew that terrible coffee at home?"

"We use the same brand as you, believe it or not," said Michael. "Whenever passengers complain, we always say 'it's the terrible airplane water,' but everyone knows it's the terrible airplane coffee."

"Diedre spends the entire flight cramming stuff into large Ziploc bags that she brings from home. She waits until my back is turned, and then *crinkle, crinkle,* something else disappears. This went on for hours in both directions! I thought the noise would drive me crazy. And the worst thing is: she steals shit before it even *becomes* a leftover! Like today, we served large, beautiful salads at lunch. Each one is garnished with three pieces of chilled asparagus. So I unwrapped fourteen salads for her and set them on the counter. I turn around for thirty seconds to get the bread out of the oven, and *crinkle, crinkle*: there's no asparagus anywhere. I said, 'Diedre, where's the asparagus?' And she said, 'Oh, no, baby boy, That's all for *me*.' I said to her, 'The salad contents are printed right on the menu. I think the passengers will notice.' And she waved her hand and said, 'Don't get all excited. I'll tell 'em that LAX catering screwed up. It happens all the time.' Then right in front me, she slipped a box of Lindt chocolates into her tote bag. She didn't even try to hide it! 'It's Teacher Appreciation Day at my daughter's school tomorrow,' she said." He snorted. "I happen to know that her daughter is a sophomore at NYU."

"You serve Swiss chocolates, on a *domestic* flight? We serve mini Hershey Bars—to Europe!"

"Do you even get the point of this story, Michael?"

"Yes, I'm sorry. Please continue."

"So, after that fiasco, I'm plating the hot food for her to serve. I had just put roast beef, mashed potatoes, and green beans on plates for three passengers at once. Everything was perfectly cooked, mind you. All I had to do was add the *au jus*, which was my next step. She looks over my shoulder and barks, 'Where's the sauce? It's supposed to come with sauce!' I said, 'It's in the oven, I'm *getting* it.' Well, I guess I wasn't moving fast enough for her. She shoved me aside, grabbed one of the little metal pots from the oven, and started pouring. Only it wasn't the *au jus* that she'd grabbed. It was butterscotch for the dessert service. She didn't even realize what she'd done! She hauled out all three plates and served them. And then thirty seconds later, the call lights started going off. *Ding, ding! Ding, ding!* Oh, the look on her face when she came back into the galley! I wish I'd had a camera."

"Talk about poetic justice," said Michael. "How'd she recover from that one?"

"She had to scrounge for leftover beef filets in business class. Thank God they weren't full today. Nevertheless, the passengers in first class weren't too happy with her."

"Serves her right," said Michael. "Bitch!"

"And then as soon as we were through with that bit of drama, *this* happened: a passenger from row ten came up to first class to use our bathroom. There were already three people waiting in line for business class lav, and he had to go. Diedre very rudely told him to go back to business class and wait his turn. When he balked, she actually *put her leg* up across the bathroom door to block him from using it, when it was vacant and there was no one else waiting in line. This poor guy was seventy years old and ready to pee on the carpet! It was the most ludicrous thing I ever saw! Then the two of them got into a big fight, and he demanded her name and employee number, which of course she refused to give him. And then he started asking *me* for my name! He was going to write *me* up when I wasn't even involved! Can you believe that I would get in trouble because another crewmember is acting like a jackass?"

"Yes, of course I can believe it. What did you do?"

"I told the passenger that I'd speak to him after I served lunch to the pilots. Then I brought the pilots' meal trays to the cockpit and hid up there for half an hour. By the time I came out, the guy from business was back in his seat, sound asleep. Those old guys can't remain standing forever, no matter how indignant they are."

"It sounds like you've had quite a day. Do you want a glass of wine? I was thinking of opening a bottle."

"You never have to ask *me* if I'd like wine."

"I know, honey. I'm being polite. So, were there any other crises before you landed?"

"Not a crisis *per se*. Diedre wouldn't even acknowledge my presence for the rest of the flight, other than to say she couldn't serve my 'burnt-on-board' cookies, as she called them. Of course, those cookies found their way right into her bag."

"Unbelievable." Michael poured two glasses of wine and set them on the table.

"Isn't it?" said Eric. "I will say this, though: that leg of hers came in mighty handy after we landed."

"What happened?"

"Well, during deplaning, all flight attendants are supposed to stay on board until the last passenger has left. It says so, in black and white, right in our manual."

Michael nodded. "Every airline has the same rule. Just try enforcing it."

"Bingo. While we were still taxiing to the gate at Kennedy today, this DFW commuter named Bobbie comes running up from the back, dragging all her luggage with her. We had just turned off the runway, mind you; we were still five miles from the terminal."

"Nothing unusual about that," said Michael. "Those DFW girls *have* to get home. There's a sixteen-ounce can of Lone Star Beer waiting for them at home in the fridge."

"Bobbie had disarmed her exit door as soon as we touched down, and then left it unattended. Can you imagine doing anything so stupid? If we'd had a last-minute emergency during taxi-in, a passenger might have opened that door—now with no slide attached—and fallen twenty feet to the ground. Bobbie would have been fired and maybe even gone to prison for negligent homicide. But that didn't even occur to her, because *she's* a commuter and her needs come first."

Michael shook his head in disgust. "What is wrong with these people?"

"So Diedre looks at her standing there in the first-class galley and says, 'Where do you think *you're* going?' And Bobbie says, serving major attitude, 'To catch my commuter flight, where else?' Then Diedre says, 'Oh, no, baby girl, I don't think so,' and she throws her leg across the galley entrance to keep Bobbie from leaving. Bobbie starts yelling, 'Move your goddam leg!' right in front of the passengers! And Diedre says, 'You want to take it up with a supervisor, Missy? I'll call the office right now.' So the door opened, and Bobbie just stood there fuming until the cabin was emptied out, and then we all deplaned together. She had to haul ass to catch her flight to DFW, which was at the other end of the terminal. I was quite pleased. I'm fucking sick and tired of having to stay behind while these commuters bail."

"So," Michael said, "Diedre redeemed herself in the end. Bravo. That's a great story. Here, have some more wine."

"Should we open the caviar, too?"

"No, let's save it for Christmas. If you want some munchies, there's a bag of pretzels in the pantry."

"I wonder what Diedre does with all the loot she takes, and what that hoarding business is about in general. I mean, she's too young to have lived through the Depression and she's obviously loaded. So what gives?"

"I don't know," said Michael. "'We have a couple of hoarders at Global, too. One is named Jenny. She's a big woman—big bones, big bright red cheeks, big black wig. She always works coach galley. Every flight before we start boarding, she rings up the purser and says, 'Call catering right away. We're short ten entrées.' And every single time, the purser goes running back to coach and finds the entrées wherever Jenny has stashed them. Usually, they're hidden under a pile of blankets or in an overhead bin. One time, she scooped the contents of all ten casseroles into a Tupperware container and then hid it in her wig box, which you must admit is pretty clever. I don't know what Jenny'll do though, come January. Or what the hell *any* of us will do." With a trembling hand, Michael lit another cigarette.

"What do you mean?" said Eric. "What's happening in January?"

"Global just made an announcement this morning. Come January, we're going to start selling meals in coach, instead of serving them for free."

"What do you mean, selling meals in coach?"

"I mean, if anyone wants to eat during the flight, they'll have to pay for it."

"That's crazy. What kind of airline *sells* food?"

"*My* airline." Michael's skin was ashen. Eric looked at him closely and noticed that small worry lines had begun popping up across his forehead.

"Michael, what the hell is going on at Global?"

"We're in the crapper financially, worse than any of us ever imagined. Management is cutting corners everywhere. One place they think they can save money is with catering. All those free meals cost millions by the end of the year. So they've decided to simply stop serving them. No more cheese lasagna at thirty thousand feet. But get this: It won't even be *hot* food that we'll be selling. It'll all be cold stuff—sandwiches chips and popcorn and things like that. They're even removing all the ovens from coach to save money on fuel. That's how serious they are."

"But that's just on short haul flights, right? Not on transcons?"

"Yes, dear, even on transcons. They're removing ovens in coach from the *entire* domestic fleet."

Eric was genuinely shocked. "What will the passengers say?"

"Our passengers in coach are currently spending ninety-nine dollars to travel between New York and California," Michael replied glumly. "My guess is they won't say shit. If they're hungry enough, they'll buy something. All they ever did was complain about our food, anyway. Give me another cigarette, would you?"

"Michael, why are you chain-smoking?"

"Because that isn't the only bad news. Since the service in coach is being downgraded, we'll need fewer flight attendants on every trip, system-wide."

"Don't tell me they're going to start laying people off!"

Michael nodded. "They're furloughing five hundred flight attendants on January fifteenth. *After* the holiday travel rush is over, of course."

"Are you part of the five hundred?" Eric asked, hoping that he didn't sound nervous.

"No, thank God. But I'll probably be back on reserve. Fuck! Reserve, after fifteen years of being *off* it! The waiting around for days on end... the midnight phone calls ... the shitty three-day trips to Fargo and Kansas City." He pounded his fist on the table. "Goddammit! My own company is going into a free-fall, right before my eyes!"

"Well, I'm sure you must be... grateful to still have a job," Eric said lamely, trying to quell his own anxiety. Jesus, what would happen if Global went out of business? Would Michael have to sell the apartment and move? And where would that leave Eric?

"Oh, yes," said Michael, draining his wine glass. "I'm grateful to still have a job. I'm sure that phrase will be printed in bold letters on our bid sheets from now until Armageddon, which from the look of things could happen any day now. And that brings me to my third and last piece of bad news. In exchange for preventing the company from furloughing *one thousand* flight attendants instead of five hundred, the union agreed to a temporary wage cut. My pay is being cut twenty percent, effective January first. Merry Christmas, Happy New Year, and fuck me for flying for Global Airways."

"How long is temporary?"

"Until we start turning a profit or go belly up, whichever comes first," Michael said, with a dark laugh.

"How could Global go belly up?" said Eric. "it's one the oldest airlines in existence. Your logo is known all over the world!"

"That must be what they said at Atlantic Coast, right before they went out of business. Weren't there some ACA people in your training class?"

"Two at least," said Eric, thinking immediately of Anthony and Ginny Jo.

"I don't think I could start all over again at another airline," said Michael. "I just couldn't do it."

"Let's take it one day at a time, and hope for the best," said Eric. He suddenly felt guilty for something over which he didn't have the slightest bit of control: the fickle hand of fate. "In the meantime, maybe you could pick up an extra trip now and then."

"Another trip? I'm already flying a hundred hours a month, and probably not making that much more money than you are. Besides, everyone's going to be scrambling for extra trips. There just won't be enough flying to go around. I'm going to have to resort to unpleasant options. For starters, I'm going to have to raise your rent."

"How much?"

"Two hundred and fifty dollars a month."

"Ouch."

"I know that seems like a lot. But when I add up my mortgage and my maintenance payments together, you're still not paying even half of what's due every month. I've been giving you a break on the rent because you're a new hire and I knew you were struggling. I remember what my life was like when I started, but I can't do anything about that now. I'm sorry, but my days of being magnanimous are over."

"I understand. I'll have to figure something out for myself. I can't pick up an extra trip either, because of that stupid thirty-in-seven rule we have at Mercury."

"Oh my God, you're such fucking lightweights," Michael said with a sneer. "You high-ass bitches at Mercury couldn't *possibly* fly more than thirty hours in seven days. It might cause dark circles under your eyes or constipation or varicose veins—or worse."

"It's not *my* stupid rule, Michael," said Eric, yanking off his tie. "Do you think I want to live in New York City on nine hundred dollars a month? Believe me, if they'd *let* me fly more hours, I would."

"I'm sorry, Eric. That was a shitty thing to say. You *are* a hard worker, and a very responsible roommate, too." He poured himself another glass of wine, emptying the bottle. "Just for that snide remark of mine, I'm only going to charge you two hundred dollars extra for the month of January."

"Thank you. I appreciate that."

"Can you live without a Christmas tree this year, even though it's your first December in New York?"

"Yes, of course. We'll have to make do with the one at Rockefeller Center."

"Christmastime in New York," Michael said wistfully. "There's no more enchanting place on earth—unless you're as broke as we are. Well, never mind. We'll take a day off together and tear the hell out of Fifth Avenue. The windows at Bergdorf-Goodman's will dazzle you, I promise! And I'll still put up some decorations, tree or no tree. And I'm still having my annual holiday party, on the twentieth of December. Only this year, for the first time ever, it'll be BYOB. You are off on that day, right?"

"Yes, as of right now."

"Good. Invite as many people from Mercury as you want. My friends from Global are going to be a glum group this year, I'm afraid." He pointed to the stack of Christmas cards on the table. "The cards that I've been getting in the mail have a decidedly false ring of cheer."

"I'll do *my* best to be dazzling at the party."

"By the way, this came for you in the mail yesterday. I forgot all about it, with all this drama going on at work." He handed an envelope to Eric. "Open it right now, would you? I'm dying to know whom *you* know that lives on Central Park West and uses engraved stationery."

Eric looked at the return address. "Oh, it's from my friend, Chaz."

"Chaz? Who is Chaz? A Calvin Klein model?"

"Don't be snarky. As beautiful as he is, he could be. He flies for us."

"Then he must have a rich husband."

"He does," said Eric, carefully opening the envelope. "You should see Chaz and Aaron together. They're both gorgeous. Oh, it's an invitation! They have an extra ticket to an AIDS fundraiser. They'd like me to come as their guest, and to be the date for a friend of theirs who'll be at their table. They invited me to a benefit at the Guggenheim last month, but I ended up flying that day and missed it. How nice of him to think of me again, even if it's at the last minute."

"*Their* table? They paid for a whole table at a fundraiser?"

"Aaron is a senior partner in a very prestigious Manhattan law firm."

"Let me see that invitation. Wow, look, it's at the Helmsley Palace! And it's being emceed by Titus Hutton!"

"Who's Titus Hutton?"

"Who's Titus Hutton?!" Michael sighed in exasperation. "He's just the hunkiest actor-singer-dancer ever to appear on Broadway! Don't you ever read Page Six in the *Post*? His picture is in there at least once a week."

"No, I only read the *New York Times*."

"Yes, and I'm sure they're impressed at the Mykonos Diner when you sit skimming the front page as you eat your five-dollar breakfast special. By the way, if you're going to be so *la-dee-da* about your primary news source, just called it the *Times,* like everyone else. Wow! The Palace on Madison Avenue! When that hotel is decorated for the holidays, it's so beautiful that it's like stepping into a fairy tale. I went there with a friend last year on Christmas Eve. We stumbled around the lobby for an hour, gawking like a couple of tourists. Then on the spur of the moment, we decided to stay for tea."

"How was it?"

"Two cups of tea and a microscopic plate of cookies cost us forty dollars—plus a tip! I almost fainted when the waiter brought our bill. But it almost seemed worth it to sit down, even for a little while, in that lovely space on Christmas Eve. And you're invited to an event there!" He stuck his finger in the ashtray and smeared ashes across his cheek. "Oh, I wish *I* were going to the ball!"

"Hold on, Cinderella." Eric's smile turned into a deep frown. "I can't go."

"Why not?"

"For two reasons. One, the dress is formal. And two, it's the same date as our holiday party."

"Is that all? Don't stress about *either.* One: you can always rent a tuxedo. I'll even knock another fifty bucks of your new rent—just for next month, mind you—to help out. And two: you're going, regardless. If I had to choose between a Christmas party in Queens and a *schmooze* fest with rich, gay men and

Broadway stars at the Palace, I'd ditch my own guests. Tell me: this friend of Chaz and Aaron's that they want you to meet—does he travel in the same circles that they do?"

"What does that mean?"

"Don't be dense. I mean, is he rich, too?"

"I assume so." Eric reread the note attached to the invitation. "His name is Kyle, and he's one of the other partners at Aaron's firm."

"Then you're definitely going. Opportunities like these don't come along every day. You're going to take advantage of it."

"Take advantage of what?"

"The chance to hook a wealthy man and make something of your life!"

"Oh dear Lord, you make the whole thing sound so predatory. It's just an invitation to a fundraiser."

"Survival in this city, in case you haven't figured it out yet, *is* a predatory business. Honey, think in the long term. Is it really your life's ambition to trudge out to JFK in that burgundy blazer twice a week until you're sixty-five? That is, if Mercury is still even around by then. The way things are going in the airline industry, who knows what'll happen? If nothing else, you should learn from my own experience. It could all come crashing down overnight, and you'll be left with squat to show for twenty-five years of dedicated service to an employer *and* a world-renowned brand name."

"Michael, I hate to be contradictory, but what's happening at Global could never happen at Mercury Airways. It's like comparing apples to oranges."

"Brother, have you got a lot to learn! Listen to me: you're going to that event. End of discussion."

"All right, I'll go. Will you at least help me pick out a tux?"

"You bet."

"Is there a rental place here in the neighborhood?"

"Rent a tuxedo in Queens? Are you mad? We'll go to Manhattan tomorrow. In the meantime, get showered and changed. We're going out tonight."

"Where to?"

"To the diner for a bite to eat and then to Pinocchio's. It's two-for-one tonight, and I feel like tying one on."

"Should I even be seen at Pinocchio's? What if word got out that I was slumming with locals in an outer-borough gay bar?"

"This will be your swan song. And it's strictly social, mind you. Tonight, I want you to stay away from those locals with big, black mustaches and hairy chests. I know what a weakness you have for them."

"Says who?"

"Honey, we live together. I see who comes staggering out of the bedroom at three in the morning after you've been out on the prowl."

"Well, yes, it's true. I do have a thing for hairy men and everyone knows it."

"Nevertheless, you're going to keep your nose clean." He eyed Eric critically. "I've got a lot of coaching to do before the big night, if you're going to pull this off."

"Oh, God. I have a feeling this will be an exhausting experience."

"Go with the flow. I could use the distraction, and you could do with a bit of cultural enlightenment."

"Me?! What am I, the village idiot?"

"Hardly. You're attractive and very bright. But you can't coast forever on your cute ass and your high school knowledge of French Impressionists. You'll thank me after you've reeled in that millionaire."

"I know I'm going to regret this, but OK. I'm putty in your hands."

"Wonderful," Michael said, grinning. "To quote the great Dolly Levi: 'just leave everything to me.'"

CHAPTER 27

Raising Funds

"May I help you, gentlemen?" asked the desk clerk.

"We have a reservation," said Jim.

"Under what name, please?"

"Sizemore. Jim Sizemore," Jim replied with an air of disbelief. He was a regular at the Plaza Hotel and known by the entire staff. "Where's Jean-Luc? He usually checks me in."

"He's on vacation. My name is Eduardo, and I'll be happy to assist you. May I have your credit card, please, Mr. Sizlack?"

Jim slapped down an American Express Platinum card. "It's *Sizemore*."

"I'm so sorry, Mr. Sizemore," Eduardo said, as he typed. "Please forgive me. Would you like two keys, gentlemen?"

"Yes, we would," Anthony said eagerly.

"Would you like assistance with your luggage?"

"No," said Jim. "That's not necessary."

"Enjoy your stay then," said Eduardo, never taking his eyes off Anthony. "And please let me know if there's anything at all that I can do for you."

"Yes, *we* will," said Jim, grabbing the key folder. "Thank you."

"Is something the matter?" Anthony asked as they walked toward the elevators.

Jim sighed. "Does every single service person that we encounter have to ogle you like you're an overstuffed cannoli?"

"Hey, sometimes they do the same thing to you, right in front of me. Those nineteen-year-olds see your handsome face and that salt and pepper hair, and they think, 'Oh, Dad—' "

"Don't say it. Please. Not today."

"Don't say what?"

"The D word."

"All right, I won't. But that's what they're thinking." As they waited for the elevator, Anthony slung the garment bag over his shoulder. "Jesus, this is heavy."

"Anthony, be careful with that. I doubt that we'll have time to get anything pressed before tonight."

"OK, OK, got it. By the way, why didn't you want someone to help us with our luggage?"

"Because between the two of us, I think we can manage two Rollaboards, one garment bag, and one tote. We're only here for the weekend."

"I know. But I thought that all the extra service was part of the whole Plaza 'premium guest' experience for you."

"I have other things on my mind today," Jim said, as the elevator door opened. They had to step aside to allow a boisterous family of six, all wearing matching Santa hats, to exit.

"Oh, God!" said Jim, as they stepped into the elevator and the door closed. "Tourists!"

"What are we?" said Anthony.

"We are *not* tourists. We're here on business."

"Oh, I forgot." They exited on the tenth floor and turned left. "There's our room, Jim."

Jim sighed as he put his key card in the lock. "I can't wait to lay down. Four A.M. is just too damn early to get up in the morning."

"Welcome to my world." Anthony followed him through the door and immediately started looking for a place to hang the garment bag. "Oh," he said, looking around the room. "This isn't a suite."

"No, it's not."

"Don't we usually stay in suites?" he asked, as he hung the bag in the closet and then carefully removed their evening wear.

"I'm sorry, Mr. Rockefeller, but you'll have to make do with a standard room for the weekend. This is what happens when you book at the last minute."

Anthony opened the drapes. "There's not even a view of the park."

"Christ, please don't sulk." Jim kicked off his shoes and stretched out on the king-sized bed. "If you want a view of the fucking park, go for a walk. It's right across the street."

"I think I will. You need a timeout, obviously."

Jim sighed. "Let's not start the weekend like this. Let's try to get some pleasure out of being here."

"I'm Sorry, Jim," said Anthony, feeling embarrassed. After all, he wasn't the one paying for the trip. "I was being obnoxious."

"Thanks for admitting it."

"This is a great room. And we'll have a wonderful time together. There's no one I'd rather be here with more than you. I wouldn't care if we were at the Holiday Inn."

Jim laughed. "You don't have to go into overdrive." He covered his eyes with his hand. "Do you mind closing those curtains? That sunlight's hitting me right between the eyes."

"No." Before pulling the curtain closed, Anthony examined Jim's face closely. He looked tired and pale. There was a slackness under his jaw that Anthony had never seen before. "Honey, do you feel all right?"

"Yes, I'm just beat, that's all. I'm going to take a nap." He patted the mattress. "Why don't you come and lie down with me?"

"I'm a little restless. I would like to go for a walk in the park. And maybe stop somewhere for a bite."

"You should have had breakfast on the plane with me this morning," Jim said drowsily.

"Thanks, but I've had enough airplane omelets to last a lifetime. Do you mind if I go out by myself for a while? I'd love a pastrami sandwich from the Carnegie Deli."

"Of course not. Bring me back half. Hey, if you head for the park afterward, stay out of the Rambles."

"Don't worry. It's thirty-five degrees outside. I doubt that anyone will have his dick hanging out in this weather." He grinned. "Besides, I'll have pastrami breath." As he reached for his leather bomber jacket, the phone rang.

"Get that, will you?" said Jim.

"Sure." He picked up the phone. "Hello?"

"Hello, this is Eduardo at the front desk. Is this Mr. Sizemore?"

"No, this is Mr. Bellini."

"Oh, hi!" The clerk's voice brightened. "Is everything satisfactory in your room?"

"Yes, fine, thank you."

"Wonderful. May I speak with Mr. Sizemore, please?"

"Just a moment." He covered the phone. "Jim, it's the front desk. They want to speak with you."

"Whatever they're offering, I don't need it. Take a message, would you?"

"Mr. Sizemore isn't available right now," Anthony said into the phone. "May I take a message?"

"Well, it seems that there's a slight problem with… I'd rather speak to him personally, Mr. Bellini, if I may."

Jim was already asleep and snoring faintly. "I'm afraid that he can't come to the phone right now."

"I see. In that case, would you please ask him to call me back or stop by the front desk at his earliest convenience?"

"Will do."

"Thank you, Mr. Bellini. If there is *anything* that I can do for you, please let me know."

"Thanks," he said curtly and then hung up the phone. God, could the guy be any pushier? What does he think, I'm gonna slip downstairs and let him blow me behind the front desk?

He scribbled a note for Jim and set the alarm clock for five P.M. Then he put on his jacket and gloves. It wasn't quite cold enough outside for a hat. Besides, he'd let his hair grow longer for the winter. It was just the right length now, and he wanted to show it off. Before he left the room, he stopped to check himself out in the mirror. He looked good—damned good. He didn't need a nap, or to close his eyes for even five minutes. He was still buzzing from the surge of energy that he'd felt the moment the plane touched down at La Guardia. After an absence of six months, he was finally home—with no family obligations. All of New York City is right outside that door, he thought, and I'm not going to miss one fucking thing.

***

Anthony walked across Central Park South, deeply breathing in the cold, crisp December air. What a welcome change that was; back in Dallas, it was still in the high 70s and a muggy in the afternoon. The Christmas decorations at Neiman-Marcus had seemed out of step with the balmy weather.

All the frantic activity on the street was a welcome change too. Horns honking, taxis screeching to a stop, and every corner packed with hordes of pedestrians waiting impatiently to cross. People were actually out of their cars and *walking* from point A to point B—unfathomable in Texas—even though many were doing it at a snail's pace. You could always tell the locals from the tourists. Locals dodged around the tourists with great exasperation. 'Would you just move the *fuck* out of my way?' was written across every New Yorker's face. Tourists, on the other hand, lollygagged with every step. They looked up or left or right, but never directly in front of them. Well, why shouldn't they gawk? thought Anthony, as he chest swelled with hometown pride. New York is the greatest city in the world. It's impossible to take it in all at once.

There was one direction, though, in which everyone seemed to be looking, and that was right at Anthony. Both tourists and locals stopped in their tracks, jerking their heads and bumping into each other, without so much as a "Pardon me!" as he passed by. He loved the dumbstruck look that he generated. That kind of attention was a rush that he never tired of, whether it was from a desk clerk, a passenger in first class, or one of Jim's clients. Anthony believed that he could have any man in the world, and rightly so. But Jim was the only man he wanted—or so he thought—since they'd met last June. Lately, Anthony had started second-guessing his choice… even though he couldn't pin down the exact reason. Jim had so much to offer: looks, brains, a successful business, and a pile of money in the bank. What's *not* to like about this setup?

Maybe the problem was *where* they lived. Dallas was nice, but… if only they could live here instead! They could take advantage of everything that New York had to offer—world-class architecture, the best restaurants, the hottest trends in art, and the most gifted performers on earth. Yes, of course they could experience all these things whenever they chose to travel *to* New York… but it wasn't the same thing as *living* here.

Unfortunately, Jim's life and career were both tied to Dallas. He was well known nationally as a designer, but his business was firmly established in Texas. All of his most important clients lived there. Anthony had accepted that fact from the very beginning. And really, what could he possibly have to complain about? He had the kind of life that his friends in New York could only dream of. He lived in a 5,000 square-foot home that had been featured in *Architectural Digest*. The household staff took care of every imaginable domestic chore; Anthony never had to lift a finger. Whenever he wanted to venture out, he had his choice of several luxury vehicles, including the Ferrari. That was his favorite car, and the only one he drove to work. Christ, talk about making an impression! He loved to watch other crewmembers—especially the pilots—do a double-take when he came roaring into the employee parking lot. Fortunately, thanks to Jim's VIP status and his connections at crew scheduling, Anthony only had to fly a few trips a month. (If there ever was a big shakeup in that department, Anthony's life would change dramatically—and not for the better. But really, what were the chances of that happening?) He also enjoyed a circle of attractive, wealthy and influential friends, all of whom he'd met through Jim. And to top it off, he had a wallet stuffed with credit cards that had no preset spending limit. Jim was very generous; he never questioned a single transaction, whether Anthony was at home or away on a layover. Anthony never even had to open a bank statement to check their account balance; money was just always *there*. When he added it all up, he'd been an idiot to want anyone else. So why, all of a sudden, was he beginning to have doubts?

The entrance to Central Park was so crowded that even Anthony started to feel overwhelmed. Maybe he'd venture south on Fifth Avenue and look at the tree in Rockefeller Center. He hadn't done that since he was a kid. Then he thought of the millions of camera-wielding tourists who'd be jockeying for the same view and decided to head in the other direction. There was a famous landmark that he wanted to see while he was in the city anyway. He turned around and walked west for several blocks and then turned north on Central Park West. Ten minutes later, as he reached Seventy-second Street, his heart began beating quickly. Directly across the street stood the imposing façade of the Dakota—one of the most iconic and exclusive apartment buildings in the world. Anthony had fantasized about living there ever since the first time he'd seen it. That dream, however, would never be realized. Even with all his vast holdings, Jim could never afford to live in the Dakota. That type of Manhattan real estate required a completely different level of wealth, prestige, and connections. But, man… just to think about strolling through the gated courtyard… entering the lobby… nodding a discreet hello to Yoko as she stopped to get her mail…

"Magnificent, isn't it?" a male voice said. Anthony came out of his reverie and noticed a man standing right next to him. He was tall—even taller than Anthony—and had a head full of blond, curly hair. He was broad-shouldered and so solidly built that he looked as though he'd just stepped off the cover of *Sports Illustrated*. He wore a Harvard sweatshirt and a pair of sweatpants. The sweatpants were cut off at mid-thigh and revealed massive quadriceps and sculpted calves that were covered with blond fuzz.

"Yeah," said Anthony. "That's the exact word I'd use to describe it. You know, I've walked by here a thousand times, and every single time I have to stop and look for a while."

"I know what you mean," said the man, moving closer. "To tell you the truth, I'm a little in awe of it."

"I wish we could see more of the architectural details of the roofline from down here on the street. Man, what I wouldn't give to get up there and see it all closeup."

"That can be arranged—if you should happen to meet the right person."

"Such as who?"

"Such as me." He smiled. "I can give you a guided tour. I know this building very well."

Oh, yeah, right. "How would we get in?" Anthony asked, playing along.

"With these." The man reached into his pocket and pulled out a set of keys. "Front door, apartment door… they're all here."

"Are you're trying to tell me *you* live in the Dakota?"

"Yes, I do."

Anthony laughed. "Let me guess: dog walker? Personal trainer? Picking up some papers for your boss? Or maybe you're watching the place for your grandmother, who just left for Palm Beach for the winter."

"Wow, so suspicious! You must be a native New Yorker." He reached into another pocket and pulled out a money clip. "Will this do?" he said, passing a card to Anthony.

Anthony looked at it carefully. It was a New York State driver's license. *Steven Gregory Endicott. One West Seventy-second Street. New York, NY, 10023.* Holy shit: this guy was the real deal. "What do you know," Anthony said, trying to sound casual. He knew when it was important *not* to seem impressed. "And it doesn't look like it's been tampered with, either." He handed the license back. "So, tell me, Steven, *do* you live with your grandmother? Or maybe somebody else who went to visit his own family for Christmas? Someone whose parting words were: 'Don't bring anyone home while I'm gone'?"

"Call me Steve. And no, I live alone." He put one hand on Anthony's shoulder and pointed with the other. "Right there. Fourth floor, the windows on the corner."

"Park view. Hmm, that's nice, Steve."

"You know my name. Aren't you going to tell me yours?"

"Anthony." They shook hands. "Jesus, that grip of yours!" Steve's grip was ferociously strong. "What do you do, Steve?"

"I hang on to a tight to a pole, all day long. Two of them."

"Excuse me?"

"I ski."

"You mean, professionally?"

"Semi-professionally. Mostly on weekends. I'm a partner in a law firm. That takes up Monday through Friday." He leaned against the flagstone wall. "I'm a speed skater, too."

"Well, that explains those big legs of yours."

Steve crossed one leg over the other. "Yeah, they're pretty big all right."

"Do you have any gold medals to show me?"

"One or two. I'll show you whatever you want. Where do you live, Anthony? In Chelsea?"

"No, I used to live here. I live in Dallas now. I'm just visiting for the weekend."

"That's nice," said Steve. "There's no place like New York at Christmastime. Especially if you have the right person to share it with."

"I'm here with someone, Steve." Fuck it, he thought. A direct approach is always best.

Steve nodded. "I thought you might be. Your body language speaks volumes. It doesn't matter to me, though." He rubbed his arms. "Jesus, the temperature has really dropped since I l left the house. I'm freezing out here." He started running in place, causing the lump in his pants to move from side to side.

Anthony couldn't help staring at Steve's crotch. It was nice to feel hypnotized by somebody else for a change, instead of the other way around. By someone taller, bigger and stronger... A stranger who might take him upstairs, get him naked, and take full charge... A man like Steve, who might shove Anthony's face into his sweat-stained, musky jock strap and make *him* do the worshipping for a change.

"So," said Steve. "I hate to pressure you, but I have a holiday event tonight that I have to start getting ready for." He stared right into Anthony's eyes. Jesus, Steve's eyes were so blue! And the skin on his face was taught. There were no wrinkles around his eyes—unusual for an outdoor athlete. His jawline was firm. And that hair... that beautiful, blond curly hair, without a single strand of grey in it.

Do you want to come up?" Steve casually pulled up the t-shirt under his sweatshirt. He had rock-hard abs and a trail of darker blond hair that went all the way from his pectorals to his waistline. "I have a lot more to show you."

"Give me ten more seconds to make up my mind."

"I'll count for you. One, two, three, four, five…"

Oh, fuck! What do I do *now?*

"Six, seven, eight, nine… ten." Steve dangled the keys. "All right, handsome. What did you decide?"

***

Anthony checked his watch as he got off the elevator. It was six o'clock. Fuck! he thought, as he raced to his room. How could it already be six o'clock? He opened the door as quietly as possible. If Jim was—please, God—still asleep, he didn't want to disturb him. But no such luck: the lights were on and water was running in the shower. As Anthony entered and took off his jacket, he heard the water being turned off.

A minute later, Jim walked into the room, wrapping a towel around his waist. "Where the *hell* have you been?"

"I'm sorry, Jim. I lost track of the time. There was so much to see. The tree in Rockefeller Center, and the windows at Bergdorf's, and—"

"I'm *starving.* I haven't eaten since breakfast. I was going to slip downstairs and get something, but I was waiting for you. Where's my pastrami sandwich?"

"Your what?"

"My half of a pastrami sandwich. You said you were going to the Carnegie Deli for a sandwich, and I asked you to bring me back half."

"I'm sorry. I ate it all."

"You ate an *entire* pastrami sandwich from the Carnegie Deli? That's like two pounds of meat."

"I'm really sorry. It was very selfish of me. Once I got started, I just couldn't stop."

"That's one hell of an appetite, Anthony," Jim said, his voice full of suspicion. He walked over to him, nostrils flaring, and stood so close that they were nose to nose. His lip curled. "You don't smell like fucking pastrami to me!"

Anthony quickly turned away to look for a menu on the desk. "Do you want me to call room service?"

"Room service?! We haven't got time for that. We're meeting people for drinks in an hour! I'll have to raid the mini bar." He grabbed a candy bar and tore the wrapper off. "Here we go! Ten bucks for a Milky Way, that's just *dandy!*"

Oh, thought Anthony, this is going to be a *great* night. "I'd better get in the shower."

"Give me five more minutes to finish in the bathroom. Then I'm getting dressed and going downstairs for a drink. Meet me in the bar at six forty-five, and not one minute later."

"I thought we were meeting people for drinks."

"So? I'm having a drink *beforehand*. Do you mind?"

"No, I don't mind." Anthony kicked off his shoes. "What time did you order the car for?"

"Car? We're not even ten blocks away. We'll take a taxi or walk."

"All right. As soon as you're through in there, I'll jump in the shower. I'll make it as fast as I can."

"Don't rush on *my* account," said Jim, storming back to the bathroom. "but do me a favor while you're in there. Scrub yourself hard. Everywhere. *Twice.*"

Oh, fuck, thought Anthony, as Jim slammed the door. Fuck, fuck, fuck!

***

At 6:40, Anthony went downstairs and headed immediately for the bar. Jim was nowhere to be seen. Shit, he thought, he's left without me! Anthony panicked and started racing through the lobby. Maybe I can catch him before he gets into a cab. He heaved a huge sigh of relief when he saw Jim standing at the front desk speaking in a hushed tone to Eduardo. As Anthony stepped closer, he saw Jim handing another credit card to the clerk. "I'm sure it's just some damn technical problem. I'll have to call American Express on Monday."

As Eduardo made eye contact with Anthony, Anthony discreetly gestured for him not to acknowledge his presence. Eduardo returned his gaze to Jim's face and smiled politely. "Of course, Mr. Sizemore, not to worry. I was merely following my manager's instructions."

Anthony walked up to the front desk, acting as though he'd just arrived. "There you are, Jim. I thought you'd be in the bar."

"I had to take care of a small problem," said Jim, with a big smile on his face. "Let's go. If we can get a cab, we'll be there right on time." He steered Anthony to the front door. "My God," he murmured. "Do you know how beautiful you look in that tuxedo?"

Talk about a change of attitude, thought Anthony. "Thanks, you too."

"How I love walking into *any* event with the world's most handsome man on my arm. Lucky me."

Funny, thought Anthony. You'd think after six months that I'd be able to tell if he's sincere.

The doorman got them a taxi right away. As they got in, Anthony noticed that Jim didn't give him a tip.

"Where to?" asked the driver.

"The Palace Hotel, Madison and Fiftieth."

"I thought we were meeting people for drinks first," said Anthony, as the taxi started moving.

"We are," said Jim. "We're meeting Doug and Alphonse in their room for a quick drink and then we'll all head downstairs together."

"Oh. Are you looking forward to tonight?"

"As much as I usually look forward to this kind of thing."

They rode in silence through the heavy Saturday night traffic. Jim stared straight ahead, tapping mindlessly against the plexiglass partition that separated them from the driver.

"Yes?" said the driver, turning around.

"What?" said Jim. "Oh, nothing. Just a nervous habit." He looked out the window and checked the cross street. "Actually, yes, there is something. Stop the car right here, please."

"We're still three blocks away," said the driver.

"I know that. Just *stop* the car." He reached for his wallet as the driver pulled over to the curb. "Come on, Anthony."

Anthony climbed out of the car without saying a word and waited for Jim to pay the driver.

"Let's walk," said Jim. "I had a double Scotch in the bar. It hit me fast. I need a few minutes to clear my head."

"Fine."

"And there's something important that I need to discuss with you."

"If it's about this afternoon, Jim, I'd rather wait until—"

"It's not about this afternoon. It's much more serious than that."

What's more serious than being accused of fucking around? Anthony wondered. Then a more distressing thought occurred to him. Only one crisis caused more stress to in a relationship than infidelity, and that was a financial crisis. Was it possible, even *conceivable*, that Jim was having money trouble? In a flash, all of Jim's odd behavior started making sense: the mood swings, the sudden penny pinching, the standard hotel room, the taxi instead of a limousine… and the declined American Express card. That was the card that Jim used for business expenses. Oh, fuck me, what else *could* it be? "All right, Jim," Anthony said as calmly as he could. "Let's walk."

"Do you have a cigarette?"

"Yes, but why do you ask? You hate it when I smoke."

"I know. I quit years ago. But once in a while, I still want one. And this is one of those times."

Anthony handed him a cigarette and a lighter.

Jim lit a cigarette, took a deep drag and then slowly exhaled. "Oh, God!" He stopped on the sidewalk. "That first rush. How can something so bad for you be so fucking wonderful?"

"What do you want to talk about, Jim?"

Jim took another long drag. "Anthony, it's is very, very important that we show a united front tonight, both as business partners *and* life partners."

"We always do. Why should tonight be any more important than usual?"

"There'll be someone at our table tonight who may become a new client. A *very* important new client. That's the reason that we're here this weekend. Not for this goddam fundraiser."

"I know about the new client. Kyle McAdams. You told me all about him yesterday."

"We *have* to make a good impression and land that job immediately. It's worth a great deal of money. I want the contracts signed by Monday, before we leave for the airport."

"A signed contract in two days? Nobody in this business gets a contract signed that fast, especially right before the holidays. I've been around long enough to know that."

"Don't argue with me! This is exactly what I was talking about just a moment ago! I need Kyle McAdams to like us, to fucking *love* us, and to love *you* especially."

"What do you mean by that?"

"I mean, be extra nice to him. As nice as he wants you to be. He's seen your picture and you're all that he talks about. I need you to do whatever you can to help seal this deal."

Anthony tried to keep a steady hand as he lit a cigarette of his own. "If you're suggesting what I *think* you're suggesting…" he said, as smoke poured from his nostrils. "The answer is: go *fuck* yourself." He turned and started walking back toward the hotel.

"Listen to me!" Jim grabbed him by the arm. "Don't start acting like the last goddam virgin in America. Especially after this afternoon."

"How do you know what I did this afternoon?"

"What do you think I am, a fucking *moron*? When you came back—an hour late, I might add—you had another man's *dick* on your breath. Your whole body *reeked* of sex. Christ, you didn't even bother to take a shower at his place! Do you know how that made me feel, today of all fucking days?! After everything that I've done for you, everything I've given you! You're lucky that I haven't pushed you into moving traffic."

"You want me to go? I'll go. I'll catch the last flight to DFW tonight and clear out before you get back."

"You're not going anywhere." Jim's grip was like a vice on Anthony's arm. "This job is *vital* to the future of our business. It could be worth more than a million dollars, plus a lot of referrals to other new clients in New York. It means a huge amount of cash heading our way—fast. And believe me, we *need* it."

"Explain to me, Jim, why you need so much cash so fast that you're willing to whore me out to get it."

Jim finally let go of his arm. "We're in trouble, Anthony."

"*We're* in trouble?"

"Yes, we are. Half of the business belongs to you, remember? Your name is on everything, right alongside mine. I wish I didn't have to drag you into this, but you're the one who insisted on being given fifty percent of—"

"Exactly what kind of trouble are we in?"

"Cash flow trouble. I'm over-extended on every line of credit that I have. The bank is calling for a big loan payment by next Wednesday and I don't have it."

"How much do you owe them?"

Jim wouldn't look him in the eye. "Five hundred thousand dollars."

"I don't believe it," said Anthony, shaking his head. "Say that again."

"You heard right the first time."

Anthony almost vomited. "How can you owe the bank that much money?! I've seen the goddam books. We're making a profit of over two million dollars this year!"

"You've seen *one* set of books. Every business owner has two. And in case you haven't noticed, we live a pretty lavish lifestyle. Where do you think the money comes from to pay for it?"

"Bullshit. We live in Dallas, for Christ's sake, not on Park Avenue! And I've only been with you since June! There's no way we burned through that much cash in six months."

"All right, it's all *my* fault. That's what you want to hear, isn't it? OK, here are the facts: I made some very bad investments last this summer. Some stocks that I thought would make a fortune ended up being a huge pile of shit. It was a stupid, *stupid* gamble, and I lost. I needed money fast after that, so I took out a second mortgage on the house."

"Without telling me?!"

"I didn't need *your* permission. The deed to the house is the one thing that your name isn't on. Things went from bad to worse. We had a couple of big clients who were slow to pay this fall. We may have to take one of them to court. Carter Buckley still us a thousand of dollars, that *bastard*, and I've known him for twenty years!" Jim was talking a blue streak now. "So then I had to start dipping into the client accounts. Jesus, I only did it a couple of times, I swear! But there still wasn't enough cash coming in to put the money back, so then I had to—"

"Whoa, whoa, back up a minute! What do you mean you started 'dipping' into client accounts?"

"Clients open up checking accounts for me all the time. That way I can buy furniture or artwork or pay for contractors up front, without having to get everything approved one item at a time. It makes life easier for everyone."

"Especially for a fucking con artist like you! Jesus, Jim, what have you done to us? I fell for you like a ton of bricks! I believed *everything* you told me about yourself! And now you're telling me we're *broke?* How could I have been so fucking stupid?!"

Before Jim could answer, his cell phone rang. Anthony couldn't believe it when Jim reached into his coat pocket. "You're going to answer that? *Now?*"

"Yes, I am. It may be our hosts. Fuck, we're late!" He took a deep breath and spoke calmly into the phone. "Hi, buddy ... yes, we're on our way, I'm sorry we're a little behind schedule. It just couldn't be helped ... Yes, all right, we'll meet you in the ballroom. We'll be there as quickly as possible ... yes, we're looking forward to meeting everyone, too. Bye!" He slipped the phone back in his pocket. "Can I have another cigarette?"

"Here, keep them. I have a feeling I won't be able to afford cigarettes or anything else from now on, thanks to you and your financial *genius.*"

"Listen to me, Anthony. *Listen.*" He was pleading now. "We can pull this off. I can get us *out* of this hole, I know I can, and I can do it fast. But it has to start with one new high-profile client, and I need your help to get the ball rolling. Everything is at stake: the house, the cars, the business, our money, my family's money—even my family's fucking *name.* Come on!"

"You're out of your mind. The only thing I'm doing is getting myself out of here and getting a lawyer—my *own* lawyer—as fast as I can."

"Anthony, if you don't help me, I'll have to declare bankruptcy. And if that happens, I'll kill myself."

"You wouldn't do that," Anthony said, even though he could tell by the look of desperation on Jim's face that he very well might.

"You don't know me as well as you think you do. Isn't that obvious, after what I've just told you? I *would* kill myself. I'd take a gun and blow my brains out, right in front of our closest friends at the next Sunday brunch. Think of the legal mess that you'd be in *then.* And I won't be here to help you untangle it."

"Jim, please..."

"It looks like you have two options. I think sticking with my plan is the better of the two." He looked at his watch again. "We're out of time, Anthony. I need to know if you're in. Otherwise, we're out of business and both in deep, deep shit. What's your decision?"

Fuck! Once again, it was the only word that Anthony could think of. Fuck, fuck, *fuck!*

CHAPTER 28

The Fabulous Fake

"Eric," said Michael, "are you almost ready? It's five-thirty."

"I'll be out in a second."

"The suspense is killing me. Can I have one of your cigarettes?"

"Yes. They're on the coffee table." Eric stuck his head out of the bedroom door. "Michael, I'm a little worried. Smoking is getting to be a habit with you. Just like knocking back a few shots of Jamison's at four o'clock every afternoon."

"Thank you, Carrie Nation. Get back in there and don't come out until you're ready to walk out the door. I want the full *GQ* cover man effect."

"I just have to tie my shoes." Eric heard a kitchen cabinet door creaking, and then the clink of a bottle being set on the counter. Well, at least today, Michael had waited until after sundown. "Here I come." He walked into the living room.

"Oh, my gosh!" said Michael.

Eric grinned from ear to ear. "It fits me nicely, doesn't it?"

"You were *born* to wear a tuxedo. Especially Armani. It was worth the extra money you spent to rent it."

"Thanks for loaning me your oxfords." Eric looked down at his feet. "They're so shiny I can almost see myself."

"Well-polished oxfords always look so much better than patent leather. Patent leather screams, 'I'm an usher at my cousin's wedding.' I have something else for you to wear, too." He held up a gold wristwatch. "My Cartier tank watch. I bought it on a layover in Hong Kong years ago, when I had a lot more money in the bank."

"It's stunning!"

"Put it on."

"Oh, no, I couldn't."

"Eric, come over here and put this on right now! You are *not* wearing your Timex with a tuxedo."

"This is unbelievable," Eric said, as Michael slipped the watch onto his wrist and fastened the clasp. "I've never felt so elegant in my life."

"Promise me you won't lose it! I may have to hock it to pay the mortgage when Global crashes."

"I promise."

"And I have something else for you. This cigarette case."

"Is that real gold?"

"Yes, indeed. Eighteen-karat."

"No! I'm sorry, and I appreciate the offer, Michael, but I have to draw the line somewhere. If I leave the house with both of those, I'll be so nervous that I won't be able to think about anything else. Besides, I'm going to smoke as little as possible tonight. People are starting to look down their noses at smokers, even in New York."

"You *will* take both. I insist. I want everything about you to make a statement tonight." He started transferring Eric's cigarettes to the gold cigarette case. "What time is it?"

Eric checked the time on the Cartier. "Five forty-five."

"Don't turn your wrist so self-consciously, Eric. Remember, to you it's just your everyday watch."

"Speaking of which, what do I say if someone asks me how a flight attendant, making eighteen thousand dollars a year, can afford Cartier?"

"They shouldn't ask. One's salary should never come up in casual conversation. It's vulgar. Any man who notices your watch should assume that it was a gift from an admirer—and that you're worth it." Michael stepped back and looked at him. "You look fantastic, like a young European nobleman! I can just see you gliding into the lobby, stopping to casually admire the holiday decor, and then slowly walking up that grand staircase to make your entrance into the ballroom. They're going to be enthralled."

Eric blushed. "I hope so. Well, I guess I ought to get going."

"Not yet." Michael wagged his finger. "You don't want to be the first one to arrive. It'll make you seem overeager. Do you want a shot of Jamison's to quell those butterflies in your stomach?"

"No, thank you."

"I think I'll have another one." He refilled his shot glass.

"Michael, another one already? You're going to be drunk before your guests even arrive."

"Eric, in one hour I'm hosting a holiday party for twenty-five co-workers. Some of them are about to be laid off. Most will drink to excess. And I guarantee you that every single one is taking prescription meds for a major anxiety disorder. So I think that as the host of this soirée, I'm entitled. Now, let's have one last review before you leave. Tell me, which current Broadway musical would you graciously decline to see, even if you were offered a free ticket in the orchestra section?"

"*Cats.* Not now, not ever. Strictly for Midwestern tourists."

"I said 'graciously'. You can be selective without being a snob. By the way, *Phantom of the Opera* would have also been an acceptable response. Who is Le Corbusier?"

"A Frenchman and one the most important architects of the twentieth century. His modern conceptual designs led to both the German Bauhaus movement and the American Universal Style. Incidentally, Le Corbusier is a French expression meaning 'raven-like one'. His birth name was Charles-Édouard Jeanneret."

"*Mon Dieu!*" said Michael. "The way those French syllables just roll off your tongue—you're giving me a hard-on. In what year was his design for the United Nations completed?"

"Is that a trick question? The Secretariat Building, which serves as headquarters for the United Nations, was designed by an international team that *included* Le Corbusier, along with Oscar Neimeyer and Wallace Harrison. It is a perfect example of universalist architecture. Construction was started in 1947 and completed in 1952."

"Very good. What was the last art exhibit that you saw?"

"Austrian Fine and Decorative Arts at the Neue Gallery on Fifth Avenue."

"There's no need to say that it's on Fifth Avenue. Everyone worth their salt knows where the Neue Gallery is. What were your impressions?"

"I was deeply moved by the superb craftsmanship, the elegance of design and the innovative use of classic materials."

"That's a good answer, but try to speak a little more naturally. You sound as though you've been memorizing a guidebook."

"Well, duh!"

"Now, finally, what is your favorite building in New York?"

"I'm always torn between the Flatiron Building and the Chrysler Building. They're both so deeply embedded in our collective psyches. But in the end, for me, it's the Chrysler Building. It just… *soars*."

"Oh, that's good! I like the way your eyes get misty when you say that. Besides, it's a perfect answer: everyone is a sucker for the Chrysler Building. I'm proud of you, Eric. I have no doubt that you'll be able to hold your own tonight." He stood up and opened the hall closet. "Don't forget your overcoat."

"*Your* overcoat, you mean. God, it's beautiful! Where did you get this?"

"Barney's. I picked it up at their once-a-year sale." If there was a bargain to be had in New York City, Michael was the first to know about it. "You're lucky that we wear the same size. Besides, you can't walk out of here with that *schmata* you bought at Sears last week."

"It's a nice, warm jacket, and it only cost fifty dollars. I'm trying to live within my means."

"Honey, this is the northeast. By the end of December, you are going to need a *real* winter coat, or you'll freeze to death."

"I know. I'll worry about it then." He slipped into Michael's overcoat. "I feel like an imposter. The only thing I'm wearing that belongs to me are my socks and my underwear."

"So?" Michael adjusted the coat around Eric's shoulders. "If I know men, and I think I do, they'd just as soon see you wearing nothing at all."

"Will you wait up for me?"

"Of course! I'll want to hear all about it. Here, take these gloves, too. You'll need them. It's going down to the thirties later." As he gave Eric a quick hug, the intercom buzzer rang. "Who the hell could that be? I'm not even dressed yet." He pressed the intercom button. "Yes, Desmond?"

"One of your guests is on her way up," said the doorman.

"Jesus Christ," said Michael, rushing to stash the bottle of whiskey and dump out the ashtray. "An hour early? Is she out of her mind?" A moment later, the doorbell rang. "Get the door, would you, Eric? I need a Scope rinse!"

Eric opened the door and was surprised to see Dee Dee standing in the hallway. It was the first time that he'd ever seen her out of her threadbare Global uniform. She was wearing a sequined navy-blue dress and silver pumps. A large shopping bag was dangling from each hand.

"Hi, Eric!" said Dee Dee. "What're you doing here?"

"I live here," he replied, trying not visibly recoil from her bourbon breath. "Since last July. Michael is my roommate."

"You're kidding! What a small world! All the times we've taken the Q10 together, and I never knew we had a mutual friend."

"Come on in."

She wobbled across the thresh hold. "Oh, gosh, I'm not used to wearing high heels anymore. Would you take these, please?" She handed him the shopping bags.

"Dee Dee!" said Michael, bounding into the room. "Happy holidays! What's all that you brought with you?"

"You said it was BYOB. I wanted to make sure we didn't run out."

"Are you kidding? With that stash, we'll be able to go 'til dawn."

"I hope you don't mind that I'm a little early. I had a few nips while I was getting ready, and all of a sudden it seemed lonely in my apartment."

"I don't mind," said Michael, with a phony smile plastered on his face. "You can keep me company while I finish setting up the buffet."

Dee Dee's chin quivered. "I didn't want to say anything, you guys, but I'm upset. I had to put Fee down last week."

"Oh, no!" said Michael.

"Fee was one of my cats, Eric. Thank God I still have his brothers Fi, Fo and Fum. But they're not adjusting to it any better than I am."

"Bless your heart," said Eric. "I'm so sorry for your loss."

"Thank you. Eric, you look fantastic. Michael said 'dressy,' but I didn't know it was black tie."

"Eric's not staying," said Michael. "He has a function to attend in Manhattan. In fact, he's leaving right now."

"Oh, my God," said Dee Dee. "Remember, Michael, when we used to get invited to big events? We were so *young* then." She plopped herself down on the sofa. "That seems like a lifetime ago." A tear rolled down her cheek. "Everything's changed now."

Eric started to offer her his handkerchief, but Michael shooed him away. "Eric, go! Fashionably late is one thing, but an hour late is inexcusable."

"You look beautiful, Eric," said Dee Dee. "Hey, can I get a picture of the two of us before you leave?"

"I'd love to," said Eric, slipping off his overcoat.

"You haven't got time." Michael opened the front door and shoved him into the hallway. "Come on. I'll walk you to the elevator."

"That was rude," said Eric. "Can't you see how upset she is? She just wants her picture taken with a handsome, young man. It would be a nice holiday memento for her."

"Oh, *brother*. Talk about a letting few compliments going to your head! I'm doing you a favor by keeping the two of you separated. Do you really want to waltz into that ballroom reeking of Shalimar? She practically bathes in it."

"Christ, I didn't even think about that. Thank you!"

"Good night and good luck. Now, go!"

***

Eric boarded an express train bound for Manhattan. The subway was even more crowded than usual on a Saturday night; there were hordes of people on their way to parties and other events. He looked at the Cartier watch and relaxed. It was only 6:15. Good. He'd still arrive with time to spare. Maybe I can stop someplace for a quick drink, he thought, and then decided: No, I shouldn't meet my date with liquor on my breath. That would make a poor first impression. I'll just walk around for ten minutes or so and collect myself.

He was slightly dismayed a few minutes later when the train stopped at 67th Ave, which was a local stop. "Ladies and gentlemen, this is the conductor. Due to track work, all Manhattan-bound trains are running on the local line and will be making all local stops."

Damn, Eric thought. Local trains take forever to reach Manhattan. He checked the time again and was dismayed to feel the watch catching on something. It was then that he noticed the coat's silk lining was frayed and had starting to pull away from the sleeve. Oh, no! He tried to tuck it back in carefully. Well, thank God it was only a few inches wide. Who would even notice? He'd have to be extra careful with the watch, though. He fingered it nervously. Was it his imagination, or was the clasp a tiny bit loose? No, it wasn't his imagination. It *was* loose. What if it were to slip off his wrist without him realizing it? That would be a disaster. He remembered a short story he'd read in college about a pretty but thoroughly middle-class French woman named Mathilde who desperately aspires to move into better social circles. Her devoted husband manages to wrangle an invitation for them to attend a dress ball. Mathilde is despondent over having no jewelry of her own to wear, and so she borrows a beautiful diamond necklace from a friend. To her horror, she loses it coming home from the party. Rather than tell her friend the truth, she borrows a fortune to buy a replacement and then spends years in punishing servitude to pay off the debt—only to find out later that the necklace had been a piece of costume jewelry. Eric had no intention of following in Mathilde's tragic footsteps.

He was, however, being given a singular opportunity. If he made a good impression on Chaz, Aaron and their friends, this evening could be his foray into a whole new world: one of wealth, privilege and prestige. He remembered the casual way that Chaz talked about their various homes, including the apartment on Central Park West. Eric had never personally known anyone that rich and was frankly a bit envious. What is it like, he wondered, to never have to worry about money? To *dine* out instead of eating out. To buy the best tickets available for the opera without giving a thought to the cost. To travel in first class as a paying passenger, rather than standing by as an employee for any available seat in coach. In reality, he had no idea what that kind of life was like. But if he played his cards right, he might find out.

The subway car was getting more and more crowded at each subsequent station. And it was starting to get warm. Eric stood up, folded the coat neatly in his lap, and sat back down.

"*Hoo haw!*" An older woman sitting across from Eric nudged her seatmate. They were both wearing glittering evening gowns under their coats and had carefully teased hair. "Look, Mildred, how *nice* he looks! When's the last time you saw a young man wearing a tuxedo?"

"It's been so long, Beverly, that I can't even remember," said Mildred. She smiled at Eric. "Where are you going?"

"To a fundraiser."

"Oooh!" said Beverly. "Is it a bachelor auction? Because if you're in the lineup, you're gonna raise a lot of money! Mildred, can you imagine the bidding war over *him*?"

"Oh, yes," said Mildred. "Tell me, young man, is it too late for us to buy a ticket?"

"I'm afraid so," said Eric.

"That's too bad! Well, good luck just the same. My gosh, this car is crowded," said Mildred, yanking her coat out from underneath the man who'd just sat down on it.

"Yes," said Beverly, "but it's nice to see people all *fahputzed* for a change. Everyone's gotten so goddam casual about the way they dress. Young women especially, like my daughter. It's like she's getting ready to leave the house and she thinks: 'Why should I make an effort? Who's gonna notice?' I wanna tell her: Believe me, darling, people notice. *Men,* in particular, will notice."

The train made its last stop in Queens. The subway car was packed now. Everyone seemed to be in good spirits though, as they chatted about their plans for the evening. Eric started to get excited. Soon the train would pass under the East River. A few minutes later, Eric would arrive at his destination and his magical night would begin.

"Stand clear of the closing doors," said the conductor, as the bell rang. The doors closed halfway and stopped. "Ladies and gentlemen, *please* stand clear of the closing doors." Eric looked around. There was no one standing in the doorway.

"You people in the last car, stop holding the damn doors!" said the conductor.

Beverly sighed. "'It's always the people in the last car."

The bell rang again. For a third time, the doors closed halfway and stopped. This went on for several more minutes.

"What the hell is going on here?" an elderly man asked no one in particular. He stuck his head out of the car and looked toward the back of the train. "There ain't nobody holding the damn doors. Let's go!"

"Ladies and gentlemen, this is the conductor. We are experiencing a minor mechanical problem with the doors. We hope to have the problem resolved soon and to be moving shortly. Please be patient."

"*Oy,* such *mishegoss!*" said Beverly. "No matter how hard you try, you can't get anywhere in this city on time!"

Fifteen minutes later, the doors were still open and no further announcement had been made. As holiday spirits began to fade, people started getting cranky and fidgety. The subway car was even warmer now. Eric took out a handkerchief and blotted his forehead. He was mortified to see that he had rubbed off a little face powder.

"Oh, is it *warm* in here," said Beverly, patting her hair nervously. "I wish I'd brought a fan. How long is *this* going to take?"

"Don't get all excited," said Mildred. "We'll get there when we get there."

"But what if we're *late?* You know how Sophie treats latecomers. Don't you remember what happened at *Rosh Hashanah?*"

"She can serve the first course without us. For heaven's sake, Beverly, it's a dinner party, not a Broadway show. It's not like they have to wait for us to ring up the curtain."

Ha! Eric thought. That's what *you* think. I have an entrance to make at 7:30! Somebody get those damn doors closed and get this train moving!

But the doors didn't close, and the train didn't move, and everyone just sat and sat and *sat*.

***

At 8:30, Eric's train finally arrived at the 53rd Street station. He ran up the stairs and toward Madison Avenue. He forced himself to take deep breaths and to walk at a regular pace. He couldn't help being late and he surely wouldn't be the only one. I am calm, grounded, and—*goddammit!* I'm going in the wrong direction! He spun around without even looking and nearly collided with the people behind him.

"Hey, dude, watch where the *fuck* you're going!"

"Sorry!" he mumbled, flying past them. He reached the corner of Madison and Fiftieth Street a few minutes later and arrived at the hotel. He entered the lobby, looked at the directional signs, and ran straight up the staircase on the left. Halfway up, he slipped and almost fell, but grabbed hold of the banister just in time. Shit! he thought. I'm going to kill myself if I don't calm down.

He paused on the landing to collect himself and then then walked slowly to the top of the staircase. Directly in front of him was a registration table staffed by a young blond woman and a man who appeared to be in mid-thirties. Printed volunteer name tags identified them as Alyssa and Benjamin. Benjamin was trim and dressed in an elegant charcoal suit. He had wavy dark hair, with just a few flecks of grey in it and little *woosh* in the front that made Eric think of Tin Tin.

"Good evening," Eric said. "I'm here for the benefit."

"May I see your ticket, please?" said Alyssa.

"Ticket? I don't have one."

"You don't *have* one?" she said. "I'm afraid I can't let you in without a ticket."

"But I was invited!"

"By whom?" she asked imperiously, as though he'd wandered in from the street.

Eric composed himself on the spot. "I'm a guest of Aaron Rosenstein. My name is Eric Saunders."

Benjamin looked at seating chart on the table in front of him. "Yes, I have your name here. Table ten," he said. "But you'll have to wait just a moment. Someone's making a speech right now."

"Thank you," said Eric, heaving a sigh of relief. He moved to stand by the entry door and folded his hands in front of him.

"Excuse me," said Benjamin. "Wouldn't you like to check your overcoat?"

"What? Oh, yes." Eric hurriedly pulled it off. "Who do I give it to?"

"Carol, the coat-check volunteer, has stepped out for just a moment. I'll take it. Give it to me and I'll be right back with a claim ticket."

"Thank you. That's very kind."

Benjamin disappeared around the corner and returned a moment later. "Alyssa, it looks like Carol will be gone for longer than we thought. Do you mind taking over the coat check until she comes back, just in case there are other late arrivals?"

"Oh, *all right*," Alyssa replied. "But I'm not standing in that closet for any longer than that! These heels are killing me." She left in a great huff.

"Here's your claim check, sir," said Benjamin. "And here's something else you may want to hold onto."

Eric almost fainted as Benjamin handed him a watch. "Oh my fucking God!" he blurted. "Michael's watch!"

"Something borrowed?" Benjamin asked with a grin.

"Yes."

"Me, too." He showed Eric his French shirt cuffs. "These gold cufflinks belonged to my grandfather. My parents would murder me if I lost them, so I know just how you feel." Benjamin had the most soulful brown eyes that Eric had ever seen. And his smile was completely natural. He slipped the watch onto Eric's wrist. The touch of Benjamin's hands on his skin gave Eric a tingling sensation. "This must have gotten caught in the sleeve when you were taking off your coat. The lining is a little bit frayed on the right sleeve."

"I know," said Eric. "I was hoping that nobody else would notice."

"I wouldn't worry too much about it. I'm glad you didn't lose that watch, though."

"Thank you, Benjamin. You saved my life."

"My pleasure. Now, let me see what's going on in there." He opened the door and took a peek inside. "The coast is clear. Enjoy yourself tonight, Eric. And by the way…"

"Yes?"

"You look great." He smiled. "Kill the people."

Eric entered the ballroom and was immediately overwhelmed by the opulent décor. Two grand chandeliers hung from the ceiling and gleaned a shimmering pattern of light on the guests below. Alternating sections of the pale grey walls featured recessed panels, delicate gold leaf design, and classical paintings of lovers in courtship. Huge silver candelabras formed the centerpiece of each table. At every place setting, cut crystal glassware sparkled like a jeweler's window. The entire room was bathed in soft, golden light. Mirrored French doors with Palladian arches multiplied the hundreds of formally dressed men into a thousand. Eric felt as though he'd stepped out of his own life and into an Edith Wharton novel.

The room was oval; there were no corners and no point of reference for its beginning or end. As a Richard Rodgers waltz began playing, the three-quarter tempo only added to Eric's confusion. He became frozen where he stood, having no idea where to find the Rosenstein party. If only he'd asked Benjamin to direct him to table 10! Should I go back outside, he wondered, or ask a passing waiter? Then he noticed light from one of the chandeliers shining on the head of man with light-blond hair. It was Chaz, sitting at a large round table across the room. He had a tight smile on his face and was discreetly waving his hand to get Eric's attention.

Eric replied with a nod and beamed his most sincere smile. I must be past the point of being fashionably late, he thought. He kept smiling and began slithering through the mire of black ties and chatter. Late or not, this was his big moment. He knew that he mustn't appear rushed, or anxious, or try too hard to apologize for his tardiness. He had simply arrived.

Aside from Chaz, there were eight other men at the table. As he came closer, he noticed Chaz' partner, Aaron, seated on the left. Eric recognized him from the pictures in Chaz's photo album. He was even better looking in person. Past the empty chair on the right (presumably Eric's), there was a nice-looking man with thinning hair and a freckled face. He appeared to be engrossed in conversation with two handsome men sitting to his right. Eric almost tripped over his own feet when he realized that the two men were Anthony Bellini and Jim Sizemore.

"Eric!" said Chaz. "I'm glad you're here. We'd almost given up on you."

"I'm so sorry that I'm late," said Eric. Before Chaz could say anything else, Eric smiled at Aaron and held out his hand. "You must be Aaron. It's a pleasure to meet you. I'm Eric Saunders. Thank you so much for including me."

"We're glad you could make it," said Aaron, gripping Eric's hand.

"I'm afraid you've missed the cocktail hour, and the appetizer and the salad," said Chaz, still wearing the tight smile, "but they're just about to serve the main course, so the evening isn't a total loss. Let me introduce you to everybody."

"Please don't get up," said Eric, still smiling. "I wouldn't want to interrupt your meal."

"This is Mark and Tim, and Rod and Damien." It was obvious that they were two couples. Nevertheless, they greeted Eric warmly and then resumed eating their salads. That left just one free male at the table. "Eric," said Chaz, "I'd like you to meet Kyle Wilkerson."

Kyle stood up to shake Eric's hand. "It's so nice to *finally* meet you."

"Likewise, Kyle."

"And surprise, surprise!" said Chaz, chirping like Billie Burke in *Dinner at Eight*. "I had *no* idea that you already know each other, but here they are—all the way from Dallas—Anthony and Jim."

Anthony made a big point of getting out of his seat to give Eric a hug. "It's good to see you, Eric."

"You too, Anthony," Eric said half-heartedly.

"Hey, nice to see you again, Eric!" said Jim. He gave Eric a bear hug and then slapped him on the back. "Do you believe this, buddy? What are the chances of us old friends running into each other here tonight?"

"Only in New York, as we say." It took every ounce of strength that Eric had to maintain his composure.

"Sit down, everybody, please," said Chaz. "Eric, let's get you a drink. What would you like?"

"A vodka and tonic, please." Eric carefully unfolded his napkin and laid it on his lap. He took a moment to study the arrangement of silverware on each side of his charger. Thankfully, it wasn't a very complicated setting. It was then that he noticed everyone at the table was drinking wine. "On second thought, Chaz, I'll have red wine." He was very grateful when his glass was filled almost immediately. Now, if there's a God in heaven, he prayed, I won't knock it over.

"So, what happened to you?" said Kyle. "I thought that I'd been stood up." He smiled, but his tone indicated that such a thing could never happen to him. "Did you get lost?"

"No," said Eric. "I left my house in plenty of time. I came via subway and we got stuck in a station for almost an hour. I thought I'd never get here." Such a typical New York experience, he thought. It could happen to anyone.

"Why didn't you just go upstairs and get a taxi?" asked Kyle.

"You can't get a taxi on the street in Queens," said Eric. "There aren't allowed to operate there. It was either wait for the train to move or walk across the Fifty-Ninth Street Bridge, in which case I wouldn't have arrived until breakfast. So, Kyle, Chaz told me that you and Aaron are—"

"Queens?" Kyle's smile vanished. "You live in Queens?"

"Yes, in Forest Hills Gardens," he replied, stressing the word 'Gardens'. If Kyle is a true New Yorker, he thought, he'll know that I live in a beautiful and historic neighborhood.

"Huh," said Kyle. "That's nice." He turned around to face Anthony. "So, Anthony, tell me about this fantastic job that you and Jim just did in La Jolla. I saw the pictures, and I was blown away by your work."

"That was a really exciting project for us," said Anthony, leaning in as he spoke. His olive skin glowed in the candlelight. "We were there for almost two months, but it was worth all the time we took. The client was very pleased with the results."

"Two months in La Jolla?" said Eric, trying to join the conversation. "Aren't you still flying, Anthony?"

"Now and then," said Anthony, never taking his eyes off Kyle. "Jim and I are quite involved in our design business."

"But how do you manage to get all that time off from the air—"

"Let's get back to that project in La Jolla," said Kyle, interrupting Eric. "I love what you guys did. I can't wait to see the plans that you come up with for my townhouse on East Forty-first Street. I have a feeling you're going to knock all the New York designers right out of the goddam ring."

"I hope so," said Anthony.

"I hate to think of you spending all that time out there just working non-stop," said Kyle. "Did you get any sun time? The beaches there are some of the most beautiful in California."

"Yeah. Almost every Sunday, we went to Black's Beach. And you're right. It was spectacular."

Of course you went to Black's Beach, Eric thought as he reached for a roll. Naturally, you'd go to the nude gay beach so that you could show off for the entire West Coast.

"Oh, yeah, I *love* Black's Beach," said Kyle. "You can really... be yourself there."

Anthony leaned back slightly in his seat and spread his legs. "I know what you mean. That was the best part."

"Do you ever go to Jones Beach, Kyle?" Eric asked lamely. "I went there a few times this summer. It was fun."

"Jones Beach? *No.* When it's ninety-eight degrees outside, I can do without the teeming, sweaty masses and their boom boxes. Not to mention the nauseating smell of their overly-spiced food. If I'm in New York for any part of the summer, I head right to the Pines."

"Oh," said Eric. "Do you have a share?"

"No, I *own* a home. Anthony, you and Jim have to come out next summer. You'd love it. My property is completely secluded. You can be yourself *there* too, if you know what I mean."

"That'd be great," said Anthony. Then he leaned over and said something to Kyle that Eric couldn't hear.

Kyle laughed a nasty laugh and squeezed Anthony's thigh.

Well, thought Eric, so much for this setup. He drained his wineglass and signaled the waiter for another, barely able to contain his anger. Fuck you, Anthony, he wanted to scream. Why are you coming on to my date? You're *taken.* Not only are you taken, but your boyfriend is sitting right next to you and doesn't even seem to mind. In fact, he seems to be enjoying it! He turned to Chaz, determined to be included in the group one way or another. "Chaz, this is such a perfect setting. I think it may be the most beautiful room that I've ever seen."

Chaz nodded. "Stunning, isn't? Louis the Sixteenth, filtered through the impressions of Edwardian New Yorkers. I love all the attention to detail, from those fantastic chandeliers right down to the delicate chairs. Did you notice the paintings?"

Eric nodded. "They're splendid pastorals. I love the sense of romance that they convey." Oh, God, he thought, as he listened to himself. Why don't I just shut up?

Chaz nodded. "I can't tell if they're Wateau or Fragonard, but they certainly bring to mind *The Process of Love*. Have you seen it at the Fricke?"

"No." Eric tried not to glare at Anthony. "But I'm glad that *somebody's* getting Fricked tonight."

"What, Eric?" said Chaz, as a waiter appeared at the table.

"Nothing. I think our dinner has arrived."

Chaz beamed as the staff began serving the main course. "This beef looks beautiful! And it will go perfectly with the Cabernet. Don't wait for everyone else, Eric. You must be starving, you poor thing."

"Not at all," Eric said, smiling serenely and thinking: Where do you think I was raised, in a barn? He observed the artful way that the food had been arranged on the plate and nodded approvingly. "Chaz, just out of curiosity, what are Anthony and Jim doing here tonight?"

"To tell you the truth, I'm not sure. I suppose that Kyle invited them. The firm paid for a table and divided the tickets among the senior partners. I still can't believe all these lawyers are here at an AIDS benefit—at a thousand dollars a plate yet! Times have changed. Even a year ago, you'd *never* have seen these men..." He paused as he received a stern look from Aaron. "This *is* such a wonderful evening! I hope it will raise a lot of money. How do you know Anthony and Jim, Eric?"

"Anthony was my roommate in training. We became very close friends... for a while. I've only met Jim twice."

"They certainly are a striking couple." Chaz lowered his voice and leaned closer. "I'm surprised that you and Kyle aren't hitting it off. I thought you'd be just his type. That's why we invited you."

"He knows I'm from Queens. Nobody in Manhattan wants to date a 7-1-8."

"Oh, come on," said Chaz, with a laugh. "I can't believe that any man would discriminate against you just because of your area code."

Eric snorted. "Obviously, you've been off the market for quite some time."

"I'm sorry there's not another bachelor at the table," said Chaz. "Except for you and Kyle, everyone's already paired off."

"I know. Thanks for trying, Chaz. I do appreciate it."

"By the way…" Chaz nodded toward Kyle, Anthony and Jim, who seemed oblivious to everyone else. "That's an interesting scenario. I can't wait to see how it plays out. In the meantime, darling, don't be too disappointed. Think of where you are tonight—in this elegant room, surrounded by all these handsome men and their huge portfolios. Savor the meal, and drink as much wine as you want. It's all paid for, so you may as well relax and enjoy yourself. And try to get to know the other men here at our table. They're all wonderful guys. Just because we're all couples, it doesn't mean we can't be friends. After dessert, you and I will grab a couple of brandies and then go circulate." He patted Eric's hand. "There have to be *some* other single men here tonight."

Eric had never felt so patronized in his life. He put down his fork and looked around the table. All the men looked relaxed and self-satisfied. They seemed to be at ease both in their formal wear and in their own skins. Eric felt like a fraud in his rented tuxedo. His necktie was too tight; he felt as though he were being strangled. But removing it at the table would be considered the height of boorish behavior. The oxfords were pinching his toes. He wanted desperately to kick them off and shove them under his gilded chair. Yes, he thought, I may as well let out a great, big fart while I'm at it.

He tried to focus on his tablemates and to show interest in every subject being discussed. As the hour progressed, the conversation jumped from one topic to another: their involvement in complex legal cases, their views on New York City politics, their second and third homes, and their plans for the Christmas holidays. No one was staying in town. They were off to sail the Greek Isles, to ski the Italian Alps or to shop in Singapore. Eric tried to keep up, but he had nothing substantial to contribute. There was no mention of the current season on Broadway, or the latest exhibit at MoMA, or architecture of any kind—not even the Chrysler Building. All of Michael's careful tutelage had been for naught. He felt invisible until Damien looked over at him and asked, "What do you do, Eric?"

"I'm a flight attendant for Mercury Airways."

Suddenly, everyone was interested. "Why is it so hard to get an upgrade these days? We have a million miles between the two of us, and first class is *always* full."

"Why don't you hold flights for connecting passengers when we're late and it's the airline's fault? We had to spend the night in LAX last year, and missed an entire day of Carnival in Sydney."

"Mercury's food is the worst. We were served a *Chateau Briand* in first class last week that was *inedible*. Why don't you hire a new chef?"

Oh, God, thought Eric. Why does this happen wherever I go? People find out what I do for a living, and suddenly it's open season. I should have saved myself the trouble of dressing up and worn my uniform instead! He noticed that neither Chaz nor Anthony responded to a single question about the airline. Why would they? After all, they weren't *real* flight attendants. They were trophy spouses. They were like the Connecticut housewives Eric knew who showed up once a year to don an oxygen mask and then spend six hours thumbing through *Town and Country*. Eric made the usual banal responses until the subject had been exhausted and then reached into his pocket for the cigarette case. Screw it, he thought, as he started to light a cigarette. I don't care what any of them think of me anymore.

"Sorry, Eric," said Chaz, taking the lighter from Eric's hand. "This is a non-smoking event. You'll have to go downstairs."

"Of course. Pardon me, gentlemen." He'd never been so relieved to get up from a table. Free at last, he thought. I'll smoke a cigarette, come back for a Courvoisier, and then politely excuse myself and go home. I should probably be sure to leave before midnight. God knows what will happen to my clothes when the clock strikes twelve. He quickly made his way to the exit and started walking down the staircase. He didn't bother stopping for his overcoat. The fresh, cold air would feel wonderful.

"Hey, Eric, wait up."

Oh, *no*. He recognized the voice immediately. As he reached the landing, he turned around and saw Jim coming down right behind him.

"You're not leaving already, are you?" said Jim, oozing fake charm.

"No. I'm going to have a cigarette."

"Good idea. I'll join you."

Oh, ducky, Eric thought, as Jim followed him. That's just fuckin' *ducky*.

They walked into the courtyard and lit cigarettes. "Beautiful, isn't it?" said Jim, looking up at the façade.

"Yes," said Eric. "The Italian Renaissance style is wonderful… although I do think that the brownstone gives it an unnecessarily austere appearance."

"Really. What a keen observation," said Jim, with a bemused expression on his face. "Did you study architecture in school?"

"No, I have a B.A in Psychology from U.T. Austin. But I have many interests. Architecture is just one of them."

"U.T. That's a good state school. I went to Rhode Island School of Design."

"I'm surprised you didn't say Harvard or Yale."

Jim snorted. "My alma mater is one of the most prestigious design schools in the country. A private school education facilitates exposure to influential people and vital networking opportunities. My career path was set before the end of my sophomore year, I'm pleased to say. Those opportunities simply don't exist for the students of *public* universities."

What a pompous ass, thought Eric. He's trying to get under my skin, but I'm not going to give him the satisfaction. "Did you know, Jim, that this wasn't originally built as a hotel? The Villard houses were a series of six mansions, all built on this site by Stanford White for Henry Villard. Villard was a German immigrant who became a multi-millionaire and was president of the Northern Pacific Railroad."

"Yes," said Jim, noisily exhaling smoke. "Any first-year design student knows that."

"Well, did you know that he only lived here for one year? He lost his entire fortune when the Northern Pacific went bankrupt. Millions of dollars' worth of his own stock went right down the drain. Terrible, isn't it? He and his family had to practically flee from an angry mob that gathered around the house afterward. They were investors in the railroad too, and lost everything."

Jim doubled over as though he'd been gut-punched. He started to stammer a response, and then took a deep breath and pulled himself upright. "You're just a font of knowledge tonight, aren't you?" he said. He hand was shaking as he reached for a silver flask in his pocket.

I've hit a nerve, thought Eric. I don't know how, but I've hit a nerve, and it feels delicious. "Well, I *can* talk about something else besides upgrades and flight delays, just in case you were wondering."

"I *wasn't* wondering." Jim took a big swig from his flask.

It was Scotch. Even in the cold night air, Eric could smell it. Clearly, all was not well in Lone Star paradise. "Tell me, what's new with you and Anthony? I haven't had a chance to catch up you yet this evening."

"Anthony and I are just fine and dandy," Jim said, smiling. "Thanks for asking."

So much for trying to press my advantage, thought Eric. "It's been nice chatting with you, Jim. I'm going back inside now. There's a brandy up there with my name on it. And there are a few people I'm supposed to meet." He walked to the corner to put out his cigarette. He was quite pleased that he'd been able to maintain his composure while having a discussion, however brief, with a man he truly loathed.

"Good luck with those introductions," said Jim. "I guess you came stag tonight, huh?"

Eric's poise vanished instantly. "No, I *didn't* come stag. Kyle was supposed to be *my* date. I'm sure you're aware of that."

"Sorry that didn't work out for you. I know how disappointed you must be. But I don't think you're his type anyway."

Walk away from this jerk, Eric told himself as his blood boiled. Just walk away, right now! But he couldn't help himself. "What's *that* supposed to mean?"

Jim sneered. "It means you're out of your league with this crowd. That should be painfully obvious to you. It's certainly obvious to everyone else. Oh, I'm not saying you can't find a boyfriend in New York, but I think you're setting the bar a little too high. I can see you nesting with a high school teacher. Or a social worker. Maybe even a therapist with a private practice in Brooklyn. You two will fall in love in a cozy, little café on Flatbush Avenue while discussing Maslow's hierarchy of needs." He was gloating now, being obnoxious just for the sake of it. "You'll buy a fixer-upper in Park Slope and find yourselves completely in over your heads. So you'll ask your lesbian friends to do the all heavy lifting. They won't mind. They *love* that kind of shit. After they finish restoring your hardwood floors and retiling the bathroom, you can invite them all over for a nice Sunday brunch." His speech was starting to slur. He wasn't just obnoxious. He was drunk, too.

"It seems you've put a lot of thought into my options," said Eric. "But as far as Kyle is concerned, I think it had more to do with the fact that you and Anthony got here *first*. Tell me, is this your usual strategy?"

"What are you talking about?"

"Three-ways. *Predatory* three-ways. Just swooping in, with your great hair and your pumped up muscles and your big dicks, and grabbing any man you choose, without any *fucking* consideration for anyone else."

"Hey, I can't help it if we get what we want, whenever we want it. That's just the way of the world. You were outclassed tonight, sport. Get used to it."

"You know what, Jim? You're an asshole. I knew that from the first moment I ever laid eyes on you. A pompous, flaming *asshole*."

"And you're a tittie baby," Jim said with glee. "And a phony too, with that ridiculous cigarette case and your Canal Street Cartier knockoff. What'd you pay for that watch, ten bucks? It's probably not even worth *five*." He took another swig of Scotch. "Go on home, tittie baby. There's nothing else happening here for you tonight."

"Fuck you, Jim! *Fuck* you!"

"Yeah, he's right! Fuck you, Jim!"

Eric was startled to hear another man's voice. It was Anthony, standing less than twenty feet away from them with an overcoat hanging on each arm.

"What are you doing out here?" said Jim.

"Looking for *you*. Kyle wants to skip dessert and go right to his place."

"Success!" said Jim, raising his arms like Rocky Balboa. "I knew you'd come through, Anthony." He grinned drunkenly. "Baby, I love you."

"Congratulations," said Eric. "I hope you three will be happy together."

"Don't jump to conclusions, Eric," said Anthony. He glared at Jim. "I *don't* love you, Jim. In fact, right this minute, I hate your fucking guts. What line of bullshit are you trying to feed my friend?"

"I'm just teaching him a few cold facts." Jim took another swig. "He needs an education."

"I heard everything you said to him. And Eric's right. You *are* an asshole. You think *you* outclassed *him*? Bullshit! Why don't you tell him the real reason I made a move on Kyle?"

"You keep your goddam mouth shut," Jim said menacingly.

"I'm sorry we screwed up your date, Eric," said Anthony. "Here's what really happened: Jim and I are in deep shit. Our business is about to go bust, and it's all his fault, but he came up with a great idea for saving the company. Kyle saw my picture in an article about the La Jolla project. He's been hocking us for weeks to arrange a business meeting. That's why he invited us here tonight. He wants to hire us for a big job. He has more money than God, and he's willing to give us a big pile of cash up front. He's also interested in fucking me. He made it very clear just now—that's part of the deal. So, to save us from bankruptcy, Jim has decided to whore me out. Real class act, don't you think?"

"That's a lie!" Jim shouted. "That's a goddam lie!"

"It's the *truth*," said Anthony. "And I have no choice but to go along with it. I own half the business now, and I'm liable for whatever shit goes down. So I'm fucked, literally, no matter what I do. *That's* what our life is like right now, Eric. Impressed?"

"You *bastard!*" said Jim, seething. "I ought to kick your sorry ass all the way back to Texas."

Anthony was unfazed by the threat. "You'd better calm down if you want me to play this thing through to the end. Our whole future is riding on my ass, remember?"

Jim grabbed his coat. "I'll wait for Kyle in the lobby. Meet us there in five minutes."

"I'll be there when I'm good and ready. I want to talk to Eric first."

Jim pointed at the Rolex watch on his wrist. "Five minutes!" he said, as stormed off.

Anthony and Eric stood silently for a few minutes.

"I'm sorry, Anthony. I had no idea. I thought your life with Jim was velvet."

"It seemed like that, for a good long while. Man, talk about deluding myself."

"I'm glad you have a solution for saving the business, even though it seems like a very unpleasant one."

"Don't try to sound so polite. I'm *letting* myself be whored out." Anthony shrugged. "I'll live. It's just… it's that look they get in their eyes when they're fucking you, and they know they own a piece of your soul. It's so goddam degrading." He looked at the ground. "Let's talk about something else."

"All right. How's Sammy? I haven't heard anything about him since the last time I saw you at JFK."

"Sammy died."

"Oh, no!"

"He hung on for about a week in the hospital, and then he died from internal injuries." Anthony was struggling to keep from crying. "It almost killed my mother. She worried about him all the time, despite what she would say whenever his name came up in conversation, but I don't think she ever expected *that*."

"Why didn't you call me?"

"How the hell was I supposed to call you? I didn't have your phone number. I gave you *my* phone number the last time I saw you, and then I never heard from you again."

"I'm sorry. I was so angry that day that I threw the card away."

"I figured." He sighed. "I'm sorry I was such an asshole, trying to buy you off with that check. Guilt money. God, was I being stupid. I was so caught up in my new lifestyle that I couldn't even think about giving it up. Lifestyle: how I hate that fucking word." He lit a cigarette. "I miss you, Eric. I wish we could be friends again."

"I don't see how. We live in two very different worlds."

"Not for much longer, buddy."

"How do you mean?"

"I'm getting out of this mess with Jim and getting my ass *back* to New York, where I belong."

"How?"

"I don't know how. But I will."

"Anthony!" Jim yelled from the entryway. "It's time to leave."

"I gotta go." He stubbed out the cigarette and reached for his wallet. "Here's my new card. This is a private cell phone number. Jim doesn't even know I have it. Don't tear it up this time. Call me when you can and we'll take it from there."

"I will. I promise. I miss you." Eric hated to admit it, but it was true.

"Come here for a second." Anthony took Eric in his arms and squeezed so hard that Eric thought he would suffocate. "I love you. I hope I'll see you soon."

"We'll figure something out. I love you, too, Anthony. Good luck." He watched Anthony walk away, with his head held high and his back perfectly straight. Anthony *would* pull through, somehow. He always bounced back from calamity. But for the first time since they'd met in April, Eric didn't envy him in the least.

Eric took a moment to enjoy the beauty of the courtyard and then walked back into the lobby. As he started to climb the staircase, he was filled with gratitude. Whatever I have and whatever I've accomplished so far, he thought, I've done it all on my own and it's mine. No one can ever take it away from me. And that counts for a lot. My life, just as it is, is pretty damn good after all.

As he reached the top of the stairs, he heard a lively Cole Porter medley playing and felt as though the evening was starting all over again. He anticipated the cognac that he was about to enjoy, and the introductions that Chaz had promised to make. He checked the time on Michael's watch and smiled. It was still well before midnight. Anything was possible.

CHAPTER 29

"I Have Never Seen Snow"

"This a South Ferry-bound number one train," said the conductor. "Next stop: Christopher Street."

Five minutes later, Denny got off the train, walked up to the street level, and sighed contentedly. It was a just the kind of winter day in New York that he loved. The temperature was in the thirties. A frigid wind was coming off the Hudson River; he could feel it blowing all the way over to Seventh Avenue. Huge, heavy clouds were getting darker by the minute. There would be snow today, for sure; he could feel it. And he looked great in his brand-new leather bomber jacket.

He debated whether to duck into the Italian coffee shop up the street but decided against it. It was already 11:55 and he was supposed to meet Eric on the corner at noon. Eric was maddeningly punctual and expected the same of everyone else. But, Denny thought, if punctuality is the only flaw I can find in my best friend's character, then so be it.

He was startled to realize that he thought of Eric as his best friend. He couldn't even remember the last time he'd allowed himself the luxury of *having* a best friend. Male flight attendants were a notoriously fickle group, and those stationed in New York carried it to the extreme. They often lived their lives like straws in the wind, ready to blow from one city to another without a single thought for the consequences. Their lack of desire to put down real roots hampered Denny's social life year after year. He had lost track of the number of friendships that he'd started and endeavored to maintain, only to have someone drop a bomb within six months: "Denny, I'm in love with a man that I met on a layover in Rio de Janeiro. I'm moving down there to live with him and I'm going to commute to JFK."

"Let me get this straight," Denny had replied, incredulous. "You're going to spend ten hours on a red-eye flight from Rio to JFK, probably crammed into a middle seat in coach, just to turn around and work a ten-hour flight *back* to Rio the next night—all because of a man?"

"Not just any man. The *perfect* man. Here, look at this picture! Isn't he gorgeous? He could be a porn star for Kristen Bjorn Studios."

"He already is a porn star. He played the lead in *Asses Ahoy!* I have it on DVD. And believe me, his ass *was* ahoy—from the opening credits right through to the end."

"Don't rain on my parade, Denny. I have the whole thing worked out. I'll use a trip trade service to back up all my trips. I'll only have to commute up to JFK once or twice a month."

"Yeah, and after one month of doing that, you'll look like the living dead."

"I'll make it work. Just watch me."

"OK. Good luck with that…"

"I'm sorry, Denny," said another friend, "but I can't stand New York for even more minute! I hate the freezing winters and the stifling summers. I hate the traffic, the noise, and the garbage. I hate the panhandlers on every street corner, and the homeless people stinking up the subway. I'm *done*. I'm transferring to L.A. I've already bought a car, found a roommate in West Hollywood, and a hired personal trainer. Don't worry, we'll still be friends. We'll see each other on layovers. And you're welcome to visit whenever you like."

Sure, sure. Have a nice life…

"I'm transferring to Miami," the most recent defector had said. "You cannot believe how many beautiful men there are down there! Brazilians, Cubans, Jamaicans, Dominicans. They have *huge* uncut dicks, and they're always ready to get off—even the straight ones! I found a studio in a high-rise that's only a block from the Twelfth Street beach. Except for putting on my uniform to go to work, I'll never have to wear anything again besides a Speedo, flips-flops, and Coppertone. And I'll be tanned all year round!"

My, what lofty personal goals you've set. *Adios, amigo…*

Eric, on the other hand, was staying. Denny was sure of that. He'd never met anyone who was so enchanted with the Big Apple. Eric spent every single free day exploring New York, from the Upper West Side to the Staten Island Ferry and everywhere in between. He could walk for hours on end with only a guidebook, a bottle of water and a bag of salted nuts in his knapsack. After only six months, he seemed to know more about the city than Denny himself. And Denny had lived there for over five years! Eric was a keeper. He was a hardworking crewmember, a loyal friend and an occasional fuck buddy—one with absolutely no strings attached.

"Hi, Denny," said Eric, waving from the bodega a few doors down.

"Hi, sweetheart." They gave each other a big hug. "Eric, what are you wearing?"

"This is my new winter coat."

"That's *not* a winter coat. It's a corduroy jacket. It's thirty-five degrees today."

"I have a heavy sweater on underneath. And new gloves and a wool scarf. I'm fine."

"And I'm telling you, that's *not* warm enough. After lunch, we're going to the army-navy store down the street to buy you a real coat."

"I can't afford another coat."

"Then I'll buy it for you as an early birthday present."

"We'll see."

"Listen," said Denny, "are you starving?"

"No, I had a late breakfast."

"Good. I promised to look in on a friend, and I'd appreciate it if you'd come with me."

"Sure. Is it anyone I know?"

"Do you know Zack Pendergast?"

"Oh, yes! I flew a transcon with him last June. He was working the lower lobe galley. Just between you and me—I know you can keep a secret—he initiated me into the mile-high club."

Denny's heart skipped a beat. "Did he?"

"Yes! It was fantastic! God, what a hottie! I'd love to see him again. Where does he live?"

"He's about a ten-minute walk from here, on Hudson near Jane Street. I told him we'd stop by around twelve-thirty." He looked at his watch. "It's only twelve o'clock now. We have a little time. Let's pop into that coffee shop."

"Good idea," said Eric, shivering. He pulled his jacket zipper up all the way. "It *is* freezing today."

"I told you. I'm buying you that new coat whether you like it or not. You can't go running around New York in January dressed like the Poor Little Match Girl."

"Butch me up a little, would you? Make it Raggedy Andy."

"Whatever."

"There's a seventy percent chance of snow today," Eric said excitedly. "Do you think it *will* snow?"

"Yes. Look at the sky. See how low and heavy those clouds are? I'm sure they're bursting with snowflakes—great, big, fat ones."

"I hope so! This will be my first time."

"First time for what?"

"To see snow."

"You've *never* seen snow?"

"Nope, not where I'm from in Texas. We get a little freezing every couple of years, which shuts the city down completely, but I've never experienced an honest-to-goodness snow storm. I can't believe it didn't snow *once* during the entire month of December."

"Then you're in for a treat today, my friend. Come on, let's go inside."

They entered the coffee shop, which was surprisingly crowded for a weekday. Denny steered them to a table in the corner. They took off their coats, sat down and ordered two cappuccinos. "Do you want to share a cannoli or something?" Denny asked.

"No," said Eric. "I'm within a pound or two of my weight limit. It's all muscle, but I still don't want my supervisor hassling me about it."

"Weight limit? What are you talking about? Aren't you off probation?"

"Yes, but Pumpkin Head still puts all of us on the scale once a month."

"Not anymore, he won't."

"What do you mean?"

"There was a special union hotline update yesterday. I guess you haven't heard it yet. The union and the company have agreed to scrap the weight limit for flight attendants."

"*What?*"

"The hotline said that both parties are spending too much time and money dealing with the issue. The company keeps suspending people without pay or going to the extreme of firing repeat offenders. The union spends months fighting to get their jobs back. It's a ridiculous waste of time, money, and energy. Just a few months ago, the company made a thirty-year flight attendant go through initial training all over again as a condition of re-employment. It's total bullshit. No other employee group at this company has a weight limit, including the pilots."

"But we have to keep the weight limit! How else will you make sure that people stay looking trim and professional?"

Denny shrugged. "They'll have to be self-motivated, I suppose."

"Well, *that* leaves out at least fifty percent of the flight attendant corps."

"Eric, please don't use expressions like 'the flight attendant corps'. It makes it sound like you went through the Charm Farm in 1948. Anyways, I have something more serious to discuss. It's about Zack."

"Oh, right. You never mentioned why we're going to see him. Was he on that flight to Miami last week that hit severe turbulence? I heard at least half the crew got injured. A woman in the galley had a cart fall on top of her. It broke her leg in two places!"

"Zack isn't injured. He's sick."

"Sick with what?"

"It's 1991. I mean, it's 1992 now. What do you think?"

"You mean… HIV?"

"Worse. He has full-blown AIDS."

The color drained from Eric's face. "Oh, Jesus Christ!" he blurted. "I had sex with him, Denny! *Twice!*"

"Calm down," Denny said, as ten heads swiveled in their direction. He lowered his voice to a murmur. "Did you let him fuck you without a condom?"

"No, we jacked off together in the galley. And I sucked his dick. And then, that evening, we had a three-way with a pilot that he knows. But nobody got fucked. It was just oral sex and kissing and poppers and dirty talk. God, Zack's a *great* dirty talker."

"If he didn't fuck you," said Denny, "then you have nothing to worry about. Nobody gets HIV from sucking dick. If that were the case, we'd all be dead by now."

"Oh, *shit.*" Eric buried his face in his hands. "I'm so sick and tired of thinking about this goddam disease every time I have sex."

"We're all sick of it. But since you're probably in the clear, let's focus on Zack instead. How long has it been since you've seen him?"

"Actually, not since that one time I flew with him last summer."

"Then you should prepare yourself for a shock. He just got out of the hospital—for the second time. He's lost a lot of weight, has zero energy, and he's extremely pale."

"Does he have… please tell me he *doesn't* have KS. I can't bear to think of that beautiful man covered with awful purple lesions."

"No, he doesn't have KS, thank God. His last trip to the hospital was for pneumonia. He's wiped out physically. I don't know how long it will be before he can come back to work. Or if he even wants to come back. You know how vicious people can get when they start to suspect that another crewmember has HIV."

"No," said Eric. "To tell the truth, I don't."

"Then I suggest you start opening your ears when you're around the Bible thumpers instead of tuning them out. You won't believe the hateful comments that spew from their lips. I have more compassion in my pinky toe than all of *them* combined."

"If Zack has been out of work for so long, how is he able to pay his rent?"

"He's using sick time, but that won't last forever. His mom sends money whenever she can. Fortunately, he has a lot of good friends here at the base. We're helping him out with food, utility bills, and pocket money. Although we're getting stretched a bit thin with so many guys in the same situation."

"Tell me what you and I can do for him right now."

"We're going to pay a social call. We're going to smile and tell him how good he looks, even if it's a lie. We're going to kiss him hello and drink out of his glasses and use his bathroom. We're not going to behave like those assholes who treat AIDS patients like lepers. Think you can handle it?"

"Of course I can," he said indignantly. This won't be my first time, Denny. I'm not a kid, you know."

"I'm sorry if I sounded condescending."

Eric drank the last few drops of his cappuccino and started into the bottom of the empty cup. "I don't suppose we can pop in somewhere for a drink before we see Zack?"

"No, no drink beforehand. Not today anyway." Denny stood up and put on his jacket. "Today, my friend, we're going to deal with *real* life for a change."

***

"This is the place," said Denny, stopping in front a plain six-story brick building. He pressed the buzzer for apartment 6E.

It took a few minutes for Zack to respond. "Who is it?" His voice sounded feeble.

"Hi, Zack. It's Denny and Eric."

"Come on up. Do you still have the extra key I gave you?"

"Yes, it's right here in my pocket."

"Would you mind checking the mail, please?"

"Will do," said Denny. He took out the key and opened the door. He and Eric entered the small, dreary lobby. There wasn't a stick of furniture in it or a single piece of artwork on the walls. There was just enough room for a wall of mailboxes next to the staircase. The linoleum floor had been recently mopped and smelled of disinfectant. The light fixture on the ceiling was cracked and covered with a layer of grime.

Denny opened Zack's mailbox. It was stuffed with medical bills, a magazine wrapped in plain brown paper, and a few get-well cards. Zack would be very grateful for the cards and the magazine; the bills would be another matter. "Let's go." He started walking up the stairs.

"Where's the elevator?" Eric asked.

"There isn't one in this building."

"He has to walk up *six* flights of stairs every time he comes and goes?"

"Yes. This is how you afford to live by yourself in the heart of it all."

"Look at the carpet on the staircase," said Eric. "It's worn through in patches. And the paint is peeling on the walls. It's probably lead paint." He sighed as he followed Denny up the stairs. "Living in this building would depress me to no end."

Denny shrugged and kept climbing. "We can't all live in the splendor of pre-war Tudor in Forest Hills Gardens."

"Don't be snarky."

"I'm not. But you can't have it all. Location trumps everything else. Besides, his apartment is very nice. You'll see."

Denny had to stop to catch his breath on the fourth-floor landing. Eric, who had recently quit smoking again, was fine.

"Do you know what I just realized?" said Eric. "We're walking in empty-handed. Shouldn't we have stopped for some flowers or something?"

"I brought him flowers a few days ago. Believe me: he'll be happy just to have some company. That's what he wants more than anything. Come on, let's go."

They reached the sixth floor and walked to the end of the hallway. Zack's apartment door was slightly ajar. Denny knocked anyway. "Zack?"

"Yeah, come on in you guys."

They walked in to an empty living room.

"I'm in the bedroom," said Zack. "I'll be right out."

Eric and Denny sat down on the sofa. There was a stark contrast between Zack's lobby and the interior of his apartment. The living room was decorated with classic mid-century modern furniture. Zack had purchased it himself, piece by piece. The walls had been recently painted, and the original crown molding had been beautifully maintained. The curtains, done in a bold plaid pattern, were drawn around a large picture window next to the sofa. From the sixth floor, they could see a small but pretty park at the corner.

Denny noticed Eric doing a double-take when he saw a piece of homemade artwork on Zack's refrigerator. It was collage of naked men culled from porn magazines. Each model had been placed in such a way that another man's erect penis hung just an inch or two away from his face. The graphic images seemed strangely out of place in an apartment that had a coffee table covered with prescription medication bottles, and a portable oxygen tank in the corner. The oxygen tank was uncomfortably close to a dried out, six-foot tall Christmas tree that was still decorated and that should have been taken down weeks ago. The carpet underneath the tree was covered with a thick layer of dead pine needles. One tiny spark from a heavy-footed passerby would turn the apartment into a raging inferno.

"Hi, guys," said Zack as he shuffled into the room wearing pajamas, a bathrobe, and slippers. He was still painfully thin, Denny noticed, but his color had improved. He'd started growing a beard, which helped to mask the deep hollows in his cheeks. "Sorry to keep you waiting, but I was getting my laundry together. Can I get you guys something to drink?"

"You can give me a hug first. That's what you can do," said Denny.

"Oh, that'd be nice," said Zack, opening his arms wide.

"I want one, too," said Eric, waiting his turn.

"Absolutely," said Zack. He hugged Eric and patted his back. "You have no idea how good it feels to hold a man after all this time." A deep, hacking cough suddenly overcame him. "Uh oh, I think I've been on my feet a little too long." He sat down in an armchair, attached a cannula from the oxygen tank to his nostrils and took several deep breaths. "That's better. I can't tell you how happy I am that you're both here. Thanks for coming, Eric."

"I was sorry to hear that you were ill," said Eric. "I'm glad that Denny asked me to come with him."

"I guess I look a little different than you the last time you saw me, huh?"

"A little," said Eric.

"A *lot*," said Zack. "I lost over twenty pounds. I've put a couple of pounds back on since I came home. I'm trying to eat as much protein as possible. Maybe in a few weeks, I can start going back to the gym."

Denny and Eric nodded politely.

"So, you made it upstairs from the lobby," said Zack. "Quite a hike, isn't it? I can't believe I used to do it all day long, without even thinking about it. And with my luggage yet!"

"That must be how you got those beautiful legs of yours," said Eric.

"Not so beautiful now," said Zack. He seemed self-conscious and pulled his bathrobe tightly around him. "Too skinny. If I could just get back to the goddam gym. Right now, I can't even get to the lobby."

"But you *will*," said Denny. "You'll just have to give yourself time."

Zack looked off into the distance. "Time is pretty much all I have right now."

"That's not true," said Denny. "You have a beautiful apartment, which you're still able to live in independently. You have health insurance, excellent medical care, a job to go back to when you've recovered, and friends who care about you. That's more than a lot of other people have right now."

"I know. I'm sorry. I constantly have to remind myself to get off the pity pot. I am grateful for all these things."

"You *do* have a beautiful apartment," said Eric.

"Thank you," said Zack. "You'd never know it from the street, or from that godawful lobby! I think it was designed that way on purpose to keep burglars away. One look inside and they must figure there's nothing here worth stealing."

"I like your artwork," said Eric. "Especially your collage. Those are some of my favorite models."

"Oh, that," said Zack, laughing. "It's been up there for so long I don't even notice it anymore. I need to take it down before my mother comes to visit next week."

"Your mother's coming? That's great," said Denny. "How is she getting up here from Florida?"

"My supervisor authorized a pass for her," said Zack. "Isn't that wonderful? Technically, no one can use your travel benefits when you're out on medical leave, but Phillip Hendry made an exception for me."

"Pumpkin Head did something nice for somebody?" said Denny. "I don't believe it."

"He's bent over backward for me," said Zack. "Everyone in Flight Service has gone out of their way since I got sick. I wish you'd them give a break, Denny. They're not all terrible people just because they work in the office."

"You're right," said Denny. "I don't know why we automatically knock down management whenever they come up in conversation. Force of habit, I guess. I'm glad they've been so helpful. Speaking of help, would you like us to take down your Christmas tree?"

"No, thanks. That's my project for later this afternoon. My buddy's going to help me with that."

"Your buddy? Which buddy?"

"My buddy from GMHC. He comes over once a week and helps me with whatever I need. He's such a great guy! He knows a lot about psychology. He's talked me off the ledge a couple of times. I've felt a little desperate during the past month." An uncomfortable silence followed this admission. "Oh, where are my manners? I offered you a drink and then forgot all about it. I have iced tea and seltzer and ginger ale and even vodka if anyone wants a cocktail."

"Well, since you offered," said Eric. "I'd love a vodka and—"

"You and I will both have plain seltzer," Denny said, as he got up. "What can I get for you, Zack?"

"Would you bring me a bottle of Ensure from the fridge? I'll take a chocolate flavor if there's one left."

"Sure." Denny walked into the kitchen, removed beverages from the refrigerator and opened a cupboard to get out glasses.

"Don't bother with the glasses," said Zack. "There's a stack of plastic cups right there on the counter."

"I am *not* drinking out of a plastic cup in your home," said Denny. "This isn't beer bust at the Eagle."

"I wish you would use plastic," said Zack. "It's easier for me to throw everything away after company leaves than to stand at the sink washing dishes."

"I'll wash them for you myself before we leave," Denny said resolutely.

Zack slumped in his armchair. "Oh, Denny, stop it. Would you please just *stop it?*"

"Stop what?"

"Stop acting like the model 'friend of the AIDS patient.' Everyone who comes by to visit me runs through the same routine. I know it by heart. Brave face, kisses, hugs, lots of physical closeness, no fear of personal contamination. The next thing I know, you'll be making a big point out of using my bathroom before you leave. I just can't *stand* it!" His face contorted as he fought back tears. "I'm *sick!* I'm probably dying. And no one but my GMHC buddy, whom I barely know, will let me even *talk* about it!" Zack started sobbing and cried so hard that he began to choke. "Oh, oh God!"

Denny rushed to his side. "Eric, get me some Kleenex or something while I reset his oxygen!" Turning the valve on the tank, he raised Zack's oxygen's level to the highest possible setting.

Eric returned a moment later. "No Kleenex. This was the closest thing I could find." He handed Denny a clean kitchen towel.

Denny took the towel and knelt next to the chair. He started to wipe away Zack's tears, along with a giant blob of mucous from his nose.

Eric knelt on the other side and patted him gently on the back. "Honey, you've got to calm down and catch your breath. Shh … shh … shh …"

Denny shook his head. "Let him cry it out, Eric. It's good for him. Zack, go ahead and cry all you want. We're not going anywhere. And you can talk about whatever you want. And we'll listen."

"Thank you… I'll be OK. I just need to… catch my breath. Eric, would you open a window, please? It's so goddam hot in here all of a sudden."

Denny felt his forehead. "I hope you're not starting to run a—"

Zack jerked Denny's hand away. "No, I *don't* have a fever." He stopped crying and took several deep breaths. "I can't control the heat in the here! The radiator handle broke off right before Christmas, and the super hasn't come to fix it yet." He wiped his eyes with the towel. "Denny, would you get me that Ensure, please?"

"Yes, of course."

"And make Eric a cocktail if he wants one. That'll be the day when someone can't have a goddam cocktail in my house. There's a bottle of Smirnoff in the freezer. Help yourself."

"You bet," said Denny. "Eric, do you want a double? I'm making a double for myself."

Eric looked mortified. "Don't be vulgar. A single will do."

Denny came back into the living room with all their drinks on a tray. He waited for Eric to clear a space on the table and then put the tray down. Then he reached for the Ensure bottle and started to crack it open.

"For heaven's sake!" said Zack, grabbing it from him. "I can do that myself."

"Sorry."

The three of them quietly sipped their beverages. "Good cocktail," Eric finally said.

"The Ensure is pretty tasty, too," said Zack. "But it gives me terrible gas for a few hours after I drink it. I'd hate to subject you guys to that."

"Don't worry," said Denny, with a grin. "We'll be cleared out long before then. No, I'm kidding. As I said, we'll stay as long as you want. So, do you want to talk about anything?"

"Well, I'm… I'm lonely." Zack looked as though he were about to start crying again. "I never thought I'd say that living in New York, but it's true. I mean, my mom calls every day, and friends call to check on me, but it's not the same thing as *being* with people. I'm so grateful to you, Denny for coming every couple of days, and it's wonderful to see you, Eric, even though we just met that one time. But if you could get some of the other guys to come over and see me, I'd appreciate it."

Denny nodded. "Of course I will."

He and Eric waited for Zack to continue, but Zack seemed to be holding back. "What else is going on, Zack?" Eric asked.

"I miss flying!" he blurted. "Oh, God! I miss it so much! I miss packing a Speedo for Miami Beach in December, or a sweatshirt for San Francisco in the middle of July. I miss bidding for the next month's schedule and finding out where I'll be going. I miss putting on my uniform and checking myself out in the mirror before I leave, and getting cruised in the subway on my way to the airport. I miss heading to bars with a group of hot men and walking in like we own the place." He did start crying again, but not as forcefully this time. "I miss the passengers, even the crazy ones. Even the jerks in business class, because I always had funny stories to tell about them at parties. I miss *everything*: the camaraderie and the cat ladies and the commuters, too."

"You miss the commuters?" Eric asked. He couldn't help himself.

"Yes, I miss the commuters. Because even with all their annoying habits, they're part of your crew. There's *nothing* like being part of the crew. It's the most wonderful thing in the world to get on an airplane and make instant friends and take off for somewhere—anywhere! And we take it for granted. We *all* do. We constantly complain about management, and the bid sheet, and early sign-ins and the all-nighters. We bitch about flying on holidays, and four-legged days on the Ultra Jet, and three-day trips to Cleveland and El Paso. What I wouldn't *give* to walk out of here with a suitcase and head for Cleveland or El Paso! There's no other job like it in the whole world. Then one day, bam! Just like that, you're grounded. It *sucks*. I wish every single, goddam day that I was back at work."

"Then," said Eric, taking his hand, "you'll just have to get better, Zack, so you *can* come back and fly with us."

"Maybe I can," said Zack. "Maybe I can get my strength back and put weight back on and come back to work, even if it's just a few months." He let go of Eric's hand and looked him straight in the eye. "Eric, I don't want to beat around the bush. Have you had an HIV test recently?"

"No. Not for about three months."

"How about you, Denny?"

"It's been about a year."

"Well, you should both get one and find out what your status is. We all take too many chances. We leave New York and get drunk on free booze that we steal from the plane and then get drunker in the bars so that we can forget about AIDS. Who could blame us for wanting to forget for a few hours? The problem is that when we get that fucked up, we become careless and make bad choices. And those choices have serious consequences."

Oh, boy, here we go again, thought Denny. "It's a *virus*, Zack, that you probably picked up years ago. I mean, come on: you didn't go out and intentionally get sick."

"I know. I just want all my friends to start being more careful. There's more to life than hunting for dick on layovers."

So sayeth the man whose refrigerator is covered with gay porn, thought Denny. "Well, if you'll excuse me for a minute, I *am* going to use your bathroom, because I have to pee. And I'm going to use your hand towels too, so there."

"There's a basket of paper guest towels on the window sill," said Zack. "Now, after that, would you mind clearing out? My buddy will be here in fifteen minutes, and I want to wash my face. I don't want to be a mess *every* time that he comes over."

"Sure," said Eric. He reached over and kissed Zack on the forehead. "Honey, you are a little warm. Would it be terrible if I suggested that you take your temperature? Where's your thermometer?"

Zack sighed and reached into the pocket of his robe. "It's right here. I have to do it so often that I've started keeping it in my pocket." He stuck in the thermometer his mouth.

"Do you want a couple of aspirin from the bathroom?" asked Denny.

"Let me take my temperature first," he mumbled.

Denny used the bathroom and washed his hands. As he was drying them, he noticed that a handicap grab bar and a seat had been installed in the shower. It looked just like a nursing home bathroom. Jesus, how old was Zack? *Maybe* twenty-five? The gravity of the situation hit Denny like a tsunami. He suddenly wanted nothing so much as to get out of that apartment and back onto a crowded city street full of healthy-looking, mobile men. Thankfully, when he came back into the living room, Eric already had his coat on.

"My temperature is perfectly normal," said Zack, smiling. "Forgive me for not getting up. I'm glad that you came to see me. I'm sorry that I got so emotional."

"You don't have to apologize," said Eric. "And from now on, Zack, I'll be here for you whenever you need me, as a friend." He wrote his phone number down and left it on the coffee table. "It's a 7-1-8 number, but I'm right across the river, you know, not in a foreign country. Use it."

Zack laughed. "Thank you, Eric."

Denny kissed Zack on the cheek. "And you know you can count on me. I'll make some calls and get some other friends to come and see you."

"Great. I appreciate it. I'll see you soon. Bye, guys, and thanks again."

Denny headed down the stairs so quickly that Eric could barely keep up with him.

"What's the rush?" he asked.

"I need some air," Denny replied. As soon as they were outside, he lit a cigarette. "Do you want one?"

"No. Not after watching Zack struggle to breathe. That was something, what he said about missing flying so much."

"Yes." Denny exhaled loudly. "It was like a monologue from an *Airport* movie—with a screenplay by Larry Kramer."

Eric looked shocked. "What a cold-hearted thing to say. Were we in the same apartment just now?"

"I've heard that speech the last three times I came to visit him. You were a new audience. Hey, check out *that* hot man," he said, as a motorcycle rider came down the street wearing a leather jacket and boots. He had a splendid physique. His face was obscured by a helmet, which made him even more intriguing.

"He's hot, all right," said Eric.

To their surprise, the man pulled into an empty parking space right in front of Zack's building. After turning off the engine, he took off the helmet and stashed it under one arm. His hair was brown and wavy, with just a few flecks of grey in it. He nodded a friendly hello to Denny and Eric, and then he slung a backpack over his shoulder.

"Oh, my God!" said Eric. "It's Benjamin!" He rushed over so quickly to greet the man that he almost knocked Denny down. "Hi, Benjamin! Do you remember me? My name's Eric Saunders. I met you at that AIDS benefit last month."

"Oh, sure I remember. The wristwatch." He laughed. Benjamin has a great face, Denny thought. He had big brown eyes and long lashes, just like Eric. His complexion was beautiful. Even in the middle of January, his skin had a warm, olive glow. "It's good to see you, Eric. You know, I tried to say goodnight on your way out that evening. But you were leaving with someone and didn't notice me, I guess."

"I was?" Eric blushed, thinking about the man he'd met just before he left the benefit. "Oh, that's right. I did leave with someone."

"How did that work out, by the way?"

"It didn't. As it turns out, he wasn't my type."

"I could have told you that," said Benjamin. "He wasn't special enough for you."

Eric started giggling and looked as though he might go into a swoon right there on the sidewalk. Denny decided to intervene before Eric made a complete fool of himself. "Hi, Benjamin," he said, extending his hand. "My name is Denny Malinovski."

"Benjamin Kaufman. It's nice to meet you."

"Do you live on this street, Benjamin?" Eric asked.

"No, I live in the East Village. I'm visiting a friend in this building."

Denny suddenly put two and two together. "This is none of my business, but is it Zack Pendergast, on the sixth floor?"

Benjamin looked taken aback. "Yes. Why do you ask?"

"We're friends of his, too," said Eric. "We fly with him at Mercury Airways. We just saw him."

"Are you his buddy from GMHC?" Denny asked.

"I really shouldn't answer that question, but since you're his friends, and since he did mention my name... yes, I am his buddy from the agency."

"That's great," said Denny. "While you're with him today, Benjamin, maybe you could get him to focus on the future. He spends too much time dwelling in the past. It's not good for him psychologically."

"Thanks for the suggestion. I'll keep it in mind, but I like to let him process whatever he wants to process." He looked at his watch. "I've got to head upstairs or I'll be late. Nice to meet you, Denny. And nice to see you, Eric. Play safe, you guys."

Denny watched Benjamin run up the stoop. His ass looked great in a pair of Levi 501 jeans. A moment later, he disappeared inside the building.

"Look at this bike!" said Eric, lovingly touching one of the handlebars. "It's a real Harley Davidson!"

"I didn't know you had a thing for motorcycle men."

"I have a thing for *that* motorcycle man."

"Funny, you didn't show it," Denny said sarcastically.

"I wonder if he's the marrying kind."

"Eric, what are you talking about? You've met him *twice*."

"I know. But I have a feeling I'm going to meet him again." He took his notepad and a pen out of his knapsack. "Benjamin... *Kaufman*. I'll see if he's in the phone book."

"There are probably a thousand Benjamin Kaufmans in the New York City phone book."

"So? I'll look at the map in the front section and find out the exchange for the East Village. It's three digits, how hard can it be?"

"You're really going to call him? Why? For all you know, he's already with someone. I'm *sure* he is. You think a sexy East Village-type like him, with a Harley, is sitting at home on a Saturday night, waiting for the phone to ring?"

"Probably not. So I'll call on a Tuesday. But one way or another, I'm going to see him and go out with him. And really get to know him."

Denny shook his head. "I don't like this, not one bit."

"What do you mean, you don't like it?"

"I'll tell you what I mean. I didn't like that goofy look you get in your eyes when you talk to him. You've been flying for less than a year, and your career is just starting to take shape. You should be single and not worrying about anyone but yourself. You certainly shouldn't be getting involved with a nine-to-fiver. I guarantee you that it'll be trouble. In one month, he'll start pressuring you to fly any kind of crappy schedule that you can hold, just as long as you have weekends off to spend with him and *his* friends. And then he'll want you to start flying Chicago turns, so that you're home every night by dinnertime."

Eric laughed. "As if I'd ever willingly bid a month of Chicago turns."

"Your *own* needs and your *own* friends should come first right now, and you should keep it that way for the foreseeable future. It just makes sense."

"Oh? Are we talking about *my* needs, Denny? Or yours?"

Denny lit a cigarette to avoid looking Eric in the eye. "Wise guy," he finally said. "All right, do what you want. But if this does go anywhere, do me a favor: make it a long engagement. At least five years."

"Why?"

"Because that's how long it will take before I have the strength to break in another new best friend."

"Oh, darling, we'll always be best friends."

"Yeah, right. Do you know how many times I've that one before?"

"I'm hungry. Should we go get some lunch now?"

"Yes, why don't we—"

"Look, look!" Eric shouted. "There's a snowflake!" He swiped at the air. "There's another. And another!" The sky was suddenly full of them. "It's snowing! It's snowing!"

Denny was so moved by the look of pure joy on Eric's face that he almost cried. "Come on," he said, suddenly determined to make this special event even more special. He hailed a passing taxi and pushed Eric inside as soon as the driver stopped.

"What's going on?" said Eric.

"Driver, we're going to the corner of Seventy-second and Central Park West," send Denny. He turned to Eric. "I'm taking you to Belvedere Castle. It's the best place to be in New York during a snowfall. You can practically see the whole park from there. And it's beautifully peaceful and quiet. We'll probably have the whole place to ourselves. Then we'll go to a great little French café I know on the Upper West Side for hot chocolate and lunch. My treat."

"Oh, my God," said Eric, grinning from ear to ear. "Am I lucky to have a friend like you!" He opened the window and caught a few snowflakes on his glove. "Look, Denny!" He stared at his glove in wonder. "They're so big that you can actually *see* the shape of the snow crystals! Just like the ones I used to cut out of folded paper in the first grade. It's like magic!"

Denny laughed. "It is magic!"

"Look at how fast this shit is coming down, from out of nowhere!" said the driver. He wearily shook his head. "The roads are gonna be a shit show by rush hour today. And tomorrow, the whole city will be one, big fuckin' dirty *mess*."

"We'll worry about that tomorrow," said Denny. He was in no mood for a negative spin on anything else. "For right now, sir, just take us to our castle."

CHAPTER 30

Making a Date

"Hello?"

"Hi, Zack, it's Eric. How are you?"

"I'm OK. Much better, in fact. I'm off the oxygen tank and breathing on my own."

"That's great news! Congratulations."

"Thanks. I thought that I would hear from you sooner. It's been a couple of weeks since you and Denny came over."

"I'm sorry, sugar, I'm on reserve this month, and it seems like they're flying me almost every day. Did your mother make it into town all right?"

"Yes, she's been here for about a week."

"How's the visit so far?"

"Wonderful. It's nice to have her here. She just made us banana French toast. That was always my favorite breakfast when I was a kid."

"Nice! How is she coping with those six flights of stairs?"

"No problem. She's a runner, so she's in great shape. I don't think she minds at all. She's going out right now to do a little grocery shopping for us. Hang on a second, Eric. Mom, don't forget the list. It's right there on the kitchen table. Would you pick up some Diet Coke, too? … I know it's bad for me. Just buy a one-liter bottle, OK? … See you in a while. Take your time and enjoy the beautiful day … OK, Eric. I can talk now. Whew!"

"Is everything all right over there?"

"Oh, yes. It's just a little too much togetherness. I love her dearly, and it's wonderful having her here. But this is a small apartment and she hovers."

"How much longer is she staying?"

"Another week. She has to go back to work next Monday. She used her vacation time to come here, so of course I'm very grateful."

"It sounds like you could use a little time by yourself, though."

"Oh, my God! Just to have an hour to watch some porn and jack off would be heaven."

"Tell you what: I'm flying to L.A. today and I'm back tomorrow afternoon. Why don't I come over on Wednesday and take her out to lunch and a movie?"

"Would you? That'd be great. She hasn't seen much since of New York on this visit, except for the inside of this apartment. I appreciate the offer."

"It's my pleasure. By the way, how's Benjamin?"

"Benjamin who?"

"Your buddy from GMHC. We met him outside your building that day we came over. Actually, I'd met him once before, at a benefit in December."

"Oh, that Benjamin. He's not my buddy anymore."

"What happened?"

"He was assigned to me on a temporary emergency basis. He just started a master's degree in social work and didn't feel like he could do both at the same time. That M.S.W. program has a pretty heavy workload. I'm getting a new buddy next week."

"Where's he going to grad school? NYU?"

"No, San Francisco."

Great, thought Eric. That explains why his phone number is disconnected. "Did he leave you his contact information?" he asked casually.

"Nope."

"I wonder how I could get in touch with him."

"I guess you could call the Buddy Program at GMHC. But I don't know if they'd give out a volunteer's personal information. What did you want to talk to him about?"

"I was thinking of volunteering myself. I wanted to ask him a few questions about being a buddy."

"Bullshit. That's a *huge* commitment. You can't fit that into your schedule right now. Just admit it: you like him."

Eric could feel himself turning pink. "What makes you say that?"

"Eric, you're *so* obvious. But I don't blame you at all. First off, he's *hot*. Oh, man, the way he looks in that leather jacket and those Frye boots! Second, he's a down to earth, genuine person—the salt of the earth, as my mom would say. And third, he's actively doing something to help fight AIDS. That alone gets him five gold stars."

"Yeah, he's a dreamboat all right." Eric sighed. "Too bad about the move to San Francisco. California is a long way from New York."

"So? Hook up with him on a layover once in a while, if he's interested. It's not like either one of you has time for a boyfriend right now."

"We'll see."

"So, who's on your crew today?"

"I don't know yet. I just got assigned to the trip an hour ago. I hope they'll be some real senior New York stews who've been flying for twenty years. I love their stories about partying with Halston at Studio Fifty-four, and movie stars leaving lines of coke for them in the first-class lav."

Zack laughed. "I don't know if those stories are true or just recycled. When it comes to their former glory days, the senior gals all love to tell tall tales."

"I don't care if they're true or not. I've had it up to here at this point with Westchester homemakers, commuters from *anywhere*, and lazy straight men. Get this: on my last trip, this 'dude' told me that he didn't answer call lights because nine times out of ten the passengers hit the button by mistake. I was up and down the aisle the whole flight, while he sat parked in the last row with a surfing magazine!"

"Sorry you've had such a difficult month. Just remember, you could be in my shoes."

"I know. I'm not complaining. I'm just mouthing off."

"What time is your sign-in?"

"Noon."

"It's ten-thirty. You'd better get going."

"Oh, Christ, I had no idea it was so late. Good thing I'm packed and dressed. I'll talk to you soon."

"You won't forget about taking my mom out on Wednesday, will you?"

"Of course not. I'll call to confirm a time with her when I get back tomorrow night. Find out what movie she wants to go see and where it's playing nearby."

"I'm afraid it'll be a Julia Roberts flick. Can you handle that?"

"It's her day, Zack. Whatever she wants to do is fine by me. I'll talk to you tomorrow." As Eric hung up the phone, he looked at his watch and decided that he had five minutes to spare. He pulled out the phone book, quickly found the number he was looking for and dialed it.

"Gay Men's Health Crisis. How may I direct your call?"

"Hello, may I speak to whoever is in charge of volunteers in the Buddy Program?"

"One moment, please. I'll transfer you." After a brief pause, someone picked up the phone. "Buddy Program, Dottie Klein speaking."

"Hello, Ms. Klein. My name is Eric Saunders, and I'm wondering if you can help me. I'm trying to reach a volunteer who recently left the program. His name is Benjamin Kaufman."

"I see. Were you a client of his, Mr. Saunders?"

"No, I'm more of an acquaintance. I understand that Benjamin recently moved to San Francisco and was wondering if he left a forwarding address or phone number."

"I'm afraid that I can't give out that information. It's against agency policy."

"Oh, I'm very sorry to hear that," he said, unable to hide his disappointment. There was just *something* about that man. How would he ever find him now?

"Are you with another agency, sir?" she asked.

"An agency? No, I'm not. I'm a flight attendant for Mercury Airways."

"A flight attendant for Mercu—oh, *that* Eric! Can I put you on hold for a moment, Eric?" Her tone was suddenly very casual. Benjamin must have mentioned his name to her!

"Sure."

"Bill," he heard Dottie say, "could you come here for a moment? I need to ask you something about…" She lowered her voice, and then he heard music playing as he was put on hold.

Dottie returned to the line a moment later. "Thanks for waiting, Eric. If you give me your contact information, I'll be happy to pass it onto to Benjamin the next time I talk to him. How's that?"

"That'd be great! Thanks!" He gave her his home phone number and mailing address. "Thanks for your help, Miss Klein. I greatly appreciate it." He hung up the phone, threw on his coat, and left the apartment with a bounce in his step that had been missing for a while.

***

In operations, he signed in for his trip and pulled up the crew list for his flight. Oh, what luck! Sylvia and Jacques were working in first class. Eric was working in coach, but at least the three of them could have dinner together. I'm fortunate, he thought. I could be on my way to Buffalo right now. Instead I'm flying a transcon with two good friends. And Sylvia Saks loves telling stories. He hurried to the departure area, anxious to see his friends. As he neared the security checkpoint, he stopped dead in his tracks. Two VIP agents were escorting an Italian movie star through the terminal. Everyone stopped to watch her pass by, some with their mouths wide open. She was beautifully dressed in a bright pink wool crepe dress and kid leather pumps, with an Hermes scarf casually knotted around her neck. A sable coat was folded over her one arm; a leather handbag dangled from the other. Soft, chestnut curls cascaded down to her shoulders. Her face glowed with health and vitality. Eric noticed that she wasn't merely walking through the terminal. She glided, as though she were hovering an inch or two above the ground. She smiled as people made eye contact with her. Eric tried not to gawk, but he couldn't help it. He had met many celebrities in his short career, but more often than not, he was disappointed in the way that they presented themselves. Women rarely bothered to put on a full face of makeup and their hair, just like everyone else's, was shoved into a ball and secured with a plastic clip. Men came to the airport unshaven and dressed as though they were on their way to a Lakers game. Both sexes hid behind dark sunglasses and wore baseball caps jammed low on their foreheads. He knew that it was a justifiable attempt to travel incognito. Who could blame them for trying to avoid being hounded by the public? But that strategy invariably backfired, especially when an entourage of sycophantic personal assistants trailed behind them. Today was different. It was a joy to see someone radiate such poise, beauty, and pure magnetism. She was a star. An old-fashioned, honest-to-goodness *movie* star—and she stopped right in front of him! "Hello," she said, smiling at Eric. "How are you today?"

"*Buongiorno, Signora,*" he replied, thankful at that moment that he could actually form words. *"Vado bene, grazzie. E lei?"*

"Ah!" she said, smiling even wider. *"Parlate italiano. Bene!"*

"*Un po',*" he replied with a laugh. And then she was gone. Oh my God! he thought, as his heart pounded in his chest. Who do I call? Who do I stop and call to tell them that I was just within two feet of *Sophia* and that she spoke to me? But there wasn't time. If he didn't hurry, he would be late for his flight.

He arrived at Gate 12 and checked in with the agent, who wore the chronically weary look of all senior agents who worked at Kennedy Airport. "Hi, Eric. The airplane's still at the hangar," she said. "They're fixing an oil leak on the number one engine. It won't be here for another thirty minutes, so you may as well get a cup of coffee and relax."

"Thanks, Theresa. Do you want one, too?"

"Nah, thanks. I'm coffeed out. I've been here since five this morning." She looked at the sea of disgruntled passengers standing in line before her and pulled Eric aside. "My God," she muttered. "You'd think the world was coming to an end because we're delayed for thirty minutes. I'm ready for a cocktail as soon as I get these bozos on board and then clock out for the day. I already called my husband and told him to have a pitcher of martinis ready by one P.M. *sharp.*"

"Gotcha," said Eric. He looked around for Sylvia and Jacques, but they weren't there yet. Grateful for the extra time, he decided to get coffee and a sandwich. When he returned twenty minutes later, he was surprised that Sylvia and Jacques still hadn't arrived. Hmm, he thought. Sylvia is never late. There must be traffic in the midtown tunnel. Other members of the crew, however, had arrived. He waved to two pretty women whom he recognized by face. After they waved back, he discreetly checked their names on the crew list. Renata and Edith were dedicated buddy bidders who flew together month after month, year after year. They flew only transcons, worked only in business class, and for the most part spoke only to each other. Like many buddy bidders, they had developed their own private system for communicating in the presence of others. Theirs involved hurried whispers, secret hand signals, and barely perceptible changes of facial expression. They left their cabin for one reason and one reason *only*: to assist in a medical emergency that was too close in proximity to ignore it.

There were three other flight attendants at the gate who, by default, had to be Eric's co-workers in coach. He checked their names on the crew list. Dan, Missy, and Jeanie were engaged in a lively debate about the relative merits of cats versus dogs. Dan handed them a photo album. Oh God, thought Eric, here we go: it's time for the pet parade. Missy and Jeanie took it from him and began eagerly flipping through the pages, making cooing and squealing sounds. Without interrupting or stopping to introduce himself, Eric quietly took a seat in a vacant row. He had learned, after his first month on the job, to never show interest in others' photo albums. To do so meant being taken as a virtual hostage and tortured with long, rambling stories that were invariably about one of three topics:

The first was weddings—invitations, ceremonies, and receptions; bridal showers, bridal gowns, and bridal bouquets; maids of honor, bridesmaids, and bridesmaid dresses. Planning a wedding took a minimum of twelve arduous months—if not longer. The stress involved seemed to bring out the worst in people. It also brought out the cattiest remarks about friends and family members. "What was she thinking!? With her body type, a strapless chiffon gown is *not* the way to go. That poor thing looks like a rhino cooling her hide in a giant vanilla milkshake!"

The second topic was children: pregnancies, births, birthday parties, first communions, school pictures, school plays, and school sports. (Truth be told, Eric didn't mind flipping through photos of teenaged athletes. Some of them were very handsome and took great pride in their physiques.)

The third topic was household pets of every shape, size and variety. On this subject, Eric stood his ground. He had neither the 'cat' gene nor the 'dog' gene and could tolerate only so much emotionality about either species. He was particularly opposed to photos of cats dressed in holiday outfits. Rumors of this type of photo album were legendary, but they did exist. Eric had been forced to look at one earlier in the month when he was assigned to work an all-nighter back to JFK with a Los Angeles-based crew. That particular album was the pride and joy of a septuagenarian named Eudora Lee who lived alone in a condominium in Redondo Beach. She had converted her one-car garage into a refuge for the many cats that she had adopted over the years. At one point, to the dismay of her neighbors, the count had risen to a total of forty-five. "So, what's wrong with *that*?" Eudora asked Eric indignantly. "I'm giving these poor souls a loving home, two meals a day and regular veterinary care! And it is *my* garage, after all!" Then with a withered hand, she proffered the album. It would have been rude for Eric to decline; she was a *very* senior flight attendant. Eudora's menagerie featured a fat tabby dressed in red velvet ("That's St. Nicholas! Doesn't he look jaunty in his Santa suit?") and a calico draped in red, white and blue ("That's Lisa, my Little Miss Liberty. I call her Lizette on Bastille Day, and Liesel during Octoberfest! She loves it!"). There was also a sleek, white Siamese in a brocade vest perched in a straw basket filled with jelly beans and Cadbury eggs. ("That's Petey. He was my Peter Cottontail every Easter Sunday for fifteen years. I lost him last spring—on *Good Friday*, if you can believe it! It just about broke my heart!")

By the time that she'd shared her last sad tale ("This is H.R. Fluffenstuff. The Lord took him from me too soon!"), Eric wanted to cry. My God, he thought, this is her life! After providing an appropriate amount of time, interest and sympathy, he had passed the album back to her and reached for a textbook. "I'm going to study my French verbs for a while, Eudora. I'm working with a private tutor, and I have an exam tomorrow." What a smooth liar I've become, he thought. He sat and read until dawn, as there wasn't a single passenger awake in coach. Eudora spent the next four hours floating up and down the darkened aisle like a phantom. She was desperate to find someone—*anyone*—to engage in conversation. She seemed almost giddy when it was time to start waking passengers for landing. "Good morning, sir! Please fasten your seatbelt and raise your tray table! What's brings you to New York today? … Oh, isn't that lovely! … Me? *I'm* going to Central Park to feed some hungry cats!"

Oh, well, Eric thought. I can't expect excitement every single time I come to work. He hated to admit it, and he would never say it out loud, but flying for a living was often a very mundane experience.

"Hi there, are you going to L.A.?"

Eric looked up and almost lost a bite of his food. The captain standing in front of him was the best-looking pilot that he'd ever seen. He was over six feet tall and built like an Olympic athlete. His uniform blazer tapered perfectly from his broad shoulders to his trim waist. The legs of his pants had also been tapered and fit very snugly against his thick, muscular legs. Eric was shocked. In the ultra-conservative world of airline pilots, wearing tapered pants was unheard of. His white shirt was starched and perfectly pressed and contrasted beautifully against his copper-colored skin. He had wavy salt and pepper hair, a thick mustache and light green eyes. "I'm your captain, Jake Alexopoulus."

"Hi. Yes, I am going to, uh, L. A.," he stammered. "My name is Eric."

They shook hands. The captain's grasp was warm and firm.

"Mind if I join you while we wait for the plane, Eric?"

"No, of course not, have a seat."

"Thanks." Jake put down his luggage and rested his uniform hat on top of his kit bag.

"I guess this is our first time flying together," said Eric, as Jake sat down next to him.

"That's right. But I've seen you around," said Jake, with a wink.

"Really," said Eric, "what do you know?" He looked down on the pretext of putting away the other half of his sandwich. Please God, he prayed. Whatever happens, don't let me start giggling like a twelve-year-old girl.

"Excuse me, guys," said Theresa. "I'm sorry to interrupt you, but the plane is finally here and you can get on now. They cleaned and catered it while it was at the hangar, so you should be able to get out of here fairly quickly. Eric, Flight Service called for you. Sylvia and Jacques are running very late. Would you mind setting up the first-class galley for them?"

"No, of course not," he said.

"Can we start boarding in about ten minutes?"

"Sure."

Jake reached for his uniform hat and put it on. "Let's go, buddy."

***

Sylvia and Jacques finally arrived, five minutes before departure. "Oh, thank God we made it!" she said, throwing her luggage into the closet. "That goddam midtown tunnel! It'll be the death of me, wait and see." Jacques shoved his suitcase into an overhead bin and then ducked into the lavatory, apron in hand, without saying a single word. Sylvia gave Eric a quick peck on the cheek. "Did you get my message?"

"Yes. I set up the galley, served pre-departure drinks and passed out menus. They seem like a very nice crowd up here."

"You're so *delicious* I could eat you alive. Now, can you get this old lady a glass of ice water, please? How's my hair? I haven't even had a chance to look in the mirror."

"Perfect, but you might want to touch up your lipstick."

"*Oy vey!* It's always something!"

Theresa walk through the door with final paperwork. "Ready to close up, Sylvia?"

"One sec." She grabbed a lipstick and a compact mirror out of her purse. "Eric, honey, call the back and get an all-clear from them, and then stick your head in the cockpit and see if the captain's ready."

Eric called the crew in coach and then went into the cockpit. "Hey, guys are you—"

"One minute," said Jake, holding up his hand. "We're right in the middle of our checklist."

Eric waited patiently for Jake and Adam, the first officer, to finish. "Can we close up, Jake?"

"Yeah, we're good. Get the cockpit door, would you, Eric?"

"Sure. See you in the air." He closed the door and stepped back into the cabin. "We're good to go."

"Great," said Sylvia, waving goodbye to Theresa as she closed the entry door. Then she picked up the interphone. "Flight attendants, prepare your doors for departure. Eric, do you mind getting 1R for Jacques?"

"No problem." He armed the door and spent a minute tidying the counter. "Is Jacques coming out of the bathroom before takeoff?"

"Let's let Jacques alone for the moment."

"Is everything all right?"

"No, *bubbee*, I'm afraid it's not."

"I'm sorry to hear that. Maybe I can perk up his spirits at dinner."

Sylvia shook her head. "Sorry, but we can't join you today. We have a very unpleasant task to attend to."

Eric was shocked to hear her stifle a sob. Sylvia never became emotional—while in uniform, anyway.

"You'd better head to the back, Eric. I'll fill you in later. Thanks for all your help."

"You can always count on me, Sylvia."

"I know. And I love you for that. See you in a bit."

***

"Ladies and gentlemen, we're currently number three for takeoff and will be airborne within just a few minutes. Flight attendants, please prepare for takeoff."

Eric was in his jump seat next to the aft door. He sat with his feet flat on the floor and mentally conducted his thirty-second safety review. He had made it a habit of doing so since his very first flight; he never wanted to be caught off guard in an emergency.

His three co-workers, in contrast, seemed casual about their safety-related duties. Dan leaned against the galley counter. He was engrossed in a magazine called *Guns and Ammunition* and sipped coffee from a mug stamped with the NRA logo. Obviously, he and Eric would have nothing in common. Missy and Jeanie sat together in the middle jump seat across from the galley. Missy was knitting a sweater. A huge knapsack at her feet overflowed with supplies, including an extra set of long, sharp needles that protruded from a side pocket. Jeanie was rummaging through a tote bag that she had placed in the aisle. Both items should have already been stowed. However, blocking a pathway with their luggage seemed of no great concern to either crewmember.

"Here it is!" said Jeanie, pulling out a copy of *People*. She showed the cover to Missy.

"Oh, my God!" said Missy. "I've been *dying* to read that issue. I was hoping a passenger would leave a copy behind today."

"I bought this at Hudson News," said Jeanie. "I just couldn't *wait*."

Eric glanced at the magazine. The man and woman featured on the cover were a married couple who were both country music stars. Eric recognized their names, but he couldn't name a single one of their million-selling songs. This fact alone gave him a certain amount of satisfaction.

Jeanie shook her head. "My God, she has been through so much with him!"

"I know!" said Missy. "This is his third time in rehab. Why does she stay with him?"

"She'd be *so* much better off on her own!" said Jeanie. "I don't know why she doesn't just go solo."

"Poor thing, she just can't help it," said Missy. "She's really in love with him and says she'll stick by him no matter what. 'For better or for worse', she said on her wedding day, and she meant it. And then, of course, she has to think about the twins."

Jeanie nodded. "Kelly and Kendra. They're just precious, aren't they?"

Eric couldn't help rolling his eyes. He never understood fans who discussed the private lives of celebrities as though they were close, personal friends. Missy and Jeanie were a special breed of flight attendant. They never picked up a book or a newspaper or even (God forbid), the union newsletter. And the contract vote was only a month away! Their preference was for glossy periodicals—chockful of photos—that promised to bring the reader into the homes and hearts of America's brightest stars. They were "people who need *People*," as Denny would say derisively. Eric sighed. It was going to be a long flight.

"I know why she stays with him," said Dan, as he strapped into his jump seat. "I bet the dude is really good in bed. Women will put up with a lot of shit if a guy's good in bed." He sat with his legs spread far apart and rested one hand on his thigh. "Know what I mean?" he asked, with a leer.

"Oh, Dan!" said Missy, tossing a skein of yarn at him. "Like you know anything about *that!*"

"I know quite a lot about that, sweetheart—and I'd be happy to show you sometime."

"Ha! You just try it, Mister. My husband's with NYPD. He'll blow those puny little balls of yours right off."

A passenger in the last row turned around and glared. "Do you people *mind?* My five-year-old daughter is sitting right next to me!"

Oh, brother, thought Eric, as his temples started throbbing. I may need one of Denny's Little Helpers to get me through this day. He prayed that he still had a few of them left in his tote bag. He needed to make an appointment *toute suite* with Denny's doctor to get his own prescription.

The aircraft came to the end of the taxiway and made a 180-degree turn. A moment later, the takeoff roll began. Eric sat straight up. The takeoff was still his favorite part of the flight. The 767 started lumbering down the runway but quickly picked up speed. As both engines revved up to maximum power, the plane began streaking down the runway, and objects outside the window became a blur. A moment later, the nose lifted. And then they were airborne, heading out over the water and making their first climbing turn.

During this critical phase of flight, Eric's co-workers may as well have been lounging on a sofa in operations. Missy knitted, Jeanie read, and Dan slurped coffee. "Look at this!" he said, holding out the magazine. "I could take out trespassers in two seconds with this mother fucker—and legally, too! I'm gonna add this gun my collection right away."

Jeanie groaned. "Oh, *Dan!*"

Eric stared straight ahead. He had nothing at all to say.

***

As soon as the service was finished in coach, Eric headed up to first class. Let *them* deal with the passengers back here, he thought. They probably won't even notice that I'm gone. He nodded hello to Renata and Edith as he passed the business-class galley. They briefly looked up to acknowledge him and then returned to a shared copy of *Vanity Fair*. Their heads were so close that they almost touched.

In the first-class galley, Sylvia was clearing off the dessert cart. "Hi, sweetheart," she said. "Are you hungry? I have a few beef filets left over, and there's plenty of salad."

"No, thanks anyway. Do you have any coffee?"

"I just made a fresh pot. Pour yourself a cup and pour one for me, too, with just a little cream." She patted the empty jump seat next to her. "Come, sit."

"Where's Jacques?" he asked, as he sat down.

"He's sleeping underneath a blanket in the last row. I gave him half a Valium, and he went out like a light. Thank God I have a few empty seats today."

"Now I'm really worried. What the hell is going on with him?"

She sighed. "It's awful. We're going to Long Beach to say goodbye to a dear friend of ours. He's more than a dear friend: he's Jacques' ex-lover."

"Oh, no!"

"We've known him for years. Bill used to fly for us. He was based out of L.A. and was everybody's favorite flight attendant. He went out on medical leave a few years ago. I've rented a car for the day so that we can drive down there, and I have no idea what time we'll be back. That's why we can't join you for dinner."

"Is it… does Bill have…?" He couldn't bring himself to say the word AIDS. It was just too many times in one day.

"No, it's not AIDS," said Sylvia. "It's almost worse. He's at the end stage of ALS—what they used to call Lou Gehrig's disease. He's trapped in his own body. He can't sit up, eat, talk or even move his eyes. It's a fucking horror show. Forty-five years old. The last time I saw him, I almost burst into tears. I can't help but wonder: where the *hell* is God these days? Is he out to lunch? Or walking on the moon?"

"Oh, Sylvia, that's awful. What a tragedy!"

"It won't be much longer, thank goodness. That's the only saving grace. You know, when Bill first got the news, he was determined to spare himself the worst of it and take his own life. A death with dignity, on his own terms. But he waited too long, and then all of a sudden it was too late. We thought about taking matters into our own hands. But I spoke with my husband—he's an attorney—and there was nothing we could do without getting ourselves into serious legal trouble. Jesus, the laws in this country are fucked."

"Were Bill and Jacques together a long time?"

"Yes. Fifteen years. They met in training and fell madly in love with each other. I thought they'd be together forever, but Jacques—" She stopped herself in mid-sentence. "Never mind. It's not my place to say anything else. Jacques will tell you himself someday if he ever feels close enough to open up."

"I don't know if that will ever happen," said Eric. "He's warm with me, but never really lets his guard down."

"You're a very perceptive young man." She reached for a napkin as a tear slid down her cheek. "I'm so *fucking* tired of watching people die that I could scream. If it's not AIDS, it's ALS or breast cancer or pancreatic cancer or some other goddam thing. Sometimes I don't think I can do it anymore." She took a deep breath, as though she were steadying herself. "But we have to. We *have* to show up for people because they need us and it's the decent thing to do." She looked off into the distance. "Jesus, where did the time go? That's such a clichéd thing to say. But it seems like just yesterday that I had my wings pinned on at training. It's so strange. Once you hit fifty, everything starts to speed up. You can't even keep track of the time anymore."

"My mother says that all the time." He looked out into the cabin. "I think Jacques is waking up. I see a head peeking out of the blanket. I should probably head to the back and give you guys some privacy."

"No, stick around. We need to talk about something else, even if it's just for a few minutes."

"Yes," said Eric. "A little escape might be good for everybody."

Sylvia stood up. "I think I'll have some ice cream. Sugar always does the trick for me. And besides, it's too early for a drink." As she reached for a dish of ice cream, the crew phone rang. "Hello, this is Sylvia … Hi, Jake … Sure, hang on, I'll send Eric up. One second." She hung up the phone. "The F.O. wants to use the lav and stretch is legs. Why don't you go up front and keep Jake company for a while?"

"I'd love to," said Eric, thinking: that's exactly the kind of escape that I need.

"I thought you would. He is handsome, isn't he? Ask him if he wants a sundae. The dry ice is melting, and this ice cream will all be soup in about ten minutes."

"Will do." He entered the cockpit as Adam opened the door and stepped out.

The captain smiled and gestured toward the co-pilot's vacant seat. "Make yourself comfortable, Eric. How's the flight so far?"

"Fine, except that my co-workers in the back haven't stopped talking long enough to take a breath since we let JFK."

"Occupational hazard," said the captain, with a grin. "Anything else the matter? You look kind of down."

"I've got a terrible headache. And a pain in my left shoulder. I must have slept funny last night." He peered through the windshield at the desolate terrain below. They were in the middle of nowhere, seemingly far removed from every other human on earth.

And then suddenly, Jake's hand was on his shoulder, kneading it. "Jesus!" said Jake. "You've got a knot there that's the size of an egg. You need a good rubdown, son."

Eric's started to get a strange, tingling sensation in the pit of his stomach. He wasn't sure why, but it seemed to have something to do with the captain calling him "son." He slowly turned to look at him. Jake's profile was magnificent. He had a prominent brow and a large, beautiful nose that perfectly suited his face. The fine lines at the corner of his eyes only added to his rugged appeal. His mustache was thick and shot through with silver, just like his hair. "A massage would be great, Jake," he said.

"Oh, hang on a second." He looked down at the instrument panel. "I have to make a little twenty-degree turn."

Eric looked at Jake's enormous hands. They were deeply tanned, like his face. Eric imagined Jake's hands squeezing him all over and got an instant hard-on. "Jake," he said, trying to control the sudden dryness in his mouth. "Do you know where I could get a good massage?"

"Sure do. There's a Chinese guy about a quarter-mile from the hotel. He gives a great massage, and he has a special crew rate of only sixty bucks for a whole hour. You can't get *that* in New York."

"Oh, thanks." Eric instantly felt foolish for misreading Jake's cue. "But that's not really in my budget."

"Pretty new, aren't ya?"

About eight months."

"They're not paying you much, are they?"

"No. But I'm not here for the money."

"Oh? What are you here for?"

"New experiences."

Jake laughed. "I remember being a brand-new flight engineer fifteen years ago. I didn't have a pot to piss in. I shared a crash pad with nine other new guys in Kew Gardens. One bedroom, one bathroom, and no AC. Sometimes in the summer, it was so friggin' hot and so damn crowded that by eight o'clock at night, we'd all be hanging out in the living room in just our skivvies. Ten men going through a case of beer, debating which one of us had the smelliest armpits, and praying that we'd get a called out for a trip the next day."

"That doesn't sound very pleasant," said Eric, thinking just the opposite: Ten fit, restless, semi-naked pilots sitting around in a cramped living room... getting drunk and swapping stories about the women they'd scored with recently... egging each other on for all the dirty details. It would only be a matter of time before someone said, "Hey, I've got a porn tape that you guys have *got* to see. This blond chick takes it from every position you can think of. Somebody turn on the player while I go get it from my suitcase."

"Yeah, dude! Put it on!" another pilot would say. "I'll get another round of beers from the fridge." Twenty minutes later, the sexual tension in the room would be unbearable. One thing would lead to another. "A circle jerk, just like when we were teenagers! Fuckin' A!" Of course, whatever happened next would never be shared outside the walls of that crash pad...

Eric had a raging hard-on now and couldn't leave his seat even if he wanted to. He tried to think of something else. "By the way, Sylvia wants to know if you want a sundae before they melt."

"No, thanks." Jake slapped his rock-hard belly, resulting in an audible thud. "I work too hard for this shit to eat *that* shit."

Eric decided to test the waters again. "Looks like you've got a nice six-pack, Jake. What's your secret?"

"Planks every day, no bread or pasta *ever*, and lots and lots of cardio."

"Looks like you lift weights, too."

"Oh, yeah. Seems like I spend half my life at the gym. It's worth it though. Don't you think?" He made a fist, causing his bicep to swell up as big as a grapefruit.

"Yes, sir." All right, thought Eric. Jake is either interested in me, or he's a raging narcissist. Either way, I can think of nothing but seeing him shirtless.

"So, what are you doing on your layover today?" Jake asked.

Eric shrugged. "Going to the hotel gym, and then out for a cheap dinner, I guess."

"That gym at the hotel sucks," said Jake. "It's small and cramped. They've got no free weights, just a shitty universal machine that's always missing a pin to set the weight you want. And the girls will be in there blaring Oprah at full blast on the TV, with a running commentary on everything she says. You won't be able to hear yourself think. Why don't you go to L.A. Fitness across the street?"

"They charge a fifteen-dollar day rate. The hotel at the gym is free. I'll have to suck it up and make sure I've got fresh batteries in my Walkman."

"Don't do it, Eric. I have a membership at L.A. Fitness. You can come as my guest."

"Really?"

"Sure. Unless you're into Oprah, too. Maybe you are."

"No, I'd much rather come with you."

"Good. Today I'm doing a chest, legs and about forty-five minutes of cardio. I usually don't do some much in one day, but I pulled a hamstring last week and I've been slacking off."

"Today's my chest day, too," said Eric thrilled at the idea of being the captain's gym buddy. "And I always finish with some cardio."

"We'll work up a good sweat and then head for the steam room and sweat some more. You like steam, son?"

"Oh, yeah."

"Me, too. After my workout, I love sitting in a steam room, just letting it all hang out." He said this with a wicked grin on his face that did nothing to ease Eric's throbbing erection.

"Sounds good," said Eric.

"Of course, the manager at L. A. Fitness is a little uptight. In *his* sauna, you can't sit around naked."

"You can't?" Fuck, what is this man trying to do? Torture me?

"No, over there you've got to wear a least a jockstrap. Did you bring a jockstrap?"

"No, I didn't."

"Don't worry, I have a spare that you can borrow. It should fit you just right. It's a size medium, plain, white Bike-brand jockstrap."

If he says the word 'jockstrap' one more time, thought Eric, I'm gonna cum right in my pants. "What time do want to go, Jake? Is four o'clock good?"

"You've got yourself a date," said Jake. He picked up the crew phone as it rang. "Jake here ... yeah, I'll tell him." He hung up the phone. "They need you in the back for another service."

"Uh... OK." He stood up and put his hands in his pockets, trying to hide his erection. Thank God for my apron, he thought.

"Son?" said Jake.

"Yes?"

"Let's keep our plans to ourselves, OK?"

"Yes, sir."

"Good boy. See you at four."

CHAPTER 31

Playing with Fire

Eric arrived at L.A. Fitness promptly at four o'clock wearing his tightest jeans, a tight black t-shirt and a New York Mets cap. In his gym bag, he had a muscle shirt, ankle socks (to show off his calves) and the skimpiest pair of gym shorts that he owned. He anxiously checked his watch every thirty seconds. By 4:05, he started getting nervous. *Where the hell is Jake? I hope he didn't change his mind. If he stands me up, I'm going to be so mad that—*

"Hey, buddy! There you are."

Eric turned around. Jake was standing behind him in the doorway, wearing onion-skin shorts, a white muscle shirt, and the biggest pair of sneakers in the world. His chest and shoulders were carpeted with salt and pepper hair. He was the personification of a sexy Daddy.

"I thought we were meeting inside," said Eric. "How long have you been here?"

"A few minutes. I was right inside the door, enjoying the view. Ready to start pumping iron?"

"Yes, sir."

"Then let's get you signed in and head for the locker room. I brought that jockstrap for you, by the way." He squeezed Eric's shoulder. "Let's go get you dressed, son."

Eric instantly felt the same strange, excited feeling that he'd experienced a few hours ago in the cockpit. "Yes, sir. I'm ready."

***

Once they started their work out, Jake was all business. His chest workout was grueling, and he forced Eric to match him set for set. By the time they got to the dumbbell press and finished three sets, Eric felt utterly spent. "That's it, Jake. I don't think I can do anymore."

"You can, and you *will*," said Jake. He added ten more pounds to each side of the barbell. "Don't worry, I'll be right here to spot you."

Eric looked up. Jake was leaning over him with his arms spread and his fingers resting lightly on the barbell. His sweaty armpits were so close that Eric's face that he could smell their musky, intoxicating odor.

"Come on, son. Push!"

Eric looked up at the deep cleft in Jake's chest. That was all the motivation he needed. Using a strength that he didn't know he had, he completed a set of twelve reps with no strain at all.

"Good job!" said Jake.

Eric crawled out from under the barbell. "I can't believe I was able to lift a hundred pounds," he said, feeling very proud of himself.

"But you *did.* Do you *feel* it? Do you *feel* that burn?"

"Yes, sir!"

"Good." He put Eric's hand on his chest and flexed his pectorals. "That's how you make big, rock-hard muscles like these! Now, let's head to the Smith press. It's time for some squats."

"I don't do squats. I hear they're bad for your knees. I usually alternate between the leg press and the leg lift."

"Well, today, you're gonna squat! It's the perfect lower-body exercise. You work a whole group of different muscles at one time." He spread his furry legs and flexed his quadriceps. "You like these legs, son?"

Eric eyed Jake's legs hungrily. The hell with discretion, he thought. "Yeah, your legs are fucking beautiful, Jake."

"Then let's do it."

They walked over to the Smith press. "I'll go first and show you how it's done," said Jake. He put a twenty-five-pound weight on each side of the barbell, slipped underneath it, and placed it across his upper back. "I start with lower weight for a couple of warm-up sets. Then I'll gradually work my way up to a hundred pounds. Now, pay attention: correct form is paramount. You hold the bar like this, spread your legs until they're shoulder-width apart, and slowly, slowly lower yourself as far down as you can go. Then just as slowly, come back up. Watch me."

Eric didn't have to be told to watch. His eyes were glued to Jake's lower body. His muscles were so shredded that Eric could count every single one of them. As Jake reached the bottom of his squat, his onion skin shorts rode up just enough for Eric to get a good look at his ass. It was round, rock-hard, and like every other part of his body, it was covered with hair. "I'm going to do super-sets, resting for just a minute between each one. Then we'll get to you. OK?"

"Fine. I could use a little break."

By the time that Jake had reached one hundred pounds of weight, his face was covered with sweat, and he grunted loudly with the strain of lifting such a heavy load. usually, the sound of men grunting in the gym drove Eric crazy, but he loved to hear it coming from Jake. Furthermore, he couldn't take his eyes off the pilot for even one second. Watching Jake was like watching Hercules, live and in the flesh, pushing himself to the absolute limit. He'd never met such a macho man in his life, and certainly never had the chance to work out alongside one as his gym partner.

"Whew!" said Jake, wiping sweat from his brow. "Your turn, buddy." He set up the barbell for Eric with only ten pounds on each side. "I know it doesn't seem like a lot, but we'll work on your form first and then increase the weights. Go ahead and slip under here."

Eric assumed a semi-squatting position and grasped each end of the barbell.

"All right, start going down. That's good, but arch your back a little and keep your head and neck straight. No, you're arching too much. Hang on." He stood behind Eric, placed his hands on Eric's hips, and tilted them slightly forward. "There. That's it. Keep going, keep going. I've got you."

Eric could feel the heat from Jake's hands through the fabric of his shorts. He forced himself to concentrate on the movement as he completed one set. Then Jake increased the weight on each side. As he began his second set, Jake stayed right behind him, once again placing his hands on Eric's hips. They repeated the sequence for two more sets. By the last set, Eric's leg muscles felt so strained that he couldn't do even one more rep. "That's enough, Jake. I have to stop."

"Nope. Take a quick break and give me eight reps. Or at least six. I know you can give me six. Come on, son."

"All right, I'll try." As Eric reached the fourth rep, his legs turned to jelly. "Jake, take the bar! Take the bar!"

"I have it. Good job!"

"Oh, oh Christ!" said Eric, feeling a sudden, terrible pain in both legs. "I've got cramps! Two of 'em! Bad ones!"

"Where?"

"Inner thigh, both legs," he gasped in agony.

"Quick, lie down here on this bench and try to relax. I'll take care of it."

To Eric's great surprise, Jake started massaging his legs all the way from his quads to his calves. He used a steady, deep pressure, and kept working until the pain had disappeared completely. When he'd finished, he left his hands resting on Eric's legs. "All better now?"

"Yeah, better. Thanks."

Jake started making lazy swirls, moving higher and higher until his fingers were only an inch away from Eric's crotch. By that time, Eric had a raging erection that he didn't even try to hide. Why bother? he thought. It's obvious that Jake wants me. Straight men don't take other men through squat routines, and then massage their legs right in front of God and everybody.

"Feel better?"

"Yeah. Feels great."

"Looks like we got your blood flowing in the right direction," said Jake, grinning.

"You sure did."

"Let's go stretch out for a few minutes to loosen our muscles. What do you say?"

"Whatever you want to do is fine by me."

A moment after they'd begun stretching out, a third man joined them on the mat. Eric wasn't surprised; the man been watching them from the corner of his eye ever since he'd first entered the gym. He was about twenty-five, blond, and handsome in a clean-cut, all American way. He had a beautiful body that was shaved smooth to show off every bit of his musculature. Even his armpits were shaved. I bet that he shaves his crotch too, Eric thought with disdain. To make matters worse, he preened front of the mirror between each exercise, apparently infatuated with own image. Eric couldn't stand shavers *or* preeners.

"You guys had a real work out today, didn't you?" the man said.

"Yup," said Jake. "That's what we came for."

"I admire your dedication," he said. "It shows."

"Thanks," said Jake.

"My name's Mark."

"Hi, Mark. I'm Jake. This is Eric."

"Nice to meet you guys." His eyes bored into their crotches.

"Same here," said Eric.

Jake kept his gaze focused on Eric's face. "I think we're about finished. See you around, Mark. Eric, are you ready?"

"Yep."

"Let's head to the locker room and get on with the rest of our day."

"See ya, Mark," said Eric.

"I sure hope so." Mark looked disappointed, but Eric didn't feel the least bit sorry for him. It was good for everyone to get turned down now and then— especially those self-absorbed men who thought they could have any other man they wanted.

Eric followed Jake into the locker room. They headed to the back and sat down on benches across from each other. Jake immediately pulled off his shoes and socks. His feet were enormous—easily a size 13—and as hairy as the rest of him. Then he ripped off the sweat-stained muscle shirt. His nipples were dark brown and as big as quarters. Eric followed suit and then just sat there and looked at Jake. And he could tell that Jake was enjoying it.

"Man, that steam is gonna feel good!" said Jake, as he started to shuck his gym shorts.

"Sorry, guys," said an attendant, who was passing through the locker room with a stack of clean towels. "The steam room is out of order today."

"You're kidding. No steam?"

"No steam. You can shower to your heart's content, but the steam room is closed. We have a part on order. It won't be here for a least a week."

"Damn," said Jake. He and Eric sat looking at each other. Every part of their bodies was soaked with sweat. Jake's chest hair was matted down and swirled into complicated patterns that had Eric hypnotized.

"Well, what do you want to do?" said Eric. "Should we hit the shower?"

"No, I don't want to take a shower," said Jake. He reached for the sweaty tank top and started to put it back on.

"You're getting dressed?" said Eric.

"Uh huh."

"You mean… that's *it?*" He heard the indignation in his voice but couldn't help it.

Jake laughed as he reached for his socks. "O, ye of little faith. No, that's *not* it. We're both gonna get dressed."

"I can't put my clean clothes back on right now. I'm so funky that I can smell myself."

"I know. I can smell you, too. And it's *good*. Now, here's what I want you to do. Put those shorts and that muscle shirt back on, and then pack up the clean clothes you wore over here in your gym bag. Give me a ten-minute lead, and then come back to the hotel and meet me in my room. I'm in 345."

"I can't walk across the street in these shorts. Half my ass is hanging out!"

"That's the whole point," Jake said with a grin. "Let's see if you stop traffic."

They heard someone clearing his throat, and both turned. Mark was standing at the urinal, shirtless. His gym shorts were pulled down, and he was lazily stroking himself. His penis was as beautiful as the rest of him, but as Eric had suspected, all of Mark's pubic hair had been shaved off. Why on earth do men do that to themselves? he wondered. No matter how big their dick is, it made them look like prepubescent boys.

"Eric," said Jake, "let's focus."

"Sorry."

"Now, once you get back to the hotel, do *not* go to your room and shower first, and whatever you do, don't take off that jockstrap. Come directly to my room. I'll leave the door open a crack, and the Do Not Disturb sign on the door handle." He leaned closer and started running his hand up Eric's thigh. "You don't need to knock. I'll be waiting for you. Just let yourself in and lock the door behind you. You got that, son?"

Eric groaned. "Yes, sir."

"Hey, you guys," said Mark, walking up to them with his dick in his hand. "I couldn't help overhearing. You interested in making it a threesome?"

"We're flattered," said Jake, "but no, thank you."

Mark wasn't deterred in the least. He stood there stroking himself, seemingly mesmerized by the sight of Eric and Jake sitting sweat-covered and half-naked on the bench.

Hey, do you mind?" said Jake. "I already told you: we're not interested."

"OK." Mark pulled up his shorts. "You can't blame a guy," he said, as he slunk over to his locker, one row away.

"Now, one more thing, son," said Jake, speaking softly. "No more calling me 'sir.' You know what I want to be called, don't you?"

"Yes. You want me to call you Da—"

"Ssh." Jake's eyes darted to Mark, who was straining to hear every word. "Let's save that until we're alone."

"All right. Will you do something for me, Jake?"

"Sure, what?"

He murmured into Jake's ear. "Leave your uniform jacket and hat out where I can see them."

Jake laughed. "Sure. I get you." He quickly finished dressing. "See you in ten."

Mark trailed Jake with his eyes as he walked out of the locker room. "Jesus Christ," he said to Eric. "That is the hottest fucking man I've ever seen."

"I know," said Eric, thinking: and just for today, he's all mine.

***

Eric didn't stop traffic, but he did get a friendly wave and few honks as he waited for what seemed like an eternity at the crosswalk. That was one thing about being a pedestrian in L.A.: you could grow old waiting for traffic lights to change. He crossed the street, entered the hotel lobby, and quickly made his way toward the elevator. He debated whether to stop by his room first to brush his teeth at least, and then decided against it. If Jake wanted a natural man, that's what he was going to get. The elevator finally stopped on the lobby floor. As he entered it, he ran right smack into Dan, who was stepping out.

Dan eyed him critically. "Where've you been?"

"At L.A. Fitness, across the street." He held his gym bag in front of his crotch.

Dan shook his head as he stepped out. "Dude, for God's sake, this isn't West Hollywood. Go put on some pants."

Eric started to feel embarrassed and then thought: up yours. While you're in some crummy sports bar knocking back a pitcher of Miller Lite, I'll be in the captain's room, sucking his dick. "Have a good time, Dan," Eric sang out as the elevator door closed. He impatiently pressed the button for the third floor, hoping that no one else from his crew would be waiting for the elevator once it stopped. He was in luck: when the door opened on Jake's floor, the coast was clear. He was so nervous as he made his way down the hall that sweat dripped from his armpits. The door to room 345 was cracked open and held in place by one of Jake's enormous sneakers. Trembling, Eric pushed the door open, picked up the sneaker and stepped inside.

The room was almost entirely dark; there was a sliver of light coming through the closed bathroom door. He made sure that the Do Not Disturb sign was secured to the outside handle and closed the door. He set Jake's sneaker and his gym bag on the floor and gave himself a moment to adjust to the dim lighting. The last thing he wanted to do right was trip over a suitcase.

The radio next to the bed was tuned to a country-western station with the volume set on low. As Eric's eyes adjusted to the dark, he noticed that the sliding mirrored closet door had been left open. Inside, Jake's four-striped uniform jacket was hanging next to a pressed white shirt with epaulets on the shoulders. His hat, with the Mercury Airways logo embroidered on it, was placed on a shelf. Seeing those items in the captain's darkened hotel room, within an arm's reach, gave Eric such a raging hard-on that his penis popped right out of his shorts. He heard a groan and turned to look at the bed. Jake was lying shirtless in the middle of the bed, with a sheet pulled up to his waist. The white waistband of his jockstrap gleamed like a beacon. His breathing was so low and steady that Eric thought he might have fallen asleep. He hesitated, not sure what to do next when Jake slowly pulled the sheets down to his mid-thigh. Eric gasped. The mound in Jake's jockstrap was the size of a catcher's mitt. Eric crept closer to the bed, in such awe of the semi-naked man that he couldn't speak.

Jake groaned again and rolled over on his left side. "That you, son?" he asked sleepily.

Eric tried to reply, but his mouth was so dry that nothing came out. He worked up a little saliva and managed to say, "Yes, Dad."

"Oh, good. I'm taking a nap." He patted the mattress. "Come on, son, and join me. Let's sleep for a while."

As Jake began softly snoring, Eric peeled off his sweaty muscle shirt, shorts, and socks. He left the jockstrap on, enjoying the sensation of his hard dick pushing against the cotton pouch. The room reeked of male sweat—both his and Jake's combined. The aroma was more intense and more powerful than a double hit of poppers.

Eric slipped into bed, pulled up the covers, and nestled against Jake's hairy back. As his body came in contact with the pilot's, he went into a state of pure bliss. He gently brushed his lips against the back of Jake's neck and thrilled at the salty taste of his skin. Jake grunted but otherwise remained still.

Eric couldn't tell whether he was asleep or just pretending. He put his hand on Jake's leg and started slowly moving it upward. He could feel the heat emanating from the overstuffed pouch only inches away from his hand.

Suddenly, the sexual tension that had been building all day reached the breaking point. He couldn't wait another minute; he *had* to touch Jake's cock. He slipped his hand through the waistband and squeezed. Jesus Christ! The captain's dick was huge, uncut and dripping pre-cum. But touching Jake's penis wasn't enough. He had to see it, in all its glory. He started to pull the massive phallus free of the pouch that could barely contain it. As "You're Cheatin' Heart" played on the radio, Eric thrilled to the fact that he was living out one of his greatest fantasies: sex with an older, handsome, hairy and very well-hung pilot.

Suddenly, Jake's hand clamped down on Eric's. "What are you doing?" he demanded, in a tone that froze Eric's blood.

"I'm... I'm..." he stammered.

"What the hell do you think you're doing, son?"

Oh, thought Eric. He's serious about the role-playing. That's OK, I'm game. "I just wanted to... touch it, Dad."

"Touch what, son?"

"Touch your penis."

"Oh, that's what you wanted? Since when does a son crawl into his father's bed and start playing with his penis?"

"I thought you wanted me to touch it, Dad."

"Oh, yeah?" Jake let go of Eric's hand. He rolled over on his back and rested his hand behind his head. The gesture made his bicep pop up once again like a grapefruit. "What gave you that idea, son?"

"The way you were showing off for me at the gym."

"Maybe I was showing off a little. You like watching me do squats, don't you, son? You like looking at your dad's big, hairy legs and his meaty hairy ass, don't you?"

"Yes, Dad, I do."

"What else did you like, son? Tell me."

"I like the way you got a big bulge in your jockstrap when were in the locker room."

"Yeah? You like this big bulge, son?"

"Yeah, I like it, Dad."

Jake leaned up on the pillows and spread his legs. "Then take it out, son, and get a good look at it."

As Eric released Jake's penis, it sprang straight up to the ceiling—all nine inches of it. "Oh my God, Dad."

"Go ahead and touch it, son."

Eric squatted in front of Jake and reached for his penis. His hand barely fit around it.

"Use both hands, son, one over the other, and start pumping it slowly… slowly… yeah, that's it, just like that. You like looking at my dick, don't you, son?"

"Yes, Dad. It's the most beautiful dick I've ever seen."

"I'm glad to hear you say that. You know where that dick is going, son?"

"In my mouth, Dad?"

"That's right, son. And where else?"

"I don't know, Dad…"

"Yes, you do, son. Where else is it going?"

"Up my ass?"

"That's right, son. After you suck on it for a while, I'm gonna slide it right into your beautiful, creamy white ass."

"Dad, it's too big. It will never fit."

"You leave that to me, son. I'll make it fit. You ready to take it in your mouth?"

"Yes, Dad. I'm ready."

"You ready to worship it, son?"

"I'm gonna worship *all* of you, Dad."

"All of me?" Jake swung his legs over the bed and stood up. He started flexing like a bodybuilder as his colossal dick swung back and forth.

"Yes, Dad, every inch of you."

"Then get down on the floor, son, and get started." He reached into a drawer in the nightstand and pulled out a small towel. "Here. Put these under your knees. You'll be down there for a while. I don't want you to get carpet burns."

Eric kneeled in front of him, opened his mouth as wide as he could, and reached for Jake with both hands.

"No hands," said Jake, reaching in the drawer again.

Before Eric realized what was happening, Jake had grabbed his hands, pulled them behind his back, and locked them into a pair of metal handcuffs. The clicking sound thrilled Eric so much that his sphincter started to throb. He was now at the mercy of the god-like man standing before him.

"Go on, son." Jake stood with his arms crossed and his cock bobbing up and down. "You know what to do."

Eric leaned forward with his mouth open. Jake began to slide his cock in slowly, inch by inch. Eric opened as wide as he could, amazed that he could fit Jake's penis inside his mouth. And there was still more coming! His jaw began to ache as it stretched beyond its natural limit, but he ignored the pain. Here was the moment he'd been waiting for all day. He'd never felt so mentally and sexually connected to another man. Nothing mattered beyond the experience of swallowing Jake. Eric closed his eyes and thrilled to the sensation. Who knew when he left for JFK that morning that this is where he would end up?

"Look up," said Jake, grabbing a handful of Eric's hair. "Look up at me while you suck my cock, boy."

As Eric looked up to gaze lovingly at Jake, he was suddenly thrown off balance. Jake was grinning at him, but there was a sinister expression on his face. Eric wasn't sure what would happen next, but suddenly he was afraid.

"That's it boy. Now you're gonna get *all* of it." As Jake thrust his hips forward, the head of his penis moved past Eric's tonsils. Then, with a final thrust, it was all the way down his throat—and he couldn't breathe. He started gagging and tried to pull away.

Jake grabbed him by the back of the head and put his other hand around Eric's throat. His grip was like a vice.

Eric couldn't get even a molecule of oxygen into his windpipe. He couldn't move his head or use his own hands to push himself away, either. He started to panic, horrified at the gurgling sounds coming out of his throat.

A moment later, Jake relaxed his grip and pulled out. He grabbed his penis and started to stroking it in front of Eric's face. "Look at that, baby," he said, slowly pulling back on the dark foreskin to reveal the pink, monstrously swollen head underneath. "You want some more?"

"Yes, but wait! Let me catch my—"

Before he could finish the sentence, Jake shoved his cock back down Eric's throat and grabbed the back of his head again.

Tears were streaming down Eric's face, blurring his vision. He was suffocating in a sadistic sex ritual that he'd never experienced before, or even imagined. As his eyelids closed and he began to lose consciousness, Jake released his grip and said, "Good boy. *Good boy.* Take a break, son."

Eric dropped against the side of the bed, choking and gagging, desperate for air. When he could finally breathe, he was revolted by the mixture of fluids gushing out of his nose and mouth. "What... what the fuck are you *doing*, you *maniac?!* I couldn't *breathe.*"

"That's the whole point, son. It's a breath control game. It heightens the experience of going down on a man."

"Game?! I thought you were going to choke me to death!" He started sobbing even harder. The entire experience, which he'd been craving since the moment he first met Jake, was now ruined.

Oh, baby! Oh, no!" Jake grabbed a towel and started wiping Eric's face. "I wasn't trying to hurt you, I swear." Jake pulled Eric's head against his chest. "Please stop crying. Son, listen to me. Your dad knows what's he's doing. I wouldn't have let you go on even one second longer." He gently stroked Eric's hair. "I would never hurt you."

"How am I supposed to know that?"

"I thought you knew what I was doing. You seemed like you were ready for anything, once we got started. You didn't even flinch when I put those handcuffs on you."

"These goddam handcuffs. Take them off, right now! My wrists are starting to go numb."

"Sure, sure." He opened the drawer by the bed, brought out the key and unlocked the cuffs. "We'll forget all about these," he said, as he put them back in the drawer. "Unless you change your mind later."

"I don't think that's going to happen. I want to go wash my face," said Eric.

"Sure," said Jake. "While you do that, I'll pour us a drink. I think we could both use a shot."

"What do you have?"

"A bottle of single malt Scotch."

"Pour me a big shot. I'll be right back." He walked into the bathroom, horrified by what he saw when he looked in the mirror. His face was puffy, and his eyes were bloodshot. His hair was going in four different directions. There were visible red marks on his neck. He grabbed a bar of soap and a washcloth and turned the cold water on full blast. By the time he finished washing up and then dried off, he felt a little calmer and steady enough to walk back into the room. Nevertheless, he knew what he was going to do: give Jake back his goddam jockstrap, get dressed, and get the hell out of there.

Jake was leaning against the pillows, holding a glass of whiskey in each hand. "Feeling better?" he asked.

"Yeah. I'm sorry if I overreacted, Jake. But I don't think this is going work out. So I'm going to get dressed and—"

"Eric, please stop. There's no need to apologize or to get indignant. I'm sorry if I hurt you. We won't do that kind of oral sex anymore if you don't want to. Please come back into bed and stay with me for a while."

Fuck, thought Eric, as he looked at Jake. He knows he went too far, he's trying to make up, and he's still the sexiest fucking man I've ever seen. Eric started getting an erection again. He couldn't help himself. Well, he thought, what's another thirty minutes?

As Eric lay down next to him, Jake lazily swung one hairy leg over Eric's and handed him a glass. "Here. This'll make you feel better, I promise. Let's take five and relax."

Eric took a large sip and almost had a coughing fit.

"Whoa, son!" said Jake. "Twelve-year-old Scotch is made for sipping, not gulping. Let's kick back and enjoy it."

A few quiet minutes passed. "This is nice," said Eric, as he began to relax. "I don't even like Scotch, but this is going right to my brain."

"It's having the same effect on me. Come here, baby, and put your head on my chest."

Eric snuggled next to him. This part was nice: to lie with Jake, to drink his Scotch, and watch the pilot's huge, hairy foot rub against his own smooth, pale one. The contrast was very sexy. Christ, the whole damn scene was sexy! Two lustful men: one older and more mature, the other younger and craving new experiences... an afternoon together in a darkened hotel room, with no one around to disturb them or judge them... the freedom for Eric to explore whatever hidden desires came to mind, and a guiding hand to help fulfill them... *this* was pure heaven. As he snuggled closer, "I'm so Lonesome I Could Cry" began playing on the radio. "What is this?" he asked. "Is it the all-Hank Williams station?"

"They're doing a tribute session this afternoon," said Jake. He took another sip of Scotch. "I just love ol' Hank."

"I was never much into country-western music," said Eric.

"This isn't country-western, son. It's honky-tonk."

"Yes, I know. I can tell by the twang of the electric guitar."

Jake shifted a little and looked at Eric. "Should I try to find an all-Madonna station?"

"Not necessary."

"This song is one of my favorites. Just listen to him, Eric. There's such honesty in his lyrics and his voice."

"You're right," Eric said, once the song was over. "I guess I never thought of him that way." He set his empty glass on the nightstand and started running his hands through Jake's chest hair.

"That feels good," said Jake. "Will you stay?"

"Yeah, I'll stay."

"You wanna play some more? We won't do anything that you don't want to, I promise."

"Yeah, I'll stay. But let's bring it down a notch or two. And please use my name once in a while. The daddy-son stuff is hot, but I can't keep it up for the whole night."

"Fair enough, Eric. And you can call me Jake. Or Captain. After all, I'm not your dad, but I *am* your captain. And I do like the way that sounds coming from a handsome, young man like yourself." He sat up, drained his glass and put it on the nightstand next to Eric's. "We'll have some more of this later. No sense in getting stone-drunk right now." He rolled over on top of Eric and gently stroked his cheek. "Do you like to kiss, Eric?"

"Hell, yeah."

Jake leaned down and kissed him on the lips, coaxing his mouth open. Jake's face, already covered with a five-o'clock shadow, was scratchy, but Eric didn't mind it. Jake's lips were full, soft and sensual. Eric loved feeling all the different sensations at once: the scratch of Jake's stubbly face, the smell of Scotch on his breath, and the electric excitement of their naked torsos rubbing together. The alcohol helped him to relax even more and spurred a new willingness to touch, smell and taste everything.

Jake guided Eric through every square inch of his body: his rugged face, his sculpted chest, his massive arms and sweaty armpits, and his flat, hard belly. He let Eric slap it over and over; Eric loved the thudding sound that it made. He slowly guided Eric down to his rock-hard dick, letting him squeeze it and stroke it. He showed Eric how he liked to have his heavy testicles firmly tugged and then forcefully sucked. Then he rolled over, hugged a pillow and spread his legs.

"Jesus," Eric murmured as he looked at Jake lying prostrate on the bed. "Oh, Jesus Christ." Jake's muscular ass was covered entirely with sweaty, dark fur.

"You like that, son?"

"Yeah, I like it, Dad."

"Want to see more, son?"

"Yeah, show me more, Dad." The role-playing had taken on a new intensity. In his mind, Eric was transported somewhere else. He felt that they could be father and son, locked into an illicit yet thrilling bond that both had been craving all their lives.

Jake leaned over and spread his cheeks open. With his thick, hairy fingers, he pulled his cheeks apart to show Eric the smooth, pink cleft of his sphincter. A primal part of Eric's brain took over. As his tongue came in contact with Jake's musky asshole, he became blind with animalistic desire. He dove in as far he could go. As the intensity built, Jake groaned and spread his legs even further apart.

"Do you have a condom?" Eric asked hoarsely. "I want to fuck your ass, right now."

"Yeah," said Jake. "But I don't get fucked. I only top. Besides, now it's my turn." He sat up, flipped Eric over and began his own uninhibited exploration of his partner's body. An hour later, they knew each other's sexual desires as well as they knew their own. Eric was in heaven, and so enamored that he lost all sense of time and space. If he had his way, they'd stay wrapped in each other's arm for the rest of their lives.

Jake hoisted Eric's legs over his shoulders and slipped a finger into his throbbing asshole. "Look how open you are, son. Goddam, that's beautiful. You ready for me to fuck you, son?"

"Oh, yes, Dad. Fuck me." He wrapped his arms around Jake's neck. "But please go easy. Do you have any poppers?"

"Yeah, but I want you to try to take it on your own first. I know what I'm doing, and I'll go very slow." He reached into the drawer again and took a tube of lube, a bottle of poppers, and a condom. He deftly opened the package and rolled the condom down his dick. Then he started slipping it slowly, a little bit a time.

Eric tried to open up as much as possible. "Oh, Jake... I want it. But it's too big. It's too damn big!"

"That's because you're fighting it, baby. Come on, breathe as deeply as you can. It's gonna feel so fucking good when it's all the way in, I promise."

Eric struggled to accept him, but his body said no and started to push Jake out. "Jake, give me a hit of poppers, please! That's the only way it'll work."

"All right, baby." He unscrewed the cap and held the bottle under Eric's left nostril. "These are from London. Their called Jungle Juice and they're the real deal. Take a big hit... good boy. Now the other nostril... now one more through your mouth. Let's get you all gooned up, boy, and ready to take that big, fucking dick all the way."

Eric felt the top of his head come off. His entire body went limp and he could think of nothing but being fucked. "Ready... ready, Dad." Before he knew it, Jake was in all the way. He was fucking him, rocking him, kissing him, and running his tonguing over his face... dripping sweat onto Eric's torso and whispering obscenities in his ear.

Jake had incredible stamina. Every time that Eric's ass started to tighten up, the bottle of poppers magically appeared under his nose. After half an hour, he pulled out and flipped Eric over. "Look at that," he said. "Look at that sweet, round ass in that jockstrap!" He ran his hands slowly over Eric's butt cheeks. Then he grabbed the waistband of Eric's jockstrap with one hand, and with the other hand began slapping his ass repeatedly. The stinging sensation of Jake's strong, wide palm only added to Eric's pleasure. Then Jake breathing became very short. "Turn over again, son," he groaned. "I'm really close. And I want to see your face when I cum inside you."

Eric immediately turned over on his back. Jake had the poppers ready and put the bottle under Eric's nostrils. "Big hits, come one, big hits, baby, I want you ready for it." With a single thrust, he entered and started pounding. As he pounded faster and faster, he grabbed Eric's dick and pumped it with the same intensity. "You ready, baby? You ready for it?"

"I'm ready... I'm ready... give it to me, Jake! I can't hold off any longer. I'm gonna cum. I'm gonna cum!"

"Here it is, boy. Take it!" He slammed into Eric, roaring into his ear. "Take my fucking load!"

Eric felt Jake's dick begin to pulse in the deepest part of his being as his own orgasm exploded all over Jake's abdomen. His eyes rolled back into his head and he felt himself floating up to the ceiling. Jesus, he thought, this really is like going to heaven...

Afterward, they stayed together for a long time with Jake's penis still inside. Eric couldn't believe it, but Jake was still hard. He tried to shift around it a little. "Jake..."

"You ready for me to pull out?" Jake asked groggily.

"Uh huh."

"OK… slowly… slowly… here we go."

"Oh God! Easy, easy!"

"There. I'm out." He pulled off the condom and dropped it on the floor. "Do you want to go get cleaned up?"

"No. I can't move. Don't *want* to move right now. Stay on top of me."

Drenched in sweat, Jake collapsed on top of him. The pressure of his bodyweight was exquisite. "Let's stay just like this for a while," said Eric.

"We've got to eat sometime. Aren't you hungry?"

"Shh. Please don't talk, Jake."

"OK." They both fell into a deep sleep from which they wouldn't wake for several hours.

***

The phone rang and rang. It was the most intrusive sound in the world. Eric opened his eyes. He was in a pitch-black hotel room and had no idea where he was. Out of habit, he reached for the phone.

Someone slapped his hand away. "My room. I'll get it."

That's right, he thought, I'm with Jake in his room and just had the best sex of life. He sat up. Jesus! He was a sticky, smelly mess. "Jake, could you bring me a—"

"Shh, be quiet," Jake said, as he picked up the phone. "Hello? … Oh, hi, sweetheart. How are you? … You're kidding … no, that's great news, what a coincidence. Just tell me what time to expect you … All right, I'll be here. See you then." He hung up the phone. "Oh, fuck," he said as he snapped on the lamp next to the bed.

Eric shielded his eyes from the light, feeling sure that the encounter was about to come to an abrupt end. "Who was that?"

"Sorry, Eric, but there's a change of plans, and I need you to be cool about it."

"Cool about what?"

"Hang on a second." He picked up the phone and dialed. "Could you connect me to housekeeping, please? Thank you … Good evening, I'd like someone to service my room—a whole set of clean towels, fresh sheets on the bed, clean the bathroom, the works … Great, can you be here in about thirty minutes, but not before then? … Thanks, I appreciate it."

"Jake, what the hell is going on?"

"My wife is on her way here."

"Your wife? You have a *wife?*"

"Yes. She was supposed to be in Seattle tonight, but she got reassigned to fly to L.A. and she'll be here in an hour and a half."

"Reassigned? You mean, you not only have a wife, but she's a *flight attendant?*"

"Yes. That's why I need you to be cool. If I didn't think you could be, I would never have hooked up with you in the first place." He snapped his fingers. "Come on, buddy, let's get moving."

"Did you just *snap* your fucking fingers at me?"

"I'm sorry. I don't mean to be rude, but I'm running short on time. Jesus, this room reeks of poppers!" He reached for the window sash. "Thank God the windows open."

"What about dinner?"

"Another time, I promise. Listen, would you mind showering in your room? I need to get my shit together before my wife arrives."

"You're kicking me out without even letting me wipe myself off?!"

"Oh, for Pete's sake!" He walked into the bathroom and came with a dampened washcloth. "*Here*. Now come on, be a buddy and help me out."

Eric tried to control himself, but he was trembling with rage. He cleaned himself as best he could and threw the washcloth on the floor. "I can't believe you *used* me like this."

"What do you mean, used you? You've been coming on to me all day like a bitch in heat. You're a hot little fucker and you got me! It was great fun, we had great sex, and I hope it will happen again sometime. But right now, I have to get back to my real life, so let's not make a big deal about it."

"Your *real* life? You cheated on your wife with me! Not only that, she's one of my co-workers! What am I supposed to do if I ever fly with her? I can't even fucking believe you're married to *a woman!* What kind of straight man travels with lube and poppers and a fucking extra jock strap to share?"

"Eric—oh shit!" Jake stepped on the used condom and bent over to pick it up. "I'm glad I found this before the maid did." He went to flush it down the toilet and then came back into the room. "Eric, how long ago did you come out?"

"Six years ago. What difference does that make?"

"Then by now, you should know all about men having sex just for the fun of it. That's what we do, whether we're married or not, and we do it without any big emotional hang-ups. Besides, my wife flies for another airline, so I doubt that your paths will ever cross. Now please be cool, get your stuff together, and let me do what I need to do. Come on, be a buddy." He tried to sound brusque, but there was a pleading look in his eyes.

You're full of shit and you know it, thought Eric. But he said nothing, as there was no point. He got dressed and grabbed his gym bag. "Good night, Jake. Thanks for the great afternoon."

Jake looked relieved. "Goodnight. Hey, take that jock strap if you want. You can wear it next time you work out. It'll be a souvenir of our hot afternoon together."

"A souvenir? What kind of loser do you think I am?" He threw it on the bed. "*You* keep it." He didn't look back as he slammed the door closed. In the fresh, clean air of the hallway, he could smell himself and he stunk to high heaven. Now I *really* hope I don't run into anyone from the crew, he thought, as he headed for the elevator. He decided to play it safe and take the stairs instead. He looked at his watch. It was already eight o'clock, and pick-up was at seven the next morning. Well, so what? he thought. The night's not a total loss. There's still time to shower, clear my head, grab a bite, have a great, big cocktail and try to make sense of what just happened. *This* is one for the goddam books, that's for sure! As he reached the second floor and entered the hallway, he heard the elevator open behind him. Without turning around, he started walking quickly toward his room.

"Eric, is that you? Hey, Eric! Wait up."

It was Jacques. He was red-eyed and stumbling toward Eric, carrying a brown paper bag.

"Where are you running off to?" Jacques asked as he caught up with him.

"My room. I'm just coming back from the gym."

"Gym?" Jacques sniffed him. "Bullshit. You reek of poppers and lube." He sniffed again. "And Scotch. You've been drinking— and fucking." His voice was slurred. "Now, *whom* were you fucking? That's what I'd like to know."

"That's none of your business."

"OK, OK. I'm glad to see that somebody's getting it these days." He patted Eric on the shoulder. "Not to worry, sweetheart, your secret is safe with me."

Eric had never seen Jacques in such a state. He always conducted himself like a gentleman. What on earth could have happened to make him—Oh, shit, how could I forget? he thought. He took out his room key. "Jacques, this is my room. Why don't you come in for a minute? You must have had a difficult afternoon."

"Oh, you bet!" Jacques followed into the room and took a fifth of vodka out of the paper bag. "You got a couple of glasses? Let's have a drink."

"Right there on the desk. How did it go in Long Beach?"

Jacques laughed. It was a long, bitter laugh. "How do you *think* it went? It was fucking torture. I'm never going through that shit again. Ever! How I wish I could have changed places with *you* this afternoon. Anyway, I'm through with the deathbed visits. From now on, I'll just scribble my name on a fucking sympathy card and send my 'thoughts and prayers', like every other asshole in the world."

"I'm really sorry to hear that. You must be very upset. And you've had a lot to drink. Maybe you should go lie down in your own room."

"Drink first." He took the plastic wrap off two glasses and poured them each a half a glass of straight vodka.

"All right. And then I really think you should go lie down." Fuck a duck, could this evening get any worse?

Jacques plopped into an armchair and took a big sip as he looked Eric up and down. "Fucking A! I always thought you were handsome, Eric, but I never knew what a hot body you have." He grabbed Eric's crotch. "You are fuckin' turning me *on* in those fucking gym shorts!"

Eric moved his hand away. "Jacques, you're drunk."

"Of course I'm drunk. You'd be drunk too, if you had the afternoon that I did. You know what else I am? Horny as hell, that's what. It's been months since I had sex. You interested? I *know* you are, you've always been interested in me." He stood up and kissed Eric on the neck. "I don't mind sloppy seconds. Sometimes, that's the hottest kind of sex. That sweet, little hole of yours will pop right open."

"Get *off* me, goddamit! You're drunk!"

Jacques reeled back as though he'd been slapped in the face. "I'm sorry. That was shitty thing to say." He looked ashamed. "It's been a long time since I tried to hit on somebody. I don't know how to do it anymore—especially these days."

"I understand." Eric took the glass out of Jacques' hand. "Go to bed. You've had enough to drink. You're going to feel like shit when you wake up, and we have a flight to work tomorrow morning."

"No, we don't have to work. Didn't you hear? Crew scheduling called. Our flight canceled, and we're deadheading home on the three P.M. flight tomorrow."

"Then you should go to sleep for a while. I'm going to shower and get dressed. If you're still awake when I ready to leave, we can go out for dinner together."

"Not hungry. We stopped on the way back from Long Beach."

"I'll see you tomorrow then."

"Eric, please come and have a drink with me when you get back. *Please.* I can't be alone tonight. I need to be with another gay man, even if you just hold my hand or let me cry on your shoulder. No, on second thought: I *don't* want to cry. No more fucking tears. What I want is to get even drunker than I am right now, forget about everything, and have a few laughs. I promise not to lay a finger on you. What do you say? It's either that or I'll jump in a cab to go bar hopping in West Hollywood, and God knows *what* will happen then."

Eric sighed. Jacques was drunk, but he was a decent man and a friend— even if not a very close friend. If he went traipsing off to West Hollywood in his inebriated state, he might not it make it back to the hotel at all. "All right. I'll come and knock on your door around nine-thirty when I get back from dinner."

"Yippie! We will have a party after all."

"At this point, I'm ready for a few laughs too, but that's all, Jacques. I won't take advantage of your vulnerability. We'd both regret it tomorrow."

Jacques grinned. "You know what, Eric? You are what Sylvia would call a real *mensch*. Do you know what that means? It's a Yiddish word. It means a human being—a person of integrity and honor."

That's wonderful, Eric thought ruefully. Of all the things I'd like to be known for, I get to be known as a *mensch*. He swallowed the vodka in one big gulp, enjoying the stinging sensation as it went down his throat. "Well," he said, "I guess it's better than being known as a *schlemiel* or a *schlimazel*."

CHAPTER 32

Two Tickets to Paradise

"Hello?" Eric said into the phone at home on a mid-February morning.

"It's Denny. What the hell are you doing answering the phone without waiting for the code ring? You're supposed to be listening for two rings, then a pause, and then another call immediately afterward."

"Sorry, I wasn't thinking. I'm trying to pack and leave the house early to get to JFK. The whole borough of Queens is an unholy mess today because of the blizzard."

"Well, don't do it again. The company is short flight attendants. Commuters haven't been able to get in for the past few days, and crew scheduling is reassigning people left and right. Once they get you on the phone, if they want to send you someplace else, you're screwed. Why don't you and your roommate get caller ID, like everyone else I know?"

"It costs an extra ten dollars per month. It's not in Michael's budget right now."

"He can't afford ten bucks for something that vital? Oh, brother. It sounds like Global Airways is going to go 'tits up' any day now."

"It's not funny, Denny. He's back on straight reserve with twenty-five years' seniority. He's barely able to pay his bills."

"That's gotta suck. Well, are you ready for V, baby?"

"I am so ready for V!"

"This is going to be the party of the year," said Denny. "I still can't believe that you were able to score us two tickets."

"It pays to be nice to passengers in business class. Ha! Did you ever think you'd hear me say that? *I* can't believe that you were able to get me off a two-day Cleveland trip and onto the L.A. flight today so that we could go together."

"That's why I only deal with Jerry Genualdi. He's the Tiffany of trip trade services in New York. But you're going to owe him a favor, to be called in whenever he wants. Where are our tickets for V, by the way?"

"They're already packed in my tote bag."

"Double-check. If you leave them behind, it's not like you'll have time to run back home and get them."

"I just checked myself for the third time this morning. They're in a zippered compartment right next to my crewmember ID, so stop worrying. What are you wearing tonight?"

"I had a red leather harness custom-made on Christopher Street. I'm wearing that with a white thong, red rugby socks, and my police boots—and nothing else. I'm ready for action. What about you?"

"Nothing so extravagant: a cropped red muscle shirt, white briefs, and white sneakers. Simple, but sexy."

"I bet you look hot in that muscle shirt."

"I do. I haven't had a single gram of carbohydrates in three weeks, and I've been pumping iron and doing crunches like crazy. By the way, someone you know is going to be there tonight."

"Please don't tell me it's Pumpkin Head."

"No, of course not. What would Pumpkin Head be doing at an event like that? It's Anthony Bellini."

"That asshole?"

"He's not an asshole."

"Excuse me, but what were you calling him five months ago when he left you high and dry in Queens to move in with that sugar daddy in Dallas?"

"We made up at Christmastime. His relationship with Jim turned out to be a total disaster. Jim, as I knew all along, was the *real* asshole."

"Are you gloating? I swear I can hear you gloating over the phone."

"Just a little. At any rate, Anthony's in the process of untangling himself from Jim and their business *mishegoss*. It's very complicated legally. But he hopes to be back in New York by this summer, if not before. I'm glad that he's coming back."

"You forgive too easily. I'm going to have to bite my tongue when I see him. I'd just as soon tell him what a self-centered prick I think he is, but I'll keep the peace for your benefit."

"I doubt that we'll actually see him. He has a VIP ticket. You and I are in the general admission section."

"How did he swing a VIP ticket without Jim paying for it?"

"I don't know. Some connection or other. Listen, I've got to leave now or I'll be late."

"I'm walking out the door now too. Meet me by the first-class ticket counter at ten A.M. Do *not* go up to operations under any circumstance. We're keeping a low profile today. We'll sign in for our flight at the gate. Remember, once they nab for you for a reassignment—"

"Denny, you're starting to sound like a broken record. I'll see you at ten!"

He hung up the phone, grabbed his luggage, and left the house. As he opened the front door, he was almost knocked over by a blast of frigid Arctic wind. He stepped back inside and wrapped his scarf around his head, all the way up to his eyeballs. Jesus Christ, this was *real* winter! Three days previously, a blizzard of epic proportions had hit the East Coast, dumping a foot of heavy, wet snow all the way from Washington, D. C. to Boston. The storm had utterly paralyzed New York City; all three major airports were closed. The airlines had sporadically resumed operations just last night, but according to the morning news reports, flights were now departing as scheduled. The sky was bright and clear; Eric was sure that his trip to Los Angeles would leave on time. His only challenge would be getting to the airport. Thankfully, the superintendent had cleared the walkway in front of the building. The sidewalks and streets, however, were a mess. The beautiful white flakes that Eric had so gleefully watched tumbling down at the height of the storm had now become a filthy mix of soot-blackened snow littered with dog feces and cigarette butts. To make matters worse, constant foot traffic over the past two days left treacherous pools of slush at every street corner. Wheeling his suitcase was impossible. He had to carry his luggage by hand all the way to the subway. By the time he reached the station, he feared thought his arms might fall off. He waited for a stream of riders to clear the staircase before he proceeded and took extra time walking down. One false step could land him at the bottom of the wet, slippery staircase with a broken leg… or worse.

He exited at Kew Gardens and got on a longer than usual line for the Q10 bus. Everyone wore heavy winter coats, thick gloves, hats pulled down over their ears, and scarves wrapped around their heads. Together, they looked like a conga line of colorful mummies. Being New Yorkers, their well-arranged layers didn't impede them in the least from complaining about the miserable weather. Eric said nothing and waited patiently for the bus. Many of the other riders were on their way to work a daily shift at the airport; they would have to deal the same issues going home. Eric, on the other hand, was escaping. One of the great joys of being a flight attendant was being able to leave New York during a bout of inclement weather and jet away to a more favorable climate. Accordingly, he had no complaints. After a twenty-minute wait, the bus finally pulled up to the corner and the driver opened the door.

"Can you come closer, please?" asked a woman at the front of the line. "There's a lake of slush between us and the door."

"I can't come any closer," said the driver. "My wheels'll get stuck."

The woman sighed and deftly jumped from the sidewalk onto the first step of the bus. Eric tried to do the same, but with his bulky luggage, he slipped and landed feet first in the icy water. "Dammit" he yelled. "Look at this! My shoes and socks are drenched!"

The driver wasn't fazed in the least. "What do want me to do about it?"

"You *could* bring this bus closer to the sidewalk," he said, as stepped up to the fare box. "Somebody's going to get killed."

"Mister, you're holding up the line. Do you want to go to JFK or not?"

"Yes, I'm *going*!" Eric paid his fare, grumbling all the way to the back of the bus, and sat down. Within seconds, his feet felt frozen solid. At least I can change my socks when I get off the bus, he thought. But I'm stuck wearing these wet loafers the whole flight. My white sneakers, unfortunately, won't go with the uniform.

The usual forty-five-minute ride took well over an hour. Thankfully, when they reached JFK, the bus stop in front of the terminal was clean and dry. His shoes squished as he walked into the building. He needed to change into warm, dry socks—and fast.

Denny was waiting for him near the first-class ticket counter. "Hi. What's with the sourpuss?"

"My feet are soaking wet. I need to change my socks right now."

"There's a bathroom right over there. Leave your luggage with me. Jesus, look at this place, Eric! It's like a refugee camp today."

Denny was right. Army-style cots were strewn from one end of the terminal to the other. They were occupied by weary families, many with small children, who looked as though they would willingly pay a million dollars to get out of New York. They had been stranded by the hundreds of flight cancellations caused by the storm. Their only travel option now was to be placed on the standby list of an oversold flight, trying in vain to reach their final destination. "Poor bastards," Eric said. "This is one of those times when I'm very grateful to be working crewmember. At least no one can take my jump seat away from me."

"You said it. Come on now, Eric. Chop-chop."

Eric went to change his socks and returned five minutes later.

"Feel better?" Denny asked.

"How about: slightly less miserable."

"That'll do. Hey, can I see our tickets?"

"Jesus, Denny, stop hocking me. I told you: I have them."

"I know you have them. I just want to *see* them."

"All right, hang on." Eric reached into his bag and took out two red leather envelopes. Inside each, there was a white leather invitation embossed with a stylized red heart and a large red V.

Denny read the text aloud. " 'V. February 14. Los Angeles, California. Admit one.' Hey, there's no address on here! Just a phone number."

"I know. Do you see that serial number at the bottom of each of each ticket? I had to call the phone number and read them off to one of the hosts. He wouldn't give me the address and start time until he confirmed that we were on the guest list. That's how exclusive this party is."

"Cool! This is going to be *the* gay party of the year! And it's about damn time that we celebrate something."

"I know, and I—oh, crap!"

"What's the matter?"

"I need to go to operations."

"What for?"

"Someone bought me a bottle of Jungle Juice in London and left it in my mailbox. I'm not going to V without a nice, fresh bottle of poppers. There's sure to be a designated play space somewhere."

"Problem solved," said Denny. "We'll get someone else to pick it up for you."

As they headed to the security checkpoint, a desperate-looking man stopped them. "Excuse me. Are you the crew for the Orlando flight?"

"No, sir," said Eric. "We're going to Los Angeles."

"Where the hell *is* the crew for the Orlando flight? The agents at the ticket counter said they're not here yet. The flight was supposed to leave an hour ago."

"I don't know why they're not checked in yet, sir. We're not the crew schedulers, and we have to sign-in for our own flight. Come on, Denny."

"Don't you walk away from me when I'm talking to you. We've been trying for *two days* to get out of this fucking airport! My kids are going crazy! Your goddam airline isn't even *feeding* us!"

"Sir," said Eric, "we—"

"Ignore him, Eric," said Denny. "We're going to be late." As they walked away, the man continued to rage about his terrible treatment at the hands of the airline.

"Good God," said Eric. "Does he think he's the only person who's been inconvenienced? There are at least a thousand other people camped out here."

"Forget it. Let the Orlando crew deal with him. They'll be the *real* poor bastards! Let's go stand near the elevator for a few minutes until we see someone who can pick up your package." A moment later, a handsome flight attendant carrying a Harrods tote bag walk by them. "Good, here comes my friend Dave Gregory. Hey, Dave! How are you?"

"Hi, Denny, good to see you."

"Where are you headed?"

"I'm going to London this afternoon. I'm super early. You?"

"I'm going to L.A. on the noon flight."

"L.A.? Oh, my God, you're still on *domestic?*"

"Yes, for the time being. Dave, can you do us a favor? This is my friend, Eric. He has a small package in his mailbox that he needs for our trip. Would you mind getting it for us while we wait here? We're trying to avoid getting reassigned. Eric's the junior man on our flight today, and we have big plans in L.A."

"Oh, yes, honey," said Dave. "I know all about reassignments when 'screw' scheduling is short. I went through that myself many times when I was junior. No problem. What's your last name, Eric?"

"Saunders. It should be a bottle, about this size, wrapped in a small manila envelope."

"O.K. I'll be back down in ten minutes, after I sign in and pick up my purser paperwork."

"Thanks, Dave."

After Dave went up in the elevator, Eric said, "Why did he ask you that question the way he did?"

"What question?"

"About our trip. He said, 'You're still on *domestic?*' as though you were being forced to repeat the sixth grade."

"Oh, you know how those international stews are. They're a bit uppity about their overwater status—even if they're flying the Caribbean, which believe me is nothing to be uppity about."

Dave returned a few minutes later. "Here you go." He handed the package to Eric and grinned. "I think I know what that is. A little 'juice,' baby boy?"

"Something like that."

"I thought so. Jungle Juice is the best. You can't find anything comparable in the States. I'm backed up on orders for all my friends, which is why I'm flying London this month. Well, you guys have a good trip. Nice to meet you, Eric."

Eric and Denny proceeded to the gate. To Eric's surprise, Jeanie, Missy, and Dan were on the crew, and he was once again working with them in coach. Jim and Ted, whom Eric hadn't seen since his first month of flying, were working with Denny in business class. As it turned out, they had tickets to V too, which was fortunate. They could all share a cab from the layover hotel to West Hollywood and back; the round-trip fare would be less exorbitant. The purser, who was a harried-looking woman named Daniella, raced through the pre-flight briefing and then dismissed the crew to prepare the cabin for immediate boarding.

***

"Some storm, huh?" said Dan, as the aisles filled with passengers. "Even in Denver, I can't remember the last time we got this much snow so quickly. Good thing I was already here, or I'd never have made it in."

"We were buried out in Long Island," said Missy. "I didn't think that Jeanie and I would make it to the corner, much less all the way to Kennedy Airport."

"You know, there's a fifty percent chance of more snow tonight," said Dan. "I saw it on CNN just a few minutes ago. I hope we don't get stuck in L.A. But if we do, I'm just going to commute home on the first available flight to

Denver. Why hang around for a couple of days trying to get back into *this* mess?"

"We'd better NOT get stuck in L.A.!" Missy said. "I have childcare issues. I have a sitter for one night and one night *only*. And Jeanie's daughter has a dance recital that she's been rehearsing for weeks. We have to be back tomorrow."

"Oh, Christ, thought Eric, here we go: the *special needs* stewardesses.

"Jeanie," said Missy, "Your husband works for the city, right? Go call him from the gate phone and get an updated weather report. If there's even a remote chance of getting stuck out in L.A., I'm getting off this plane right now and going home."

"Well," said Eric, "I'm going to be flexible and go with the flow, which is what I promised to do when I got hired. So what if we spend an extra day in Los Angeles? It's better than coming back to this misery."

"Hey!" said Missy. "Was I talking to *you*, Eric? No, I was not." She stood with her hands on her hips. "I know you think you're better than everyone else, the way you roll your eyes at us and walk through the cabin with your nose in the air. But it's time to get *over* yourself. We don't *all* live in some crappy, little apartment in Queens. We don't spend our free time thinking: where's the best gay bar to go for Happy Hour, and how does my ass look in these new jeans? We have *real* lives. We have husbands, children, aging parents, and more responsibilities in one day than you have in an entire month. So stop acting so superior and mind your own goddam business."

"Thanks for enlightening me, Missy," Eric said, smiling serenely. "I'll remember that before I consider saying anything else to you."

"That's a good idea," said Jeanie. "You need to consider other people's needs once in a while."

"Damn straight," said Dan.

"You've all made your point," Eric said. "There's no sense in beating a dead horse. I'm going to see if business class needs a hand with pre-departures. I'm sure that you can manage without me until after takeoff."

***

To everyone's relief, the flight left the gate on time. The ground crew had done an excellent job of clearing the taxiways and runways. The airplane proceeded quickly toward the assigned takeoff runway. Eric stood in the business class galley chatting with Denny as Denny methodically latched compartments closed. "Hey, Eric, double-check me, would you? I don't work this galley very often, and I'd hate for something to come flying out of the ovens during takeoff."

Eric checked the compartments one by one. "Everything looks good. God, can you believe it? In six hours we'll be in L.A., and later tonight we'll be on the dance floor with some of the hottest men in the world!"

"I knew it would work out," said Denny. "God is always on our side, despite what the Evangelicals say. How's it going in the back today?"

"Those two Long Island girls tried to serve me some attitude, but I didn't give them the satisfaction of a reaction."

"Good for you. You'd better go and sit down. We should be taking off any minute now."

As Eric reached his jump seat in the back, the crew phone rang. "I've got it," said Dan, picking up the phone. "Hi, this is Dan … oh, really? Dammit! … Yes, I'll tell everybody." He hung up. "That was the captain. We have to go back to the gate. There's a small maintenance issue that has to be checked out. He wanted to give us a heads up before he made a PA."

Eric strained to listen to the captain's announcement over the collective groaning of passengers. There was an indicator light in the cockpit that had to be reset. It was a simple procedure that would take no more than fifteen minutes. A mechanic was already standing by at the gate. If everyone would please be patient, they'd be on their way to Los Angeles in no time.

Eric heaved a sigh of relief. They taxied back to the gate, and the door was opened almost immediately by an agent. The agent made a PA asking everyone to remain seated; they'd be on their way very soon, and everyone would make their connecting flights in L.A.

Denny came walking toward the back of the plane. "Whew!" he said, when he reached Eric's jump seat. "I got worried when I heard we were going back. Sometimes, even simple mechanical fixes can turn into three-hour delays—in which case we'd be screwed for tonight."

"What're you doing in L.A. tonight?" said Jeanie.

"We're going to the biggest gay party of the year," Denny said. "For once, we'll be able to do something on an L.A. layover that doesn't involve choosing a lettuce at the Souper-Salad buffet. You'll have to get along without us this evening, ladies."

"*Woo hoo!*" said Eric.

"You see! That's exactly what I was talking about!" said Missy. "Why do you gay guys think you're so superior?"

"So we're a little excited," said Denny. "Geez, what's up your ass today?"

"I've had it, that's all. You should start your own goddam airline… with a rainbow flag covering the tail, and a box of condoms in every seat pocket."

"That's a good idea," said Denny. "At least our layover hotels would be in a decent location for a change."

As Denny turned to leave, a new voice came over the PA system. "Flight Attendant Saunders, please contact the purser ASAP. Thank you."

"What do you think that's about?" Eric asked as he picked up the crew phone.

"Don't answer!" said Denny. "The only reason they'd be paging you now would be to reassign you!"

"Oh, fuck!" Eric dropped the phone as though it were a piece of molten metal.

A moment later, the page was made again, more urgently this time. "Flight Attendant Saunders, please come to the forward entry door and bring all of your luggage." Eric recognized his supervisor's voice. "It's Pumpkin Head! What do I do?" he asked, panic-stricken.

"Hide in the bathroom," said Denny. "Pretend you didn't hear the announcement. If he comes looking for you, I'll tell him that you're sick."

Eric jumped into the bathroom and locked the door. They *can't* do this to me... not after all this trouble... not after I spent weeks getting myself in the best physical shape of my life... not after Denny worked a miracle to get us on this trip together... not after I've spent an entire month on the Ultra Jet, going from one depressing rust belt city to the next, laying over for twelve hours in dreary airport hotels. This party is the only thing I've had to look forward to all winter. I can't even fly anywhere on my goddam free passes, because I've got no money to pay for a hotel once I get there! *They just can't fucking do this to me!*

There was a loud knock on the door. "Eric, It's Phillip. Are you all right in there?"

Oh, shit. He couldn't stay in there forever. He opened the door.

"Why didn't you answer the page?" Phillip asked sternly.

"I was in the bathroom, as you can see. I'm not feeling well."

"That's strange. According to your co-workers, you were perfectly fine five minutes ago, and bubbling with excitement about your layover plans."

It was then that Eric caught the look on Missy and Jeanie's faces. Their eyes were shining. They were both five seconds away from bursting out laughing—at Eric's expense.

"You've been reassigned," said Phillip. "We're short one flight attendant on a narrow-body trip. They can't leave without the FAA minimum crew, and the flight has already been delayed by several hours. Let's go."

"Who didn't show?" Eric demanded. "Was it a *commuter* who couldn't make it in?" He could picture the scenario: a woman from upstate who was at home with her kids in Rochester, helping them out of their wet snowsuits and heating a pot of cocoa on the stove. 'Too bad I couldn't make my commuter flight into JFK, but that's what new hires are for, ha ha ha! Besides, I wouldn't have missed this day with my kids for anything in the world...'

"Yes," said Phillip. "But that is beside the point. You're the most junior person on this crew and therefore the first person subject to reassignment. You've been around long enough to know that. Now, I need you to take immediate action. Either take your luggage and report to Gate 12 or call in sick and go home. I assure you, though, that if you take the latter course, there will be a thorough investigation into your sudden, dubious illness, which may result in disciplinary action."

"Then I guess I have no choice."

"See, Eric?" said Missy, who couldn't be more pleased with this turn of events. "It's just like you said—it's all about being flexible and going with the flow. That's why they hired you, remember?"

Eric turned away. He knew that if he so much as looked at her, he'd sock her right in the jaw.

"I don't suppose any of you would consider going to that flight in Eric's place?" Denny asked in desperation.

Jeanie snorted. "Um, *no*. I don't think we're in the mood to do you any favors for the two of you today."

"Let's go, Eric," said Phillip. "I'll wait for you up front."

Eric tried to look stoic as he gathered his luggage, but in reality, he was about to cry.

"Let me give you a hand," said Denny. "I'll carry your coat for you."

"Thanks, Denny." The one true friend I have right now in this world, he thought. And now all of our pain-staking plans are ruined.

As they reached the business-class galley, Denny tapped him on the shoulder. "Before you leave, could I have my ticket, please?"

"What?! You mean you're going to V… *without* me?"

"Well, it *is* a perfectly good ticket. And I am on the guest list already. I'm sorry you can't go, but there's no reason why we should both we screwed. Besides, I'll give you a detailed report next time I see you. You know what a good storyteller I am. It'll be almost as good as being there."

Eric opened his tote bag and threw the tickets on the counter. "Don't bother, Denny. Go drink yourself into a stupor, screw a hundred men in the playroom, and come back home with a raging case of the clap for all I care. But whatever happens, keep it to yourself. I don't give a flying *fuck*." He ignored Denny's pleas not to be angry with him and continued walking toward the front of the plane. A mechanic was in the cockpit, signing off the log book. The flight to L.A. would leave in just a few minutes, and Eric would not be on it. If only there'd been no stupid indicator light, if only they hadn't returned to the gate… if only… if only. What a useless fucking phrase.

"Eric, pick up the pace, please," Phillip said as they walked up the jet bridge.

Fuck you, Eric thought. I'll crawl all the way to that goddam gate if I want to. "Where am I going?"

"You're going to be number two on the Ultra Jet to Orlando with a very nice thirty-three-hour layover there. Think of how many New Yorkers wish they could say *that* today!"

Eric almost tripped on the carpet. "Orlando!?" he sputtered, blind with rage. "That's right." There was a faint trace of sympathy in Phillip's voice, but at this point it, didn't matter. Nothing mattered now. "Orlando."

***

Two young, impeccably-groomed flight attendants stood up immediately as Eric passed through the boarding door. They were both as shiny as new copper pennies. "Hi!" said the young woman. "You must be Eric. Are we glad to see you!"

"I'm Simon, and this is Jane," said the young man. "We just graduated from training last week. This is our very first flight."

Eric eyed them critically, even though they both looked adorable. "I can *tell* that you're new. Who else would be on this *stupid* trip but a couple of new hires?"

Jane and Simon exchanged a nervous glance. "We checked all the emergency equipment," said Jane. "Everything is in order. Can we start boarding? The passengers are very anxious to—"

"I don't give a damn *what* you do." Eric threw his suitcase into an overhead bin and slammed it as hard as he could. What a wonderful noise it made! "You two can deal with everything during boarding. I'll be in the coach galley setting up, with the curtain closed."

"No problem," said Simon, puffing out his chest. "We're ready for anything."

Oh, that delicious new-hire enthusiasm. Eric couldn't wait to squelch it. "And may I suggest," he said, "if you know what's good for you, that you *do not* disturb me until boarding is complete and I need to arm my door."

"Not to worry," said Jane.

Eric could see actual fear in their eyes. He'd never experienced that before and decided, on the spot, that eliciting such a response from two twenty-year-old greenhorns was delicious.

"Aren't you going to meet the captain, at least?" Simon suggested.

"The captain," Eric said, sounding more obnoxious by the second, even to himself, "can come to the back and introduce himself to *me*."

***

During taxi out, Eric and Jane performed the safety demo while Simon read the announcement over the PA system. His voice was as smooth and professional as a radio announcer. Eric could hear the satisfaction in Simon's voice as he went about performing his essential task as the number one flight attendant. As Eric perfunctorily pointed out the exits and demonstrated the proper use of the oxygen mask, he took great pleasure in the fact that no one was paying the slightest attention to anything that Simon said.

As he and Jane strapped into their jump seats in the back of the plane, she tried to make friends again. "We're going to dinner in Orlando tonight if we can scrape enough money together between the two us."

Oh, thought Eric. That perennial new-hire poverty. Should I tell her that she won't escape that for at least five years?

"We're going to Red Lobster," Jane added. "Would you like to come with us?"

"Red Lobster? You want me to come with you to *Red Lobster*?"

"If you like."

"*Fuck* Red Lobster!" he exclaimed, loud enough for the last ten rows to hear.

Jane looked as though he'd hit her with a raw flounder. "Never mind," she said, turning away from him. "Forget that I even asked."

***

Without verbally offering lunch, Eric slapped a snack basket down on each open tray table. *Slap, slap, slap.* He never knew that making noise could be so enjoyable. He pulled out another rack and dropped it on top of the meal cart with a loud metallic thud, and then pushed the cart back to row 20.

"Excuse me," said a woman in row 18. "You skipped me."

Eric didn't make eye contact with her. "You didn't have your tray table down," he said loudly enough to make every person within earshot pull down their tray table immediately.

"Well, I would *like* one," she said. "Can I please *have* one?"

He handed a basket to the closest passenger. "Would you pass this up to that lady in row eighteen with the, *ahem*, 'blond' hair, please?"

"Well," said the woman. "I never!"

"Yeah," said Eric. "I just *bet* you've never…"

"Eric!" said Jane, from the beverage cart a few rows in front of him. She was overwhelmed by having to prepare drinks for one hundred and thirty passengers on her own. "There's no vodka in here."

"There isn't?" he said. "Sorry, I guess the kitchen is out of vodka today."

"Out of vodka? How could the kitchen be out of vodka?"

"I don't know. Sometimes, they just run out."

"What'll I do?"

"Offer them gin, or go see if Simon has vodka to spare up front."

She tucked a loose strand of hair behind her ear. "Are you going to help with me with these drinks?"

"Yes, when I finish the meals!" he snarled. "You don't see *me* complaining because I have to serve all the meals by myself, *do you?*"

A passenger next to him stood up. "I can't believe this. You are the rudest steward I have ever met in my life!" Eric recognized him immediately. It was the desperate man from the inside the terminal who'd stopped him near the security checkpoint. "First you keep us all waiting for *three* hours in the terminal what you do God knows what—"

"Do you even know what you're talking about, sir? This isn't even my goddam flight!" said Eric. "I was *supposed* to be going to L.A."

"How dare you use such language in front of my children. Do you know who I am?"

"Yeah, you're the bozo who complained that we weren't even feeding you. Well, I'm feeding you *now*." He dropped three baskets at once on the man's tray table.

"What is your name?" the man demanded.

Oh, thought Eric, the old scare tactic. Don't even bother, buddy boy. "My name is Eric Saunders. S-a-u-n-d-e-r-s. Base: La Guardia."

"And what's your employee number?" said the man, clicking a pen.

"You don't need my employee number. I'm the only Eric Saunders in the entire company."

"Your supervisor will be hearing from me, that's for sure."

"Good! I can't wait!" said Eric. "It'll be my first bad letter. I'll frame it and hang in my living room." He looked up and down the aisle. "Does anybody *else* have a comment to make?" No one made eye contact with him—except Jane, who stood with her mouth open, horrified. "I didn't think so," he said, ramming the cart five rows further back. "Moving on!"

***

"Welcome to Orlando!" said the desk clerk at the hotel, with a warm smile.

"Thanks," Eric said snidely. "We're *thrilled* to be here."

She handed Eric the sign-in sheet. "Don't forget your free cookies," she said, gesturing toward a basket of individually wrapped chocolate chip cookies on the counter.

He rolled his eyes. "Someone else can have mine. I don't *want* it."

The clerk's friendly smile disappeared. "Enjoy your stay, sir," she said curtly.

Eric grabbed his key and headed straight to the elevator, leaving Jane and Simon behind. "What time do you want to go to dinner?" he heard Simon ask Jane.

"I don't even want to go to dinner anymore," Jane replied in a muffled voice. "I've never been so tired in my life. He was such a…" Her voice faded away.

"Wait here for me for one second," said Simon.

As Eric waited for the elevator, Simon came around the corner. "Hey, Eric, hang on for a second. I want to talk to you."

Eric pressed the elevator button again. "Whatever it is, you should have brought it up on the plane. I'm on *my* time now."

"Yeah, I would have, but I wanted to wait until we were alone. I just wanted to tell you that I think you're an *asshole*. In fact, you're the biggest asshole I've ever met."

"What the—"

"I may be a new hire, but I'm not an idiot. My mother's been a flight attendant for thirty years and my father is a captain. I knew that I'd meet some jerks on the line—I've heard all their horror stories—but you take the cake. Who the *fuck* do you think you are, anyway? The goddam CEO? Do you know that you made Jane cry? She was up in my galley after the service was over, crying her eyes out. This was our very first flight. It was supposed to be something special, a flight that we'd always remember. Well, we'll remember it all right, but not for any *good* reasons. I don't know what your fucking problem is or what great plans you had that got ruined when you were reassigned, and I don't care. But I suggest that you change your attitude completely before the return flight. Otherwise, when we get back to base, I'll march straight into the office and tell them all about our 'great' first flight and the contribution that you made to it. I know that you're off probation, but that doesn't mean that there aren't any consequences for your behavior. You're not even fucking *senior!* I can tell by your employee number that you've been flying for less a year."

"Fine. I'm sorry. How's that?" Please, he thought, fairly itching to get on the elevator and away from Simon. Let me get to my room and crack open a couple of vodka minis, and I might make it until midnight.

"That's not good enough," said Simon, standing with his arms folded across his chest. "You be down here in the lobby at nine A.M. tomorrow to apologize to both of us, and then you're treating us to breakfast. Understood?"

"Yes, it will be my pleasure."

"Good. We'll see you in the morning."

The elevator had finally arrived, thank God. Eric hopped in immediately.

Simon reached in and pressed the hold button. "By the way," he said. "You can get good and tanked on all that booze you swiped from the plane. But don't *ever* steal all the vodka again on a packed flight, full of angry people, and then expect your co-workers to cover for you. 'The kitchen must be out of vodka.' Even Jane didn't buy that bullshit story—and neither did the passengers. Think about *that* while you're knocking 'em back tonight."

Eric felt as though he'd been punched in the stomach. He grabbed the railing and tried to keep from hanging his head in shame. And it wasn't just because of his appalling behavior on the plane. It was also because he was being chewed out, and rightfully so, by a twenty-year-old co-worker with five minutes of seniority. "Please forgive me," he croaked. "I'm truly sorry that I ruined your first flight."

"So you say. Let's just hope that you're still as contrite when you wake up tomorrow morning. We'll see you in the lobby at nine."

"O.K. Goodnight, Simon."

"Goodnight."

***

Eric jumped out bed the next morning and fell to the floor in a tangle of sheets, bringing the ringing telephone with him. Oh, fuck! he thought, I'm late! I've missed breakfast with Simon and Jane. "Hello?" he croaked into the receiver.

"Good morning. This is your scheduled wake-up call. Have a wonderful day and thank you for choosing the Doubletree Orlando."

It was 8:30. Thank God, he had just enough time to jump in the shower and make himself look presentable. He has a brutal hangover. As he hung up the phone, he noticed a can of spilled club soda and ten empty vodka minis on the nightstand. He'd drunk all ten of them. Of course he had. What else was new? He also noticed a blinking red light on the phone, indicating that he had a voice mail. He must have been so drunk that he never heard the phone ring. I'd better check it just in case it's from Simon. Perhaps he and Jane have made other plans.

The message was not from Simon; it was from Denny. "Hi, Eric. I'm glad we talked last night and I'm glad that you're not mad at me anymore. I called again this morning and asked the operator to be sent right to your voicemail. I knew you were going to be up late, and I didn't want to wake you too early this morning. I still think it's ironic that neither one of us made to L.A. yesterday. Christ, I can't wait to get out of this fucking hotel in Chicago. We're out by the airport in the middle of nowhere. I could have gone into the city last night, but it was eighteen degrees and there was a foot of snow on the ground, and it just wasn't worth the effort. Anyway, I've thought about what you said, and I think your idea is a good one. You and I both need a major change. I have your passcode and I already took care of processing the computer entry. Hopefully, we'll hear something soon from crew planning. Anyway, I'll call you when I get back home—whenever the hell that is. I hear New York is still a mess. Have a good flight if you do get out of Orlando today. I'll see ya."

Eric hung up the phone in a daze. He'd talked to Denny last night? He couldn't remember a single word of the conversation. *Why* hadn't Denny made it to L.A.? Was it weather, a mechanical, a medical emergency? His daze turned to panic as the last part of Denny's message started to sink in. What idea of his was Denny talking about, and why was it a good one? If it involved using Eric's work passcode, it had to be something significant—and whatever it was, Eric didn't have a clue. Another night of blackout drinking, he thought. This one might have consequences, and I don't even know what the hell they are. In a fit of anger, he slammed the empty minis off the nightstand. The phone rang again. He grabbed it. "Hello, Denny?"

"No, this is Simon. Is this Eric?" At least his tone was cordial.

"Yes, good morning." He cleared his throat and made sure that his voice was upbeat. "How are you, Simon?"

"Fine. I'm just calling to see if we're still meeting at nine for breakfast."

"Yes, of course. I'm jumping in the shower right now. I'll be there on time."

"Good. We'll see you then. Don't forget: you're treating."

"I remember. See you in thirty minutes."

He jumped into the shower and turned the water on icy cold to make himself sober up. After thirty seconds of that torture, he turned it to hot and started scrubbing himself furiously. He'd smoked last night, too. He could smell the nicotine coming through his pores, even as he scrubbed. Fuck! he thought, trying to remember he'd told Denny to do with his passcode. What kind of trouble have I gotten myself into *now?*

CHAPTER 33

The Wheeler-Dealer

"Hi, sweet cheeks," said Denny, walking up to Eric in operations at JFK.

"Hey! What are you doing here?"

"I'm going to L.A. with you and Ginnie Jo. Last minute trip trade."

"Oh, great!"

"I was supposed to go to Phoenix today." He shuddered. "Phoenix."

"Which cabin are you working in?"

"Business class, with Ginnie Jo. I see you're in coach. Want to swap positions?" Denny asked hopefully.

"No. I avoid that cabin like the plague, especially on flights to Los Angeles."

"You know that you're working with Pavonia and Darcy today—the commuters. From DFW. They're going to make you crazy with all the commuter chit-chat—not to mention that unbearable twang."

"No, they won't. I've learned to tune it all out."

"Since when? You're the most noise sensitive person I know. You change subway cars if someone starts cracking their gum."

"Not anymore. It's a brand-new me. I've started transcendental meditation."

"Well, let's see how long that lasts."

"Besides, it will give me a chance to talk about the contract negotiation. I'm a 4-1-1 Rep for the union, you know. I want to make sure that people know what's going on."

"I applaud you for doing that. I don't have the patience. How's it going so far?"

"OK. It's strange, though: people seem to either be very well informed or they know nothing at all—except for galley gossip, which is invariably five miles north of the truth."

"It's always easier to make shit up than to read the union newsletter, even though it's mailed to their house every month."

"God willing the union has their current mailing address, and that they bother to read it," said Eric. "We have competition."

Denny nodded. "*People Magazine*. It's hard to put down the Sexiest Man Alive issue. I read that one myself."

"They *should* pay attention to what's happening. Alice Jacobson is a fantastic union president. She and the negotiating team have been working night and day for months on our behalf. We're this close to reaching a tentative agreement with the company on a new contract, which will then go to the membership for a vote. Every flight attendant needs to know what they'll be voting for—or against. And I don't want anybody screwing up my chance for a better salary, just because they're pissed off that Arbor Day won't be a paid holiday. God willing, we'll get a decent raise and I can finally stop applying for food stamps."

"Yes, God willing," Denny said, without much enthusiasm.

"I'm trying to keep a positive attitude. But truth be told, I'm not expecting much from these *gonnifs* in management—without a fight."

"*Gonnifs*," said Denny," nodding his head. "Thieves. That's a perfect Yiddish word to describe the people who run this airline. Obviously, you've been reading Sylvia Saks' old pamphlets from Kinderland."

"What's Kinderland?"

"A leftist summer camp in Massachusetts. It was very popular with Jewish families from New York, back in the day. They used to call it The Little Red Summer Camp. Is Sylvia planning a workers' revolt?"

"Don't laugh," said Eric. "I feel like revolting. Do you have any idea how many times I've applied for food stamps since I started working here? And I'm denied every time. My monthly salary is exactly twenty-five dollars too high. I'm living in New York on a starvation wage, paying federal, state *and* city taxes, and I can't even get government assistance."

"I know. I tried it too when I was new. It's a *shanda*—a disgrace. That's intentional on the company's part. They set the salary just over the legal limit for us to qualify. Otherwise, how would it look in the papers? 'Employees of a major American corporation can't even afford a loaf of bread.' Their feeling is: if you're that hard up, steal some liquor money. Then if you get caught and get fired, it's your own damn fault. They'll just hire someone new to replace you for less money."

"You see?! That kind of fucked up corporate mentality is exactly what I'm talking about."

"Hey, Eric. Watch that big mouth. You never know who's listening."

"Denny Malinovksi, are you afraid of management?"

"No. It's you I'm worried about. You need to learn to play your cards close to your chest." Denny nodded toward the managers' office. "Haven't you read *The Art of War*? You should never let them know what you're thinking."

"Ha! They're the ones who should be worried. There's strength in numbers, and there are twenty thousand of us. Twenty thousand angry people, including senior stews who are just as fed up with this company as the new hires. If this negotiation doesn't go well, it may even come down to a strike."

"Strike?!" said Ginnie Jo, joining them. "Who's going on strike?"

"Eric and Emma Goldman," said Denny.

"Did the union call a strike?" She looked wild-eyed. "How is that possible? We haven't even voted on a new contract yet!"

"Nobody has called a strike," said Eric. "We're just talking about the possibility of one."

"Oh, thank God. I wouldn't want to go through that shit again. Once was enough." She shook her head. "Crossing the picket line at ACA was the biggest mistake I ever made."

Denny and Eric exchanged a wary glance. As much as they liked Ginnie Jo, it was awkward at times to be friends with a former scab. "Let's not get all excited," said Eric. He showed her his union rep pin. "I'm just trying to make sure people are informed."

"Good for you. I bet you're a great one. Hey, Eric, I'm in business class today. Any chance you want to—"

"Don't bother," said Denny. "I already tried. He said no."

"Well, it never hurts to ask," she said. "Who's the purser today?"

"Candice Manion."

"Oh, good. I like her. She never minds coming back to deal with those jackasses when they start pushing me over the edge. And today especially I have no patience for them."

"Do you feel all right, Ginnie Jo?" said Eric.

"Yeah. Why?"

"You look tired."

She sighed. "I had a late night last night. I should have gotten to bed earlier."

"Earlier?" Eric looked at his watch. "It's two o'clock in the afternoon."

"Who are you, my mother?"

"No, I just worry about you."

"Oh, that's sweet." She kissed him on the cheek. "Thanks, honey. I'm glad that someone does." She looked at Denny imploringly. "Denny, you're gonna have to look out for me today. If even one of those assholes snaps his fingers for a wine refill, he's gonna lose them."

"We'll get through it," said Denny. "But I'll be curious to see who flips their wig first: you or Eric. He's working with the commuter brigade in coach. Who else is back there with you, Eric?"

Eric looked at the crew list. "A woman named Lana Everhart."

"Jackpot!" said Denny. "You'll be flipping before we reach Chicago."

"Is Lana a commuter too?" Eric asked casually.

"No, but she doesn't really work. She loafs for six hours. You might find yourself pulling double duty on this flight."

Eric pursed his lips. "We'll see about that. So, what do you guys want to do today? I thought that maybe we'd take the bus to the Santa Monica Pier."

"Sorry, babe," said Ginny Jo. "I'm good for Dealer Dan's and dinner near the hotel, and not much else. I don't have the energy."

"Oh, please don't make me go to Dealer Dan's," said Eric.

"What's wrong with Dealer Dan's?" said Ginnie Jo.

"Eric has never been there before," said Denny. "He prides himself on it."

"I just don't see the point in having an orgasm over a bag of peanut-butter stuffed pretzels," Eric said. "There has to be more to life."

"Get over it," said Ginny Jo. "My wine supply at home is running low, and it's too dangerous to take it off the plane right now. It's contract time. They want someone to fuck up. They're dying to make an example out of somebody to scare the bejesus out of the rest of us. For the time being, everybody needs to keep their noses clean."

"Well," said Eric. "I'm glad that somebody's reading the union newsletter! Thank you, Ginnie Jo. As a token of appreciation, I'll go to Dealer Dan's with you."

She rolled her eyes. "Your martyrdom for the cause is very noble."

"Yeah," said Denny. "Isn't it just?"

***

At five minutes before boarding, Eric was the only flight attendant in the coach cabin. He had checked all the emergency equipment, set out all the pillows and blankets, and examined the entire cabin for garbage that cleaners might have left behind. By the time that he started scooping up a pile of Cheerios smashed into the carpet, he had worked himself into a frenzy. Why the hell, he thought, am I doing the work of three other people who should already be here? He stopped mid-scoop to answer the crew phone.

"Hi, Eric. It's Candice. The catering rep is here and wants to know if you're missing anything back there."

"I wouldn't know," he replied testily. "I'm not working the galley today, and I haven't had time to check catering. I've been taking care of everything else since I'm the only one back here."

"I know, honey. I'll talk to the coach girls as soon as they get there. In the meantime, would you mind checking the catering? If you are missing anything, it's better that we know now, instead of halfway across the country."

"All right. I'll do it. But those girls better get here fast."

"Don't worry, we can't leave without them. Oh, here they are, with the passengers right on their heels. Thanks for doing that, honey. I'll make it up to you, I promise."

A moment later, Darcy and Pavonia came rushing down the aisle. Darcy, as usual, looked neat and tidy. Her buster brown haircut always maintained its shape, even under the most adverse weather conditions. Pavonia, on the other hand, was a mess. She wore her wall of fried blond hair exactly as she always did: piled on top of her head and pinned with a large plastic clip. Raggedy tendrils were spilling out everywhere. If I were a supervisor, Eric thought, I'd come up behind her with a pair of scissors and chop that mess right off her head, just like they did to Ginnie Jo in training. As satisfying as that image was, he said nothing aloud. It was pointless. No matter what grooming missives came from headquarters, some flight attendants couldn't be bothered to make an effort.

"I cain't believe we made this flight!" said Pavonia. "We like to never get here. First of all, there were twenty other non-revs ahead of us on the standby list. We ended up having to take jump seats in the coach galley. For three hours we sat on those damned jump seats!"

Oh my God, thought Eric. They can't wait even one minute before they start sharing the minutia about their commute. As if I give a damn!

"It was ridiculous!" said Darcy. "This first-come, first-serve business on the standby list is bullshit! Commuting flight attendants should come first. We're trying to get to work."

Well, Eric wanted to say, if you just *lived* where you *work*, it wouldn't be an issue. Besides, the first-come, first-serve policy is the only fair way to assign free seats to employees to the standby list. He knew from experience, however, that it was useless to broach that topic, too.

"And then we had terrible thunderstorms at DFW this morning," Pavonia added. "There's always thunderstorms at DFW. You cain't win for losing!"

Just ignore them, thought Eric. Let it go in one ear and out the other.

"Then we had to wait forever to get takeoff clearance," said Pavonia, "and *then* it took forever to get here to JFK from La Guardia."

Darcy sighed. "We would have been on time, Pavonia, if we'd just taken Queensborough Car Service. I mean, there was a driver available right there in front of the terminal."

"I told you, Darcy, I am not getting into any car with a driver who wears a diaper on his head."

"I think you mean a turban," said Eric. "Was he a *sikh*?"

"If that means 'Middle Eastern terrorist,' then yes, I'm sure he was."

Oh, brother, thought Eric. Can anyone be that stupid?

"Stop whining, Pavonia, and just get in here and help me set up," said Darcy, stepping into the galley. Pavonia followed right behind her. Darcy grabbed the curtain and yanked it closed.

"Hey there!" A voluptuous brunette wearing spike heels came teetering down the aisle. She wore an emerald-green pashmina draped around her shoulders that clashed violently with her uniform. "I'm Lana."

He immediately wrote her off. "Eric," he said.

"Good to meet you. Geez, I'm sorry I'm so late," she mumbled, "but I had to get the kids off to school and get my get husband off to work, and then there was an accident on the Whitestone Bridge, and I..."

Eric strained to understand her as she chewed a wad of cinnamon gum. "…and then I was halfway here when I realized that I'd left my ID badge at home!" She draped her pashmina and blazer over the last row of seats. "Anyway, where should I put my luggage?"

Eric took a deep breath. He knew from reading the crew list that Lana had been flying for at least ten years. How could she not know something as basic as where to put her luggage? "In an overhead bin, I guess, like the rest of us."

Chomp, crack. "There's no closet back here?"

"No, there isn't a closet," he said, wondering if she had even been on an airplane in the last ten years.

She struggled to lift her suitcase overhead, shifting her weight from one wobbly leg to another, and then suddenly let it drop to the floor. "Hey, Aaron, can you help me put this up?" She made a helpless face. "It's really heavy."

Without answering, Eric ducked into the lavatory, slammed the door closed, and locked it. The clicking sound of the locking mechanism was deeply satisfying. God dammit, he thought, I should have traded with Denny. Working in 'bitter' class couldn't be as bad as this. He leaned against the counter and spent three minutes breathing in through one nostril and then out through the other. Once he felt sufficiently calm, he opened the door and stepped back into the cabin. Both aisles were already full of passengers.

"Never mind about my suitcase," said Lana. "A passenger helped me put it up."

"Good," said Eric, smiling. "That's what they're here for, after all."

"It was that hot guy, right there," said Lana, pointing to an attractive young man in a sailor uniform. "He was glad to help. You can always count on the men of America's Armed Forces. Hey, Aaron—"

"It's Eric."

"Sorry. Hey, Eric, where's my jump seat on this bird?"

Eric flared his nostrils. He couldn't help it; it was either flare his nostrils or wring her neck. "Try looking in the station assignment chart in your *manual*. It's all there, in black and white—anything and everything you may need to know about doing your job today."

"Wow, you're a little uptight. Are you a new hire?"

"No," said Eric. "Are you?" Without waiting for a reply, he ducked into the lavatory again. Slam, click! Breathe in, breathe out, breathe in, breathe out. It was useless. Oh, fuck this shit! Maybe I have one of Denny's little white pills in my bag. I always swore I'd never take one on the airplane, but maybe just this once, to get me through this flight…

***

Once the plane had leveled off at cruising altitude, Eric stood up. It was a little bumpy at 30,000 feet, but to not too bumpy to walk around. He felt deliciously calm, thanks to Denny's pill. He was still alert, just in case anything out of the ordinary happened. But like magic, the muscle relaxer had taken the edge off his anxiety. He reached into an overhead bin and took out two bags of headsets.

"Eric," said Darcy, as she put on her apron. "Do you and Lana mind selling headsets on our side? Pavonia and I have a little more setting up to do before we can start the service."

"No problem." He placed one bag in the empty last rows of seats and waited for Lana to come to the back from her over-wing jump seat. She appeared a moment later, still wearing her spike heels, grabbing onto seatbacks as she made her way to the back of the plane. I won't be surprised if she falls right off those fucking shoes, thought Eric. He passed a bag of headsets to her. "Do you mind doing headsets on the other side? They're still setting up the galley."

"Sure. How much do we charge for headsets these days?"

"Five dollars."

"Wow, that much? The last time I sold one, I think it was two dollars! How much are mixed drinks, by the way, in case anyone orders one?"

"Beer, wine and liquor are all five dollars."

"Wow." She shook her head. "We used to sell Bloody Mary's for a buck a pop on the 747! And we sold hundreds of 'em!"

Eric looked at her in wonder. Mercury had not operated a 747 domestically for at least ten years. "Exactly how long has it been since you worked your last trip?" he asked.

"I can't even remember. I only fly one trip a year. That's what the FAA or *somebody* requires. I drop all my trips every month. It took me forever to pack today!"

"Do you have another job?"

"Nah, I'm just so darn busy all the time, with the kids and all. Who has time to fly?" She winked. "Good thing my husband makes a lot of money!"

There you have it, he thought. A rich bitch from Connecticut who doesn't have to work, has no idea what's going on here, and probably doesn't even care. I'll bet that her union newsletter is at home buried under a stack of Bergdorf Goodman catalogs.

"Let me just change into my flats and we can get started," said Lana. She reached for her tote bag and unzipped it. "Oh, dammit! I put them in my suitcase this morning." She opened the overhead bin where the suitcase was jammed inside. "Can you help me—"

"I'll start on the left-hand side," said Eric. "You start on the other side whenever you're ready."

"So much for team spirit," said Lana. She tapped the sailor on the shoulder and smiled. "Sir, I hate to ask you to get up, but would you mind…?"

***

That afternoon, Eric sat in the hotel lobby impatiently waiting for Denny and Ginny Jo. Even though he had quit smoking for an entire week, he was dying for a cigarette. Thank God that Denny and Ginny Jo still smoke, he thought. Maybe they'll let me bum one. And perhaps we can stop someplace for a quick drink before we head for Dealer—

"There you are," said Denny, stepping off the elevator, with Ginnie Jo right behind him.

"What do you mean, 'there you are'?" Eric snapped. "I'm right on time. We said four o'clock. It's now four-fifteen."

"Oh, did we say four o'clock? I could barely understand you, you were in such a rush to get to your room today. And you didn't say a word on the van. So, how did it go in coach?"

"Just as you said it would. I dealt with it," said Eric, lying through his teeth. "How was business class? Were they demanding wine refills from takeoff to landing?"

"On the contrary," said Ginny Jo. "It was one of the best flights I ever had. We both got fifty-dollar tips from this guy in the last row. He loved us!"

"How nice for you."

"So dinner is on us," said Denny.

"Good," said Eric. "Can we skip Dealer Dan's and go right to dinner?"

"Nothing doing," said Ginny Jo. "We're going right now. We'll drop our goodies back at the hotel after we finish shopping, and then we'll go to dinner. I'll even buy you a bottle of wine to take home."

"Well, that's something at least," said Eric.

"Did you get to talk about the contract negotiation?" Denny asked.

"Yes. Darcy and Pavonia were surprisingly well informed. They know each step in the process, and what will happen if we vote 'no' on a tentative agreement. It means we go right back to the drawing board and start the process all over again from scratch. Lana, on the other hand, doesn't know shit. She doesn't even know the name of the union president. I loathe people like her."

"I'm with you, Eric," said Denny. "That's the problem with flight attendants who drop all their trips. They have no stake in anything. They're usually senior, so they hold the best trips and best vacations. They keep their flying benefits and insurance, but they don't ever work and they never have a clue as to what's going on. The next time Lana shows up, it will probably be the day that we go on strike. She's so clueless she won't even know she's crossing her own picket line!"

"That set up is ridiculous," said Eric. "What other major corporation would allow it to exist? Either you work here or you don't. I don't know why the company allows people to stay on the payroll when they don't work for years at a time. If I were in charge—"

"Boys," said Ginny Jo, "you're giving me a headache. Let's do our shopping and then go have a nice drink somewhere. And just for a little while, let's talk about something else."

The trio walked silently the rest of the way to Dealer Dan's, which was in a strip mall several blocks from the hotel. "I can't believe you've never been here before, Eric," said Ginnie Jo.

"Well, I haven't. The last thing I want on a layover is to be trapped in a crowded space with a gaggle of flight attendants."

"What about the Midnight Sun during Happy Hour?" said Denny.

"That's completely different."

They entered the small cramped store, which was a madhouse of activity. Eric was instantly put off by the kitschy décor and horrid staff uniforms. All the employees wore a tuxedo shirt under a garish emerald-green vest with buttons designed to look like a pair of dice. Their bowties and sleeve garters were the same shade of green. The aisles were chockful of frenzied shoppers who squealed with delight as they grabbed item after item and them into overflowing shopping sounds. The sound could be heard every few seconds, all over the store, as favored items were snatched up. Chips, dips, salsa and a mind-blowing variety of hummus seemed to make up the bulk of their purchases. Two-dollar bottles of wines disappeared from crates before the stockers could even put them on the shelves.

"I recognize a lot of these people," said Eric, pointing. "She's based in New York, and she's based in New York, and so is he."

"I think every customer in this store is a flight attendant," said Denny. "You can tell just by looking at them."

"Christ, what a scene!" said Ginnie Jo, taking cover behind Eric and Denny. "We should have had a drink first."

"Hey, this was your idea," said Eric.

"Let's grab a bag of chips and three bottles of wine and split, OK? I'm about to break out in hives."

"What kind of chips do you want?" said Denny. "They sell five hundred different kinds."

"Just get some—"

"Good afternoon, ladies, and gents!" a man's voice boomed over the PA system. "And welcome to Dealer Dan's! This is your lucky day, shoppers! In just a few minutes, at five o'clock sharp, we're gonna play Spin the Wheel, hosted by yours truly, Dealer Dan himself!"

A collective shriek of excitement went up. It was so loud and sustained that Eric had to cover his ears.

"So make your way toward the Magic Wheel, shoppers, and let's see which lucky Club Card member is going to win—and win big! I mean, *really big!*"

Carts were abandoned *en masse* as a horde of people rushed to the front of the store. "Jesus," said Eric. "What is this, *Let's Make a Deal?*"

"Hey, Denny!" said a cute redhead as he raced by them.

"Oh, hi Jason." Denny grabbed him by the arm. "Hang on a second, let me introduce you to my friends, Ginnie Jo and Eric. They're based in New York, too."

"Nice to meet you. Aren't you guys coming to play? Last week, a woman on my crew won a whole case of wine!"

"We're not Club Card members. We don't shop here that often."

"Then just come to watch what happens. Dan is hot!"

They followed Jason and wedged themselves into the back of the tittering crowd. A handsome blond man stood in front of a large, upright roulette wheel. He wore a visor, a green bow tie, and a vest like the other employees. But he was bare-chested underneath the vest, and obviously proud to show off his muscular body.

"Wow!" said Denny. "Look at those arms! They're like Popeye's! So that's Dealer Dan, huh?"

"In the flesh," said Jason. He sighed. "What I wouldn't give to lick that man from head to toe."

"And he's here every week?"

"Yes, but you never know on which day. He likes the element of surprise, and so do the customers."

"What a crowd!" said Dan, beaming at his loyal cadre of customers. "I love it!"

"And we love you, Dan!" Eric recognized Pavonia's voice immediately.

"Look at your Club Card, folks. If the last three numbers match the digits that come up on the wheel, you'll win a case of Saborosa Salsa…"

"A case of salsa," someone muttered. "Is that all?"

"…and a two-liter bottle of Maravillosa Margarita mix… to go with your case of Tío Thomás Tequila!" At the mention of free liquor, the crowd went mad. Dan turned to face the spinning wheel and paused to let the crowd enjoy the sight of his beautiful rear end, which seemed ready to burst through his tight pants. Although Eric said nothing, he gawked right along with everyone else.

"Here we go!" said Dan. As everyone stood expectantly with their cards in hand, Dan spun the wheel and waited for it to stop. "One! One is the first number. Now, let me spin it once again!" The wheel came to rest on 1 again. "One again! Let's go for the magical third spin, my friends." There was an agonizing wait as the wheel slowed down and finally came to rest on 5. "One-one-five. Do we have a winner?"

A woman standing right in front shrieked, dropped her card, and fell to the floor in a dead faint.

"Now that's what I call a satisfied customer," said Dan, as he reached down to help her up.

The woman opened her eyes. When she realized that she was only inches away from Dan's bare chest, she looked as though she might faint again. The crowd gathered around her, ostensibly to help her up. In reality, they were only trying to get closer to Dan: to shake his hand, to stroke his massive arms, or make a playful grab at his blond curls.

"OK, I've had enough," said Eric. "Let's get back to our cart, get our stuff, and get the hell out of here."

As they reached their cart in the red wine aisle, another commotion was taking place near the back of the store. Darcy flew by them and came to a screeching halt next to Pavonia, who was shopping for white wine one aisle over.

"Darcy," said Pavonia, "what do you think about Chantilly Chardonnay? It's only three dollars for a bottle. I don't care for that two-dollar wine."

"Never mind that!" said Darcy. "Do you know who's here? Wilma Cherrywood!"

"Oh, my God. Are you serious?!"

"She's here on a layover. So are Kimmy Sue Connelly and Bonita Ivers. And guess what: we're gonna have a C. of C. meeting right here! Today!"

"A C. of C. meeting! And we're here for it! I can't believe it! Praise Jesus!"

"Kimmy Sue has already arranged a space for us with the manager of the hotel. He's going to let us use a vacant conference room for free!"

"What time does it start?"

"In thirty minutes. Let's pay for our stuff and get out of here!"

"Wait a minute now. We need to pick up some extra goodies. We can't just walk into that meeting empty-handed."

"I've got plenty, let's go."

Before Pavonia and Darcy could even turn themselves around, other shoppers came whizzing by, all talking excitedly about "the meeting… the meeting … *the meeting!*" In a matter of seconds, news of the event had spread through the store like a wildfire.

"Come on," said Denny, grabbing four bottles of wine. "We're going."

"Thank you!" said Eric. "I cannot take another minute of this place or these people!"

"No, I mean we're going to that meeting."

"Forget it. I am not going to a Church of Christ meeting," said Eric. "I got enough of that Fundamentalist crap growing up in Texas. You two go on without me. I'll have dinner alone."

"No, no, no," said Denny. "It's not a religious thing. C. of C. stands for Circle of Commuters. It's a system-wide support group for flight attendants who commute. I can't believe you've never heard of it. Darcy Usher is the head of the New York chapter."

"Why on earth would I want to subject myself to even ten minutes of that?"

"For pure entertainment value. You won't believe the crap they talk about!"

"I'm game," said Ginny Jo," as long as they're serving drinks. I could use a good laugh."

"It's BYOB," said Denny, "but we're more than covered. Come on, Eric. We're already buying you a bottle of wine and dinner. You should be there anyway, to take notes."

"To take notes for whom?"

"For the negotiating team. You want to take the pulse of the membership, right? You want to know what people are really thinking? Well, just wait until you get a load of this group."

"But how would we even get in the door? We're not commuters."

"We'll fake it. We'll show up at the last minute and take seats in the back. All the diehards will be sitting up near the front. If anyone says anything, let me do the talking."

"Oh, all *right*," said Eric. "But I know I'm going to regret it."

CHAPTER 34

A Meeting of Like Minds

The C. of C. meeting was held in the Pacifica ballroom. A middle-aged woman wearing a tan pantsuit and a large gold crucifix around her neck was seated at table just outside the entrance. A hastily written name badge identified her as Bonita Ivers—one of the organizers mentioned at Dealer Dan's. She eyed the trio suspiciously. "Can I help you?"

"We're here for the meeting."

"Where are y'all based?"

"We're from New York," said Eric

"That's funny," Bonita said. "I've been based in New York for five years, and I've never seen any of you at a meeting before. Or on a standby list at the airport, for that matter."

"That's because we're just *thinking* of becoming commuters," Denny said smoothly. "We've had it with living New York."

"New York is a swill hole," said Eric. "It's the noisiest, filthiest—"

"We like being *based* in New York," said Denny, interrupting Eric before he went overboard. "It's great to be off reserve and to hold a beautiful schedule. We just don't like living there. We miss our families and friends back home."

Ginny Jo nodded. "I miss my pastor and my church most of all. I feel so… unmoored lately. I have to get back home. I want to try it *your* way," she said with all the piety of a true believer.

Bonita handed them a clipboard. "Sign in legibly, please. Make sure we have your home address and phone number. And make a name tag for yourself before you go in. They're right there on the table. What did you bring for your contribution?"

"This." Denny reached into his Dealer Dan shopping bag and pulled out a bottle of wine, an economy-size bag of blue corn chips, and a large tub of guacamole.

Bonita laughed. "Good Lord! I have never seen so much Chantilly Chardonnay in my life. It seems like that's all anyone is going to be drinking today. Well, set your goodies on the table in the back and take a seat. We're starting in just one minute."

They entered the room and took seats in the second to last row. There were approximately two hundred people in the room. Over the general din, Eric could make out snatches of conversation: lonely nights spent sleeping in operations… missed birthdays, anniversaries, and soccer games… Mercury's absurd, antiquated system for placing employees on the airport standby list on a first-come, first-serve basis. His head started to throb. He gulped his plastic glass of Chardonnay and made a beeline for the refreshment table for a refill.

"What'll you have?" asked the flight attendant who was staffing the table. He was a stout young man with tortoiseshell eyeglass frames. His name badge identified him as named Craig W. from Chicago.

"White wine, please."

Craig filled Eric's glass. "There you go."

"Could I have some of those?" He gestured toward the bags of chips and bowls of dip arranged on the table.

"Those are for later," Craig replied. "People make too much noise otherwise. Nobody can hear the speaker over the crunching."

Eric took his wine and took a seat next to Denny and Ginny Jo. A moment later, he felt a tap on his shoulder. "Eric?"

He turned around and saw pregnant Rebecca, whom he hadn't seen since their adventure in Miami. She appeared to be at least six months pregnant. "Rebecca! How nice to see you! It's been… months."

"I know." She patted her baby bump. "A lot has changed since the last time I saw you."

"Where's Dick?"

Rebecca shook her head sadly. "We're not together anymore. Once he found out I was pregnant, he left me. I guess he thought it would interfere with our 'spontaneous' lifestyle. I thought about having an abortion, but I couldn't go through with it. I'll have to raise the baby without him."

"I'm sorry to hear that. You guys were such a great couple."

"I thought so, too." She laughed bitterly. "Just goes to show you never *really* know someone until the chips are down."

"Are you still living in Brooklyn?"

"No, I couldn't possibly raise the baby alone in New York. I'm back living with my folks in Pittsburgh."

"You mean… you're a commuter now?"

"Yes, on Mercury Express. We only have three flights a day to La Guardia. And it's *murder*."

He took out a pen and scribbled his number on a piece of paper. "Here's my number. If I can ever do anything for you—"

"Ladies and gentlemen, if everyone will take a seat, we'll get started," Eric heard a woman say from the front of the room. She had a babyish voice. She must be a very young commuter, thought Eric: a new hire who spent six months in New York and raced right back to Paducah once she got her travel benefits. Her boyfriend, Mack the mechanic—who had been her sweetheart since the second grade—had probably told her to come back home and start commuting to work—or quit flying altogether.

Denny nudged Eric. "Get a load of the group leader," he said.

Eric turned to face the front of the room. The blue-eyed woman standing there in a sundress and sandals was definitely not a new hire. She had a haggard face, sun-bleached hair, and skin that was the color of a saddle. Eric immediately assumed that she was from Florida. Another one who's spent twenty-five years baking in the sun, he thought.

The speaker cleared her throat. "Welcome to our impromptu meeting of the Circle of Commuters. My name is Kimmie Sue Connelly. I'm the chairperson of the Miami chapter."

"Florida: I knew it," Eric whispered. "All that's missing is the flip-flops."

"Aren't we all lucky," said Kimmie Sue, "to have the sisterhood—and brotherhood, hi, guys!—all gathered together in one place on this beautiful day!" Her childlike voice contrasted so sharply with her appearance that Eric had to stifle a laugh.

The crowd enthusiastically applauded her opening remarks. "The Lord Jesus gave us this day!" shouted one attendee.

Kimmie Sue smiled and looked around the room. For just a moment, she made eye contact with Eric. At that moment, his blood ran cold; it was like staring down an alligator as it surfaced in a swamp. There was nothing behind her eyes. *Nothing*. The plastic cup of wine slipped out of his hand and fell to the floor.

"We have a lot of ground to cover and some sensational speakers. We're here to support each other and to share our experiences. And even more importantly, to enlighten others about what we go through as commuters."

"Oh fuck," muttered Ginnie Go, standing up. She quickly headed for the refreshment table and returned with a glass of wine in each hand.

"A few months ago," said Kimmie Sue, "in our quarterly newsletter, we decided to have a contest to find the flight attendant who has the absolute worst commute. We received hundreds of entries and spent weeks pouring over them." She shook her head wearily. "Let me tell you, friends: I didn't know that it was possible for one human heart to break so many times. Pittsburgh to New York... Bangor to Miami... Champagne-Urbana to Chicago... Waxahachie to L.A. Planes, trains, buses and automobiles. The stories just kept coming and coming and *coming!*"

Darcy left her seat and joined Kimmie Sue. "And for our co-workers who *don't* commute," she said, "they are gonna *start* hearing these stories, even if I have to tell 'em twenty-four hours a day!"

Kimmie Sue grabbed Darcy's hand. "That's my girl! For those of you who don't know this incredible lady, her name is Darcy Usher. She commutes from Killeen, Texas via DFW and she is the chairperson of the New York chapter.

She's a real dynamo and has worked tirelessly on our behalf for over five years. Darcy, would you take the honor of introducing our first speaker?"

"I'd love to," said Darcy. "Folks, the winner of our contest goes to such lengths to get to her base city that we almost couldn't believe what we were reading. But in our hearts, we knew it had to be real. When we found out that she was here in Los Angeles today, we knew that we had to bring us all together to let her tell her story in person. Some of it you might find hard to listen to. But it's the truth. And that's what we're after: the truth! Please welcome Wilma Cherrywood."

The crowd applauded as a woman with neatly pinned-up auburn hair and green eyes stepped up to the front of the room. "Well, hello there," she said. "My name is Wilma Cherrywood. I'm originally from Duluth, Minnesota but transferred to Miami five years ago, when Mercury opened a new crew base there. We were delighted to make the move. My husband, Dale, and I had just had it with the weather up north and were thrilled to be living someplace where you could actually see the sun during the winter months. Then, just about a year after we moved, Dale was offered a job with a company based in Barrow, Alaska. It was an excellent opportunity for him career-wise, one that we felt that we couldn't pass it up. As far as *my* employment was concerned, there aren't many jobs available for women in the northern-most city in Alaska, unless I wanted to drive a snow plow. Can you imagine me doing that?" she asked. The crowd chuckled as they shook their heads. "So I decided to keep flying and commute. Here's an example of what I do to get myself to work at Miami International Airport:

"My commute starts three days before the day of my actual trip. I get up at four A.M. and start the coffee—Dealer Dan's Wild Woman Blend is my favorite. While it's brewing, I dress to the mournful sound of grey wolves howling outside. As I pour the coffee into my Sears thermos and pack food for the journey, Dale gets the Huskies and the sled ready. We only have one car, so I had to find an alternate method of transportation to get myself to Anchorage for the first leg of my commuter flight. As I settle myself into the sled, Dale ties my luggage to the back and lays a bearskin across my lap. I give him a sweet goodbye kiss through the flap of my face mask, and then with a cheery "Mush!" off we go! Destination: the Yanomacko tribe, five hundred miles and ten hours away. I am captivated, as always, by the moonlight shining on the snow-covered fields. The silence is broken only by the occasional ringing of my satellite phone as my co-workers call to trip trade with me. Hallelujah, someone wants my La Guardia turnaround on the tenth! Dale will be so happy! That's one less trip to worry about this month. I stop at the halfway point to give the dogs a rest, and to nourish myself with carefully prepared snacks. It's usually Dealer Dan's 'Dang, This Is Delicious!' dried fruit and nut mix. If I'm really hungry, I'll have a baby penguin filet or two, which I can cook in a jiffy on my kerosene mini stove. The coffee and snacks are scrumptious, and I wish that I could take a longer rest, but I have no time to dilly-dally. I must reach my destination before nightfall. I arrive just as the evening meal is about to be served. It's always such a joy to see other human beings after my long journey! I am warmly greeted by the children, who lead me by the hand to the dinner table in the main hut. After feasting on fresh fish, caught through the ice by the older boys, and freshly baked bread slathered in seal butter, I am led to the ceremonial hut. Inside, I am disrobed, tenderly bathed, rubbed down with fragrant oils, and presented to the tribal chief for his sensual pleasure."

The audience gasped *en masse*, but Wilma continued without missing a beat. "Dale would probably not like that part, but there are no hotels nearby and I can't sleep outside with the dogs, for heaven's sake! Besides, they throw in the meals free of charge. The next morning, after a hearty breakfast, I wave goodbye to my wonderful hosts and then I'm off again.

"By the next evening, I am securing the dogs to post in the employee parking lot of the Anchorage International Airport. I know my that friend who works in the guard house will take good care of them until I return. I hop on a bus and am whisked away to the main terminal. The agents who work at the ticket counter there are so sweet! They never charge me an excess baggage fee to check my sled. I've had so many altercations with flight attendants about stowing it on board that I don't even bother trying anymore. I attempt to sleep during the all-nighter to Seattle, but sometimes I'm just too keyed up. So I always bring my knitting or a couple of catalogs or some inspirational literature. They all seem to have a soothing effect. By the next morning, a little worse for wear, the day bed in the ladies' room at Seattle-Tacoma Airport is calling my name and I ready to claim it as my own.

"After a quick nap, I am off on the Mercury flight to Miami, via Chicago O'Hare. Miami Operations is a madhouse, as always, and I need some shut-eye before my oh-six-hundred sign-in the next morning. If it's too noisy or crowded in the crew lounge, I take out the leftover baby penguin filets and heat 'em up on my trusty mini stove. That clears the area fast! After a good night's sleep, it's a quick sponge bath in the lav of the closest Ultra Jet, and *voilà!* I am fresh as a daisy and ready to greet my passengers! At the end of my trip, I do the same commute in reverse back to Barrow. By the time that I get home and get the dogs tied up, I'm bone tired, absolutely exhausted. Sometimes I don't think that I can stand to commute for even one more trip. But then Dale's at the door to greet me, and I smell something heavenly cooking on the stove, and I'm getting reacquainted with our other animals, and suddenly it's all worth it and I'd never live anywhere else. And that's my story."

Wilma nodded humbly and took her seat as the crowd gave her a round of thunderous applause. A few of the attendees sat with their arms crossed, glaring at her, but only a few. While sympathetic to Wilma's plight, their high moral character would never permit such an illicit arrangement.

Darcy stood up and addressed the crowd again. "Thank you, Wilma. I knew we made the right choice when we selected your story for first prize. Now, I think I see high and mighty judgement in *some* of your eyes, but let me remind you what the Bible says: 'Judge not, lest ye be judged.' I'm sorry to say that our second and third prize winners could not be here today. So what we'd like to do now is—"

"Wait! I have a story to tell!" All eyes turned to Pavonia as she stood up. "May I?"

"Of course," said Darcy. "Ladies and gentlemen, may I present my buddy bidder, fellow-commuter from Killeen, and my best friend in the world: Pavonia Lee Rickerson."

Pavonia stepped forward and took a deep breath before she started speaking. "A few months ago, I decided to give up my crash pad in Kew Gardens. I don't have to stay overnight in New York that often anymore, and I couldn't see any reason to keep paying two hundred dollars a month for a bed I rarely slept in. So I thought that on those rare occasions when I did have to spend the night, I'd sleep in operations. Frankly, I was glad to save the money. But then that very first month, I had several very late arrivals into New York, and by the time I got to ops, all the chairs were taken. I didn't mind making a bed for myself on the floor. But the purser from my flight, who is also a commuter, was sleeping on the floor right next to me. I had to spend the whole night watching his wiener flopping in and out of his boxer shorts! And when he wasn't flipping and flopping, someone else was farting and belching. After two trips, I began to regret my decision. Then, one day, this woman struck up a conversation with me on the Q10 bus. She worked for a new airline that flew primarily Eastern European routes and mentioned that her landlord was looking for a couple of commuters. He'd lost a few tenants unexpectedly and wanted to replace them as soon as possible. She hinted that the rent would be more than reasonable, so I agreed to go over and see the place that very afternoon.

"Well, it wasn't the coziest crash pad I'd ever set foot in, but it was right on the bus line to JFK, and the rent was only one hundred dollars a month, and it was females only. So I moved in the very next day. Everything seemed OK at first. I noticed, though, that the other girls in the apartment didn't fly very often. They just sat around in their bathrobes all day waiting for crew scheduling to call them. I figured they were on reserve and didn't want to bother having to change again if they got assigned to a trip. They didn't have much to speak of in the way of their own wardrobes anyway. Just odds and ends shoved into those big, striped heavy-duty plastic bags that you buy at the dollar store. That was their regulation crew luggage, believe it or not! They were facinated by my Rollaboard suitcase. Sometimes, they'd spend the whole afternoon wheeling it around the apartment. The poor things, they didn't make much money and couldn't afford to go anywhere or do anything. Just to be nice, I'd tried to strike up a conversation occasionally, but they weren't very talkative. I figured they were embarrassed because their English wasn't very good. But boy, could they communicate whenever I brought food home! They 'd circle like vultures, no matter what I set on the table. It got to the point where if I wanted to eat in peace, I'd have to lock myself in the bathroom with my headphones on and my music playing full blast to drown out the sound of their pitiful cries. 'Food! Please! Give us food!'

"The second week, I came back from a trip at one in the morning and found, to my horror, that the landlord had brought six more girls into the apartment. Not only that, he'd moved all six of them into my bedroom! Boy, was I steamed! I marched right upstairs to his apartment and started banging on the door. Some woman, who was obviously expecting her boyfriend, opened it wearing nothing but her bra and panties underneath a filthy bathrobe. She dropped the cigarette that was dangling from her mouth and started screaming, 'Mikael! Mikael! Girl from downstairs vants to see you!' After much shouting back and forth, the landlord finally staggered to the door, swigging vodka right out of a bottle. He listened to me rant and rave for about thirty seconds. Then he shrugged his shoulders and said, 'Vat you vant for a hundred dollars a month?' Then he slammed the door right in my face! I was so mad I couldn't even see straight! I stomped back downstairs, only to discover that my belongings had been ransacked by those awful girls. If they weren't forcing their big buttocks into my clothes or applying my makeup in the bathroom mirror, they were drinking my wine and eating my baked-on-board cookies. That was the last straw. I was moving out! I packed up what I could salvage and was heading to the door when suddenly someone kicked it in. It was the police! They shoved us all against the wall and handcuffed us. As it turns out, Mikael wasn't running a crash pad. He was running a whorehouse out of the apartment upstairs! Can you *believe* it!"

The entire first row recoiled in shock. Bonita closed her eyes and mumbled over her crucifix.

"All the neighbors were standing around on the sidewalk, watching as we were shoved into police cars and taken to the precinct for booking. I have never been so embarrassed in my life. I couldn't reach any of my friends. I couldn't even get a union rep on the phone! The only thing that saved me was my crewmember ID and a frantic phone call to my supervisor, and even then, it took two days and a sworn statement from her to get me released! The police initially didn't buy my story. They kept saying that nobody could be that stupid, but I guess they got tired of me crying and banging my head against the bars. They finally released me around midnight. Having nowhere else to go, I took the Q10 bus to JFK and headed for ops. And wouldn't you know it: there was the wiener man, flipping and flopping, just like before! I turned my face into the pillow and cried myself to sleep. It was the worst experience of my whole life. Which brings me to the whole point for telling my story: where the hell was my union rep? I've paid my union dues every month for the past five years! And they left me high and dry in a jail cell full of foreign prostitutes! I could have been sent to prison or deported!" Then she burst into tears. Darcy led her to a seat and offered her Kleenex and a glass of wine. Even though the audience was clucking in sympathy for her, Pavonia sat down and hung her head in shame.

"Trials... trials and tribulations!" shouted a woman, jumping up. "And pain! *Lord*, our *pain! We* know. We know all about it. *They're* the ones who don't know... and they act like they *don't* want to know."

"But they're *gonna* know!" yelled Craig W. "Oh, yes, sir, they *are!*"

Kimmie Sue paced back and forth in the front of the room. Then she stopped and slowly turned to face the audience. "I'll tell you why you couldn't find a union rep, Pavonia: it's because the union doesn't give a damn about commuters! If they did care, they'd have done something about our plight by now. They say it's our choice to commute, and then they leave us high and dry whenever there's a crisis. Well, *we're* the ones who get to make a choice now. And our choice is going to have huge effect, and I mean *huge!* I have some information that I think you will all find very interesting. And I'll share with all of you once I have your undivided attention." One reptilian glance at the first row was all it took to quiet them down. "I am pleased to report that just thirty minutes ago, the union and the company reached a tentative agreement on a new contract."

"What the hell?!" Eric shouted. "That's impossible. How would *you* know that?"

Kimmie Sue found him immediately in the crowd and smiled. "We have a few good friends on the inside."

Eric stood up. "My name is Eric Saunders. I am a 4-1-1 rep for the union. You don't have the authority to make that announcement, even if it were true. Only the union president should—"

"Oh, it's true," said Kimmie Sue. "And I have some juicy details to share with you right now. There's a nice pay raise for every seniority level."

At the mention of a pay raise, Eric's heart started to soar.

"Unfortunately," said Kimmie Sue, "there isn't a single provision for commuters in the agreement."

"Nothing?!" shouted Darcy.

"Nothing," said Kimmie Sue. "More importantly, there's no provision for giving us the right to automatically be placed at the top of the airport standby list if we're commuting to work or commuting home. So I have sad news for the union president. All of her hard work was for naught. Because when our ballots come in the mail, we'll all be voting a great, big NO."

The crowd rose to their feet. "Vote no! Vote no! Vote no! Vote no!" they began shouting in unison. Someone behind Eric was shouting so loudly that he had to plug his ears with his fingers. He turned to see Rebecca, who was yelling louder than all the others. Her face was purple, and both of her fists were raised high in the air.

Kimmie Sue and Darcy reveled in the uproar. They smiled at each other and joined hands.

"Let's get out of here," said Eric. "I have to call union headquarters right away before this thing gets out of control. I'll meet you guys in the lobby in half an hour." He raced out of the room.

"Yes, let's get out of here, Ginnie Jo," said Denny. "I've had my fill. I wish Eric wouldn't get so worked up over nothing. There are more of us than there are of them. They'll never get the numbers they'd need to screw us over on the vote."

Ginnie Jo grabbed her purse and drained her fourth glass of wine. "Don't be so sure of yourself. I have a terrible feeling that those whack jobs might suddenly become a force to be reckoned with." She looked back once as they left the room, and shuddered. "I think we may be in for one *hell* of a bumpy ride."

CHAPTER 35

The Slippery Slope

On a dreary Sunday in March, Ginnie Jo entered Terminal 10 at JFK with mixed feelings about her assignment. She was happy to leave the frigid East Coast for two days. This year, it seemed like winter would never end. She was glad to be flying to Seattle, which was one of her favorite destinations. Even if it was raining cats and dogs, there was always something interesting to do there. And she always looked forward to working with Eric. There was never any drama when he was on the crew. Unfortunately, Brick Fisher was also on the crew. She knew that at some point, he'd start spewing vitriol at her for crossing the picket line during the strike at ACA. She wasn't thrilled to be working in coach on the 757 either. With a capacity of 170 passengers, and one narrow aisle, it was sure to be a tight and trying day. Screw it, she thought. I'll have to try to get through the day moment by moment.

She signed in and headed to her gate, stopping for coffee along the way. As she waited in line, two flight attendants in front of her were arguing about the recently failed vote on the new contract. One of them had voted yes and the other had voted no; they were both adamant about their choices. Ginnie Jo sighed. There would probably be a lot of bickering on her flight today. Voter turnout had been unusually high; people had talked of nothing else in the weeks leading to the date when the ballots were counted at union headquarters. She remembered the impromptu Circle of Commuters meeting that she had attended in L.A. and wondered if their grassroots effort had been the real reason for the 'no' vote. She'd have to ask Eric about it. She could always depend on him to have facts at his fingertips.

Naturally, Brick would be running his big mouth about the vote, but he'd just be blowing hot air. Ginnie Jo could never understand why Brick had become a flight attendant in the first place. He woke up every morning angry at the world and went to sleep at night the same way. He hated every passenger on sight, as well as everyone in management. And strangely enough, he loathed every union rep, too. Anyone in a position of leadership in the union was in Brick's crosshairs, including departmental reps, the negotiating team, and the national officers. After being with the company for only one year, Brick had tried to run for union president in a brazen attempt to seize control. But he was so full of rage, so poorly informed about the issues, and so obviously unqualified for the position that he received only twenty-three of the fifteen thousand votes cast. Brick's humiliating loss—and the ridicule that followed—left Ginnie Jo with a feeling of pure joy. What's more, he'd brought it all on himself. That made it even more gratifying.

She arrived at the gate and waited for Eric. When he showed up five minutes later, he looked as crisp and professional as ever. Eric liked to be the perfect flight attendant. She couldn't fault him for it though, because he loved playing that role so much.

"Good morning, darlin'," he said walking up to her with a smile as wide as Texas.

"Good morning, handsome. Hey, I forgot to ask you last night: do you have any plans for the layover, or can we do dinner?"

"I have no plans. We can do whatever you want."

"Oh, good, I was afraid you'd drop me like a hot potato and rush up to Capitol Hill to party with the boys."

"No, I'm flying San Francisco the rest of the month. I'll have my fill of partying then."

"A whole month of San Francisco? At our seniority? How did you manage that?"

"Jerry Genualdi is doing my schedule now. He's fantastic! Whatever I hold, he trades it away and gives me transcons instead."

"I want some of that action! Can you get me hooked up with him?"

"Sorry, honey, but he's not taking any other new clients now. I was able to slip in because he and Denny are close friends. And one of Jerry's very senior clients died"—he lowered his voice—"*on the airplane.*"

"What happened?"

"She had a massive heart attack on the way to Los Angeles, an hour after takeoff."

"Oh, no!"

"Yes. She fell right on top of the caviar cart and then hit the floor with her face covered in caviar, sour cream and blinis. The crew tried to revive her, but it was too late. And get this: while they were performing CPR on that poor woman, some jerk in first class starts yelling that she's ruined his caviar course."

"God, what asshole."

Eric pursed his lips like Sylvia Saks. "He was an upgrade, naturally."

"That woman who died—how long had she been flying?"

"Class of 1941. She started her career before airplanes were even pressurized. Can you imagine? For her first decade, she probably never flew above ten thousand feet."

Ginnie Jo shuddered. "I hear about this kind of thing happening more and more often—super senior stews dropping dead in flight. We'd both better find rich husbands... and fast! When it's my time to go, I will *not* be wearing this fucking uniform."

"You said it. Anthony had the right idea. He snagged a rich husband right away. Unfortunately, he snagged the *wrong* rich husband."

"What's up with Anthony, anyway?"

"He's putting in for a transfer to New York. Hopefully, he'll be back by the beginning of June."

"You must be happy."

"I am."

A moment later, a young flight attendant approached them. "Hi, Eric!" she said in a sing-song voice. "Guess what? I'm going to Seattle with you."

"Oh, terrific," said Eric. "Ginnie Jo, this is Chrissy. Chrissy, this is Ginnie Jo."

Chrissy was a pretty blond with a long ponytail, who possessed the whitest teeth that Ginnie Jo had ever seen. Obviously, she was not a smoker. Ooooh, Ginnie Jo thought. Six hours to Seattle without a smoke. It's getting harder and harder. I should quit like Eric did, and avoid those terrible in-flight cravings.

As Chrissy hijacked the conversation and started rattling off her layover plans, Eric began nervously tapping his foot. He reached into his tote bag and took out a toiletry kit. "I have to run to the bathroom for a second. Would you two mind keeping an eye on my luggage?"

"No problem," said Ginnie Jo.

Chrissy smiled at Ginnie Jo. "Do you like Seattle?"

"Sure, who doesn't?"

"I'm so excited that I get to see my family today. I'm from Seattle, and I hardly ever get this trip!"

"That's nice."

Eric returned a few minutes later and sat down, looking decidedly more relaxed.

"Who's working as the coach galley today?" Chrissy asked.

"His name is Brick," said Eric. "He isn't here yet."

Chrissy set a large white box on a vacant seat. "I'm hoping he can keep this in the chiller for me. They're some muffins for my family from our favorite bakery in New York."

"There isn't a chiller on this plane," said Eric. "We could put them on top of an ice drawer though, with a towel underneath so that the box doesn't get damp."

"Oh, that would be awesome!" said Chrissy. "These are the most amazing muffins in the world! When my mom and my sisters came to visit last summer, we used to wake up at four o'clock every morning to be the first customers in line. We'd be like, 'Good morning! We'll take every single muffin in the display case!' The owner thought we were kidding, but we weren't!"

"Well," said Ginnie Jo. "that's *one* way to spend a New York vacation."

"Oh, don't worry!" said Chrissy with a laugh. "We partied in New York, too! My family has incredible stamina. My mom and my sisters are *amazingly* beautiful women. They have men buy drinks for them all night long!" She made a pouty face. "I'm the ugly duckling in the group. I guess every family has one."

"That's absurd," said Eric. "You're a beautiful young woman."

Ginnie Jo could tell that Eric was smitten by Chrissy's appearance. He always favored flight attendants, male or female, who looked as though they came from central casting.

"I wish I could show these muffins to you!" said Chrissy. "But the knot is tied so tightly I'm afraid that if I try to untie it, it'll break it. Oh, wait, I know!" She picked up the box and slid her finger through the side, creating a small opening. She brought her nose close to the box and inhaled. "Just *smell* these muffins! You've never smelled anything so amazing in your life!"

Oh, fuck, thought Ginnie Jo. This woman is going to work my last nerve—and Eric's last nerve too. She took a quick whiff. "Very nice."

Chrissy passed the box to Eric. "Oooh," he said. "They smell *delicious*. Which bakery are they from?"

"It's called Moist. It's on Eighty-ninth Street near First Avenue, right around the corner from me."

"What kind of muffins are they?" Eric asked, sounding genuinely interested.

Ginnie Jo looked at him in disbelief.

"They're a mixed assortment: corn, blueberry, cranberry, peach, pistachio, chocolate, chocolate chip, poppy seed, bran, and—oh darn it!"

"What's the matter?" Eric asked.

"I left the accompaniments in operations!"

"What accompaniments?" said Eric.

"The homemade jams and butters to spread on the muffins! They're from Moist too, and they're the best part! They're in a separate bag. I must have left it in ops. I can't show up at my mom's house without them! There'll be a riot!" She stood up, panic-stricken. "Do you think I have time run back and get it?"

"Oh definitely," said Ginnie Jo, who was anxious to get rid of Chrissy as quickly as possible. "Don't worry. We'll take your suitcase onto the plane for you."

"Where are you working today, so we'll know where to stow your bags?" Eric asked.

"I'm in coach."

"Great!" said Eric. "So are Ginnie Jo and I!"

"Oh, yeah, great, thought Ginnie Jo. Six straight hours with Chatty Chrissy. That's just what I wanted.

***

As boarding began, Chrissy greeted passengers at the door, while the purser, Amanda, set up the first-class galley. Eric and Ginnie Jo were busy in the back of the plane. Brick arrived one minute before the first passenger boarded, threw his luggage overhead, and grunted at Eric. He ignored Ginnie Jo completely. Fine with me, she thought. The less that asshole says to me, the better. As Brick pulled his apron over his head, he accidentally knocked his toupee to one side. Without missing a beat, he set it straight and continued to tie his apron strings. Ginnie Jo ducked into the bathroom and flushed the toilet to cover the sound of her laughter. Jesus, how could any gay man walk out of the house wearing that atrocious rug without making sure it was glued down? She composed herself and came out of the bathroom.

Eric was in the galley with Brick. "I checked off all the special meals for you, Brick. We have thirty. They're all here."

"Thanks," Brick said curtly. He put his hand on the curtain. "Do you mind? I need to concentrate while I'm setting up and I can't do it with the two of you back here."

"Not at all," said Eric stepping out of the galley. "Just let us know if we can help you," he added, as Brick yanked the curtain closed.

"Hey," Ginnie Jo whispered. "What the hell is up with you?"

"What do you mean?"

"Why are you being nice to that asshole?"

"Crew harmony is essential," he replied robotically. "I want a smooth flight today, so we'll have to put aside our differences for the next six hours and work as a team."

"Are you for real?"

"Yes, of course."

"Geez, what drugs are you on today?"

"Ha ha. Oh, look, that woman in the aisle needs help with her suitcase. I'm sure it's much too heavy for her to lift it by herself."

"So? Let her gate-check it. Lifting passenger luggage is not part of our job description—despite what they think."

Eric made a clucking sound. "Oh, Ginnie Jo, you've been flying too long. You stay right here. *I'm* going to be of service to our valued customers."

She grabbed him by the arm. "Why are you talking like that?"

"Like what?"

"Like a goddam Stepford Wife!"

"I'm simply conducting myself as a professional." He straightened his tie and headed up the aisle. "Madam, may I help you with that suitcase?"

Weird, Ginnie Jo thought. This is fuckin' *weird*.

***

After the safety demo, the coach flight attendants sat strapped in their jump seats in the rear galley. Ginnie Jo and Chrissy were on the righthand side; Eric and Brick were on the left. Crissy sat with a large shopping bag from the Moist Bakery on her lap. It with full of dozens of tiny jars which she lovingly examined one by one.

"I'm so glad that your accompaniments were still in ops," Eric said.

"Me, too!" said Chrissy. "There would be hell to pay if I showed up without them."

"What kind of accompaniments do you have?" Eric asked.

Oh, fuck, thought Ginnie Jo. Here we go!

"I tried to get one of every kind," said Chrissy. "There's strawberry, blueberry, cranberry, blackberry, apple butter, orange marmalade, lemon curd, and kiwi. The kiwi jam is new. *Plus,* I have assorted butter flavors. I forget exactly which flavors I got today. I was in a bit of a hurry, but I think I have at least four different kinds."

"Wow," said Eric. "That's a staggering variety of accompaniments!"

If he says that word one more time, Ginnie Jo thought, I'm going to bash his head against the wall.

"I know! There're so many choices!" said Chrissy. "You know what'll be, like, so funny? It's when we sit down at the breakfast table. There's always a big pot of Starbucks coffee brewed—my mom *always* has Starbucks coffee in the house. She's a real Seattleite. She pours us all a cup of coffee, and then we sit there staring at the muffins, jams and butters all displayed together on one enormous platter and try to decide what goes with what. I mean, is it, like, redundant to put cranberry jam on a cranberry muffin? Or is that just *wacky?*"

"That's an interesting question," Eric said. "I never thought of it before."

"Right?!" said Chrissy. "Should we mix and match the muffins and jams, or play it straight? I can never decide."

Ginnie Jo squirmed, as this conversation was taking place over her head. Is it too early for me to sneak a Scotch and soda? she wondered.

"And then," Chrissy said, "what if you *do* have cranberry jam on a cranberry muffin? Is cranberry *butter* on top of a cranberry jam on a cranberry muffin just, like, *too much*? We spend so much time trying to decide exactly *how* to eat them that before you know it, the coffee is cold and it's time for lunch!"

Brick groaned as he turned the pages of the *Daily News.* "That's fascinating, Chrissy. It sounds like you're involved in a regular Manhattan Project."

"Oh, Brick, you're such a *meanie!*" said Eric. He wrinkled his nose like a rabbit, which made Ginnie Jo's skin crawl. "Chrissy, it sounds like a great way to start the day, and tomorrow I'll want a full report on how it played out. Promise?"

"Promise!" said Chrissy. "You're so sweet, Eric! I've always liked you, ever since the first minute I met you."

"I like you too, Chrissy. I think you're just a super stew!"

As Eric and Chrissy beamed at each other, the newspaper curled in Brick's hands. Ginnie Jo stifled a giggle. It's *so* easy to get Brick riled up! she thought. I think I'll have some fun with him today. Then, as she watched Eric smile serenely at Chrissy, with his head tilted pertly to one side, she felt sweat break out on her forehead. This is beyond weird, she thought. Eric is nice, but not that nice. Something freaky is going on and I'm find out what it is—come hell or high fucking water!

***

To Ginnie Jo's surprise, the lunch service went very smoothly. Their destination had something to do with it, of course. Seattle passengers were the most easy-going people in the world. But it also had to with the energy level of the cabin crew. Any time that a call light went off, Eric and Chrissy were like jackrabbits running to answer it. Ginnie Jo gave up even trying to respond. Brick, of course, never stepped out of the galley once the service was over. He watched with disgust as Eric and Chrissy chased each other up the aisle to answer a call light at row 10. "People pleasers," he muttered.

"You said it," said Ginnie Jo.

"What the *fuck*," he said, scowling. "Was I talking to *you?*"

"I don't know, Brick. *Were* you talking to me? There's no else here but me."

He looked as though he wanted to bite off his tongue. He stomped into the corner, sat down, and buried his face in the newspaper.

Eric and Chrissy came back a moment later. "Well, I think everybody has what they want, for a while at least," said Eric. "Let's eat. What's left back here?"

"We have both choices," said Brick, without looking up. "Cheese lasagna and beef with red pepper sauce, in the oven on the left."

"Beef with red pepper sauce sounds good!" said Chrissy.

"I'd stay away from that if I were you," said Eric. "It'll give you terrible gas! I know. It happened to me two days ago on the way to San Francisco. I couldn't even leave my hotel room for twelve hours. It produces the foulest-smelling—"

"Hey, Fart Man!" said Ginnie Jo. "We *get* it: stick with the pasta!"

Chrissy and Eric roared with laughter and then quieted down once they started eating.

"So," said Chrissy, with her mouth full of lasagna, "what's the deal with the new contract? Did it get voted in?"

"No, it was voted down," said Eric. "We have to go back to the drawing board and start all over again."

"How could you *not* know that, Chrissy?" said Ginnie Jo. "The result was announced two weeks ago. Don't you read the union newsletter or listen to the hotline?"

"I moved a few months ago, and I haven't had time to update my mailing address," said Chrissy. "And I can never remember the darn phone number for the hotline."

"It deserved to get voted down," said Brick. "It was typical, piece-of-shit first offer from the company. They'll have to do way better than that to get me to vote yes."

"You know what I heard?" said Chrissy. "I heard the commuters were going to band together and vote it down because the company wouldn't change the pass riding policy and put them at the top of the standby list. Is that what happened?"

"Commuters don't have that kind of power," said Eric. "It was voted down for several reasons. Although there was a nice pay raise included, the company was going to raise insurance premiums so high that it would negate the pay raise. They also wanted new-hires to fly straight reserve, instead of one month on, one month off, as we do now, in which case they'd all starve to death. And they wanted to make onerous changes to the work rules that would make our lives miserable."

"It sounds like you really know what you're talking about, Eric," said Chrissy.

"He does," said Ginnie Jo. "He's a 4-1-1 rep for the union and he's on the local strike preparation committee."

"Strike?" said Chrissy, wide-eyed. "Are we going on strike? When?"

"No, we're not going on strike, not for a long while at least," said Eric. "There are a lot of other steps that we have to go through first. Anyway, the company just started contract negotiations with the pilots, so we're on hold now— probably for a good, long while. Nevertheless, we're taking action. Starting in April, we're going to do informational picketing at each base once a month."

"What's that?" said Chrissy.

"We walk a picket line in uniform in front of the terminal. We carry signs and pass out leaflets. It lets the public, the media *and* the company know that we mean business. I should get your phone number, Chrissy, so you can join us if you're not flying that day."

"Count me in too, Eric," said Ginnie Jo. "I'd be happy to participate."

"Are you serious?" said Brick. "Do you think we'd even *let* you on a picket line, whether it's an actual strike or even informational picketing? We don't *want* you there." He pointed at her in disgust. "You were a scab once, and I bet you'll be a scab again. When we do go on strike, I'm sure the company can count on you to walk right across the picket line and get those fucking airplanes in the air."

Ginnie Jo was so angry that she could barely speak. But before she had the chance to say anything, Eric set down his fork and pulled the galley curtain closed. "You listen to *me*, Brick. Whatever happened in the past, Ginnie Jo is a dues-paying member of *our* union now. She has apologized repeatedly for the mistake that she made at ACA. And if she wants to join us and show support for *our* union and *our* co-workers, neither you nor anyone else will stop her. We need as many people as possible to be informed, to be aware, and to participate. If the shit hits the fan and we do go on strike, we'll need every hand on deck to shut this airline down and get the contract that we deserve. Not to mention, *I* am on the local strike committee, and you are not. You couldn't get a seat on *any* union committee, because you're an obnoxious son of a bitch and the laziest flight attendant in New York and everyone know it." He leaned in close. "So, let me suggest that in the future, you think twice before you open your big mouth and say something stupid. Do you understand?" Although Eric's face was only inches from Brick's, his manner was utterly calm, as though nothing in the world could ruffle his feathers.

"We'll see about that, asshole," said Brick, storming out of the galley. "I'm going up front."

"Wow, that was some speech, Eric!" said Chrissy. "*You* should run for union president the next time that we have an election. You'd have my vote for sure."

"Thank you, Chrissy."

Ginnie Jo took a deep breath before she spoke. "Eric, I appreciate what you just said. But in the future, please let me fight my own battles. I don't need a big, strong man to stick up for me. I can take care of myself."

It was the first time that day that she had seen a crack in his demeanor. "As you wish," he said. He reached into his tote bag and took out his toiletry kit. "Excuse me." He stepped into the lavatory and slammed the door closed.

"Wow," said Chrissy. "That was a little strange, don't you think?"

"Yeah, a little strange, all right."

Fifteen minutes later, he still hadn't come out. A long line was forming in the back of the plane, as there were only two lavatories.

"Should we check on him?" said Chrissy.

"I'll do it," said Ginnie Jo. "Excuse me, sir," she said to the man in the front of the line. She knocked on the door. "Eric, it's Ginnie Jo. Are you all right in there?"

A moment later, the door opened. "Yes, I'm just fine." He smiled at the waiting passengers. "Sorry to keep you waiting, folks. Just a tad of airsickness." He walked back into the galley and put away his toiletry kit. "Is it time for the water service yet?"

"Not yet," said Ginnie Jo. "We need some more plastic cups. Chrissy, would you mind getting some from first class?"

"Not at all. I'll be right back."

Eric sat in his jump seat and smiled serenely. He looked as though he were Queen Elizabeth, about to review the troops. Then his eyelids started to droop, and a moment later his head fell against the wall with a *plunk*.

"Hey!" said Ginnie Jo, trying to rouse him. It was no use. He was out like a light. She shook him harder. He finally sat up, looking at her with glassy eyes. "Listen to me," she said. "The last row is empty. Go take a seat, cover yourself with a blanket, and don't say another word for the rest of the flight. If anyone asks, I gave you a Dramamine for your airsickness and it knocked you out."

"All right," he said groggily, as he stood up and stumbled to the last row.

"I think I know what's going on, Eric, and we'll talk as soon as we get to the hotel. In the meantime, you have *got* to maintain. Can you do that?"

Why, of course I can!" he said, giggling. "I can do *anything!*"

"What you're gonna do is sit there and *shut up*, or else you'll be in big trouble. Got it?"

"Got it."

She fastened his seatbelt to keep him from falling forward and threw a blanket over him. What the fuck, she thought, as she stared at him, shaking her head back and forth. *What the fuck?*

***

Ginnie Jo entered Eric's room with two Scotch minis and a can of club soda in her purse. "Got a glass?" she asked.

"Yep, right there on the desk. I was just about to make myself a drink." There were two vodka minis next to the glasses on the desk.

"Are you sure you should?"

"Yes, why not?"

"I think you know why not. I'll cut right to the chase, Eric. What are you on?"

"What do you mean, what am I on?"

"Don't play dumb with me. You're popping pills—*at work*, for Christ's sake! I wanna know what they are."

"All right, don't get all excited. I'll show you." He pulled out three prescription bottles and set them on the desk. "I've been to see Denny's doctor several times. I told him about all the issues I'm having, and he prescribed these."

"Well, what are they?"

They're my dolls," he said proudly.

"Your dolls?"

"Yeah, you know, as in *Valley of the Dolls*."

She rolled her eyes. "I don't think you can legally use that term without being sued for copyright infringement."

"They're my little helpers, then."

"But what are they *for*?"

"They're for all different kinds of things." He picked up a bottle and opened it. "These little green pills are for a generalized anxiety disorder. They put me in an instant state of bliss, but they make me very loopy. I have to be very careful about where and when I take them. The round, white pills are muscle relaxers. They're great for strained muscles, back pain, and taking the edge off when I can't take something as strong as the green pills. And these tiny little, oblong ones are sleeping pills. I like these the best." He shook the bottle. "Hear that little tinkling sound? Nothing else in the world sounds like that." He shook the bottle again. "I love that sound. It means that I'll never suffer from insomnia again. Dr. Rosenbaum wrote me a prescription without blinking an eye. He has a lot of patients who are flight attendants, so he's very well versed in the wacko hours that we keep."

"Flight attendants are *supposed* to be able to work wacko hours. It comes with the territory."

"Yes, but everyone has personal limits. Take me: if I'm working a red-eye back from the West Coast, I can stay up all night with no trouble. But the pre-dawn sign-ins on the East Coast kill me. How am I supposed to go to bed at eight o'clock and fall asleep right away, just because I have a four A.M. wake-up call the next morning?"

"Ever heard of Tylenol PM? Or melatonin?"

"Surely you jest. Tylenol PM does nothing for me. And don't even bother suggesting melatonin. It's pointless." He picked up the bottle of sleeping pills. "This is the only way to go."

"Do you know how addictive those are?"

"Yes. I only take them when I have an early sign-in."

"That's what everybody says in the beginning. I know. Been there, done that. Done all of them, as a matter of fact."

"Then you know how great it feels to go to the pharmacy and pick up a whole stash of meds."

"What do you mean by that?"

"It means you're *covered*, in all aspects of your life."

"Explain it to me."

He sighed. "I mean that no matter what New York City throws at you, there's a way to cope with it instantly. Here's an example: for the past few months, the constant noise has been driving me crazy. The horn honking and the wailing sirens and those goddam jackhammers that never stop. Not to mention drivers who blast rap music with their car windows rolled down.

Sometimes I'm afraid that my eardrums will shatter. And then there are the loud talkers—they're the worst. Jesus Christ, can *anyone* in New York speak in a simple conversational tone? Everyone yells when they're talking—all the time! And I'm not singling out any one group, in case that's what you're thinking. I'm including everyone. Let's say you're sitting on the subway during rush hour, and there are two *dumbassimos* from Howard Beach—which is the *dumbassimo* capital of the world—at the other end of the car, talking loud enough to wake the dead. It makes me insane! God, I used to love New York accents, but anymore, they just set my teeth on edge. And then let's say there's another guy, sitting right across from you, cutting his nails—*in public*— making that little click-click sound with the clippers. Who the fuck carries a nail clipper on their key chain? Don't these men have mothers, wives or girlfriends to tell them that's something you do at home—in the bathroom? And then those 'clipper' men let their nail parings fall wherever they may, either on the floor, on their lap, or the seat next to them. Pigs. *Pigs!* Looking at those nail parings makes me want to throw up. And then let's say at the *other* end of the car, there's a woman who's proselytizing at the top of her lungs all the way from the Upper West Side to the Far Rockaway. And of course, she's doing 'the list' over and over to try to convert as many people as possible. 'God doesn't care if you are black or white, God doesn't care if you are young or old, Gold doesn't care if you're a man or a woman, God doesn't care if you're a sinner or a saint, God doesn't care—' "

"I get it!" said Ginny Jo. "I live in the same city that you do. What does that have to do with you popping downers like they're Skittles?"

"Because sometimes it's either take a pill or shove a stranger into a poll at the next stop. I did it that once. I rammed a proselytizer as hard as I could to get her to shut up. Then I bolted off the car and up the stairs before she had a chance to identify me." The color drained from his face. "It frightened me. My own behavior frightened me. I've never done anything like that in my life."

"I notice you're not ramming the Italian guys from Howard Beach or the man with the nail clippers."

He shrugged. "The Howard Beach guys run out of steam eventually, and the man with the clippers only has ten fingers. The Jesus freaks, on the other hand, are relentless."

"I see. Tell me: have you ever thought of just getting a decent pair of headphones or taking a cab?"

"Cabs are too expensive. And headphones are completely impractical. I can't wear headphones at work when a flight attendant is yacking non-stop about nothing for three days in a row. I simply cannot cope with that anymore."

She shook her head. "You're on a slippery slope, my friend. What if you get drug tested at work?"

"I never worry about that. In the first place, if I test positive, I have a written prescription. In the second place, we only get drug tested at the end of a trip, so I rarely take anything on the return leg. Timing is everything."

"Why did you feel the need to take a pill today?"

"Oh my God, did you work the same flight that I did? I've been trapped on a plane with Chrissy before. She never shuts up! She's the queen of minutia— the way she prattled on and on and on about those goddam muffins. It's insanity!"

"What the hell, you encouraged her."

"She would have done it anyway. If I take one of these, you see, I'm able to *cope* with it."

"Eric, I've lost track of the number of times you've used that word since this conversation began. But your 'coping' skills leave a lot to be desired. I think you have two options: learn to tune it out like the rest of us, or transfer to DFW where you can drive yourself everywhere you need to go barricaded inside your car."

"DFW? Are you insane? I could never live in Texas again!"

"Then you've put yourself in an impossible situation. I mean, come on! You knew that New York was going to be crowded and noisy. You wanted to be based there. You talked about it non-stop in training. What did you think it would be like?"

"Stimulating—but not *that* stimulating."

"I get it. But listen: popping a pill every time that someone sneezes is going to set you on a path of serious trouble."

Eric put his medications away. "I don't understand why you're making such a *gonsa meghilla* about this."

"A *gonsa meghilla*? Who are you, Henny Youngman?"

"Doctor Rosenbaum teaches me a few new Yiddish phrases every time I see him. I've built up quite a vocabulary. Believe me, it comes in handy if you're *schpotzeering* on the Lower East Side and want to pop in someplace for a *nosh*."

"*Oy vey.* We're getting off topic here. I still think you should—"

"Darling, do I say anything when you show up a six A.M. with Scotch on your breath? No. I keep mum and feed you peppermint Lifesavers all day. Let's consider this topic closed, please. I appreciate your concern, but I'll know when I've gone too far."

"All right, Whatever. I've had my say."

"Thank you. I feel like having my cocktail now. Is that all right?"

"God forbid I should stop you."

He poured two minis into a glass and took a big sip.

"You're drinking vodka straight now?" she asked.

"I like it straight. I love to feel the burn as it goes down."

"Oh, boy." She shook her head again. "Slippery slope... *very* slippery slope."

CHAPTER 36

People on the Edge

The next day, after landing one hour late at DFW, Ginnie Jo and the rest of the crew were racing through the terminal to catch their connecting flight back to JFK. "Should we stop for food?" Eric asked.

"There's no time," said Ginnie Jo. "I don't want to miss this flight and get stuck here overnight. The less time I spend in DFW, the better."

The gate area was crammed with a mob of anxious people; the flight was obviously going to be full.

"Hi," said Amanda, as they approached the gate. "We're the outbound crew."

"You're late," the agent snapped.

"That's not our fault," Amanda snapped right back. "If you'd bothered to check, you'd know that we just landed half an hour ago—at the other end of the terminal. In the future, send a driver with a cart to pick us up if you want us here on time."

"Oh, sorry. You're right. I should have checked."

"Forget it," said Amanda. "Just give me the preliminary paperwork and let us get the hell out of here." No one, it seemed, wanted to spend any more time than necessary in DFW.

"Let's plan on boarding in five minutes," the agent asked.

"Don't *rush* us," said Amanda, clearly exasperated. "I'll call you from the jet bridge when we're ready."

Once on board, the cabin crew was stowing their luggage when Amanda's voice came over the PA system. "Could I get everybody up front for a quick briefing with the captain, please?"

They all sighed and trudged up first class, where the captain stood waiting. He was short and squat, with a large belly that hung over a gaudy western belt buckle. Ginnie Jo looked at his feet. He wore cowboy boots with pointed toes that looked just as tacky with his uniform as the belt buckle. Ugh, she thought. He's DFW-based, for sure.

"Hi," said the captain. "My name's Dave. I'll make this fast because I know the agent wants to board right away. I just wanted to give y'all a heads up. We might have a rough ride going into to New York tonight. There's a nor'easter that will probably be arriving right around the same time that we do."

"Oh, shit," Ginnie Jo muttered.

"It's a fast-moving storm," the captain continued. "It could be completely gone by the time we get there, or it could be sitting right over the airport. I won't know until we get closer to JFK. But I will say this: if I come over the PA and tell you to sit down, I want you to sit down immediately. Does everyone understand?"

"Yes, sir," said Amanda. "What kind of winds are you expecting?"

"Right now, about sixty miles per hour."

"Oh, *shit!*" This came from Brick.

"That exceeds the maximum allowed for this aircraft or any aircraft, for that matter," said Dave. "But as I said, we'll see what happens when we get closer to the East Coast. Conditions can change very quickly with this kind of storm. If the winds die down and we can land, we're going in. Tim, the first officer, is based in New York, but I'm from DFW. I don't want to get stuck overnight in New York. I'm supposed to deadhead back on the last flight to out of JFK tonight."

"In case we have to divert, what's our alternate?" Brick asked.

"Hartford," said the captain.

"Well, if the storm is sitting right over JFK during our final approach, we *will* divert to Hartford, right?" Brick asked. Ginnie noticed that he was sweating profusely. "Surely you won't try to land if it's not safe."

"That's why we *have* an alternate," Dave said with great condescension. It was obvious that he didn't like having his authority questioned—especially by the cabin crew. "Don't worry, I'd never put anyone's life at risk. But remember, this is a 757. It's built like a flying tank. She can take anything that Mother Nature throws at her and come out just fine. Any other questions?"

No one raised their hand.

"Good. Then let's start boarding."

***

During taxi out, the coach flight attendants were unusually quiet. Eric finally broke the silence by asking, "What's a nor'easter?"

"I was wondering the same thing," said Chrissy.

Ginnie Jo and Brick exchanged a nervous look. "I forget that you're both new," she said. "A nor'easter is a particular type of powerful, late-winter storm that we get on the East Coast. It can move up the seaboard either slowly or quickly. It's not exactly a hurricane, but it usually has very high, rotating winds.

Sometimes there's snow, sometimes there's rain. Either way, if you're flying around a nor'easter, be ready for turbulence—and I mean *horrible* turbulence."

"Did you just say, 'horrible turbulence'?" Eric squeaked.

"Yes," said Ginnie Jo. She could see no reason to sugarcoat what lay ahead. If anything, she should prepare them for the worst. "Nor'easters can produce anything from moderate chop to severe turbulence."

"Ooh, a roller coaster kind of ride!" Chrissy said with delight.

"I *hate* roller coasters," said Eric.

"Then you'd better get out your rosary beads or something else to occupy your mind," said Ginnie Jo. "That's exactly what it could be like tonight."

"I'll be right back." Eric left his jump seat, reached for his toiletry kit and went into the bathroom.

Shit, thought Ginny Jo. There he goes again, reaching for those goddam pills. What the hell *can* he cope with anymore?

"Turbulence never bothers me," said Chrissy. "I love roller coaster rides." She raised her arms high up over her head. "It's like, *woohoo!* Look ma, no hands! I'm ready for the next big drop!"

Brick looked at her as though she were insane. "Have you ever *been* in severe turbulence?"

"Well, I don't know if you'd call it severe. But I've had some very bumpy rides since I started flying last fall, that's for sure."

"You would know if you've ever been in severe turbulence," said Brick. "It's not a fucking joke. Pilots can lose control of the plane and people get hurt. A few have even been killed. Usually, we're the ones who get injured because we're not strapped in. Listen to me, Chrissy: if it gets bad, don't even bother doing a seatbelt check. Just come back here and sit down."

"Yes, sir," she said, with a crisp salute.

As Eric returned and sat down, the captain announced that they were next in line for takeoff.

Ginnie Jo pictured the pilot sitting at the controls with his belt buckle, his cowboy boots and an arrogant look on his face. The image made her shudder. "I don't like him," she said. "I don't like him, and I don't *trust* him."

"You don't trust the *captain?*" Eric said.

"*No.* I don't like that macho shithead attitude. He's the kind of pilot that will try to land in a major storm, no matter what. It's all about his ego: challenging himself, the airplane, and the weather to 'get the mission accomplished,' in pilot-speak. That's when accidents happen—serious accidents that could have been *avoided.*"

"I agree completely," said Brick. "The expression 'pilot error' immediately comes to mind."

Ginnie Jo was shocked. It was probably the only time in her life that Brick had agreed with her about anything.

"Let's make sure that we're all on the same page," said Brick. "Once it starts getting bumpy, we stow the carts immediately and strap in. And we don't get up for any reason, even if there's a medical emergency. I'm not taking any fucking chances with our safety, just because *he's* willing to. Agreed?"

As the takeoff roll began, they all nodded in unison. "Agreed," said Ginnie Jo.

***

"Eric," Ginnie Jo repeated for the third time as they collected dirty meals trays, "you're going too slow. Let's *move* this cart."

"Sorry," said Eric. "I was answering a question for a passenger."

"No, you weren't. You were staring off into space. And what is it that you keep reaching for in your shirt pocket?"

"My flight insurance."

"What do you mean?"

He leaned over the cart. "A little something to keep me calm when the severe turbulence starts," he murmured.

"You're not serious? You can't handle a little turbulence?"

"A little turbulence, yes. But not *that* kind of turbulence. I went through it on one of my training flights and I've been terrified of it ever since. I know myself. I don't want to start freaking out in front of the passengers."

"What's that you're saying about turbulence, young man?" asked an elderly woman who was straining to hear their conversation.

"It might get a little bumpy tonight, that's all," said Ginnie Jo. "Come on, Eric we have a least ten rows to go and I want to get this cart stowed." She looked up the aisle. "What the hell is Chrissy doing?"

Eric turned around and looked. "She's at the front of the cabin, offering coffee from a tray."

"What is she, an idiot? Why is she serving hot coffee now when at any minute we could—"

"Ladies and gentlemen, this is the captain speaking. We're starting to pick up some light chop from that storm that's headed up the East Coast. I'm turning on the seatbelt sign. Flight attendants, please take your seats as quickly as possible."

"That's all the warning I need," said Ginnie Jo. "Let's roll." They started to move the cart back to the galley, despite the protests of passengers who tried to hand back their dirty meal trays. Ginnie Jo shook her head repeatedly. "Did you hear what the captain said just now? He told us to *sit down*. We'll come back for them later." They had to push the cart around a man who stood, rather stupidly, near the galley. "Sir, take a seat. It's going to get very bumpy."

"I'm waiting for the bathroom."

"You can use the bathroom later. Sit *down*."

The man rolled his eyes as he opened the bathroom door. "You people are always such alarmists. Do you know how many miles I've flown on this airline? *Millions.* We're going to have a little chop, the captain just said. I *know* what a little chop means."

"Have it your way, mister. Don't say we didn't warn you."

Brick was waiting for them in the galley with an empty space for the cart. "Put it here," he said, as he quickly latched compartments closed. "And then let's sit down. Where is Chrissy?"

"She's—" Before Ginnie could complete the sentence, they all rose off the floor together, stayed suspended for a few seconds, and then hit the galley floor. The plane had dropped at least one hundred feet. "Fuck!"

"Sit down, sit down!" Brick shouted as they scrambled for their jump seats. "Ginnie Jo, lock down that beverage cart across from you! I missed that one."

She tries to reach for the pull-down handle that would keep the two-hundred-pound cart from rolling out and smashing into them, but it was impossible. She instinctively propped her feet against the cart to keep it in place. Her feet slipped off as the plane dropped again—this time even more steeply—and she was thrown across the jump seat.

"Oh, God," said Eric. "Oh, my *GOD!*"

"Chrissy—where the hell is Chrissy?" said Brick, as passengers began frantically pushing their call lights.

Ginnie Jo looked up at the small mirror mounted on the galley wall. "I see her! She's on the floor!" Passengers seated next to Chrissy's prone body were waving wildly toward the back of the plane. She could tell by their terrified expressions that Chrissy was injured. "Shit! I think she's hurt. At least somebody has enough snap to hold her down with his feet, thank God." She reached for the interphone and dialed first class. "Amanda, this is Ginnie Jo. Three of us made it to our seats in time, but Chrissy got caught out in the aisle. She's on the floor, and I'm pretty sure that she's badly hurt. Someone is holding her down so that she doesn't hit the ceiling. Let's hope that he can *keep* her down. Would you let the captain know while I make a PA? Thanks." She switched over to the intercom. "Ladies and gentlemen, due to the severe turbulence, we cannot get up for any reason. Please keep your seatbelts fastened, and please keep our co-worker secured on the floor until we can safely get her to a seat." She hung up the phone and held tightly to her shoulder harness. There was nothing to do now but ride it out. Jesus, the plane was all over the sky! During severe turbulence, there was no worse place to be than in the back of the aircraft. The fuselage was so long and skinny that it was always ten times worse than up in the front. It felt like someone had grabbed the jet by the nose and was slamming it up and down and then side to side. It was a terrifying experience. Just when she thought the ride couldn't get any worse, it did. In unison, they were all lifted from their jump seats, forced against their shoulder harnesses, and the then shoved back down. It happened over and over. She looked at Eric, who was white as a sheet and holding onto his shoulder harness for dear life. He finally let go long enough to reach into his shirt pocket, with a trembling hand, and take something out. Between two fingers he was clutching a white pill. As he raised his hand to his mouth, his hand shook so much that he dropped it. He watched in horror as it rolled underneath a cart and out of reach. He started to unfasten his seatbelt.

"No!" said Ginnie Jo. "Let it go! You have to learn how to deal with this shit or stop flying, and that's all there is to it. Come on, be a man." She reached over to give him a reassuring pat on the shoulder.

"Don't touch me!" said Eric. "Don't touch me and don't talk to me!" He stared straight ahead, closed his eyes, and started hyperventilating so furiously that she feared he would pass out.

"Eric, Slow down your breathing! You're just making it worse."

"I'm trying, *I'm trying* to calm down!" he said, with his face scrunched up.

She could tell that he was trying not to cry. Brick, on the other hand, wasn't as stoic. He sat with his face turned against the wall, balling like a baby. Jesus, she thought, am I the only one who here can hold it together in a crisis? To make matters worse, that kind of fear was contagious. It could have every passenger in hysterics in a matter of minutes.

She decided to ignore both men and concentrate on herself. She rested her hands on her lap, stared straight ahead, and forced herself to control her own breathing. The cacophony all around her was unbearable: the engines revving up and slowing down as the pilots repeatedly changed altitude… the garbled announcements from the cockpit that weren't the least bit reassuring anyway… the shrieks of fear from the cabin… the sound of passengers retching into barf bags… the pounding against the galley wall. Wait a minute. Pounding? Where the hell was *that* sound coming from? Then she remembered: Mister Frequent Flyer with the million miles, who'd insisted on using the lavatory. Now he was trapped in there and probably scared to death. She tried turning her ear toward the wall and imagined that she could hear him crying, too. Well, good. He *deserved* to be scared. She pictured him on the toilet, with his pants pulled down, grabbing onto anything he could to avoid being thrown off. He had probably shit all over himself and was too embarrassed to try to get out. Ginnie Jo was in the throes of the ultimate crewmember fantasy: the comeuppance of the non-complaint passenger. Oh, how she would enjoy watching him crawl back to his seat—*if* he could get out of the goddam lav before the plane landed. The thought of his plight amused her so much that she started laughing. Well, anything to take her mind off the turbulence…

Suddenly, it stopped. They were in smooth air, and they were flying straight and level. Was it over, or just a brief interlude before it started all over again?

"Ladies and gentlemen, this is the captain. We have been cleared to land at JFK. We'll be on the ground in fifteen minutes. Flight attendants, please prepare for landing."

Ginnie Jo immediately left her jump seat and went up the aisle to help Chrissy. As she approached, Chrissy was writhing in pain.

"She hit her mouth on the armrest when she fell," said the passenger who had held her down. "I think she broke a few teeth. You'd better have the captain radio ahead for paramedics and an ambulance."

"Thanks for keeping her safe," said Ginnie Jo. She'd never had more gratitude for a passenger in her life. She knelt in the aisle to help Chrissy get up. As Chrissy turned her head, Ginnie Jo had to avert her eyes. Blood was gushing out of her mouth. Oh fuck, those beautiful teeth! God knows how much time and money it'll take to make her smile look normal again.

The man reached into his pocket and showed her a flight attendant ID badge. "My name's Scott. I'm based in New York and off duty. Is there anything else I can do to help?"

"Yeah. Are you qualified on this airplane, Scott?"

"Yes, I am."

"Then take her jump seat in the back and assume her duties for landing and taxi-in. We'll have to strap her into your seat. Give me a hand, would you?"

"Of course." After they had strapped Chrissy into the seat, Scott clipped his ID to his lapel and headed to the back. "I'm on my way. Do you want me to call up front for you?"

"No, I'll do it in a second, thanks." She ran to the closest lavatory and brought back a huge stack of paper towels for Chrissy. Then she called Amanda on the interphone. "Were you able to reach the cockpit?"

"No! I've been trying to call them since this shit started a half-hour ago. They won't pick up the goddam phone!"

"Then start banging on the fucking door until they open it. We have an emergency back here! Chrissy broke a few teeth on an armrest, and she's bleeding profusely. God only knows if she has broken facial bones, too. Tell him to call ahead for paramedics and an ambulance. And tell him to make a PA asking the passengers to stay seated until the paramedics have removed her from the plane."

"Anyone else hurt back there?"

"No, I'll have to pull Brick and Eric off the ceiling, that's all. By the way, there's an off-duty flight attendant who offered to help us. He's qualified on the 757 and he has his ID with him. He's taking Chrissy's jump seat for landing."

"What quick thinking, Ginnie Jo! Leave it to *us* to take charge. Oh, am I gonna give that captain a piece of my mind!"

"Just wait! I'm gonna rip that gaudy fucking belt buckle off and beat him with it for flying us through that shit. Amanda, one more thing: it's imperative that he files a severe turbulence report before this plane goes anywhere else tonight. If he doesn't, the company will make Chrissy use her own sick time to cover lost time while she's out of work, instead of coding this as an injury on duty and paying her full salary. Make *sure* he knows that."

"Wow, you think of everything. Not to worry, girl. I'm on it."

***

As soon as the plane had blocked in at the gate, Ginnie Jo raced up the aisle toward Chrissy. Amazingly, she had to fight passengers who were already trying to remove their luggage from the overhead bins. "Sit down, sit down! Didn't you hear the announcement? We have an injured crewmember. Paramedics are coming on board, stay out of their way!"

The paramedics came down the aisle a moment later with a wheelchair.

"Which hospital are you taking her to?" Ginnie Jo asked.

He mentioned the name of the hospital which was closest to the airport.

She nodded. "Got it. We'll be there as soon we can," she said.

Chrissy was sobbing uncontrollably. Ginnie Jo leaned down to stroke her hair. "Honey, don't worry, you're safe now. We won't let you go through this alone. We'll be there as soon as we can."

Chrissy tried to speak but couldn't. Keeping her mouth covered, she feebly pointed to the overhead bins that were chockful of luggage.

Ginny nodded. "We'll bring your luggage. Your purse and your suitcase are right next to mine in the back."

Once Chrissy had been wheeled off, Ginnie Jo stepped out of the aisle. As the passengers walked past her, they stared straight ahead, looking numb. Ginnie Jo nodded goodbye to the few who made eye contact with her. There seemed to be nothing to say. As soon as the last passenger left, she ran to the front of the plane. Amanda was standing with her hands on her hips and a look of disbelief on her face.

"Where is he?" Ginnie Jo demanded.

"He's gone," said Amanda.

"Gone? Gone *where?* To the hospital with Chrissy?"

"No, gone to catch his deadhead flight! He grabbed his suitcase and kit bag and ran off right behind the paramedics."

"What?!" It was unfathomable. The captain had left an overwhelmed crew and a plane full of traumatized passengers to fend for themselves. After a crisis, the captain was *supposed* to stay with them to provide reassurance and leadership. That was part and parcel of the job.

"The first officer is still here," said Amanda, "but you better catch him quick. He looks like he's getting ready to leave, too."

With her eyes ablaze, Ginnie Jo stormed into the cockpit. "What the fuck? How could you let Dave leave?"

The first officer shrugged. "He's the captain."

"Did he file a severe turbulence report?"

"No, he didn't. That would take the airplane out of service. This flight is going to Miami in forty-five minutes, and it's full. The company isn't going to lose that kind of revenue when we didn't even suffer a lightning strike."

"Did he know about Chrissy's injury?"

"Of course. Who do you think called for the paramedics?"

"And does he know that if he doesn't file a severe turbulence report, she'll have to use her sick time instead of the company paying for an IOD? Does he *know* that? Does he even fucking care?"

"You'd have to ask him, I guess," said Tim.

"Then *you* should submit the report."

"Sorry, the captain is the only one who can do it. Company policy. Looks like your friend will have to do some extra legwork to get this covered as an IOD."

"She's not just a friend. She a member of this crew, and *you* two were responsible for her safety—for everyone's safety. What were you thinking, taking us through weather like that? Why didn't we divert to Hartford? Are you that fucking incompetent? You should both have your licenses revoked."

Tim wiped sweat from his forehead. "You know, you're getting a little shrill. Sometimes, we don't have any more advance notice about turbulence than you do. Once in a great while, people get hurt. It *happens*."

"You know what, Tim? I'm gonna get a lot shriller when I walk into the chief pilot's office tomorrow and tell him exactly what happened on this flight."

The pilot pulled a business card out of his kit bag. "Here, I have his number. Why not call him right now?"

"I have to go to the hospital with her right now. But I tell you what: you'd both better be available for an official company debrief with the entire crew. Otherwise, your name is going to be fucking mud at this base."

He shoved his maps into his kit bag. "Now you're threatening me. Should I include *that* in the debrief?"

"Just be there, Tim. It's the least that you can do."

"I'm sorry that this flight was so traumatic for everyone, but we *did* land safely after all."

"No thanks to Cowboy Dave, or to you. I wonder what the FAA would have to say about your flying skills if I called them and reported you."

At the mention of contacting the FAA, the pilot turned stone-faced. "This conversation is over." He put on his hat and left the cockpit without saying another word.

***

As Ginnie headed toward the back to retrieve her luggage, Brick was already halfway up the aisle. His eyes were bloodshot from crying so hard. "Are you guys coming to the hospital with me to see about Chrissy?" Ginnie Jo asked.

Brick shook his head. "I can't," mumbled. "I'll call her tomorrow. I have to get home to my dog right now and just be still for the rest of the night."

"So much for crew unity."

He put up his hand. "Please, not tonight, Ginnie Jo. I'll see you at the debrief—if I'm still working here. This may have been my last flight. *Ever*. Good night."

As she reached the back, Eric was putting his blazer on. He seemed to be moving in slow motion, but he at least he was moving.

"How are you?" she asked.

"I'm OK. I survived. But I hope I never have to go through anything like that again."

"I'm really proud of you for not taking a pill. I know how hard that was. Are you coming to the hospital with me?"

"Yes, of course. How will we get there?"

"We're taking a cab. I'll pay."

"What about Chrissy's luggage?"

"We'll bring it with us. She'll need some clean clothes when she finally gets discharged— whenever that is. Let's head for the taxi stand."

***

As they settled in the back seat of the cab, she noticed that Eric was trying to stop his hands from trembling. "I don't know what's the matter with me," he said. "I just can't get them to stop shaking."

"It's the adrenaline rush from the turbulence," she said. "It might go on for a while, and you may feel like shit for a couple of days. It's pretty toxic to have that level of adrenaline coursing through your body. Look, see?" She held out her own trembling hand. "I've got it, too." She thought about the nightmarish patients they would encounter in the local emergency room—stabbings, gunshot wounds, drug overdoses—and wished that she had taken a few Scotch minis from the plane. "Hey, Eric, do you have your stash with you or is it with the luggage in the trunk?"

"They're all right here," he said, patting the tote bag on his lap.

"Let's each have one of those little green ones. We've got a long night ahead of us, and it might not be pleasant."

"Good idea," said Eric, opening his bag immediately. "A little green pill is just what the doctor ordered."

Chapter 37

A Word of Warning

Six weeks later, on a Sunday morning in April, Eric was signing in for his flight when he heard his name called. "Hi, Eric!"

He turned around and was delighted to see Chrissy wearing her uniform. "Hey, you!" he said, hugging her tightly. "Does this mean you're back to work?"

"Yes, this is my first trip. I'm going to San Diego today."

"I wish I was going with you. I'm off to Orange County—dullest city in America."

"After Tulsa."

"That's true. But tell me about you. Do you feel well? You look wonderful."

"Thanks. Yes, I'm much better now. The orthopedic surgeon did a great job. It was tough going for a while, but I had great support from the union and all the flight attendants in New York." She shook her head. "That flight... that goddam, *terrible* flight from DFW."

Eric looked at her closely. Something about her had changed, but he couldn't quite put his finger on it. "I'm sorry that you couldn't attend the debrief with us, but we did stick up for you at every turn."

"I know, and I appreciate it. I heard that the pilots didn't show."

"No, *neither* of those chicken shits showed up, after everything they put us through. And I know that the captain never filed a severe turbulence report."

"I was out of work for over a month. I had to use up all the sick hours I'd accrued. And you wouldn't believe the medical bills that are still coming in—I owe thousands and thousands of dollars! You know what my supervisor said? She said, 'You should have sat down the minute the captain told you to, Chrissy.' I said, 'Yes, but I was in the aisle, and there was a cart between me and my jump seat. I couldn't sit down.' And she said, 'Nevertheless, you must always follow a captain's directive immediately. When I told her that I may have to declare bankruptcy because of the medical bills, she said, 'There really is nothing I can do for you. If you think you've been mistreated, you can always grieve it through your local union rep or file a claim with Workers Compensation.' And then I was dismissed. Needless to say, I've already filed a case with Workers Compensation *and* found a good attorney."

"Assholes," said Eric. "They're such assholes. You know, the story of what happened to you spread like wildfire throughout the whole system. No one could believe that an injured flight attendant could be treated so terribly. Everybody is pissed off. Last week, five hundred people showed up for informational picketing. And that was just in New York."

"I know. I saw your picture in the paper. I loved the raised fist. By the way, that new haircut looks great. It's a whole new you."

Eric grinned. "It's called a jarhead."

She nodded. "You look just like those old pictures of my dad when he was in the Marines. Well, I'd better get down to my gate."

"I should get going, too. But first, I have to see *my* supervisor. Pumpkin Head has called me in for a meeting."

"Oh, crap, do you know what it's about?"

"Yes, I have a pretty good idea, but I'm sure I can handle it. By the way, there's a big weather system moving across the Midwest today. Watch out for bumps."

"I know. I'll be checking the weather forecast before every single flight from now on. Thank God I'm working up front today." Her face turned pale. "I'll never get caught in the aisle that far from a jump seat again, *ever*. Just between you and me, I feel completely differently about the job now. I don't think I'll ever be the same. Do you know what I mean?"

That's what had changed. Chrissy had lost her ready smile and light-hearted spirit. "I know," he said. "Me neither. In fact, my attitude about everything has changed."

Chrissy smiled weakly. "Who knows, maybe we'll bounce back one day."

"Yeah, maybe. Keep the faith."

"Have a good flight."

After Chrissy left, Eric walked down the corridor and tapped on his supervisor's cubicle. "Hi, Phillip. You wanted to see me?"

"Oh, yes, Eric." Phillip gestured stiffly toward the empty seat in front of his desk. "Sit down, please." Phillip's complexion, usually as pale as a glass of skim milk, was crimson from the top of his forehead down to his fingertips.

"Where'd you get that... tan?" Eric asked.

"You mean second-degree sunburn? I went to St. Maarten with friends last week and fell asleep at Orient Beach. I'm this color everywhere, all over my entire body—if you know what I mean."

It wasn't like Phillip to make such an off-color remark. Was he trying to act buddy-buddy to lure Eric into a false sense of security? Supervisors were famous for using that tactic. And then the minute your guard was down— bam!—they hit you with an infraction. "You look as though you're about to pass out, Phillip. Why didn't you call in sick today?"

"Because I am a member of management. I'm required to be here to help maintain the operation. We don't use our sick time frivolously, like *some* work groups do. I wouldn't dream of calling in sick for a hangnail or a hangover."

Eric ignored the last remark. His own attendance record was spotless. There had to be some other reason why Phillip wanted to see him. But Eric was smart enough to smile and play dumb.

Phillip pointed to a straw basket heaped with candy. "Would you like some jelly beans? A malted egg? A chocolate bunny? They're Lindt chocolate—the best in the world."

"No, thanks for the tempting offer, but I'm trying to stay off sugar." He patted his flat stomach.

Phillip smiled. "Yes, you're still as fit and trim as the first day you reported to me." Then he sighed. "I wish I could say same for the rest of the flight attendants in my group. I *knew* that dropping the weight limit would be a mistake. I protested over and over, but no one ever listens to me. Naturally, it took no time at all to prove that I was right. I can't believe how many crewmembers are literally bursting out of their uniforms. By the way, are you wearing a new hairstyle?"

"Yes."

"That's quite a different look for you."

Eric nodded. "A bit more updated." Eric's days of wearing puffy hair were over. Besides, he was getting cruised by a whole different type of man now.

"I think it's a tad severe," said Phillip. "Perhaps you should let the sides grow in a bit to match the top."

"I checked the grooming regulations. This haircut falls within company guidelines for male employees," he replied evenly.

"I'll double-check those guidelines. In the meantime..." Phillip folded his hands together. "I saw that there was quite a commotion at JFK while I was away."

Here it comes. "I'm not quite sure to what you're referring."

"You're not?" Phillip reached into a stack of papers and pulled out a copy of the *Post.* "Perhaps this will refresh your memory." He flipped the paper open to the business section and set it on his desk. In a picture that took up half of the page, hundreds of uniformed flight attendants were carrying picket signs in front of Terminal 10. Eric was standing right in the middle of the group with a megaphone in one hand. His other hand was raised high over his head, clenched into a fist.

Damn, thought Eric. That really *is* a great picture. "That wasn't a commotion, Phillip, it was just informational picketing."

"If it wasn't a commotion, why did you need a megaphone?"

"There were five hundred people out there. We had to maintain some type of crowd control. Surely you wouldn't have wanted us to block passenger access to the terminal."

"It was a little rowdier than mere informational picketing. I understand that flight attendants were sharing confidential company stories with the press. And that others were chanting such witticisms as: 'We're going to shut this motherfucker down.' "

"I don't recall hearing that particular chant."

"I'm shocked, Eric. This sort of activity reflects very poorly on you and all of your co-workers."

"This sort of activity is permitted under Article Fifteen of our current contract. Additionally, we had secured all the requisite permits from the Port Authority. Everything was completely legal."

"Are you all *that* unhappy here, Eric? Most people would consider yours a dream job. Think about the benefits you have: fifteen or more days off a month, a regular paycheck, health insurance, layovers at luxury hotels, free limos, crew meals, the ability to fly anywhere in the world for practically nothing. And that's just for starters."

Yes, and what about the *cons*? Eric thought, such as a starvation wage with no significant pay raise in sight; the nightmare of being on call 24/7 for days on end; pathetic crew meals—how can they call that a meal?—and eight-hour layovers at dreary airport hotels; twelve-hour duty days that were worth only six hours of actual flight pay; obnoxious, drunken and demanding passengers; an archaic IOD reporting system that resulted in people being stuck with medical bills that should be paid by the company...

The list of flight attendant grievances was endless. But Eric wisely chose not to engage with his supervisor. "On matters that pertain to the contract negotiation, Phillip, it's not really appropriate for us to discuss them. I let my negotiating team speak for me." He looked at his watch. "I should get to the gate if I want to board on time, so if there's nothing else—"

"Actually, there *is* something else. I'd like to discuss *this.*" He placed a document on his desk.

Eric knew right away that it was a letter from a passenger. "Is that an orchid?" he asked casually.

"On the contrary. It's an onion—one that stinks to high heaven, I might add. I believed it's the first one you've ever received. Take a look."

Eric scanned the letter. He recognized the name at once. The passenger was a famous TV producer and one of the vilest people that Eric had ever met. Just the memory of his pock-marked face, rat-like eyes, and sour breath made Eric want to throw up. Son of a bitch, he thought. He said he was going to write me up, but after the way that *he* behaved, I didn't think he'd have the nerve. Eric read the letter passively, making sure there was no trace of reaction on his face.

He had learned this technique from Denny months ago. When he had finished reading, he looked up. "This is a completely inaccurate account of what happened."

"Is it? Then suppose then you tell me your side of the story."

"Mr. Adelman spent the entire flight—in first class, mind you—with his dirty, bare feet pressed against the headrest in front him. The passenger sitting in front of him complained, naturally. I politely asked Mr. Adelman to lower his feet, but he refused. In addition to having no regard whatsoever for other passengers, his raised feet prevented me from being able to serve the woman seated next to him. The only way that I could serve her, without having those filthy feet right in front of my face, was to pass all service items on a tray behind Mr. Adelman's head. As the woman reached for her Bloody Mary, we hit a bump. She accidentally knocked the glass off my tray, and it spilled all over Mr. Adelman. It *was* an accident, of course." And we had a wonderful laugh about it later in the galley, she and I. But there's no reason to bring that up now.

"That Bloody Mary ruined a six-hundred-dollar shirt and a nine-hundred-dollar pair of pants," said Phillip. "I have a copy of the claim form that he submitted to headquarters."

"That is a bogus claim. JC Penny makes neither V-neck t-shirts nor sweatpants in that price range."

"Are you getting smart with me?"

"No. I am merely stating the facts. The tag of his t-shirt was showing when he sat down."

"So now you're accusing one of our premium passengers of lying."

"No, I am relating the facts of the matter: Mr. Adelman boarded the flight wearing a white V-neck t-shirt, a pair of stained grey sweatpants, and rubber shower thongs. He slipped them off immediately and sat with his feet propped up, as I have already stated, and *kept* them there for the entire six-hour flight to Los Angeles. I will put up with a lot from passengers, but I will *not* put up with bare feet in my face, especially *these* bare feet." He reached into his tote bag, pulled out an envelope and placed it on Phillip's desk.

"What is this?" said Phillip, opening it.

"This is a shot of Mr. Adelman at his seat: nasty bare feet, sweatpants and all."

"Who took this picture?!"

"I did. For heaven's sake, don't have a heart attack. I was standing behind the last row. Nobody *saw* me take the picture."

"This is appalling! Perhaps you are unaware of the high value that we place on the goodwill of our premium passengers, especially those who've attained the status of… *Almighty Titan*." He whispered the designation as though it were sacrosanct. "Not to mention the extraordinary revenue that they produce."

"I know all about the value of 'premium' passengers—and the level of obsequiousness that you expect from us when we interact with them." He loved the momentary look of confusion on Phillip's face. As pompous as he was, words with that many syllables were simply not in his vocabulary. "That's a rather unreasonable expectation, given the boorish way they interact with us."

"That is beside the point. There are repercussions for the way in which you conduct yourself while on duty, and—"

"Phillip, as far as I am concerned, this discussion is over," Eric said calmly. "Tell those sycophants at headquarters to respond any way they want. Send him a check for fifteen hundred dollars and reinforce his infantile behavior. I guarantee you, though, it only means even more outrageous demands in the future. You're creating a cadre of in-flight monsters for us to deal with and it will only get worse as time goes by. As for that letter: if you choose to take this baseless complaint any further, I'm not saying another word. I'll schedule a meeting with the local union rep for the three of us, and we'll take it from there. If she can't resolve it, I'll grieve it all the way up to the president if I have to." He stood up. "Now, my flight is boarding in fifteen minutes. Are you going to keep me on the trip or remove with pay and send me home? Those are your options, per the contract." Eric could see that Phillip's blood was boiling—even under his sunburn. Tough shit, he thought. I'm not a new hire anymore; he can't fire me at a moment's notice without cause. I have contractual rights and I'm going to exercise them.

"Go to your flight," Phillip said, through gritted teeth

"Is that letter staying in my personnel file?"

"I haven't decided yet."

"Fine. I'll call the base chair."

"As you wish," said Phillip. "But let me give you a word of warning, Eric. Watch your back. You should *all* be watching your backs, all the time. And remember that in the end, management will always win. We run this show, not you."

Eric had to bite his tongue to keep from making a sarcastic reply. But why ruin a great performance? "Thanks for the heads up." He reached into the basket for a Cadbury egg. "And have a Happy Easter."

***

As Eric walked down the jet bridge, he realized that he hadn't pulled up a crew list. No matter—he'd learn everyone's name at the briefing. As entered the plane, he was pleased to see Leander checking the emergency equipment in first class. That was a pleasant surprise. He hadn't flown with Leander in quite a while. Leander wasn't the most exciting person in the world, but he was friendly, dependable and never caused any trouble. By this time, Eric had learned that a drama-free flight was more important than anything else. "Hi, Leander, it's great to see you. Are the coach flight attendants here already?"

"Yes. They're parked in the last row."

"Did you meet them? What are their names?"

"I did, but I've already forgotten. All I can remember is that they're both brand-spanking new and very impressed with themselves. You'll see."

Eric picked up the phone and pressed intercom. "Could I get everyone up front for a quick briefing, please?" A few minutes later, he and Leander were still alone in first class. Eric looked down the aisle and saw that the new hires hadn't budged. His hackles were immediately raised. Even if they were new, they should be aware of basic crew courtesy. He picked up the intercom again. "I need the two of you up here for a briefing *now*." Why waste time being conciliatory? He was the number one, and he wasn't putting up with any nonsense.

A moment later, they begrudgingly arrived and introduced themselves as Thomas and Julia. Thomas was rather nice-looking with a head of thick, blond hair. He wore the short-sleeved summer shirt, even though it was a cool spring day. He had altered the sleeves to show off his biceps. Where are we, thought Eric, Miami? Julia wore her hair short and her eye makeup heavy. She had a sweater wrapped around her waist and wore scuffed clogs. Clogs, Eric thought with disdain. They were known universally as the footwear of choice for flight attendants who'd given up on life. It usually took years for that to happen—not a few of weeks.

Eric introduced himself. As he ran through the pre-flight briefing, Thomas and Julia avoided making eye contact with him and whispered back and forth with their hands covering their mouths.

"I beg your pardon," Eric said. "Am I inconveniencing you?"

"No, we got all the pertinent information," said Thomas. "We're just not used to having a briefing go on for so long."

"You may return to your cabin now," said Eric. "We'll start boarding in one minute."

"God," said Julia, with a look of disgust. "I can't *believe* we have to work today."

"What's so special about today?" Leander asked.

"It's Easter Sunday. I missed church this morning, and now I'll have to miss dinner with my family. My grandmother baked a ham and made a coconut Easter Bunny cake. That's my favorite."

"I'm missing the holiday day with my family too," said Thomas. "I didn't even get one lousy jelly bean this morning."

"Perhaps the hotel will offer Easter dinner," said Leander. "They're pretty good at doing something special for crewmembers on the holidays."

"A hotel dinner on Easter," Julia said with a sneer. "Why don't we just pool our money and head out to the Golden Choral?"

Eric pursed his lips. It was a bad habit that he'd picked up from Sylvia Saks, but he couldn't help himself. "Tell me, how long have you two been flying?"

"Tomorrow is our two-month anniversary," said Thomas. "We were in the same training class."

"If you're this upset about having to work on Easter," said Eric, "I hate to think what you'll do when they call you with a three-day reserve trip on Christmas Eve."

"Christmas Eve?!" Julia's hand flew up. "Oh, *no sir!* That's *not* going to happen!"

Eric and Leander exchanged a look. It clearly said, 'Thank God I'm not in the back with those two today.'

"Here come the passengers," Eric said. "It's time to go to work."

***

After they had served lunch and made ice cream sundaes for sixteen first-class passengers, Eric and Leander sat down on their jump seats for the first time since takeoff.

"Do you want me to get the pilot trays ready?" Leander asked.

"We'll get to them in a little while," said Eric. "We need a five-minute breather. I haven't flown with you months. How's your love life?"

"I haven't had much time for that. My mother isn't well. I spend most of my days off flying to Louisiana to look after her."

"I hope it's nothing serious."

"She was diagnosed with Parkinson's disease a few years ago. It's only gone downhill since then."

"I'm sorry to hear that. Is there anyone else besides you who can take care of her?"

"My older sister lives nearby, but she works twelve-hour shifts as a nurse and has four kids. There's only so much that she can do." He sighed. "You'd think those two new hires would be a little more carefree. What are they, twenty years old? If missing Grandma's bunny cake is the biggest goddam problem in their lives today..."

"Did you get that sense of entitlement?" Eric asked.

"Did I get it? They *reek* of it. Well, screw' em. They'll get over it. What about you, Eric? Do you have a steady boyfriend yet?"

"No, it's impossible with my schedule. I end up working a lot of weekends, and that's when boyfriends want you to be home. It'll be this way for a good long while until I get some more seniority. I'm not complaining, though."

"When you do get lucky, are you playing safe and always using condoms?"

"Of course."

"Whatever happened to that guy from GMHC you were so hot for?"

"Oh, you mean Benjamin. I just met him a couple of times. He moved to San Francisco in January to start graduate school. I haven't seen him or heard from him since. I finally got *his* number and called him, but I guess he never got my message." Or just wasn't interested, Eric thought.

"That's too bad."

Eric shrugged. "Maybe I'll bump into him on a layover. I always keep my eyes open."

"It would be good for you to settle down. I hear you've become quite the party boy on your San Francisco layovers. That can get you into all kinds of trouble."

"Exactly what have you heard?"

"I won't go into any gory details. But remember, you can't be too careful these days."

"Whatever you've heard, it's galley gossip and nothing more. If I had a dime for every time that I actually went home with a guy, I'd—" He looked up as a passenger from coach came walking toward them. She wore a two-piece suit with a silk scarf pinned to the neckline of her jacket. Her lips and her fingernails were painted fire-engine red.

"I'm sorry to bother you," she said, "but could I please get a cup of coffee with milk and two sugars?"

"Sure," said Eric. "Let me brew a fresh pot, and I'll bring it to you. Where are you sitting?"

"I'm in 34C."

"Bless your heart," said Leander. "You didn't have to come all the way up here for that. The main cabin galley is just two rows behind your seat."

"I know," she said, "but the flight attendants aren't in the galley right now, and I don't want to go rummaging around on my own."

"Are they in the aisle?" Eric asked.

"No. Your colleagues are parked in the last row with headsets on, watching the movie. Quite a few passengers still have trays in front of them. I can tell that some want to get up to use the lavatory. May I ask who's in charge here?"

"I am," said Eric. "My name is Eric. I'm the lead flight attendant today."

"Let me suggest, Eric, that you have a chat with your co-workers. This isn't the kind of service that people expect from this airline."

"I agree. Thank you for letting me know. I'll be right back." He opened the curtain and was shocked by what he saw. The coach cabin was littered with dirty trays, coffee cups, plastic glasses and piles of newspaper. At least ten call lights were illuminated. The passengers seated beneath the call lights looked as though they had been waiting a long time for a flight attendant to respond. One customer after another tried to pass refuse to him as he walked down the aisle.

"I'll be with you in just a moment… I'm sorry the delay," he said over and over. By the time he reached the last row, he was ready to kill. Thomas and Julia *were* wearing headsets, with their eyes glued to the video monitor in the ceiling. In the seat between them was an enormous bag filled with Easter candy. The carpet beneath their feet was littered with colored foil wrappers. Eric stood there, waiting for them to remove the headphones. They didn't even look at him. He finally gave Thomas a hard tap on the shoulder. "What do you think you're doing?"

Looking highly annoyed, Thomas took off his headphones. "We're on our break."

"A break on a domestic flight is defined as sitting in your jump seat for fifteen minutes once the service is over—which it obviously is not. Your cabin looks like a hobo camp. And under no circumstances does a break involved watching the movie."

"International flight attendants get *two-hour* breaks, and they can watch a movie if they want," said Julia.

"This is not an international flight," said Eric. "The rules are different on domestic. Read your contract."

"Well, that *sucks,"* said Julia. "I mean, we're working a holiday not even getting paid any overtime!"

"Damn straight," said Thomas.

You punks, thought Eric. He reached over and pulled their headsets jacks out of the sockets. "Get up right now. I'm blocking this row for the rest of the flight. First, you're going to finish picking up this cabin. Then you're going to remain in the galley in case a passenger comes back and needs something. You *will* answer call lights and be available to passengers because that's your job. I don't care if today is Armageddon. And if I see you sitting in a passenger seat again, there's going to be big trouble. Understand?"

"Dude, who do you think you are, our supervisor?" said Thomas. "You're not even the purser on a widebody. You're just the number one. You don't have any authority over us."

Eric could see that passengers in the immediate area watching the conversation intently, including the woman who'd come up front to ask for coffee. "I see we're addressing this behavior none too soon. Let's step into the galley—*now.*"

They reluctantly got up and followed him.

Eric pulled the curtain closed. "You're both still on probation, right?"

"Yeah, so what?"

"Do you remember the term 'restriction of output' from when you were in training? You must: the instructors bring it up at least five times every day. It means loafing when you're on the clock."

"Oh," said Julia. "You mean, like, when I'm on the clock earning *jack shit* pay?"

"That's precisely what it means," said Eric. "Just for the record, I'm earning the same wage that you are, so don't try that argument with me. In case you've forgotten, restriction of output is a terminable offense while you're still on probation."

"What does terminable mean?" Thomas asked.

"It means you can be fired on the spot and the union can't do a damn thing to get your job back. If you want to keep your new jobs long enough to get *off* probation, then get into the aisle."

"Oh, yes, massah," said Julia. "I'll do whatever the white man tells me too. They didn't tell me I'd be working for Simon Legree today."

"I won't even dignify that with a response," said Eric. "If you have anything else to say about working conditions on this airplane, take it up with the captain. I guarantee you that he won't be on your side." As he opened the curtain, he almost collided with the woman from 34C, who was waiting to use the bathroom.

"I couldn't help overhearing your conversation," she said. "Thanks for coming back to address this issue. I'm on these planes all the time, and I've never seen the service so poorly executed. I'd like to commend you on your leadership skills."

"Thank you. Is there anything else that I can do for you, Miss...?"

"My name is Elizabeth, and no thank you. You probably want to get back to your own cabin. I'll stop up front to say goodbye after we land."

***

"What's going on back there?" Leander asked when Eric came back.

"Those two lazy, snot-nosed new hires are copping an attitude, that's what's going on."

"I bet you set them straight."

"I certainly did. I don't think we'll have any more trouble from them."

"Good. Now, what are we doing on our layover today?"

"We're going to find someplace to have a drink and pretend that we're not the only homosexuals within a hundred-mile radius. God, is there any place in the country more heterosexual than Orange County?"

"No, there isn't. It's funny. We always say, 'we are everywhere,' but you really have to beat the bushes to find another gay man in O.C. Well, at least we have each other. And it's only for one night."

"Amen to that."

***

Eric and Leander were stationed at the front door as the passengers deplaned. "Goodbye... goodbye... thank you for flying with us." At the end of a long flight, it took a fair amount of energy to smile and say goodbye almost two hundred times. As the last few stragglers reached into the overhead bins for their suitcases, Eric and Leander started gathering their own luggage. "I should say goodbye to Elizabeth," said Eric, as he saw he walking up the aisle.

"Who's Elizabeth?"

"That woman from the back who came up for coffee."

"Oh, you mean Miss Lips and Tips."

"What'd you say?"

"Lips and tips. Didn't you notice how her red lipstick and nail polish matched exactly? Along with her hairdo and shoulder pads, she looks like she could be the stewardess from a 1984 recruitment poster."

In a flash, it all came together in Eric's mind. "Oh, shit. Lips, tips, big hair! You don't think she's a supervisor, do you?"

"Let me check the final paperwork and see how she's listed." He scanned for her seat number. "No, she's a non-rev. She may be a flight attendant supervisor, but if she is, she's off duty, so there's not much she can do. Just turn on the Saunders charm and send her on her merry way."

Eric put on his most sincere smile as Elizabeth approached. "It was very nice having you on board, Elizabeth. I hope you enjoy your stay in Orange County."

"Thank you. Do you mind if I pop into the cockpit to say hello to the captain?"

"No, go right ahead." He watched Thomas and Julia coming up the aisle. "Doesn't Thomas have a uniform blazer?" he asked.

"Oh, no," Leander replied. "Heaven forbid he should walk twenty feet anywhere without showing off his biceps." He looked at Thomas again and shrugged. "He's cute, but he's not all *that* hot."

"I know, but he thinks he is."

"Are we going?" asked Julia. "I'm ready to get off this damn airplane."

"In just a second," said Eric. "There's still one passenger on board."

A moment later, Elizabeth stepped out of the cockpit. Eric immediately noticed that she had a company ID badge clipped to her jacket. "Oh, good. You're all here," she said. "For those of you whom I haven't met, my name is Elizabeth Hartsfield. I'm with Flight Service in Chicago. Please put down your luggage. We're going to have a debrief right now."

The captain nodded to the crew as he and the co-pilot walked past them. "Eric, we'll see you at the hotel," he said.

"We're supposed to go with them," Leander said to Elizabeth. "We're staying at the same hotel."

"Transportation will be provided for you and Eric once we're finished here. As for you two—" She gestured to the new hires. "You're deadheading back to JFK in an hour."

"What do you mean?" said Thomas.

"You're both being removed from service."

"Removed from service... *why?*"

"Where shall I start? Violation of uniform and grooming regulations, your less than stellar attitude, and restriction of output. As I heard Eric mentioned to you, that in of itself is a terminable offense."

"You mean we're being *fired?*"

"Yes. Please hand over your manuals, ID badges, and wings."

"With all due respect, Ms. Hartsfield," said Eric, "are you allowed to perform supervisory duties when you're traveling on an employee pass? It's not as though you announced that you were on board to do a check ride."

It was the wrong thing to say. She lost all pretext of professionalism and looked as though she enjoyed exercising her authority. "We may conduct supervisory duties whenever and wherever we choose. Rules are *rules*. Eric, I'll need a written statement from you as a witness." She gave him a sheet of paper. "Please start writing immediately. I want this all wrapped up before boarding begins." She snapped her fingers. "Thomas and Julia: your wings, please."

As he unpinned his wings from his shirt, Thomas burst into tears. Eric had to look away and focus on the blank page in front of him. You *idiot*, he thought. To throw away your career away just because you had to work on Easter Sunday...

***

"I don't believe it," Leander said for the fifth time, over drinks. "I just don't believe it!"

"I couldn't believe it when Thomas started crying. I thought that would be a very gratifying thing to watch after they were so rude to me, but it wasn't."

"No, of course not. It's one thing to put the fear of God into people. But to fire them on the spot like that. It's outrageous!"

"I felt like a traitor writing that witness statement. But she saw everything. What choice did I have?"

"I know she's management, but she could at least have given them a warning this time and let it slide."

"A warning," Eric muttered. "Shit, I just remembered! 'Watch your backs.' "

"What's that you said?"

"I had a meeting with my supervisor this morning about a bad passenger letter and the contract negotiation. Things got a little heated. Right before I left, he said, 'You should all be watching your backs, all the time.' Mother *fucker*, do you think this whole thing was a setup?"

"Maybe. I put nothing past management. But even so, those two should have known better. I didn't say boo to anyone while I was on probation. It would never even have occurred to me to park my ass in the last row for an hour. It took a whole year before I realized that people were stealing liquor and headset money. That's how naïve I was."

"Thank God I didn't take any booze off the plane today. If Elizabeth had done a bag check, I'd be deadheading back to JFK, too."

"You know what this means: until we get a new contract, we're at war with management. And it's only the beginning. You know how they love to throw their weight around and remind us who's in charge. Things will get a hell of a lot worse before it they get better."

"I'm afraid you're right, Leander."

"So just for today, let's enjoy ourselves while we can. I'd like another drink."

Eric signaled for the waiter, who brought them another round and then stood by the table to chat for a few minutes. He mentioned in passing that he was a ballet student and only worked at the restaurant part-time.

As the waiter walked away, Eric noticed one of the obvious benefits of daily ballet classes. "There is no ass in the world like a ballet dancer's ass," he said. "He's a hot little fucker—younger than I usually like them, but he's hot."

"He's cruising you," said Leander.

"I know. I like it. It's fun to flirt."

"Go for it," said Leander. "I bet you'd have a good time with him."

"No, I wouldn't leave you to fend for yourself."

Leander waved his hand. "Don't worry about me. I'm gonna get a good buzz on and then go back to the hotel, order room service, and be asleep by nine o'clock. Besides, at this rate, who knows how long we'll keep having this kind of opportunity? We could be fired tomorrow for looking cross-eyed at an Almighty Titan."

"You're right. I'm going to tell him which hotel we're in and ask if he wants to stop by."

Leander laughed and downed his drink. "I had a feeling you would. And I'm sure he'll say yes. Another conquest for the Infamous Flight Attendant Saunders."

"Do me a favor and keep this to yourself. This is no one's business but mine."

"Hey, honey, I just listen to gossip, I don't spread it. Don't worry about me. *My* lips are sealed."

CHAPTER 38

The Balm in Gilead

Dexter Ludlow, the New York Flight Service Base Manager, walked to the podium at the front of the conference room and tapped on the microphone. "Ladies and gentlemen," he said, in his most officious voice, "thank you very much for coming this afternoon. It is now one o'clock. If you'd please take a seat, we'll begin right away."

For once, no one had to be corralled into sitting down. Phillip Hendry, one the last people to enter the room, quietly took a vacant seat in the fifth row. The room was packed with supervisors from all three New York area airports. On the table in front of each attendee, there was a report entitled *The State of the Airline: An In-depth Review of the Operation.* Six months in the making, the report detailed the strengths and weaknesses of each hub in the system. By now, everyone in the room knew that the review of New York was not a favorable one. Some supervisors glanced nervously at the thick stack of paper, praying that their name wasn't mentioned within. Others, with big smiles frozen on their faces, kept their eyes glued to the front of the room. Maxwell Cutler sat a table next to the podium, scowling. His presence was not a good sign. When the CEO left headquarters to attend a local flight service meeting, the news had to bad indeed. As a latecomer rushed in and took off her coat, he bared his ferocious teeth. The harried woman looked as though she might faint.

"I know that we have a lot of information to go over," said Dexter, "but Mr. Cutler would like to make an opening statement. Please give him your undivided attention."

Nah, thought Phillip, as he applauded along with the other supervisors. I think that I'll jump up and start singing "Get Happy" instead.

Maxwell Cutler was over six-feet tall and had a lanky frame. His thick grey hair was cut close to his head. He wore heavy black-rimmed glasses, a charcoal suit that looked as though it came off the rack from Filene's Basement, and black wingtip shoes. Cutler was a heavy smoker with teeth that showed it. Even from five rows away, Phillip could smell the stale cigarette smoke that famously trailed him everywhere he went.

As the CEO stood up and took over the podium, Dexter hovered nearby. He was overdressed by comparison in a three-piece suit, a shirt with French cuffs, a floral print tie, and calfskin loafers. Dexter spent a fortune on his professional wardrobe. He had begun his career as a reservations agent, then become a cargo supervisor and then a passenger service manager. Six months ago, despite having no experience with the flight attendant group, he had been promoted to Base Manager of New York—the second-largest hub in the system. Dexter made it clear to his subordinates, on a regular basis, that this assignment was merely a pit stop on his way to a high-level position at headquarters. Dexter was "going places." Phillip, who seemed to be going nowhere, couldn't stand the sight of him.

"Ladies and gentlemen," said Mr. Cutler in his deep, gravelly voice, "let's get right to the point. We have a serious problem on our hands." He lit a cigarette, ignoring the No Smoking sign posted near the door. Dexter hastily improvised an ashtray by pouring two inches of water into a coffee mug, and set it before him on the podium. "After fifty years of being known as the greatest airline in the world, we've started slipping. No, forget slipping: we're going right off a goddam cliff. Twenty-five percent of flights are late. Complaint letters are at an all-time high. Customers are abandoning us left and right for other carriers, taking millions of dollars in revenue with them. You know as well as I do that once they leave, they *never* come back." He paused to let his last remark sink in. "After doing a great deal of research, we have determined that the problem lies right here in *your* department—with the flight attendants. And which base has the highest number of complaints? *New York City.*" He paused again. "This is the financial capital of the world and one of our most important hubs. Nowhere else in the system do business travelers pay such a high fare for premium service. They expect a lot for their money, as well they should. And what do they get in return? *Nothing!*" He pounded his fist, sending a collective shudder through the room. "Flight attendants barely offer the service they're supposed to. They cut corners everywhere, and then they sit on their asses for hours on end, flipping through magazines and yacking. They don't even bother to answer call lights. A passenger has to ring the damn call light ten times before someone responds, and when they finally do respond, it's always with an eye roll and a smart-ass remark. To make matters worse, in the twenty years that I've been here, I've never seen crewmembers take such little interest in their appearance. We've got thousands of front-line employees who look like hookers, sad sacks, and bums. Everywhere I go, I see stiletto heels, clogs, and sneakers. Since when are any of those considered regulation footwear? Women's hairstyles are atrocious. They don't even *comb* their hair. It looks like they roll out of bed in the morning and right onto the plane. And incidentally, the males are no better: ties are missing, they're unshaven, they wear their hair like it's 1968. While walking through the terminal here today, I saw a young man with a ponytail. Yes, a ponytail! His shirttail was hanging out, and he was wearing headphones He was oblivious to everyone, including a passenger who tried to ask him for directions to baggage claim. When I stopped him to address his grooming, he looked at me slack-jawed as though he had no idea who I was and said, 'Dude, I'm off the clock.' " He grunted. "I demanded to see his crew ID. Needless to say, that flight attendant is now off the clock *permanently*."

Oh, great, thought Phillip. Another fight with the union over a crewmember who's been 'unjustly' terminated. How many more people can we fire in one year?

"Now," said Cutler, picking up his coffee mug and taking a sip, "I—goddammit!" He sputtered as he drank a cupful of ashes and water, and then threw the cup to the floor. As it shattered and pieces went flying, the entire first row cringed. The CEO's temper tantrums were legendary. He had reportedly thrown a chair through an office window one Christmas Eve when the sick list climbed past fifteen percent and, as a result, flights packed with holiday travelers began canceling. Dexter bent down to pick up the pieces and then resumed his post, acting as though nothing out of the ordinary had happened. "Now, you people are charged with managing the flight attendants—their grooming, their performance, and their conduct. Obviously, you're not doing that. What I want to know is: what the hell *do* you do?"

Everyone suddenly became very busy smoothing hair, fumbling for pens, and looking anywhere but the front of the room.

Phillip remained calm. Whatever he did at work, he was merely following the base manager's instructions. Screw it, he thought. I'd love to watch Dexter squirm. He raised his hand. "I can tell you what we do, sir. We attend lots of meetings."

"And what do you do during these meetings?"

"This week, we spent three days doing team-build exercises. We split up into groups. Each table was given a blank poster board and a set of colored markers. We wrote the word 'Mercury' vertically and then had to find a word or words corresponding to each letter that we could associate with good customer service. 'M-motivated, E-excellence, R-raring to go, C-committed,' et cetera. Afterward, a leader from each table presented the finished product and then we shared our thoughts as a group."

Cutler glared at Dexter. "*This* is how you spend your managers' time?"

"It was a dry run," Dexter said, visibly withering. "We're anticipating doing the same training for all the flight attendants here in New York. It seems many of them have moved away from the goals they stated during their interviews and initial training. We want them to *recommit* to those goals. It's a refresher course that I'm calling Ready to Rise."

"You've got to be kidding," said Cutler. "We have thousands of flight attendants in open revolt, and you want them to come in and play with Magic Markers? What are you running here, a crew base or kindergarten?" He turned to the supervisors and jabbed his finger at Phillip. "When is the last time you did an observation ride or walked through the terminal to do a grooming check?"

"At least three months," said Phillip. "Unfortunately, with all the meetings that we have to attend, the pie charts we have to create, the conference calls with headquarters and the daily reports, there isn't enough time in the day. We're tethered to our desks, more or less."

Cutler flared his nostrils. "I can see that some changes need to be made here, and fast. Now, I want to know why the flight attendants are so unhappy and what it will take to get them back on track." As Dexter started to speak, Cutler silenced him. "No, I don't need to hear anything else from you. I want someone who has the guts to tell me exactly what's going on here."

Phillip raised his hand again. "They want a new contract, and they want it now. Compared to flight attendants at other airlines, they feel that they're underpaid. They're physically exhausted from fourteen-hour duty days. And they're hungry because we don't provide them with either sufficient crew meals or the time to buy food between flights. A three-ounce can of tuna, a pack of saltines and on orange just doesn't cut it. So, in a nutshell, they want a pay raise, a decent night's sleep, and a reasonable duty day."

"A pay raise is out of the question. We can't increase our costs right now. If anything, it's imperative that we *cut* costs across the board. Read the goddam report! We're hemorrhaging money, along with every other airline in the country. I don't think that you *or* they understand: the survival of the company is at stake. Don't they read the newspaper? Global is going into liquidation any minute now. There'll be five thousand laid-off attendants banging on our door. Quite frankly, in this economy, *our* flight attendants should consider themselves fortunate to have a job, travel benefits and health insurance. Has anyone mentioned that to them?"

Phillip remembered his recent conversation with Eric Saunders. 'You should be grateful to have...' How ironic to hear his own words coming out of the CEO's mouth.

Cutler lit another cigarette. "I want one good idea from somebody that will improve morale around here that doesn't cost a goddam dime. Somebody had better come up with something right now."

"I have an idea," said Phillip.

"Let's hear it. Stand up and tell me your name." He turned to Dexter. "You—grab one of your Magic Markers and write this down."

"My name is Phillip Hendry. I'm a supervisor here at JFK. To appease the flight attendants in the short term, and as a gesture of good faith, I propose that we dedicate a space in operations for flight attendants to post pictures of themselves."

"That's a *splendid* idea," Dexter said condescendingly. "Anyone else?"

"Shut up," said Cutler, without even turning his head. "Go on."

"In the mailbox room in Flight Service Operations, there is an entire wall covered from top to bottom with only two things: notices about rules and regulations, and copies of bad passenger letters. It infuriates them every time they walk by it. If we take all that down and give the space to them, they'll have something positive to focus instead: themselves. As an added incentive, we can give them one of these." He reached into a shoulder bag and pulled out a Polaroid camera. "We have two hundred of these cameras left over from a promotional campaign with a local travel agency that just went out of business. Right now, they're collecting dust in the sales office. We can put out an email and give them away to the first two hundred flight attendants who respond."

"How is this supposed to solve all our problems?" asked Cutler.

"It won't solve all of our problems. But in the short-term, it will benefit us. One, it's a positive step toward morale building. Two, it's a freebie. Flight attendants love freebies. Three, these are Polaroid cameras. The film is included, so there'll be no developing costs. Four, it will provide them with instant gratification. In case you haven't noticed, flight attendants as a group are not good at delaying gratification. Five, if they know that hundreds of co-workers will be looking at their pictures every day, they'll be motivated to renew focus on their grooming. They'll want to look their best."

"This plan sounds like a temporary distraction to me," said Dexter.

"There is merit in distraction," said Phillip. "Besides, there is a long-term benefit which may not be readily obvious to them but should be crystal clear to us."

"Such as?" said Cutler.

"As time goes by and the wall starts to fill up, there will be competition for space. There is nothing so good for the company and so bad for the flight attendants as competition among themselves. The long-term benefit for *us* will be a strategy known as 'divide and conquer.' I assure that it won't take long. They'll be at each other's throats within a month, and we won't have to lift a finger for it to happen."

A slow grin spread over Cutler's face. "I have just one question for you, young man. Why aren't you working at headquarters?"

As Dexter turned purple with rage, Phillip beamed. Maybe, he thought, *I'll* be the one who's going places.

***

Two weeks later, Eric walked into operations at JFK. After he signed in, he stepped into the mailbox room and noticed a cluster of flight attendants chatting excitedly in front of a wall that was half-covered with photographs.

"What's that?" he asked Sylvia Saks, who was also checking her mail.

"The balm in Gilead," she said.

"Huh?"

"Didn't you read your company email this week?"

"No, I was out with the flu. This is my first trip back."

"Flight Service has taken down the rules and regulation notices, and bad passenger letters, and is dedicating that space to us."

"For what?"

"To put up pictures of ourselves doing whatever we want: sightseeing, modeling a new pair of work shoes, getting hoisted into an overhead bin. As long as it's work-related, it's OK. Shots of kids and pets are forbidden, thank God. We get enough of that crap on the plane."

"What the hell is the point?"

"Isn't it obvious? It's a distraction from the *mishegoss* about the contract."

"Whose bright idea was this?"

"They had a slew of Polaroid cameras sitting around for some reason, so they gave them to us for free."

"Oh, please. Who would fall for such an obvious ploy?"

"Those cameras were snapped up in less than twenty-four hours. There was near riot. I know, I was here when they gave out the last one. Now every base in the system is demanding the same thing, and the company is more than happy to comply."

"This is ridiculous. It's not what we want or need. What we *need* is a new contract."

"You overestimate your own kind."

"Ha. We'll see how long this bullshit lasts."

"You may live to eat those words, sweetheart."

***

The wall was phenomenally popular. What started as a few people shyly putting up pictures became an overnight sensation. It began, naturally, with international flight attendants documenting their European layovers. The customary four-hour nap, previously a necessity after working a grueling transatlantic flight, became a thing of the past. Crewmembers changed out of their uniforms and hit the ground running for hours of frenzied sightseeing. Paris was ceded the prime spot at the center of the wall. The Eiffel Tower, the bridges across the Seine River, and Notre Dame Cathedral went up first. Westminster Abbey, Big Ben and the Tower of London came next, followed by the Colosseum in Rome, *Las Ramblas* in Barcelona, the *Puerta del Sol* in Madrid and the *Grande Place* in Brussels. A photo of any locale was not complete, however, unless a flight attendant was in the picture. A sumptuous dinner in a four-star restaurant followed sightseeing. The number of wine bottles on the table far exceeded the number of crewmembers. It was imperative to have a glass of wine in one's hand at all times; being photographed at dinner without one was considered *déclassé*. These multi-course feasts nearly bankrupted the more junior international flight attendants. They were accustomed to making twenty-five dollars stretch for an entire layover, which in of itself was an impossible feat. But if they wanted to be included in the picture, they had to play the game. They'd be mortified if their worldly senior colleagues found out that they usually dined on fast food. MacDonald's was everywhere, thank God. If even that was too expensive, they bought a sandwich and a can of beer and consumed both sitting on a secluded park bench, their faces hidden by a hat and dark sunglasses.

Photos of South America quickly followed. Domestic flight attendants looked enviously at their co-workers sunbathing among the beautiful, nearly naked Brazilians on Copa Cabana Beach. In Buenos Aires, they posed in front of the *Casa Rosada* and Eva Peron's family crypt in *La Recoleta* Cemetery. In the afternoon, they ran back to the hotel for tango lessons from dashing instructors wearing obscenely tight pants.

Not to be outdone, domestic flight attendants in San Francisco snapped pictures of themselves on the Golden Gate Bridge, at Fisherman's Wharf, and in front of the celebrated Castro Theatre. In Miami, they flocked to the trendy gay bars and sandy shores of South Beach. There, they could find almost as many handsome Brazilians as there were in Rio de Janeiro.

In Los Angeles, there was simply the beach—and nothing but the beach. As they had no layover hotels anywhere near Beverly Hills or Hollywood, there was no other no place else of interest in which to be seen. Then someone came up with the idea of having himself photographed in the white wine aisle of Dealer Dan's. He pinned it on the wall along with the caption: "A world of endless possibilities!" Being shown choosing a good bottle of reasonably priced wine proved so popular that it became a rite of passage. However, this elicited nothing more than a sneer from the European jet-setters. "A California Chardonnay: can you *imagine?*"

In New York, the city of real endless possibilities, no one took pictures. As a cost-cutting measure, all New York layovers were shortened to twelve hours or less and crewmembers were sent to the La Guardia Marriott. Everyone fumed. Why bother to bring a camera? Who would lower himself to being photographed at the Unisphere—in *Queens?*

There was only one drawback to having your picture taken for the wall: someone else had to be there to take the picture. Friends soon became impatient with each other, as the Polaroid shots had to be taken over and over until they came out right:

"No, I said a *three-quarter profile* shot. This one is straight on! I'm all nose, and you can't see my jawline at all. Do it again."

"Not yet! I'm waiting for the wind to come back up. I want my hair moving just so in the breeze."

"Should I put my hand on my hip and toss my head back, or just put my hand on my hip, or just toss my head back?"

"Oh, my God, I know we're in Covent Garden, but could you wait until there *aren't* a million tourists walking behind me?"

"I knew I should have worn the Andrew Christian trunks instead of the Speedo. The Andrew Christian trunks have built-in crotch support, and my dick looks *huge."*

As people tired of catering to their friends' needs, they began occasionally retreating to solitary exploits. Pictures of omelets in the hotel coffee shop became popular for a while, when it was just too damn hot to walk to IHOP (although everyone knew that a short stack of strawberry pancakes topped with whipped cream simply "read" better). For some, whatever lay just beyond their feet—be it the shoreline, the hotel pool, or their actual bare feet propped on a hotel pillow— was an easy, albeit lazy, subject. That lasted until galley gossip started spreading about which co-workers groomed their feet properly and which ones did not. "Look! There's a great, big piece of black sock lint stuck under his toenail. And *she* has a bunion that's the size of my fist!" Hotel room shots were also popular among the slam-clickers who spent the layover drinking alone in isolated bliss. They woke up the next morning with wretched hangovers, but still wanted something to show for their time away from home.

A bloody hand, mangled by a runaway beverage cart, was a hot topic of interest for one afternoon. It was followed the next day by a broken leg in a plaster cast—the result of an encounter with severe turbulence. People seemed to rouse themselves from a deep slumber as, once again, the subject of being injured on duty reared its ugly head. But the awakening lasted for less than forty-eight hours. Despite management's pledge not to interfere, the offending photos were taken down in the middle of the night. Any such similar photos, posted afterward, disappeared within the hour.

As the weeks went by, competition for space on the wall became exceedingly fierce. One afternoon, a flight attendant named Craig Edelstein moved a picture of Rosemary Licata at the Trevi Fountain from its coveted spot at the center of the wall. He tacked hers to the bottom and replaced it with a picture of himself at Disneyland. Unbeknownst to Craig, Rosemary was one of the most senior people at JFK. Whenever she was in operations, she hovered around the wall like a hawk guarding its nest. When she was away, a cadre of senior friends assumed the task for her. A friend of Rosemary's jumped on Craig and told him, in no uncertain terms, that that the center space was reserved for senior international flight attendants *only*. Craig stated that being seen in front of Sleeping Beauty Castle was a life-long dream; that the photo of Rosemary had been up for almost a month; and that furthermore, any space on the wall was open to everyone, domestic or international, regardless of seniority. Co-workers in the vicinity immediately came forward and took sides. Voices were raised; threats were made.

The manager on duty was summoned to settle the dispute but wanted no part of it. "I don't have time for this," she said. "The wall was Phillip Hendry's idea, not mine. He is out of the office until next week. You'll have to wait until he gets back on Monday. In the meantime, I'm barring anyone from entering that room. It will remain locked until further notice. If you need to check your mailbox, you may enter one at a time—but only with an escort from management."

An entire week without posting on the wall! It was preposterous! For the next seven days, people talked of nothing else:

"Isn't it just like the international flight attendants to be so self-centered? They already get everything: the best trips, the best vacations, real layovers in the best hotels, and extra pay just because they can shove people onto a raft in the middle of the Atlantic Ocean. It's not fair!"

"Oh, those *domestic* people. As if anyone wants to look at them shopping for toilet paper at Costco. Do you believe some of them *bid* that layover specifically, to go to Costco? They buy a slice of pizza at the food court, and a twelve-pack of Angel Soft to lug home and *that's* a good layover for them! Could you imagine them shopping in London? They probably don't even know how to exchange money. Hell, they probably don't even know what foreign currency *is!*"

Tempers reached the boiling point when the manager announced that Phillip's return would be delayed by a week. He was still in meetings at headquarters. It was later revealed that management had spent an exhaustive two weeks trying to decide, city by city, if they could transport crewmembers to and from hotels on public buses—for a minor and reimbursable sum of money—rather than provide hired vans, which was a major expense. It would save the company millions of dollars each year, but was it really feasible?

After an anguishing two-week wait, Phillip returned and announced his decision. "The center space is reserved for the international division. As seniority dictates every other facet of the job, this ruling is in line with company policy. However, pictures must be stamped with a date and taken down after two weeks. Additionally, during December each year, the center space will be allocated to the domestic division."

Phillips verdict only further incensed the entire base. "What about the European Christmas bazaars?" screamed the senior flight attendants. "The beautiful white lights, the delicate, handmade ornaments, the carolers in authentic holiday dress, the cups of steaming mulled wine? Those are the best shots of the year!"

The squabbling intensified to the point that flight attendants were barely speaking to each another. Their pictures and their location on the wall became paramount in their minds, to the exclusion of everything else. Eric and the other union reps threw their hands up in frustration as co-workers stopped reading the union newsletter and attendance at monthly meetings dropped precipitously. "This is absurd!" Eric wailed. "Doesn't anything *matter* to people anymore, besides that goddam wall?" His cries fell on deaf ears. It was apparent that being envied by others did matter more than anything else.

***

"You see," Phillip said smugly to Dexter, as he packed up his desk for a new high-level job at headquarters. "It's just as I predicted. They're at each other's throats. The wall is all they ever think about. They've even stopped complaining about the bid sheet. *This* is how you divide and conquer, my friend. And on another positive note, compliance with grooming regulations has improved one hundred percent. Hair, makeup, hosiery, shoes—from head to toe, they all look marvelous. People spend hours preening in front of the mirror before they come to work, just like when they were new hires. Mr. Cutler is quite pleased, as you can imagine."

"And what will you do when they get tired of that goddam wall?" Dexter asked. "This won't last forever. At some point, they'll remember that they still don't have a pay raise or anything else you said they wanted."

"One step at a time, Dexter," he said as he sealed the last box. "Just take it one step at a time."

CHAPTER 39

Where or When

Eric stepped off the elevator at noon to sign in for his flight to San Francisco. He was grateful to find operations blessedly quiet. Even the mailbox room was nearly empty. The fury over the wall seemed to have run its course at last. People still posted pictures occasionally, but they were no longer obsessed by it twenty-four hours a day. Thank God, thought Eric. Maybe now we can get everyone to focus on the contract again.

Denny arrived a few minutes later. His skin was pale, and he had dark circles under his eyes. He looked utterly worn out.

"Hi," said Eric. "Late night last night?"

"Yes. Very."

"Were you at the Eagle?"

"No. I was somewhere else."

"You look like you're about to drop. Are you sure you're up for Happy Hour today?"

"Of course." He rubbed the back of his neck. "Let's go in the break room. I could use a cup of coffee before we head downstairs."

They walked into the break room, which was occupied by two male flight attendants.

"Oh, hi guys," said Denny. "This my friend Eric. Eric, this is Tyson and Angel. They're flying with us today."

Tyson was tall, handsome, and broad-shouldered. He had glossy hair and wore silver rings on all his fingers. His fingernails were rather long for a man, Eric noticed, but at least they were clean. Angel was much shorter, but just as solidly built. He had a shaved head and a small dark goatee. A heavy silver keychain was attached to a belt loop on his left side; the end of the chain disappeared into his rear pocket. He wore thick black leather bands on both of his wrists. Instead of dress shoes, he wore combat boots.

Oh, please, thought Eric. Combat boots with the uniform? Talk about trying too hard to look butch. "Nice to meet you, guys."

"Same here," said Tyson.

"An all-gay crew in coach," said Angel. "How cool is this? It almost never happens."

"I *love* it!" said Tyson. "I'm like, hey, *bitches!* Get out of the way!"

"You said it, baby!" said Angel. "The boys are back in town!" They hugged each other and dissolved into a fit of laughter.

Eric tried not to wince. It was a little early in the day to be making such a ruckus.

"We'll see you guys at the gate," said Denny. "We're going to pop over to the food court. Come on, Eric."

"See you down there," said Eric. As they walked to the elevator, he said, "I thought you wanted a cup of coffee."

"I do."

"Why not have it in the break room? Coffee's free in there."

"I need to talk to you, and I thought we'd be alone. It's kind of hard to have a conversation with those two around. They're so loud."

"Thank God you said that. I thought it was just me, being my usual uptight self. They don't seem like regular transcon flight attendants."

"They're not. They usually fly the Caribbean. They resigned from international and came back to domestic for a few months to take a break. Caribbean flying is hard, especially in the summer. That crowd will really wear you out. By the way, Tyson loves to tell stories about altercations with passengers. If it gets to be too much, walk away and go visit another cabin."

"Oh, great. Just what I wanted today."

Denny sighed. "It's six hours out of your life. You've been flying for almost a year now. Learn to cope already."

They walked into the food court, which was nearly as deserted as operations. "Do you want a coffee?" asked Denny. "My treat."

"Sure. Milk, no sugar. Thanks."

Denny returned a moment later with two cups of coffee.

"So, what did you want to talk to me about?" Eric asked.

"I have some bad news."

"Don't tell me they took away our downtown San Francisco layovers next month! That's the only trip I like on the entire bid sheet."

"It's a little more serious than that," Denny said, in a tone that gave Eric a sick feeling in the pit of his stomach.

"What is it?"

"I hate to be the one to tell you, but Zack died last night."

"What did you say?" It seemed silly to ask Denny to repeat himself, but Eric couldn't believe what he had just heard.

"I said, Zack died last night."

"What are you talking about? I just spoke with him two weeks ago. He sounded fine."

"Maybe he was fine two weeks ago. But things happen very quickly with this disease. He was rushed to St. Vincent's Hospital on Monday with pneumonia again. They put him on IV antibiotics, but his poor body was just too tired to fight it. He died at one o'clock this morning."

"Why didn't he call me? He knew he could count on me to be there."

"He could barely talk. When he realized how grim the situation was, he asked his doctor to call his mother and Sylvia Saks. Those were the only numbers he had memorized. Sylvia called me yesterday. Thank God I got the message."

Eric was furious. "Why didn't *you* call me, Denny? I was sitting at home, drinking wine and watching *Saturday Night Live*. I could have been there."

"Dying isn't something you necessarily want an audience for."

"Please don't *lecture* me," Eric snapped. "I'm not an *audience*. I'm his friend."

"I'm sorry, Eric. We kept hoping he'd pull through. But he went so fast. His mother didn't even make it in time. She's arriving this afternoon. Sylvia, bless her heart, is going to meet her at La Guardia and bring her back to her apartment, like she's done a hundred times before for other families. She's amazing. If Jews could be canonized, she should be named the Patron Saint of PWAs when she dies."

"Oh my God, I wish I'd been at the hospital with you." He felt suddenly guilty. "I could have done more for him. I could have called every week, rather than every *other* week. I could have visited more often." Instead, he thought, I metered out my "support" on a biweekly basis and felt so proud of myself for doing so. What the fuck am I doing with my free time, anyway?

"Be glad you weren't there," said Denny. "No matter what the doctors did, Zack couldn't catch his breath. He suffered terribly. It was fucking awful to sit in that chair next to his bed—like watching someone be tortured. Jesus, I've never wanted to be somewhere else more badly in my whole life. Even the morphine wasn't helping. At midnight, they finally slipped something under his tongue. That did the trick. He quieted down, his breathing became less labored and then he just… died."

"Oh, my God." Eric didn't know what else to say.

"I'm sorry to break it to you right before a flight, but I didn't want to tell you over the phone, and I wanted you to know before Tyson and Angel. They knew him too, even though they weren't close friends."

"Thanks for telling me. I'll have to call Zack's mother at Sylvia's as soon as we get back tomorrow. Have the funeral arrangements been made?"

"No, of course not. He just died twelve hours ago. His mom isn't even here yet."

"Sorry, that was silly. It's one of those questions you automatically ask, I guess."

"Eric, you're white as a sheet. Are you sure you'll be OK to work today?"

"Yes, of course. It's just a shock, that's all. Thank God we're not full in coach today. And thank God I'm not working in business class. After that terrible news, I'm in no mood to put up with nonsense from the Titans, Almighty or otherwise."

Denny looked at his watch. "We'd better get down to the gate. By the way, the debrief is gonna be in my room today. Everyone's bringing their own booze. Just grab whatever you want from the liquor cart."

"Who is everyone?"

"Angel and Tyson will be joining us. We'll have a few drinks together before we head out to the Castro."

"You mean, we're hanging out with *them* today?"

"Yes, this was decided last week, before you traded onto the trip. They called to invite me and I couldn't say no. Besides, we all hang out at the same bars. We're bound to run into them at some point."

"I wish I had known. I'd have made other plans."

"Come on, loosen up. They're not that bad. If you can get Tyson to talk about something other than passengers, he's a pretty funny guy. So is Angel. Besides, you don't want to spend the day sitting alone in your room. What good is that?"

"Spare me your Sally Bowles philosophy of life. I'll let you know later what I decide to do."

***

The coach cabin was half-empty, which was odd for a Sunday in June. However, what should have been an easy service became a Herculean test of Eric's patience. Tyson and Angel ignored the station assignment chart in the manual, and both insisted on serving drinks. Their seniority and inflexibility relegated Eric and Denny to the meal carts. Eric was stuck working with Tyson and was mortified by his unprofessional behavior. The words 'Sir' and 'Madam' were not in Tyson's vocabulary. He addressed passengers by their seat assignment and barked at them when they didn't immediately respond to his query. "Hey! Row 23, window! I *asked* you what you want to drink." Eric had to look away as Tyson slapped a napkin and beverage on each tray table. Maybe thought Eric, he's pissed because no one's ordering liquor and he was counting on some ready cash for his layover. But no, that wasn't it. He was just as rude to a man who ordered a double Scotch and soda and promptly handed over a ten-dollar bill. Tyson snatched the money and shoved it into his apron pocket. Eric prayed that it wouldn't reach the point where a passenger would demand Tyson's name. Normally in such situations, Eric would say, "It's right there on his apron." But Tyson, who had apparently been asked for his name many times over the years, had taken a black marker and covered it up. To Eric's relief, by the time the service was finished no one had asked. Thank God that's over, Eric thought, as he stowed the last dirty meal cart and washed his hands. Now I can relax and eat my lunch in peace.

He took a leftover meal tray and settled in the last row with his food, a bottle of water and a copy of *Men's Fitness*. A young mother in the row ahead of him was watching the movie with her one-year-old son curled up on the seat next to her. The baby had been very cranky and noisy during the first two hours of the flight. He'd finally quieted down and was sleeping. This was the time of flight that Eric liked best. All the passengers were in their seats, reading or watching the movie. No one was ringing the call light to ask for a fifth drink or coming to the back of the plane to do yoga postures. All flight attendants loathed yoga devotees who tried to align their spines near the galley. When attempting Downward Facing Dog in that cramped space, the passenger's rear end, sheathed in skin-tight stretch pants, was invariably thrust in their faces.

Eric finished his chicken with rice. He had just reached for his magazine when he realized that he was physically and emotionally exhausted. The news of Zack's death was too sudden to process. I can't think about it right now, he thought. I'll get too upset. As he felt his eyelids starting to flutter, he put down the magazine. He felt a sudden chill in the cabin and slipped into his blazer, and then leaned back against the headrest. Ten minutes, he thought. I'll close my eyes for ten minutes. Then I'll find Denny, and we'll make our plans for the evening...

Five minutes later, he was jolted awake by a harsh voice coming from the galley. "So then she tells me she's supposed to get free drinks 'cause she's a 'frequent flyer.' Frequent flyer my ass. And I'm like, '*Hello!* You're in *coach!* You gotta *pay* for drinks back here, same as everybody else.'" It was Tyson's voice, without a doubt. In the two hours that Eric had known him, he'd learned that "I'm like, *hello!*" was Tyson's favorite expression. That phrase was invariably accompanied by a sneer that defied the laws of physics: one eyebrow raised all the way to his hairline, and the opposite corner of his mouth open wide enough to see his molars. The effect was so horrifying that the first time Eric saw it, he thought that Tyson was having a stroke. Denny had to grab the interphone out of Eric's hand to stop him from paging for a physician.

"Was that the same woman who wanted you to put her bag up before takeoff?" That was Angel speaking.

"Mmm hmm. I looked at her and said, 'Hello! Is that your carry-on luggage or my carry-on luggage? 'Cause if it's *your* luggage, you're supposed to lift it, not me.' And she said, 'It's too heavy for me to lift. Why don't you do the job that you're *paid* for?' And I'm like, '*Hello!* For your information, we don't get paid *shit* here on the ground for all this work we're doing. And while we're on the subject, my name isn't Kunta Kinte and I *ain't* your damn slave.'" He snapped his fingers. "Then I turned and walked away."

"Ha! Good one, Tyson! You sure told *her* what to do."

"Hey, what d'you *think* I'm gonna tell her? I ain't playing with these *fools*."

The baby woke up and started crying. The mother, clearly exasperated, looked toward the back of the plane and waved at Eric. "Excuse me. It took me two hours to get my son to sleep, and I was hoping he would *stay* asleep. I don't know what's going on back there, but would you please ask your co-workers to lower their voices?"

"Yes, ma'am." Eric walked to the galley, knowing before he even opened his mouth that any attempt to quiet Angel and Tyson would be an exercise in futility. "Hey guys, that lady with the baby would appreciate it if you would keep it down."

"Keep what down?" said Angel.

"Your voices."

"We're just talking," said Tyson. "Where does she think this is, a library?"

"No, she doesn't think it's a library. But we can hear every word you're saying back here."

"If she don't want to hear what we're saying, tell her to put on some damn headphones."

"She's trying to keep the baby asleep so that he doesn't start crying and bother everyone else in the cabin."

"This is *our* galley," said Tyson. "I'll talk whatever damn way I want to."

Jesus fucking Christ, thought Eric. How did these two ever get hired? "I know it's your galley," he said, trying to keep his voice modulated, "but do you have to talk so loudly? They can hear you all the way to business class. They don't *want* to hear you, and frankly neither do I."

Tyson eyed Eric's buttoned blazer. "I tell you what, Maria Von Trapp: mind your own damned business. I don't need you coming back here and telling me what to do."

"You're making it my business, because I'm the one who has to deal with the passenger that you're bothering. All that I'm asking you to have some basic consideration. She doesn't want to spend the next two hours hearing you mouthing off."

"If she don't like it," Tyson said with the sneer, "she can pick up her baby and move."

"That's right," said Angel. "There are at least twenty empty seats closer to the front. We don't have to fucking whisper just 'cause there's a baby on board."

Eric considered going up front to ask the purser to intervene. Screw that, he thought. I'm not going to be bullied by two assholes who have no manners. "Fine," said Eric. "I'll let *you* give the passenger that suggestion. She's in 28F. I'm out of here." He stopped by the woman's seat. "I did my best. I brought your concern to their attention. I shouldn't have to apologize for my co-worker's behavior, but I am. Let me suggest that you ring your call button and address them directly."

"What?! That's absurd. Who is the purser today?"

"Her name is Sue."

"Please tell Sue I want to speak with her immediately." She showed Eric her embossed Almighty Titan membership card.

"I'll give her the message." Eric never thought he'd appreciate the day when an Almighty Titan decided to throw her weight around. But this was an exception. He'd be delighted to deliver the message. Sue was the ultimate in no-nonsense pursers. Eric knew that she'd straighten out those jackasses in two seconds.

He went to first class, where Denny was sitting on a jump seat eating a steak with mashed potatoes. "Hey! Nice way to leave me alone in the back with those two jerks, Denny."

"I'm just taking a break, like you were doing in the last row. I'll be back in a minute."

"Where's Sue?"

"In the cockpit."

Eric picked up the interphone and dialed the cockpit. "Hi, this is Eric. Can I speak with Sue, please?" He explained the situation to her. She stepped out a moment later, looking peeved.

"Goddammit," she said. "And just when the captain was about to invite me to dinner. There's nothing I hate more than having to put out other people's fires. I knew those two were trouble the minute they came on board. I wish those hard-core Caribbean flight attendants would *stay* on the Caribbean. We don't need their big mouths or their bad attitudes over here on domestic." She took off her apron and put on her blazer. "Have you ever thought of becoming a purser, Eric?"

"Yes, eventually."

"Well, here's survival tip number one." She pointed to her purser wings, which were larger and featured a more substantial design. "Whenever you have to settle a dispute, always put on your sheriff's badge. It's a good visual. It reminds them that you're in charge." She left the galley with a determined look on her face.

"I like her," said Eric.

"Me too," said Denny. "Sue doesn't play around."

She returned ten minutes later. "I don't think you'll have any more trouble with them, Eric. Tyson and Angel want to apologize to you."

"Apologize?" Eric said in disbelief.

"Yes. I suggest that you graciously accept it, and that the three of you try to get along for the rest of the day. You too, Denny. Break's over. I want all four of you back in your cabin."

"Yes, ma'am."

"Thanks for taking care of that, Sue," said Eric.

"It was nothing. I told them that if they couldn't conduct themselves as professionals, I'd call Flight Service when we land and have them removed from the return trip tomorrow. Not to mention, I'm sure that the last thing Tyson wants in his file is another bad letter. He probably has hundreds. The next one could be the straw that breaks the camel's back." She picked up the interphone. "Now let me try to salvage that dinner invitation from the captain. I'll see you boys on the ground."

***

Neither apology seemed very sincere, but they did apologize. "We just can't help it sometimes," Tyson said. "On the Caribbean, we have very high stress levels, and we're used to being able to blow off some steam."

"Let's start all over again," said Angel. "Besides, we have a kick-ass afternoon ahead of us. It's gonna be fun. I haven't been to the Castro in years."

"We're gonna get *wild*, child!" Tyson said at the top of his lungs.

"Tyson! What did Sue just tell you?" said Angel.

"Oops, sorry." He grinned and whispered, "We're gonna get wild, child!"

***

The last portion of the flight was quiet, for which Eric was extremely grateful. "So, are we all squared way about the layover?" Denny asked as he and Eric prepared the cabin for landing.

"I'll compromise," said Eric. "I'll skip the debrief because I want some time to myself this afternoon. But I will join you guys in the Castro for Happy Hour. Angel and Tyson did finally pipe down, and I don't want to be a spoilsport."

"Good. What time do you want to meet us?"

"Let's meet the corner of Castro and Eighteenth at six-thirty. We'll take it from there."

"Deal."

***

As Eric walked down Castro Street, he saw the trio waiting for him. Denny was wearing 501s, a leather jacket, and Doc Marten shoes. Angel also wore a leather jacket, along with camouflage pants, his combat boots and the silver keychain. Tyson was in a tight black t-shirt, acid-washed jeans, and flip-flops. The late afternoon sunlight bounced off his silver rings. Eric looked at Tyson's feet. Mercifully, he did not have silver rings on his toes.

Tyson was talking as he lit a cigarette. "...and this homeless dude, who reeked so bad I wanted to vomit said to me, 'Hey, brother, can you give me some money to buy a beer?' And I'm like, '*Hello!* In the first place I'm *ain't* ya damn brother, and in the second place, I *work* for a living! Fuck off.' "

"Those fuckin' homeless people," said Angel. "They're so aggressive here, especially near the hotel. I think most of them are psychotic."

"You'd have to be psycho to take a dump right in the middle of the sidewalk," said Tyson. "You gotta watch every step to make sure you don't slip in a pile of someone's shit. I'm like, hello! Even in New York, the homeless don't do that." Tyson saw Eric and waved. "Hey, Maria! Glad you could make it."

Eric tried to appear happy to see them. It was his decision to come, after all.

"You're late," said Angel, looking at his watch. "What have you been doing?"

"I bet he's been sniffing around, trying to pick up a man right on the street," said Tyson. "You know how those buttoned-up boys: they're always looking for it!"

"I'm exactly five minutes late," Eric said. "I just got off the bus at the corner."

"Where were you this afternoon?" Denny asked, lighting a cigarette.

"I went out for a walk in Pacific Heights."

"Oh, God, it's been years since I've been up there. How was it?"

"Wonderful," said Eric. "It was a beautiful day. The sun was out, and the streets were quiet. There's no more beautiful architecture anywhere in this city." Not to mention, he thought, I thoroughly enjoyed my own company and would have been happy to spend the entire day by myself.

I thought you might change your mind and come to the debrief."

"No, I didn't change my mind." He forced a smile. "But I am here with you now, as promised."

"Everything all right, girl?" said Angel. "You still seem uptight. Maybe a great, big cocktail is what you need."

"Or maybe a great, big something else!" said Tyson, fingering the enormous bulge that ran down his pant leg. The trio burst out laughing. Tyson's tumescent penis was hard to miss, even at a distance. A trio of men passing by turned around to ogle him, which he relished. "That's OK, men. Get a *good* look at it!"

Eric noticed that all three of his co-workers were weaving slightly. Just looking at them made him feel seasick. "How much have you all had to drink?"

"Enough to feel *good*," said Denny. "Let me tell you, after six hours on that plane, I needed to get a little buzz on. You usually do too, Eric. I'm glad you came to join us." He looked around and sighed happily. "How *lucky* are we to be here? There's nothing better on a Sunday afternoon than being in the Castro for Happy Hour… even if it's the *dregs* of Happy Hour. The sun is going down soon. Nevertheless, you can still feel adventure in the air."

Oh, yeah, thought Eric, as he watched a boney young man with sunken cheeks and a cane struggle to walk up the street. He had a large poster tucked under one arm, which made the effort more difficult. He wore a Giants baseball cap pulled low on his forehead, as though he was trying to avoid the stares of onlookers. I'm sure that poor guy can't *wait* for the adventure to start.

"Where do we want to go first?" said Angel.

"They always have good videos at the Midnight Sun," said Denny.

"Oooh, I love that!" said Tyson. "I mean, all they have to do is start with wire hanger scene from *Mommie Dearest* and I'm rolling on the floor."

"I'm down with that!" said Angel. "My favorite is *Female Trouble*. What's the name of that fat chick with the big hair who wants cha-cha heels for Christmas?"

"Dawn Davenport," said Denny.

"That's right, Dawn Davenport!" said Angel. "I love that scene where Dawn starts yelling at her mama 'cause she *didn't* buy her the heels, and then she pushes her, and the Christmas tree falls over on her. Whenever I see her mama lying there cryin', I'm always like, 'Hey, bitch, you wouldn't *be* under the tree if you'd just bought your daughter the damn shoes she wanted!' Now listen, guys, I don't want to spend the whole evening there. After we get good and drunk at the Midnight Sun, I want to head over to a bar where there are men looking for action."

"*After* we get good and drunk?" said Tyson. "Girl, what do you think we are *now?*" Tyson and Angel shrieked so loudly that Eric had to turn away in embarrassment. Christ, he thought. If only Denny and I had arranged to meet someplace on our own. We could have a few quiet drinks, maybe raise a glass to Zack, and then go cruising on our own. These two loudmouths are going to scare off every man in the place.

"I'm good with the Midnight Sun," said Denny. "Come on, Eric. We'll ask them to play a few scenes from *Whatever Happened to Baby Jane?* That'll get you in the mood."

"I love that movie, too!" said Tyson. "When Blanche start pressing that buzzer ten times in a row trying to get Jane's attention, I'm always like, 'Hello! Bitch, why do you have to *overdo* it? That crazy sister of yours gonna come charging upstairs with a lunch that you sure as hell *won't* want to eat!'"

Angel started croaking *I've Written a Letter to Daddy* and twirling around like Baby Jane on the beach. A small group of men on the sidewalk started applauding.

Tyson laughed, lit another cigarette and shouted, "Sing it, bitch!"

"That's it. I've changed my mind," said Eric, zipping up his jacket. "You guys have a good time. I'll see you tomorrow." He started walking back up to Market Street.

Denny followed him and grabbed his arm. "What is your problem today?"

"Those two. *They* are my problem. I'm embarrassed to be seen with them."

"I don't get it. It's OK for you to do your Karen Black *Airport '75* impression in the galley for the thousandth time, but it's suddenly not OK when Angel does Baby Jane in the Castro?"

"No, that's not it." He sighed. "Give me a cigarette, would you?"

"You haven't smoked in three months."

"I know that. Just give me one and let me collect myself."

"All right, but just one."

"Hey, are you guys coming or not?" said Tyson. "My buzz is starting to wear off."

"You go on ahead," said Denny. "I'll be there in a few minutes."

"Fine," said Angel. "Eric, why don't you head up to the Glass Coffin on the corner to hang out with the other tired old men and we'll see tomorrow. Let's go, Tyson."

Eric heaved a sigh of relief as they left.

"Make it fast," said Denny. "My buzz is starting to wear off, too. What's going on with you?"

"Don't you understand? One of our friends *died* less than twenty-four hours ago. Didn't you tell them that? Zack was only twenty-five years old. I don't think we should be partying like it's 1999."

"Would you rather we go up to Grace Cathedral and light a candle for him? That won't bring him back."

"No, I don't think we should *schlep* all the way up there. But we should find some way to show a little bit of respect. When I was a kid and someone died, my mother wouldn't even let us turn on the TV."

"Is Zack the first person you've known who's died of AIDS?"

"Of course not. I've known three people. Wait, Zack makes four."

"I've been living in New York for five years. I can't even keep track of the number of people who've died. Shit, if I added up all the guys from Mercury alone, I'd start crying and never stop. You weren't here for the worst of it in the late eighties. Every other day, somebody was going out on medical leave and never coming back. I've spent hours on the phone with agencies, brought food to their houses, washed shit-covered bedsheets, gone to hospitals, held their hands and watched them die. Sylvia did it, Jacques did it, we've *all* done it. A lot of times, there wasn't anyone else to do it. We dealt with their families, too. Some of their parents were angels: Christians in the true sense of the word. Others didn't even know their sons were gay and didn't want anything to do with them. Family values my *ass*. It all comes down to finding out that their son likes to suck cock. When that happens, they feel perfectly justified in abandoning their own children—those sons of bitches." He lit a cigarette and smoked furiously. "So, I think I've done my share and that I'm entitled to enjoy myself and forget about AIDS for a few hours. Agreed?"

"I'm sorry, Denny. I don't want this to turn into pissing party about grief. Tyson and Angel just seemed so callous about it all."

"Tyson's brother died last year. Angel's lover died six months ago. They've been through hell. You can't expect them to go through life every day like the walking wounded. Everyone deals with grief in their own way. Sometimes, you have to pretend that just for one damn day, the plague *isn't* happening and party like it *is* 1999. Maybe there'll be a cure by then. I hope so. Otherwise, I'll wake up one morning and find myself locked up in the psych ward at Bellevue." He put out his cigarette. "Well, my buzz is officially gone now, and I want to get it back on. I'm going to meet Angel and Tyson at the Sun. Do you want to come?"

"Maybe a little bit later. I think I'll walk around for a while and wait 'til the crowds thin out."

"Suit yourself. If we're not there, do a quick tour of the bars we like. We'll be in one of them. Otherwise, I'll see you at pick up tomorrow."

"Thanks, Denny. I'm sorry if I got all high and mighty."

"I'm used to it. You wrote the book on high and mighty. Oh, get that look off your face. If your best friend can't point out your faults, who can? I mean it: you're very quick to judge, Eric. Think twice before you make assumptions about people. Just a suggestion." He kissed Eric on the cheek. "I'm off. You do whatever you want that will make you feel purposeful today. Call me later. I should back before eleven."

"Would you give me a few cigarettes?"

"No. I only have half a pack left. If you're going to start smoking again, buy your own. I'll see you later."

***

Eric reached Market Street and tried to decide which way to go. The sun was starting to go down and the temperature was dropping rapidly. He was glad that he had brought a warm jacket. As he reached the corner, he noticed a large group of people gathering, including the skinny young man with the poster tucked under his arm. He was trying to manage both the cane and the poster while trying to put on a denim jacket. One or the other kept slipping out of his grasp. Eric walked over to him. "Here, let me help you," he said, taking the poster.

"Thanks," said the young man. "That's very nice of you."

Eric looked at the poster. A handsome, young man's face was printed on both sides, along with his name and the years of his birth and death. 'Chuck Lynch, 1959-1992'. He then noticed that other people in the area were carrying similarly printed signs.

"What's going on?" Eric asked.

"It's an AIDS memorial march from the Castro to City Hall." He pointed to the poster. "Chuck was my best friend. He just died a month ago."

"I'm sorry. What's your name?"

"Kenny."

"Hi, Kenny, I'm Eric. Tell me, do you have to live here to participate in the march?"

"No, anyone can join us."

"When does it start?"

"In about fifteen minutes, once it's dark outside. It's a candlelight march. The candles look good in print and on TV."

"Gee, I don't have a poster to carry or a candle."

"You can share Chuck's poster with me if you want to. It gets a little tiresome carrying it all the way to City Hall. And you can get a candle from one of the volunteers. They're the folks wearing the white baseball caps with the red ribbon stitched on the front."

"I'll be right back," said Eric. He walked over to a volunteer who was kneeling next to a large box of tapered candles. "Excuse me, may I have a candle, please?"

"Sure." The man looked up. "Eric?"

Eric's heart skipped a beat. He had known for months that this moment would happen. He just didn't know where or when. "Benjamin!"

Benjamin had a look of disbelief on his face. "What are you doing here?"

"I'm on a layover. I'm a flight attendant, remember?"

Benjamin jumped up and grabbed him in a big bear hug. "Am I happy see you!"

"You are?"

"Of course. Why wouldn't I be?"

"I called you months ago and left a voicemail with all my contact information. I never heard back. I just assumed that you were either busy with graduate school… or not interested."

"I'm sorry, Eric, I never got the message. My first roommate here turned out to be very unreliable. I've moved since then, and have my own place now. Believe me, if I'd known that you called, I would have called you back. Are you in town by yourself today?"

"No, I'm here with my best friend, Denny. Do you remember him? He was with me when I met you in front of Zack's house last December."

"Vaguely."

"He's with two other rowdy flight attendants from our crew. They're getting drunk at the Midnight Sun. I don't feel like partying today." He winced as he heard himself use the word 'party' as a verb. It sounded so juvenile. "Oh, my God, I just remembered! You were Zack's buddy from GMHC."

"How is he?" Benjamin asked, as he resumed passing out candles.

"He got pneumonia again earlier this week and he... he didn't make it. He died early this morning. He'd been back in the hospital since last Monday. I didn't even know that he was there." He struggled not to cry, but the tears came anyway.

"I'm sorry to hear that." Benjamin hugged him again. "I was hoping that Zack would beat the odds, but he was very, very sick during the brief time that I knew him." He opened a knapsack and handed Eric a travel-size packet of tissues. "Keep that. I have plenty more."

"Do you always travel with that much Kleenex?" Eric asked.

"I do whenever I'm involved in one of these marches. We *have* to share our grief. That's what binds us together. Then right before we get to City Hall, we get angry. And then we start to make some noise, which is the real purpose for all this. We make noise to get help for the community. Will you walk with me today, Eric?"

"I'd like to, but I think I just made a new friend. His name is Kenny and he seems to be all alone. I think he could use some company." Eric looked for Kenny and pointed him out to Benjamin.

"Then the three of us will walk together," said Benjamin. "How's that?"

"That sounds wonderful."

"Give me a hand passing out the rest of these candles, would you? The march is starting in ten minutes."

***

By the time they were ready to step off, and Eric had introduced Kenny and Benjamin to each other, the crowd has swelled to several hundred people.

"How are all these people going fit on the sidewalk?" Eric asked.

"We're not," said Kenny. "We're taking over Market Street. It's been closed off to traffic, just like for the Gay Pride Parade and the Halloween Parade. Believe me: those two occasions are a lot more fun. But this is more important." He sighed. "Chuck and I used to have so *much* fun. We did everything together. God, I miss him." He gave Eric an impromptu hug. "I'm glad that we met, Eric. I'd have hated to do this alone. None of my other friends are here today." He pointed in the direction of 18th Street. "They're all down there. I think they're suffering from battle fatigue."

Eric thought of Denny. "I hear you. I'm glad we met, too."

"Anyway, after the march, you and Mr. Hunkeroo should do whatever you want. I don't want to be a third wheel, understand?"

"We haven't even made any plans yet."

"If you don't yet, I'm sure you will by eight o'clock tonight."

Benjamin blew on a whistle that he kept on a string around his neck. Eric had learned that he wasn't just a volunteer; he was one of the event organizers.

"Time to light candles, everyone," he shouted. A hush came over the crowd as Market Street was suddenly filled with the light from hundreds and hundreds of candles. Eric could see marchers stretching all the way to Church Street and beyond.

Benjamin turned to Eric, who was just about to light his candle from Kenny's. "Wait, Eric. Let me do that." He lit Eric's candle, and then his own. They paused for a moment and gazed into each other's eyes. Oh my God, thought Eric. I've just found my purpose in life.

"Come on, you guys," said Kenny. He held the poster of Chuck high over his head. "Let's get this thing started."

"Give me one second," said Benjamin, as another volunteer stopped him to ask a question.

"Listen, Eric, I don't know what your situation is," said Kenny, while Benjamin spoke to the volunteer. "But if you don't hook up with Benjamin tonight, you're out of your mind. He's gorgeous, and he's crazy about you. I can see it in his eyes."

"I'm not jumping into anything," said Eric said, certain that he was going to jump—feet first. "But I promise to let you know how it all turns out."

CHAPTER 40

Halfway to the Stars

By the time the march ended, the crowd had surged to almost a thousand people. Eric and Kenny stood with their arms around each other as Benjamin made an impassioned speech from the steps of City Hall. He reminded everyone to stay focused, to stay in the fight, and to love one another. Afterward, Eric and Kenny waited patiently on the street as people came up to thank Benjamin for his speech and for organizing the march.

Benjamin kept making eye contact with Eric and Kenny, indicating that he'd join him as soon as he could. As the event wore down, some people left almost immediately. Others stood around trembling with emotion, as if they had no idea what to do or where to go next. Despite their commitment to their friends and their community, no one knew when the next shoe was going to drop... or on whom it would fall. At one point during the march, Kenny had become so overcome with emotion that Eric and Benjamin had to help him walk for two blocks. But he seemed all right now.

Eric was feeling emotional, too. But more than anything, he was hungry. The last time that he'd eaten was hours ago on the plane.

"How do you feel?" Benjamin asked, when he was finally free to join Eric and Kenny.

"Better," said Kenny. "I'm so happy that I met you guys today. Thanks for carrying me. I'm afraid that I would have had to turn around halfway to City Hall otherwise."

"Is anybody hungry?" asked Benjamin.

"Yes, I'm starving," said Eric

"Let's get something to eat," said Benjamin. "Kenny, why don't you join us?"

"I'd like to, but I'm exhausted. This event wore me out. I think I'll go home and be quiet for the rest of the evening. But I'd like to stay in touch with both of you. Eric, be sure to call me next time you're in town. We can do something more upbeat next time. I'm ready for some fun."

"I'd love to."

"OK, I'm gonna hop on Muni and head back to the Castro. I'll see you, guys."

"Looks like it's just you and me," said Benjamin.

"Yup. Where do you want to go?"

"How about back to my place? I'll make us some spaghetti. I've got a *Bolognese* sauce recipe that'll make your toes curl—in a good way."

"Sounds great. Where do you live?"

"On Telegraph Hill, just a few blocks from Coit Tower."

"How do we get there, by bus?" He reached into his pocket to see if he had bus fare.

"No, I'll drive us. I'm parked right around the corner. This way." He slipped his arm around Eric's waist, as though it were the most natural gesture in the world.

"Did you trade in your Harley for a car?"

"No, I brought the Harley with me."

"You drove a motorcycle all the way across the country?"

Benjamin laughed. "Are you kidding? Jews don't ride motorcycles cross-country. My mother would have a heart attack. I shipped the bike and flew here—on Mercury Airways, by the way."

"I wish I'd been working that flight. Would I have made *you* feel like someone special in the air."

"I asked the cabin crew if any of them knew you, but they didn't. They were San Francisco-based."

"You're kidding! You asked about me?"

"Yes. You made quite an impression the two times that we met. But I think you knew that. Here we are." They stopped in front of Benjamin's gleaming motorcycle.

"Do you have an extra helmet?"

"Yeah, right in here." He unlocked the rear seat, where an extra helmet was stowed in a compartment underneath and handed it to Eric.

Faced with the reality of the situation, Eric was suddenly nervous. "Uh… I've never ridden a motorcycle before."

"Then this should be a real treat for you."

"What do I do?"

"Watch me get on first. You always want to mount from the left side, where the kickstand is, so you don't tip the bike over." Before he mounted the bike, he leaned over and flipped down small metal bars on either side. "These are the foot pegs. There's one on each side, as you can see. Just step on the one on the left, swing yourself over, and put your right foot on the other one." He patted the backrest. "You can lean against this, but you'll probably be more comfortable wrapping your arms around my waist." He climbed on the bike. "OK, you can get on now."

Eric strapped the helmet to his head, feeling conspicuous in front of passersby. "I guess we're going to go via the Embarcadero and ride around by the wharf where it's flatter, huh?"

"That'd take too long. I want to get you home now. We're taking the direct route."

"You mean, we're driving *uphill?* Is that even legal here?"

"Of course. Besides, I want to give you the grand tour, and my golf cart's in the shop."

Eric felt the color drain from his face as he imagined himself zooming up the incredibly steep streets. "I'm sorry, I can't do it. I have a morbid fear of being smashed to bits at the intersection of Powell and Bush." He took the helmet off and handed it to Benjamin. "Just give me your address. I'll take a cab."

Benjamin smiled. "There's no need to be afraid. I've ridden this bike all over Manhattan and San Francisco and I've never had an accident. I would never do anything that would put you in harm's way. If you start to feel overwhelmed, just squeeze twice hard on my waist and I'll stop the bike at the next corner. Do you trust me?"

He looked into Benjamin's big brown eyes. This was one of those moments in life that required a leap of faith. In an instant, his fear lifted like a morning fog. He knew that he would be in good hands. "Fuck it. Let's go."

Benjamin was in sure command of himself and the bike. The next twenty minutes were the most thrilling that Eric had ever spent in San Francisco. Buildings passed by in a blur as they raced uphill and downhill at what seemed like a break-neck speed. To Eric's surprise, he wasn't the least bit afraid. They could have ridden across the Golden Gate Bridge and back, and Eric wouldn't have minded at all. But that thrill would have to wait for another layover.

Benjamin turned onto Chestnut Street and slowed the bike, stopping in front of a pretty, three-story mission-style house. It was painted yellow and had a tiled roof. The yard, surrounded by a beautiful wrought iron fence, was full of bright red wild flowers. "This is my house. Hop off, Eric, it's easier for me to park by myself."

Eric waited for him on the sidewalk, trying to stop his legs from trembling after the ride. "This whole house is yours?" he asked in disbelief.

"No, it was subdivided into apartments years ago. I have a tiny one bedroom on the third floor—at least, for the next six months, it's mine. It's a sublet."

"What a great neighborhood to live in. It's so peaceful up here. Hey, look at that!" In the clear night sky, a full moon was rising above Coit Tower. It was a postcard-perfect view. "Can we see the moon from your apartment?"

"No, my windows face north. I have an even nicer view. Come on up." They walked through the front door. The lobby floor and the staircase were covered with lovely blue-and-white tiles. "Hold onto the banister," said Benjamin. "These steps are slippery. They should be carpeted, but covering up tiles in this type of house is *verboten.*"

As they reached the third-floor landing, Eric could hear the irritating sound of a dog yelping and scraping a door.

"Christ, I hope the dog walker didn't pull a no-show," Benjamin said, and then loudly whispered, "Brody, be quiet!"

Oh, God, he has a dog, thought Eric. Be nice to the dog. If you want to make a good impression, try your best to be nice to the dog.

"Here we are," said Benjamin, opening the door. A black Scottish terrier was waiting impatiently inside. Benjamin immediately picked the dog up and tried his best to sooth it. "Hello, sweetheart, I'm home. Did Karen forget about you? Oh, no, she left a note. Good. I'm going to put you down for just a minute. Eric, this is Brody. He's a little territorial, so don't try to get friendly too fast. Let him come to you and check you out. Here, give me your jacket." He hung both of their jackets in the entryway closet. The top shelves were stuffed with boxes of Christmas tree lights, ornaments, and a large tree stand.

"I thought you were Jewish," said Eric.

"These belong to Vincenta, the woman I'm subletting from. She's working in London for a year. But I might put up a tree next Christmas. All Jewish men love Christmas trees because growing up, we never had them in our own homes."

Eric stood calmly as Brody toddled over and started sniffing his shoes. The apartment was small, but it was nicely furnished with a sofa, a club chair, and interesting framed prints on the wall. A bookcase was filled with an impressive array of gay-themed literature. Two entire shelves were filled with CDs. A small roll top desk occupied one corner. There was just enough room on top of the desk for a computer and a few framed photographs. "You have your own computer? Nice."

"That's essential. I do so much writing that if I didn't have it, I'd spent my life on campus waiting to use one of theirs. Do you want something to drink? I have a bottle of Chardonnay in the fridge."

"That'd be fine."

Benjamin handed Eric a box of doggie treats. "Here. Offer one or two of these to Brody while I open the wine and get dinner started. You'll be an instant friend if you let him have two, but no more than two, please. Do you want to put on some music? The CD player is right over there."

"Sure. Anything in particular?"

"No, choose whatever you like."

Eric sorted through the collection of jazz artists, vocalists and original cast recordings of Broadway shows. With the exceptions of *Evita* and *Jesus Christ Superstar*, Andrew Lloyd Weber was blessedly absent. Thank God, thought Eric. I couldn't bear trying to make love to the score of *Phantom of the Opera*. "How about the Ella Fitzgerald Collection?"

"Sure, Ella is good anytime."

"Vincenta has great taste in music," Eric remarked.

"Those are all mine. So are the books. She took hers to London. I've found that wherever people live, they're more comfortable when they're surrounded by own things. Have a seat. I'll be right out."

Eric sat down on the sofa. To his surprise, Brody walked over to him started trying to climb up. His short legs prevented him from reaching the seat. What the hell, thought Eric. He pulled the dog into his lap and started petting it. I'll give it a try.

Benjamin came into the room with two glasses of wine and a small tray of cheese and crackers. "Well, look at that!" he said, grinning. "You've made a fast friend. That's unusual—and a good sign."

I'll be all right, just so long as he doesn't try to lick my face, thought Eric. But boy, if he does… ugh, dog lips! Thank God there are toothpicks on the cheese tray. Otherwise, I'd have to get up and wash my hands after petting him.

"Cheers," said Benjamin, as he and Eric raised their glasses. "Welcome to my home."

"Thanks. It must be nice living up here. Although it is a little far from the Castro."

Benjamin laughed. "Yes, I guess it would seem far to the party boys of the airlines. There's a lot more to living in San Francisco than just the Castro. Between classes, my field placement and my volunteer work, I don't have much free time. When I do go out, I usually head to SOMA. It's easier to park my bike there."

"I haven't spent much time in that neighborhood. I've never explored the leather scene. Anyway, I don't have boots or chaps or even a vest. I'd be a little out of place."

"That's all just a costume, as far as I'm concerned. I'm more interested in making real connections with people. It's easier when we're not playing dress up. Come with me and I'll show you what makes it worthwhile living up here. Bring your wine glass." He walked Eric to a closed door. "This is my bedroom. I keep the door closed because Brody is never allowed in here. Well, almost never." He opened the door. Benjamin's bedroom was furnished with a double bed pushed against the wall, a nightstand with a reading lamp, and several shelves of books. The walls were painted light blue. The bed, covered with light blue sheets and a seafoam green comforter, looked tranquil and inviting. The only artwork on the wall was a large, somewhat faded quilt protected by a glass frame. "That's beautiful," said Eric. "I wonder where it came from."

"My grandmother made it. It was one of the few things she was able to bring with her when she left Romania. Wherever I go, it goes with me. Now let me show you something else." He opened the drapes, exposing a floor to ceiling window with a breathtaking view of the bay. A small French door on one side of the wall led to a patio.

"Oh my God, how beautiful. Can we go outside?"

"Sure. It might be a little chilly. Do you want your jacket?"

"No, I don't need it."

They walked outside, wine glasses in hand, and stared at the view. They could see lights from boats in the water, and Alcatraz and Angel's Island. If they turned hard to the left, the could see a partial view of the Golden Gate Bridge. "It's perfect," said Eric. "If I lived here, I'd probably never want to leave."

"It is wonderful to come home to at the end of a hectic day. See, I have a little table and two chairs. I like to have my coffee in the morning out here. I'm Cancer. Being near the water soothes me instantly. I'm glad you like it."

Eric shivered as a sudden breeze came up. "It is a little chilly."

"Come here. I'll warm you up." He took Eric's glass from his hand and set both their glasses on the table. Then he took Eric in his arms and hugged him. "I'm so glad you're here. I kept hoping I'd run into you again. What were the chances of running into each other an AIDS march here in San Francisco when you live almost three thousand miles away?"

"Pretty slim chances, I guess."

"It must be fate. I'm a great believer in fate." He cradled Eric's face with his hands and kissed him. His lips were soft and warm. They kissed for so long that by the time they finished, they were both shivering from the cold. "Let's go inside," said Benjamin. He led Eric by the hand back into the bedroom and closed the patio door. Brody had slipped into the room and made himself comfortable in the middle of the bed. "Brody, out," said Benjamin, scooping him off the bed and carrying him back into the living room. "Let me feed him. It'll take one second. You wait right here."

Eric sat on the bed and took off his shoes. He'd never felt so comfortable in someone else's apartment. As he wondered what it would be like to see the sun come through the picture window in the morning, Benjamin came back in and closed the door. "I turned the music up a little bit so that we can hear it in here. Is that OK?"

"Yes, of course." He stood up as Benjamin walked over to him.

"Do you mind waiting a little while for dinner? I promise to feed you before the night is over."

Eric nodded. Without saying a word, they started unbuttoning each other shirts, slowly at first until hunger took over, and they both ripped each other's shirt off and let them drop to the floor. Benjamin's torso was just as beautiful as Eric had imagined it would be. His chest was well-defined and covered with salt and pepper hair. His biceps popped as his arms encircled Eric's waist. The feeling of their bare chests touching describable. A few second later, their jeans and underwear came off. They stood admiring each other, completely naked, for the first time.

"Jesus, you're beautiful," said Benjamin. "I can't remember the last time I wanted to be with a man so much."

"I know. Me too."

Benjamin took Eric's nipples in his hands and squeezed them gently. Eric's nipples were wired directly to his dick and balls. He was so excited that he feared he might ejaculate before they even got started. "Hang on one second," he said, his voice hoarse with lust.

"Yes, let's negotiate what we're both comfortable doing," said Benjamin. "It's important. Oral sex is cool. No cum swallowing, and no fucking without condoms. I'm fine with anything else."

Eric became even more excited. It was rare that two men could negotiate safer sex directly and honestly without killing the mood. "Agreed. Let's go."

Leaving the curtains open, Benjamin pulled down the comforter and the sheet, and then and pulled Eric onto the bed with him.

As Eric felt Benjamin's naked body against his, he knew that this was exactly where he was supposed to be. The feeling was so overpowering that the corners of his eyes became wet, and tears plopped down on Benjamin's chest. They were tears of happiness, a thing that had only happened to him one other time in his life.

"Why are you crying, sweetheart?" Benjamin whispered in the dark.

"I don't want to say. This is our very first time together. I don't want to scare you off."

"It's all right," he said, gently stroking Eric's penis. "Tell me."

"Because..." he struggled to speak. "Because I feel like I'm *home*."

Benjamin climbed on top and looked into Eric's eyes. The smell of his skin was so sexy that Eric felt as though he were drunk. "I know, baby. Whenever you're in San Francisco, and we can find the time to get together, you *are* home. But let's take it one step at a time, OK?"

***

The next day, as he sat in the hotel lobby waiting for the rest of his crew, Eric felt as though as he were in a daze. The night and the following morning with Benjamin played over and over in his mind. They'd had sex before dinner and after dinner, and again the next morning. The intensity hadn't diminished a bit over the twelve hours. It was the most satisfying sex that he'd ever experienced.

"Hey, Eric." It was Denny, standing in front of him. "Where've you been?"

"I've been sitting here, waiting for the van. I guess the driver is running late today."

"The van has been parked outside for ten minutes and we're all on it, waiting for you."

"Oh geez, sorry." He walked outside with Denny and boarded the van. "Good morning, everybody. Sorry to keep you waiting."

"There you are, glad you could make it." The purser pointed to her watch. "It's not like you to be late, Eric."

"Just one those days," he said with a shrug. He'd spent hours waiting for other crewmembers to board vans. So what if he was late for once? He took the only vacant seat, which was toward the back next to Denny. Tyson and Angel, who were in the last row, barely raised their heads to acknowledge him. "What's up with them?" Eric asked. Denny.

"They have sinister hangovers. I was smart for once and left at twelve. They closed the Midnight Sun and took a cab two in the morning. Speaking of last night, what happened to you? We went to five different bars in the Castro and never saw you once."

"I ran into Benjamin." Oh, how he loved saying that name!

"Benjamin who?"

"Benjamin Kaufman. Remember? Zack's buddy from New York. We met him once in front of Zack's apartment, right after he got out of the hospital."

"Oh, yeah, Motorcycle Man. What's he doing in San Francisco?"

"He's living here while he's going to grad school. He's getting a master's degree in social work."

"What a coincidence. So, what'd you guys do?"

"We did a candlelight AIDS march from Castro to City Hall and then went back to his place for spaghetti *Bolognese*."

How was it?"

"It was the best sauce I've ever had in my life." He giggled. "We had it again for breakfast."

"I see. I'm glad that one of us got lucky. Well, it's a long ride to the airport. Give me all the details. How was he in bed?"

"Sorry, no details."

"What do you mean? We always share details."

"Not this time. I don't want to talk about Benjamin like he's some guy I picked up at Headquarters for a one night stand."

"Whatever. I can tell by the look on your face that it was good."

"It was more than good. I'm in love."

"That fast, huh?" said Denny, looking doubtful.

"Yep."

"Let me guess: your next step is going to be transferring to San Francisco."

"Don't be ridiculous. It's one thing to say I'm in love. It's another to think about packing my bags and moving to California. What kind of reckless person do you think I am?"

"A flight attendant, that's what kind. You don't know how many times I've seen this happen."

"Jesus Christ," said Tyson, finally lifting his lead. He gestured toward the front of the van, where the other flight attendants were talking even more animatedly than usual. "Would someone please ask them to keep it down? I'm trying to get some sleep!"

"Look who's talking!" said Sue.

"I know, I know," said Tyson. "Payback is a mother-fucker."

Sue laughed. "Here, you can borrow this." She passed him a Walkman with a pair of headphones attached. "This is a nice piece of classical music by Debussy—one of my favorites. It'll take you right to dreamland. Just be sure to have your act together by the time we get to the airport. I'm in no mood to clean up one of your messes today."

Tyson grunted a "thank you" and put on the headphones.

"They *are* loud today," said Eric. "What's going on?"

"I guess you didn't read the newspaper this morning.," said Denny.

"No, I was otherwise engaged."

"Oh, girl, who do you think you are, Loretta Young? Just say you were fucking this morning!"

"What was in the paper?"

"Big news. It's just a rumor, but it has been confirmed by two anonymous sources. Mercury Airways is getting set to either merge with or acquire Global Airways."

"What?!"

"Global is in worse shape than ever. They're not teetering on bankruptcy this time. They're getting ready to declare Chapter Eleven in a few days. We're moving in and absorbing the company before anyone else does. Mercury is now going to be the biggest airline in the world."

Eric immediately thought of his roommate. "Oh my God, that's great news! It means Michael will be coming to work for us! And think of all the places they fly to that we don't. We'll double our international routes. No wonder everyone is excited!"

"Listen, do Michael a favor: don't be so excited when you get home tonight. Sometimes these things turn out to be a big mess. It takes months, if not years, to integrate two airlines. There're a lot of steps involved: dealing with bankruptcy judges, getting DOT approval, protests from other airlines who want a slice of the pie—and that's just for starters. Sometimes things don't work out the way everyone expects them to. Michael has been through a lot in the past couple of years. Don't get his hopes up unnecessarily. When you get home today, be cool about everything."

"That's good advice, Denny. Thanks."

As the van pulled onto the southbound freeway and the crew finally settled down, Eric's thoughts returned to his unforgettable night. He was in love, no question about it. He'd never met a man like Benjamin before: mature, open, giving of himself, and loving. But there was no sense in rushing into anything. Benjamin had his hands full with graduate school, and they did live on opposite sides of the country.

But Eric was a flight attendant. Mercury operated six flights a day between New York and San Francisco. Eric could finally hold those layovers, now that he'd been flying for almost a year. And on days off, he could jump on a flight to SFO whenever he wanted. If he was patient, and let the relationship take its natural course... Somehow, it would all work out.

CHAPTER 41

"Nothin' But Good News"

Anthony sat in the breakfast nook of his new apartment and enjoyed every sip of coffee as he took in the view outside. It was a bright, dry June day; a sweet summer breeze floated in through the open window. If I were still in Dallas, he thought, it would be a hundred degrees already and I'd be sweating to death. At eleven A.M., Central Park West was already jammed with New Yorkers enjoying the outdoors. There were nannies pushing strollers, joggers stretching out before they headed into the park, men in short-shorts heading for the Rambles, and clumps of tourists with cameras hanging around their necks. Tourists often gathered in front of Anthony's building. The Dakota was one of the most photographed edifices in the city. He remembered the many times that he had stood on the street, looking wistfully at the gate and wondering which famous resident he might see entering or leaving. Now, *he* was a resident. He loved the stares that he got whenever he left dressed for work. "Did you see that? A flight attendant in the Dakota. What is this world coming to?"

He faintly heard Steve call him from the bathroom and set down his coffee cup. The apartment was so large that they couldn't hear each other from one end to the other. He walked through the kitchen and dining room and into the living room, which he stopped to admire. Steve had excellent taste. Many of the staid, fussy furnishings that he'd inherited from his grandparents had been sold before he moved in. There wasn't a needlepoint cushion or a Dresden figurine to be seen. The new furniture, from the tufted black leather sofa and suede club chairs to the glass and chrome coffee table, was manly and modern. His grandparents' art and book collections, however, remained firmly in place. Most of the books were first editions of great pieces of literature. The bulk of the magnificent artwork had been purchased during the core period of the European Modern Art movement. Steve's friends and business associates all coveted the framed paintings and drawings.

He walked down the hallway and into the bathroom, where Steve was shaving. The sight of his lover's naked, six-foot frame filled him with desire. Steve's cock bobbed against the sink as he deftly moved a razor across his face. Anthony was so turned on that he had to reach for Steve's heavy balls and cup them in his hand.

"Hey, not while I'm shaving!" said Steve, laughing. "You want me to cut myself and bleed all over the place?"

"Come on, just a quickie before I leave for my lunch date."

"Can't. The partners and I are meeting a new client at noon, and I have to be there on time." He rinsed his face, dabbed it with toner, and gave himself a once-over in the mirror. Anthony loved the fact that it was always a quick once-over. As beautiful as Steve was, he never preened. There was no need for him to do so. "Come and talk to me while I get dressed."

They walked into the bedroom, where Steve's clothes were already laid out. He slipped into his underwear and tugged black socks over his thick calves. Then he put on a starched white shirt and reached for a pair of gold cufflinks. He didn't need an undershirt. Even when he perspired, he never had body odor. On the contrary, his pheromones drew everyone to him. He selected a red tie with tiny silver polka dots; that was about as daring as he would get when dressing for work.

Anthony admired the charcoal suit hanging on the valet stand. All of Steve's suits were made to order. It was impossible to buy one off the rack that fit his forty-four-inch chest and thirty-one-inch waist. He slipped into creased trousers and gleaming wing-tip shoes, and carefully brushed his jacket before he put it on.

"So, today is the big day," said Steve, as he placed a stack of files into his briefcase. "Where are you meeting your friends for lunch?"

"Chez Henri on West Sixty-eighth Street."

Steve whistled. "Isn't that a bit rich for your co-workers?"

"It's a special occasion. They've all been saving their pennies. It was Eric's idea. He made the reservation. I'm kind of surprised. I thought for sure that he'd pick 'Twenty-one' or Sardi's—one of those real New York institutions."

"Who else is coming?"

"Rose and Geneviève. They just transferred here from Chicago. We all met in training and became good friends. I haven't seen the girls since we graduated last June. Well, that's not true, I saw Rose once on a flight, but I was with Jim and I didn't have a chance to talk to her."

"It sounds like you're going to have a wonderful reunion. I wish I could join you."

Anthony shook his head. "The airline talk would drive you crazy in about five minutes. I do want you to meet them though, especially Eric. We've had our ups and downs, but for the most part he's been a very loyal friend. You'll meet him soon, I'm sure."

Steve looked at himself in the full-length mirror, frowned, and adjusted his tie. "Does he know about your new living situation?"

"He will. I'm meeting him early for a drink before lunch."

"How do you think he'll take the news?"

"He'll be fine. I think he's adjusted to living in Queens. He didn't even mention the possibility of us getting an apartment together when I told him I was moving back. Besides, he's head over heels in love. All he cares about is being able to hold San Francisco layovers so that he can be with his new boyfriend."

Steve pulled a credit card out of his wallet. "Why don't you let me treat everyone to lunch today?"

"No, we've all been flying for a year now. We can afford to splurge once in a while. Thanks for the offer, though. Hey, I just remembered: today is the anniversary of our graduation from the Charm Farm."

"The Charm Farm. That's such a funny name for the airline training center. As if *you* needed any more charm. Where are you meeting him?"

"Downstairs at the corner, at noon."

"I thought you wanted to break the news to him gently. Don't you think that might overwhelm him?"

"No. Eric loves landmark buildings. That was his idea too, since we're eating in the neighborhood."

"Well, I'm off. Do I get a hug before I leave?"

"As if you had to ask." Even fully clothed, the sensation of Steve's body pressed against his filled Anthony with uncontrollable lust.

"What are you doing after lunch?" Steve asked, pulling himself away.

"I'm going out to Queens to see Eric's place and meet his roommate, and then I'm taking my folks to dinner. They live just a few blocks away."

"Do you remember how to get to Queens on the subway?"

"Of course I do, you fucking snob. I was born there, you know."

"OK. I have a training session with Mike at the gym after work, so I guess I'll see you here at home tonight." He rubbed his palm over Anthony's ass. "Don't eat too much today. This summer weather makes me horny as hell, and I'll want to fuck your brains out tonight, probably a couple of times."

Anthony grinned. "You kill me. No one would ever know that under that starched shirt there beats the heart of a rutting sex pig."

"I know. I like it that way. See you tonight."

***

As Anthony stepped out of the elevator and into the lobby, he was pleasantly surprised to see of the building's most famous residents walking toward him. It wasn't the first time that they'd crossed paths, but seeing her up close always gave him a thrill. The actress was older now and had thickened in the waist, but her carefully styled hair and her whiskey-dipped voice were unmistakable. He was even more surprised when she smiled and greeted him. "Hello," she said. "Beautiful day, isn't it?"

"Yes, it is. There's nothing like early summer in New York." Oh Christ, he thought. You'd think even I could come up with something more original.

"I thought that damned winter would never end. You're new here, aren't you? I've seen you coming and going a few times."

"Yes." He held out his hand. "My name is Anthony Bellini."

She introduced herself, even though it was hardly necessary. "It's nice to meet you, Anthony. We can always use a few more young, good-looking men in this building. Sometimes, there are too many old farts milling around the lobby to suit my taste."

Anthony laughed and wished her a good day. As he stepped into the courtyard and walked toward the gate, he suddenly felt pleased with himself. He wasn't a tourist gawking from the corner. He was a resident—and a neighbor of the actress. That's what neighbors did; they exchanged pleasantries in the lobby, even though they'd never dream of inviting each other into their homes. That was New York City, and Anthony wouldn't have it any other way.

He walked to the corner and waited patiently for Eric. He saw him from a block away. Eric was sprinting up the street, as though he didn't have a minute to spare. He was wearing chinos, loafers and a black Ralph Lauren polo shirt that fit him perfectly. Eric had spent a great deal of time at the gym during the last year. His perennially puffy hair was gone. Now he wore it buzzed short on the sides and a bit longer on top. He looked like a sexy, young marine making his way up the street. He caught the attention of several passersby but seemed oblivious to their stares. That was one of the things Anthony liked best about him. Although he had developed in a handsome, well-built man, he wasn't the least bit arrogant. Eric remained a genuine, down to earth person.

He waved excitedly at Anthony from across the street. Too impatient to wait for a green light, he ran into the intersection, dodging a taxi driver who cursed him through the open window. "Oh, go fuck *yourself!"* Eric shouted right back. He reached Anthony, grabbed him in a big bear hug, and refused to let go. Anthony finally had to pull himself away.

Eric smiled at him with tears in his eyes. "I can't believe you're finally back. It seems like a dream."

"It's no dream," said Anthony, handing him a handkerchief. Anthony knew what to expect and had come prepared for an emotional reunion. "I'm back for good."

"How long have you been here? I kept missing your calls. I'm on reserve this month and I've been flying for days on end."

"A few weeks. I've been busy getting settled."

"Where are you staying?"

"Here in the neighborhood."

Eric was wide-eyed. "In *this* neighborhood?"

"Uh huh," Anthony said casually, as though they were chatting on a street in Astoria. "Let's go get a drink and I'll tell you all about it."

"Fine. Where to?"

"There's a great little bar just a few blocks from here."

"Lead the way. I'm glad we have a chance to catch up one-on-one before we meet Rose and Geneviève. God, I still can't believe Geneviève was able to pry Rose out of Chicago and away from that cop she's been seeing."

"We'll get the details later," said Anthony, guiding him down the street. "First I want to hear all about this guy that you're seeing in San Francisco."

"I'm not just 'seeing' him. We're a couple. I'm in love."

"I know, you told me. But, geez, Eric, a million other gay men live in New York. Couldn't you have met someone here? It's such a typical flight attendant thing to date someone who lives all the way across the country."

"*Ach*, New York men," said Eric, waving his hand dismissively. "They're impossible, except one: my boyfriend, Benjamin. He *is* a native New Yorker— from the Lower East Side yet. He's living in San Francisco temporarily while he's in grad school. He'll be back in a year."

"That year will go by in a flash. Look how quickly the past year flew by. Well, this is the place," said Anthony, stopping in front of a building with a beautiful Art Deco facade. He led Eric into a bar on the ground floor where a Nancy Wilson song was playing softly in the background. Her classic rendition of *Guess Who I Saw Today?* was one of Anthony's favorites. "Let's get a table instead of sitting at the bar. It's easier to talk. Should we order champagne?"

"Let's wait for lunch to order champagne. I'll take a vodka and soda."

"Vodka before champagne?"

"I'm just having one," said Eric. "Besides, vodka has practically no calories. I'm very careful about everything I put in my body these days."

"I can tell. All right, I'll have the same."

They sat in a booth and ordered two drinks. "Well, let's get right to it," said Anthony. "Tell me all about Benjamin."

Eric gave him just the basics so that he wouldn't have to repeat the whole story at lunch. But he did open his wallet to show Anthony a picture of Benjamin that was already worn from being handled so often. Benjamin was handsome and appeared to be in his early thirties. He had short, wavy brown hair with a few streaks of silver and an olive complexion. He was solidly built and had beautiful brown eyes and a natural smile.

"Nice," said Anthony. "I like that little tuff of hair in the front."

"Just like Tin Tin, the Belgian comic book character. I love it."

"I know who Tin Tin is. Does he have a white dog named Snowy, too?"

"No, he has a rather nervous Caryn terrier named Brody. I'm trying to make friends with him, but I don't have the dog-lover gene, as you know. I'm more like Lucy Van Pelt whenever Brody's lips get too close to mine."

Anthony looked at the picture again. "What's his last name?"

"Kaufman."

"Is he Jewish?"

"Yes."

"I always knew you'd end with a nice Jewish guy."

"Why do say that?"

"Because that's your destiny in life. Don't look at me like that. There's nothing wrong with it. You were born to fall in love with a *mensch* who'll treat you like gold, won't give you any bullshit, and won't put up with any from you, either."

Eric laughed. "You just described him to a T."

"Is he funny? Most Jewish guys have a great sense of humor."

Eric nodded. "He's one of the funniest people I've ever met. We laugh all the time—when we're not screwing our brains out. The sex is incredible."

"*Mazel tov.* I hope you're happy."

"I am."

"How's your living situation?"

"It's great. I can't wait for you to meet Michael this afternoon. I couldn't have asked for a better roommate. It's been a rocky couple of years for him. He flies for Global, and you know what a mess that airline has been in. Their senior management has tried everything to avoid yet another trip to bankruptcy court. It's been hell for the employees—especially the flight attendants. They've had to bear the brunt of passengers' anger over every silly thing that the airline has done to save pennies here and there. Now that Global is merging with Mercury, he's like a kid on Christmas Day. He has a bottle of champagne chilling in the fridge, so let's not get too drunk at lunch, OK?"

"Deal. So you're happy to stay in Queens? For the time being, at least?" It was important to ask—and to get verification—before Anthony shared his news.

"Yes, I have too much on my plate to consider moving right now. Although—now listen, don't you dare breath this to the girls. I would consider transferring to San Francisco if Benjamin, for some reason, decides to stay there after he graduates. It would be impossible now—he's much too busy to have a live-in boyfriend, and things are just fine the way they are now. Anyway, I'm sure he'll want to move back. New York is his real home, he always says." He finished his drink. "Jesus, we've spent all this time talking about me, and you haven't told me a word about yourself. What's new with you?"

"Well, since you asked… I've met somebody too."

"What?! You're kidding me. You've only been here for two weeks."

"I met him when Jim and I were here for that benefit in December. His name is Steve."

"You met him then? How? I'm surprised that Jim let you out of his sight for even five minutes."

"It's a long story."

"What does he do?"

"He's an attorney. A very successful one."

"Naturally. I figured he wouldn't be a civics teacher at P.S. 123." There was a tinge of sarcasm in Eric's voice.

"Listen, if it weren't for him, I'd still be tangled up legally and financially with Jim, and I'd still be in Dallas. I'm damn grateful to him."

"Do you have a picture?"

"Yeah." He showed Eric a picture of the two of them seated together on their sofa.

"God, he's gorgeous," said Eric. "I wouldn't even know what to say to a man who's that good-looking." He looked at the picture more closely. "Hey, wait a minute. Is that a Matisse on the wall behind you?"

"Yes."

"That's not a print, is it?"

"No, it's the real thing."

"And where was this taken?"

"In our living room."

"*Your* living room? You mean, you're already living together?"

"Yes, we're trying it out."

"Where is your apartment?"

"Where you met me, at the corner of Seventy-second Street and Central Park West."

"Which corner? Northwest or Southwest?"

"Northwest."

Eric looked stunned. "You're living in the Dakota?" he sputtered.

"Yes."

"Well, I don't know what to say."

"How about: 'Congratulations, I hope it works out for you.' "

"Congratulations. I hope it works out for you," Eric said with a minimum of sincerity. "Is he rich? Never mind, that's a dumb question, of course he's rich. You wouldn't be with a man who isn't. Frankly, I'm surprised that he's not the CEO of a Fortune 500 company."

"What's with the wisecracks? Jesus, we've been reacquainted for less than an hour, and you're already getting huffy about me meeting someone new. Are you jealous? If you are, just say so and let's move past it."

"No, I'm not jealous. It's only that… you just came back! I thought we were going to be friends again. Now I'll probably never see you, except for running into you in operations once in a while. That is, if you're still flying. Has he asked you to give up your job yet? I'm sure he has. He doesn't look like the type to sit around all weekend while you're on a thirty-three-hour layover in Denver."

"No, he hasn't. In the first place, he's very secure with himself. And in the second place, I'd never be with someone who couldn't cope with my job. And stop worrying about you and me. Of course we'll still be friends."

"I don't know how. We'll be moving in completely different circles. I'll be roasting a chicken and braiding challah bread for dinner on Friday night, and you'll be directing the caterer where to set up for your A-list-gay sit-down dinner party."

Anthony sighed. He hated to admit that Eric was painting a fairly reasonable picture, but he wasn't about to give in so soon. "You're not being fair. Meet Steve and give him a chance before you make any snap judgments. That's all I ask."

"All right. I'll try to keep an open mind."

He looked at his watch. "We should pay up and go. By the way, do me a favor and get rid of that get that sourpuss before we meet the girls. There's so much good stuff happening right now. Don't be a downer."

"You're right. Today is special, and I won't ruin it for everyone. Happy anniversary, by the way."

"Same to you, buddy. We'll have a nice toast at lunch. Now let's get going."

***

"Hi, we have a reservation for four. The last name is Saunders."

"Right this way, sir. The rest of your party is already here." The *maître'd* led them past the ornately decorated bar and into the dining room. Rose and Geneviève were waiting at a corner table with expectant looks on their faces and a bottled of champagne in a silver bucket. They jumped to their feet, greeting Eric and Anthony with hugs and joyous yells, to the surprise of the restaurant's usual well-heeled patrons. Eric responded just as effusively. It was such typical flight attendant behavior that Anthony had to look at the floor. Then he let go of his embarrassment. Get over yourself, he thought. Hell, this *is* a joyous occasion. He hugged the women too, genuinely pleased to be reunited with his friends.

As they sat down and all started chatting at once, Anthony took a moment to observe them. Rose had put on a little bit of weight, but she was still beautiful. It was hard to believe that she was the same awkward woman from East Texas that he'd met a year ago. She'd been friendly from the start and excited about starting a brand-new life as a flight attendant. But she was self-conscious about her six-foot height and was used to hiding behind what she thought were Plain Jane features. In classic "stewardess school" tradition, she'd been transformed by the airline from a brunette into a striking blond. Rose wore expertly applied makeup that brought out her green eyes and flawless complexion. Her hair was pinned in a *chignon*, which accented her long, lovely neck.

Genevieve had worn a pixie haircut cut a year ago. Now, she wore soft, blond curls that gently framed her face. That was the only thing that had changed about her. Even after a year of living in the Midwest, her voice, her smile and her mannerisms were still wholly French.

As the quartet chatted excitedly, the waiter opened the bottle and poured champagne into four flute glasses. Anthony could see that Eric was bursting to make a toast.

Eric finally picked up a knife and tapped it on his glass. "Quiet, everyone, please. I want to make a toast."

"Not too emotional, please," said Geneviève, dabbing the corners of her eyes, "unless you want me to make a complete fool of myself."

Eric picked up his glass. "I've never been happier to be reunited with old friends. And never been happier to do it in such a special place. The past year has been a challenge for all of us—"

"Brother, you can't *imagine* what a challenge!" said Rose.

"Shh, let him finish," said Geneviève.

Eric smiled and continued. "But we made it through the first year, living different lives in three very different cities. Now we're finally together where we should have been from the beginning. I hope that you'll be as happy here as I am. I love you all, and I'm thrilled at last to be able to say welcome to New York City."

"Here, here!" said Geneviève. "Everybody drink!" She signaled to the waiter. "You may as well bring us another bottle, *monsieur*. I think we're going to be here for a while!"

***

They were so busy catching up that the waiter had to ask them three times if they were ready to order. Once they'd made their choices about lunch—Jesus, these prices! I may have to kick in a little extra, thought Anthony—they settled down. Anthony was pleased to learn that Rose and Geneviève had secured an apartment in Manhattan—on the Upper East Side, no less.

"It's a tiny studio," said Geneviève.

"I don't know how they can even call it a studio," added Rose, laughing. "It's more like we're sharing a closet."

"But it's ours," said Geneviève. "No sub-letting for us this time and ending up in the boonies three months later, like in Chicago. We paid the first and last month's rent and our name is on the lease."

Anthony mentioned that he was living on the Upper West Side and didn't elaborate any further.

"That sounds nice," said Geneviève. "Are you close to Central Park?"

"He's not just *close* to it," Eric blurted. He lives right across the street from it, on Central Park West!"

"What's the big deal?" said Rose. "Where would expect him to live, down in the Bowery? I'm happy for you, Anthony. And I'm guessing there's a very nice man involved."

"Thank you, Rose. Yes, there is a nice man involved. Now let's talk about you. The last time I saw you, you were gaga over a Chicago police officer."

"With big muscles and those beautiful furry arms," said Eric. "I met him on the plane the same day that you did, remember?"

The mood at the table changed suddenly. "The officer ended up *not* being a very nice man," Geneviève said.

"Please, Geneviève. Let me tell them." Rose started to speak but seemed to be having trouble finding the words. Geneviève squeezed her hand, which seemed to calm her. "It's important for me to able to talk about this openly. For the better part of the last year, I was in an abusive relationship."

"Oh, Rose!" said Eric. "I'm sorry to hear that. He seemed so…"

"I know. Handsome, protective, and utterly charming. He was protective, all right. He was a control freak who tried to keep me completely under his thumb. He spent nine months 'checking up on me' both at home and while I was on layovers. And when we were alone, he never stopped reminding me that I was practically his personal property."

Anthony asked the question that he knew was on everyone's mind. "Did it ever get physical?"

"Just once. That was all it took. You can't imagine how difficult it is to find yourself in that situation— and to get out of it. But I did, thanks to Geneviève, a support group, and the help of a good therapist." She paused. "That's all I want to say for the time being. But let me tell you, I know all the warning signs now. And I *want* to be open about it so that I can help other women in the same situation. You wouldn't believe how often it goes on, even at our own company. Suffice to say that for the foreseeable future, I'm happy to be footloose and fancy-free." She smiled. "That's it. Someone else can talk now. Geneviève, don't you have some news you wanted to share?"

"I'm seeing someone," she said. "It's only been a few months, so I don't want to go into too much detail. It may not go anywhere."

"Come on," said Rose. "We're among friends. You said just this morning that you wanted to tell them."

"I'm dating a pilot."

"A pilot?" said Eric. "That's the last thing I would have expected in a million years. Please tell me that he doesn't wear those little zip-up boots with his uniform."

"Hardly," said Geneviève. "Why would you even suggest that?"

"Sorry," said Eric. "You'd never allow anyone to park a pair of boots under your bed. I bet he's good-looking, though. What's his name? Is it Bill? Ted? Mack? Joe? Hey, did you guys ever notice that practically all pilots have one-syllable first names?"

"Her name is Janet," said Geneviève. "She's a first officer on the 737. We met working a flight to Rochester, New York, of all places. We discovered that we have a lot in common, and we're getting to know each other. Is there anything else you'd like to know?"

Eric was speechless, which Geneviève seemed to find amusing. "I don't believe it. Eric Saunders is at a loss for words."

"Congratulations," said Anthony. "Janet must be a special woman. I hope it works out for you."

"Why didn't you tell us you're a lesbian?" Eric said. "I mean, *us*, of all people. Were you afraid that we'd judge you or something?"

Geneviève sighed. "You gay American men, with your coming out announcements and rainbow flags and labels. Do I have to have a label? Can't I just be in a relationship?"

"Well, sure," said Eric. "I'm just surprised, that's all."

"Now, listen, you two," said Geneviève, looking at Eric and Anthony. "This is very important. I want to be discreet about this. No, let me rephrase that: I *have* to be discreet about this relationship. Our co-workers, for all their supposed worldliness, are not as open-minded as you may think."

"I think you're being unfair," said Eric. "With the exception of one trio of Evangelicals based in New York, I've never heard a single homophobic comment from a flight attendant."

"Maybe not to your face," said Rose, "but you'd be amazed what they say behind your back. I was on a flight to San Francisco last month. A guy on the crew was reading the *Bay Area Reporter* on his jump seat. One of the girls reported him for reading pornography at work."

"The *Bay Area Reporter?* How ridiculous. That's just a local gay newspaper."

"He was thumbing through the massage ads in the back, which I suppose could be considered sexually suggestive," Rose explained. "Some straight women are even more intolerant of lesbians than they are of gay men. You can't imagine the vicious remarks they make. All I can say, boys, is that you should be leery of any co-workers who read the Bible on their jump seat. Especially the ones who think AIDS in a punishment from God for having gay sex. They'd love to be able to get rid of gay co-workers. *All* of them."

"It's even worse among the pilots," said Geneviève. "Janet's work life is hard enough. She often has to deal with captains who believe that women don't belong in the cockpit, period. Can you imagine how much more difficult it would be if they knew about her personal life?"

"Yes, I can imagine," said Eric. "This is a very enlightening conversation. Amazing, too, when you think that a lot of gay men come to work in this industry partly because we think it'll be a safe environment for us. I mean, 'male flight attendant.' The whole world expects us all to be gay."

"I don't want to spoil things for you," said Geneviève. "That wasn't my intention. But I don't think you should go around with blinders on, either."

"You've spoiled nothing," said Eric. "I appreciate your need for discretion. And you can count on that from us. But I'm dying to meet her. When do you think that will happen?"

"Soon," said Geneviève. "Give us a little more time. Goodness, I'm not used to talking so much about myself." She saw the waiter approach the table with a tray. "*Et voilà*, here comes our beautiful meal!"

***

Two hours later, Anthony and Eric exited the subway at 71st Street in Forest Hills and walked upstairs. As they reached the street level, Anthony winced. The neighborhood had not changed; the neighborhood would never change. The same drab six-story red brick apartment buildings… the same bodega, the same bagel shop and pizza stand… the same frail, elderly residents in huge, wrap-around sunglasses, wearing mismatched clothes. They were all leaning on walkers, waiting with healthcare aids to help them cross the street. "Which way?" said Anthony.

"Straight down Seventy-first and into the Gardens. God, this corner is always mobbed. But it is nice to live so close to the subway." He led Anthony south under the trestle of the Long Island Railroad station. As they continued, Anthony was surprised to remember what a difference just a few blocks could make. They were now in the Gardens—a mix of expensive private homes and charming Tudor-style apartment buildings. They turned right on Dartmouth Street. After walking half a block, Eric stopped in front an elegant apartment house that looked it had been constructed for a period English film set. A long brick path led to a carved oak door with small, leaded glass windows.

"This is it," Eric said proudly.

"Wow," said Anthony, genuinely appreciative of the design. "This is like the Forest Hills version of the Dakota."

"Thank you, that's nice to hear," said Eric, as they walked to the front door and entered the lobby. "We have an elevator, but let's take the stairs. It's only two floors up and it's good for my quads."

They reached the landing on the second floor. The terracotta floors were spotlessly clean. The white walls looked as though they'd just received a fresh coat of paint. "Come on," said Eric. "I'm ready for another bottle of champagne. Besides, Michael is just dying to meet you. His tongue practically falls out every time he sees your picture." He pushed open the front door with a big smile on his face. "Hi, Michael! I'm home! And look at the hunk I brought home with me! This is—" Eric stopped in his tracks. The apartment was so dark inside that it seemed like the dead of night. The curtains were closed and there were no lights turned on. Eric opened the door wider to let in a little light.

Anthony could make out the shape of a man lying on the sofa. On the coffee table next to him was a half-empty bottle of Scotch and an ashtray full of cigarettes. On the CD player, Sarah Vaughn was moaning about being jilted by a man she thought would love her forever. Something was *very* wrong.

"Welcome home," said Michael, half sitting up. "Who's this?"

"This is Anthony. Remember I said I'd bring him by?"

"I forgot." Michael clumsily stood up and put out his hand. He was drunk. "Nice to meet you."

"Same here."

"Why is it so dark?" Eric asked.

"I like it that way," said Michael, practically falling back down.

"Do you mind if I open the drapes?"

"Yes." Michael turned on the lamp next to the sofa. "How's that?"

"Better."

"Michael, what's the matter?"

"Nothing. Just the knife in my back, that's all."

"I thought we were having a party."

"A party? What is there to celebrate?"

"The merger, of course."

"Oh, that. I guess you haven't heard the latest news."

"It didn't fall through, did it?"

"No. But there's been a change of plans. Your airline is buying all our international routes, but they're not taking any of our airplanes—*or* employees."

"What are you talking about?"

"A friend from the union called me today. They've been trying to negotiate a deal with Mercury for the past twenty-four hours, and they failed. He wanted me to know before I heard it on television. In court today, your company swooped in like a vulture and picked up our international routes for a couple of hundred million dollars. They just wanted the route authorizations, though. They don't want our tired, old airplanes or our tired, old flight attendants or pilots. Anyone with more than forty years of seniority will stay on payroll and maintain what's left of the domestic operation. I don't even know if they'll call it Global anymore. What's the point, if the airline never leaves the country? The rest of us are getting pink slips. We're free to apply off the street as new hires. That's a good laugh. Me and my broken down old friends starting all over again, as if your airline would even *consider* hiring us." He kept saying "your airline" as though Mercury was Eric's personal property.

"Well, that's *some* good news," said Eric, fumbling for words. "You're a Spanish speaker. They're always looking for Spanish speakers."

"I haven't spoken real Spanish in twenty years. I don't think that being able to say, '*¿Desea* Coke *o Sprite?*' qualifies me as a Spanish speaker."

"Well, I'll help you brush up. I'll even coach you through the interview. I'm sure I can write a letter of reference for you. I have a friend who works at headquarters, and—"

Michael reached over and threw the ashtray off the coffee table. It shattered, leaving shards of glass and a heap of cigarette butts on the pristine Persian rug. Eric jumped back. Anthony didn't even flinch.

"Don't you *get* it?" Michael shouted. "They don't *want* us! They don't want our torn rotator cuffs, our bad lower backs, our hips that need replacing, our varicose veins or our fallen arches. They don't even want to see a single strand of grey hair! Mercury is going to hire a thousand more twenty-somethings like you to take our place. Meanwhile, the dinosaurs at Global will limp along with a pathetic domestic route map of ancient 727s and DC-9s, until that gets eaten up by another carrier or just shuts down altogether." He laughed darkly. "At least they'll get a paycheck for a little while longer. They're tossing the rest of us out on the street, without even a severance package. I'm getting nothing! After twenty-five years of giving my blood, sweat, and tears to the company, I AM GETTING NOTHING!"

"I'm very sorry, Michael. I don't know what else to say."

"Don't say anything. Just get out, both of you, and don't come back! I'll pack up all your shit and leave it in the lobby. You can pick it up later. Now get the FUCK out of my house!"

***

As they walked to the sidewalk, Eric started to dry heave. "Oh my God, I think I'm gonna be sick!" He hurried to the curb and leaned over.

"No, you're not." Anthony immediately pulled him upright. "I'll be damned if you're going to toss up a *boeuf bourguignon* that cost you forty-five dollars. Come on, take a few deep breaths and clear your head."

"What'll I do? Where will I go?"

"The first thing we're going to do is get a drink. Is Pinocchio's on Queens Boulevard still open?"

"Yeah." Eric pointed. "It's that way."

"Let's go." They walked to the boulevard and turned right. Eric didn't make a sound; Anthony practically had to push him all the way. They stopped just once for Eric to buy a pack of cigarettes. They entered the bar where disco music from the Seventies was blasting for the three patrons inside. The bartender wore a white ribbed muscle shirt. He had a thick black mustache and wore a large crucifix on a gold chain. Oh, Jesus, thought Anthony. It's like stepping back in time twenty years. But thank God this bar is open. He nodded hello to the bartender. "Two martinis, please. Very dry and each with triple olives."

"I don't like gin. Make mine vodka," said Eric.

"Sometimes gin is the only thing that will do the trick," said Anthony. "This is one of those times." They munched olives in silence for a few minutes. "You know what this reminds me of? One of our last weeks in training. The day that we got our base assignments and found out that you were going to New York and I was going to DFW. Remember how flipped out we were?"

"Flipped out? They may as well have dropped a bomb on us." He lit a cigarette. "It's been a whole year since that fiasco. You'd think by now that my life would be more settled." He sighed. "I don't suppose there's a spare bedroom for me at your place? Or a small corner in your living room where I can tuck my futon? I promise to roll it up in the morning."

"Nope," said Anthony, lighting a cigarette for himself. "I promised not to come home with any excess baggage."

"Oh, so that's what I am now? Excess baggage?"

"Calm down. I was just trying to lighten the mood."

"Thanks. You're a *riot*, Alice."

"Maybe you can work out something with Rose and Geneviève."

"In their studio apartment? It's more like a closet, remember?"

"Well, you probably wouldn't ever all be home at the same time."

"Anthony, I'm too old to share a studio. Furthermore, I would never live on the Upper East Side."

"Then I think you should let Michael cool off and call him in a few hours."

"Michael, at this moment, is probably throwing all my things into a big pile in the lobby."

"Where do you think we are, Jersey City? People don't do that sort of thing in co-op buildings like yours. The doorman would be all over him in five minutes. Listen to me: give him time to cool off—and sober up—and call him, or just go back home. You still have a key, don't you? I doubt he's has time to change to locks. You guys will work something out. Besides, if he is getting a pink slip, he'll need to keep a dependable roommate—one like you who pays the rent on time."

"But why would he want me to stay there? It would be like pouring salt in a wound every time I put on my uniform." He sighed. "Maybe I should think about transferring to San Francisco now."

"And do what? Crash on Benjamin's couch while he's going to graduate school? That'd be just great. I'm sure he'd love the four A.M. phone calls from crew scheduling."

"It's summertime. He doesn't have any classes right now."

"Don't even think about, buddy, if you want that relationship to go anywhere in the long-term. You'll doom it from the start. You haven't even made friends with his dog yet."

"Oh, I forgot. Dog lips."

"I need to meet my folks in about an hour. Let's enjoy our drinks and then when you're good and relaxed, you can call home. If Michael still won't let you in, I'm sure my mom would let you crash on her couch. She remembers you, and she likes you. If you don't want to do that, I'll ask Steve if you can stay at our house—for one night only. But I don't think the situation at your house is that dire. Michael's not the first person to lose a flying job. He'll adjust. We all do."

"That remains to be seen." Eric jumped off the bar stool as his pager went off.

"Jesus," said Anthony. "Don't tell me you're on call for tonight. You're half-drunk already."

"No, I don't start my reserve shift until tomorrow night. Why the hell would crew scheduling be calling me right—" He looked at the phone number. "Oh, shit. It's Michael."

"Good. He probably wants to apologize."

"Yeah—or to tell me that he's ripped my uniform to shreds and buried my wings under the azalea bushes. What should I do?"

"Finish your drink and then give him a call. And stop worrying! I have no doubt that your current housing situation is secure."

"I'm glad you were here this afternoon. Otherwise, I'd have spent the last hour running around the Gardens with my hair on fire."

"You Texas queens. You just love being dramatic, don't you? Have another martini."

"Nope. One is enough for me." He smiled and finally looked like was starting to calm down. "I'm really glad that you're back, Anthony. I've missed having you in my life."

"Me too. And don't worry us moving in different circles. You can always count on me."

"Good." He picked up his martini glass, which still had a quarter-inch of gin in it. "Here's to us, old friend."

CHAPTER 42

The Unlikely Event

An hour later, Eric nervously entered the apartment, unsure of what he would find. He was relieved to see that the lights were on, the windows were open, and the carpet had been cleaned. Michael sat at the kitchen table, drinking a large mug of coffee. His fit of rage seemed to have passed. He smiled weakly at Eric. "Hi," he said.

"You OK?" Eric asked, perching on the edge of the sofa.

"I'm better. Just having a little trouble focusing my eyes. Please come and sit with me over here. I promise I won't bite. There's fresh coffee if you want some. I just drank half a pot myself."

"No thanks," said Eric. He walked into the kitchen and sat down. "I just had a martini at Pinocchio's."

"I owe you a big apology."

"Well, you must have been—"

"Please let me finish. I behaved abominably in front of you and Anthony. I'm sorry about that. I was so looking forward to meeting him. He must think I'm the world's biggest asshole."

"Anthony used to fly for Atlantic Coast. He's been in your shoes."

"That's no excuse. I know this was a special day for you and your friends, and I shat all over your happiness. But Eric, you can't imagine how awful it is to have the rug pulled out from under you. I was so hopeful about the merger. It was the first time I've been hopeful about anything in a long time. And now…" He looked down at the table and started to cry. "Now I don't know what the hell I'm gonna do. There was a part of me that kept hoping this day wouldn't come, but in my heart of hearts, I knew it would. If it weren't for airline deregulation, we might still have had a chance. But truth be told, I saw the handwriting on the wall at least five years ago. There was no way for us to compete with bigger, stronger carriers. I should have tried to get on with another airline then. But the idea of starting all over again was just too much. Fear of the unknown, I guess." He took a deep breath and dried his tears on a napkin. "At any rate, it's certainly not your fault, and I don't hold you personally responsible. Please forgive what I said. I don't want you to move out. You're the best roommate I've ever had, and to kick you out because I lost my job would be cruel." He looked up at Eric. "Do you forgive me, and will you stay?"

"Yes to both," Eric said immediately. "You've been such a good friend, Michael. If you hadn't taken me in last fall, God knows where I'd be right now. Probably still living in that hellhole in Kew Gardens with fifteen miserable roommates."

"Good. Let's shake on it."

"Fuck the handshake. Give me a hug."

Michael hugged him and kissed him on the cheek. Then he sniffed him. "Have you started smoking again?"

"Yes. I bought a pack the minute I hit the corner."

"Good. Let's have one. I lost mine in the ashtray incident."

After they each lit a cigarette, Eric said, "Michael, I want to ask you something, but I don't want you to get upset."

"If you're going to ask me not to increase your rent again, please don't ask right now. We'll to see how quickly I can find another job." He sighed. "There's a Help Wanted sign in the window of the Mykonos Diner. Maybe I'll pop over there tomorrow."

"No, Mildred Pierce, you are *not* going to start waitressing at the diner. Nor are you going to start baking pies at home for the diner to supplement your tips."

"Do you have any other ideas?"

"Yes. I want you to apply to be a flight attendant at Mercury. Wait, hear me out! You are only forty-five years old. You don't have fallen arches, varicose veins, or a grey hair on your head."

"That's only because I have no hair *left* on my head."

"You're experienced, fit, and have an excellent work record. If anyone from Global is going to get hired, it will be you. I'll do everything I can to help you. Unless most flight attendants who say they have a friend at headquarters, I *do*. I've only been flying of a year, but a letter of reference from me would carry some weight… I think. Will you at least consider it?"

There was a long pause before he responded. "All right. I'll consider it. Try as I might, I can't picture doing anything else, as impossible as that sounds. Will you really help me brush up on my Spanish?"

"Yes. Starting tomorrow, we'll speak nothing in this house but Spanish, no matter how hard it is for you."

"Deal. Listen, I still have that champagne in the fridge. Do you want to—"

"God, yes! It's either that or we go to Pinocchio's, and I can't make two appearances there on the same day."

"Then open it and get out two glasses while I pour out this coffee. We'd better think about food at some point, too. I haven't eaten all day."

Eric took the bottle of out of the fridge, popped it open with pure joy, and poured two glasses. "To the future: yours *and* mine," he said as he raised his glass.

Michael nodded. "I hope you'll always remember this day. I love you like a brother, I and don't mean for this to sound bitchy. But do remember this, in case one day the shoe is on the other foot."

"What do you mean?"

"I mean, *your* good fortune could change at some point, and Mercury Airways could be in the same position that Global is now."

"How is that even remotely possible? Mercury is now going to be the biggest airline in the world. I don't mean to gloat. It's the truth. That's why I want you to come work there. You'll have job security for the rest of your life."

"That's what I thought twenty-five years ago when I started flying for Global. But a lot can happen over the years. The price of fuel goes up, management makes a few bad decisions, or there's suddenly political unrest in half of the countries on your route map. I'm no psychic, but history had a way of repeating itself. Hell, something could happen one day that's so disastrous it could put the entire airline industry on the verge of collapse."

"Let's talk about that later," said Eric. "We can't drink champagne and worry about the future at the same time. *Ésta noche, vamos a disfrutarnos.*"

"Come again?"

"Tonight, we are going to enjoy ourselves."

"*Sí, sí, que buena idéa.* Hey, did you hear that? My Spanish coming back already!"

Eric smiled and raised his glass again. "*¡A la futura!*"

***

Later in the week, after three straight days of sitting reserve without the phone ringing, Eric finally got a call. "Hello, Eric. This is John from crew scheduling."

"Hi, John." John was one of Eric's favorites in the department. He knew the kind of trips that Eric liked and did his best to hold one aside for him whenever possible.

"I know this is short notice, can you make the one P.M. departure from JFK to San Francisco?"

"Sure. Is it long layover, by any chance?"

"How does thirty-three hours downtown suit you?"

"That suits me fine!"

"I thought you might like that. Sign-in's at noon."

"I'll be there. And thanks!"

"Enjoy yourself. But don't get into any trouble. Your buddy, Denny, is on the flight too."

"Not to worry. Thanks again." He raced into his bedroom to pack a suitcase. Then he called Benjamin, who answered the phone sounding sleepy. "Hello?"

"Hi honey, I know it's short notice, but I just got assigned to an extra-long layover in San Francisco. I'm arriving around four. Are you free tonight or tomorrow?"

"Sorry, sweetheart, but I'm leaving the house at noon today for a three-day AIDS conference in San Diego."

"Ah, dammit! Well, let me think for a minute. Maybe I could check flight schedules from San Francisco and meet you down there."

"Don't go to all that trouble. I'm one of the facilitators, and I'll be tied up the whole time. Besides, what if you can't get back to San Francisco in time for your return flight? You'd get a missed trip."

"I didn't think of that. I was just so excited about seeing you."

"I'm disappointed too, but you're flying here next month, right?"

"Yes, I just got my July schedule a few days ago. I have six long San Francisco layovers."

"OK, so we'll see each other then. Do you have any friends on the flight that you can hang out with?"

"Yeah, Denny's with me."

"Then I'm sure you won't be lacking for something to do. Why not go the Castro for a few drinks and dinner? You haven't done that in a while."

"There's an idea."

"Crap, look at the time! I have to get off the phone. I need to shower and pack. Give me a call when you get back home. And have a good time with Denny. Remember, you're not an old married man—yet."

"OK, I will. I love you."

"I love you, too. Have a safe flight."

***

In operations, he was pleased to run into Sylvia Saks, whom he hadn't seen for months. To his great delight, she was the purser on his flight. "Is Jacques with us, too?" he asked. That would be the icing on the cake.

"No, he has a terrible summer cold. You're filling in for him. Are you OK with working the first-class galley position?"

"Sure. I've done it lots of times."

"Good. I'll see you down at the gate. I need to stop by the ATM and get some cash. Don't rush. We'll probably be delayed. That fog outside is thick as pea soup. I just checked, and our inbound aircraft is still out there circling somewhere over the Rockaways."

"Do I know anyone else on the crew besides Denny?"

"Chaz. He's working in business class."

"That'll be nice."

"Edna MacAllister is on here, too."

"Oh, fuck. The world's biggest pain in the ass."

"And the world's biggest *schnorer,* too. Don't let her even step into the galley if I'm not there. She'll help herself to anything that isn't nailed down."

In addition to being a chronic pilferer, Edna MacAllister was the most self-centered flight attendant that Eric had ever met. She insisted on being the first person on and off the van when traveling to the layover hotel. That was her *modus operandi* to reach the check-in desk before everyone else and ensure that she got the best room available. Edna felt that her advanced seniority entitled her to the best of everything—at the expense of every other person on the crew. She never considered anyone else's needs or wishes. As a result, Edna usually spent her layovers on her own. "Well, screw her. It'll still be a nice trip."

"I'm looking forward to it myself. I haven't been to San Francisco in ages. You know how much I like that noon flight to L.A."

"Why the change?"

"I snapped last week when this big jerk put his disgusting bare feet up on the bulkhead wall, right in front of my face, and wouldn't remove them. I lost it! I swear, that crowd to L.A. gets trashier every day."

"Was it a certain flabby, entertainment-industry type with little red rat eyes and a pock-marked face?"

"Yes! my God, how did you know?"

"Been there, done that. It's my dream in life to see one of those assholes try to evacuate when there's a fire in the cabin. I want to watch him running toward the exit with his feet in flames."

What a vivid image. Do thoughts like that occupy your mind very often?"

"Just once in a while. Is that wrong?"

"No. It's *my* dream in life to strap a loud cell phone talker into a chair in a brightly lit room, and then force her to listen to her own voice recorded on a loop. It will play hour after hour, at top volume, until she goes stark-raving mad. Oh, it feels good to admit that."

"You know what they say: we're only as sick as our secrets."

"Then I'll have more to share with you later. One involves a screeching toddler with inattentive parents, a roll of duct tape and a dark, locked coat closet."

"I have a feeling we won't lack for topics of conversation today."

"See you downstairs."

As Eric signed in for his trip, he was suddenly filled with happiness. My life can't get better than this, he thought. I've been flying for a whole year already, and I'm firmly established here at this base. I've made wonderful friends with people that I wouldn't have met anywhere else in the system. Granted, I've flown a lot of crappy trips with layovers in towns so dull I can't even remember where I was or how I passed the time. But everyone has to pay their dues, and I'm fortunate to have paid mine so quickly. We're still hiring flight attendants, and there are so many new hires coming to New York every week that I'll be off reserve soon and holding a line every month. And to top it all off, I bid San Francisco for July and held it. I can see Benjamin every couple of days. He grinned to himself and thought: My life as a flight attendant is exactly the way that I wanted it to be.

"Hey," said Denny, jumping onto a computer next to him. "Jesus, I'm making sign-in by one minute. The bus got stuck in the mid-town tunnel for a half an hour. I was sweating bullets. I've already had two late sign-ins this month. Whew! Done!"

"Ready to head downstairs? I'm hungry. Let's grab a burger."

"Let me check my company email first."

"All right, I'll print a copy of my schedule for July while you're doing that." Even though the next month hadn't started yet, it would be gratifying to see those six downtown San Francisco layovers plotted on his July schedule. He entered the code in the computer and eagerly tore the page from the printer.

"Hey, look at this!" Denny yelled. "I got it!"

Eric couldn't respond. He stared at the sheet of paper in a daze. Four of the San Francisco trips had disappeared. What the *fuck?* "Denny, look at this. Half my schedule is gone. Where the hell did my trips go?"

Denny looked over Eric's shoulder and pointed. "That's a training removal code. Did you check your company email? I bet you got it, too!"

"Got what?"

"The proffer!"

"What the hell is a proffer?"

"Pull up your email, and I'll show you. See, it's right there. 'Flight Attendant Saunders: you have been awarded the proffer to JFK International effective August first. Please check your schedule for overwater training dates and subsequent trip removal. If you have any questions, please contact Crew Planning.' Isn't that great? I'm in the same training class with you. We're going together, just like we planned! Goodbye, Columbus and hello, London!"

"I don't want to go to international. I want to stay on domestic. I held San Francisco next month. I'm *dating* someone in San Francisco! How do I get out of that training class and get my trips back?"

"You can't get out of it. Once you put in for a proffer and hold it, it's irreversible."

"But I didn't put in for a proffer to international."

"Yes, you did."

"No, I *didn't*. I'm calling the crew planner right now."

"Oh, no you're not. Come here with me. We need to discuss this in private." He dragged Eric into the break room. "You don't remember, do you?"

"Remember what?"

"An Orlando layover… and a late-night, heart to heart conversation during which certain important decisions were made."

"No. I've only had one Orlando layover in the past six months, and you weren't with me."

"Exactly. It was Valentine's Day. We were supposed to go to that party in L.A., but at the last minute, you got reassigned to the Orlando flight. You were fit to be tied and furious with me."

"Yes, I remember that, but I'm drawing a blank about the rest."

"I didn't make it to the party either. We lost an engine ninety minutes out of New York and had to make an emergency landing in Chicago. The plane went out of service, so we laid over in Chicago and deadheaded home to the next day. I called you from hotel. We were both royally pissed, but at least you weren't pissed off at me anymore since I didn't make it to the party either. Is any of this ringing a bell? Maybe not, because when I talked to you, I could tell you were three sheets to the wind."

Eric couldn't remember a late-night conversation, but he suddenly remembered the voicemail that he had from Denny when he woke up the next day. "Go on."

'You *don't* remember, do you? I can tell."

"No, I don't remember. I must have been talking to you in a blackout."

"I'm not surprised. You do that more often than you think and it's not pretty. Anyway, we both said we couldn't stand the shitty domestic schedules for one more minute and had to have a major change. I suggested that we try to go international. You jumped all over the idea. I said I would put us on the standing proffer list. You gave me your passcode and told me to take care of it for both of us, which I did. You *can't* call Crew Planning and tell them that you gave me your passcode because that's a corporate security violation. We could both get fired. So, you're going to international."

"But what about Benjamin and me?"

Denny sighed. "You can see Benjamin on your days off. You're a flight attendant, remember? You can go anywhere you want, whenever you want. For a small service charge, the world is your oyster."

"It would be nice if you had mentioned to me, during that heart to heart, that once you put in for a proffer and hold it, you can't change your mind. You *know* how important this relationship is to me. Are you jealous, Denny? Are you trying to come between Benjamin and me?"

"What is this, sixth grade in the girls' locker room? I don't give a shit if you have one boyfriend or ten boyfriends. I did what you *asked* me to do. Incidentally, you might try to show a bit of enthusiasm. Most other one-year flight attendants would give their right arm to go international. You're a French speaker, for Christ's sake. That's one of the reasons you held the proffer at your seniority. You'll be able to hold Paris. The Ultra Jet will be a thing of the past. We don't fly that shitty airplane on international. You'll be on widebodies all the time, and flying to *Europe*. Jesus, what else could you ask for?"

"I'm a Spanish speaker, too. I may get stuck flying the Caribbean."

"Oh, you poor thing. Having to spend your day on the beach in San Juan, surrounded by sexy tourists and hot local men who are always looking for action. My heart bleeds for you."

"I still wish I had the chance to my change mind. I mean, of course I want to fly overseas eventually, but not right now."

"Then in the future, I suggest that you avoid making major life decisions when you're blind drunk. Now are you going to pout about this all day, or we going to have fun?"

"Yes, we'll have fun. We have to. God knows when I'll see San Francisco again."

"You're only locked into international for six months. If you really hate it, you can resign and go back to domestic. Once you get a taste of the good life, though, I doubt that you'll want to go back. No one ever does." He looked back at the computer screen. "Our plane just landed. Let's head for the gate. Let me pull up the crew list. Oh, hey, look at this! Jake Alexopoulus is our captain today. Have you ever flown with him? He's the hottest pilot in the whole system!"

"Yes, I've flown with him." As if I could ever forget that layover!

"Man, what I wouldn't give to be naked and alone in a hotel room with *him* for a couple of hours. I bet the sex would hot, hot, hot. Too bad he's married."

"Yeah. Too bad."

***

On their way to the gate, Eric heard a familiar voice call his name. He turned around and was delighted to see Rose, Geneviève and Ginnie Jo in uniform. "Hey! What a nice surprise! Denny, these are my friends from training, Rose and Genevieve. Ladies, this is Denny. Where are you going today?"

"We're on the one o'clock flight to Chicago," said Geneviève. "Isn't that ironic? We just moved from Chicago, and now we're going back, with a twelve-hour layover at the airport."

"Just as well," said Rose. "We have tickets to see *Phantom of the Opera* tomorrow night—in the orchestra section, fifth row!"

"How did you swing that?" Eric asked.

"They're compliments of a passenger that Geneviève met on a flight from Miami yesterday."

Geneviève smiled. "It pays to be nice to strangers. You never know who you may be talking to."

"It's wonderful that you're all flying together today," said Eric. "Is Anthony on the trip, too?"

"No," said Ginnie Jo. "Rose and Geneviève are up front, and I'm stuck in the back with Brick Fisher, of all people."

"How delightful," said Eric. "I know there's no love lost between you two."

Ginnie Jo shrugged. "He's been OK ever since ever that turbulence incident. There's nothing like the fear of a fiery death to bring sworn enemies closer together. I just hate working in the back of that goddam Ultra Jet. It's so claustrophobic, and I can't stand that my jump seat is right between the bathrooms."

"We're on the 767 to San Francisco today," said Eric.

"*Quelle chance!*" said Geneviève. "What a wonderful trip."

Denny looked at his watch. "We'd better be going, Eric. You know how Sylvia hates it when we're late for her briefing. Nice to meet you both, and Ginnie Jo it's always a pleasure to see you. Don't torture Brick too much."

"Eh, it's a two-hour flight," said Ginnie Jo. I can handle him for two hours. You guys have a good trip. And play safe if you go out tonight, which I know you will."

***

Passengers were still coming off the inbound aircraft when Denny and Eric arrived at the gate. The entire outbound crew was there, including the pilots. Jake walked up to Eric and shook his hand. He was as casual as could be, acting as though they'd never spent an afternoon in his hotel room having sex. Well, no matter. All Eric had to do was cook the pilots' meals. He didn't even have to talk to them if he didn't want to.

Chaz looked as handsome as ever. "Nice to see you, Chaz," said Eric. "How's Aaron?"

"We're great," said Chaz. "We just got back from the most fantastic trip. A group that we belong to rented a villa in Tuscany for two weeks."

"Which group is that?"

"An international gay nudist group."

"I guess that could be interesting—or not, depending on who else is there."

"Oh, it was interesting, all right. It's is a very exclusive group. To join, you have to submit a recent photo and have your measurements verified."

"What measurements?"

"Length and girth. The founders are very strict about that, but we both made it in easily."

"Well, that does indeed sound exclusive."

Chaz and Denny exchanged a wary look. "Hello, Neely," said Chaz. "Still hooked on booze and pills?"

"Hello, Ivana. Still hooked on your cheating ex-husband's alimony payments?"

"It's been months since I've seen you, Denny. I heard the police pulled a corpse from the river near the Christopher Street pier last week. They suspect an alcohol-fueled gay cruising scenario that went tragically wrong. I was hoping that it wasn't you."

"I never go cruising near the Christopher Street piers," said Denny. "That's strictly for tourists— and Upper West Siders like you—looking for a cheap thrill. I stick to the East Village. I like real men."

"OK, OK," said Sylvia, who'd had enough of this banter. "Let's get this show on the road." The crew gathered their luggage and made their way to the jet bridge door.

Even though a sign indicated that the flight would be departing thirty minutes late, passengers were already lining up to board. Some of them glared impatiently at the crew.

"You may as well have a seat, folks," said Sylvia. "It's going to be at least fifteen minutes before we can start boarding."

The first passenger in line, a short, rotund man with a bald head and a thin black mustache, sneered at her. "We wouldn't *have* to wait if you people would move your asses a little faster."

Jake, who was printing the flight plan, immediately looked up. "What was that you said to my crew?"

The fat man seemed taken by surprise. "I suggested they move a little faster, that's all."

"I'm quite certain you told them to *move their asses*. Isn't that right, Sylvia?"

"Quite right, Captain," she said, trying to keep a straight face.

"Are you interested in traveling with us today, sir?" said Jake, looming over the man. "If so, I suggest that you apologize right this minute. Otherwise, you're going nowhere."

"You can't speak to me like that. I'm an Almighty Titan."

"I don't care if you're the President of the United States. You either apologize or go buy a ticket on another airline. I won't put up with this kind of rudeness toward my crew—or anyone else on this flight."

Everyone in the boarding area watched the scene intently, waiting for the passenger's response. "I apologize," he said. His face was beet red. Eric couldn't tell whether it was from anger or embarrassment, but it didn't matter. A moment like this was a dream come true.

"Apology accepted. Sylvia, let me know if you have further trouble with this gentleman. I can't imagine that we will, but just in case."

"Aye, aye, Captain. Come on, kids, let's go."

Eric was delighted to be working in the first-class galley. He would hardly come in contact with the passengers at all, which was a welcome reprieve. Sylvia raced through her preflight briefing so that everyone could begin setting up their cabins. A moment later, as she was arranging the newspaper cart, the crew phone rang. "Hello, this is Sylvia … oh damn, all right, I'll tell them." She pressed the PA button. "Hey, everybody, the safety demo tape in stuck in the machine, so we're going to have to do a live demo in the aisle. Check your safety manual right now to verify your assigned position. And please get your equipment out of the demo bag *before* we start. I don't want one of those Keystone Cops situations as I'm trying to deliver the PA. Thank you."

This announcement was met with a collective groan. Even though it was as fundamental to the job as doing seatbelt checks, everyone loathed doing a manual demo. A moment later, a rail-thin woman with short, spiky grey hair came up the aisle.

"Look out, Sylvia," said Eric. "Here comes Edna."

Edna entered the galley and stood with her hands on her hips. "FYI, Sylvia, I am not doing a manual safety demo." Edna was a heavy smoker. Her voice was so deep that it sounded as though she was speaking from a bottomless hole in the ground. "I'm senior on the crew. One of the junior kids can do it for me."

"What's the big deal about doing a manual demo, Edna? You've been flying for forty years. We didn't even *have* a videotaped safety demo until the early Seventies."

"Exactly. I've paid my dues, and I'm *not* doing it."

"Let's make a deal," said Sylvia. "Eric will do the demo for you in coach. In exchange, you don't come up here once during the entire flight. I don't even want to see, hear or smell you until after we land. Now beat it."

The second that Edna opened her mouth to reply, Sylvia cut her off. "End of discussion, Edna. Get out of my sight."

Edna marched off in a huff. "That woman has been a pain in my ass for thirty years," said Sylvia. "I can't believe that someone hasn't followed her to Fisherman's Wharf and fed her to the sea lions. Sorry, Eric, I shouldn't have volunteered your services without asking you first."

"I don't mind," said Eric. "It will be my one appearance in the aisle today. After that, I'm going to hide behind the curtain and eat all the *canapés*. Hey, do you think we'll get out of here today with this fog? I can't see a damn thing out the window."

"Well, nothing's canceled so far. I'm sure it will take forever to taxi out, but Jake will put the pedal to the metal once we're airborne. He's in a hurry to get there. He and his wife are celebrating their wedding anniversary."

"Oh, are they?" said Eric, his face betraying nothing.

"Yes. Shirley left earlier, on the ten o'clock flight. They managed to take off, so unless it gets a lot worse, we're going."

Jeff, the first officer, stepped out of the cockpit. "When you guys have a chance to brew some coffee, will you bring a cup to Jake, please? Cream, no sugar. I'm gonna pop into the lav for a second."

"Do you mind, Eric?" said Sylvia. "I have to call cabin service for some hangers."

"No, I don't mind." He poured the coffee and took it to the cockpit, where Jake was busy loading the flight plan. "Here's your coffee, Jake."

"Thanks. How've you been?"

"Fine."

"Good. Got exciting plans for your layover today?"

"Denny and I are going to hang out."

"That's nice."

"I understand that you're celebrating your wedding anniversary tonight." He shouldn't have said anything, but he couldn't help himself.

"That's right. I made a reservation at a cozy French place not far from the hotel."

"I hope you have a *wonderful* time."

"Thanks. Sorry, Eric, I wish I could chat, but I've got to finish this before we push back."

"No problem," said Eric, turning to leave. I don't fucking believe it. He's not going to acknowledge it even when the two of us are alone together.

"Hey, Eric," said Jake. "You and I are cool, right?" There was a hint of anxiety in his voice, which Eric found gratifying.

"Yeah," he said, stepping out of the cockpit. "We're cool."

***

As the plane began moving away from the gate, Sylvia delivered the usual pre-takeoff announcement. Eric joined the other flight attendants in the aisle to perform the safety demo. He could see Edna seated on the aft jump seat. She was reading a magazine and looked very pleased with herself. He thought about giving her a good glare, but decided not to. He wouldn't give her the pleasure of knowing that her behavior affected him in the least. As a psychology major, he had tried several times to ascertain the root cause of her sense of entitlement, but it was pointless. Edna would never change. She was just one of those people.

As he held up the safety briefing card and pointed out the emergency exits, he noticed that, as usual, no one was paying attention. That no longer bothered him, like it did when he was a new hire. If there's ever an actual emergency, he thought, they'd better be able to think fast. He had just slipped the oxygen mask over his face when he heard a cell phone ring behind him. *That* still bothered the hell out of him.

"Hello … yeah, I'm the plane. Did you get that memo I left for you?"

Eric swiveled around to see who was talking. Naturally, it was the fat man who'd been rude to Sylvia. He removed the oxygen mask and walked over to the passenger immediately. "Sir, you have to turn that phone off. We're away from the gate, and you can't use it right now." It was then that he noticed the man was sitting in the exit row. An extension was attached to his seatbelt, which strained over the girth of his enormous belly.

"This is a very important call," said the man.

"It doesn't matter," said Eric. "Turn that phone off right now. Incidentally, why are you sitting in an exit row? You can't sit here if you require a seatbelt extension. You must be able to respond immediately in the event of an emergency."

"Hang on a minute," the man said to the caller. He glared at Eric. "I've just had about enough of you people for one day." He jerked a thumb toward the back of the plane. "Your co-worker brought me the extension and didn't say a word about me sitting here."

"Which one?"

"The old one."

Edna! "That must have been an oversight on her part."

"It doesn't matter. I'm not moving. I need the leg room."

"There's an empty row right in front of you. You can move there."

"That seatback doesn't recline because of the exit behind it. I *have* to be able to recline."

"Sir, you are in violation of at least two Federal Air Regulations. You cannot use your phone once we leave the gate, and you cannot sit in an exit row if you require a seatbelt extension. Either you get off your phone and move out of that row, or I call the captain. If you choose the latter, we'll go back to the gate and have you removed."

"Bullshit. What's your name?"

"Oh, no, we're not playing that game today. Obviously, you've made your choice." Eric marched up the aisle, picked up the nearest interphone and called the cockpit. "Hello, Jake this is Eric. I have a safety of flight issue." He explained the situation and received the response he had anticipated: if the passenger did not comply, they would return to the gate. He walked back down the aisle feeling gleeful at the prospect of removing the fat man and was disappointed to see that he had moved out of the exit row.

He showed Eric his phone. "See? It's turned off. You happy now?"

"Your compliance is appreciated," Eric said, his voice dripping with sarcasm. He turned and walked back toward first class. As he passed, a young woman in the first row of coach anxiously waved at him.

"Can I help you, Miss?"

"Yes, thanks. Sorry, I'm a bit of a nervous flyer." She pointed out the window. "Is it really safe taxiing around here and taking off in this weather?" She tapped the window, through which Eric could see nothing but a mixture of drizzle and thick, grey fog. "How can the pilots even see where they're going?"

He knelt in the aisle next to her seat. "I understand why you're anxious, but there's nothing to worry about. The pilots are required to have certain visibility minimums before they can leave the gate. Plus, ground control has a radar system in place. They know where every airplane is on the taxiways and runways, and keep them spaced a safe distance apart. I promise you that we wouldn't be leaving if it weren't safe to do so."

"OK, if you say so. Would you mind bringing me a vodka and tonic? It would help to calm me down."

"Technically, I'm not supposed to…" He looked into her eyes, which were wide with fear. He leaned over and whispered to her. "Yes, I'll bring you one. But if anyone asks, it's just water, OK?"

"Deal. Thanks a lot!"

He brought her the drink and continued his way back to first class.

Sylvia and Chaz were just sitting down in their jump seats. "How's the crowd in business class today?" Sylvia asked.

"The usual," said Chaz. "Believe me, I'd much rather be working up here. Any chance you want to trade positions, Eric?

"Thanks for asking," Eric replied, "but I'm quite happy to be working up here with Sylvia."

As he strapped into his jump seat next to Chaz, Denny walked into the galley. "Hey, do you guys mind if I take a bottle of water for myself? We're already running low in the back."

"Up there," said Chaz, gesturing toward a compartment above his jump seat.

Denny took a bottle. "Thanks. I'll come up and visit later. Working in coach is going to be a joy today. Sylvia, do I have your permission to tell Edna to go fuck herself?"

"As if you had to ask."

"Thanks, see you later."

"Eric," said Sylvia, "I meant to ask you: who were those two beautiful blond women I saw you and Ginnie Jo talking to?"

"Two friends from my training class. They just transferred to New York. They're out there somewhere on an Ultra Jet bound for Chicago."

They heard the squawk of the PA system. "Ladies and gentlemen, this is the captain speaking. We are currently number three for takeoff and will be airborne in just a few minutes. Flight attendants, please prepare for takeoff."

"Here we go," said Sylvia, as a single chime sounded in the cabin. The plane made a full turn and moved into position for takeoff. A moment later, they were rolling.

"Goddammit," said Chaz, unfastening his seatbelt.

"What's the matter?" said Sylvia.

"Denny left that compartment unlatched. There's a whole insert of large water bottles in there."

"Make it quick," said Sylvia, as the roar of the engines increased. "We're moving."

"I know," said Chaz, as he jumped up and reached for the latch.

Eric mechanically pulled his seatbelt and shoulder harness tighter. Given the weather, it was probably going to be a bumpy takeoff. A split second later, his felt his head fly forward and then smash back into the headrest. Then he heard a noise so loud that he was left momentarily deaf. He felt the explosion that followed more than he heard it, as a bright orange light suddenly filled the galley.

After that, everything happened in slow motion. He saw the insert come flying out of the compartment and smash into Chaz's face, and then saw Chaz go flying across the galley. Sylvia screamed as he slammed into the wall and fell to the floor, immobilized. She and Eric immediately jumped out of their seats. Eric could smell the smoke before he even saw it. He looked in the cabin. To his utter disbelief, passengers in first class were standing up and pulling suitcases out of the overhead bins. "No bags!" Eric shouted. "Leave them!"

"This is the captain." Jake's voice was loud, clear and authoritative. "Do not, I repeat, do NOT use any left-side exits. Flight attendants: evacuate immediately!" As the evacuation horns starting blaring, Jeff burst out of the cockpit holding a fire extinguisher.

Eric started to shout his commands, then stopped. At that moment, there was no way out of the front of the plane. They couldn't use the left-hand door, and Chaz's body was blocking the door on the right. This would not be a textbook evacuation. The crew would have to improvise moment by moment.

Sylvia pointed to Chaz's crumpled body. "Jeff, you and Eric have to move him! He's blocking the only usable exit that we have up here! But be careful!"

As Eric and Jeff moved Chaz away from the door, Eric had to turn his head. Chaz's face was swollen to twice its normal size and covered in blood. Eric couldn't even tell if he was still alive.

"I'll get the 1R door," said Sylvia. "We'll get Chaz out before it's too late." In an instant, the galley was full of frantic passengers. "Eric, hold the people back while I try to open the door!"

Eric put up his hand, fingers spread wide. "Stand back! Remain calm!"

Sylvia stepped in front of the door and assessed conditions outside. Miraculously, it seemed safe enough to open the exit. She pulled up on the handle. Within seconds, the door opened. The escape slide inflated and appeared to be firmly in place. "Jump and slide, jump and slide, leave luggage! Jump and slide, jump and slide, leave luggage!" She looked over the heads of fleeing passengers and made eye contact with Eric. "Go back, elevate on a seat if you can, and do flow control. Send people to the window exits or rear exits if they're usable."

Eric was out of the galley in a flash, as Sylvia continued her evacuation commands. "Jump and slide, jump and slide, no luggage. Drop that goddam suitcase, sir! Your life is more important! Jump, jump, JUMP!"

"Move, move, move!" Eric shouted, as he tried to make his way down the aisle. It was a stupefying scene: people were still trying to get luggage from the overhead bins and from under their seats. "No bags!" he yelled at the top of his lungs. "Leave them! Get up and get out!" The acrid smoke burned his nose and eyes, but at least he could see to the back of the plane now. Two window exits and one rear exit on the right side were being used. People seemed to be following instructions rather than trampling each other. He could see a flight attendant at the window exits commanding passengers to step through and slide down the ramp off the back of the wing. The window exits were a painfully slow way out, but at least they *were* a way out. As he reached the middle of the plane, the fat man, still buckled into his seat, was sobbing and waving his arms and legs like a toddler having a tantrum. "Help me, help me!" he screamed. Despite the urgency of the situation, Eric had to stifle a laugh. The man looked like Baby Huey. Eric reached over to unbuckle the seatbelt and forced him to stand up. "Get up and get out! There's an exit right behind you."

"I can't!" said the passenger, pawing at his tears. "I won't fit!"

"Then go to the back and exit via the main door. Move, move, move! You're blocking the aisle!" A few minutes later, once his cabin area appeared to be under control, he ran back to the front of the plane, which was empty except for Sylvia, Chaz, and the pilots. "We've got to get out of here right now," said Jake, his face covered with sweat. "Eric, you and Sylvia go down. Then Jeff will go, and then I'll come down with Chaz. He's breathing and has a pulse, so he might have a chance. You two stay at the bottom to help catch him. I don't want him hurt any more badly than he already is."

Eric watched Sylvia go down, and then he jumped into the slide. Before he had time to blink, he was on the ground. Jeff followed him down. He and Eric stayed at the bottom of the slide to help safely catch Jake and Chaz.

Jake slid down with Chaz secured between his legs. "We've got to get away from here, in case this thing blows. Let's carry him as far as we can."

As they moved away from the airplane, Eric heard the blare of sirens and then saw the lights of the fire trucks coming toward them. From out of nowhere, dozens and dozens of rescue personnel appeared and raced to help the passengers and crewmembers. Some passengers, who appeared to have escaped without a scratch, sat on the tarmac in a dazed state. Others were badly injured and begging for help. It was like watching a scene from a disaster movie. But it wasn't a movie. It was real: the unlikely event that had a one-in-a-million chance of ever happening aboard a commercial airliner.

Eric sank to his knees and started to dry-heave, fighting an overwhelming urge to vomit. Sylvia was by his side in a flash. She had lost heels going down the slide and stood next to him in her stocking feet. "It's all right. We did good. I'm fairly sure that everyone got off. And they're already getting Chaz into an ambulance. He might make it."

"What the fuck just happened?"

"A runway incursion. We hit another airplane… or they hit us. It's too soon to tell."

"Was it one of ours?"

"I'm afraid so. Don't look, Eric. It's very bad."

He *had* to look. As emergency vehicles continued to arrive, the crash site, still enveloped in fog, became more brightly lit. From the right side, the 767 appeared to be intact. He could only imagine what the left side looked like. Just beyond the nose, he was horrified to see the unmistakable tail assembly of a Mercury Airways Ultra Jet. It has been shorn off, and lay bent and blackened on the ground. "Was it the Chicago flight?"

"I think so. Honey, I'm sorry, I know your friends were on there."

"What about our crew?"

"I just saw Denny hand off a baby to a fireman. He seems OK. And you *know* Edna was the first one out of her fucking door."

"Any chance of survivors on the Chicago flight?" Eric asked tersely.

"I don't know yet. It looks like the back of that plane got the worst of it. Maybe the crew seated up front managed to get out. Come on, let's try to round up everybody from our flight. We had one hundred and twelve souls on board. Can you help me do a passenger and crew count?"

Eric couldn't budge.

"Eric, did you hear me? Oh, my God, sweetheart, did you hurt yourself going down the slide? Do you need help getting up?"

It was unfathomable: Geneviève, Rose and Ginnie Jo, gone just like that. The Ultra Jet was a flaming hull of scorched metal. It would be a miracle if anyone got out alive. To even try to cope with such a staggering loss was unfathomable. Before he could open his mouth to respond to Sylvia, everything went black as his brain started shutting down. He seemed to be floating high above the crash site, away from the heat and smoke and the horrible smell of burning jet fuel. He faintly heard Sylvia calling his name… and then, there was just nothingness.

To be continued...

Coming up next:

We can't *wait* to say, "Bonjour, Paris!"

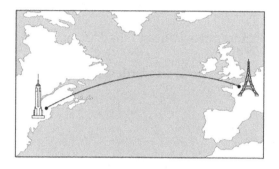

STEWARDESS BOY 3:
Je m'appelle Stewardess Boy

A novel by Henri Gustave

For all the latest details, stay tuned via our website:

www.stewardessboy.com

or

Facebook: www.facebook.com/stewardessboy

Instagram: stewardessboy2

and Twitter: @BoyStewardess

About the author

Henri Gustave works in the aviation industry and lives in the borough of Queens in New York City. *Stewardess Boy 2: The Wilder Blue Yonder* is his second novel. His first novel, *Stewardess Boy*, is available in paperback and Kindle at:

www.amazon.com

Readers may contact him directly via email:

henri@stewardessboy.com

About the illustrator

Rae Crosson is a New Jersey-based illustrator. You can see more of his work at the following websites:

http://www.greetingsfromcrazyville.com

and

https://rae-crosson.format.com/illustrations

Acknowledgements

Thanks to all my silver-winged friends, who have been so supportive of my writing. Being repeatedly asked, "When is that sequel finally coming out?" has motivated me to complete the second installment in the series.

Special thanks to Sue Alberti, Karen Kelley-Altes, Mark Arcarisi and Tim Johnson, Jerry Arko and Hank Baker, Michael Aylett, Michael Berning, Steve Berridge, Gina Blakely, Georgette Botti, Bruce Bridgeford and Pierre Hamel, Bob Brach and Tad Donovan, Randy Brooks, Robert Buckner, Mathew Craig, Kevin Dalton, Jerry Genualdi, Charles Gustina, Donald Hartsfield, Rob Hoffman, Jeffrey Holland, Brian Hooks and Scott Shoup, Florence and Samantha Hue, Ken Koc, Michael Letizio, Salvadora Lorelli and Monte Lavner, Nance Lynch, Jacqueline Martell, Leo McLaughlin and Alex Mullens, Michael Napolitano, Jeff Pharr, Shane Pfeiffer, Robert Rapport, Mickey Rodgers, Sheryl Stapp, Chuck Sweeney, Karen Varley, and Eddie Wall.

I'd also like to thank a few non-airline friends I've made along the way: Deiby Reele and Bill Wilson, Mark Leach, Jeff Elgart and Mark Rotenstreich, and Ron Glick and Donald Reidlinger.

For years of support and encouragement from the very beginning, much love to Patricia Grossman and Helene Kendler, Kiki Nesbitt, the Beckwith family, the Licata family, the Smith family... and to my own family, from whom I learned to have a sense of humor and many other invaluable life skills—Louise, Simone, Fran, Christian, Steve and Raymond.

34164744R00325

Made in the USA
Middletown, DE
24 January 2019